The Hall of Records Trilogy

By John Schroeder

Acknowledgements

It seems no one ever writes a book by themselves. It takes the help of many to edit, proof, format and graphically design a book from cover to cover. The fact that this trilogy is truly three books under one title helps to explain why it took me nearly ten years to ready the manuscript for print. Finally, it is time to thank all those people for making this book possible.

No one else but my wife, Stephanie, has been with me from the start to the finish of this book. The only reason she is not listed as the co-author is that she asked me not to. It started at lunch one day when I described an idea that popped into my head. She started taking notes and those notes became the basis for resonant frequency technology, the science fiction answer to the many seemingly magical devices used throughout this book. As I wrote the rough drafts, her proofing and editing made the story far more readable and entertaining. She constantly encouraged me to stay with this decade long project. She is my greatest love, my best friend and cherished companion for life. No one could ask for a better spouse, and I was incredibly lucky that she agreed to marry me some 38 years ago.

Three other people were instrumental in getting this book into print. They are David Stipes, Mary Travis and Joanna Schildt. David wrote the introduction to this trilogy and helped me resolve the complex timelines and maintain the story's continuity over the three parts. Mary Travis spent countless hours editing and proofing and even rearranging the order of the story to improve the flow. While I have lost track of Joanna Schildt, she was so helpful for most of this process that I wanted to acknowledge her contribution as well.

The feedback I received from others may have seemed small to them, but the impact was greater than perhaps they know. Annie Kloss, Steve Bobbitt, Bill Schroeder and Greg Clarke all offered their time and sage input on how to make this a better book.

Introduction

Humanity is often at its worst when we are motivated by revenge. This is especially true when old disputes between sovereign nations approach the point of no return. Conflicts like this escalate toward war when personal agendas for wealth and power are fueled by that desire for vengeance. Can civilization be saved from annihilation because of the extraordinary efforts of a few key people? The answer to that question is found in The Hall of Records trilogy. Indeed it is a work of fiction, but this epic story is told using the same real-world scenarios that are reported in the news on a daily basis.

John Schroeder is the dynamic author who takes us through three grand adventures that offer a glimpse of our future. John and I have been friends for over 50 years as, quite unknowingly, life prepared him to become a writer. While our paths were rather different, we both shared a love and preference for the philosophy given in the psychic readings of the mystic Christian Edgar Cayce.

Over the years, John and I often spoke about how to live up to our personal ideals despite the values of a secular world. I had my challenges in Hollywood and John had his as an entrepreneur, college professor and executive director of a large church. We were often faced with the choice to stand up and do the right thing or take self-serving shortcuts. It was always a joy and pleasure to talk with John about the Edgar Cayce ideals and principles and watch him, without fail, take the high road to measure up to his own ethics and ideals in spite of the difficult circumstances.

As John moved through life searching for ways to live up to his beliefs, he was drawn to connect with a wider audience online with his books and videos. I watched John grow as a writer and as a person as he explored the deeper questions that many of us ask ourselves. His greatest joy is to share his understanding of the Edgar Cayce philosophy and principles with those who wish to spiritually learn and grow.

Through his books and videos, John found a platform where he could express his perspective of the Cayce principles and how to apply them in real life under the most adverse circumstances. He initially planned for part one of this trilogy to stand on its own as one book. He soon realized that a second book was needed to complete the study of the human experience in adequate detail. It became obvious that books one and two investigated the physical and mental trials and successes of humanity, but yet another book was needed to address the spiritual aspect of our lives.

The overall question asked in this trilogy is what happens when we rise and stay true to the best that is within us? Can the worst of society transform to bring mankind back from the brink of destruction? Within these thrilling stories, John's epic adventure follows a few central characters who come from both sides of goodness, to see if we will ultimately measure up to such a monumental task.

John's ability to apply profound understanding to physical, mental, and spiritual situations provides stories of exciting jungle adventure, geopolitical espionage, and philosophical science fiction.

As a follower of John's life and books, let me encourage you to join our explorers in some of the most dangerous and beautiful areas of the earth in search of answers to the world's deepest mysteries and profound spiritual questions. These adventures are great fun to read if only for their riveting entertainment. But for those who are open to it, this trilogy will reveal personal insights worth incorporating into our daily life. How often do we have a chance to study life's greatest mysteries in such an entertaining way?

David Stipes
Visual Effects Artist
Glendale, Arizona

The Hall of Records Trilogy

Part 1

Through the Valley of Death

Chapter 1

Private First Class Wiley kept the truck's window wide open to let the cool desert breeze kick-start his brain. The coffee cup he kept trading for the gear shift also helped to clear his head. He looked at his watch again and sighed. It was 3:24 am, only three minutes since the last time he'd checked. Wiley knew another hour of unpaved roads lay ahead before they would arrive at the depot. Per regulations, Private Shaw was riding shotgun along with him. Despite the bumpy ride and rules against it, Shaw was fast asleep with his cap pulled down over his eyes.

Wiley looked in his rearview mirror for the headlights of the other "deuce and half" 2½ ton M-35 truck that followed convoy style behind him. Both he and Private First Class Mendez, the other driver, had navigated this hazardous route through the northern Israel desert many times before, but a cargo of high explosives always upped the stakes.

Suddenly, the truck's frame hit the ground hard as Wiley's right front tire bottomed out in a pothole. He quickly recovered control of the truck, but his coffee was a goner. To his amazement, Private Shaw managed to sleep on undisturbed. Wiley kept driving but the pothole really had his adrenaline pumping. He had to remind himself that C-4 is quite stable and wouldn't explode even if the truck had turned over. Then he smiled and wondered which would be worse, the C-4 igniting or his commander's explosive reaction if this load wasn't delivered on schedule. He leaned forward in his seat determined to keep a closer eye on the road.

These oh-dark-hundred transport missions always put Wiley in a bad mood. He usually made his deliveries to the remote supply depot around 10:00 am, but the Israeli weather forecast for that morning said a heavy storm was due in just after sunrise, and so here he was. He glanced longingly at the spilled coffee on the floorboards and considered what else he could do to stay awake.

Wiley thought back to his great run of luck the night before. His favorite entertainment was playing cards, and his favorite casino was located in Alumot just southwest of the Sea of Galilee. He was up several hundred when he remembered this early morning mission was only a few hours off. When Wiley said he had to leave because he was scheduled for an early run, the other guys were relieved. He was always a good poker player, but that night he had won several hands on the river (the last card drawn) in Texas hold'em poker. Wiley wished now he could trade a few of those winning hands for a good night's sleep.

***

Wiley, peering ahead in the darkness, could tell something wasn't right about 50 yards in the distance. Instead of the usual tire ruts in the dirt road, there was a five-foot section that looked cultivated like someone had planted a garden. He stopped in front of the odd patch of dirt and shook Private Shaw's shoulder to wake him. Shaw pulled off his cap and looked around. He was still disoriented and had no idea why they had stopped.

The two-way radio crackled and the voice of Mendez came through from the other truck. He asked what the holdup was. Wiley responded that there was something wrong with the road and to keep an eye out. Mendez started to switch frequencies to call ahead to the depot while his passenger, Private Reynolds, reached for his rifle. It was already too late.

Using the cover of darkness, two men had quietly moved up along the sides of the rear truck and slammed the butts of their rifles through the open windows into the faces of both men. Mendez and Reynolds were out cold when they were pulled from the cab and forcefully thrown to the ground. They were stripped of their Army Combat Uniforms - ACUs - and quietly executed with brutal bayonet jabs.

Unaware of the violence behind him, Private First Class Wiley left his diesel engine running and the headlights on high beams as he stepped out to investigate the smooth patch of road. Private Shaw, still only half awake, grabbed his rifle and begrudgingly slid out of the truck to join Wiley. They both stared at the recently graded dirt and wondered if they should check it for buried explosives. The answer became obvious a moment later.

A single rifle shot rang out over the sound of the idling diesel engines. "Don't move!" yelled a threatening voice from behind them. The words were spoken in English, but with a distinctly Arabic accent.

Wiley couldn't believe it. He had heard of terrorist activity within the borders of Israel, but he had never heard of a face-to-face assault on an American military convoy. The significance of this raced through his mind as he automatically put up his hands to show he held no weapons. Private Shaw reluctantly let his rifle fall to the ground. At first, all they could see was the front of their truck surrounded by darkness. Then they saw a man walking toward them silhouetted by the truck's headlights.

Wiley couldn't see the man's face, but he could tell he carried an AK-47 rifle from its outline. The man spoke quickly with a thick Arabic accent.

"You are now prisoners of war captured by the army of Mohammed's Faithful. If you do everything I say, you may survive this night."

Wiley and Shaw realized this whole thing had been a trap to get them to stop. Feeling a little stupid and very scared, they both knew surviving this ordeal was unlikely.

The hijacker continued, "You two will complete your mission as ordered. You will drive these trucks and my men to the supply compound. We leave now."

He pointed his AK-47 at Wiley and motioned for him to get into the driver's seat. Shaw was pushed from behind toward the second truck. He caught his breath and hesitated when he saw Mendez and Reynolds lying dead on the road. One of the hijackers jabbed at Shaw's ribs with the barrel of his rifle to keep him moving.

Wiley just stared as one of the hijackers handed the man, who was obviously their leader, Mendez's ACU shirt and cap. He kept Wiley at gunpoint while the man in charge put them on. Wiley was filled with dread as he started to piece together their plan. Anyone would assume this hijacker was a soldier in the U.S. Army because he was clean shaven and wearing a United States military uniform.

Wiley knew he and Shaw were out of options. By the different voices he could tell there were eight or more hijackers. He figured their plan was to infiltrate the supply depot by posing as soldiers riding shotgun while the others stayed hidden in the back of the M-35s. He couldn't see any way to stop them that wouldn't get himself and Shaw killed. Even if they tried and failed, the hijackers would still have the trucks to do whatever they had planned.

The more he thought about it, the more Wiley knew he had to count on the compound's 100 soldiers and security protocols to keep this situation from getting any worse. He knew that once the trucks were in sight of the gate the guards would radio him. Then he was expected to either give the "all-clear" or use the code phrase to signal trouble. Until then, he would do his best to stay alive.

***

Colonel Achmed Mansur, Commander of Mohammed's Faithful, heard the report from Hakim on the radio that the trucks had been successfully hijacked without incident. The American hostages were cooperating, so far, and had resumed driving toward the compound. He added that the drivers knew their front seat passengers had hand guns trained on them along with AK-47s from the other soldiers hiding in the truck beds. Colonel Mansur told his men, hiding in the hills that surrounded the supply depot, they had less than an hour to be ready.

***

Amon was the best sniper among the 150 soldiers in Mohammed's Faithful. He silently prayed to Allah for help as he anxiously watched the American guards at the front gate of the compound. From his position in the nearby hills, he could see their attention was focused on the two military trucks headed directly for them. One of the guards picked up a radio and Amon was intensely alert. They didn't always do security checks, so the next minute would be critical to the success of their mission.

Setting aside his binoculars, Amon picked up his M-40 sniper rifle. He motioned for his fellow sniper, Abel, to do the same as they made ready to teach these infidels a lesson they would not soon forget. Months of careful planning would be wasted, along with the lives of many of Mohammed's Faithful, if all did not go well at the

5

gate. If the approaching trucks were not allowed to enter the compound, may Allah guide their aim to ensure a glorious victory.

The real question, Amon knew, was if the drivers would try to take heroic actions once they arrived at the front gate. If so, then it was his and Abel's job to shoot the guards as their fellow soldiers inside the trucks killed the drivers. Assuming it came to that, they might still enter the compound and complete their mission.

***

The radio crackled inside Wiley's cab. The gate guard was calling for confirmation that everything was copacetic as the trucks approached. Wiley looked at the man holding the gun and told him that if he didn't respond, the guards would not let the truck enter and would call for backup. The soldier pointed a .45 caliber pistol at Wiley and nodded toward the radio.

"Gate security, this is M-35 leader. We are on final approach and everything is A-OK," said Wiley.

The gate guard asked him to repeat and Wiley did as requested. With a quick "10-4," the soldier signed off and went inside the guard shack. The terrorist riding shotgun inside the cab relaxed, but Amon could see through his scope that the soldier from the gate was making a phone call. The second soldier at the gate took a defensive stance and waited as the truck approached.

As Wiley pulled up to the gate, both soldiers quickly assumed positions at the corners of the truck's front bumper with their M-16 rifles at the ready.

"Are you okay in there Wiley?" the guard who talked to him on the radio asked.

Wiley responded without looking at him, "I told you I was A-OK before and I'm A-OK now."

Just then, a wicked crack whipped through the air that sounded like the sizzle of lightning before the boom. The first guard was falling to the ground when the crackling sound came again. The second guard fell where he stood from the sniper's round fired 500 meters away. The two soldiers in the cabs didn't hesitate and shot both Wiley and Shaw simultaneously. They opened the drivers' doors and pushed the Americans out to take up their positions behind the steering wheels.

Wiley's luck continued to hold. The bullet smashed through his right arm with the humerus bone deflecting its path away from his vital organs. His injuries were limited to a broken arm and a couple of cracked ribs. He would survive this night, but Private Shaw was already gone.

***

Amon warned Colonel Mansur that the guard at the gate had probably sounded the alarm to bring help. Mansur ordered Amon to let the truck drivers know and to get ready for the assault. Amon notified Hakim that he had perhaps 60 seconds until American reinforcements arrived. Hakim jammed the truck into first gear and floored the accelerator to smash through the gate.

The concrete barriers that were attached to the rolling gates held off his first assault and even the second as he reversed the truck and tried it again. On his third attempt, Basir, the driver of the second truck, pulled up beside him. Pushing together, the barriers tipped over and the M-35s were able to shove them and the mangled gate forward. After forcing the concrete barriers ahead for another 20 feet, they had enough room to maneuver away to do some real damage.

Hakim's mission was to destroy the fuel reserves, but they no longer had the element of surprise. He turned left and headed toward the far west end of the post. He saw Basir turn right to take out the ammunition storage facility located to the east.

***

Captain Rob Norton was the Officer in Charge of security during night duty. He was at his desk when the call came in from the front gate that Wiley had given the "A-OK" signal. That was the verbal security code indicating they were in serious trouble. He told his sergeant to sound the general alarm and contact HQ to let them know what was happening. There were only two other soldiers on duty with him and just one Jeep parked outside. Rob knew he couldn't wait for reinforcements. Keeping the M-60 machine gun loaded and firing was a two man job, especially with the Jeep on the move. Captain Norton decided it was better if he drove. He prayed they could get to the gate before all hell broke loose.

As they exited the building, Rob heard the rifle shots and knew they were already too late. The Jeep was still 100 yards out when he spotted four bodies lying on the ground near the guard shack. Then he saw two trucks split up after smashing through the security gate with one of them heading straight for him. According to the delivery schedule, the deuce and half trucks were supposed to be carrying C-4 explosives but he had no idea how many men were inside, nor how heavily they were armed.

Captain Norton's Jeep was also equipped with the standard four M-16s, eight extra pre-loaded magazines for the rifles, and four MK II grenades. The C-4 would not explode if only hit by bullets or shrapnel but the grenades would set it off for sure. Norton knew their best bet for this fight was the Jeep's mounted M-60 machine gun. He gave his men the order to fire and they obliged. The oncoming truck's radiator emitted several clouds of steam as the bullets ripped into it. The windshield shattered as well, but it was unclear if the driver was hit or not. He could have ducked below the dashboard purposefully driving blind until they passed the Jeep.

The M-35 truck was picking up speed as it crossed in front of them, so it was a good bet that the driver had survived. Worse yet, terrorists in the back of the deuce and half started shooting. Two rounds hit just above the knee of one of Norton's soldiers and his right leg was blasted from his body as he toppled over the side. Norton spared a split-second to glance back at his injured man while the other soldier continued to return fire with the machine gun. The rounds ripped through the truck's metal sides and canvas covering. The pattern of bullet holes was tight enough that the terrorists in back had probably all been hit. Only the dense C-4 itself could have stopped any of the M-60 rounds from killing them all.

The truck turned right and was clearly headed for the fuel depot at the far end of the camp. Norton got on the radio and informed anyone listening that there were two M-35 trucks loose in the compound being driven by enemy forces. He announced his location just behind the truck that was headed for the fuel depot. He warned that the other truck must have a different target, probably the ammunition storage warehouse, and to make sure as hell it was stopped before it got there.

8

***

Now the entire compound was awake and moving quickly. The facility was more or less a half mile square and the majority of the buildings were only one story. From most vantage points in the camp the two M-35 trucks could be seen racing to their explosive destinations with American forces in hot pursuit. The good news was that their heaviest armament was already positioned in front of the fuel depot and the ammunition warehouse. The compound was designed to defend against this scenario though no one expected it to ever happen on an American base inside of Israel's borders.

Hakim was doing his best to keep the truck moving toward their goal. He could see the fuel depot's storage tanks directly ahead. He floored the accelerator, kept his head as low as he could and shouted to the soldiers in the back that they were almost to the target. In an exalted prayer he yelled, *"Allahu Akbar!"*

Indeed those were his last words.

***

The two men on guard duty at the fuel depot could already see the fast-approaching M-35 truck. They were stunned, realizing that this was not a drill. Their training took over as they armed and aimed two LAW-72 rockets at the approaching vehicle. They had heard the trucks were carrying C-4. They also knew that the LAW rockets had enough incendiary force that the C-4 would ignite upon impact. Still, that would be nothing compared to the explosion that would occur if the terrorists reached their intended goal. They fired on the truck the moment they confirmed their range to the target.

Both rockets left a trail of smoke from the M-72 launchers all the way to the approaching deuce and half. The resulting explosion knocked everyone to the ground within 100 yards. A few seconds later it happened again, but this time hell was unleashed from the other side of the base. It seemed the soldiers protecting the ammunition warehouse had also hit the bull's eye. Moments passed with the phantom ringing in everyone's ears as the only sound they heard.

The hush lasted about five seconds until the entire compound realized they had successfully stopped the attack. A cheer started at one end of the camp and spread to the other as the soldiers shouted their relief at having repelled this assault. They had no idea that hijacking the trucks had turned into a ruse to distract the Americans from the real danger. With 150 heavily armed soldiers of Mohammed's Faithful running quickly to surround the compound, the real assault was about to begin.

***

Mansur had chosen well to select Amon and Abel as the snipers who would take out the guards at the gate if needed. The primary plan had a reasonable chance of succeeding, but the Colonel considered all contingencies when preparing for battle. His past experience had taught him that, so he was not surprised when only the hijacking went according to plan.

The Americans would never know just how much preparation went into this mission. It started with Mansur knowing when to intercept the trucks. They would have perhaps three hours to organize once word was received of the early morning special delivery. To learn when an early morning shipment was scheduled, Mansur had planted an operative in the poker room of the casino to keep an eye on Wiley. It took more than a month to identify him as a regular driver for the target camp as well as his weakness for gambling on cards. The operative was able to immediately notify Mansur that Wiley had a pre-dawn run to make. They confirmed from other sources that the cargo would be high explosives like C-4 or even Semtex. There was only one route from Wiley's military base to the remote supply compound. All that covert preparation had been just the beginning.

Another challenge was how to get the drivers to stop the trucks without damaging them. Mansur's plan was pure genius it was so simple. They would smooth the tire ruts from the road with just a couple of shovels and rakes. He knew that even at a distance and at night a good driver would spot such a contrasting difference in the dirt road. They would become cautious in case landmines or tire spikes had been concealed there.

The truth was that if the infidel soldiers had ignored the graded section in the road and kept driving, the hijacking would have turned into a chase. That would have ruined the advantage of surprise because the Americans could radio ahead to the compound. Had that happened, they would have settled for the capture of the trucks' cargo. But the driver had spotted the graded section of road and stopped as they had hoped. Mansur's careful planning assured no one had time to send a radio message to the base. Just as important was that the trucks and their load were in perfect condition.

From there, everything fell apart. The guards at the front gate figured out something was wrong and called for reinforcements. The trucks did not easily clear the concrete barriers at the main gate, which forced them to engage in a bloody firefight all the way to their targets. And then to be within sight of their respective goals only to be abruptly cut down was tragic but not unexpected. Once the hijackers' mission had gone awry, Colonel Mansur's plan shifted to take advantage of the confusion. In fact, now he was counting on it.

***

The LAW-72 rockets fired from the fuel depot ignited the C-4 cargo causing a tremendous shockwave and fireball. The Jeep, Captain Norton and the soldier firing the M-60 machine gun were blown backward by the fiery explosion just ahead of them. Norton looked around and saw that his man had been crushed underneath the vehicle. Norton was thrown clear, but he was badly burned and he could see the jagged ends of his left shin bone sticking through his calf muscle.

Rob Norton got his hopes up for a brief moment when his fellow soldiers started cheering. He too thought they had successfully stopped the attack. But from the bonfire of the C-4 explosion, he could see that enemy combatants were lining up around the security fence of the camp. He tried to yell out a warning but he couldn't make himself heard.

Rob recognized the finality of these last moments. He would not be going home to his wife and baby boy. All the plans he had made for when this tour was over were about to end. He felt shamefully responsible for failing to repel this attack. Now, neither he nor his brave soldiers would be going home to their families.

Heavy machine gun fire and mortar rounds started exploding throughout the compound. The Americans quickly understood this battle was not over. The enemy had them surrounded and caught with their pants down. Norton watched in helpless anger as a mortar round finished what the hijacked M-35 truck had started, the annihilation of the fuel storage tanks. The tremendous explosion was echoed moments later when he saw and heard the ammunition warehouse being destroyed in the distance.

All Norton could do was pray, but he knew it was too late. He couldn't help but think, "Why? What possible motive could these terrorists have for targeting this remote location inside Israel's borders?" Through his agony, he also realized that this could signal the beginning of a war. The U.S. would not take this unprovoked attack lightly.

All those thoughts ceased abruptly when he saw the machine gun's tracer rounds headed his way. One of the bullets savagely ripped through his right side and he knew the end had come. He would bleed out in seconds if nothing else happened to kill him sooner. He tried to picture his wife and son as consciousness faded. His last words were barely audible as he whispered, "I'm so sorry..."

***

Colonel Mansur's personal goal was to destroy the fuel depot and ammunition warehouse with a minimum of casualties to his own troops. Although Hakim's and Basir's men were willing to die to strike this tremendous blow against the American infidels, the primary plan had been for those men to survive.

There was flat desert for 500 meters surrounding the camp that was under constant, automated surveillance. If they attacked by force, his 150 men would be easily detected and wiped out before they could breach the perimeter. Mansur decided the better way to destroy the two targets was by stealth of a few men while using his other troops and firepower to provide cover for their escape. However, the moment the trucks met trouble at the gate, Mansur knew those brave men were finished.

His backup plan was a direct assault on the entire compound using the diversion of the two M-35s to surround it unnoticed. Once his troops had safely reached the security fence, Mansur's men more than completed the mission with brutal and overwhelming firepower. There was nothing left standing inside the compound when Mohammed's Faithful received the signal to cease fire.

The trickiest part of the mission was still ahead of them. That was to move his soldiers and equipment out of harm's way in less than 30 minutes. Months before, a clean escape out of Israel seemed impossible. But Mansur devised a way to pull it off and perhaps make further missions into Israel equally promising.

Their quickest exit from Israel would be the Jordanian border, about seven miles to the east of the supply depot's location. The faster they left Israel, the more likely that re-tasking U.S. satellites and deploying Israeli troops to search for them would fail. An impressive tunnel network had been secretly excavated underneath the Israel/Jordan border over a period of months. The area was uninhabited because it was nothing but sand, dirt and rock. The underground facility Mansur built was large enough to hide his soldiers and their complement of equipment, although they were limited to using Jeeps and trailers that would fit in the tunnels.

Twenty minutes after their attack on the compound was over, the first vehicles quietly disappeared into the tunnels leading to the Jordanian border. What was left of the original 150 soldiers would stay hidden underground for a few days before returning to civilization on foot in small groups. Their departures would be spread out over time and different exit routes would be used to avoid being of notice. All the equipment and ordinance would remain hidden underground, hopefully ready for the next mission.

Chapter 2

Matthew Alexander fumbled over the objects on his nightstand with confused annoyance. He was only three hours into what he had hoped would be a full night's sleep. As his mind struggled for consciousness, he mistook the second ring of the phone for an alarm clock. By the third ring he had it figured out. He put the handset to his ear and mumbled, "This had better be good!"

"Mr. President?" the nervous voice began. "Mr. President, I am told that you will want to attend a briefing at the White House."

"You've got to be kidding," Matt complained immediately. "We just got to Camp David."

"Mr. President, there's been an unprovoked attack on an American supply base in Israel," the voice continued. "The National Security Council members are gathering to meet you in the Situation Room as soon as you can join them. Marine One is standing by."

Now Matt was wide awake. "Was this another biological attack?"

"I don't think so, Mr. President. There were few survivors to infect. That's everything I know for sure. Can I tell the White House staff when to expect you?"

Matt hesitated and then asked, "Is Erin, I mean the First Lady, awake yet?"

"I'm not certain, Mr. President. Do you want her notified of the situation?"

"No! Don't tell her what happened, just wake her and give her the option of coming back to the White House if she chooses. I'll be ready to go in fifteen minutes." And with that, Matt hung up and headed for the shower.

***

Erin Alexander and Murray were already waiting on board Marine One when Matt climbed the steps into the helicopter. Erin was scratching Murray's ears and he wagged his tail seeing Matt walk in. He was amazed that she still looked beautiful and put together with so little notice that they had to leave. When he wasn't summoned out of a deep sleep in the middle of the night, Matt was handsome enough to be an older male model. He was sure he looked awful, but his focus was on the attack in Israel. Thank God there were no reporters or photographers around to make matters worse.

An aide checked to make sure POTUS (the President of the United States) and FLOTUS (the First Lady) were secured in their seats. Murray also allowed himself to be buckled in with a dignified turn of his head. The aide then signaled to the pilot they were ready to go.

As Marine One lifted off and veered toward the White House, Erin asked, "What is it this time? It had to be bad if they interrupted your vacation plans in the middle of the night."

Matt didn't answer her. He was lost in his own thoughts of how to react to this latest assault. He still didn't know the details, but at least it wasn't another biological strike. Matt wondered if it was a good or bad sign that these escalating attacks had a sudden change in tactics.

Erin asked again in a louder voice, "Matt, can you tell me what's going on?"

Matt couldn't ignore her any longer. "I really can't. I don't know much and I don't know if I can share anything as yet. I'm headed for a briefing with the NSC. I'll know what I can tell you after that."

Erin knew this conversation had ended. She was hardly surprised that he would hesitate to fill her in on what was happening. She typically learned more roaming the halls of the White House and overhearing the staff's casual conversations than she ever got directly from her husband. "How the hell did we ever wind up like this?" Erin wondered to herself. They used to be best friends and closest confidants. Keeping the First Lady in or out of the information loop was any President's prerogative because there were no official rules on the issue. Matt had clearly made his choice.

She still loved this man but she no longer felt like he was her friend. They used to have so much in common but they'd grown apart as he ascended to his position as the most powerful political leader in the free world. She remembered his charming sense of humor and playful attitude from their early years together. Erin realized that in a very real sense Matt was cheating on her. Not with another woman but with the voters and the media. Erin knew the only occasions when he seemed like his old self were when other people were in the room.

They used to share everything together but that had eroded with each election Matt won and every new state secret he learned. In one sense, she was glad about that. Erin stayed out of politics because she had little patience for making back room deals and voting against one's conscience. Her husband was a masterful politician but what had that cost them as a family? Whenever she made mention of the growing distance, Matt changed the subject or didn't respond at all.

Still, Ronald Reagan was the only divorced U.S. President and his divorce was final long before he took office. Erin had already decided she would make the most of it and continue in her role as a good First Lady. She really wanted what was best for Matt and the country. If she had to put her own happiness on hold for three more years, or even a second term, then so be it. Erin consoled herself with the fact that being the First Lady allowed her to have a greater impact on the people and projects that were important to her.

A short time later, Marine One touched down on the south lawn of the White House. Murray ran on ahead knowing a dog treat would be waiting inside. Matt and Erin also exited the helicopter and, as usual, went their separate ways.

***

The pressure felt by everyone in the Situation Room of the White House was intense. Over the past year, American forces had suffered several escalating attacks including two with biological outbreaks persisting after the skirmishes. As with the prior terrorist strikes, there was sparse evidence found to link a militant group or government to the attack in Israel. The major loss of life combined

16

with the previous use of biochemical weapons could not be allowed to go unanswered. If the U.S. response to these attacks was not handled properly, it could mean all-out war in the Middle East.

The only face missing from the members on the NSC committee was the Director of National Drug Control Policy, Gil Kowalski. He was in South America at the moment and not typically involved in military matters unless illegal drugs were involved. General Martin McComb, Chairman of the Joint Chiefs of Staff (JCOS), was concluding his initial briefing on the horrific massacre in Israel.

The General added, "I hate to admit it, but they've crossed a line this time I never thought they would. I can't imagine what these terrorists believe warranted the annihilation of our supply depot, especially one located inside Israel's borders. I recommend that our response be unmistakably strong to discourage any such future actions against us."

Secretary of Defense Steve Lombard offered a different point of view. "Would a strong response bring them back to reality or perhaps escalate matters? I agree that we can't be seen as indecisive or hesitant in dealing with these continued acts of aggression. However, what can we do now that won't be used as cause to make matters worse?"

The room settled into an uneasy silence. Matthew Alexander looked up to see everyone staring at him waiting to hear his thoughts. He suddenly felt dizzy and began to notice an unusual glow around Steve Lombard. It somehow sparked a daydream of his earlier self. A younger Matt would have considered ways to respond peacefully without appearing weak. He once believed that all conflict could be resolved without violence. That perspective, he knew now, was naïve. A few decades in national politics would harden anyone and you couldn't become President of the United States by being naive.

Matt's Chief of Staff, Michael Simons, broke the silence hoping to give his boss more time to consider his options. As Michael calmly recapped where things stood at the moment, Matt was doing his best to focus. He saw the same strange luminescence surrounding Michael that had enveloped Steve Lombard just a minute before. The radiance shifted and it appeared as if there was a figure of a man standing just behind Michael in the strange light.

Matt forced his attention back on the meeting. He was embarrassed that he had allowed his thoughts to wander at this most critical time. Once he refocused on the other people in the room, he found that the luminescence had vanished with the feelings of dizziness. He mentally reviewed his position on the Middle East considering this latest attack.

He felt he could no longer trust several of the Muslim politicians in the Middle East to keep their extreme factions in check. He knew that some Muslim leaders were good and honorable men. The problem was that the altruistic thinkers among them were few in number and certainly not in control of their governments or people. Matt concluded he had exhausted all reasonable options to achieve peace without violence. Perhaps it was time to take off the gloves and show the terrorists what they were really up against.

President Alexander decided it was time for decisive action. He did not mince words as he set the course for their next steps. "I am leaning toward a response that sends a stronger message than they might expect. We have endured an increasing number of terrorist attacks against our people and allies over the past year. The two biological outbreaks were quickly contained, but by any definition they constitute the use of WMDs. While the governments of these countries have declared they want peace, they seem to turn a blind eye to the terrorist factions among their people who continue to attack civilian and military targets. Allowing these groups to organize and train within their borders must be defined as an act of complicity and aggression against America. The action we'll take, once we can confirm who is responsible, should put any government that aids these terrorists on notice that it stops now! So I'm ready to hear what you people think will best send that message."

Secretary of State Joan Hartley was the first to voice her thoughts. "If you're serious about sending a strong message to any government complicit in these attacks, then our response cannot be limited to a surgical strike against the terrorists who annihilated the supply depot. Chances are the people who actually did this have gone in a hundred different directions by now. They know their best defense against our retaliation is to disperse and disappear."

The President thought for a moment before asking, "What do we know of the terrorists' escape? Have we been able to track them? That would certainly help identify our options for a proper response."

General McComb was waiting for this question but he didn't relish answering it. "The moment we received word of the attack, we scrambled our jets. We also re-tasked the satellites covering that area to detect any movement of personnel in the vicinity. The Israelis deployed ground troops but were unable to pick up the trail. Our best guess is that they are still in hiding within a ten-mile radius of ground zero and doing a damn good job of it. We don't believe they could have moved outside of that radius in the time allowed."

Matt looked to George Salazar, Director of the CIA, for his opinion. George nervously cleared his throat knowing he had nothing. "We have few operatives in northern Israel who aren't specifically focused on Syria, Lebanon or various terrorist cells. While many groups have already claimed responsibility for this attack, it seems likely that only someone with the resources of a government or a larger militant group like Hezbollah could have pulled this one off. As usual, the terrorists who didn't do it are the ones who claim the credit. We're working quickly to get a better grip on this. Since our fly-bys and satellites have been unable to track the retreat of the attackers, we are sending investigators to the scene in search of forensic evidence to determine where they went. A heavy storm that already moved through the area has made that search much tougher."

Steve Lombard interjected with a question for the President. "I am certain we will figure out who is behind this. We may be able to tie them to the biological attacks as well, but just how strong a response are you proposing once we identify those involved?"

The room stilled. Matt knew his next words could be the most important of his life. His younger self would have prayed fervently for the answer but he now felt that politics had little to do with God. He had even begun to doubt if God existed in the first place. But that wasn't the question before him. Everyone in the room wanted to know the magnitude of the United States' response.

"Let me be clear," said the President. "They started escalating this conflict by resorting to massive deadly force as well as using WMDs. Therefore, there is nothing in our arsenal that is off the table."

There was no misinterpreting that statement. If Matt didn't have their full attention before, he had it now. "We need to know who is accountable for all the recent terrorist acts. We need to learn where their training bases are as well as the names of their leaders and where they meet. We also need to know where the funding and logistical support for these terrorist activities is coming from. I have no doubt that part of the investigation will lead to militant factions in the Muslim world. But it is time to establish what links exist between the sovereign governments of the Middle Eastern countries and the abominable groups who commit such monstrous acts. If it turns out that one or more of these governments are using these militant groups as their henchmen to hide their involvement, God help them!"

The President stood indicating the meeting was over. The room quickly erupted into side conversations discussing and arguing the implications of what he had just said. Matt knew it was better to let them all chew on it for a while before they regrouped.

He had taken just a few steps when he began to feel dizzy again. He shook it off and kept walking through the door of the Situation Room. He realized that Michael Simons had asked him something but he had not heard the question. Matt couldn't ignore the mounting ache in his left arm coupled with the sensation of a tightening band around his chest. The pain became more intense as he recognized the serious nature of his symptoms.

He turned and said, "Mike, I think you'd better get me to a doctor, now!" Matt managed to sit down in a nearby chair before he slumped forward and fell unconscious to the floor.

Chapter 3

Matthew Alexander was aware he was neither asleep nor awake. He searched his memory for a word until it came to him. He was in the 'hypnagogic' state. He laughed to himself for recalling that word from his college days. He tried to remember where he was supposed to be. How long had he been like this? Why hadn't his assistant prompted him to get ready for his next meeting? And then he remembered the chest pains and collapsing in the chair.

When he opened his eyes, Matt found he was back in the Situation Room, but it was not the same. He vaguely remembered seeing that odd luminescence surrounding his Chief of Staff and Secretary of Defense as they spoke. The entire room now had that same incredible glow.

"Hello! Can anyone hear me?" Matt called out in confusion.

There was no response. In fact, Matt couldn't hear anything. He was surprised at the absence of any sound coming from the overhead lights and wall-mounted video monitors that surrounded him. Matt tried again, "Is anyone here?"

A voice responded but it seemed to come from inside his mind rather than from an outside source. "Of course. I have not left your side since you collapsed."

Matt spun around trying to locate the person talking to him. He hesitated when he realized his instantaneous 360-degree turn to scan the room should have been physically impossible. Out of frustration he yelled, "Where are you?"

The voice responded, "I am right here with you. Just focus on my words and you will begin to see."

Matt vaguely remembered hearing this voice before. Then something very bright started moving in his peripheral vision. He tried to track the motion but whatever it was moved so quickly he couldn't follow it. In frustration he cried out, "Can you hold still? How can I see you if you keep avoiding me?"

The clear voice, mellowed with humor, chimed, "Now that's an interesting perspective! If you can accept for a moment that it is you who has been avoiding me, you will begin to understand the truth of why you are here."

Matt tried to make sense of the words. He closed his eyes and willed himself to calm down. When he opened them again, the details of the room faded while the strange luminescence formed into a familiar person standing directly in front of him.

The voice was now coming from the man. "Nicely done! It's been a while since you have been able to focus this well. It is good that you have for we have much to discuss."

Matt impatiently asked, "Who are you? Where am I? And what are you talking about?"

Then he suddenly recognized the man. Though the voice was different, the face he saw was his own.

The man replied, "You can call me Amelius. You agreed to this meeting and the agenda long ago. As to where you are, that's a tricky question from a human perspective. Your body is being cared for by three exceptional doctors, and they will see you recover remarkably. Your mind is anywhere you want it to be. Right now, you have chosen to be here with me."

Matt hesitated, trying to take it all in. He couldn't think of anything else, so he asked, "Why do you look like me?"

Amelius answered, "How I appear to you is a combination of both our preferences. Seeing me as yourself is meant to help you relax and have more trust in what I have to say."

"And you say I agreed to this meeting?" Matt asked.

"Yes. Even before you were born we both saw the certainty of this critical juncture once you became the President. You knew you would need encouragement to stay the course and achieve a most extraordinary goal."

"I've already seen and agreed to all these things?" Matt asked, vaguely feeling in his gut it was true. "You make it sound like I was predestined to be President and yet I had some choice in the matter."

22

"Indeed you did!" said Amelius. "You were chosen by many and you agreed to accept this pivotal role in earth's history, or future, depending on how you look at it. That does not mean predestiny ever trumps your free will. Nothing is stronger than free will."

"And so what is it that I already agreed to do?" Matt pressed again.

Amelius smiled and said, "You are in a unique position to channel the best and worst of humanity into a wonderful outcome. You have the desire and ability to make choices where everyone wins instead of trying to take advantage of others' weaknesses and that can change the course of humankind."

Matt was unconvinced. "Exactly what choices are you talking about?"

Suddenly the space around them changed as Matt began to receive his answer. It didn't come in words. He felt like he was living inside of an epic movie as he witnessed the various responses, one after the other, that the United States might choose in retaliation to the recent terrorist attacks. He was shown how each of these scenarios would play out, from the historic changes down to the forgettable differences his choices would bring. A feeling of profound sadness overwhelmed him as the scenes before him slowed and then stopped.

Matt asked, "How am I supposed to know which of those is the right response? Some scenarios lead directly to a world war while others inevitably bring terrible suffering that would likely result in a world war anyway. What difference does it make which way I choose?"

Amelius answered gently, "Indeed those are your choices as things stand at this moment. But you stopped before seeing all of the possibilities. There are opportunities still available to you if you can persevere in patience despite all that may seem to go wrong along the way."

"Show me!" said Matt.

The holographic scenes resumed where they had left off. This time Matt saw that happier outcomes were possible, although unlikely. Regardless of which direction he chose, he saw how difficult it would be to stick with the decisions he would have to make in order to succeed. If he failed, he could just as easily cause a world war instead of prevent one.

"And what if I can't do this?" Matt asked. "You can see that it will create a disastrous conflict with three members of the National Security Council if I change directions now. I have already told them I want to deliver a stronger response than even they expect."

Amelius laughed, "You spoke the truth, but the convincing strength of your response will come from within you rather than from any military aggression. Be not afraid of this. I am with you every step of the way."

"I saw that the scenarios with happier results require a profound commitment from my wife Erin. Why does she have to play a role in all this? You must already know that I keep the challenges in our relationship separate from the challenges I face in running the country."

Amelius answered softly but firmly, "This is very important for you to understand. Repairing your relationship with Erin is as a microcosm of the enormous global task before you. At a later time, another like me will help and guide you in your relationship with Erin."

Despite everything Amelius had just shown him, Matt feared that healing his relationship with Erin was less likely than achieving world peace. His mind was spinning with all he had just experienced. He barely noticed the random shifting of his thoughts as he drifted back into a deep sleep.

***

The next time he opened his eyes he saw Erin. She stood next to his bed frantically gesturing to the doctors that he was awake. He reached for her hand but realized his whole body was weighed down with wires and tubes. He tried to say something to her, but his voice failed him. He coughed and that caught her attention.

"Well, I guess your heart has made you stronger!" she said.

Matt managed to whisper, "What?"

"Isn't that what they say? That which doesn't kill you makes you stronger? The doctors said your heart was beating erratically for three or four minutes."

He mumbled, "So I'm okay now?"

Erin couldn't hold back a guarded laugh. "They say there is no damage to the heart muscle and all your vital signs are good. It was a moving blood clot rather than a full blockage in the arteries that started the episode, but you seem to be out of danger for now. The question of permanent damage is still up in the air because the doctors couldn't tell if your brain was deprived of oxygen. How do you feel?"

Matt finally understood his situation and simply replied, "Tired."

"Well, you've been in bed for the past twenty-four hours when they weren't removing the blood clot or running tests. Still, I'll bet you are tired after all you've been through."

Matt nodded off again remembering the bizarre dream that started with his heart attack. He foggily recalled an extensive briefing with detailed video for each response scenario. Some of it had to do with the recent violence in Israel. Some of it concerned his marriage to Erin. He understood that every bit of the dream was important but, for the life of him, he wasn't sure why.

As Matt went back to sleep, Erin sat down again with the book she'd been reading. She took a moment to thank God for bringing her husband back from the brink of death. She prayed that he would make a full recovery while secretly wondering if that would be in the best interests of the nation and the world.

Over the years, their political views had drifted in different directions. They had started out together with closely aligned perspectives on most everything. They wanted to share their vision of an even greater America with the world. Erin watched as Matt's political career skyrocketed by winning election after election. Outwardly, he seemed happy and ever more the personification of 'the people's choice.' Inwardly, she saw him change from being an altruistic visionary to a cynical pragmatist. She watched as he increasingly traded his vote for agendas he didn't support in order to secure the backing he needed to advance his political agenda and office. And as he pulled away from her politically, she could see that their relationship was coming apart as well.

For a couple of years now, their marriage had existed as just another political convenience. They 'lived in separate rooms' in every sense of the phrase. She was determined not to divorce him while he was active in politics, but their marriage had become a dull shadow of the love and friendship they once felt for each other. Erin had tried to tell Matt he had lost his way by allowing his ambition to become President to justify the means he used to get there. He had snapped back that she simply did not understand. His goal in making all these 'deals with the devil' was to put him in a position where he was beyond anyone's grasp. Once he was elected President, he'd never again agree to anything he didn't truly support.

Erin had tested that promise the day after Matt's inauguration. She overheard him speaking on the phone to a senior Representative from California in an effort to get his proposed legislation passed through Congress. It was the same old story; they promised support for each other's bills even though neither of them believed in the worthiness of the other's legislation. When Erin reminded Matt that he could and should stop compromising his beliefs now that he was President, he told her to "stay out of it." And so she had remained distant in body, mind and soul until the heart attack forced her to step up and be a supportive wife in his time of need.

***

As Erin remained at Matt's bedside in the ICU, his dreamlike memories of his time with Amelius became clear again. One of the important scenes Matt witnessed was intended to remind him of the love he and Erin shared. He reminisced about the first time they spoke to each other after being paired up on a college science project.

"So are you conservative or liberal?" he asked with a broad smile.

"I'm neither. My name is Erin," she replied coldly.

Matt realized he was so intent on impressing this beautiful woman with his political savvy that he had completely forgotten to introduce himself. He tried to think of something that would help

26

him recover from his botched first impression. The painful silence between them turned to embarrassment.

He began to stutter, "I, I, I was hoping to start over with a witty comeback, but I've got nothing. You're obviously better at this so help a guy out. Is there any chance I can still impress you?"

"What's in it for me? I think it's much more fun to watch you squirm," Erin shot back, appreciating his discomfort and starting to enjoy the exchange.

"Matt Alexander," he said wryly as he offered her his hand.

She took it gracefully and answered, "I know who you are. You've done an annoying yet very effective job of plastering your name and face on every bulletin board across campus. Clearly either politics or marketing is in your future."

"So, can I count on your vote?" he asked with a grin, trying to change the subject over to his comfort zone.

"Seriously? I vote that we stay focused on this class and getting an 'A' on this project." Erin was warming to Matt's charm, but she refused to show it.

He quipped, "So you're a bright lady who never got a 'B' in her life? Lucky me! But what if I'd rather have your vote than an 'A'?"

Erin visibly softened and said, "If you continue to show up, I'll make sure our team gets an 'A.' And just so you know, I don't believe politicians have the answers we need to make a better world."

Hoping he still had a chance with her, Matt asked, "Do you drink coffee, Erin?"

***

Matt suddenly flashed forward to the ICU room to see Erin still waiting at his side. He found himself floating in the upper corner of the room and realized he was out of his body. He felt great despite his brush with death. Looking down, he remembered saying he was tired before he closed his eyes to sleep.

He was surprised to find he could clearly read Erin's thoughts as if they were his own. She was reminiscing about the

27

more notable moments of their relationship. Erin remembered how happy they were when they first met in college. Matt winced at the flood of sad emotions that followed her next thoughts. She was regretfully thinking how different her life could have been had she declined that fated cup of coffee.

Chapter 4

President Alexander walked into the Situation Room some nine days after his not-so-graceful exit. The members of the NSC all stood to applaud his return. Matt humbly took his seat visibly touched by the sincerity of their reception. He gratefully thanked them and asked them to be seated. "Thank you all for your concern, patience and support over these recent days! Now what have we learned since our last meeting?" he asked with reassuring strength.

CIA Director George Salazar was first up in the briefing. "We sent in ground investigators to collect any forensic evidence that would prove who was behind the attack in Israel. There has been nothing definitive as yet mainly because there has been so much evidence to evaluate. Most of the equipment and weapons used by the terrorists originally came from the United States. It's not unusual for American made weapons to be used against us. However, weapons manufactured in Russia, China and France were also part of the forensic arsenal gathered in trying to prove who was behind the assault.

"We had better luck locating where the attackers had gone after they razed the supply depot. With the help of the Israelis, finding the trail the terrorists took heading east was not difficult. However, the storm that passed through the area within hours of the attack made it almost impossible to determine their final destination." Salazar added, "By now the terrorist troops have likely disbursed and gone to their homes rather than staying together as a military unit."

Secretary of Defense Steve Lombard stepped in to cover Salazar's disappointing lack of progress. "We have satellite intel of increased civilian travelers just over the Jordanian border in the general vicinity of where we think they went. We believe most if not all of the people moving about the area over the past week are mostly made up of the terrorists who attacked the compound. The movement of these pedestrians was meant to appear as if it was random but we have narrowed our search grid because of this unusual foot traffic. A careful evaluation of this area should soon yield results. We are hampered by the likelihood that they were all

29

temporarily sequestered in an underground facility located inside Jordan's border. Knowing now to search for a hideout below ground, it shouldn't be long before we find the entrance tunnels, hopefully on the Israeli side of the border."

President Alexander suggested that diplomatic channels should be used to contact the Jordanian government. They would need permission to conduct a search for the terrorists within Jordan's sectors of the grid once they had proof of their presence. Then he looked at Secretary of State Joan Hartley, and asked, "What is the mood and feeling of the major powers in the Middle East? What do they expect us to do?"

Joan replied, "Your recent health challenges have made everyone nervous. Apparently there were leaks that all options are on the table in responding to these attacks once the culprits and targets are identified. No one wants to make a war out of this but there are many who think violence against our posts in the Middle East will not end until they understand America will no longer tolerate these attacks. Vice President Jefferson calmed the waters while you were in recovery but now the world is waiting to hear directly from you."

Matt went on record, "Eric, I want to thank you for the outstanding job you've done over these past days. I can't imagine where we'd be now if you had not kept such a steady hand on things while I was getting back on my feet." The Vice President blushed a bit at the praise and nodded his acceptance. Matt continued, "This may sound odd, but in some ways the timing of my episode could not have been better. It gave me and the government leaders involved a chance to let our fears fade and tempers cool. I'm almost relieved to learn that my willingness to leave all options open regarding our retaliation was leaked. No doubt hearing that raised the stakes but it also has everyone thinking this has gone too far. So now, General McComb, what do you suggest we do in response?"

The JCOS Chairman instantly felt the weight of the world on his shoulders. "Our best guess from what we know now is that an extremist group of trained terrorists known as Mohammed's Faithful was responsible for this heinous attack. Despite the probable underground bunker that made possible the terrorists' escape, we don't believe the Jordanian government was involved. The area in question is fairly close to the Syrian and Lebanese borders. So it is

30

possible either of their governments could have been helping Mohammed's Faithful in the attack and to escape undetected. We have yet to conclusively prove any of this, but if we need a 'best guess scenario' to bounce around, a partnership between Syria and a militant faction of between 100 to 250 soldiers is a reasonable start."

Matt asked, "Are there any other governments besides Syria, Lebanon or Jordan who could have been involved in this?"

McComb answered, "That's still hard to say. We haven't been able to rule any of them out but the one with the most to gain and least to lose over this seems to be Syria so far."

"Is there a name for the region where our supply depot was situated? I've seen its location on the briefing maps, but what's the nearest city or landmark that a tourist would recognize?" Matt said looking at the video monitor with a map of the region.

McComb hesitated but then answered, "As you can see, there are no nearby cities or towns. We purposefully choose our supply locations to remain out of the spotlight while still being accessible by air and ground. The compound itself was on the east end of Israel's infamous Jezreel Valley."

Matt had to ask, "Why do you say infamous? I've been to Israel a few times and I don't remember much being said about the Jezreel Valley."

General Martin McComb took off his glasses and wiped them as he tried to look casual. "The Jezreel Valley's modern name is neither well-known nor infamous, really. However, in biblical times it was called Armageddon."

The people in the room collectively held their breath. The history of that name and place was known to all. President Alexander attempted to break the tension by saying, "Then let's see what we can do to make the best of what happened in the Jezreel Valley rather than using it as an excuse to fulfill an ancient doomsday prophecy!"

There was an excited reaction to Matt's revised directive. They were largely relieved that WMDs weren't automatically included in the response scenario. There were also a few in the room who were not pleased with this development. They were tired of terrorists and fanatics taking advantage of the United

States' endless forgiveness born of a desire for peace. They believed that "peace was possible through force" if key groups were eliminated leaving only the right people in charge of the Holy Land.

***

Today had been one of the most frustrating days General McComb could remember. He thought the President was about to give the green light to shut down terrorism once and for all in the Middle East. He couldn't understand what changed his mind. He had no idea why the President was wavering, but McComb knew in his heart the country couldn't afford to let this perfect opportunity pass.

He poured a tall drink of single-malt scotch and sat back in his oversized easy chair to assess the situation. McComb knew that Director of National Intelligence Rick Newman agreed the time to strike was now. By the look on CIA Director George Salazar's face at today's meeting, he was probably the angriest guy in the room when POTUS set a new direction for their response strategy. McComb decided he would arrange to meet with Newman and Salazar. He was sure that together they could steer things back in the right direction. McComb drifted off to sleep reviewing their options.

As his subconscious mind took over, he was soon dreaming. Martin first sensed he was weightless and then he took off like a rocket. He looked around and couldn't make sense of his surroundings. He felt like a bubble floating up from the bottom of the ocean but he wasn't wet despite the sensation of rushing water. He then catapulted out of the stream landing abruptly without feeling the impact.

Martin found himself in a nondescript room with three other people. He recognized two of the men, Rick Newman and George Salazar, but the third man was unknown to him. There was an intense glow to the man's presence that made him appear to be dressed completely in white.

The unknown man was the first to speak, "Welcome! My name is Halaliel. The important events of today have brought us together to discuss the critical choices before you."

George Salazar responded, "You said your name is 'Ha lay lee al? Uh, okay. And what do you know about today's events?"

McComb and Newman were just as confused as Salazar.

Halaliel smiled and said, "My name is as unique as it is ancient. As to what I know about the President's NSC meeting, well, there's very little I don't know."

All three mumbled their objections, but Halaliel held up his hand and added such an authoritative look that they all fell silent. "You three are in the dream state together and this place is apart from the earthly realm you call home. Your minds often travel away from your body while sleeping but you rarely remember what occurs. That's because your conscious mind can't remember what it doesn't understand. Instead, you often wake remembering what happened as if it were just a dream. While correctly interpreting dreams can reveal the guidance contained in the symbolism, those messages are easily ignored in the waking state."

Salazar couldn't help but ask, "If we won't remember what you're about to say, why are we here?"

Halaliel smiled and said, "I personally feel this meeting will change nothing. Allowing your conscious mind to be directed by the subconscious requires a willingness to listen to your inner guidance. The three of you, in your waking state, are so threatened by your perceived enemies that you quit listening to the unobtrusive voice of your subconscious long ago. However, in the surprising event that you take my advice to heart, it will save you and the world much suffering.

You already know that the President is about to reveal an extraordinary response to the attacks against your country. I suggest you three support it to the best of your abilities."

Newman and McComb asked the same question, "What, exactly, is he planning to do?"

"The details are not yet defined because much is still undecided by your President. However, it will not be the aggressive response you had hoped for," Halaliel confided.

Salazar angrily said, "And so you are suggesting we stand by and let these terrorists do anything they want to us when we can so easily wipe them off the face of the earth? What kind of message will that response send?"

"That violence only returns violence and so it must cease. How that cycle is broken depends a great deal on the three of you," he warned with a bit of a challenge in his tone.

They listened as Halaliel explained the possible choices and outcomes they would soon face. When they awoke the next morning, each man vaguely remembered having disturbing dreams. No matter, with the morning's first cup of coffee and a look at the headlines, the dreams were soon forgotten.

Chapter 5

Special Agent Ross was in charge of the team of CIA operatives tasked to track the terrorist soldiers' escape. It was nighttime and progress had been painfully slow because of the storm that moved through the area shortly after the strike. Even though surveillance planes and a satellite search had begun within thirty minutes of the attack, the terrorists' exit plans remained a mystery. That was why the CIA agents were spending most of their time at the Israel/Jordan border nearest the supply depot's location. It was the most likely exit point from Israel given that they had so little time to disappear. It simply would have been impossible for the terrorists to have made it to the border of Syria or Lebanon without being seen in the time it would have taken them to get that far.

Two hundred miles above the earth, a KH "Keyhole" imaging satellite relayed pictures to Ross and his team via the National Reconnaissance Office - NRO - headquartered in Chantilly, Virginia. This particular satellite had been in orbit for thirty years but could still identify objects as small as five square inches at ground level. There was also cutting edge technology assisting in the search. A highly classified satellite telescope developed by Boeing had been tasked to relay images from beneath ground level.

This process requires a helicopter with a shielded X-ray generator installed between its landing struts. It uses technology similar to "painting" a target with a local laser to accurately guide a missile attack. Ross' helicopter team could paint a twenty foot by twenty foot area of land when flying forty to fifty feet overhead. The reflected X-rays from underground allow the Boeing satellite above to 'see' up to fifteen meters beneath the surface, depending on the density of the soil.

Trying to find a tunnel entrance hidden among the many hills and valleys in this terrain was like searching for the proverbial needle in a haystack, but Ross was sure it was only a matter of time until they found it. He knew the tunnel had to be there and they had already covered seventy-five percent of the search grid's sectors. With the increased pressure he was receiving from CIA headquarters in Langley, Virginia, Agent Ross hoped this would be the day he could deliver.

Special Agent Culver called Ross on the radio. He had located numerous faint tire tracks still visible despite the recent storm. Ross contained his excitement, knowing this had happened many times over the past few days with no luck in finding the terrorists. Culver asked for X-ray satellite support of the area. Ross ordered the helicopter to Culver's location and told the pilot to stand by for orders to paint the area. Then he instructed the support team at NRO to focus the Boeing satellite's telescope on the same coordinates Agent Culver had just given. When both teams were ready, he gave the go-ahead to proceed. A minute later the images began to appear on Ross' laptop.

He had received many such scans over the past several days and by now he had a good deal of experience identifying the natural underground terrain. Then he saw it. The green still-shots on his laptop showed an underground passageway close to the tire tracks. Once they located any section of the underground passage, pinpointing the elusive entrance to the tunnel was easy.

The team at the NRO asked him to guide the helicopter along the tunnel's coordinates to find the entrance. The pilot reminded Ross that a complete scan would require that they enter Jordanian air space. Ross gave him the approval to proceed knowing their people had already cleared that through the proper channels. The Jordanian government had been only too happy to demonstrate their cooperation, especially since the terrorists' assumed exit through their border implied they were involved in the attack.

The images continued to update on Ross' laptop and he could see that the other end of the tunnel emptied into a much larger room, still completely below the surface. In fact, the room was so large that the twenty foot by twenty foot X-ray pictures showed only a small portion of the underground chamber. He was able to make out many of the vehicles and trailers parked inside to confirm they had found the right place.

While his laptop connection could only handle downloading still images, the NRO was receiving real-time video. They informed Ross that the subterranean room and tunnels appeared to be abandoned, though it would take hours of careful scanning to be sure. He told them that searching the premises for any stragglers could wait. The priority was the find the entrance and gain access to the underground chamber.

***

It was just after midnight in Israel marking the tenth day since the terrorist attack on the U.S. supply depot. Agent Ross was frustrated that he was still unable to provide any answers. However, the time spent searching had not been wasted. The backhoe they'd requested was now on site along with construction work lights and a generator to dig at night. That was exactly what Ross needed to avoid further delays. The backhoe quickly disposed of the camouflaged wall that had completely sealed the entrance to the tunnel leading to the underground complex. He then sent in three two-man teams to recon the area and hopefully capture any terrorists who might still be there.

The main access tunnel had been dug to follow the path of least resistance around naturally occurring boulders. The twisting passageway was perhaps 250 yards long compared to the 120-yard straight shot from the entrance to the large underground room. They knew to watch for booby-traps at all points in and around the area. That made progress slow but no one minded being careful considering the risk.

It would probably take them forty-five minutes to be sure the tunnel was safe all the way to the large chamber. Ross surmised the only reason these vehicles were still there was because the fanatics couldn't remove or destroy them and remain undetected. That made the odds of this complex being wired to blow somewhere near 100 percent. He knew he had the best trained men in the world for this job. They just had to be careful to make sure they got what they came for without casualties to the team.

***

Sadad was struggling through his third day of solitude in the underground bunker. Everyone else had already left the hideout and headed for their homes. He was the last remaining soldier of Mohammed's Faithful who had volunteered to keep watch over the weapons and vehicles stored there. He thanked Allah that even though this was perhaps the loneliest mission imaginable, at least it was not designed to end with his suicide. He volunteered after

Colonel Mansur assured him that he could fulfill this important assignment and still safely return home to his family.

The entire chamber had been set with explosives, as had the vent shafts leading to the surface. These vents allowed the vehicles to run for brief periods without suffocating the soldiers, as long as they wore gas masks. Sadad's job was to remain in the underground complex for up to two weeks keeping watch for intruders. If the Americans and Israelis had not found their hidden location by that time, they likely never would and all that equipment could be used again someday. If they did manage to find the hidden chamber, it was Sadad's job to detonate the explosives and bury the equipment and infidels under tons of dirt and rock.

He remembered his exact instructions in case this place was discovered. "When the infidels are within 20 meters of the chamber, start the laptop's three-minute countdown that will detonate the explosives. Once activated, the timer cannot be turned off but the infidels won't know that. There is a ladder installed in the nearby ventilation shaft so you can escape on foot leaving the intruders behind to die."

He was perfectly vigilant during the first two days of his mission. He barely slept and had set the laptop computer to emit a tone every thirty minutes to remind him to check the area. Colonel Mansur had told him it would take longer than those thirty-minute intervals for any intruders to enter the chamber. He knew they were trained to check for trip wires and buried mines in the winding tunnel. If Sadad obeyed his instructions, he would soon be home with his family knowing he had served Allah well in their fight against the infidels. However, that intensity of vigilance was difficult to maintain and the hours of solitude in that dark underground chamber took their toll. He began to deviate from his instructions in self-defense of his sanity.

The camera at the opening of the Israeli tunnel was remotely connected to the laptop. He would be able to see anyone coming if they breached the camouflaged wall blocking the entrance to the complex. He didn't have a camera in the other tunnels leading to Jordan, but the odds were negligible that any of the infidels would enter from the Jordanian side. Since there were no lights in the walled-up tunnel, all Sadad could see on the monitor was a dark screen. However, if the wall blocking the entrance was breached, the camera was light-sensitive enough to show that intruders were coming, even at night. He had more than enough charged batteries to last two weeks and the laptop had been modified to allow him to change batteries without having to reboot the computer.

Sadad's first departure from his orders was to use the computer for spiritual enlightenment rather than security. He tried watching religious videos that were stored on the hard drive but he quickly tired of those and moved on to read the *Qur'an* and a little of Riyad al-Sâlihîn, the most revered Islamic holy books. They too did not hold his attention for long, so he started playing variations of the card game solitaire. Being a good Muslim, Sadad avoided any gambling games that were considered to be *makruh,* because gambling is sinful according to Sharia law. He found he enjoyed playing a solitaire game called free cell. As he continually tried to improve his score in the game, he became less diligent in checking the camera for signs of intruders. His need to keep himself entertained after this long period of isolation in the dark was the flaw in Colonel Mansur's otherwise excellent plan.

It was a little after midnight and Sadad had been playing free cell for hours. The ongoing music programmed into the computer game had become quite annoying. He was not good with computers so he felt a little pride when he clicked on something that made the music stop. What he didn't realize was he had also muted the regular alarm beeps to wake him from his short naps.

***

Agent Ross' backhoe team had just breached the walled-up tunnel entrance. Sadad was sleeping soundly as the special agents quietly moved in to clear any explosives. Almost immediately, they found the camera monitoring the tunnel's entrance. They determined it was strictly for local use but they could only guess if anyone was watching. They destroyed the camera and moved on with the assumption that anyone inside now knew they were coming.

Almost forty minutes after the CIA teams had begun clearing the tunnel, Sadad woke up with a start. He saw the laptop screen patiently waiting for him to resume the card game. He realized he had slept far too long and immediately switched the monitor from the game to the tunnel camera. The screen was dark, as usual, but it

39

didn't look the same as it had before. There were some English words displayed on the monitor that he had not seen before. The laptop was programmed for the Arabic language, but the camera's monitoring software was not designed to tie into the operating system's translation software. The words said, "No Input Signal." Sadad didn't know for sure what those words meant, but he feared the worst.

Grabbing his AK-47 rifle, he moved quickly toward the tunnel on Israel's side of the large chamber. He needed to be sure intruders had come before he activated the detonation timer. To set it off unnecessarily would only alert his enemy where to search and they would probably catch him escaping in the process. He mentally reviewed each step of the plan. He would activate the timer from the laptop computer. He would keep the laptop where the infidels were sure to find it. Then he would escape up the ladder to the surface.

Mansur was sure the infidels would expect the underground chamber to be wired with explosives. Although the detonation timer could not be turned off, Mansur had installed a second software program to confuse them. The computer screen would show a timer counting down as well as an icon labeled 'Abort.' Clicking on the icon would stop the timer on the laptop's display but do nothing to stop the total destruction of the chamber and tunnels.

Colonel Mansur made Sadad repeat how important it was that the infidels immediately find the laptop after starting the countdown. The ruse would give Sadad time to escape. However, if the laptop survived the destruction, the enemy might be able to use it to connect Mohammed's Faithful to other attacks on American targets. The Colonel was angry that his personal laptop was the only one that had both the hardware and software to fulfill this mission. He regretted having to give it up for the cause. Sadad assured Mansur he would do his job and that the laptop would be demolished one way or another.

***

Special Agent Ross was near the tunnel entrance following his teams' progress as they cleared the way. He was still calculating the implications of the remote camera they found just inside the concealment wall. Their X-ray satellite intel indicated no people

40

were moving inside the underground chamber. He knew that was not a certainty, but the more time that passed without any signs of life from within, the better he felt. The agents were using night vision goggles (NVGs) rather than flashlights. They were working well and Ross heard the lead team confirm that they could see some vehicles off in the distance.

Agent Culver was in charge of the lead team that had first entered the tunnel. He rounded the last bend in the path and peered through his NVGs into the gloom ahead. He saw a faint light revealing an underground chamber filled with vehicles. He radioed for everyone to hold their positions and maintain silence while he verified the source of the light. As he watched, the shadows danced around revealing that the light source was moving. In fact, the shifting silhouettes indicated that there were two probable light sources. One was fixed while the second light source was probably a flashlight held by someone moving about in the chamber. Culver determined that the person inside would be far away by now if any of the remaining tunnel was booby-trapped. He decided to act immediately.

He dove headlong into the chamber and rolled to an upright position behind a nearby Jeep. He looked toward the lights and realized he had been right. On a small table about fifty feet off to his left was a TV or computer monitor providing a steady blueish glow. Culver briefly saw the flashlight resting on a table just before his view was blocked by a man taking a seat in front of the screen. Soon he heard the tapping sounds of a keyboard filling the room.

Culver understood that whatever the other man was typing was more important to him than escaping with his life. That made his next move more logical than suicidal. He charged directly for the silhouette as he raised his M-5 rifle to fire. Suddenly, the light from the monitor and the flashlight were gone. Agent Culver fired a three-round burst into the darkness. He could still hear the man's feet scrambling on the floor which meant he had probably missed. Culver slowed but continued to move cautiously forward as his eyes and NVGs readjusted to the darkness.

He covered enough ground to reach the small table where the man had been a moment before. There was an AK-47 lying on the floor and a laptop sitting on the table with the lid closed. Culver looked around for the other man. He saw him sitting motionless with his back to the excavated wall of the cave. He understood that the faint green glow from his NVGs was probably the only thing the man could see.

He was unsure if the man had used the computer to call for help or to set off a bomb, but waiting to find out was not an option. He pulled out an M-84 stun grenade. He yanked the pin and yelled "FLASH BANG" as loud as he could and threw it directly at the seated man. The other agents within earshot would know to cover their eyes and ears to avoid being disoriented by the brilliant flash and gigantic "BOOM" that shook the chamber.

Culver reset his NVGs and looked around. He saw that the man was now lying on the floor clearly bewildered and shaking his head to clear it. Culver took a moment to open the laptop to see what the man had been doing. The screen showed a timer counting down with less than three minutes remaining and his heart nearly jumped out of his chest. Just beneath the timer was an icon with a large typed word in both English and Arabic. The icon read, 'Abort.'

Culver radioed to Ross what he'd found and urged everyone underground to evacuate immediately. Ross made Culver's suggestion an order and the men quickly retreated toward the tunnel entrance. Having nothing to lose, Culver clicked on the abort icon and the timer stopped counting down with 2:07 left to go.

***

Sadad had never been so scared in his life. He had faced death in battle before, but he had never felt as alone as he did right then. Having discovered the intruders were mere meters from entering the main chamber, Sadad knew he had only seconds to set the timer and escape through the ventilation shaft. He barely managed to start the countdown before the first of the intruders fired at him. Sadad had closed the laptop and turned off his flashlight in time to keep from being an easy target. In the pitch black of the huge cave, Sadad blindly crawled on the ground until he bumped into the excavated wall. He couldn't tell if the exit ventilation shaft was to his left or right. He assumed the American soldier would have expensive technology to see in the dark so he decided his best defense was to not move at all.

As his eyes adjusted to the darkness, Sadad could barely see a green light outlining the soldier's head in the distance. He seemed to be scanning the chamber trying to locate Sadad's position. He wasn't sure if the soldier could see him or not, so Sadad held completely still. Suddenly, the green glow moved and Sadad heard something hit the floor of the cave in front of him. Then the soldier shouted something he didn't understand. A second later a painful flash of light and concussive explosion knocked Sadad over nearly causing him to pass out. After a moment, he realized he was only dazed rather than injured.

As he regained his bearings, Sadad observed that the soldier had the laptop open and was speaking on his radio. The faint light from the monitor allowed Sadad to locate the exit ladder to his right. He knew he had to kill this American if there was any chance of escape. He had lost his rifle in all the confusion but he still carried a Russian F-1 hand grenade on his belt. Despite the danger to himself, he decided to use the grenade knowing he would either escape or die heroically.

Sadad pulled the pin and tried to toss the grenade directly at the American. He was still so disoriented that his aim was off by perhaps five meters. However, when it comes to hand grenades, accuracy is not crucial. The soldier dove for cover the moment it hit the ground.

Sadad rushed for the ladder. The grenade's shrapnel would kill him just as easily as it would his intended victim. He prayed that the laptop would be smashed beyond recognition because he wasn't stopping for anything. As he climbed the rungs of the ladder, he counted the seconds expecting the grenade to kill them both at any moment. He got to ten before realizing his escape plan was working better than he had hoped. The F-1 was so obsolete and depleted that it wouldn't have exploded any time in the last decade. His unintended deception of the defective grenade had saved his life but that meant the soldier was still alive as well.

Sadad climbed the last few steps up the ladder and cleared the vent shaft. The sun was not up yet but he could see bright lights off to the west. They were probably the work lights the soldiers used to breach the tunnel's entrance. He had no idea how much time remained before the chamber and access tunnels were destroyed, but he knew he did not want to be standing on top of them when that happened. He set a fix from the North Star toward Syria hoping to get out of sight before the soldier below caught up to him.

***

Agent Culver was sure his life was over. He watched as the terrorist threw a hand grenade in his general direction. He knew the thing would explode in seconds and automatically dove to the ground. He curled up in the fetal position and was on his third or fourth "Oh My God!" before he realized nothing had happened. The grenade was a dud. Feeling a little foolish now, Culver stood up as he reset his NVGs once again. He saw the man's legs ascending a ladder up one of the vent shafts. Culver grabbed the laptop and shoved it in his backpack before following the terrorist. "I'm in pursuit of a suspect up a vertical shaft!" he yelled into his radio.

As he reached the surface, the light of the stars would have been more than enough to see through his NVGs. However, the distant glow from the work lights at the tunnel entrance made for easy viewing all around. From the way he was moving, Culver could tell the other man was still disoriented from the flash bang grenade.

He yelled, "HALT!" to the fleeing man and fired a warning shot. It came much closer than he had intended as it ricocheted between the man's feet. The man stopped running and held up his hands in the universal gesture of surrender. Agent Culver radioed to Ross that he had a prisoner in his sights on the surface approximately 300 yards northeast of the tunnel's entrance. He requested backup and added that he could not be sure there weren't more enemy personnel below. Culver slowly approached the man who had just tried to kill him. He directed the man to get on his knees in English. The man didn't comply. Culver heard him speaking in Arabic as he drew closer.

***

Sadad knew this was the end of both him and the soldier. He would not survive this mission but he hoped that he had succeeded in doing Allah's will. There couldn't be more than a minute left before the explosives below killed him and the infidel who was probably about to shoot him regardless. Sadad felt like he had failed his family and Colonel Mansur. Why hadn't he done what he was told? He let his boredom and laziness get the better of him and now he would have to pay for that with his life. He heard the soldier yelling to him in English and all Sadad could do in return was to pray aloud. He began with the standing *raka'ah* prayer of the *Salah*. He hesitated to go on to the second prayer. That would require him to bow as he recited the words. Instead, he looked at the approaching soldier and defiantly uttered, *"Allahu Akbar!"*

A moment later the timer expired and so did the underground network beneath them. The U.S. satellite imagery captured the initial explosion and subsequent implosion of earth as the chamber and tunnels breathed out and then collapsed. The few agents who were still below ground died quickly under the weight of the crumbling earth. Others were incinerated by the blast that pushed through the tunnels and vent shafts with the force of a flame thrower shooting fire more than 100 feet into the dark night. Both Agent Culver and Sadad lost their footing as the ground shifted like quicksand. The earth beneath them roared and collapsed as the dirt, rocks and boulders remixed to form a new foundation below. When the ground stopped shaking and the desert was quiet once again, Agent Culver and Sadad were both badly injured and trapped in the crushing debris.

Sadad could neither move nor breathe. He could only watch as Culver mustered the strength to pull his backpack up through the dirt. He wanted to ensure that the laptop would not be ignored when he was found. The breathing room he gained by removing his backpack served to keep him alive until help arrived. The last thing Sadad saw was the laptop spilling out of the backpack that was now next to the soldier's face. Sadad knew he had failed because both the infidel and that cursed computer would survive this ordeal to reveal their secrets.

Chapter 6

The NSC meeting in the Situation Room was interrupted by an aide with a written message for the President. They had just resumed discussions regarding their response to the attack on the compound in Israel when the intel they had been waiting for finally arrived. President Alexander handed the note to George Salazar and announced the briefing would continue in 5 minutes with an update from Director Salazar. After all, it was his CIA agents who tracked down the evidence and the location of the bunker where over 100 terrorists had hidden and dispersed without detection.

The members of the NSC received identical dossiers containing photos and a synopsis of the evidence collected thus far. George was on the phone with Special Agent Ross who despite his injuries was able to bring them up to speed on the investigation that continued on site. Within minutes, Director Salazar and the other members of the NSC were ready to continue the discussion.

George cleared his throat and read aloud the summary he had just received from Agent Ross. "This morning at approximately 1:00 am local time in Israel, Agent Ross and a team of CIA special agents discovered what they believed could be the entrance to an underground bunker. Their mission was to locate the terrorists who annihilated our Jezreel Valley supply depot seven miles west of the Jordanian border. With the permission of Jordan's government, Agent Ross' men breached the camouflaged tunnel entrance and proceeded to investigate the underground complex. Apparently the terrorists had already evacuated the bunker except for one. Had our people not found this underground location, it is certain the equipment would have been used again by the terrorists at a future date.

"At around 1:45 am local Israel time, the lone insurgent activated a detonation timer and attempted to escape to the surface before the resulting explosion. An agent was able to recover a laptop computer probably used to facilitate the destruction of the complex. Unfortunately, the resulting explosion killed the man we believe was responsible for destroying the bunker. All of the injured were transported by air to a nearby medical facility in Nazareth. The laptop is already being couriered to Langley where a forensics team will determine if they can recover any incriminating evidence."

President Alexander asked if this meant they were any closer to identifying with certainty those responsible for the attack on the supply depot. He could tell that his inquiry had deflated George's enthusiasm, which in itself was an answer.

"Mr. President," he replied, "we don't yet know the answer to that question. However, I am confident that from the physical evidence already recovered and the intel we'll glean from the laptop, we will soon know who was responsible. I can add that nothing we've found so far negates our working scenario that the group known as Mohammed's Faithful is responsible for the attack."

Vice President Eric Jefferson commented, "We initially discussed that there may be Syrian support for the terrorist activities of Mohammed's Faithful. However, I thought all the violent factions moved elsewhere once the Syrian government became unfriendly toward them. In light of that, what makes you believe the Syrian government is helping Mohammed's Faithful?"

Secretary of Defense Steve Lombard responded. "You are correct that Syria's government has taken steps to improve its reputation with the non-Muslim world. Distancing themselves from terrorist organizations and officially inviting them to leave the country allowed for an easing of international sanctions and increased foreign aid that was desperately needed to quell the civil unrest among their citizens. However, it's thought by many that those outward changes were better described as 'cosmetic' to achieve a goal rather than indicating an authentic position against terrorism. Syria, along with Lebanon, still has major issues with Israel over territorial disputes concerning the Golan Heights. They like it when militant factions torment their enemies. In those cases, the Syrian government looks the other way and even offers certain groups whatever support they need."

Eric then asked, "Do we really believe that the Syrian government would risk the gains they've made to help destroy our supply depot in Israel? Where is the advantage in taking that chance?"

Steve conceded that was a good point but the answer required an understanding of their history. "The war with Israel in

1967 is still being waged in the minds of many who fought and were defeated. Some of those angry young soldiers have become the military leaders of those same embarrassed countries. For them, what we call the 'Six Day War' of 1967 was only one battle in a war that is ongoing.

"Syria continues to be quite aggressive and outspoken in their loathing of Israel. They would love to see the U.S. withdraw military support from the Jews. If they can frustrate us enough to reduce or even abandon our military presence in the Middle East, then Syria, Lebanon, Iran and others could organize together and really give Israel a run for their money."

Matt added, "So we may well have government backing of terrorist activities in this case." He turned to General McComb and asked, "In light of these developments, what is the recommendation from our military leaders as an appropriate response to the attacks on our bases in the Middle East?"

As Martin began to outline a series of retaliatory strikes aimed at isolating the perpetrators, Matt found himself mentally drifting away from the subject at hand. He wasn't tired and he'd been off all medications except blood thinners for a few days now. He found himself again reliving the experience after his heart attack. He had not been able to fully recall what happened that day, but he knew what he'd been shown was very important to the decision he was about to make.

While his gaze was fixed on General McComb, Matt remembered he had attended some kind of briefing with just one other person. That unusual man patiently showed him the long history of Middle Eastern conflicts. The 3-D scenes he witnessed went well beyond the images he was used to seeing in a briefing. Strangely enough, he found he was able to feel the emotions of every person affected by thousands of years of war and unrest. He could sense the distrust, the anger, even the hate on both sides of every conflict. It wasn't just the ongoing struggle between the Jews and the Muslims he experienced. He came to realize that kind of negativity was part of every religious and political conflict in the history of the world. To personally feel the suffering of each individual on the planet was overwhelming. It was also quite compelling that something had to be done to resolve it.

Matt pondered what he was told during that odd encounter. He was beginning to think it might have been a near-death experience or NDE. However, he'd never heard of anything like what he'd been through. He wasn't shown the wonders of heaven or deceased relatives from his past. The focus of his NDE, if that's what it was, seemed to be on what he could do now to make things better in the future.

The stranger who had briefed him agreed achieving a peace-loving world was a near-impossible goal as things stood today. He had explained that while most everyone agrees that peace among all nations is preferred, many harbor a deep-seated desire for vengeance because of the sins committed against them and their people. He had also suggested this was because humankind has little faith in the righteousness of outsiders. For thousands of years all conflicts in the Middle East could be summed up as 'us against them.'

From this new and unusual perspective, Matt began to see that violent solutions only attract more violence. Each transgression only amplifies our desire for vengeance and that helps us believe we are ridding the world of evil. Such a vicious cycle, because it feeds itself, can last forever.

Matt realized General McComb had stopped talking and all eyes were on him. They thought he was shaking his head to McComb's proposed response scenarios. Their worried expressions conveyed concern that he might still be recovering from his health challenges regardless of his doctors' consent that he could return to work. No one knew what to say, so they awkwardly waited as they stared.

Matt decided to plunge right in with his revelations by posing a question. "Is there any response we can agree upon among ourselves that would be so clearly appropriate that everyone in the world would agree we've done the right thing?" The members of the NSC looked at each other as they silently wondered where POTUS' question was leading.

"If we were able to conduct a strike where only those responsible for the attacks against us were killed, would there be 100 percent agreement around the world that our response was correct?" Matt paused for effect and then continued, "I think it is safe to say that whatever 'appropriate response' we come up with, there will be those who think we have no right to retaliate. Others will feel we didn't go far enough. But either way, the conflict will continue as before and the violence will probably escalate. If no correct 'appropriate response' exists, then what can we do that will make things better?"

Fred Shapiro, National Security Advisor, blurted out in surprise, "Are you suggesting we do nothing about this?"

"Certainly not, but aren't we here to make decisions that take us toward our ultimate goal of peace? The question becomes one of deciding if peace really can be achieved through force. We have thousands of years of history that indicate violence doesn't work to achieve peace in the long run."

White House Chief of Staff, Mike Simons, had never heard his friend and boss speak this way in their many years together. He asked the obvious question, "What are you proposing we should do?"

Matt appreciated that Mike had provided the perfect lead-in to introduce his new strategy. "We've all been spinning our wheels trying to figure out how to put the toothpaste back in the tube. I believe that conflicts between nations won't be healed by using violence to achieve peace. What we need to do is establish our mutual points of agreement and build on those to achieve greater and sustainable solutions that will work to the good of all."

The silence in the room was as profound as the implied challenge the President had just placed before them. Matt could feel the questions swimming around in the room, albeit unspoken. Questions like, "What points of agreement?" "Don't the Muslim nations largely believe that all infidels are abominations before Allah?" "What about the families of our soldiers who have died over there? Don't they deserve to see justice done to those who murdered their sons and daughters?" "The Muslim nations don't trust us. They don't respect us. They believe America is nothing more than a spoiled child who has not been around long enough to understand how the world works. In perhaps a thousand years the Americans will mature, but they have a long way to go before they have the right to sit at the table with their elders."

Matt reflected on what he believed was the real conflict. He decided this was the time to start being completely transparent and lay all his cards on the table. "Let's forget about the past for a moment. We all know the real issue is the long-term economic survival of the Middle East nations." He paused to look around the room. Matt was thankful to see they were still listening with interest. Feeling optimistic, he continued. "These countries currently rely on crude oil to supply as much as ninety percent of their revenues from exports. Since those desert nations have little else to sell to the rest of the world, the clock is ticking when it comes to establishing their permanent place in the global economy.

"If the Middle East nations don't manage to shift into sustainable products and services in say the next fifty years, the world's need for energy will be forced to look elsewhere to protect their own long-term interests. If we want to find lasting solutions to the conflicts in that region, offering them hope for a prosperous economic future is a great start. Giving them reason to trust in our good intentions is crucial. Figuring out how to get all nations to recognize that each person in the world is a valued member of our shared family is the key."

The entire NSC was stunned. They all wondered what had happened to their President since his heart attack. His proposal was the kind of talk that sounded good after many drinks with a close friend, but this meeting was about hard reality. These terrorists played for keeps as well as by different fundamental rules. Many of the NSC members feared that if Matt actually went down this road that it would further disrupt the ongoing Middle East conflicts as well as the continuous flow of oil to the U.S.

President Alexander could see they all needed to take a break to think about what he had said. He told the NSC members that each person would be polled for their best suggestions when they reconvened in a few hours.

***

George Salazar was a teenager when he was told that his father, Major George Salazar Sr., had been captured in Vietnam. The whole family was counting on a prisoner exchange to see the patriarch of the Salazar household returned home. The Paris Peace Accord did arrange the release of all remaining American soldiers, but George's father was not among them. The Vietnamese government records briefly stated that "he died in captivity."

51

When George became an adult, he had already chosen his career. He wanted to join the CIA. He never spoke of his real motivation for this, but the family knew he was still looking for his father. He hoped that working for the CIA would give him the access and contacts he needed to find and bring his dad home.

It turned out that George had a real talent for his job. He was an excellent agent who always managed to complete his missions. When he became a team leader, his successes continued and so did the promotions. He became known for his creative solutions to tricky problems and his excellent record gained him a lot of leeway to complete his missions.

George was quickly promoted to a level where he could investigate his father's "missing in action" status in Vietnam. He discovered that sketchy records of his father's imprisonment existed from the first months of his capture. Years had passed without further status reports in any of the CIA's files. George became convinced that his father might still be alive and let his superiors know what he'd discovered.

Despite his pleas for help, no one wanted to open up that can of worms with the Vietnamese government. George pushed the matter until he was called on the carpet and told he'd have to let the matter go or face disciplinary action. Outwardly, he heeded the advice and no longer mentioned his father to anyone. Inwardly, he vowed to rise high enough in the CIA's ranks to discover the truth and rescue his father if he was still alive.

Years later, when he became the head of the CIA, George learned it had not ended well for his father. Unofficially, he contacted people outside of normal channels who knew of his father's imprisonment. Their information was that Salazar Sr. remained captive in Vietnam even after the Paris Peace Accord had arranged for the release of all American prisoners. George's father had been so brutally tortured by his captors that releasing him to be displayed to the international media was not an option. He died, still in prison, a few years after he should have returned home.

George knew there was nothing he could have done personally to rescue his father, but there were many in the United States government who could have saved him. An intense resentment filled George that was focused on the Washington bureaucrats who were too timid to do the right thing. It wasn't just his father's welfare, but the entire country that had been damaged by our government's lack of action in Vietnam. George swore he would never put politics or his own career ahead of the welfare of the country.

***

Dr. Jerome Westcott was in charge of digital forensics at CIA headquarters in Langley, Virginia. The damaged laptop computer had been brought directly to him from the site of the underground bunker in Israel. He was assured that before the battery ran down, this old beat up laptop had been functional. Not only was it several years old, but the power supply and battery configuration had been modified from the manufacturer's original design. The challenge now was to make sure he connected the right voltage and amps to power it back up without frying any of the components. He heard that agents had died getting this laptop from the terrorists. Failure to download the data stored on its hard drive was not an option.

Jerome removed the battery from the laptop and applied a low voltage trickle charge to revive it. Over several hours, he increased the voltage slightly until the indicator showed it was fully charged. He took the necessary readings and set his lab's power supply to match the battery's optimum output. He then fired up the laptop with a new hard drive that was compatible with the existing motherboard. He was not misinformed. This unit was fully functional when it had enough juice.

Next came the most important step. Dr. Westcott made a cloned image of the laptop's hard drive. The original drive would contain traces of deleted files that were not recoverable from a copied drive. If he could get the cloned drive to boot up without something going wrong, he would then try it with the original hard drive.

He clicked the icon telling his test computer to boot off the copied drive. After a few moments, the operating system logo appeared. Then the drive started to execute a command that was hidden deep within the boot sector. It was programmed to reformat itself to remove all files or traces of files it might contain if it was ever rebooted.

Dr. Westcott quickly cut the power and the monitor went black. It was a good thing he took this precaution or he might have lost everything. The bad news was that this project would take far longer than he originally estimated to salvage the recoverable data off the hard drive. He would have to dissect the boot up sequence's machine code to safely locate the self-destruct program hidden within. He did not look forward to reporting this delay to the Director. Jerome thought Salazar had been in a really foul mood lately.

Chapter 7

Matt needed some time to reflect and rest up for their next NSC meeting and the Oval Office was not the best place to relax. Instead, he walked through to the White House residence. He settled on the couch in the family room trying to make sense of his own thoughts. He was asleep where he sat when Erin walked in a few minutes later. She took a seat at the other end of the couch, careful not to wake him. The stress of recent events was also taking its toll on Erin. She too had trouble focusing her thoughts as she drifted off to sleep.

***

Matt realized he was back in the nondescript room again. The other man looked like Amelius at first glance, including the glow around his body, but there were subtle differences. The next moment Erin was at Matt's side looking bewildered at having arrived so abruptly.

"What? Wait...what the heck is this?" she said looking around in all directions.

"Welcome! My name is Ariel. You don't remember me quite yet but we have worked together before."

Matt was quicker to find his bearings and asked, "Where is Amelius?"

Erin looked at Matt and stammered, "You know what's going on here? Who is Amelius and who are you?" she said pointing toward Ariel.

"There is nothing here that threatens you," said Ariel. "Our work together in the past was the same as it is now; repairing your relationship. You were once the perfect couple as both soulmates and the best of friends. Now you don't trust each other, you don't respect each other and you rarely agree on anything."

"Amelius said something about you the last time I was here. So you're a marriage counselor or something?" Matt asked.

"The 'or something' is closer to the truth, but I accept the role of counselor as things stand between you now," Ariel answered.

Erin was clearly bewildered and frustrated. "Am I the only one who doesn't know what's going on here?"

Ariel smiled, "You will soon remember our previous encounters. Relax and allow your subconscious mind to acclimate as it takes control. While you are in physical form, that is to say, when you are awake, the subconscious mind is often blocked out by the conscious mind."

Matt groaned, "I'm remembering all right. Every time we've met like this in the past, things only became worse back on earth."

Erin too was beginning to remember. Ariel had been trying to help them work through the conflicts in their relationship. At the end of those sessions, her heart would become light with hope. Then they would wake up and go back to 'business as usual.' In fact, tensions were often worse because they became even more frustrated with each other. "And so here we are again. Why should we expect anything to improve given our history with these sessions?"

That's an excellent question!" Ariel went on to explain, "The challenges in your relationship are temporary and not without purpose. Matt chose to go down a different path in order to become the President. You stayed the course you were on and that disagreement caused most of your conflicts. Neither of you was right nor wrong in this. But now you can, and should, come together despite the suffering each has caused the other. You truly are soul mates and it is time to heal this earthly rift in your relationship."

"All our talks turn into fights. What makes you think we can heal our marriage now when things have only become worse over time?" Erin said with frustration.

Ariel answered patiently, "In the same way that people often wait until just before a deadline to accomplish an important task, you two have arrived at that point. Matt's heart attack, the conflicts in the Holy Land, the lack of agreement among members of the NSC, and the challenges in your marriage have all converged to bring this unique opportunity to fruition. If you do not heal your relationship at this juncture, you won't be able to successfully navigate that which is about to unfold in your lives. The well-being and happiness of literally billions of people are riding on your decision."

As Ariel's words echoed in their minds, their vision was filled with scenario after scenario of the choices they might make in the near future. None of them were easy and all of them were frightening, even those with the best outcomes imaginable. There was a real chance that another world war would be the result if they diverged from a very narrow path of choices. Perhaps the scariest part was having so much responsibility for seeing the plan through this critical period. They had to remember how to love and trust each other again as they had in the early years of their relationship. They had seen the potential of a better life play out into the future and agreed this was what they both wanted, but the harsh truth of the 'real world' conspired to push them apart each day of their waking lives.

Matt asked skeptically, "What can we do differently this time so that we heal these old wounds and become best friends again?"

"That is a hopeful step forward for it is the first time you've thought to ask me that question," beamed Ariel. "Your subconscious mind is in control right now and it is ideally the guide of your conscious mind on earth. Like an architect, we are here drafting the plans for your earthly lives and relationship. But a design is only as good as the actual contractor who puts the structure together."

Erin cut in, frustrated, "Didn't you say that the subconscious mind is usually blocked by the conscious mind when we're awake? How can the subconscious be our guide if our conscious mind never lets it be heard?"

"You make an excellent point," soothed Ariel. "It takes practice to listen to our inner voice, our conscience, but like exercising a muscle, the more you make use of it, the stronger it grows. You have been working on this for years and it is now time to put your love and trust into action. You must believe that you are ready if this is to succeed."

Matt was clearly distraught as he responded, "Even the best scenarios and choices you showed us place Erin in real danger, in some cases to the point of her being killed! How can I possibly respond patiently and peacefully when she is in great danger?"

"Matt, you are unique in that you are humankind's best chance at walking the narrow path you see before you. You are correct that Erin faces the possibility of great danger, but if you don't succeed and she does die in the effort, it would be a blessing. If you fail, no one will want to be on earth for the horrific violence that follows. You know you do not desire to start a world war no matter what happens, so focus on that and you will be constantly guided to persevere in this laudable quest. Erin volunteered for this solemn mission long ago and she may yet survive to help you achieve a lasting peace," Ariel said with conviction.

Erin started to ask another question, but the room began to fade as someone nudged her shoulder.

***

Matt woke to find Erin sleeping next to him on the couch. He shook her gently. She sat up and rubbed her eyes as he moved toward the door.

Erin said, "You don't have to leave. In fact, I came here to talk with you."

He started to cut her off with a typical sarcastic response. Something made him stop from saying out loud, "The last thing I need right now is another of your one-way conversations where 'we' explore my shortcomings." Matt reconsidered what to say. If he was honest with himself, he knew deep within that it wasn't all her fault that they had grown apart. He rarely responded to her observations; and that meant that her unintended monologues were as much his fault as they were hers. He laughed ruefully to himself when he admitted the truth. He remembered thinking it would be easier to negotiate a lasting peace in the Middle East than to restore the loving relationship he once had with his wife. Then something flashed through his mind. He didn't understand why, but somehow he knew that avoiding this talk would have dire consequences.

"What did you want to talk about?" he asked cautiously, softening his tone.

"I hear you made quite a statement in the NSC meeting this morning." Matt just nodded. Erin continued, "Are you really considering a change in Middle East policy and strategy at this crucial point?"

"It seemed appropriate to me," he replied. "Nothing else was working."

"Would you be revealing state secrets by telling me what you have in mind?" she asked.

Matt laughed. "Actually, my new strategy for resolving the challenges in the Middle East is to do away with state secrets." He described his proposal to the NSC members to help wean those countries away from their dependence on oil exports. He outlined his vision for all nations to achieve such peaceful prosperity by truly trusting each other. This could be accomplished by pursuing only win/win scenarios for all concerned on each issue. Trust would be built by all nations living up to their agreements and accepting all people as equal members of the same family.

Surprised, Erin had no quick response for him. She too was wondering about Matt's change of heart, so she asked, "What happened since your heart attack to change your mind like this?"

Matt winced hearing the question that no member of the NSC had dared to voice. He hesitated to discuss it knowing her deep disappointment with him simmered on so many levels. Still, if he couldn't be honest about this with Erin, who else could he trust to help him see this through? If transparency was truly the answer, he had to trust that his vision for a peaceful world could start with the woman he had married.

He tried again to fully recall his extraordinary experience after his collapse. He started to describe the unusual briefing with the man in glowing white when a tremendous feeling of déjà vu washed over him. He had already experienced this same conversation with Erin. It was playing again like a familiar movie. The man in the odd room had shown this particular scene to Matt to encourage him to persevere in accomplishing a difficult task. Matt understood that the choices he and Erin were about to make would affect many events that had yet to unfold.

He did his best to explain what he was thinking and feeling as well as what his conscience was guiding him to do. Erin listened intently but gave nothing away in her body language or expression. Matt wondered aloud if she thought he was going crazy.

Her reply surprised him. "Honestly, this is the first time you've sounded like a sane person in years. I don't know what to think of your briefing room experience or what that man showed you, but I do think that you just offered a logical approach to resolving the Middle East conflicts. I'm not saying it will succeed. It probably won't when you look at every event and attitude that would have to align in the world for your plan to work. That doesn't change the fact that starting over fresh and helping everyone to succeed is the best way to achieve world peace."

Matt felt his eyes moisten as he realized she was with him instead of against him on this. How many years had he felt that Erin just didn't understand what it took to succeed in politics? For how long had he been shying away from deep conversations with her because she no longer saw things as he did? It felt good to be on the same page as his wife. He had forgotten that her moral compass was usually spot-on accurate.

***

When the President returned to the Situation Room, everyone stood but there was no round of applause this time. He could tell by their expressions that this was going to be a tough meeting. If he read the room correctly, their concern wasn't necessarily that they disagreed with his suggestion. Like Erin said, the plan could work in theory, but all odds were against it. They took their seats and waited for Matt to begin.

"A lot has happened today. We uncovered vital intel on the terrorists. We opened discussions that could change our entire strategy and policies for the Middle East. I know this has been quite a reversal from where we started just over a week ago and that's why I want to hear from each of the NSC Directors and Statuary Attendees. I want to hear your thoughts on how you think we should proceed. Let's start with Eric."

The Vice President cleared his throat, sighed and quietly began. "Mr. President, the concept of starting over by establishing our mutual points of agreement and developing fresh ideas with an emphasis on trust is a good one. We have think-tanks that recommend such an approach all the time and not just for resolving conflicts in the Middle East. The reason those recommendations have never been implemented is because they won't work unless

60

everyone agrees to play by the same rules. In my opinion, the majority of the people living in the Middle East, including the moderates, see no reason to 'play nice' with infidels.

"I believe that your ideas have merit and should be explored further in hopes that they might work someday. However, in light of all I just said, I do not feel the Middle East is a good place, nor is this a good time, to test a new strategy for achieving peace."

Secretary of State Joan Hartley spoke next. "The Vice President has articulated much of my thinking as well. I might add that I'm not sure what 'points of agreement' we could build upon with terrorists who believe non-Muslims are an abomination before Allah. Setting religious beliefs aside, few countries would define world peace in the same way let alone agree on how we might get there."

Secretary of Defense Steve Lombard added his opinion. "Mr. President, it will be almost impossible to get terrorists to trust that we are being completely honest and have no hidden agenda to take advantage of them with this new approach. I believe they would only agree to your proposal if they thought doing so would relax our guard. The Vice President was correct when he implied that the U.S. has become the ultimate infidel to many of the Muslim people. If they believe that making peace with us is tantamount to making peace with the devil, can we really expect them to deal with us honorably?"

General McComb continued on the theme. "I have to agree there. It's not just trying to get the people of the Middle East to trust us; it's trying to get all of us to trust them in return. I know I'm not going to have faith in any agreements we make with Middle Eastern leaders until a long list of grievances have been addressed first."

Director of National Intelligence Lieutenant General Richard Newman spoke next. "I find I can't remain unbiased in this either, sir. My days are spent finding and stopping people who would take great pleasure in killing off every single American and believe they are doing Allah's will in the process. Just because we decide that the violence has gone on long enough does not mean everyone else will agree. Secretary Hartley made a great point that few nations will define world peace in the same way. Even if we could agree on a definition, the chances of everyone agreeing on a process for achieving global peace would be slim at best."

Director of the CIA George Salazar added, "Like Director Newman, I work to frustrate the plans and efforts of terrorists on a daily basis. At any moment there are literally thousands of people thinking of how they might kill us. Getting people with that mindset to think seriously about achieving a true and lasting peace is a wasted effort. They are far too committed to vengeance and justice through killing off their enemies for me to believe they will change their ways now."

Gil Kowalski, Director of National Drug Control Policy, was last to speak. "I regret I was unable to attend the meeting last week because I was in the Yucatan peninsula with a dozen of my South and Central American counterparts. It sounds like I missed a lot." Everyone laughed lightly at his understatement. "Like so many others here, my responsibilities keep me in constant touch with some of the worst criminals in the world. One thing I will say about most of the drug lords, they make decisions according to their own best interests. In my experience, the President's proposed strategy has a slim chance to succeed. We have to convince everyone involved that this peace initiative will make them richer and happier without putting them in greater danger. Figure out the points of agreement that lead to that goal and you just might be on your way to a viable new strategy."

The room fell silent again as they waited to see how the President would respond to the overwhelming lack of support for his proposal. Matt too was silent but his mind was racing. He was not surprised by their skepticism, in fact, he had agreed with them just days before. He needed to show that a peaceful response did not ignore all their opinions and sage advice. He knew from experience that he needed to adequately address all their concerns. Once there were no more objections, the only alternative left would be to support his proposal. Just as the silence was becoming uncomfortable, he was suddenly inspired.

"Actually," Matt began, "I'm glad to see that we have so much agreement already on such a controversial topic. My own thoughts on the main issues, namely trust and seeing the enemy as part of our larger family, were echoed in most of the opinions expressed around this table. I was especially interested in Gil's comments because I think he offered the key to everyone's objections. The new approach I'm talking about must begin with convincing everyone they will ultimately be better off helping my proposal to succeed."

"Can you give us a specific example, Mr. President?" said Eric Jefferson, who was a bit surprised Matt was still pursuing this line of thinking.

"Of course. In fact, let's start with our own challenges between conservatives and liberals. Let's say that a new bill is brought before Congress that would provide better food, housing and medical care for underprivileged children. We can all guess where the lines would be drawn in debating this issue. The conservatives would be against it and the liberals for it. Each side would end up thinking the other is wrong, either for wasting money and raising taxes or for being stingy and having no compassion for those in need. The usual negotiations to get such a bill passed would bring out the worst in all of us. We would become polarized in our positions and attempt to massage the bill until it doesn't really accomplish anything. The inevitable bad feelings make it tougher for opposing sides to trust each other with every new debate. It's easy to see that we already have tough challenges at home, albeit without the violence, when compared to the Middle East."

The leaders around the table mumbled their mixed reactions to the President's example. Where he was going with this was still anyone's guess.

Matt continued, "I think it's safe to say that it would be impossible to get 100 percent agreement on the bill in question using the same arguments and process we always have. But, what if we approached this differently? What if we invited all of Congress to a meeting where we lined up ten homeless children who would be helped by the proposed legislation? What if we took a vote among the 500-plus elected officials asking which of those kids should be denied better shelter, food and health care? Do we think anyone would deny them such help on principle? Since we still have underprivileged children, it becomes clear that our system is flawed in accomplishing that laudable goal. That is what I mean by starting out fresh by finding our points of agreement."

They nodded their general accord, at least in the example he provided. Who would want America's homeless children to go without food, shelter or proper medical care? Still, finding just one point they could agree upon would not resolve all the other underlying issues involved in making that happen.

Matt was encouraged by the change he could see in their faces. "The real conflict is not whether or not we should all help these kids to have a better life; it is in how we can best accomplish that goal. Once we are clear everyone is willing to help, we can move on to asking better questions such as; 'Who is best equipped to make it happen?' 'How do we fund this effort?' 'If we could start fresh, what solutions would make this a win/win for everyone concerned?'"

Joan Hartley interjected, "Mr. President, this is an interesting exercise on paper, but in the real world your approach is unrealistic. We can't simply undo overnight the long standing political processes that have made us who we are today. Cumbersome as it may be, working within the system is still the best way to go about organizing all the power and money it takes to help the children you mentioned."

Matt recognized that Jane's slight shift in the topic indicated he was making progress. "Perhaps, but let's go back to our situation in the Middle East. Suppose tomorrow everyone on the earth unilaterally agreed to stop all violence for twenty four hours? And then what if we all agreed to extend the peace for a second day, then a third and so on? Hypothetically, this could happen tomorrow without passing any legislation. In many ways, our 'long-standing system' of doing things the way they've always been done is an addiction we must overcome. We continually stand in our own way to avoid change instead of achieving our most important goals. Much like alcoholics in a twelve-step program need to decide for themselves not to drink for just one more day, the world could change its violent ways immediately if each individual agrees to try."

Matt pointed to Director Kowalski noticing he had a point to make. "My job in the war against drugs helps me to understand a lot about addictive behavior. Addicts fall off the wagon all the time, even when they are in rehab. How many 'violence addicts' worldwide does it take to fall off the wagon before things return to what I hesitate to call normal?"

"That's a valid question," Matt said, "but see how quickly it takes us back to familiar old fears and patterns. Perhaps a better way to phrase the question would be, 'When so many people support righteous retribution against their enemies, how does a peace initiative ever get started?' Clearly one side has to go first and not second-guess themselves while setting a peaceful example."

General McComb argued, "That approach won't work. The Muslims will never stop using violence against us unless it's out of fear of our reprisals. Don't forget that to them we are infidels and deserve whatever damage and suffering they can inflict upon us."

National Security Advisor Fred Shapiro interjected, "I feel compelled to add my two cents here considering that I have deep family roots in the region. General McComb has said that achieving a peaceful coexistence between Muslims and infidels won't work. I recall that in 1947 India and Pakistan became free sovereign nations largely through civil disobedience aimed at Great Britain. The Hindus and Muslims fought fiercely among themselves, but the gentle leadership of Mohandas Gandhi had a remarkable effect on all sides of those conflicts. My point is that President Alexander's peace initiative has a precedent that eventually worked between the British, Hindus and Muslims."

Matt took back the floor at this point saying, "Thank you for that reminder, Fred. Perhaps we don't have to reinvent the wheel here. We can scrutinize what Gandhi did right less than 100 years ago. It wasn't perfect but it was far better than an all-out war to resolve their differences. Asking ourselves, 'What can we do today to improve on his success?' is a great example of framing better questions.

"Actually, I'm going to leave all this as 'questions to ponder' for the moment. I want everyone to consider what has been shared for our next meeting. I find this subject fascinating, but there is a lot more to running this country than pursuing peace in the Middle East. I'm late for several meetings on domestic issues. We'll pick this up tomorrow."

Chapter 8

General McComb, Lieutenant General Newman and Director Salazar shared a limousine ride to their next meeting. That would be a briefing on developments from the evidence discovered in and around the underground bunker in Israel. The four-star General set the tone for the discussion. "Have you ever heard a bigger load of crap in your life? Alexander thinks the peaceful resistance trick Gandhi pulled in India will actually work again in the Middle East. Does he really believe we can ever trust a terrorist?"

George Salazar added, "I was thinking the same thing, but he is apparently convinced his plan will work."

Rick Newman's agreement made it unanimous, "It does seem to be a recipe for disaster with no upside for the U.S. I wonder what 'come to Jesus meeting' happened after his heart attack to make the President change his mind? It seems like he's done a one-eighty on us."

McComb said, "I don't care if God Himself came down to set him straight. Trying to achieve peace through trust and nonviolence is a temporary fix at best and just damn unrealistic. I'm guessing it will take a lot more murder and mayhem before he comes to his senses and changes his mind again. It felt like we were so close to doing the right thing just a few days ago but now we're back to square one."

"So what are we going to do about this?" Newman asked.

Salazar replied, "We know it's just a matter of time before the President sees the error of his ways. His peace initiative won't succeed no matter what we do. But I think the passive approach he prefers can actually be used to help speed things along. I believe he will quickly discover the wisdom behind aggressively ending all Middle Eastern conflicts."

McComb and Newman had the same question, "What did you have in mind?"

"In the CIA, we specialize in circumventing terrorist plots before they become reality. We often arrest or otherwise remove the key people before they can carry out an attack. What if, in the spirit of cooperative nonviolence, we just sit back and watch for a while? Even if a vast majority of the countries agree to a policy of nonviolence, there will always be someone who sees this as the perfect time to make themselves heard. The idea is to rectify the President's good, albeit misguided, intentions before he goes too far. I want to nip this in the bud before he announces this plan publicly and tries to sell it to the world."

McComb and Newman pondered this. The approach had merit. After all, Salazar's suggestion was in keeping with the nonviolent intent of the President's proposal and it could make the point quickly. They also knew that it would be Salazar and his people who would catch the heat if things backfired. They couldn't see any downside to the plan.

"I like it," said McComb. "How long before we might see some tangible results?"

"It would probably become noticeable within a few weeks. And understand that I will continue to stop any activity that might interfere with the greater good of the United States."

Newman asked, "Don't you think others might become suspicious once you lower the level of surveillance on these groups?"

Salazar smiled in response. "Not really. I just have to keep rotating my people to cover different activities. I can leave unnoticed holes in our surveillance for short periods so that certain groups will be temporarily off our radar. Their violent acts will seem to occur despite our efforts to stop them instead of passively allowing some tragic events to run their course."

All three men considered the implications. Salazar's plan would serve to show the President the error of his ways by not interfering with the militant factions of the Middle East. They each sincerely felt this was a bold but necessary step that had to be taken for the good of the United States. They rode the rest of the way in silence as their car passed well-known Washington landmarks, each lost in his own thoughts.

***

Riding quietly in the limousine, McComb found himself remembering one of the worst days of his life. He did this frequently enough that it bordered on obsession. That day had proved to define him and his bias against a peaceful approach toward the radicals of the Middle East. Until that day, he had believed in peace through strength and that the role of the military was one of deterrence rather than aggression.

He had won many honors on the battlefield as a young officer in Vietnam, a Silver Star with Valor among them. When his son Martin Jr. said that he too wanted to follow his father's path into the Army, General McComb supported him all the way. He wished now that he could take it back.

Martin Jr. had quickly risen to the rank of Major and specialized in G2 intelligence at the battalion level. His 3rd Battalion, 187th Infantry Regiment, also known as the Iron Rakkasans, was scheduled to pull out of Iraq in a few months. So in August, Major Martin McComb, Jr. was part of the team training the newly organized Iraqi troops to take over all counterinsurgency efforts in the coming months. He oversaw the "checkpoint training" near Yusufiyah to keep terrorists and their murderous ordinance from getting inside the larger cities.

Just before noon on that terrible day, a bus rolled up behind the queue of vehicles approaching the checkpoint. The old school bus was painted an ugly off white with flat house paint. 'Saint Boniface Catholic School' was crudely stenciled in black block letters on the sides to identify the alma mater of the young teenagers inside. There were very few non-Muslim schools in Iraq so this bus caught everyone's attention. Major McComb became interested and walked over to investigate.

A soldier instructed the driver to step out of the bus while telling the teenagers to remain seated. Once the driver was outside, the other soldiers went about the task of inspecting the vehicle for any explosives or passengers who didn't belong. Major McComb was curious enough to question the driver directly about the school. Mustafa didn't speak English but did his best to answer McComb's questions through an interpreter.

Apparently he had only worked for the school a short time. He admitted that it was "just a job" and laughed politely when asked if he was Catholic. The school specialized in educating teens who were orphaned by the war and it was funded by several Catholic churches in the United States. When asked where the priests or nuns were, Mustafa indicated their car had broken down in the last town but he expected them to catch up soon at this checkpoint. He then asked if they could wait for their arrival as long as he parked the bus out of the flow of traffic. The soldiers had finished their inspection so Major McComb allowed Mustafa to pull the bus over to the side to wait for the priests to arrive.

The teenagers poured out of the hot bus and stood in the meager shade it created. The light breeze and fresh air made standing outside preferable to remaining seated. Major McComb kept an eye on the continuing vehicle inspections while he asked more questions of Mustafa. Martin Jr. was fascinated with this country and wondered what life was really like for an Iraqi national who lived in this war-torn land of violence. Mustafa seemed unconcerned with religion or politics while doing his best to earn a living wherever there was work to be had.

A few soldiers who were not currently inspecting vehicles also gathered around to listen and enjoy the break from their routine. There may have been as many as forty men and boys crowded together in the stingy shade of the bus. Mustafa said via the translator that he didn't believe life in Iraq would always be full of security checkpoints and violence. He told them he was certain that peace would eventually come to his country because that was Allah's will. When McComb asked him how he thought there could ever be peace here after thousands of years of violence, Mustafa took that as the sign he'd been waiting for.

***

In his mind, Mustafa flashed back to the events of that same morning. He managed to punch a small hole in the oil line of the priests' car without anyone seeing him. By his calculations, it would break down before reaching their destination, the history museum in Yusufiyah. As they were passing a small town, the car's engine froze up from the lack of oil. Convincing the priests to let Mustafa proceed and wait for them at the main checkpoint while they acquired another car was the key to his plan. He would have a good reason to wait by the checkpoint if none of the clergymen were with him.

Two of the priests had volunteered to ride on the bus, but Mustafa assured them there was no need. An air-conditioned car could easily catch up to the aging bus and it was surprisingly hot that day. The teenagers were used to the climate so it was not such a hardship on them. The priests relented with a promise from Mustafa that he would wait for them at the checkpoint and return if they didn't show up within an hour or two.

He couldn't believe how well his plan was unfolding. The American and Iraqi soldiers did not seem suspicious of him and they even became friendly. Their rapid questions seemed to be out of genuine curiosity rather than an interrogation of one whom they did not trust. When more of the soldiers edged closer to hear his description of life in the villages of Iraq, Mustafa prayed for a sign that he was indeed doing Allah's will.

Suddenly, the priests' car pulled to a stop behind the school bus and they walked over to join the crowd. The American Major had just asked Mustafa a question that told him the time had come. The Major wanted to know how a lasting peace could ever come to Iraq. Mustafa had been taught since he was young that infidels, people who did not believe Allah was the one true God and Mohammed was His prophet, were the reason why there could be no peace. Once everyone believed in the loving ways of Allah, peace would be the natural result. However, the infidels must be eliminated in order to attain peace on earth.

Mustafa decided this was the perfect time to detonate the C-4 explosive vest he had concealed under his loose shirt. If he could wipe out forty or fifty of the infidels while serving the will of Allah in such a holy way, he was assured of attaining heaven.

He looked around at the group and then directly at Major McComb. He said in Arabic, "All you need to know to achieve peace in Iraq and throughout the world is *Allahu Akbar*!" Before the interpreter could translate "God is the greatest," Mustafa pulled the detonator pin and his vest exploded. The blast killed thirty-two people, including himself and Major McComb, while injuring twenty one other men and boys.

***

General McComb shook his head to end his morbid reverie. He took a deep breath and released it slowly to clear his mind before exiting the limousine with Newman and Salazar. He had pieced together the story of his son's murder from the survivors of the attack at the checkpoint to Yusufiyah. The soldiers had treated the terrorist with polite kindness and a sincere desire to understand life from his perspective. They dropped their guard because they trusted that the bus driver's intentions were simply to help the orphaned teenagers as he earned a living for himself.

How could anyone who felt the pain of cruel attacks like this ever believe there could be trust between enemies, let alone a lasting peace in the Middle East? Martin McComb had lost his son learning that hard lesson. He would be damned if he'd let his fellow Americans suffer as he had if he could stop it. Surely the only way to achieve true peace in the Middle East was to eliminate the terrorists and anyone who supported them. If these animals could be captured, tried in a court of law and jailed, that would be acceptable to him. If they died resisting, McComb would not lose any sleep over their deaths. Killing terrorists was simple justice for having caused the deaths of so many innocent people, including his son.

Chapter 9

Matt was in the White House residence living room. With him were Vice President Eric Jefferson, Secretary of State Joan Hartley and Secretary of Defense Steve Lombard. He had called them together informally to answer their questions offline and let them know what he planned to do next.

"Eric," he began, "why don't you start us off? Ask me anything that's on your mind with regard to the situation in the Holy Land."

"Mr. President, you seem to have made a complete reversal of the position you took just prior to your medical scare. You started out saying WMDs were on the table. Now it seems a peaceful response is your intention. Where are we really headed?"

"That seems to be the question on everyone's mind," Matt observed. "The truth is that life-threatening experience caused me to review my goals and priorities, not just personally, but from a strategic and tactical perspective for the country. Being the leader of the world's most powerful army does not help me look for peaceful solutions when we're provoked...quite the opposite in fact. My time off after the heart attack helped me remember an old saying: Just because we have the ability to beat up every other country in the world doesn't mean we should.

"Years ago, when I was first elected to Congress, I worked hard to win the hearts and minds of my constituents and even my enemies. I realize now how lazy I became thinking I didn't have to win over anyone as long as I could overpower them into submission. That was a mistake and I deeply regret it. The good news is that I've found myself again and now resolve to keep my eye on the ball."

Joan said, "Saying our response might include WMDs put the taste of blood in the mouths of some very powerful people on the NSC. How do you propose to gain their cooperation after the events in Israel got their blood boiling in the first place?"

"The truth is I can't do much about that. I can admit I was headed in a direction that needed to change. I can also meet with them privately, as we are doing now, to see if we can come to an agreement that will give my nonviolent policies a chance."

Steve frowned, "And what will you do if they don't come around?"

"I'm not against firing anyone for insubordination," Matt replied, "but they are all good people who deserve to be a part of this historic effort to change the world. If they choose to oppose my peace plan, I'll have to deal with that as it comes."

Eric asked, "So what is our next step? Do we just ignore the biological attacks and the destruction of the compound in Israel? That was the most aggressive threat against our people since 9/11."

Matt paused for a moment and chose his words carefully. "There is a huge difference between doing nothing and using only amicable means to accomplish a goal. I am prepared to personally meet with the leaders of the Middle Eastern nations to present my vision for a peaceful world. And I intend to do this immediately. I still want our investigators to positively identify the guilty parties involved in these attacks. However, my future plans will focus on encouraging and inspiring those who distrust and hate us more than establishing blame."

Joan was shocked, "You mean you're going to ask the Muslim leaders to come to the U.S. to meet with you with little or no notice? Most of them will appreciate the chance to publicly decline your invitation using the media to do so."

Matt made it clear he was serious. "I will not ask them to come here. I plan to go to the Middle East, unannounced, and meet with each of them on their turf. I am resolute when I say that 'full disclosure' is our best chance to win their respect, trust and cooperation. The usual political positioning games must be set aside to give peace a proper chance to work."

Now Steve expressed surprise. "Go there unannounced? Word is bound to get out and make you an easy target for perhaps a million angry people who would love to see you dead. Are you sure this is a good idea?"

"Absolutely! I will keep my itinerary secret and strictly need-to-know regarding how long we'll be there, how we'll be traveling, and where we'll be staying. If Osama Bin Laden can hide from us for more than a decade, I'm sure we can figure out how to keep me out of harm's way for a few days even with Armageddon nearby. I am willing to use whatever means necessary to stay off everyone's radar while I am in the region, including disguising myself and using my doubles. My sincerity and faith in this plan cannot be conveyed properly unless I am face-to-face with the people I am asking to trust us."

Joan, realizing that she would be at the President's side for the duration of this risky plan, asked, "Just how do you expect the heads of state of all those countries to react when you show up on their doorsteps without warning?"

"The 'unannounced' part is intended to serve many purposes," Matt replied. "First, we issue a press release that says our Secretary of State is going overseas to meet with her Middle Eastern counterparts while I am resting at Camp David. The press will not expect to see me for a few days so the cover story is plausible enough. Joan, you will work quickly to set these appointments and I will accompany you, in disguise, to each one. When we are behind closed doors with as few witnesses as we can manage, I'll reveal my presence and ask to speak alone with the head of each country in turn. I intend to personally present my vision for the future and how we will get there together without fanfare or media coverage."

Eric quipped, "I may want to be President someday but I don't want to get there like this. It seems suicidal to expose yourself in this way, especially under such precarious circumstances. This may sound indelicate, but just what will we do if they manage to assassinate you on this trip?"

"The Office of the President," Matt stated, "is not just a person, it's an ongoing position. You need to be ready to take over in case the worst happens. I am confident that you will do a great job if anything does happen to me, but I have no plans of dying on this trip. If I wasn't positive that this will work, I wouldn't take such a risk.

"Eric and Joan, I need you both to arrange the private meetings and prepare an announcement for the media. Steve, I'll need you to help me explain this to Generals McComb and Newman as well as to George Salazar. You have a better relationship with them, especially in light of my new strategy."

"I'll set that up for tomorrow morning," Steve assured Matt.

"But first," Matt sighed, "I have to explain it to Erin."

***

When they said their good nights and left him alone, Matt walked over to the door that led to the master bedroom. Erin was still awake and reading a book as he entered.

"How did today go?" she asked.

"About as well as it could, I suppose." Matt exhaled loudly and sat down next to her on the side of the bed. "I need to bring you up to speed on a few things that are coming up."

He described his idea to secretly travel to the Middle East while telling the media they were going to Camp David for a few days. Matt was doing his best to reassure Erin that he was in little danger if they followed his plan to keep his trip quiet until he returned. She didn't say a word the entire time. When he finished, he gave her his best presidential smile as his way of giving her the floor.

"And you want me to stay at Camp David keeping the reporters occupied until you return?" she asked.

"I wouldn't have put it quite like that, but essentially yes," Matt replied sheepishly.

"I have a better idea. I think I should go with you on this trip. I know I'm not part of the political meetings, but I want to be with you the rest of the time. You said yourself that it should be safe and I support wholeheartedly what you are trying to do. You will need all the moral support you can get and someone has to keep an eye on you in case you have any more health problems. You say you have no plans to die over there...well prove it by taking me with you for all those reasons and more. Hey, it's the Middle East. Women are barely noticed. I'll keep myself respectfully covered up and no one will ever know I was there."

Matt didn't have much room to argue with her. He rarely did. He had always admired her wisdom, judgment and quick mind. As much as it worried him that Erin would also be put at risk, he had to admit that having her along would mean a lot to him. She would be an excellent sounding board for the challenges that would inevitably arise.

"Okay," he said quietly. "But you must do exactly what the security detail tells you to do. We will not be following the usual travel protocols. Our doubles will fly Marine One to Camp David and 'be seen' until we return. We have to do whatever it takes to remain anonymous so we will travel as support staff personnel. If any of the wrong people learn where we are, our lives and the mission will be in great danger."

Chapter 10

The next day Generals Martin McComb and Richard Newman and Director George Salazar sat in the Oval Office. President Alexander had called the meeting but he turned the floor over to Secretary Lombard after the requisite greetings and pleasantries.

Steve began, "I know it was quite a surprise when the President announced his intentions to respond without violence to the attack on our supply depot in Israel."

The nods and looks on their faces made it clear he had hit that one on the nose.

"I can assure you," Steve continued, "that President Alexander has an aggressive plan to help this shift in policy succeed. Completely unannounced and without following the usual protocols, the President will covertly travel to key Middle Eastern cities and remain anonymous until he is face-to-face with the leaders of each nation. Then he will personally present his strategy and ask for their support."

Martin couldn't help himself and blurted out, "That's crazy, Steve! They'll kill him the moment they get the chance. Even if he survives the first meeting, his life will be in constant danger once everyone else knows where he is and how he's going about this." The two Directors nodded in agreement, glad that McComb had said what they were thinking so they wouldn't have to.

"I'm sitting right here, Martin" Matt interjected hoping to lighten the mood. "I believe your assessment of the danger involved may be exaggerated. Security is hardly going to be ignored and this new policy requires my meeting personally with the Muslim leaders if we are to give it a realistic chance. They are more likely to be persuaded if I show them the proper respect. I have every intention of living to see this plan through. If peace is ever to prevail in the Middle East, and everywhere else for that matter, someone has to go first. This is a very assertive response, in some ways even more so than the ones you proposed."

"Who else knows about this?" asked Richard.

Steve answered, "Just us, Joan Hartley, the Vice President and the First Lady. The fewer people who know the details of this plan, the better. Even I will be out of the loop regarding the precise itinerary and security details."

George looked at the President. "Is there any way we can talk you out of doing this?" he pleaded.

Matt smiled at his concern and said, "Not unless you have a better idea of how to bring peace to the region without violence. Winning their hearts, minds and trust can't happen through force or the usual diplomatic process. They will come to understand and believe just how committed I am to this plan. Without my meeting with them face-to-face, the United States and its President will continue to be seen as a force for evil rather than a trusted friend."

Martin asked, "How soon are you planning to make this trip? Can we at least have our troops ready to respond if there is an attempt on your life?"

Matt was disappointed at the question. He knew he needed to make himself clear. "I think to do that would only serve to undermine the reason I'm going there in the first place. If we show ourselves ready to strike back at the first sign of trouble, how does that engender trust and build confidence that we truly desire peace?"

"What is it that you want us to do?" Richard asked.

Steve took that as his cue. "We will, of course, need additional agents from George's people if we are to keep our security presence as low-key as possible. When traveling, the President and the First Lady will be disguised as staff members in Joan's political entourage."

McComb almost yelled, "You mean the First Lady is going on this trip?"

Matt answered him directly, "Yes, and I really don't want any more discussion about the merits of this trip. We need to work together for this to succeed rather than continue to speculate on how it might fail."

"I apologize, Mr. President," Martin said with forced calm. "I was out of line, but I am truly concerned for your safety. Rest assured your guidelines will be followed to get you back home safely."

Steve said, "We all share your concern for the President's safety, General McComb. So let's go over the security protocols for the trip."

***

Later that day, McComb, Newman and Salazar met in George's office inside Langley. They couldn't believe the situation had deteriorated this much in so short a time. They had developed a great plan. Allowing terrorists to operate freely in the Middle East by strategically ignoring certain groups would surely result in violence. But then, who would have guessed that POTUS would make this absurd trip? They realized their plan could backfire by putting the President's life at risk.

McComb was the trio's military expert but he lacked experience in covert operations. Newman's career had been focused on intelligence, but both men wanted Salazar's assessment on where things stood. "It looks like we put our plan on hold until the President returns from his trip. This whole thing could blow up in our faces if we don't keep the usual lid on things while he's exposed."

McComb shook his head. "But he is going over there with the intention of spelling out his proposal to their heads of state. There will be no way to gently retreat from this plan, especially if he is successful in gaining their cooperation. We all know that his pipe dream ultimately won't work, but he's sure it will. What can we do to show him the truth of this?"

Newman replied, "We know what convinced you, General. The fanatic who killed your son struck you at your core. You understand the brutal way they think. Without a reality check that hits him where he lives, I don't think the President will see this any other way."

Salazar had an unconventional idea. "You believe we could convince POTUS by making this personal? We could arrange an event where the people affected included someone very special to him!"

79

McComb stared at Salazar in disbelief. "George, you're seriously suggesting we allow terrorists to assassinate someone close to the President?"

"Of course, not!" George growled. "What I am suggesting is we anonymously leak information to those in the region who would do the dirty work with the absolute directive that nobody dies while making the message clear."

George continued as he warmed to his own idea, "What if we let slip where the First Lady will be at a time when we're certain POTUS is somewhere else safe and protected? I believe that once FLOTUS has been, let's say kidnapped, it won't matter that she was returned unharmed. The President will be furious and abandon his peace plan."

"It's treason that we're even discussing this! What makes you think that you can stop these zealots from hurting the First Lady once they have her?" Newman asked.

"I know the right person to organize this and he'll do all the recruiting," Salazar replied. "If I make it clear that a huge ransom will be paid only if no harm comes to the First Lady, he won't let us down. Regardless of what happens, we can be sure that the connection between us and the kidnappers is untraceable."

McComb and Newman sat stone-faced, both acknowledging that this was a line they had never intended to cross. Both of their consciences were saying that it was one thing to sit back and let violence unfold naturally by looking the other way. It was quite another to leak security information that would lead to the kidnapping of the First Lady, no matter how carefully it was planned and executed.

Newman said, "I can't be a part of this. I know something has to be done, but allowing this to happen is further than I am willing to go. There must be a better way."

McComb agreed, "I hear what you're saying, Richard, but I don't have a better idea. George, I can't be a part of this either."

Salazar had the same thoughts against this new plan, but he also felt that if they backed down now they were no better than the cowards who declined to help his father in Vietnam. He knew neither of these men were cowards. He realized that they really wanted him to proceed; but they also wanted to maintain plausible deniability if it all went to hell. Well, he hadn't become the Director of the CIA by allowing his covert missions to fail! He knew better than anyone how to pull this off. No one would die and the President would change his mind about the peace initiative.

Still, George could see that this new plan seemed more like the work of a terrorist than a national hero. He had to decide if the ends really did justify the means. Before he made up his mind, he thought about the worst case scenario. That clinched it. After all, who would ever suspect him regardless of what happened? He decided that he alone would take the risk. In fact, knowing he was the best man for the job, he felt proud that he could do this for his country.

"I'll drop the whole thing," he lied. "I agree that it's too great a risk to take under the circumstances."

Chapter 11

Salazar had just ended his call with Ramin. The Arabic name meant a person who brings comfort and joy. He thought that was ironic given what they were planning to do. He had known Ramin for many years as a broker for all manner of illicit arrangements. Ramin only knew Salazar by his voice and pseudonym, Amir. It was obvious that Amir was highly connected in the U.S., but Ramin would never have guessed that he was George Salazar, Director of the CIA. Amir had always been a good customer, who paid as agreed, and that was all Ramin cared about.

Amir/Salazar had a long history of employing Ramin to find people who would do anything if the price was right. He typically handled the details for any job he accepted, but Amir said this one was special. He wanted someone kidnapped and he didn't care if Ramin kept the ransom money. Ramin didn't care if this abduction was about revenge or politics. He only cared that it paid well. He eagerly asked for the specifics.

Amir withheld most of the details when he explained what he needed. All he disclosed was that a high level U.S. government official would soon come to the Middle East and travel to several capital cities. He would supply Ramin with the itinerary and travel plans under three conditions. The target would not be harmed at any point in the process. The person would be safely returned upon receipt of the ransom, and Ramin's crew would inflict as few casualties as possible, with zero fatalities.

Ramin assured Amir that this was possible. He would first meet with those he trusted to develop a plan. They would help recruit the right people for the job. The call ended with an agreement to speak again after the team had been confirmed and the plan developed to get Amir's final approval.

George stared at the phone in his hand in astonishment. He had just officially committed treason. His conscience was saying it was not too late to stop. He carefully considered if he really wanted to go through with this but every time he ran the scenario through his head, the result was the same. The First Lady would be returned in good health and the President would understand that fear and revenge were simply a way of life in the Middle East. Alexander's strategy for a non-violent solution would be quickly set aside for a more realistic plan. George decided that it was up to him to protect the United States from its own President and his naive ideas for attaining peace.

***

Afkar was thrilled over his good fortune. Allah was indeed smiling down upon him. Ramin had said that his information came from a very reliable source. Even with Ramin's huge commission, the wealth and prestige this job would bring was almost too good to believe. This was the kind of opportunity that changed lives.

There was much to be done and Afkar would have to assemble an experienced and dependable team of at least twenty people to ensure their success. He directed his lieutenants to be discreet in the recruiting process. The target of this abduction was promised to be a very important American. The fewer people who knew of this operation, the better.

Afkar had to design a plan that would work well under most conditions. He would receive short notice of when and where the target would be in Damascus. At the right place and time, they had to neutralize the security personnel and transport the target to a safe holding area without being followed. They would also need to remain hidden while they bargained over the ransom and details of the exchange. Normally it was easy to restrain a hostage, but not in this case. This target was not to be harmed. That meant a holding place where no amount of cries for help would attract attention. This job had more than its share of problems, but he enjoyed the challenge, knowing it would change his life forever.

The Andrews Air Force Base air traffic controller announced, "Special Air Mission 1135, you are cleared for departure on runway niner alpha."

"Roger that," said the pilot of the 747. "SAM 1135 cleared for takeoff on niner alpha." He taxied onto the runway and reminded everyone to buckle up.

The passengers included Secretary of State Joan Hartley and her usual traveling entourage of assistants and agents. Under strict instructions, no one drew attention to Matt and Erin Alexander. It was intended that none of the airport personnel, including pilots, were aware that POTUS and FLOTUS were aboard. To complete their cover, the 747's call sign was given as Special Air Mission 1135 rather than Air Force One. As far as anyone knew, President Alexander and the First Lady were already at Camp David for some rest and relaxation.

In actuality, Matt and Erin were aboard the plane headed for the Middle East. They traveled in disguise to keep their presence on the flight unknown for as long as possible. Joan's office had scheduled initial meetings with her political counterparts in four Muslim nations. Realistically it was understood that once Matt made his presence known at the first stop in Riyadh, Saudi Arabia's capital, word that he was in the region would spread like wildfire. The plan was to keep their travel schedule and itinerary unpredictable. That would minimize the chances anyone could organize an attack against them. To that end, the appointments with the various statesmen had been arranged with an open time window of four days. No country would receive much more than an hour's notice of their arrival inside of that window. While this was an unusual request, many of the heads of state of these countries were keen to prove their cooperative spirit and concern over the recent attack on the U.S. compound in Israel.

Nearly twenty Muslim nations in that region were invited to meet with the U.S. Secretary of State. Many didn't reply in a timely manner. However, Joan only wanted to meet with four of them to get the ball rolling and the right four agreed to the terms and agenda.

The secret itinerary was disclosed on a need-to-know basis only. They would first land in Riyadh, Saudi Arabia followed by Damascus, Syria, then Amman, Jordan, and finally Cairo, Egypt. Matt and Joan were relieved the leaders of these key nations graciously agreed to the odd schedule. Saudi Arabia and Egypt were chosen for their leadership roles in the Muslim world given their size, economies and friendly relations with the U.S. They would be strategic allies in developing a critical mass of support for Matt's peace plan. Syria's cooperation would be essential to winning over members of the extreme opposition. Jordan, like Syria, shared a border with Israel and worked well with capitalists, socialists and communists alike. Also, because the underground bunker the terrorists built was hidden inside Jordan's borders, a gesture of their cooperation would carry a lot of political weight.

Everyone aboard SAM 1135 took advantage of the comfortable design of the 747 to rest and to minimize jet lag as much as possible. They needed to mentally prepare for the days ahead. While planned in great detail, these unprecedented meetings had been organized quickly. They knew their lives would soon be at great risk.

***

Matt and Erin were in the Executive Suite at the nose of the aircraft directly below the control cabin. Neither was able to sleep, even though both had tried for more than an hour.

Hearing Matt's restless movements, Erin asked, "Do you want to talk about it?"

"Which part?" Matt questioned.

"Can we discuss what I can do while all these crucial meetings are going on?" she replied.

"Truthfully," Matt answered as he turned on a light, "I'd prefer that you never left this plane. Since that's not going to happen, tell me what you want to do."

"I'd really like to get a feel for how these people live. I'd enjoy taking a tour to see the residential areas and interesting places in this part of the world. And maybe do a little shopping while I'm at it," she added with a grin.

"I'm sure that could be arranged," he smiled back. "Promise that you will follow whatever guidelines the protective detail sets? The Secret Service knows how to keep you safe, but only if you do what they say," Matt reminded.

"I know," Erin breathed, sounding a bit disappointed. In truth, she was more than a little anxious about this trip. Just the thought of it sent chills up her spine, but the risk was to her husband, not her. She hoped that showing her eagerness for playing the tourist during his meetings would put his mind at ease, at least where she was concerned. After all, she really was interested in the people and culture in this part of the world. Erin had traveled much in her life but mostly as the wife of an elected official and that had always placed restrictions on what she could see and do. Maybe touring without fanfare would allow her to enjoy her visit to these mysterious and exotic places.

For his part, Matt was worried about his wife. It just didn't feel right to bring her along considering the potential for danger, and he wasn't sure why he had consented. If he was honest with himself, he was pleased by her support and enthusiasm for his plan. It felt good to make her happy and to feel the love they shared again. It seemed everything between them had changed for the better since his heart attack. He marveled that instead of losing everything, his life included, he now had the woman he loved at his side as he took on the biggest challenge of his life.

Matt was unable to shake the recurring feeling of déjà vu that he had experienced all of this before. It was as if he had already been shown what would happen on this trip. It had played in his mind like a big budget movie. And just like in the movies, he sensed disaster was coming. That should have been enough for him to call a halt to this entire trip. However, he believed to his core that if he stayed with the plan, a positive result would eventually work itself out, in spite of any setbacks.

Chapter 12

Joan Hartley stepped off the 747, onto the red carpet rolled out for her, at the Riyadh airport in Saudi Arabia. She was greeted with all the pomp and circumstance normally afforded to a visiting cabinet member of a foreign country. Matt and Erin came down the passenger stairs with the staffers doing their best to blend in. After a quick ceremony in the airport's Royal Pavilion, they were all loaded into several large black SUVs for transport to the Al Amoud Hotel in downtown Riyadh.

The hotel was situated near the King Abdullah Palace which was Saudi Arabia's answer to the White House. Joan was apprehensive about sitting down with the Saudi Minister of State, Khazin Almahdi. She was recognized for her charm and charisma, but Minister Almahdi was a well-known misogynist. Meeting with him would be challenging, to say the least.

When they were all settled at the hotel, Matt, Erin and Joan met with the head of their Secret Service detail, Wayne Thompson. They waited until Wayne assured them that the room was free of any surveillance devices before getting down to business.

Joan reviewed with them the background she had on King Tabir. "He was born in Saudi Arabia and inherited his position. He received a business degree from Yale and was an excellent student despite living the good life that America had to offer. Apparently he understood that he'd never get another chance to move freely about the world once his father passed the title on to him. So he enjoyed himself jet-setting and impressing other young, wealthy aristocrats. Once he became King, Tabir took his leadership role quite seriously. He became very devoted to his faith and gratefully earned the love and respect of his people. He was considered to be a moderate, both religiously and politically. He would make an excellent ally in reaching out to the other Muslim countries because of his sensible position on most issues."

Matt nodded. He had read most of this already in Tabir's dossier. It was no accident that he had decided to start his campaign of peace here. After all, it was the home of the mosques in Mecca and Medina, the two holiest places in Islam. Matt had met the King only once years ago at a formal function before either of them were elevated to their current positions. Bridging the gap between their two countries would be a formidable task, bordering on momentous, if they were successful.

Matt reviewed with Joan the cultural challenges they were about to face. "The United States has a history of relatively good relations with Saudi Arabia. Your position is worthy of the respect needed to get their attention. However, your gender is cause for concern given the Muslim culture, as you well know. Minister Almahdi will avoid discussing important matters of state with a woman. His misogyny should work to our advantage once he realizes the true purpose of our visit. He will be highly motivated to arrange an impromptu meeting between King Tabir and me rather than suffer through several hours of negotiations with a female." Joan smiled ruefully in understanding and shook her head that this was still an issue in the modern world.

Matt had already worked out most of the meeting's details with Joan, but he wanted Agent Thompson in the loop to ensure his security measures supported their mission. There were thirty two Americans total in the U.S. entourage. Matt, Erin and Joan were supported by three assistants and the rest were Secret Service agents. They were split into three security teams assigned to protect the President, First Lady, and Secretary of State. When POTUS was traveling outside of the hotel or palace, there were a dozen CIA agents assigned to stay close while blending in with the crowd. They had orders to keep a low profile unless an emergency presented itself.

The plan was for Joan to be accompanied by Matt and their assigned bodyguards along with four other agents. Matt would travel in the SUV with Joan using three other vehicles and the additional agents to escort them. POTUS was not to receive any special treatment, such as opening doors or addressing him with a salutation that might draw notice to him. He was to be treated as any other assistant to the Secretary of State.

With the security details nailed down, Erin's itinerary was discussed. She confirmed her desire to see the "real" Riyadh by visiting residential areas as well as taking in the main tourist sites. She reluctantly agreed that all shopping would be done in the hotel and that she would not get out of the vehicle for any reason. Erin and her assistant, Karen Moffitt, would ride with Agent Pam Selco. That arrangement positioned two agents in each of three SUVs while following the local custom that kept the females together. The idea was to appear as if there was no hierarchy to the security of the vehicles. Erin agreed to wear a modest disguise. Pam wanted the casual observer to think Joan's entourage was taking in the sights while they waited for the political meeting to conclude.

And with that, it was time to move out and test the waters of President Alexander's peace plan.

***

It was late, but George Salazar was not asleep. He was on the phone in Washington talking to Wayne Thompson in Riyadh about the security arrangements for POTUS and the Secretary of State. He tried to sound casual as he asked about the First Lady's schedule. When Wayne described the low profile measures they agreed to employ, George was confident Ramin would succeed. If they used the same protection measures in Damascus the following day, it would not be hard to "safely" abduct her with few, if any, casualties among the agents.

George had already instructed his CIA "spooks" to focus their surveillance on POTUS but be available for the First Lady if needed. They were to remain out of sight as long as nothing required their assistance. He and Wayne agreed to speak again after POTUS' meeting with King Tabir.

George then assumed his Amir persona and called Ramin. He confirmed the target was expected to be in Damascus the following day. Ramin said his people were gathered, briefed and ready to go at any time. He trusted Ramin to follow his instructions, but this was serious business. In fact, if Ramin was ever detained and questioned, George would have to make sure he didn't survive the interrogation. Salazar's conscience was relentless in urging him to stop. He did his best to ignore it. After all, the success of his plan was vital to the security of the United States.

***

Joan and Matt were fascinated by the eclectic mix of cultures and architecture as they rode to the Palace. In the U.S., buildings that were a few hundred years old were a rarity. Here, it was common to see ornate structures many centuries old comfortably sitting next to modern glass towers. There was a long history here indeed. It was no wonder the Arab world considered Americans to be arrogant adolescents rather than mature leaders advancing humanity. Matt knew he had to overcome their perception and bias if he was to have any success with King Tabir.

As the official convoy rolled up to the grand portico entrance, it was plain to see they were expected. There were many well-dressed men and women waiting with a small band underscoring the celebratory mood. Joan adjusted the silk scarf over her hair out of respect for her hosts. As she exited the vehicle and introductions were made, she could see the foreboding in her counterpart's eyes. Even from a deferential distance, Matt saw it too. He was now certain that Minister of State Almahdi would become their reluctant ally once he learned he could avoid meeting with Joan.

But when they entered the crowded Palace, Joan and Matt could see that it was not going to be as easy to arrange a private meeting as they had hoped. Joan asked their host in English if, after the media had completed their questions and pictures, they could be alone with just their assistants. At first Almahdi gave her the impression that he did not understand English, but then he smiled and declared that the press must leave immediately. Joan's bodyguard could speak Arabic and discreetly translated the announcement. Almahdi had told the media the American Secretary of State wanted them all out of the room. Joan remained silent knowing it was better to ignore Almahdi's purposeful misrepresentation.

Once the disgruntled members of the press had departed, Joan and her entourage were ushered into a large conference room. It was already filled with the usual political figures who attended such meetings. She requested that most of these people leave the room and suggested that only one assistant and bodyguard for her and Almahdi remain. She explained that the discussion was highly confidential. He agreed easily enough since he felt the fewer witnesses there were to this meeting, the better it was for him. He brusquely dismissed his people. Most of them stood and left without another word, clearly puzzled and somewhat offended. Joan wondered what he had said this time that upset them but she didn't bother to ask for a translation.

There were still more people in the room than Joan preferred but with a confirming nod from Matt, she let it go. The Secretary of State sat down at the middle of the conference table directly across from the Saudi Minister of State. They exchanged the required pleasantries before getting down to business. Joan knew her words and manner from here on would make all the difference.

"Your esteemed Minister," she began, "I must beg your pardon and tell you that the reason for my presence here today is not what it seems. I am here to shield a higher purpose between our countries than the agenda before us. I apologize that I could not tell you this before we met face to face."

He looked at her with suspicion and asked her to explain.

"The matters that need to be discussed today are above both our positions within our governments. That is why President Matthew Alexander respectfully requests the presence of the Custodian of the Two Holy Mosques, King Tabir, to join us in order to continue with this unprecedented meeting."

Almahdi was silent for a moment, obviously collecting his patience as well as his thoughts. "I regret to say that King Tabir is unavailable to meet with anyone today. I assure you that I have his full confidence in properly representing our interests regarding any topic we discuss."

Joan answered, "I humbly ask again if King Tabir would make time to meet directly with the President of the United States. We have gone to a great deal of trouble to make this as convenient for you as possible."

Her counterpart was now perplexed. He was irritated that this woman was apparently questioning his position and his right to speak for his King. He managed a diplomatic yet condescending, "I have already said that King Tabir is not available. Perhaps we should adjourn so you can rest after your long journey?"

At that moment her assistant stood up from his place behind Joan and said, "Minister, we are fully rested and I regret the secrecy required to bring me here safely. I am the President of the United States and I request that this meeting continue with only King Tabir and me at a secure location of his choosing. I ask that we meet at his earliest convenience. I am content to wait here until he is available."

The Minister was clearly shocked and looked to Joan for confirmation. Her serious expression convinced him to remain silent. He watched amazed as Matt removed the glasses and carefully peeled off the prosthetic nose, false mustache and heavy eyebrows. It was an effective disguise because, up to now, Almahdi had not given the lowly assistant a second glance. He also had no appreciation for being toyed with in this manner. The Minister angrily balked and repeated his position. "I regret that King Tabir is unavailable. Perhaps arrangements can be made for you to meet with him at another time using the proper channels and protocols!"

Matt had guessed it would come down to this and so he played his trump card. "I understand your reluctance to disturb King Tabir and I apologize for placing you in this seemingly untenable position. If you insist that the King is unavailable, then I believe you. I will do as you suggest by using the proper protocols and channels. King Tabir clearly values your judgment for you to deny my personal request without consulting with him. In the meantime, I will leave Secretary Hartley here to discuss several pressing matters of state with you."

The Minister looked horrified and his left eye started to twitch. He saw no dignified way out of this predicament. He could stubbornly stay with his original position but that meant a long meeting with this Secretary woman. Worse yet, to make no effort to contact King Tabir at the request of President Alexander would probably mean the end of his political career. Angry as he was, if he did as requested, this embarrassing meeting would become King Tabir's problem.

"I will see what I can do," the Minister announced as he quickly departed.

***

President Alexander waited forty-two minutes before King Tabir entered the royal conference room of his Palace. After offering his apologies for keeping POTUS waiting, the King turned and motioned for his people to leave them alone. Matt did the same with Joan and the Secret Service agent. He was inwardly anxious and yet pleased that this key meeting and moment was about to happen.

92

"And so, Mr. President," Tabir began, "may I ask what brings you to my humble home under such unusual circumstances?"

"Your Majesty, thank you for your gracious hospitality. I'm sure you're aware of the recent attack on our military supply depot in Israel. Justice is demanded by the families of our fallen soldiers and my advisors urge me to respond with greater force than ever before. At first, I was prepared to follow that violent path the moment we could identify who was responsible for this horrific act of aggression." Matt paused to gauge the reaction of the King. Seeing none, he continued.

"I have since reconsidered our options, knowing we all desire peace. I realized nothing good would come from seeking vengeance. No doubt the tragic attack on our soldiers was deemed "payback" for other transgressions, real or imagined, against the Islamic world. If I were to strike back at them, they would only retaliate and the vicious cycle would continue. This is just as true today as it was thousands of years ago."

Tabir simply nodded his agreement without changing his expression.

"I have decided to take a stand and allow the attack against our soldiers to mark the end of the violence. For the sake of a lasting peace, someone has to be willing to forgive and stop the bloodshed. I am no great scholar of the *Qur'an*, but doesn't Mohammed - praise be unto Him - also teach that we should '... meet the evil with good behavior'?"

The King could not hide his surprise. Not only had President Alexander accurately translated the *Qur'an*, he had also shown respect and given the proper salutation in the Prophet's honor. He replied with a nod, "It is true, what you say."

Matt continued, "Two occasions where violence is clearly sanctioned in Islam occur when your life is threatened or when you are being forcibly removed from your home. We contend that both of these offenses have been committed against the people of the United States. Some would disagree, using clever logic. Many in this region do not recognize or treat our military and political bases as our own sovereign land. That leaves the question of our right to defend our lives."

King Tabir had never heard an American politician speak knowledgeably of the sacred scripture. In his experience, any question of law had always been interpreted according to the ways of secular thinking rather than from the truth as given in the Qur'an. All of Islam knows that the truth, as the Prophet wrote down for all, has always been and will always be. Most westerners could not understand that Allah's laws always rise above those of man's design. Perhaps, he mused to himself, there was common ground between himself and this most unusual American President.

"Practically speaking, no amount of violence or vengeance will return our fallen people to their loved ones. Doesn't the Qur'an also teach that Allah - glorified and exalted is He - prefers that we pardon and overlook the transgressions against us, for God loves good-doers?" Matt asked.

The King continued to be impressed. This POTUS may not have been a scholar of the Qur'an, but he certainly knew how to approach this difficult subject from a Muslim's perspective.

"Indeed, it is so written!" answered Tabir.

"My request is simple though my ultimate goal will not be easily reached. I ask that we make great use of this unprecedented opportunity. The United States is choosing to respond with forgiveness rather than aggression. I ask you to stand with me to condemn vengeance and violence from this point forward. Those who share in this vision of peace will urge all Middle Eastern countries and militant groups to do the same." He paused to see the King's reaction.

For his part, Tabir was trying to detect the President's true motives. There was little to lose in agreeing to Alexander's proposal. Supporting such rhetoric was needed in international politics to avoid economic sanctions and to maintain a "most favored nation" trading status. So what else did this man have in mind that would be worth risking his life to come here? Tabir decided to ask him directly.

"And what else do you request of me? I see no loss if I endorse what you propose so far, but what remains unsaid between us that will be difficult for me to support?"

Matt knew they were down to the heart of it. Saudi Arabia was one of America's closest Muslim allies but they also feared economic ruin once their oil reserves were depleted. These proud people didn't accept change easily and his proposal would bring far more change than a simple cease-fire. Matt decided to unveil his new policy of transparent negotiations and lay all his cards on the table.

"I'm sure some will see this proposal as a ploy for the U.S. to gain a greater political foothold in this region. They will say our motive is merely to ensure a continuous flow of oil to the U.S. I have also heard the accusation that we hope to conserve our own oil reserves to eventually dominate the world after the Middle East runs dry. It is even believed by some that America is plotting to subdue the world to our benefit. In all of this, I can assure you we have no such plans."

Matt continued, "In truth, I believe that the greater number of peaceful and prosperous countries there are in the world, the better we will all be for it. How can we convince everyone to stop fighting? A lasting cease-fire is the first step and America is willing to forgive these attacks to demonstrate our commitment to peace. The next step is more difficult in many ways. I propose that the leaders of the Middle East educate and train your citizens to expand into new sustainable industries long before your oil runs out. We will offer all the help you desire to set up the curriculum, personnel, and infrastructure needed to accomplish this goal. However, we must all agree to abide by a reasonable timetable in bringing this vision into reality."

King Tabir sat in silence as he considered what this President had just said. Before he made his mind up on how to respond, he had one more question. "And what do you gain from all of this? Why do you care what happens to Saudi Arabia or any foreign country as long as the United States prospers?"

An excitement arose in Matt. He could feel how close they were to an agreement. He subscribed to the adage that people who are equally informed rarely disagree. With that as the goal, he was intuitively guided to again answer from a Muslim perspective.

"I believe every soul was created to live in peace. Whether we call our Creator by the name of Allah - glorified and exalted is He -

95

Brahma, Yahweh, or any of the other names we have for the 'I am that I am,' I believe we are all speaking of the same First Cause. In that sense, all such believers can be counted as good Muslims for don't we all seek love, happiness and truth while believing in the one Creator? If a person who does not perform their daily prayers is still beloved by Allah - glorified and exalted is He - who on earth should not be counted among our siblings? And if we are all of the same family, as I believe we are, then who should we consider unworthy of happiness and abundance?"

The King pondered this surprising turn trying to see if President Alexander had hidden anything from him. Oddly enough, Tabir felt he could trust this man, unlike his predecessors, especially when his words made sense. The deciding factor was simple. There was little to lose by agreeing to his peace plan. If the education of his people became a problem, he could easily deal with that when the time came. As things stood now, when the world prospered it needed more oil and that was good for his country.

"I will endorse your peace plan, President Alexander. I respect what you have said and your efforts to find common ground between our nations. I will stand with you in a joint effort to do away with terrorism and violence both inside and outside our borders. I wish you luck with your mission of peace. Convincing others to agree with you may not be as easy as it has been with me."

Chapter 13

It was barely dawn when the plane touched down on the runway of the Damascus International Airport in Syria. It was still using the call sign SAM 1135 to keep as low a profile as possible. While the elite in political circles no doubt knew that POTUS was personally traveling in the Middle East, the media had not been informed. After a private reception at the airport, the SUVs transported the American delegation to the All Seasons Hotel in downtown Damascus.

They only had a couple of hours until the scheduled meeting with Joan's counterpart at the Parliament Building. Matt was fairly certain President Maaz al-Assad already knew a face-to-face meeting with POTUS was on the agenda. Maaz al-Assad had followed in his family's footsteps since the first al-Assad came to power in 1970. If Syria was somehow complicit in the recent attacks on American forces, there would be many reasons for him to be unavailable. Matt had little leverage here, but getting Syria's support for the peace initiative was vital to its success.

Joan and Matt reviewed their notes on al-Assad's background. He came to power through an election after his brother died in a suspicious car accident. Matt thought it interesting that the al-Assad family belonged to a mystical Shia sect of Islam known as the Alawites. Only thirteen percent of Syria's population was Alawite with the more traditional Sunnis making up closer to seventy five percent. Regardless, many members of the al-Assad family have long held key positions in the government and military.

Not much is known about the Alawite religion. Their tenets are not published because they are withheld as sacred truths for its members only. According to rumor, the Alawites are described as believers in the mysticism of Islam including a belief in reincarnation. Matt knew a traditional approach to the *Qur'an* and Islam should be avoided with President al-Assad. He promised Joan he would be careful not to make assumptions about al-Assad's spiritual beliefs.

97

Erin was delighted she would soon be touring Damascus, also known as the City of Jasmine. When they arrived at the hotel, she asked for recommendations of sights not to miss on a tour. The concierge suggested the impressive view from atop nearby Mount Qassioun. The businesses alongside the mountain road near its pinnacle offered a cultural sampling of everything a tourist could want. Karen Moffitt, Erin's personal assistant, and the security detail arranged a driving tour of the area later that morning.

The First Lady's entourage loaded into three SUVs at the same time POTUS' group left for their meeting with President al-Assad. Erin's convoy headed north for Mount Qassioun as Karen recited interesting facts about its history from her guide book. It was said to be a place where Adam lived after leaving the Garden of Eden. It was described as the site of the first murder ever recorded, where Cain killed Abel. The guide book also claimed that Jesus traveled to Mount Qassioun and prayed in the caves that dotted the mountain's surface. Erin was pleased to have the chance to see all this in person, but her thoughts kept returning to Matt and his meeting with President al-Assad.

***

Ramin had told Afkar that the Americans had gone sightseeing in Riyadh so it was reasonable to expect the same in Damascus. It was hardly a surprise when Amir confirmed that the target's convoy would start their tour with Mount Qassioun. It was, after all, the most popular tourist destination in or around Damascus.

Afkar knew there was only one road up and down the mountain. That ensured the caravan would have to come and go using the same route. The twists in the road and the mountain's many caves would keep his men out of sight while still being in perfect position for the abduction. In order to have plenty of time to get set, they would wait until the target was on the way back down to make their move.

Ramin had warned Afkar that the Americans' vehicles would be armor-plated and bulletproofed. Stopping them by force would require huge firepower and that was problematic if the target was to remain unharmed. Ramin suggested using some interesting technology that combined bunker busting bombs with archery.

The sleek design of the shafts looked a lot like thick arrows or bolts used with a crossbow. In the same way that a Kevlar vest can stop a bullet, but does little to repel a knife blade, the bolts were designed to penetrate armor plating. They carried a Russian made knockout gas called Kolokol-2 and were engineered to release the fumes only after the shaft had pierced the armor. Using this specialized weapon ensured the abduction would cause few, if any, injuries.

Afkar's men were positioned on an overhang to the mountain road just out of sight of the main highway. They were instructed to fire the bolts toward the driver's seat of each vehicle. If the projectile passed through and hit anyone, only non-essential personnel would be injured rather than the VIPs. The crash barriers would prevent the vehicles from going over the edge, even after the drivers had passed out.

Afkar's men only knew the target was a woman. If there was more than one female in the group, they would have to take them all and sort it out later. Ramin would meet them at a holding facility a little north of Damascus to identify the target hostage. He would then negotiate the ransom and exchange.

Two men were stationed at the mountain top to notify the team by radio when the SUVs were preparing to leave. If any other sightseers wanted to head down at the same time, Afkar had given orders to delay them at least five minutes so there would be no witnesses to the kidnapping. More of his men would block off access to the mountain road from the main highway to ensure the same. Now they just had to wait.

Erin was glad they had taken this scenic tour of Mount Qassioun. The view of Damascus and the surrounding desert was breathtaking. As much as she wanted to walk around outside and stretch her legs, Erin had promised to follow the instructions of the Secret Service team. They knew that as long as she stayed buckled up and inside the vehicle, she was safe from most threats. The kind of firepower it would take to disable these vehicles was not easy to obtain, let alone transport, unnoticed. The Lexan windows were thick enough to repel most rounds of ammunition. The agents were fairly relaxed because they knew the real targets would be POTUS and the Secretary of State. They were all enjoying their roles as tourists even though outwardly they appeared to be "business as usual."

Wayne Thompson had put Agent Pam Selco in charge of the First Lady's security. Pam had arranged for Erin to travel incognito with a wig, scarf, sunglasses and casual clothes, similar to her assistant's modest outfit. In fact, she made sure that everyone in the group appeared nondescript so that no one drew special notice. Pam choreographed the SUVs to continually change the order in which they moved along the streets to give the impression that there was no particular importance to any one vehicle or its passengers. Going up and coming down the mountain was a little different. She tucked the First Lady's SUV in between the other two because this particular section of road was problematic to defend in case of an attack.

Pam initially objected to the trip up the mountain because of this obvious vulnerability. However, she also recognized that the real threat would be to the President and Secretary Hartley on their route to and from the Parliament building. They assumed word had already spread between governments that POTUS was in the Middle East, but none of them would be aware that the First Lady was traveling with him.

Agent Selco also knew that very few in their own government knew their travel itinerary let alone that POTUS was in Damascus. She knew information leaks were always possible, but since it was formed in 1865, the Secret Service had never had a traitor in their ranks. Pam was glad she wasn't responsible for keeping POTUS secure, knowing many people in this region hated everything about the United States. With all that in mind, she cautiously consented to the mountain tour.

On the way up, Pam was suspicious of the locals walking along the mountain road. This was a popular area for tourists and the business owners who catered to them actually lived on the mountain. The local pedestrians stared as the three SUVs drove by in a tight formation. Their curious attention increased Pam's vigilance but seeing this unusual convoy was indeed a rare sight for these people.

She watched as the city sank below her line of vision on their return from the mountain top. Pam felt better as they approached the safety of the main highway. In just a couple of minutes they would be on a six lane paved road headed back to Damascus.

***

As the SUVs navigated their way down the mountain, Afkar confirmed that all traffic was being held up at each end of the road. He also repeated which shooters were assigned to which vehicles. He reminded them to aim only for the drivers' area of the roofs and that the female occupants were not to be harmed at any point. From their elevated positions and the close proximity of the vehicles to each other, Afkar was certain his men could fire together and not give any of the drivers time to react.

The SUVs were almost beneath them and Afkar uttered a prayer to Allah for success. This would be the moment his life changed forever. He would be a wealthy man after today and he would have struck a mighty blow for Islam against the American infidels. He yelled "Atlaqa" and the shooters commenced firing.

***

Pam started to say something to Erin when she heard a sound she couldn't quite place. She looked up to see what resembled a spearhead splitting the headliner above the driver, spewing gas into the vehicle. She automatically pulled her weapon and opened a nearby compartment containing several gas masks. A moment later, a second spearhead punctured all the way through the roof painfully pinning the driver's leg to his seat. He let out a tortured yell but was mercifully rendered unconscious by the fumes.

Agent Selco knew her highest priority was to deal with the unknown gas. She couldn't tell yet if it was meant to kill them or just knock them out. She motioned for Erin and Karen to hold their breath as she handed both of them a gas mask. Karen inhaled to hold her breath and immediately passed out. Pam hoped FLOTUS remembered what to do. Putting on a gas mask is not easy, especially when you're under attack. This became even tougher when the SUVs collided. Their safety belts worked to restrain them but precious seconds were wasted as they were flung forward in their seats.

Erin had practiced putting on a gas mask only once before. Years ago she had received a brief training session on how to survive an attack while riding in a government vehicle. She kept holding her breath but was having trouble getting the mask secured around her head because of the wig. She tossed the wig to the floorboard and struggled with the mask's straps. Erin could feel the gas was irritating her nose and throat. Finally, she couldn't help but cough and then inhale. She fought for consciousness after breathing in the fumes but quickly lost that battle.

Pam had holstered her weapon and was about to clear her own mask when she saw Erin lose consciousness. The way she had peacefully gone under indicated the gas was probably not lethal. That was a small comfort but she quickly realized this was a kidnapping. Pam gambled that she had time to secure the First Lady's mask and still clear her own before the attackers made their next move.

Once she made sure FLOTUS' mask was properly sealed, Pam placed her palms over her own mask's intake filters. She was desperate for oxygen but she knew she had to completely clear out any residual vapor in the mask. She blew out all her breath as hard as she could and inhaled deeply, praying she had cleared it properly. Within seconds she knew she had failed. She could feel her consciousness fade as the small amount of gas she inhaled worked to render her helpless.

***

Afkar watched as the lead car skidded to a stop and then slowly veered into the crash barrier on the left. The second vehicle didn't stop until it rebounded off the first. The last SUV quickly stopped a few meters behind them and then all was still. Afkar could see no movement inside the vehicles, but the windows were tinted. He waited another 15 seconds to ensure the gas had done its job before giving the order for his men to advance. Then they quickly climbed down from the overhang to extract any females among the SUVs' passengers.

Afkar's driver pulled his van into position to load and transport them to where Ramin was waiting. Shaped charges were placed around the locking mechanisms at the rear of each vehicle. This would force the hatch doors open while protecting the passengers from harm. The loud BOOMs caused the three rear doors to abruptly flip up and the men watched as the gas plumed

102

out. They waited just a moment longer for the fumes to disperse and to see if there would be any resistance before entering the vehicles.

Wearing their own gas masks, Afkar's men crawled in through the back of each SUV to open all the doors. The fumes had worked well and everyone inside was unconscious. The men dragged three female occupants out of the second vehicle onto the road. Two of the women had gas masks on and a wig had been found next to one of them. Afkar guessed the one with the wig had to be their primary target but he was taking no chances.

After the females were placed on the floor of his van, Afkar and his driver immediately headed for the main road. He radioed the other two drivers to load up and follow him as soon as they were ready. They confirmed they were just pulling up to the SUVs to load the remaining team members and equipment.

Afkar's driver turned right onto the main highway heading away from Damascus. The rendezvous point was five kilometers ahead and then east for two more kilometers on a small dirt road. The unremarkable group of buildings where Ramin would meet them was not visible from the main highway. In fact, it looked like a small goat herder's ranch if seen from above. There was a barn to hide their vehicles with an underground warren of rooms where they would wait with their hostages. Afkar was pleased they had seen no other people or vehicles during the actual abduction. In fact, his team had made zero mistakes throughout the entire operation.

As they drove to their hidden safe house, he was already thinking about how Ramin would negotiate the ransom and exchange. Soon he would be a rich man and would never again have to accept such dangerous assignments. His life would be one of comfort and pleasure. Truly he was blessed, but he had earned it all the hard way.

Suddenly from behind them, a vehicle passed their van at a tremendous speed. Afkar warned his driver to beware of the black BMW sedan, knowing it was not part of their crew. They both watched as the car jammed on its brakes in the distance. Then the black sedan made a quick left turn off the highway. Their view of the dirt road the car had turned onto was blocked in both directions by small hills on either side of the highway. Afkar had his hand gun ready and told his driver to slow to a crawl as they approached the intersection. They both looked left to see what had become of the speeding BMW.

Suddenly, there was the sound of metal slamming into metal as the back of Afkar's skull smashed into his side window. Out of nowhere, a black armored Hummer had rammed into their right side door violently spinning the vehicle around. The van flipped in a circle twice before landing on its side and skidding to a stop on the crossroad. The impact caused Afkar's pistol to discharge firing a bullet through his drivers' spine and left lung. The three unconscious women were viciously flung across the back storage area of the van. When the dust settled, the women were awkwardly piled on top of each other against, what used to be, the passenger sliding door. Afkar was already dead and his driver couldn't move.

***

The day before, Colonel Mansur had been contacted by one of his men in Damascus. He reported that two of Mansur's soldiers had been recruited for a big job organized by a local mercenary named Afkar. Their mission involved kidnapping a high-level American female who would be worth a huge ransom. Mansur assumed this had to be the American Secretary of State he had heard was traveling through the Middle East. He was glad his men had accepted the job and said further instructions would be provided once they had more information.

The informant had called Mansur two hours before with the details of the kidnapping that was set for today. The abduction would take place near the bottom of Mount Qassioun as the convoy of vehicles headed back to the city. Mansur was surprised at the well thought out plan since he knew Afkar had no formal military training. Assuming Afkar's people would successfully pull off the kidnapping, the challenge would be to effectively disable the hostage vehicle on the way to the sequestered hideout. With little risk to his own men, Mansur's people could help themselves to Afkar's female hostage.

He had also learned that Joan Hartley was with President al-Assad that morning. That meant the female target would not be Hartley but he could not imagine who else it might be. He gave his two men orders to allow the lead vehicle with any hostages to drive

104

away and then kill the remaining mercenaries before they reached the main highway.

When the eighteen men were loaded up to leave, Mansur's people detonated flash bang grenades inside the vans. Both his men wore special earplugs and kept their eyes tightly closed as they turned away from the blasts. They alone had their wits about them after the grenades exploded. It was a simple matter to execute Afkar's stunned men before driving off in the vans.

The plan almost worked to perfection. Neither man had counted on the concussive force which made it impossible to see out. The windows looked like cracked ice on all sides of the vehicles. Mansur's men were forced to kick out the windshields before they could drive away.

***

The Colonel exited the BMW after returning to the main highway. He had been in the decoy car that had turned onto the dirt road. The demolished van ended up sideways on the highway's shoulder partially blocking the slow lane. When his men pried open the rear doors, Mansur saw the three women lying in a heap. They were not moving but he knew gas had been used to render them unconscious. He cursed Afkar for failing to safely secure them for transport. He ordered his men to be careful as they removed the women from the van.

Mansur knew they had to leave quickly before the authorities arrived. He cursed again as he stared angrily at Afkar and the driver through what was left of the windshield. They appeared to be dead already but Mansur wasn't satisfied. He took careful aim with his pistol and shot both men in the face. He grunted his approval at the carnage thinking these idiots didn't deserve to be pretty corpses.

The three unconscious females were then belted into the back of the Hummer before he gave the order to proceed. Mansur had prepared his own remote location several kilometers ahead where he could evaluate exactly what, and who, his hostages were.

Chapter 14

Matt and the Syrian President were at a standstill. Maaz al-Assad had no intention of supporting a peace agreement brokered by the Americans. The U.S. had little leverage to convince him to change his mind and Matt was running out of ideas. His intuition told him al-Assad had a guilty conscience and that now was the time to test it.

"Mr. President, were you aware that we recovered a laptop computer in working condition from the underground bunker between Israel and Jordan?" asked Matt.

"And what has that to do with the agenda before us today?" al-Assad asked suspiciously.

"Nothing as yet," Matt admitted, "but we have not completed our retrieval of the data on the hard drive. I am told there are incriminating files being recovered and analyzed as we speak. If the peace accord is unsuccessful, at least we'll be able to identify the responsible groups who will pay dearly for their horrendous crimes."

The Syrian leader hesitated before responding. "I know nothing about your implied accusations. Clearly you have no evidence or you would be retaliating instead of negotiating for peace."

Matt could see that he had hit a nerve but he felt that it was not the right time to press the matter. He resumed their discussion on the previous point, but he could tell Maaz was no longer listening.

President al-Assad was lost in thought over this new information. Up until then, he had been sure the Americans had not connected Syria to the recent attacks against them. The news about this laptop complicated his position. The more he considered what Alexander just said, the angrier he became with Mansur. The Colonel had decided to attack the American base in Israel without his authorization. Despite Mansur's assurances that Syria would never be blamed, the stakes were too high to accept his word alone.

Maaz also had political concerns about withholding support for the peace plan. The United States' decision not to retaliate was astonishing. Most of the non-Muslim world would agree America had a right to seek justice through vengeance, but they had so far declined. Rather than supporting the American's peace plan, al-Assad decided that it would be enough to issue a carefully worded public statement against terrorism. However, if President Alexander could prove Syria was connected to these attacks, it would change everything. He decided to conclude the meeting immediately. If the U.S. President did have evidence against Syria, ending the meeting would force him to disclose it. He stood to announce that the meeting was over but he never got the chance.

Joan Hartley rushed into the room with a flustered Syrian aide close on her heels. She begged forgiveness for disturbing them but she had to speak to President Alexander immediately. Matt was initially annoyed but realized she would not intrude unless it was critically important.

For a moment, he thought Joan might have word of conclusive proof linking Syria to the attack in Israel or the recent biological outbreaks in Afghanistan and Iraq. This would be just what he needed to motivate President al-Assad to support his peace plan. However, from the distressed look on her face, Matt could tell this was bad news. He quickly moved with her to a semi-private corner of the room.

Joan whispered to Matt that Erin, Pam and Karen had been abducted less than an hour ago. She added that there were injuries but no fatalities among the American Secret Service agents who had been charged with protecting the First Lady. Matt paled and could not hide the emotions running through his mind. He couldn't imagine why Erin or the other two women had been targeted.

Joan went on to say that the evidence collected at the scene indicated the attackers on the convoy had used knockout gas. She had no explanation for why all the kidnappers had been killed by a second group of assailants. That bizarre twist added a hijacking to the abduction. Either way, the three women were still missing. No terrorist faction had claimed responsibility nor had a ransom demand been issued.

Matt was in shock. What kind of people could commit such a heinous crime? Suddenly an overwhelming feeling of déjà vu forced its way through his seething rage. The ethereal man advising Matt during that dreamlike briefing after his heart attack had warned him of something like this. He also promised that if Matt would persevere in his efforts toward peace, then everything would turn out well. None of that mattered now. Matt was so furious that the man's hopeful prediction was quickly forgotten.

The more Matt considered what the kidnappers had done, the hotter the rage inside of him burned. He wanted the people who had taken his wife to suffer the tortures of hell! He wanted to obliterate anyone who had helped them by striking back with the full force of the U.S. military. What did they expect to accomplish by abducting Erin and these innocent women? Matt swore that if she was harmed in any way, he would personally ensure there would be no peace in the Middle East!

***

The Hummer with the three hostages turned onto a dirt road and dust plumed behind them. The main highway disappeared from sight before they came to a deserted ranch. They passed by a small house and parked under the cover of an old barn. Once hidden from view, the driver got out and walked to the other side of the vehicle. He opened the side door and ordered the nearby men to carefully unload the unconscious cargo.

All three women were gently laid out on the ground. Two of the three were still wearing gas masks. The third female had no mask and her face was white as chalk. The driver could tell she was barely alive. He had to hope she was not the Colonel's primary hostage.

Mansur's BMW pulled up next to the Hummer and he stepped out. He walked over to the three prone captives and surmised the woman without the gas mask was in bad shape. He checked her limbs then ripped open her blouse to further assess her injuries. The swelling and purple discoloration around her abdomen told him she was bleeding internally. He knew she would not be alive for much longer.

He wondered about the identities of these women and if any of them had been worth the risk and effort made to secure them. He

108

removed their gas masks to see if he recognized the other two. He didn't. Mansur had already guessed the American Secretary of State would not be among them since he had confirmed she was attending a meeting at the Palace.

He powered up his laptop with a satellite modem and logged onto the internet. He then pulled up a roster of known White House employees. Upon close inspection of the photos provided, only one of the three faces was a match to the one without a gas mask. Her name was Karen Moffitt, a personal assistant to the wife of the U.S. President. Mansur was relieved to establish that the mortally wounded woman was unimportant. His pulse quickened as he realized that one of the two remaining hostages would most likely be Erin Alexander. One of them was wearing an empty shoulder holster indicating she was a body guard. A quick internet search for a photo of the First Lady confirmed Erin's identity.

Mansur was still deciding if the First Lady's presence was fortuitous or a disaster when one of the women began to stir. He told his men to quickly place cloth sacks over all three of the women's heads. He was still contemplating how to handle this situation, but he chose not to reduce his options by allowing the hostages to see their faces.

One woman struggled when she became aware of her predicament. Her hands and feet had been bound with tie-wraps so she couldn't offer much resistance. Her movements bumped the second woman to consciousness, but she too had been bound and the hoods obscured any view of their surroundings.

Pam knew better than to say anything. Erin didn't hesitate to blurt out, "Where am I? What happened? Why am I tied up?"

Mansur ignored her questions while offering one of his own, "Which one of you is the President's wife?"

Erin realized her mistake and stopped talking and stilled her movements. The still dazed women took in the full implication of what they had just heard. They knew they were in grave danger. This man had an Arabic accent but was fluent in English. He seemed to be aware that the First Lady was among the captives. Who else had they taken hostage? And why didn't he know which of them was Erin Alexander? If she was not their intended target, then what was the reason they had been abducted?

Neither woman spoke. Karen still hadn't made a sound.

"There is no need to answer," Mansur said. "I have already learned everything I need to know."

"It sounds like you know very little," Pam exclaimed, changing her mind on remaining silent in hopes of gathering more information.

"I know that you are scared. I know that the older of you is the First Lady. I know that you are an incompetent bodyguard. And most importantly, I know that you and the silent one are useless to me."

Erin tried to sit up in alarm. "There is no reason to hurt us. We certainly pose no threat and we are worth much more to you alive than dead or harmed."

"You, Madame, will live longer than these other two, but you all must die," Mansur replied calmly. He motioned to the man standing closest to Pam who then smashed the butt of his rifle into her face. It made a sickening crunch as it dislocated her jaw. She was out cold when Mansur's men carried her and Karen out of the barn.

From the sounds, Erin was not sure what had just happened but she could guess. "You know the United States does not bargain with terrorists," Erin said defiantly.

"We both know that's not true, especially when someone like you is the hostage," Mansur countered. "Frankly, I would prefer to have taken the American Secretary of State. She could have given us much valuable information. You are useless and probably know fewer secrets about your country than I do."

Erin changed the subject hoping to gain some advantage. "Taking me was a mistake. The United States wants all Middle East nations to cease hostilities and work together to bring real peace to this region. Your actions today may well start a war that will be the end of you. Don't you realize that we came here to help?"

"We disagree. What brought you here today is America's arrogance and disregard for the freedom of other people to live as they choose. Perhaps you will stand trial as the representative for your country's crimes against Allah and his people before you die."

"If that is your intention, I would be a poor example of what you speak against. I have always supported freedom for everyone. Am I really the best person you could think of to hold accountable for the alleged crimes against you?" Erin asked.

"How clever you American women are!" Mansur spat. "Has your western culture made all its females so ill-mannered? Do you really think you are innocent of the crimes perpetrated by your country against us? Didn't you help elect your government's leaders who have committed these crimes? Does that not make you complicit in their offenses? And since you are married to the head of your government, doesn't that make you all the more responsible?"

Erin wanted desperately to reason with this man. "We cannot hold individual citizens accountable for crimes committed by their governments. If we did, then wouldn't everyone alive deserve to be convicted and sentenced?" Scared as she was, Erin wondered how people like this man could believe it was okay to terrorize innocent civilians.

"It is a waste of time to discuss such things with you," he said angrily. "Take her below while I figure out what to do with her."

***

When the phone rang, President Maaz al-Assad was surprised it was his own private line. Once he heard of the abduction from his aide, he expected the next call to be a ransom demand for the kidnapped members of the American delegation. Instead, it was Colonel Mansur urging him to have privacy before they spoke further.

Al-Assad picked up the phone in his private office and barked, "Why are you calling me?"

"No doubt you have heard about the kidnapping of the American president's wife. I intervened in that abduction and am now holding three female hostages," Mansur answered cautiously. "I had thought their Secretary of State was the intended target, but I was misled."

111

President al-Assad was stunned. "Why did you do this?" he screamed. "President Alexander has just told me some very disturbing news. He said that the underground compound between Israel and Jordan yielded a great deal of evidence that would prove conclusively who had been behind the attack. In fact, a recovered laptop was specifically mentioned. Can you tell me this computer will in no way implicate the Syrian government?"

After a moment's pause, Mansur answered, "Since the caves were destroyed, I can't imagine how they got their hands on it. But if it is ours, that computer could create much trouble for us all."

Al-Assad's worst nightmare was unfolding before him. It seemed the Americans would soon be able to corroborate far more than a shared ideology between his government and Mohammed's Faithful. Syria could become a proven accomplice in the recent biological attacks and the annihilation of the military base in Israel. He had heard rumors that the U.S. President was considering the use of WMDs in response to these attacks. By the look of him since learning of the abduction, al-Assad had no doubt that was true. It was too late to undo the damage caused by Colonel Mansur and his people. However, he would do everything in his power to keep Syria from being linked to the kidnapping of the First Lady.

What was most confusing to al-Assad was that President Alexander was here today speaking of peace rather than reprisals. Were the rumors of imminent WMDs false? Was this unprecedented personal visit some kind of perverse ultimatum where he must agree to Alexander's terms for a permanent cease-fire or face deadly consequences? The only thing al-Assad could be sure of was that this was the worst possible time for Syria to be connected to Mansur.

The Colonel had waited so long for President al-Assad to respond that he asked, "Are you there, sir?"

"I am here," he growled, "but I am thinking!"

Mansur waited with silent impatience refusing to enrage al-Assad further. Seeing the precarious position al-Assad was in, he could already anticipate what his next orders would be. He began to plan as he waited.

"First, do not hurt the President's wife. In fact, do not harm any of the hostages you've taken," al-Assad said with venom in his tone.

Mansur answered uneasily, "One has already died of injuries sustained during the abduction. That fool Afkar killed her with his carelessness. The dead woman was only an assistant, but she was a member of the President's wife's staff." He chose not to mention the body guard's broken jaw.

"*Masteje* (an Arabic cuss word)! See that there are no more mistakes! I do not care how you do it but you must release the other two today," al-Assad ordered.

Colonel Mansur considered this for a moment. "I can arrange it so that the President's wife will believe she persuaded us to spare her. I can also arrange it so that you are the hero responsible for their rescue rather than being an accomplice to their abduction. If either woman dies, it will be the fault of the Americans who are sent to rescue them."

President al-Assad didn't answer right away. From the moment he heard of the kidnapping, Matthew Alexander no longer spoke of peace. His rage-filled face was intimidating even to al-Assad. The Syrian President was curious to know what Mansur had in mind, but he also wanted to remind the Colonel who was in charge. He finally said, "Tell me of your plan. If you are wrong and I end up being anything other than a hero to this American President, I swear you will hear yourself die screaming."

Chapter 15

Erin counted thirty five steps including two switchback landings before they sat her down on a dirt floor. They secured new tie-wraps around her wrists and ankles taking away any options for escape. They never removed the hood but she could guess she was not in a pretty place.

She leaned back against a rough dirt wall and wondered if the greater danger wasn't that the ceiling might collapse from age or lack of structural support. Then the smell wafted through her hood. The scent of mold and mildew in the air had probably been undisturbed for decades. She tried not to identify other unpleasant odors but an underground outhouse was definitely involved.

Erin hadn't heard or seen anything for at least an hour since she had been moved below ground. She knew there was no use in yelling for help, since she was probably twenty feet or more underground. She kept trying to think of anything that would improve her situation rather than dwell on the frightening possibilities her immediate future might hold. Her intuition was telling her to remain calm and she'd be okay. Then her entire body would shudder as the horror of her confinement refused to be ignored. She couldn't stop her mind from racing through the scary scenarios of what might come next. She tried to focus on anything else that might be helpful.

Erin had no idea what had happened to the other people in her group who had set out on the tour with her that morning. She remembered hearing Pam's voice when she first awoke, but where was she now? She had not heard from Karen Moffitt, but their captor had implied she was with them. The crushing silence all around meant if anyone was in this underground room with her, they were unconscious or dead. She cursed herself as she realized this dark reverie was not helping.

Then noises from above followed by the sound of footsteps on the stairs alerted Erin that she was about to have a visitor. She braced herself for whatever those steps would bring. Hopefully her captor had made a ransom demand and was negotiating her release. She didn't want to think about enduring a sham trial with these extremists. When the sound of the steps stopped, she could sense the person was standing right in front of her. From her seated position on the floor, she felt very vulnerable.

"I wish to continue our discussion," Mansur said with a tone that was almost cordial. "Tell me again why you feel you are not responsible, in whole or in part, for the crimes of your country against my people."

"That's not quite what I said, but I do agree with it." Erin was surprised at this turn of events but was relieved since a conversation was better than the other things she'd imagined. She tried to see if she could see anything of the man before her, but the hood was very effective. "I said that I'm a poor example of a defendant for the transgressions you claim were made against the people of Syria. You feel that America has interfered with the freedom of your fellow citizens. If I'm to be put on trial, shouldn't the evidence against me prove what I have personally done wrong?"

"This is an interesting point you make," Mansur conceded and nodded his head even though she could not see him. "You do not believe that you should be held accountable for your country's crimes or perhaps held to a higher standard than other American citizens? After all, you are married to President Alexander."

Erin thought for a moment before answering. She was having trouble concentrating with the hood blocking most of the light and air. "I understand why you might think so, but where should we draw the line that makes one person responsible for the actions of another? That's a slippery slope where a case could be made to convict everyone alive."

"I have looked you up on the internet, Madame Alexander. I must agree that you are what you say you are, a poor representative. Perhaps the better person to put on trial is your bodyguard. After all, she is trained to kill and would certainly murder me if she had the chance."

"And so every soldier doing their job is responsible for the decisions of their country's leaders? If you were guarding your President al-Assad, wouldn't you kill to protect him?" Erin countered.

"Why do you think I am from Syria?" Mansur said coolly. "I make no such claim. However, I agree that your bodyguard was doing her job...poorly. If she was any good at it, you wouldn't be here."

"The other people who were with me on the mountain...are they okay? What have you done with them?" Erin asked.

"All of the men were left alive at the place where you were taken. I have not yet decided what to do with you females."

Erin took a shaky breath of musty air and prayed that this man was somehow willing to listen to her. "My husband is meeting with President al-Assad right now. Maybe you already knew that. His agenda is one of peace. This peace is offered by the American people even though we have suffered many recent and unspeakable attacks. My husband is doing his best to avoid more bloodshed. Do you think holding a trial is a good idea considering everything that is being done at this time in the name of peace?"

Mansur was pleased this woman was so eloquent. Her arrogance was bothersome but it could also be used to his favor. She naively believed her words could sway his opinions. That was fortuitous but there remained one awkward agenda item to resolve before he could appear to accept her arguments. "I will wait to hear the results of these peace negotiations before I decide if there will be a trial. However, someone must remain to answer the charges if a lasting peace does not endure."

With that Mansur turned and walked up the stairs, ignoring Erin's objections. He still had to arrange for the safe release of both women without being caught in the process. He also needed to eliminate any evidence that his people were connected to this kidnapping. Then there was the American woman who died. He must keep that fact hidden for at least a few days. If he was careful, he could tie up all these loose ends and make a hero of President al-Assad.

***

"How the hell do you kidnap someone and then lose them?" Amir screamed to Ramin over the phone.

Ramin had dreaded this call because he only had bad news to report. "It was as if someone knew our plan and waited for us to complete the difficult work before moving in to take the captives. Everything else had gone perfectly up to that point. Two men from Afkar's team are still missing. We don't know if they escaped, are dead somewhere, or perhaps they were helping the *Ebn Al-Sharmoota* (an insulting Arabic epithet) who stole our hostages."

Salazar, posing as Amir, couldn't believe the whole plan had collapsed. He had hoped Ramin's people would drag out the ransom negotiations for a few days. That would effectively end the President's trip and his peace plan with it. Ramin would be paid well for his efforts and the First Lady would return home unharmed if not a bit wiser. Salazar had realistically been prepared for some casualties if the Secret Service agents put up a fight, but the idea that the kidnappers would lose their hostages and be executed in the process was inconceivable.

"What are you doing to get them back?" Amir barked with contempt.

"I am making inquiries but I fear the group who did this is well connected. If they don't want to be found, then they won't be. It is my understanding that they have not yet made a ransom demand which leads me to believe they have political reasons for their interference." Ramin was glad to get all that out between Amir's ranting and personal insults.

Amir snarled, "Get back to me when you learn anything new. See if you can do something right for a change, you pig-spawned *sharmoota*." Salazar hurled the insult knowing full well it was a harsh offense to a Muslim. As he slammed down the phone, he hoped that his verbal abuse would motivate Ramin to fix this. He let out a snort and wondered aloud why he always had to clean up everyone else's mistakes.

After a moment to collect his thoughts, he considered his few remaining options. If the First Lady was injured or even killed, that would require Ramin's immediate death. It was critical that no connection could be made between Ramin and Amir/Salazar when the Secret Service started looking into this fiasco. Most of the mercenaries who participated in the kidnapping were already dead, but what if the two who were still missing had been spies and could talk if they were caught? Again, the idiot Ramin would have to die to protect Salazar's identity. But the timing was bad because he still needed Ramin for one last job.

Salazar's conscience kicked in with a vengeance as he remembered arranging for his CIA operatives to pull back from following the First Lady's convoy. Had he not held them back, they could have stopped this entire disaster. If they had at least arrived late on the scene when the second group of kidnappers attacked the first, his people could have killed them all. POTUS would have canceled the rest of his trip and no harm would have come to Erin Alexander. His goal of disrupting the peace talks would have been accomplished while his agents saved the day. He then considered that Ramin had been right about one thing. Their plans had been leaked and some very smart people used that knowledge to intervene. His conscience kept returning to his role in the fate of the First Lady. Who had taken her and for what purpose?

He suddenly realized that he'd achieved his goal regardless of how this turned out. The peace plan was dead no matter what happened to FLOTUS. Hadn't the U.S. government sacrificed his father for the good of the country all those years ago? If Erin died, it would be as if President Alexander sacrificed his queen to win the game. Salazar smiled for the first time in days. He had saved the country and perhaps the world. He felt like a vindicated hero but he had known all along that he was the right man for the job.

* * *

President al-Assad was taking a huge chance. He had agreed to Mansur's plan but it was risky. Ideally, the Colonel's proposal would undo most of the damage while winning President Alexander's gratitude for Syria's help in rescuing his wife. Al-Assad conceded he would have to support the American's peace proposal if only to survive this day. If Mansur's plan failed, they would all be dead regardless.

With the Syrian government's blessing, the American Secret Service and CIA security staff organized a makeshift command post in the Palace's conference room. The technicians nervously connected communication lines which were already receiving surveillance video of the last known coordinates of Erin's convoy. CIA Director Salazar was on the phone with Matt apologizing for the gap in their covert security. He explained that they dropped the ball by focusing on

118

POTUS rather than the First Lady. Matt's heart was vacillating between intense anger, retribution and fear of losing his beloved Erin.

Then President al-Assad quickly reentered the room. "Mr. President, I must speak with you alone. It is of great importance regarding your wife."

Matt hesitated and his heart skipped a beat. What happened? Was she safe? He wanted his security team to hear this first hand but he quickly decided he could ask al-Assad to repeat any critical information to them. He could not guess what the news would be from the look on the Syrian President's face.

"Gentlemen, please give us some privacy," he said aloud as both leaders moved away from the crowd.

President al-Assad offered the first good news Matt had heard since this nightmare began. "I believe I know where your wife was taken. I have had my best agents searching for information and their sources tell us that your wife and the two female companions are being held at a small ranch on the other side of Mount Qassioun. Once the exact coordinates are verified, I will give them to you."

"Do you have any word on their condition?" Matt asked with reserved elation.

"None, but from what I'm told, the motive was money so it is unlikely they would have been harmed as yet."

"Will you allow my security people to conduct a rescue operation inside your borders?" Matt asked.

"We have already consented to your setting up this command post. Under the circumstances, and for that purpose only, we will allow a rescue operation using your agents. Do you require any assistance from us once the location is verified?"

Matt was amazed and somewhat skeptical over the level of cooperation he was receiving from this adversarial leader. He filed that concern away for the moment and said, "I will leave that up to my security detail but I am grateful for your help if we need it."

With that, Matt motioned Wayne Thompson over to update him on this development. The coordinates came in as they talked and a live overhead image of the remote ranch appeared on the largest of the video monitors in the conference room. There were two vehicles parked outside the barn, which was no doubt hiding a multitude of sins and hostages within. It bothered Wayne that the kidnappers would leave their cars parked outside and visible from above. He doubted that they were that careless or stupid which probably meant this "mistake" was part of a larger plan.

He wanted to use the X-ray satellite to scan the buildings and perform some subterranean recon but there was little time. That would require the specialized helicopter and re-tasking the satellite they had used to locate the underground access tunnel in Israel. They could not afford the required four-hour delay and a helicopter flyover would remove any chance they had of taking them by surprise.

Wayne said his people could be on site and ready to mount a rescue mission within the hour. Matt went with his recommendation and authorized immediate action without waiting for the X-ray surveillance. Wayne began coordinating with the CIA agents to form assault teams as they geared up to leave for the site.

Chapter 16

Erin couldn't begin to guess if the sun was still up or night had come. She remembered reading somewhere that being in seclusion without interaction confused a person's sense of time and she admitted that was true. She wasn't sure if the lack of contact was good or bad. She decided that having no contact was better than a beating, rape or being put on trial by these people. So Erin counted her blessings and tried to stay positive.

That didn't last long. She started worrying about Pam and Karen. All of their lives were in danger but Erin knew she would be treated better than the other two women. She started praying for their safety, but silently doubted they would ever return home.

A noise from above caught her attention. How much time had passed? Perhaps it was the Arabic man coming down for another debate. She shuddered as she considered the possibility that he had left and his men were coming down to entertain themselves with the wife of the American president. Abject fear was making her perspire and she found it hard to breathe. As much as she hated the hood over her head, it was probably keeping her alive. Not being able to identify her captors was in her favor.

Erin strained to hear what sounded like many people moving quickly across the ground above her. That meant trouble for certain. She resumed her prayers asking for protection. Then the noises stopped completely for nearly a minute. The silence was broken by a loud pop followed by an ominous hiss.

***

Wayne Thompson's team took the lead as they swarmed the rural farm where they believed the First Lady and two other female hostages were being held. The property was abandoned except for the two cars observed earlier via satellite surveillance. His first thought was that the terrorists were hidden and planning to ambush them. He also knew the place could be rigged to take everyone out with a bomb. He had them inspect the cars first as the most likely location for hidden explosives. Both of the cars checked out clean.

The small ranch house was cleared next. It showed signs people had been there recently, but it too posed no threat. That left the old barn. The doors were open so that they could see inside. Moving in slowly, they encountered no resistance as they took up their positions. Wayne was beginning to believe everyone had left, including the hostages, but one possibility remained. He had received intel that there was an underground storage area on the property but he wasn't sure how to access it. His uncertainty made him regret not waiting for the X-ray satellite recon before attempting a rescue mission.

His team cleared the inside of the barn and Wayne signaled to the others that it was safe to approach. They had found an old wooden trap door set in the dusty floor. It was hardly hidden because it was conspicuously free of dirt. It used to swing upward on hinges but those had rusted through long ago. After making sure it wasn't rigged with explosives, Wayne had two of his men quietly remove the door. They were startled to find a body lying on the steps a few feet down from the opening. They quickly aimed their weapons at the prone figure. Luckily, they saw the black hood and that the person was bound with tie-wraps in time to hold their fire.

As they gently and silently lifted the limp body up from the steps, Wayne removed the hood. It was Pam Selco, badly beaten but alive. She was unconscious but her pulse was strong. He motioned for one of the backup teams to take her to the medical personnel standing by. Wayne guessed they had left Pam at the entrance of the stairs to test their assault skills. If his people panicked and fired on her, Pam's death would serve to shake the confidence of the entire group. As it was, finding her there would cause them to be more hesitant in case they accidentally shot one of their own. It was easy to see the kidnappers expected them and had the upper hand for the moment. Not knowing their agenda made them all the more unpredictable and dangerous. Wayne dreaded what had to come next.

If anyone was waiting below, they would know to be ready. There was dim lighting from below but Wayne couldn't see beyond the first landing of the steps. His men would not need their NVGs but it also meant whoever was down there could easily pick them off as they approached. The story of three hundred Spartans holding back literally thousands of the enemy using a similar tactical advantage made him consider other options.

He could use tear gas to start their assault; but assuming these capable abductors had gas masks and the hostages didn't, the risk of serious injury to FLOTUS ruled it out. The better option was to use a flash bang grenade to clear the way for the rescue squad. Unless it landed next to one of the hostages, they would experience no permanent damage when it went off. That option was also flawed. The grenades use a five-second fuse and are easily recognized. The captors would see it coming and have time to cover their eyes and ears before it detonated. He had to conceal what it was until it was too late to react.

Wayne decided to lead with a smoke grenade and wait fifteen seconds for the yellow haze to start filling the room. He would then throw a second smoke grenade without pulling the pin. The people below would still be able to see it was a smoke grenade and expect more to follow. He wouldn't pull the second pin because too much smoke in a confined area would work against them. If the third grenade was a flash bang, they might not expect it to cover up in time. Under the circumstances, this plan was his best option.

Wayne took out a flash bang grenade and lined it up on the ground behind two smoke grenades. His hand motions signaled his plan to the team. They were grateful Wayne was willing to do this the smart way. Not one of them wanted to be a dead hero let alone fail to rescue the First Lady.

He then picked up the first smoke grenade, pulled the pin, and tossed it down the stairs. It ricocheted off the wall of the first landing. Then came the pop followed by a yellow rush of smoke filling the space below. The hissing sound lessened as the grenade continued bumping down the second flight of steps. Wayne made sure the next smoke grenade bounced hard off the wall so the people below wouldn't miss it. With his earplugs in and the flash bang grenade in hand, he belly crawled down toward the first landing.

Wayne could hear that the dirt he pushed off the rough wooden steps was falling far below. He realized he could drop the flash bang grenade all the way down to the basement's floor by releasing it in the open space between the steps. He pulled the pin and held onto the grenade for 2 seconds before he let it go directly beneath him. Wayne covered his eyes knowing this would all be over one way or another in the next thirty seconds.

***

With the hood still covering her head, Erin couldn't tell for sure what was happening. The hissing was followed by another metallic object tumbling down the stairs. She could sense that the room was filling with smoke and she tried to hold her breath. In her panic, she inhaled as she gasped. Fortunately, the gas wasn't toxic because she could still breathe and think. Then she began to wonder if the gas was a biological agent. As she considered other possibilities, the room suddenly lit up with a tremendous flash that was so bright she saw it through the weave of the hood. An impossibly loud, concussive BOOM knocked her sideways and Erin screamed as she fell over.

Her cry forced her to quickly inhale the smoke and she began to cough. She then felt the vibration of many heavy feet rushing around her. As if from very far away she heard a distinctly American voice say, "I have one hostage alive. The rest of the room is clear!" This was a rescue rather than her worst nightmare.

"Stand by... checking for exit tunnels and trip wires," said another distant voice.

Erin could feel gentle hands cutting the tie-wraps from her wrists and ankles as the hood was carefully removed. She found herself staring through the yellow fog into the faces of people she recognized. Wayne Thompson and a few other Secret Service agents were gathered around and talking to her. One man offered her a canteen of water. At first, she was dizzy and could barely make out what they were saying. She began to realize the explosion had affected her hearing and balance. It took a minute for her head to clear enough to realize that she was okay.

"I'm not hurt," she managed to whisper between coughs. "I'm just dazed."

She vaguely heard Wayne relay the good news of her rescue over the radio. She was glad Matt would know she was safe. Her concern then turned to the others and she asked them, "Are Pam and Karen okay?"

124

"We found Agent Selco, ma'am. She was unconscious, having suffered a fractured jaw and other less serious injuries. The medics report that she should fully recover. Your assistant, Karen, is still missing. In fact, you and Agent Selco are the only two people we've found anywhere on the premises."

Erin couldn't understand why they would take Karen with them and leave Pam and her behind. The man she had debated with said he might want to put someone on trial, but why Karen? Why keep a female civilian instead of the President's wife? This thought filled her with dread. Erin was sure she hadn't talked her captor into releasing them. She was baffled at why they would let her go without holding a trial, putting up a fight, or collecting a ransom. What had they hoped to accomplish with this bizarre "catch and release" strategy? But even as she worried about Karen, she hoped Matt would persevere with his peace plan.

When Matt heard the news that Erin was safe and unharmed, he showed the proper relief and restrained elation that is expected from a world leader. Inwardly, Matt was anything but calm. He had been ready to wipe Syria off the face of the earth. He was only waiting out the rescue attempt before taking any further action. He had nearly put the world at war because he was so incensed at the mindless stupidity of these terrorists. The biological attacks, the annihilation of the depot in Israel and then to kidnap Erin while he was risking his life to bring peace to this battle-weary land was simply insane. He agreed with what everyone had been telling him. The only thing these terrorists seemed to respect was violence. The darker side of Matthew Alexander had been ready to crush them all and start over again, if anything was left of the Middle East.

But then he reflected on the outcome of the day's events. Erin was safe and on her way back to him. There were no American fatalities in her entourage, except perhaps Karen, who was still missing. At first, President al-Assad was clearly not going to support the peace plan, but he changed his tone quickly after Erin's abduction. Now the Syrian president seemed willing to bend over backwards to help make the peace plan work. With the public endorsement of Saudi Arabia and Syria, it would be easy to get Jordan and Egypt to commit as well.

Matt reflected on his near-death experience and the promise that if he would persevere in his efforts toward peace, the end result would amaze the world. He had to admit that the way this terrible day had turned out was nothing short of miraculous. The staffers were asking if he wanted to cut this trip short and return home. With Erin back safe and his faith in the peace plan restored, Matt felt he had every reason to continue on to Jordan and Egypt.

Chapter 17

George Salazar was livid. "What do you mean he's still going to meet with the Jordanian King and Egyptian President?"

Agent Thompson was conferring via secured satellite phone with the CIA Director regarding their security arrangements for POTUS' scheduled visits to Jordan and Egypt. Apparently this was the first Salazar had heard that the President's plans had not changed, despite the abduction of his wife and two other women. Wayne was surprised that Salazar was so angry. After all, the First Lady had been rescued without injury. He thought perhaps it was because Pam Selco would be convalescing for weeks or that FLOTUS' assistant Karen was missing. Still, to so blatantly oppose the President's resolve made Agent Thompson more than a little uncomfortable.

Salazar realized that he had just vented out loud to a Secret Service agent. He did his best to tone it down. "It seems like he's taken enough chances already. I would feel much better if POTUS came home where we can all regroup and do our jobs without taking such risks."

Wayne let the gaffe go without comment. "The First Lady has agreed that she will remain at the hotel for the next two scheduled stops. That frees up several agents to beef up protection elsewhere. We can nearly double the security arrangements for POTUS and the Secretary of State for the remainder of their trip."

"Well, if staying with his schedule is what President Alexander wants, that's what we'll do," George said, continuing to back off from his initial outburst. When they hung up, Salazar was as perplexed and angry as he'd ever been. He called General McComb on a secure line to see if he had any insight into the President's thought process.

"Yes, I had heard he will be completing the trip as scheduled, but I didn't get any details about his wife," McComb answered carefully.

"After the kidnapping, any sane person would have seen how futile his plans were and headed for home. I am seriously concerned about POTUS' physical and mental health since his heart attack," George said trying to calm down.

"As Richard and I said before, George, this has gone way beyond our comfort zone. The same must be true for you by now."

Salazar didn't want to chance any incriminating recordings being made no matter how secure their phone line was supposed to be. "Well maybe you're right. Let's just count our blessings and hope he's doing the right thing." George hung up and threw a briefing file across the room in disgust. Loose papers floated down harmlessly mocking him.

It was becoming clear to him that McComb had deduced he was involved in kidnapping FLOTUS. That put him at odds with McComb and probably Newman, but they could hardly tell anyone without putting themselves at risk. George knew that the President and the First Lady hadn't been close, but who would have guessed her abduction wouldn't faze him? How could POTUS so casually continue with 'business as usual' after the First Lady had almost died at the hands of terrorists?

Salazar considered what it would take to finally get Alexander's full attention. A moment later, he landed on an idea he knew would succeed where his other plans had not. What was needed was a lot of property damage and economic disruption with a minimum of casualties. POTUS would have to see the futility of his peace plan if all hell broke loose at the same instant in different locations. He knew Ramin did not have the skills or intelligence to pull this off. After all, organizing pinpoint destruction on a massive scale would require real military training, brains and talent. It was ironic that recent events had presented him with the perfect man to see this through. George would press Ramin to arrange a meeting.

***

The President, Erin and their entourage were headed back home after successful meetings with the heads of state in Saudi Arabia, Syria, Jordan and Egypt. Each of them had agreed to abide by the ceasefire pact and work together to neutralize violent factions within their borders. Matt knew the agreement was fragile at best, but it was a start.

He and Erin were resting together in the Presidential Suite of the 747. The whole world had learned of his meetings throughout the Middle East so their return flight number was officially Air Force One.

Erin had not fully recovered from her ordeal, but she put on a brave face for Matt. She was getting better each day, but the horrid memories of captivity in that awful hole persisted. She decided the best way to heal was to become her husband's cheerleader. She offered her congratulations to Matt for a job well done. "It's amazing that you even convinced Syria to agree to a cessation of violence. What a smooth talker you are! What do you think persuaded President al-Assad to go along with your vision for a world at peace?"

"At first, he was very much against my proposal. Nothing would sway him so I gambled he was involved with Mohammed's Faithful. I mentioned that a laptop and other evidence secured from the underground bunker would reveal everyone involved. Even then, it took you being kidnapped to convince him to change his mind. So he lives to rule another day and the world is better for his cooperation."

"Do you think he had anything to do with my abduction?" Erin asked, suppressing a shudder.

"I believe he was connected to those who actually did it. Maaz al-Assad is the only man who could have convinced them to simply walk away after working so hard to kidnap you in the first place. It was probably a combination of bad timing and the left hand not knowing what the right hand was up to that led to both your abduction and release."

"As laudable as your peace plan is," said Erin sadly, "it seems you are the only one who sincerely believes it can work. The other leaders either see no advantage to openly oppose it or they probably feel coerced by circumstance into agreement. That's not a great recipe for lasting success."

Matt sighed but maintained his enthusiasm. "Somebody had to go first and if everyone manages to keep the peace just one day at a time, this plan may yet succeed. I will take each small victory where I can."

129

"Do you really believe that after thousands of years of living with violence people can just forgive and forget?"

"Actually no, I don't," was Matt's unexpected response. "I think we need help and a lot of it. I think we all need a role model to show us how to break the cycle. As difficult and unlikely as this might sound, I think we need to trust each other to do the right thing. Every culture believes in some version of the Golden Rule. That's the basic point of agreement we can all build upon for a lasting peace."

"I've never heard you talk like this before, Matt, even in our early days. Can you tell me more of what happened when you had the heart attack? It was obviously profound but I hadn't wanted to press you before."

"The more I reflect on what happened, the more certain I am that it was a near-death experience. Mine was unlike any I've heard of but it completely changed my perspective. A patient, gentle stranger showed me a different world view than I've ever known. I saw the futility of the path the world has been on for many years. I was able to experience, to really feel, how others would be affected by my personal and presidential decisions. I understood the fear, pain, anger and need for revenge felt by so many miserable people. I was also shown how bright the future will be someday, but not until we collectively choose it."

Erin eagerly flooded him with questions. "You've said some of that before, but don't you think your experience was more likely a vivid dream? Who do you think the guy was that showed you all these things? And how can you be so sure of the future?"

Matt nodded his head as he said, "I've asked myself these questions more than once and I keep coming to the same conclusion; it doesn't matter. Real or imagined, it isn't hard to see we've been traveling down the wrong road. As the saying goes, taking an eye for an eye leaves the world full of blind men. A sustainable peace is clearly the better way to live."

"I'm all for that, Matt, even after what happened in Syria. But how many bad apples does it take to spoil the utopia you described? Do you really think the other nations will support your vision when the cease-fire is inevitably broken?"

"That point brings me back to my near-death experience," Matt said.

"Meaning?" Erin queried.

"I agree that it will take a miracle to stop the violence in the Middle East. If we can persevere in our efforts, I think a miracle is exactly what we'll get," Matt explained.

"Like that voice in the movie that kept saying, if you build it they will come?" Erin joked.

"Yes, I suppose so," he smiled back at her. "Every natural occurrence appears to be a miracle until we understand the science behind it. Remember the experiment we did together back in college? We filled a glass with water and slowly brought the temperature down to exactly freezing."

"I do remember. I was surprised when the thermometer showed the water's temperature was 32 degrees Fahrenheit but remained in liquid form. We figured that the thermometer was off a bit," Erin recalled. "So we kept lowering the temperature until it was at -10 degrees but there was no change."

Matt went on, "I've never forgotten what happened when we called the professor over to show him the problem. He tapped his pen against the glass and the water immediately turned to ice. He told us that all the conditions were in place to turn the water into ice but it took the energy of his tap on the glass to act as the catalyst. It seemed like a miracle, but the answer was purely scientific."

"And your point from all that is...what?" Erin asked.

"I believe the entire world is at a point today just like that glass of water. The pattern of violence appears to be unchanging but we shouldn't be deceived by appearances. I think the conditions are already in place to achieve global harmony. I'm counting on our peace plan to be the catalyst, the 'tap on the glass,' that the world needs to change," Matt said, as he searched her face for a reaction.

Erin was quiet for a long moment. "I can't figure out if you're talking about physics or psychology," she said with a confused smile. "You got all this from that near-death experience?"

131

"I can't explain it fully, but in that experience both physics and psychology blended together seamlessly. It was as if everyone's personal choices and consequences were working together as lawfully as math, physics, chemistry and music. I know that sounds odd saying it out loud. I guess it's one of those things where you just had to be there," Matt smiled back at her.

"I wouldn't tell anyone else about that experience if I were you," Erin joked. "No President has ever been impeached for being insane but you could be the first."

"I guess I'm lucky a wife can't be forced to testify against her husband!" he laughed. Then he sobered. "I'll keep all this to myself but I will also continue to do what I can to tip the world's scales toward peace. I was assured during my NDE that as we work toward peace using what we already have in hand, we will receive the help we need to succeed."

Chapter 18

At Amir's request, Ramin had been a busy man. Through discreet inquiries he located the two operatives who betrayed Afkar. He had also learned who they worked for. Ramin had little contact with Mohammed's Faithful but he had heard of their ruthless leader, Colonel Achmed Mansur. Apparently Mansur's father and uncle had been loyal to the al-Assad family since the 1970s when they first came to power in Syria. The sons in both families followed in the footsteps of their fathers.

Unlike Maaz al-Assad, Mansur never married. A military career was all he cared about and many were surprised when Achmed retired early. Actually, his retirement was at the request of the Syrian president, who had recognized that Mansur's talents for covert military operations were better used in an unofficial capacity. Since then, Mansur's off-the-record access to information, money and people was greatly sought after in certain circles. His reputation was spotless because he always accomplished the missions he accepted.

Ramin reported this to Amir over a secure satellite phone. Amir was much calmer today than the last time they spoke. He didn't comment when Ramin suggested that Mansur was the mastermind behind the recent biological attacks as well as the massacre at the American supply depot in Israel. When Ramin was finished, the silence lingered as he waited for Amir to say something.

"If you're thinking of going after Mansur," Ramin began again, "I cannot help you. He is too connected and powerful for me to take on."

Amir finally said, "I'm not thinking of getting even with him. I want to hire the man. Can you get him to call me?"

"Mansur is easy to find but he is very hard to speak with directly. He probably lives somewhere near Damascus. I know several people who can relay your request to him. Do you want me to give him this secure number to reach you?"

"Please do. He is uniquely qualified to carry out a job I have in mind for him." Amir hung up.

***

Colonel Mansur was intrigued by the message. He was sure that Ramin's connection was highly placed in the U.S. government. Knowing ahead of time when and where the President and his wife would be traveling in the Middle East proved that. And now this person, Amir, wanted to hire him to do a job. There was no reason to avoid him even if it was some sort of trap. Mansur would simply not admit to anything while he listened to what the man had to say.

Using a secure satellite phone, he dialed the number. As expected, he was instructed to leave a return number for Amir to call. Within ten minutes, Mansur's phone rang.

"I was impressed with your recent work in Damascus," Amir began.

"I was not the one who kidnapped that woman," Mansur replied carefully. He made sure to word his answer so it would be the truth. If this Amir had a voice-stress analyzer monitoring the line for lies, he should come up clean.

"You misunderstand my intentions," said Amir. "What I really want to do is engage your services."

Mansur remained politely silent. Clearly this man knew more than he was saying and he was not fishing for admissions of guilt. Perhaps it would be worthwhile to hear him out. "What do you have in mind?"

"I believe we share a common goal of divesting the Middle East of any American influence. The job I am proposing will help that come to pass."

Mansur was fascinated but hedged, "I have no interest in working for an anonymous employer. If we could meet face-to-face to discuss the specifics of your proposed mission, we might come to some sort of agreement."

Salazar anticipated this and recommended they meet at a neutral location. He suggested the Bahamas as the venue. He would appear as his alter ego Amir, make the necessary arrangements, and

134

quietly return to the U.S. with no one the wiser. They agreed to meet the following day at the Atlantean Hotel in Freeport on the island of Grand Bahama.

George knew he was getting himself deeper and deeper into this mess but there was no going back now. He could have walked away after Erin Alexander was safely rescued, but the President seemed more determined than ever to undermine America's influence in the Middle East. If he didn't do something, POTUS could potentially jeopardize U.S. security operations on every continent. In order to prevent that from happening, the next planned disruption would have to be so devastating it would be unforgivable, even for President Alexander.

***

Mansur had taken a sleeping pill before boarding the flight that would take him to the Bahamas. He wanted to be well rested when he met with Amir. As he began to dream, the scene before him had amazing clarity. He found himself sitting in a room facing a man with an iridescent white glow surrounding him. He asked, "Who are you and what is this place?"

The man answered, "I am called Halaliel." The room they were in suddenly changed and became the living room in the home where Mansur spent his youth in Damascus. "Is this location more pleasing to you? I want you to feel as comfortable as possible."

Achmed just stared at Halaliel without saying a word.

Halaliel continued, "It is important that we discuss your plans for the future when you meet with Amir. Depending on what you decide, a great many people could suffer, yourself included."

"So you know Amir?" asked Mansur. "What can you tell me about him?"

"I have already met with Amir, much as we are meeting now. He will not be swayed from a violent path that could devastate the Holy Land. That is why we are meeting now. He cannot succeed without your help. Please believe me when I tell you it is in everyone's best interests for you to reject Amir's plan."

"Will his plan stop the United States from interfering with the affairs of my people? That godless country has no business

135

dictating how the rest of the world should live. Allah has used me well to keep the American infidels from invading His holy lands," Mansur said proudly.

"I can promise you that President Alexander is a man of integrity and is sincere in his plan for peace. Despite your intentions, America's involvement in the Middle East will only accelerate. Whether that involvement is to your liking or not depends uniquely on what you decide with Amir," warned Halaliel.

"I will resist any plan that comes from the American President. I am a soldier in Allah's army. My duty is clear no matter what threats you make," he said with conviction.

Mansur suddenly awoke to find he was still seated in the jet. The landing had jarred him to consciousness when they touched down in Freeport. The details of the disturbing dream he'd just had were already slipping away. No matter, he had little time to get to the hotel before he was to meet with Amir.

***

Dr. Jerome Westcott had poured over the machine code for several days before he found the self-destruct command sequence that was intended to erase the confiscated hard drive. He carefully deleted just enough of the malicious code so it would not execute, let alone trigger, any other self-destruct programs.

He tried again to start his lab computer using the updated copy of the laptop's original hard drive. This time it booted up without a problem. Just to be certain, he ran an immediate search of the drive for any more harmful software. In fact, there was another backup program that would kick in two minutes after the computer rebooted. It was designed to reformat the disk in the event that the first program failed to completely erase the drive. It was obvious the laptop's owner was serious about security. Jerome disabled the second self-destruct program on the original drive.

This was the moment the NSC had been waiting for. Jerome clicked the icon to boot the lab computer off the laptop's original hard drive. It fired up flawlessly. As he suspected, a deep scan showed traces of files that had been deleted since the laptop was first made. Only an expert like himself - he disliked the term computer geek - would be able to recover them.

His forensic examination of the hard drive, motherboard and components showed it was originally assembled in Ireland by one of the big PC manufacturers. From the programs loaded onto it, this laptop had been used for many purposes. Arabic was the default language although it stored three versions of the *Qur'an* with search engines in all three languages. It had Islamic spiritual texts and videos that were revered by Muslim scholars. It also contained dozens of encrypted email messages that he knew would have the CIA translators and analysts salivating.

The most incriminating files he found were some that had not been deleted. He discovered three video clips he assumed came from the camera monitoring the tunnel's entrance to the underground complex between Israel and Jordan. They must have been recorded by the people testing the camera to make sure it was working. Jerome found several minutes of video showing the faces of many people and their equipment going through the entrance of the tunnel.

Using facial recognition software, he would soon identify the probable leader of the group that hid in the underground bunker. The video showed the man inspecting the camera's installation as well as everyone deferring to him as they passed. Hopefully, that would answer any remaining questions regarding responsibility for the attacks. Dr. Westcott compiled his report for CIA Director Salazar and the NSC.

***

This was the first meeting of the NSC since President Alexander had returned from overseas two days ago. The room was buzzing with conversation when Matt entered. The talking ceased as they all stood and waited for him to sit at the head of the conference table. Much of what occurred in the Middle East, including the abduction of the First Lady, had not been released to the media. In fact, very few of the people in the Situation Room were in the loop on everything that had transpired over the past week.

"I have a brief statement to make before this meeting's agenda gets underway," Matt opened. "Some of you have heard that my wife was kidnapped in Damascus and that she was returned to me unharmed in less than a day. There were serious injuries sustained by two Secret Service agents who are expected to fully recover. Sadly, the First Lady's assistant, Karen Moffitt, is still missing, but the search for her continues.

"Despite this deeply disturbing event, I would call my trip to the Middle East an unqualified success. The leaders of Saudi Arabia, Syria, Jordan, and Egypt have agreed to an immediate cessation of violence. We will work together to keep any bloodshed at bay and to dismantle any terrorist groups that attempt to disrupt our peace efforts. It is no fluke that hostilities have stopped throughout most of the Middle East since these four Muslim nations agreed to keep the peace.

"We have a report from the CIA detailing all the evidence recovered from the attack on our supply depot in Israel. We have conclusive proof that Mohammed's Faithful was responsible for the horrific assault in Israel and the biological strikes we suffered in Afghanistan and Iraq. We have confirmed the identity of the leader of Mohammed's Faithful to be retired Syrian Army Colonel Achmed Mansur. Further connections between Colonel Mansur and the Syrian government will likely be forthcoming. There are many email messages that still need to be vetted. They were all found on the laptop recovered from the underground compound between Israel and Jordan.

"I'll take a few questions before we get on with the agenda."

General McComb went first. "What I heard is that Syria's government is on board with your peace initiative but may well have been involved in the attacks against our military bases in the Middle East. Can you clarify how you intend to work with Syria if they are proven to be complicit in these assaults against us?"

"Who would have thought?" Matt said dryly. "If you remember, we already had suspicions of Syria's covert support of terrorist activities before I went to the Middle East. My meeting with President al-Assad was not random but rather specifically intended to elicit his support for the peace initiative. It took some doing, but he agreed to back my proposal for his own reasons. I can guess that they are self-serving and perhaps in hopes of garnering lenience, if he or the Syrian government are verifiably linked to the terrorists.

"With that said, the First Lady's safe return was largely due to President al-Assad's help in locating her. It is my fervent hope that, despite what has occurred in the past, all the leaders of the

138

Middle East will decide to stand for peace rather than violence. So far, Syria has turned over a new leaf and is in full cooperation with the peace initiative."

Lieutenant General Newman asked, "And what did you offer these heads of state to gain their support? It's hard to believe they would agree to your plan just because you asked nicely."

As condescending as it was, Matt gave Newman's inappropriate tone a pass knowing his answer would set the talking points for the NSC meeting to follow. "There were two major objections to overcome when I met with the four leaders. There are many reasons behind the ongoing hostilities in the region but it's my opinion they all come down to trust and economics. The OPEC nations of the Middle East fear the bleak economic future ahead once their oil reserves are depleted. So far, there is little outside help being offered to prepare for that day. Why? They believe it is because the more uneducated and ignorant the Middle East nations remain in the ways of the western world, the easier it is to dominate them in business negotiations."

George Salazar said, "There are few people in the world wealthier than the Arab leaders of oil-rich nations. But I appreciate your point about what will happen to that wealth once the oil eventually runs out. I also agree that there is little trust among enemies after so many years of deadly conflicts. That same distrust leads to fear and violence which continually feeds on itself. So we are left with a question. What makes this the best time to orchestrate yet another attempt at a lasting peace?"

Matt answered, "Have you already decided this cease-fire can't last? What better time is there for orchestrating peace than when violence is on the rise? Everyone ultimately wants to live in harmony but who is willing to go first in the peace process? We fear others will take advantage of us while we're turning the other cheek. By choosing not to retaliate for the heinous attacks against the U.S., we gained the respect of the Muslim leaders as the country that is willing to 'walk its talk.' The forgiving concepts in Christianity are also taught by the other major religions, including Islam."

McComb interjected, "But Mr. President, do you think that these Muslim leaders trust you? I can believe they'll go along with the plan until something goes wrong, but do you really expect any other nation to turn the other proverbial cheek after being attacked as America has been over the past year?"

Matt paused and sighed before answering. "No, I don't. But getting everyone to agree to stop the violence is the first step. Setting the example to prove how serious we are about peace is vital to making this work. Trust will build and peace will prevail as long as we treat each other fairly and honestly. I intend to go back and meet with the leaders of Lebanon, Iran and other nations who are still not convinced that I am committed to supporting this initiative. Once everyone is on the same side, there will be no one left to fight against."

"Assuming for the moment that all goes well and peace is maintained, how do you intend to address the long-term economic challenges?" Vice President Jefferson had long wondered about POTUS' plan on this issue. He asked the question not only to hear the answer, but also to circumvent the endless loop that was about to occur on the viability of Matt's peace initiative.

"I believe we will be asking that question for years to come, but answer it we must," Matt said with a thankful look toward the Vice President. "The Middle East cannot thrive economically, once their oil reserves run out, unless efforts are made now to develop other products and services from that region that the global market wants to buy."

Joan Hartley asked, "And what goods or services could they develop? Except for oil, cotton and some unique food products, what else do they have that the rest of the world would want?"

"Your question," Matt offered, "is a great reason why these countries are so hostile toward other nations. We buy their oil but we don't make other investments in the region, as first world economies usually do, with their major trading partners. The leaders of these oil-rich countries clearly understand they will be bankrupt once their oil reserves are depleted.

"The cure for that disease is education along with the development of new products and services that will give them a competitive advantage. I only had to point to Israel to show the economic potential they have without selling a drop of oil. More of Israel's citizens have college degrees per capita than any other country except Canada. We will work with all the Middle Eastern

140

governments to identify the potential industries they want to develop. We can help them to create a modern educational infrastructure that will bring all of their citizens up to date in the knowledge they'll need to compete as first world economies. We will encourage partnerships with private firms who are already well established in the industries in which they want to excel.

"Remember, Middle Eastern oil reserves may last for more than a century, but their easy access to oil will start to diminish around 2040. If they begin today to make the economic transformations I've outlined, they can be implemented without stress. The desired changes will come, but their economies and cultures will gradually evolve rather than suffer from too many changes too soon."

The President stopped talking and looked at each face around the table. He could tell that most were skeptical but they were not going to argue with him. He wondered how low their lack of support would sink. Rather than dwell on that unpleasant thought, he shifted gears and asked, "So shall we get on with the agenda for this meeting?"

Chapter 19

It worked well for Mansur to meet Amir in Freeport. He could avoid being seen by acquaintances who vacationed in the fine resorts of Nassau, the Bahamas' largest city. His covert activities over the years had taught him to keep a low profile. The fewer people who saw him here, the fewer witnesses there would be to connect him to Amir's next project.

"Your first time in the Bahamas, Mr. Mansur?" said a voice from behind him.

Mansur turned his gaze from the book he was pretending to read and saw a man from two worlds. He was wearing a dark business suit cut in the American style but he also wore sunglasses and a keffiyeh on his head. The headdress was mainly worn in Saudi Arabia, Jordan and Iraq, but the man didn't have an Arabic accent. His dark complexion could have been native to many places. Amir allowed nothing about his appearance to give him away.

"I have not had the pleasure before today. Should I call you Mr. Amir?" Mansur responded as he continued to search for subtle clues to the man's identity.

"There is no need to be so formal. Amir is fine. Shall we discuss pleasantries over tea or get right down to business?"

Mansur said, "I've already scheduled a flight back to Syria this afternoon, so our time together is limited."

They moved to a private table away from the tourists and waved off the approaching waiter. Mansur, quite pleased to dispense with the small talk, got straight to the point. "Please tell me what you have in mind that could rid the Middle East of the Americans."

"Very well then," Amir smiled, casually crossing his legs with the knees together as Europeans do. "You already know that President Alexander has been traveling throughout the region pushing his peace initiative on the nations of the Middle East. If his strategy succeeds for any length of time, I fear the U.S. will gain an irreversible foothold among Allah's people. This must not happen!

They characterize the proposal as offering us their western education and business acumen so that our proud nations will become sustainable economic powers without our oil. I feel certain that if we try to emulate their economic model, we will become more and more dependent upon the Americans."

Mansur asked, "And you believe President Alexander is simply using his initiative to hide an insidious plot? What exactly do you think will happen if he succeeds?"

Amir could see he was being tested but he welcomed it. "It has long been America's plan to industrialize the rest of the world while preserving their own resources and land. Do you really want our homeland to become America's pawn only to be ignored and forgotten when our oil reserves are depleted? I don't trust them and I don't believe they intend to help us. What advantage does the United States gain by doing all this? If helping us to become a sustainable world power without our oil reserves was truly their goal, it would have already happened."

Amir's answer was perfectly aligned with the Colonel's natural suspicions. Mansur didn't trust much in life, least of all the United States and its government. "Let's say you are right. What do you propose that would stop the President's plan from succeeding?"

"I believe the cease-fire would fall apart immediately if a disruptive event of major proportions happened where the financial interests of many nations would be affected," Amir said quietly, though his eyes darted around constantly behind his sunglasses.

"Did you already have a specific target in mind that would accomplish this goal?"

"I do," said Amir. "There are five essential crossing points along the Suez Canal. I have a plan to destroy them simultaneously."

Mansur almost released a low whistle. The Suez Canal had been a pivotal location in past conflicts, especially with Israel in 1967. The entire length of the Suez Canal was at sea level and that made it difficult to disrupt for very long. He knew Amir's strategy had to include such massive destruction that even the United States would be challenged to repair the damage.

"I assume the idea is to blame this incident on Israel or perhaps some western power?"

143

"Israel, correct," nodded Amir. "The plan is to take out five key crossing points along the canal route between the Mediterranean and Red Seas. There are two bridges, one tunnel, and two utility crossings spread across its roughly 200-kilometer length. Also, a railroad runs its entire length on the west bank. We can use that to transport our people and then add to the disruption when we make the train and the tracks the sixth target destroyed. Without the railroad, repairs will take months, if not years, to complete, depending on how unstable the region becomes as a result of the vast demolition."

Mansur was impressed. "I agree that such an attack would destabilize any peace effort no matter how much support was behind it, but what armaments do you have that can cause that much damage simultaneously? Also, are you sure this can be blamed on Israel?"

"Yes, I'm sure," said Amir. "I am arranging the purchase of a large quantity of the explosive Octanitrocubane which is far more powerful than HMX. It requires heat rather than oxygen to detonate. That makes it ideal for our varied crossing targets that are below ground and underwater. The satellite-controlled detonators are of Israeli manufacture and can be set to go off together. We are securing the fingerprints of some Israeli operatives in their Mossad Intelligence Unit – please do not ask me how. The prints should be strategically placed where forensic evidence teams will conveniently find them despite the damage from the blasts. There is still the question of motive, since Israel would have none. However, once the canal has been devastated, will anyone try very hard to find a motive before they retaliate?"

Mansur's excitement was growing. "I have heard of this explosive, although it was simply referred to as Cubane. If you have access to it, many challenges will be made easier. What about money, people and the other equipment needed for such a mission?"

Amir slid a USB thumb drive across the table to Mansur. "This has all the information on it that you'll need from me, as well as email addresses and secure communication algorithms, to stay in contact without being traced. You will be well compensated for organizing and executing this operation. I ask that you put together a timeline and budget for obtaining the technicians and any other equipment you'll need beyond the explosives and remote detonators."

Mansur slipped the thumb drive into his pants pocket and said, "I will consider all you have presented. If I decide to do this, where would I pick up the Cubane, detonators and evidence to plant?"

"I'll have the materials waiting near Cairo. That is nearly 170 kilometers from the Red Sea entrance to the canal. When you have everything ready on your end, we will set up a time and place for you and your men to take possession of the Cubane and anything else you need."

Without another word, Mansur stood up and left the table. In his mind he had already agreed to do this. There would eventually be peace in the Middle East, but it would not come from American interference. He would see to that.

***

Gil Kowalski, Director of National Drug Control Policy, was not enjoying his recent victories in the war on drugs. He had been focusing most of his attention on stopping the flow of illegal narcotics from south of the U.S. border. The result had been several major arrests along with the confiscation of huge quantities of drugs and cash from the Central and South American cartels. Instead of celebrating, Gil found that concentrating on that one region had only increased drug shipments from the Middle East and Asia.

He was meeting with Attorney General Deborah Voss in her office to discuss strategies to stem the flow of illegal drugs into the U.S. Gil was a man of integrity; in sharp contrast to the dealers he wanted to put out of business. His greatest challenge was how to win the war on drugs without violating the law or impinging upon anyone's rights.

"It appears illegal heroin shipments from Afghanistan to the U.S. are up significantly," he said in response to her question. "That's the region I need to work on next."

Deborah sighed and gave Gil a reality check. "Prosecuting their drug traffickers will not be easy unless they're caught here in the U.S. We have diplomatic relations with them but no extradition treaty. You can talk to their Afghan National Interdiction Unit all you want but it will be up to them to arrest and prosecute the people who manufacture illegal opiates in their country."

"Actually, I would prefer they end up in an Afghan prison, but your point is well taken. Opium has become their largest exported product. Since there are many legal uses for opium in the medical industry, it's basically impossible to shut them down." He shook his head and fell silent.

Deborah thought Gil needed a little encouragement so she suggested, "You should go talk to them face to face. That approach seems to be working for the President. Perhaps that is the first step toward a viable solution."

"I'm already scheduled to meet with officials in Afghanistan and neighboring countries in a few days. You're right that I shouldn't give up before I know what I have to work with over there. It's just that I hear the Middle East is no different from South America when it comes to government officials; welcoming favors and bribes from the drug cartels."

"Let's go back over the arrests your people made in South America. Making sure these thugs are locked up for a long time sends the kind of message everyone understands. If we can't convince the cartels in the Western Hemisphere that illegal drugs will not be tolerated, I doubt we'll have any chance in the East."

***

Ramin was speaking on his encrypted satellite phone and gave Amir an update on the explosives he had ordered. "I have the Cubane already. I acquired it from the Israeli army more than a year ago. I was lucky enough to be in the right place when their forces became more interested in what Lebanon was doing than in securing their own weapons." Ramin had been holding on to the Cubane in anticipation that it would be worth much to the right buyer.

Amir asked, "Can you get it to Cairo in a few days?"

"Just so! It is stored near New Cairo right now, so no border crossing is needed. Where in Cairo shall I make the delivery?"

"I will email the specifics to you," Amir replied. "For now, let me say that the shipment will need to be delivered to wherever Colonel Mansur says. So far, we have agreed that upon successful testing of the Cubane, it will be removed from the crate and packed into carry-on suitcases. It should not look suspicious to the casual observer. Also, a civilian Hummer will work best to transport the luggage rather than using a military vehicle. Make sure you have one on site."

***

Matt and Erin were in the White House residence after a hectic day of never-ending appointments. The living room was calm and restful, and they chatted over a glass of wine about the recent events that brought them to such a critical and exciting time in their lives, if not in history. Murray was enjoying having his ears scratched by Matt.

"Except for that part where I was kidnapped, your peace initiative is going well," Erin teased dryly.

He knew she was joking but he was not at a point where he could join in. "I think I aged a decade in those few hours before I knew you were safe. I admit that I wanted to go in guns blazing and obliterate anyone who would try to hurt you. The dangerous part was that I actually have the army to do it. I'm afraid of what I would have done if you had been harmed or worse."

"Well, I wasn't hurt, although I'm still very worried about Karen. Please let me know the minute you hear anything about her. As for the reason we made the trip in the first place, I admit that your idea could really work. Offering to be the first country to rise to the best that is within us and setting a peaceful example will go a long way toward proving your sincerity. The U.S. has been hit hard this past year and the leaders over in the Middle East know my abduction made it all very personal for you. It's easy to believe that you will strike back with a vengeance at the first sign of trouble."

Matt shook his head as he marveled that those awful events actually ended up supporting his intended goal. "It sure does seem like a lot of lucky breaks turned all those bad situations to our advantage.

"When I go back, I will miss your pep talks at the end of the day. I may call just to hear your voice. I apologize in advance if I forget the time difference," he said as he touched her cheek. "I don't know if I could have done all this without you." Matt could feel himself getting a little choked up. They had surprised each other in how hard they both worked to heal their relationship. Together, they had accomplished much more than a ceasefire. Their love was now stronger than ever because they knew it would endure.

"Promise me something?" Erin asked.

"And what would that be?"

"Promise me you'll wait at least 24 hours before you make a decision to respond in kind to any violence that may happen in the Middle East from here on?" Her expression and tone said clearly how important she thought this was.

Matt felt the same *déjà vu* experience as before. He could vaguely remember seeing this exact scene between them unfolding just as it was now. He remembered watching it like a movie being played for him during his near-death experience. He sensed that it was important for him to agree to Erin's request. He also knew that he was going to be tested on this promise in the near future.

After considering this for what seemed like a long time, he finally answered her. "Yes, I will wait a day before I make any such decisions. I already know I'll have to reach beyond my depth to maintain enough patience and trust when the time comes to keep this promise."

Erin leaned over to kiss him. Murray trotted off to his dog bed and settled down for the evening.

Chapter 20

Ramin had never wanted to meet Achmed Mansur, let alone do business with him. His reputation as a merciless killer was well deserved and now Amir had hired this ruthless patriot to do his dirty work. Ramin desired to get this transaction over with as quickly as possible.

Colonel Mansur was impressed with Amir's plan to immobilize the Suez Canal. His greatest reservation in accepting this mission was acquiring and using the Cubane. He knew Cubane was perfect for this mission, but only Ramin had any for sale. Making matters worse, the idiot knew nothing about the high-tech explosive.

That presented another problem. No one was sure how much Cubane was needed to destroy their intended targets. Mansur appreciated the irony of trying to keep a low profile while testing such a powerful explosive. He often employed the same trusted demolitions expert but the man had never before worked with Cubane. Rather than hire someone he didn't know, Mansur had to trust that his expert could safely carry out the test.

Another concern was that people might see the test detonation, even though they were miles from the nearest town. They decided it would be better to do this at night. While the explosion would be seen from a greater distance after sunset, anyone investigating the blast would not easily track where the test took place or where they went after it was over.

Ramin's warehouse was several kilometers away from the test site and had long ago become a useless building for any kind of real commerce. Its original purpose had been as a staging area for the people and equipment used to pave roads connecting New Cairo with Cairo and Alexandria. Once the highways had been completed, the construction company was glad to sell the property, cheap. Its remote location was perfect for Ramin's needs.

Mansur had ordered his people to prepare a deep hole to safely test the explosive. The pit was perhaps five meters deep by two meters wide. It would force the explosion skyward and protect them from the concussive blast. The fireball would be noticeable for a few seconds but there was little they could do about that. Since the Cubane had remained in his warehouse for a year without incident, Ramin was sure it was safe to sell. But would it perform as advertised?

The explosives expert carefully fashioned the Cubane into a sphere a little larger than a tennis ball. The detonators used for this product were specifically designed to generate enough heat to cause the Cubane to ignite without requiring oxygen. That was one of the unique features of this substance. It would blow objects up under water as well as below ground or even in outer space.

Though it wasn't very high tech, the demolitions expert wrapped duct tape around the Cubane and detonator and lowered both down to the bottom of the hole with a long length of string. The substance was supposed to be quite stable but old and careful habits die hard. No self-respecting explosives specialist would simply toss a bomb into a deep hole, no matter how stable the Cubane was supposed to be.

Once it was in place, the group of men retreated to a distance of about 100 meters to begin the experiment. The detonator was satellite radio controlled. Ramin handed the trigger device to Mansur, absolving himself of any responsibility for the test. Mansur didn't hesitate. He smiled as he lifted the cover guard and pressed the detonation button with a flourish. For a moment, nothing happened. The expert started to offer an explanation for the delay when a tremendous explosion shot flames far into the night sky. A moment later, sand particles began to rain down upon them. They burned like pin pricks as it touched their exposed skin. The falling grains of sand had become small droplets of molten glass from the heat of the blast.

None of the observers had ever seen such a powerful display from such a small quantity of explosive. Mansur was impressed and pleased as he reached for his satellite phone. Because this call had been prearranged, Amir picked up immediately.

"Did you test the Cubane?" Amir asked.

"We just did. Everything seems to be in order," was Mansur's short reply. "You can pay this man his money," and he hung up.

Both Mansur and Ramin yelled for their men to prepare to leave. As everyone rushed to pack up their gear, Mansur reflected on his disgust for men like Ramin. He hated cowards who profited from worthy causes but were afraid to get their hands dirty. Such men only believed in money and were no better than the infidels.

Ramin despised Mansur knowing he was responsible for killing Afkar and his team. After executing so many good men, he had released the hijacked hostages without receiving a ransom. It was as if Mansur was working for the Americans. Only a crazy man would do that.

***

Gil Kowalski did not feel at home in the hot, dry climate of Afghanistan. His counterpart in the Afghan government, Wajid, feigned an interest in what Gil had to say. This American would never understand the pressures of living in this part of the world. "He speaks of stopping the flow of illegal drugs into America but what do I care about that?" he thought with a frown.

Afghanistan is the largest global supplier of opiates to the medical profession and Wajid knew it had become one of their largest and most profitable exports. He hated that America wanted countries like his to take on the inherent risks of manufacturing opiates but complained loudly when some of it was used illegally.

Still, he wanted to maintain good relations between his government and the United States. Rather than divulge the identities of any illicit opium manufacturers in his country, he hoped to offer other information that would make this man go away happy. As Gil spoke on at length, Wajid appeared to be taking notes on his laptop. What he was actually doing was scanning intelligence reports of criminal activity throughout his country.

Finally, he landed on a suspicious activity memo that looked very promising. It was nothing definitive but the implications of the memo became the distraction he'd been looking for. Apparently, someone was offering an impressive fee for a dangerous assignment that would last about a week and required travel to Egypt. To recruit talent from as far away as Afghanistan could mean many things and none of them were good. Knowing of America's current push for peace in the Middle East, Wajid suspected this memo would divert Gil from his opium witch hunt.

"Do you mean to say that mercenaries in this region are being recruited to work in Egypt?"

Wajid replied, "To hear that someone is hiring mercenary talent is not so unusual. However, that they are only needed for a short time and will travel to Egypt is very much out of the ordinary."

"Would you hazard a guess as to the kind of work you think they'll do in Egypt?"

"It could be anything from the personal protection of one man to an entire military operation. Given the short amount of time they are needed, a military operation is likely. I also find it interesting that they are looking for men who do not live where the job will take place. That implies that they don't want anyone available for questioning after the assignment is done."

Gil's membership in the NSC put him in a unique position to understand the significance of this news. He quickly concluded the meeting with Wajid and excused himself. He needed to return to the American Embassy and pass the information along without delay. He didn't know how much he could trust the validity of the intelligence from Wajid but this was big enough that he couldn't ignore it.

The chief of CIA operations in Kandahar was Tom Strickland. He sat patiently listening to Gil describe his conversation with the head of Afghanistan's Counter-Narcotics Department. Like Gil, Tom didn't know how much they could trust the intel Wajid had provided, but he promised Gil he would run the information past his colleagues. Perhaps they could link this with other fragments of intelligence to make sense of it all.

Tom's first call was to Isaac, an old friend who worked for Mossad. The man worked from behind a desk these days, but he still kept up with the hot issues at any given moment. When Isaac picked up, they spent a few minutes catching up on their personal lives. When the pleasantries were out of the way, Tom asked, "What do you know about someone hiring mercenaries in Afghanistan for a short-term job in Egypt?"

Isaac answered slowly with another question, "Where did you hear that?"

Tom mentioned the ever growing chain of sources for the information and admitted it might be nothing more than rumors, given the route this intel took to get to him.

"I'm going to do some checking around here but, if this connects with some other recent events, I think the answer will be beyond both our pay grades," Isaac said.

"That doesn't surprise me, though the tip came from a member of our National Security Council," said Tom. "What do you know about this that we don't?"

Isaac's voice lowered as he said, "It's been nice talking with you, Tom. If I have anything I can tell you, I'll be in touch."

Tom knew better than to ask for more details at that point. He said goodbye and hung up.

***

Isaac walked straight into Moshe's office. Moshe was a Senior Field Agent with the ongoing assignment of monitoring any security threats arising out of Egypt. When Isaac told him of the rumored mission in Egypt, they both stared at each other. Isaac was aware that their agents had observed something quite disturbing just the night before in the desert east of New Cairo. In light of the U.S. President's peace initiative in the Middle East, he thought the recruitment of mercenaries in Kandahar for a job in Egypt might be related.

Isaac asked, "Do you think mercenaries were responsible for that explosion your agents saw in the desert last night?"

"Yes. The timing and nature of the incident coincides only too well with an embarrassing theft that occurred about a year ago." Moshe started at the beginning. "Our scientists were experimenting with a new explosive called Cubane. It was originally developed in America but they kept the formula to themselves. Apparently, it releases far greater energy per gram than Semtex or even HMX and it's just as stable."

Isaac asked, "So they had this Cubane for over a year but hadn't used it yet?"

Moshe said, "That part didn't surprise us. The stolen batch was dangerous. The damn stuff was so unstable that it would blow

153

up when dropped from just a few meters. We assumed whoever had taken it figured that out and quietly got rid of it."

Isaac said, "That's why we didn't tell anyone about the theft! So those idiots don't know it's unstable?"

Moshe nodded as he replied, "That's what we thought, but it appears we were wrong. By the way, the unstable Cubane tested with a much greater explosive force than the improved mixture we have today. Regardless, it disappeared along with the special detonators our team developed to ignite it remotely by an encrypted satellite signal."

Isaac interjected, "Did you find out who took it or where it was located?"

Moshe smiled, "We got lucky. We still don't know for sure who stole it or how, but we do know who ended up with it. A sleazy arms dealer named Ramin Acaba has it in a remote warehouse in Egypt. Last night, our two surveillance operatives who covertly witnessed that test explosion near New Cairo were able to track it down. They also confirmed the quantity they have is enough to level an entire city block in downtown Tel Aviv."

Isaac started to put it all together, "So you have the recruitment of mercenaries from Afghanistan for a job in Egypt, where you know this unstable Cubane was just tested after lying idle for a year. There is also the timing of the U.S. President's divisive peace initiative with the Egyptian government. These details isolated from each other don't mean much. Together they spell big trouble and we don't have a lot of time to react."

Moshe shook his head. "We still don't know the terrorists' target and Mossad can't announce this discovery without conceding responsibility for the stolen Cubane. That's embarrassing enough but no one will want to admit that we conduct covert surveillance inside of Egypt. Our wisest course is to turn what we know over to the Americans and let them deal with it."

"So should I inform my contact with the CIA?" Isaac asked.

"No! We must follow our chain of command and then communicate from one government head to another. I'll call my supervisor in Tel Aviv. The CIA may wind up with this eventually, but we can't start with them. No one in Mossad will want to take the blame for this mess, but there's too much at stake to not do our part to stop it."

***

Moshe kept moving higher and higher up the Mossad hierarchy, with the information that he had gathered. He was kicked upstairs each time because none of his superiors saw an advantage to becoming involved. He finally told his story to the Director of Mossad. He too did not want to be the one to bring this to Egypt's attention. However, the eminent danger, to so many, could not be ignored. He gave Moshe permission to break the chain of command and unofficially contact the head of security for the United States. That way, the number of people who knew about this would be kept to a minimum. Also, Israel's government could deny having direct knowledge, if the situation literally blew up later on.

Moshe's next call was to DNI Director Richard Newman in Washington. It took a while, but he confirmed to each new person that he had information regarding a massive terrorist attack being prepared in Egypt. Finally, his call was put through.

"Newman here. They tell me you're calling from Mossad with a report of possible terrorist activities in Egypt?"

"Yes sir, though unofficially!" Moshe replied, and he proceeded to describe the known high points of the possible threat, off the record, to the Director.

Newman surmised that George Salazar was somehow behind this despite his promise to drop any plans to disrupt POTUS' peace initiative. Newman had to do his job and that included notifying President Alexander of this potential threat to the tenuous balance of peace in the Middle East. He would consult with General McComb later regarding what should be done about Salazar.

Chapter 21

"I apologize for the short notice of this NSC meeting," began President Alexander. "It couldn't be helped. I'll let Director Newman fill you in on the latest."

Newman looked at Salazar before speaking. A moment passed between them, as they assessed what the other person knew. Salazar held his gaze steady even though he could guess this wasn't going to be good.

"Our friends in Mossad called me unofficially to offer a heads-up on a possible Middle East terrorist attack. We don't yet know where or when, but we do know that the most powerful explosive short of nuclear weapons, Octanitrocubane, also known as Cubane, will be used. We believe that the intended target is in or near Egypt. All signs point to the terrorists striking in the next few days."

The President added, "We have already alerted the Egyptian government to this potential attack. Because of our mutual agreement to fight terrorism in the Middle East, they are allowing a specialized American team to coordinate with the Egyptian authorities in stopping this threat."

Salazar decided his best defense was to take on a high profile. He asked Director Newman, "How does Mossad know this? And why are they so sure the terrorists are going to use this super explosive, you called it Cubane?"

Newman looked directly at him for a long second before responding. "Apparently, the Cubane was stolen from the Israelis about a year ago. It was by luck that two of their agents witnessed an explosion last night, most likely a test, about five miles east of New Cairo. They dropped everything and arrived near the scene in time to take pictures of the people getting into their vehicles to leave. Their night vision telephoto lens was able to take some clean photos. As the suspects left the scene, they went in two different directions. The Mossad agents decided to follow the larger group hoping they had the explosives with them. It appears to have been a good guess.

"That group ended up at a remote warehouse owned by a known arms dealer named Ramin Acaba. The agents took up a position outside the warehouse at a discreet distance. Using high-powered scopes, they were able to identify the original Hebrew warning that the crate contained Cubane. They are keeping the warehouse under surveillance, but so far the Cubane has not been moved. Before you ask, this is the first we've heard that the Israelis had lost such a large quantity of the compound."

Salazar asked, "Just how much of it was taken?"

Newman didn't bother to look at him as he responded. "Mossad admits that Ramin Acaba has enough Cubane to destroy pretty much any target we can imagine. Since the test was conducted near New Cairo, we're guessing the target is likely to be in northern Egypt.

Undaunted, Salazar asked a follow-up question. "You said the Cubane is still being stored at the warehouse location? If so, it sounds like we can stop this attack before it starts."

Newman explained, "We can't guarantee that it's still there but the Mossad agents on the scene believe that it is. They watched as it was carefully separated and packed into small suitcases. Those cases were then stored in a large SUV that is still parked inside the warehouse in full view of the agents' surveillance position.

"The terrorists will reveal the general direction of their intended target, once they exit the property. There's only one highway nearby. Turning right will take them to Alexandria while a left turn will take them to Cairo. If we go in before they attempt to transport the Cubane, we'll only have them on an illegal weapons charge instead of conspiracy. The area surrounding the warehouse is not populated and it's as good as it gets for taking them down, while risking as few casualties as possible.

Salazar had one more question. "And we believe this Acaba character is the one planning the attack?"

"We believe Ramin Acaba is the seller of the Cubane, which is a major crime. However, we want to get the buyer, too. Facial recognition software, of the stills the Mossad agents provided from the test site, has identified retired Syrian Colonel Achmed Mansur as the number one suspect."

Matt took the floor again. "I am authorizing our top Delta Force team to coordinate this mission with their Egyptian counterparts. Our people will take the lead and the risk. Egypt is not aware of Mossad's involvement thus far, so they probably believe our intel is coming through American channels. I have not lied to the Egyptian President about this, but neither do I want anyone volunteering the information, if the question does not come up. I believe a policy of honesty and transparency is the best way to maintain the trust we'll need to build upon for the future. However, for the Egyptians to learn that the Israelis are currently conducting covert surveillance on their soil is asking too much too soon, in gaining their cooperation."

Matt did not feel good about this omission of information to the Egyptian government. He would remember to discuss this integrity issue with Erin, his worthy advisor on questions of moral conscience. For now, he was choosing to be "wise as serpents yet harmless as doves."

He turned the meeting over to the NSC members and left for a pressing appointment in the Oval Office. He knew he could trust these intelligent people to develop a plan that would minimize the damage intended by the terrorists.

***

As Matt walked past the same chair he collapsed in during his heart attack, the familiar déjà vu feeling washed over him. He sat down and closed his eyes for a moment. The memory of that strange briefing returned and he recalled that this situation in Egypt was a major focus of discussion with the man in iridescent white. He had been told that if everything unfolded correctly up to this point, the success of his peace plan hinged on what they collectively did about this new terrorist threat.

For just a moment, Matt found himself reliving a portion of that experience with amazing clarity. The man had suggested two additions to the Delta Force team that seemingly made no sense. Both were archeologists who trained at Harvard; one American and one originally from Egypt. Matt didn't know either man but he now clearly recalled their names: Dr. Mark Heston and Dr. Nuri Zayd. He remembered that it was of the utmost importance to include these two men as consultants to the team in Egypt. He couldn't remember why but Matt knew their presence would be vital to the success of his peace initiative.

***

It took a moment for the NSC members to realize POTUS was back. He stood quietly in the doorway reviewing what he was about to say. The various discussions trailed off and they turned respectfully to see why he had returned. Matt spoke to Richard Newman directly. "I want you to add two civilians to the Delta Force team as advisors. They are Doctors Mark Heston and Nuri Zayd. They work for Harvard but are currently in Egypt doing research at the University of Cairo."

Newman asked, "Mr. President, what kind of doctors are you adding to the team?"

"They're archeologists."

"Uh, yes Sir. And what if they refuse?" he asked, clearly puzzled by this unusual directive.

Matt smiled and walked away with a confident, "If anyone can persuade them, it's you. Call them and set it up right away."

It was not the first time President Alexander had baffled everyone in the room. It wasn't even the first time they failed to see good reasoning behind his thinking. And the addition of two archeologists to a covert operations team, even as advisors, was by any measure nonsensical. However, as long as the two doctors agreed to follow the ops leader's instructions, there was no good reason to object to them being a part of the team.

Newman made a note of the names and continued on with the briefing.

***

Mark Heston and Nuri Zayd were conducting archeological research at the University of Cairo. They had met during their graduate years at Harvard and were now both working to translate the hieroglyphics found on ancient artifacts at various excavation sites throughout Egypt. When Lieutenant General Newman's assistant contacted them, they didn't know what to think. They were instructed to call him back on a secured line from the nearby American Embassy.

Mark was tall and lanky with a receding brown hairline that rarely saw a comb. No one would have been surprised to see his picture next to the word 'nerd' in the dictionary. His eyes seemed to change from blue to gray depending on his mood. Mark was an open book except for one secret that he did his best to hide from the world. He had a tattoo of the Sphinx on his right shoulder. The inked artwork depicted just the head of the Sphinx in vivid colors, as it had appeared in ancient times. Mark hated pain and the idea getting the tattoo made him ill. Still, he had allowed it because it was part of the hazing ceremony to join the preferred archeology fraternity at Harvard.

Nuri was raised in Cairo, Egypt but he became fluent in English to prepare him for the doctoral archeology program at Harvard University. That had been his dream since he was young. He, like Mark, had always wanted to explore the world's ancient mysteries. Nuri was 1.7 meters (5' 8") tall, with serious brown eyes and thick jet black hair that still showed no signs of graying. He always wore collared shirts that he kept buttoned to the top regardless of the weather. The strict Egyptian schools he attended required the top button be fastened when their students were in public and he never lost the habit. He had no tattoos because he refused to join Harvard's archeology fraternity when he learned that they required it.

These two had become fast friends and lab partners despite their differing personalities. Mark actually quit the fraternity after his freshman year because he didn't fit in well with the others. Both he and Nuri had been raised on stories of fantastic advanced civilizations that were responsible for building the wonders of the ancient world. Also, it was in fashion for doctoral candidates to be atheists. Mark and Nuri both believed in a God, but not in any specific religion. They described themselves as 'spiritual but not religious.' That put them on the outside of the in-crowd from their first days at Harvard, now more than six years ago.

Today, despite their misgivings, they made their way over to the U.S. Embassy in Cairo. They were surprised to find they were expected when they arrived. On the way over, they had almost convinced each other that they were the victims of some prank. Soon they found themselves in the office of the U.S. Ambassador to Egypt speaking on a secure line to Director Newman. The Ambassador stepped out of the room and closed the door.

"Gentlemen," Newman began, "the team leader in Cairo will be able to share more details about this grave situation once you both agree to come on board. Confidentiality is paramount. Let me say that President Alexander has personally asked that you two join a special team to help stop a terrorist act on Egyptian soil."

The scientists just sat there in stunned silence. Newman realized he would have to provide more information for the gravity of the situation to be understood.

"We don't know the exact target but it is conceivable that one or more of Egypt's ancient treasures is at risk. The potential threat may be against the Cairo Museum, or perhaps some treasured antiquities in Alexandria. We really don't know as yet. The point is that we need your expertise and advice and especially your presence as we work to thwart this terrorist plot."

Mark was the first to speak, "You said the President asked for us by name? I've never met the President and I sure didn't vote for him. Who are you really?"

Nuri had gathered his wits enough to add, "I guess I don't get the joke. I really don't think this is funny. Can we get back to work now?"

Newman knew this was not an easy story to believe. He regretted leading with "the President asked for you by name." He tried to redeem his credibility after such a faulty start.

"I assure you this is no joke. I was serious when I said Egypt is facing an imminent terrorist attack and that we need your particular expertise on the team assigned to stop them. If you agree to help us, I will make sure that your supervisor at the University agrees to grant you a short and immediate sabbatical."

Mark asked, "Is this dangerous? I mean, could we be hurt or worse if we decide to help you?"

Newman answered indirectly by promising that every precaution would be taken to ensure their safety. He added that if these terrible events were not prevented, the lives of many innocent people in Egypt would be threatened, including their own. Bowing to the pressure, they both reluctantly agreed to join the team.

Chapter 22

Newman had asked General McComb to meet with him after he had spoken to the two archeologists. McComb was reluctant because he could guess what was coming and he wanted nothing to do with Salazar and his schemes. He finally agreed to take a walk with Newman around Lafayette Park.

McComb opened by trying to steer the conversation away from Salazar. "So why did POTUS add those two archeologists to the Delta Force team?"

"I have no clue what that was about," Newman said with frustration. "If he hadn't given their full names and said to contact them at Cairo University, I would have thought he was kidding. As it stands, they have agreed to help. But you know I didn't ask you out here to talk about them."

McComb sighed and asked, "All right then. What's George done now?"

Newman said, "I believe he has gone ahead with his own agenda to disrupt the President's peace initiative. This latest threat out of Egypt has his markings all over it. At least he's been warned that everyone, including Mossad and the Egyptian government, is aware of the plan."

"Don't be so sure that will stop him," McComb said with alarm. "If Salazar is behind this, he can guide the terrorists through that minefield as long as no one is positive of their exact target."

Newman added, "There was something I didn't say in that briefing that's very important. The President insisted that I leave out this vital piece of information."

"Do I want to know?" McComb asked cautiously.

Newman explained, "The Cubane these terrorists have is a defective batch that is less than stable. Apparently it can blow up just from being dropped or shaken too hard. They've obviously been lucky so far, but how long will that last?"

McComb asked, "And you're saying the people who have it now aren't aware of this?"

Newman hesitated but nodded, "That's a reasonable assumption. No one in their right mind transports unstable explosives over unpaved roads. That test they held in the Egyptian desert was probably to measure its destructive power. They wouldn't have known to test it for stability."

McComb saw this development could be both good and bad. "POTUS insisted that you withhold that information at the NSC meeting? He obviously suspects information leaks. The good news is that he probably doesn't suspect you since you brought this to him."

Newman shook his head. "You didn't see his face when he gave that order. It was as if he knew I was somehow involved and was giving me a chance to make amends."

"You are not the only one he suspects since he kept the information from the rest of the NSC. That is cause for concern, but POTUS can't prove anything against us unless Salazar talks," McComb reminded him. "Regardless, it sounds like the Delta Force team has this situation covered. Is the Cubane really so unstable that these terrorists can blow themselves up driving down a bumpy road?"

Newman nodded this time. "That could happen, but the plan is to keep them on paved roads. As soon as we know whether they are headed toward Cairo or Alexandria, Delta Force will take them down before they get to any inhabited areas."

"That sounds logical to me," said McComb. "Even if the Cubane ignites, there would be limited casualties. Just how much jostling is needed to set it off?"

"The risk of an explosion was described to me as being something like the structural integrity of an egg. The shape of an egg can take a lot of pressure without breaking, if applied correctly. But dropping one off a counter will break it every time. Because the Cubane was carefully packed inside those small suitcases, it shouldn't blow up unless dropped several feet onto a hard surface or somehow sharply impacted.

"It would take something with the force of a car wreck or throwing it off the truck to accidentally set it off. You heard that

164

Mossad believes they know where the stuff is and they are not taking their eyes off it."

McComb said confidently, "We won't be connected to this no matter what happens in Egypt. Let the Delta Force team do what they're trained to do."

"But what if they catch up with Salazar and he tells them we're involved?" Newman exclaimed.

"I would keep him out of the loop as much as you can and have nothing more to do with him," McComb warned.

"But he reports to me and can effectively end our careers regardless of proof," Newman said. "With all his connections, he won't stay in the dark for long."

A thought occurred to McComb that could resolve the whole mess. "Why don't you tell Salazar that you want him in the Middle East to personally oversee the CIA's covert operations in these precarious times? He might just end up in the wrong place at the right time. Either he blows up with the terrorists or they take him out after discovering the Cubane is defective."

"That's a devious idea. And I can live with it. It gets Salazar out of the way and allows him to lie in the bed he's already made."

"What do you mean you want me to go to Egypt?" George Salazar bellowed. Lieutenant General Newman was his boss but George was livid. Newman obviously intended to put him in harm's way.

Newman pulled him up short, "I mean it George. You will leave for Cairo at once. There is a lot of confusion going on in Egypt right now that I think you are uniquely qualified to resolve. If anyone can keep a lid on the current terrorist activities over there, it's you."

Salazar considered this for a moment and he read between the lines. He had no leverage against Newman that didn't take himself down as well. He thought Newman was a coward for not following through with their original intentions, but what was to be done now?

He considered whether or not his presence in Cairo would change anything. It wouldn't if everything went according to plan and he would be in a better position to keep things moving forward, if Mansur couldn't handle it. It wasn't as if Newman was giving him a choice and it might work out for the best.

"I'm leaving now," Salazar said, rudely hanging up the phone.

***

The archeologists waited in a Giza hotel room for the rest of the Delta Force team to arrive. They hadn't learned anything more than they'd already been told back at the Embassy, so they speculated on the possibilities. They were both still wearing yesterday's rumpled clothes and Mark was getting hungry.

Nuri asked, "Why do you think they chose us to be on this team? Surely they have experts in the government who can advise them on probable terrorist targets in Egypt. What do we know about such things?"

"Nothing," Mark agreed. "I'm guessing they've already recovered some stolen antiquities and we're here to identify what's real or valuable and what's not. The terrorism threat was probably exaggerated to get our cooperation."

"Examining stolen artifacts doesn't make sense," argued Nuri. "They already have people on their payroll to do that. We need to focus on what is unique about you and me that other Egyptologists don't have to offer."

"Several things come to mind, but most of them do not make us desirable." Mark went on to catalogue them. "The Egyptian government doesn't employ us directly because we don't support their premise that the pyramids and other ancient structures were built with slave labor only a few thousand years ago. We both earned our doctorates at Harvard rather than Cairo University. Our work here is barely tolerated by the Egyptian government, for political reasons. Neither of us has a chance of getting permits to excavate significant sites in Egypt, as long as we are out of favor with the reigning archeological authorities here. Those facts don't make us very popular. If we were really their first choice, it had to be for other reasons."

Nuri sighed, "When you put it like that, this whole story being a big hoax still sounds plausible. Nothing else makes sense. But why would they want to humiliate us?"

166

Mark suddenly got a scared look on his face. "Maybe this thing really is dangerous and they picked us because the risk of being hurt or killed is so high. They aren't looking for quality Egyptologists; they're looking for expendable experts."

Nuri finally realized they had let their imaginations run wild. "Let's wait until the others get here to discuss this any further. We're jumping to conclusions that probably aren't true. It sounds like you think the Director or General, or whatever he is, was lying to us. What I heard him say was that they are taking our safety quite seriously."

They each stared off into the distance for almost a minute. Now they were both a little embarrassed they had jumped to such far-fetched conclusions based only on assumptions. Without another word, Mark picked up the room service menu as Nuri switched on his laptop.

Chapter 23

A special tone on his computer told Mansur an urgent email had just arrived. It was from Amir saying the plan had been severely compromised. He said the Americans knew a major terrorist attack would soon happen in Egypt. They knew Col. Mansur was the leader of Mohammad's Faithful and was responsible for the recent attack on the military outpost in Israel. They had the warehouse under constant surveillance and his people would be arrested the moment they drove away from the building with the Cubane. Reading this warning made Mansur smile.

He responded that all was well because he had already transported the Cubane to another location. Mansur doubted that even Ramin was aware of this. The agents who followed them from the Cubane test site thought their surveillance of the warehouse had gone unnoticed. Mansur had planned ahead by obtaining duplicates of the suitcases that contained the Cubane. Using some sleight of hand in the loading, the Hummer ended up with the empty suitcases while those holding the Cubane had been spirited out of the warehouse in a nondescript passenger car. They didn't know it, but the Mossad agents had been keeping a close watch on harmless luggage. However, Mansur did have a different sort of 'bombshell' loaded inside the Hummer. It would be quite a surprise for both Ramin and the Americans.

***

Mansur was waiting for two of his men to bring him the luggage containing the Cubane. He had to remain hidden and separate from the team until they left for Suez because the Americans might already be looking for him. He cursed Sadad for allowing the infidels to get their hands on that laptop. The security precautions he'd installed on the computer probably erased all the damaging data, but he was taking no chances.

As he waited, Mansur carefully reviewed the details of the mission and his team. Some of the members were handpicked from the soldiers of Mohammed's Faithful. Every one of those men had already proven themselves in battle. He recruited others from

Afghanistan because it was important that the people he didn't know would want to return home immediately after the mission was completed. The farther away their homes were from Egypt, the better. They were all highly trained and he was certain he could count on them, especially at the prices Amir paid.

An entire upper floor in a luxury condo complex in New Cairo had been rented by Amir to house the team. There was an impressive small scale model of the target locations along the Suez Canal to clearly diagram everyone's assignment. The five locations were to be destroyed at the same time, even though they were spread out over the entire length of the canal. The Israeli detonators could be coded to accept the same encrypted satellite frequency making this simultaneous detonation possible from anywhere in the world.

The location of his men and the Cubane were unknown to the authorities, so they were already past the riskiest phase of the mission. Hijacking the Suez train, setting the charges and blowing up the targets would be easy compared to all they had done to get to this point. Still, he'd feel better once his men delivered the Cubane to his hotel room. The final phase of the mission would begin with the setting of the sun.

***

Bashir and Kazim had been responsible for secretly moving the luggage out of the warehouse and delivering it to Mansur's hotel room in Giza. They were excited to play such a key role in one of the largest freedom fighting operations in history. Now that Mansur had the suitcases, their orders were to drive around Cairo until it was time to meet the team back at the hotel. As Bashir drove away from the hotel, they started talking about the money and notoriety this job would bring them.

Their success would be revered throughout their shrouded world of mercenaries. That meant, in the future, they would be paid higher wages. Perhaps they would be chosen to lead future missions. They enjoyed the idea of giving the orders instead of always taking them. This made both men reflect on whether or not they were ready for such responsibility. "What makes Mansur a good leader?" Kazim asked.

"We're smart. We are also fearless and will stop at nothing until we accomplish what we set out to do. Didn't we deliver the suitcases just as Mansur wanted?" Bashir said with a defiant lift to his chin. "It all comes down to one thing. If we too had some of that powerful explosive, we would be his competition instead of his employees."

"Perhaps you are right. I heard about the huge fire ball it made when they tested it. I read about Cubane online. That blast came from just a handful of what looks like C-4." Kazim cupped his hand to illustrate his point. Both men were thinking the same thing but it was Kazim who said it out loud.

"What if we remove some of the Cubane from a suitcase before we take it from the hotel to the vehicles? There is so much, surely no one would miss it."

Bashir thought for a moment and said, "We wouldn't want to carry it around with us. We must store it somewhere until we can come back for it later."

"We don't need much," Kazim added. "Perhaps the same amount as the ball they tested back at the warehouse?"

Bashir added, "We might as well each take some, if we take any at all. There is enough to destroy all the targets twice over. But how would we get it out of the hotel? We should have thought of this before we delivered the suitcases. Mansur will see everything we do, once we leave the hotel for Suez."

"Then we hide it inside the hotel and come back for it. I already know how we can do this. We drop the Cubane down the laundry chute and ask your brother Nantu to pick it up. He lives nearby in Cairo, doesn't he?" Kazim asked Bashir.

"Yes, but I don't know if he would do this for us. He deals only in drugs, not weapons."

"It wouldn't hurt to ask him. He doesn't have to know what it is exactly. Tell him we mixed the drugs together with clay to disguise them. Tell Nantu you agreed to deliver the drugs before you committed to this better-paying job. Tell him you'll split the delivery money with him, if he'll help."

Bashir had to admit that the plan would probably work. He pulled out his cell phone and called Nantu. His brother knew of the hotel, and had done business there on occasion. He agreed to go collect the "drugs" whenever Bashir called to say they had been left in the basement near or under the laundry chute.

***

Captain Paul Saunders had been put in charge of the special Delta Force team tasked with stopping the terrorist plot in Egypt. Saunders wasn't given much to go on. He knew that a group armed with unstable Cubane explosives was planning to destroy one or more high-value targets in Cairo or Alexandria. Their intel was that these were mercenary soldiers rather than religious zealots. That was good because mercenaries were driven by profit rather than wanting to die for Allah. That would make it a lot easier for Saunders' men to take them alive and avoid a huge fireworks show in the process.

Mossad operatives were keeping the warehouse under constant surveillance and stood ready to call Saunders, the moment the Cubane was moved. In the meantime, Saunders' people were staked out along the nearby highway, ready to box the terrorists in, once they turned onto the main road.

From the moment Saunders' people had deployed in Cairo, he had been keeping Washington in the loop on the mission's latest developments, and vice versa. It was a welcomed surprise when the identity of the terrorist leader was confirmed. Colonel Achmed Mansur's picture pulled from the laptop video in Israel had been positively matched to the pictures taken by the Mossad agents at the site of the test explosion in Egypt.

Additional intel, recovered from the laptop by the CIA techs, tied Mansur's actions directly to the Syrian government. There was definitive proof that Mansur had led military assaults against U.S. soldiers that deployed biological weapons, as well as destroying the supply depot in Israel. Saunders knew Mansur had to be stopped, even if it cost he and his men their lives. They all knew that outcome was possible when they signed on for this mission. Remembering that the alternative was an all-out war in the Middle East made the choice easier.

***

Saunders thought the following update from Washington had to be a mistake. He was told that two archeologists had been added to his Delta Force team. No further explanation came with the order. He called the phone number he was given to make contact with them, hoping to confirm this was a misunderstanding. Unfortunately, Mark and Nuri asked the same question he was about to ask them. "What need is there for two archeologists on this mission?" Paul sighed and told them his orders were to keep them both safe and on standby during the operation. To Mark and Nuri's great disappointment, that was the end of their briefing. They would have to console themselves with unlimited room service and a gorgeous fifteenth floor view of the Giza pyramids.

Saunders had no choice but to assign two of his men to go to the civilians' hotel room and stay with them at all times. An emergency response vehicle was also assigned to them in case the archeologists were actually needed.

***

Saunders and the rest of his men were growing impatient waiting east of New Cairo for the Mossad agents to call. The plan was to have a local Egyptian police car, with Saunders' men inside, pull the Hummer over. If the suspected terrorists made a run for it, the four vehicles led by Saunders would intercept them. If they did pull over, Saunders' men in the police car would detain the Hummer until the Humvees arrived and surrounded the vehicle. Nothing fancy, but the plan should be effective.

The problem was that the Hummer was still sitting in the warehouse, unattended. Egyptian troops had already set up a wide roadblock perimeter to ensure no traffic was allowed on the section of road where Saunders and his men were waiting. The longer they waited in the afternoon sun, the more anxious they became. They didn't know the oncoming darkness meant the waiting would soon be over.

Chapter 24

Finally, Saunders got the call from the Mossad agent that the Hummer had left the warehouse and had turned west toward New Cairo. Saunders knew their super-charged Humvees could outrun and surround the glossy black civilian Hummer. What he didn't know, was if the terrorists, with all that unstable Cubane, would choose to live or kill them all.

Saunders's people were still about five kilometers in front of the team in the Egyptian police car when they notified him that they were ready to pull the suspects over. He gave them the go-ahead and warned the men in his convoy to stay alert.

The soldiers in the police cruiser turned on their flashing lights and, to everyone's surprise, the Hummer pulled over immediately. The headlights of the oncoming Humvees could be seen in the distance as the Hummer and police car stopped along the gravel shoulder of the highway. The police cruiser's team leader radioed that they were stopped behind the suspect's vehicle. Saunders responded that his convoy was still a minute out when the Hummer started rolling backwards.

Suddenly, the Hummer's gear shift was slammed into reverse as the driver punched the accelerator pedal to the floor. The vehicle's tires spit gravel everywhere as the monstrous SUV lunged backward toward the police cruiser. The team braced for the impact that would set off the unstable Cubane.

The collision jolted the police car, pushing it backward several yards, but nothing exploded. They were shocked to still be alive. The Hummer's driver immediately jammed the gearshift into drive and the suspects fishtailed their way back onto the highway. The soldiers tried to pursue the suspects but the police car wouldn't budge. It was immobilized, with the left fender gouged deep into the front tire. The team leader radioed their status to Captain Saunders and warned that the Hummer was headed his way.

***

Saunders was amazed that the collision and unstable Cubane hadn't killed them all. He ordered his team's drivers to execute a quick U-turn. Their plan required that the Humvees travel in the same direction as the Hummer to be able to safely box in the suspects. He hoped their luck would hold in getting the Hummer to stop without casualties.

He radioed to the Egyptian roadblock to prepare for the worst. The suspect vehicle had to be stopped prior to reaching the barricade! The lives of many innocent people were hanging on Saunders' ability to end this chase now, one way or another.

The shiny black Hummer flew past the Humvees at more than 130 kph. Three of the team's vehicles let it go by knowing the Captain's Humvee was still a distance ahead of them. As the speeding Hummer approached, Saunders' driver began to match its movements so that it couldn't pass. The other three Humvees caught up doing more than 175 kph as they deployed in a U formation. With Saunders' vehicle still in front, they surrounded the Hummer, matching its speed, to cut off any chance of escape.

The men in the Hummer began to panic when they realized what was happening, but it was too late! They tried to force their way out of the moving box by swerving left and then right, but they were too close to the Humvees to break free. The scene looked like a game of close-quarters bumper cars as all four Humvees kept shoving the Hummer back into a tight formation as they continued to slow.

When all five vehicles were stopped in the middle of the deserted highway, soldiers emerged from the Humvees and aimed their weapons at the mysterious vehicle's darkened windows. In both Arabic and English the suspects were told to crawl out of the side windows of the vehicle with their hands exposed and empty. Everyone tensed as the windows were rolled down. Empty hands were shown first and the occupants of the vehicle did as they were ordered.

There were only two men inside the Hummer. Soon they were lying face-down on the road with a combat boot on each of their backs as they were handcuffed. Other soldiers quickly searched the vehicle. When they discovered that the decoy suitcases were empty, Saunders realized they'd been had.

An interrogation of the two men did not reveal the location of the Cubane, but it did explain why the men had bolted. At first, they claimed they had run because they thought they were being hijacked. As they watched the soldiers doing a thorough search of the Hummer, they decided to confess to the real reason they had tried to escape. They had been hired to dispose of a dead body that was hidden under the steel cargo plate in the rear of the Hummer. Wrapped in plastic sheeting and duct tape was the decomposing body of a woman in western clothing. She was quickly identified as Karen Moffitt, the missing Assistant to the First Lady.

A very pissed-off Captain Saunders realized this entire scenario had been choreographed to distract them from the actual mission. He had to inform his command center that the terrorists were still at large with the Cubane. Worse yet, he had no idea where they were or how to track them down.

***

Mansur was pleased his men had arrived at his hotel room in staggered order to avoid attention. Kazim and Bashir were the last to arrive. The Colonel took the lead and guided the group to the stairwell leading to the parking lot where their cars were waiting. There was plenty of time to load the small suitcases into their vehicles and convoy to the south end of the Suez Canal. He took a moment to congratulate himself on getting to this point. Commandeering the train before sunrise would be easy because most of the operators were unarmed. Setting the Cubane charges at the five strategic points along the canal would be easier still. Then Mansur would make history with the push of a button. He smiled knowing the American President's peace plan was doomed.

As the men filed out of the stairwell, the Colonel received the text he'd been waiting for. It said that the Americans had chased down the Hummer on the highway east of New Cairo. Mansur was amused because there was no evidence that tied him to the kidnapping of the First Lady or the woman's death. Ramin was their only suspect so his death would tie up any loose ends. Mansur was confident that he would eliminate Ramin before the authorities could question him.

***

Kazim and Bashir made sure they were the last to leave the hotel room. The moment they were alone, Kazim opened the suitcase and scooped up as much Cubane as his hands could hold. He formed that into a ball about twelve centimeters across. Bashir said nothing, but took only enough of the substance to make a small sphere about a third the size of the first. After he smoothed over the holes they had just created, Bashir closed the suitcase and pocketed the ball. Kazim was already headed for the laundry chute at the west end of the hallway. Bashir raced out into the hall knowing they had to move quickly to avoid Mansur's suspicion.

As Kazim reached the laundry chute, he slid the door open. Bashir watched as his friend tossed the grapefruit sized sphere into the opening. He motioned quickly to Bashir to hurry, when the unstable Cubane hit the basement floor 30 meters below.

The explosion that shook the bowels of the building sent an incredible fireball up through the laundry chute. It blasted like a flamethrower into the seventh floor hallway. Bashir watched in horror as his friend's upper body virtually disintegrated from the intense heat. A tremendous quake rose up from the building's foundation as the west end of the old hotel began to collapse.

Bashir spun away from the blast hoping to escape down the east stairwell. Time seemed to stop when he felt something strike his head. A broken brick from the explosion hit the side of his face with such force that he heard his own neck snap. His mind raced to grasp what was happening as he involuntarily dropped to his knees. He tried to feel where the brick had hit him, but his arm wouldn't respond. He died sadly confused and still pondering why the Cubane had detonated.

***

Colonel Mansur wasn't sure if he instinctively hit the ground or was thrown there, when the explosion erupted. He couldn't see the massive damage to the west side of the hotel, from where he stood in the parking lot. He correctly guessed that some of the Cubane had been detonated by accident, though he couldn't imagine how. He had the detonators with him. A quick count of the men on the ground told him that two still remained inside. That meant a

176

suitcase full of Cubane was also inside and at risk of exploding as well.

Mansur managed to get to his feet and ran back to the stairwell. He climbed the steps quickly and realized that the stairwell wouldn't be stable for long. He could hear the other hotel guests screaming and calling for help as he continued to climb. When he arrived at the seventh floor, he had to force open the door to access the hallway. He was vexed to see that, through the thick smoke, the far end of the corridor was open to the night sky. He saw a man lying face down in the hallway with a suitcase by his side. Mansur moved forward cautiously because it sounded and felt like the building was ready to collapse at any moment. When he reached the body, he could barely tell it was Bashir from the bloody mess that used to be his face.

Mansur knew he had to get the suitcase safely out of the hotel, but he had another problem. If Bashir and Kazim were identified too quickly, that information could lead the police to the entire team. A quick search of the dead man's pockets yielded his wallet and a ball of clay that Mansur immediately recognized as Cubane. The fool was trying to steal some for his own use! That partially explained the explosion and let him know not to bother looking for Kazim. He made a mental note to verify his count on the detonators.

He quickly pocketed the ball of Cubane and wallet as he picked up the suitcase. If he was lucky, the stairwell would last long enough for him to join his team outside before the first responders arrived on the scene. When he reached the ground floor, he found his men searching for him. Apparently no one had seen him reenter the hotel's stairwell. They were relieved he was unharmed and that the mission was still a go. Mansur yelled that they needed to leave immediately as he handed the suitcase with the Cubane off to Shallal, his Second in Command. They all went to their cars and turned on their radios to hear Mansur's instructions.

Police cars and fire trucks had just begun to arrive on the scene and they blocked the driveways and streets surrounding the hotel. Mansur cursed that he had opted to go with civilian cars to keep a low profile. Anything with four-wheel-drive would have made it easy to escape. Regardless, they had to leave now or abandon the vehicles. He looked around for any exits from the property. He radioed for everyone to follow him, then he slowly drove up a curb and over a landscape berm toward a possible exit. He had passed the point of turning back when he discovered his chosen route was blocked by a fire truck.

Mansur jumped out of his sedan to move the vehicle out of the way. As he had hoped, the engine was running. He jumped up into the cab and put it in gear. He had only moved a few meters when two firemen ran to the driver's door and began yelling at him. Mansur ignored them until they opened the door and tried to forcibly pull him out. He cursed their stupidity, as he shot them both. He had no quarrel with these men, but they had left him no choice.

Mansur finished moving the firetruck so that it was not only out of the way but it hid the bodies of the two firemen as well. When he made it back to his vehicle, he saw the situation had gone from bad to worse! His men had all driven in different directions, trying to find another exit. He radioed to them that they were on their own to get off the hotel property. He ordered them to meet at the backup rendezvous point in an hour and to make certain they weren't followed. With that, he slowly forced his car past the firetruck, traffic and the gawking people.

Chapter 25

Captain Saunders was hoping for a break. He felt responsible for losing track of the Cubane and failing to identify more of the terrorists or their target. He was certain that there would be an event to rival 9/11 in the next 24 hours, if they didn't catch up with these bastards.

His break arrived a moment later when the command post informed him there had been a huge explosion at a hotel in Giza. There were no other details available but Saunders knew this had to be Mansur's doing. He keyed the mic on his radio and told the rest of his team to head to Giza. He hoped he'd have more information by the time they arrived.

***

As their convoy of Humvees approached Giza, Saunders could see the bright work lights contrasting against the smoke and ash of the crumbling hotel. He wondered how much of the Cubane had detonated. Certainly not much if only this one building was damaged. But why would they detonate only a tiny portion of what they had? Was this another ruse to throw them off?

The only face Saunders knew for sure was Mansur's and that was from the facial recognition photos Mossad and the CIA had provided. He tried to figure out how Mansur would be traveling. Was he using a large team with several vehicles or was it just one dangerously loaded truck? Were they after one target or many? Would Mansur be going for the maximum loss of life, maximum financial damage, or perhaps targets that would elicit the greatest emotional impact? He assumed a man like that wouldn't settle for less than achieving all three.

***

Egypt's evening news was reporting the hotel explosion at the same time George Salazar's flight arrived in Cairo. As the jet approached the airport runway, he could see the flashing lights in the distance from dozens of emergency vehicles blurred by the continuous smoke and ash from the charred remains of the hotel.

179

He guessed that Mansur's thugs were behind the commotion and he wondered if hitting the Suez Canal was still possible after drawing that much attention.

Once inside the airport terminal, he called Mansur from a payphone. He didn't want the call to be traced back to him if Mansur had already been apprehended. The Colonel picked up after the sixth ring and Salazar immediately took on the persona of Amir.

"You couldn't wait to get started or is this all part of your great plan?" Amir began sarcastically. "The last time we spoke you said you had everything under control."

"The mission is still on but there have been complications," Mansur calmly admitted.

"I'm calling from a payphone in Cairo, so I'll get the details later. Under the circumstances, I think we need to meet. Where would you suggest?" Amir added.

"Are you familiar with our staging area outside of Suez?" Mansur asked.

"The abandoned building just beyond the city limits?"

"Yes. Meet me there an hour before sunrise. Bring Ramin for I have much to tell both of you. If I am late, I will not be coming and the operation is aborted."

Mansur hung up and calculated how he would get to the backup rendezvous point in Giza without being identified. He wanted to skirt the city and stay off the main roads but he also needed to be on the southwest side of Giza in fifteen minutes. There was no way around it. He would have to get on the Al Ahram highway to arrive on time.

Captain Saunders split his men into three groups to be on the lookout for Mansur and his mercenaries, however many there were. His best guess was that Mansur was planning to detonate the Cubane at the Cairo Museum or the Great Pyramid of Giza, or both. He ordered his people to patrol those locations in hopes of spotting any suspicious activity.

The two locations were approximately ten kilometers apart to the east and west of each other. Saunders left his driver with the museum team and decided to drive himself back and forth between the two stakeout locations. The more eyes they had everywhere looking for Mansur, the better the odds were of catching him. The streets were oddly void of traffic. The locals in this part of the world knew better than to go sightseeing once trouble started.

In the meantime, a search of the warehouse in New Cairo revealed it contained some serious weaponry but no Cubane. None of the people left behind in the warehouse, nor the two men from the Hummer, had any idea what was going on. It became clear they were hired in the past few days and were set up to take the fall for Ramin and Mansur.

Saunders tried to anticipate Mansur's next move. He figured the hotel explosion was a mistake rather than part of his plan. He heard that two of the fire fighters had been shot by a man who tried to steal a firetruck parked outside the hotel. The description was vague but it could have been Mansur himself. That would indicate the Cubane detonation was as much a surprise to him as it was for the citizens of Giza. From the description Saunders was given about the damage to the hotel, a small quantity was apparently all that had ignited. That meant if Mansur hadn't known before, he now knew that the Cubane was unstable.

Saunders saw a sedan approaching him on the Al Ahram highway leaving Giza toward the pyramids. The oncoming sedan was the only other vehicle he could see on the empty road. When they were no more than 30 meters apart, he flicked on his bright headlights to get a good view of the person driving toward him. The man automatically raised his hand to block the glare, but Saunders thought he looked like Mansur. He decided to follow that car until he was sure either way.

***

Mansur confirmed via radio that his men were already at the backup rendezvous location. He was close to the turn he would take to join them, but then an oncoming car flashed its high beams just as they passed each other. Normally, he would have cursed them and thought nothing about it, but he saw the vehicle turning around in the distance in his rear view mirror. He got back on the radio and told the team leader he had picked up a tail. He instructed Shallal to get the men and their vehicles out of sight. They should wait fifteen minutes so Mansur could lead the other vehicle away from them, then they could proceed to Suez without him. He'd shake the person tailing him and catch up before morning.

***

Shallal considered his dilemma. There was only one place to hide their vehicles completely out of sight, without getting on the highway, and that was behind a locked gate. Even if they broke the chains and parked where they could not be seen, he feared they would not remain hidden for long. If Mansur had been spotted driving alone, what chance did their five vehicles have of being unnoticed when the streets were so deserted? After dark, no one visited this area. The site of the Sphinx was a tourist favorite, but the visiting hours ended when the sun went down taking the tourists' picture opportunities with it. Mansur had ordered them to wait 15 minutes, and he knew better than to cross the Colonel.

Shallal cut the chains to the gate blocking the access path that led to the excavation pit surrounding the Sphinx. He ordered everyone to follow him in their vehicles. They went down the compacted dirt ramp that was set against the wall on one side but was open to the pit on the other. It descended at a fairly steep angle and had a ninety-degree right turn after it cleared the front of the limestone statue. The excavated pit surrounding the base of the Sphinx was perhaps 30 meters wide and 10 meters deep separating the limestone pedestal of the statue from the dirt walls.

Once they had all parked, Shallal checked his watch again. Only two minutes had passed. This was going to be the longest 15 minutes of his life. He pulled to the front of the other cars that were now parked in a straight line along the south side of the Sphinx. They were strategically positioned to make a quick exit when it was time.

As they waited, he considered how to keep the lowest profile possible. All of their vehicles had been fitted with a kill switch for their lights when a total blackout was needed. However, there was a problem with turning off all their lights. The inclined dirt road was perhaps a meter wider than the width of a standard car. It had been tough to maneuver the cars down the ramp as it was. Without any lights at all, they would have to move even more slowly as they exited or risk going over the unprotected side into the pit. He looked at his watch again. Not even three minutes had gone by. He got

182

back on the radio and ordered the drivers to kill all their lights until they were back on the highway.

At three and a half minutes, Shallal was so anxious he almost started his car to leave. He strained to hear any traffic noise from the nearby highway. He kept expecting to hear the sirens of many vehicles converging upon them. He panicked realizing this pit was only a good hiding place if no one was looking for them, and that was hardly the case.

At three minutes and forty-seven seconds, Shallal was done waiting. He told everyone to start their vehicles and to follow his lead. He put the gearshift into drive and slowly pulled forward. It was difficult to see if they were all behind him because it was so dark. He continued forward until he could see the beginning of the dirt ramp that would take them out of the pit. He had to trust that the other cars were keeping up with him.

He made the sharp left turn and continued up the narrow ramp when one of the cars behind him flashed his lights, trying to see where to make the turn. Shallal was immediately enraged. Breaking discipline like that would get them all caught or even killed. He angrily turned his head to see who it was as he grabbed his radio to warn the fool against doing that again. That was when his left front tire rolled halfway off the ramp's graded edge.

At first, he didn't notice his wheel had caught because he was still yelling into the radio. He finished his tirade by slapping the radio down on the seat beside him. He then stepped on the gas but found that the steering wheel wouldn't turn. He realized that the tire was about to drop off the left edge. He tried not to panic, as he pulled hard to the right to force the wheel back up on to the ramp. At that same moment, the car behind him bumped his fender. Though their cars hardly touched, it was just enough to crack open the gates of hell.

Shallal felt his left front tire slide off the edge of the ramp. He heard a crunching sound as the left ball joint collapsed under the direct weight of the car. His vehicle was tilting now, as it skidded on its chassis toward the pit some five meters below. In desperation, he jammed the car into reverse and tried to pull the left front wheel back onto the dirt road. At first, it started to back up just the way he wanted. Then his car bumped back into the vehicle behind him and the rear wheels lost traction and began to spin. His car resumed sliding forward along the edge of the dirt ramp. He felt the right-side wheels leave the ground as the car tipped over and began falling toward the bottom of the pit.

He thought he might be able to survive the fall depending on how the car landed. He braced for the impact, but the unstable Cubane was not to be denied.

In the blink of an eye, so many things no longer mattered. Turning on the headlights was not important anymore. Staying hidden wasn't something they'd have to worry about. The Suez Canal mission ceased to be a concern. The blast from Shallal's car set off a chain reaction of the Cubane stashed in the other vehicles. The combined explosions shook the ground as far away as ten kilometers from ground zero. Observers might assume the ominous mushroom cloud was the result of a missile strike but it was simply the largest quantity of Cubane ever detonated in one place at one time.

When the smoke and dust began to clear, what remained of the Sphinx looked more like a lump of stone than the magnificent statue it had been just minutes before. The surrounding pit was now a huge crater. The only remaining sign of Shallal and his team were shiny bits of their cars falling like hail stones mixed with debris from the statue and surrounding earth. For thousands of years, humankind had marveled at the beauty of the Sphinx. In the blink of an eye, it was gone forever.

John Schroeder – The Hall of Records Trilogy

Chapter 26

The sun was still shining in Washington when President Alexander was told the Sphinx had been destroyed just minutes ago. He barely kept the anger out of his voice to ask if the Cubane had been used. If so, it was a solid connection to Achmed Mansur. There had been no confirmation yet, but the blast was so large that the missing Cubane had to be the cause.

Matt closed his eyes, hung his head and considered the chances of his peace plan working when this event hit the world news. Realistically, he knew they were zero. His knee-jerk reaction was to prepare the U.S. military for the inevitable violence to follow. He was about to call General McComb when he remembered his promise to Erin. He swore he would not make a decision of this nature for at least 24-hours. Even when he had made that promise, he knew it would be difficult to keep. He hesitated, hung up the phone, and took a moment to reflect.

How could so few people be allowed to disrupt such unprecedented cooperation among nations? He felt an overwhelming loss knowing a lasting peace had been within their grasp. Despite everyone's best efforts toward peace, war was now the more likely outcome.

In the midst of his despair, Matt flashed on his ethereal briefing with the man dressed in white. He had been encouraged to not lose faith in the peace plan when it got to this point. He remembered this latest conflict began to escalate in the biblical battleground of Armageddon. He winced at the vision he had of the whole world metaphorically walking through that valley of death.

Through his mental anguish, a moment of inspiration flashed through his mind. He needed to figure out how to move forward without preparing for violence. Then he remembered the two archeologists he had added to the Delta Force team in pursuit of Mansur. While it was unclear at the time why he brought them on board, he realized why they needed to be at the site of the Sphinx, or what was left of it. Matt had to hope they had not been injured in all the chaos. He sent out the order that they should be the first responders to inspect the ground zero location before anyone else had a chance. He offered no further explanation knowing the answer would be clear when they arrived.

***

Captain Saunders was three kilometers away from the Sphinx when the Cubane detonated. The blinding flash, quaking road and tremendous gale force rush of wind were unbelievable. Within seconds, there was sand and other debris raining down all around him. He lost sight of the vehicle Mansur may have been driving; but that was secondary to his concern for his team patrolling the nearby Great Pyramid. He pulled his car over and looked back at the ominous glow just outside of Giza.

Saunders fumbled around for his radio that had fallen to the floor of the vehicle. He was unable to raise anyone from the team so he tried the command post. They did respond but had no information about the status of the team watching the pyramids. His men at the Cairo Museum had asked for instructions after seeing and feeling the blast in the distance. Saunders instructed them to stay alert since the museum might be next.

He then asked the command post to contact Washington and request additional orders now that prevention of this tragedy was no longer an option. They responded with a strange directive from the White House. The orders were to get the two archeologists to the Sphinx site as quickly as possible and let no one else in for as long as they could peacefully keep them out.

Saunders radioed the information to his team members assigned to protect the two civilians. He was told they were already driving in that direction. The four men had felt the foundation of their hotel shake when the Cubane exploded. From the panoramic view their hotel room provided, they could see an eerie mushroom cloud against the night sky. It hovered like an oddly shaped exclamation point somewhere above the Sphinx. Mark and Nuri had practically forced the soldiers to take them there immediately.

Saunders had an idea on how they could fulfill the orders from the White House. He told them to arrive in MOPP - mission oriented protective posture - gear as if the site were contaminated. The Cubane residue did not pose a health hazard but his men would quickly lose control of the detonation zone if the Egyptian first

186

responders were able to seal the place off. If Saunders had his people tell the local authorities that the area was lethally contaminated, no one would go near the blast site without suitable protection. They would prefer to wait until they heard it was all clear or their own protective gear was available. Saunders told the command post to update all team members of this change in their plan.

***

Mark and Nuri were heartbroken over the destruction of the Sphinx, but they began to appreciate why they were on this team. The soldier riding in the back of the vehicle with them demonstrated how to put on the MOPP gear. He assured them that there was no radiation threat from the Cubane, but there was no telling what else might have been a part of that explosion. He also told them they wouldn't have long to investigate the scene without interference from the local authorities.

The cloud over the rubble of the Sphinx was already dissipating in the nighttime sky. When they arrived at the perimeter, Saunders' own men waved them through. When the Cubane blew up, they had all been staked out on the far side of the Great Pyramid. That shielded them from the worst of the blast. They were badly shaken up for a time but had no serious injuries among them. They confirmed they would try to hold everyone else back for as long as they could.

The soldier driving pulled up as close as he could get to the blast site and parked. He quickly donned his MOPP gear and the four men proceeded to ground zero. Inside the crater was a sharply angled lump that had once been the hind end of the Sphinx. The rest had been blown away by the force of the explosion.

They made their way down the side of the crater where the Sphinx had been just minutes before. They were able to make out several odd formations revealed in the crater's walls that had been below ground. Mark and Nuri looked at each other, both realizing what these anomalies in the terrain meant. They weren't just archeologists' tunnels dug out of the dirt; they were actual passageways built to last and constructed of cut boulders for maximum support. Nuri pointed to a large breach in a particular passageway and Mark agreed that was the best place to enter. The

187

stone tunnel led in the direction where the right paw of the Sphinx had once pointed.

One of the soldiers remained at the entrance to keep watch while the other went with Mark and Nuri. With flashlights in hand, they trekked down the sloping tunnel until they came upon a 180-degree turn that headed back toward the Sphinx. The downward incline was fairly steep and it was difficult to judge how deep they were going below the original ground level. It felt to Mark as if the passage went as far back as it did forward, so they were probably now close to being directly under where the right paw of the Sphinx had been.

The significance of this was not lost on either archeologist. They looked at each other and nodded their mutual agreement of what they had discovered. In 1933, the American clairvoyant Edgar Cayce had claimed that some sort of "Hall of Records" existed at this precise spot. According to him, its eventual discovery would prove the existence of an advanced civilization from thousands of years ago. It was Mark and Nuri's open-mindedness that such things once existed that caused the Egyptian government to question their credibility as scientists.

They continued forward through the darkness, the beams from their flashlights bouncing around the walls of the tunnel. The passage turned right and led to a larger room. Just as Cayce had said, the Hall of Records would be found entering from the right paw of the Sphinx into a larger chamber centered beneath the paws. Their excitement grew as they approached an ornately carved door that had buckled and fallen away from the quaking impact of the explosion. They were able to step over the rubble into the room beyond. The soldier followed them into the room but was still watchful of anyone approaching from behind.

Once they were inside the chamber, each man was mesmerized by what it contained. Dust was floating everywhere and their flashlight beams illuminated the entire room. The frescoes on the walls were not the typical profile or side-view depictions of ancient Egyptian rulers and slaves. They were beautiful drawings of a culture, technology and architecture unknown to the archeologists. The murals looked as if they had been painted by Rembrandt for their detail and likeness to real life.

Most notable were the large stone tablets mounted on the walls setting them apart from others that were lying in pieces on the floor of the chamber. A quick count told Mark and Nuri there were 32 of the mounted tablets, eight on each of the four walls. They remembered Edgar Cayce had said much of humanity's ancient history was recorded and stored in three places throughout the world. He had predicted that the Egyptian Hall of Records would be located beneath the paws of the Sphinx. The messages contained on the stone tablets used an intricate alphabet of strange symbols that were unknown to either scientist. The rest of the room held all manner of unfamiliar artifacts that were not identifiable at first glance. Some might have been musical instruments while other objects seemed to consist of complex technology whose purpose was unclear.

Suddenly, the ground started to settle and all three men braced themselves as the quake rattled the room and their nerves. Huge cracks appeared in the solid walls and the chamber's ceiling fell to the ground in several places. When the noise and shifting finally subsided, they moved quickly knowing they might have to evacuate at any moment.

Nuri brought out a camera and started taking still-shot pictures of the wall murals and the 32 tablets. Mark started recording what he could on video of the strange objects displayed on the ornately decorated shelving that lined the walls below the tablets. The soldier was fixated on eight waist-high shiny black pedestals forming a circle around the center of the room. He approached the one closest to him and saw that it had a polished impression of a hand centered on the top. The soldier placed his right hand on the pedestal so that it matched the imprint and a strange noise filled the chamber.

Nuri and Mark both turned in surprise; their jaws dropped as a bright light filled the room emanating from the ground at the center of the circle of pedestals. As it intensified, two small objects separated from the stone floor, rose into the air and merged together. All eyes were on this new curiosity as the singular shiny object hovered about two meters above the floor. The soldier removed his hand from the pedestal but the artifact remained suspended in mid-air. Nuri finally collected himself enough to take more pictures of this amazing scene. Mark realized he had forgotten

189

he was still recording video and also aimed his camera toward the center of the chamber.

Mark approached a different pedestal and laid his hand into the impression just as the soldier had done. He could feel a rush of energy pass through his body as he pressed his hand against the polished surface. Then a focused beam of white light from the center of the floor connected with the floating object above it. When their eyes adjusted to the brightness, they could see that the beam from the floor had divided into multiple rays of light. Each ray seemed to be connecting a different device displayed on the shelves to the floating object in the middle of the room.

Suddenly, all the technology in the chamber came to life, each device adding to the spectacle with its own lights and sounds. Mark and Nuri continued capturing everything they could with their cameras. They knew this was the most significant archeological discovery in human history. They also knew they would be forced to leave this wondrous place once the Egyptian first responders arrived.

Mark's attention was drawn to a crystalline box lying on a nearby shelf. He felt compelled to pick it up. As he lifted the lid of the box to look inside, a 3-D holographic display appeared before him that filled the room. He recognized that the panoramic movie unfolding before him matched the locations shown in the fresco paintings he had just recorded. He noticed that the moving pictures changed as he faced the different scenes depicted in the wall murals. The various scenes showed demonstrations of technologies that defied modern explanation. There was a narration that went with the video, but there were too many wondrous distractions in the room to focus on what was said.

The three of them saw that the pyramids had been constructed using a device that easily levitated the huge stones. This ancient culture had also been able to produce unlimited quantities of food as well as drinking water using resonant frequency technology. No less remarkable was a procedure that apparently took place in the same room where they were standing. The pedestals were being used for healing and rejuvenation of the sick and infirmed.

Without warning, the room began to shudder. As the floor quaked, two of the tablets hanging on the walls came crashing down. Mark was so startled he dropped the crystal box, abruptly ending the show as it shattered. Objects fell from the shelves and broke into pieces as they landed. The light from the floating object faded to darkness as the room started to collapse. The soldier shouted that they had to leave and no one argued.

Both scientists powered down their cameras as they stumbled toward the exit. The soldier was right behind them when something caught his eye. The floating object had apparently dropped and skidded across the floor in his path. He reached down to scoop it up only to find that it had separated back into two pieces. He slipped them both into his pocket and emerged from the chamber just ahead of its final demise.

All three men ran through the tunnel to escape what sounded like an avalanche that came closer with each step. When they made the turn at the switchback, they realized how desperate the situation was. The crumbling passageway was catching up to them. They ran full speed staying just ahead of the dust cloud and crushing death that chased after them. To the amazement of the soldier waiting above ground, they emerged not far from where they had entered the tunnel. He had been certain they would be lost when the terrain started to quake below.

He told them the Egyptians now had their own MOPP gear and were ignoring the Delta Force team's warnings to stay clear of the blast area. They were expected to arrive on the scene at any minute. The soldier who had been with Mark and Nuri made it clear that they had found something extraordinary and could not risk having the Egyptians confiscate their cameras. The archeologists just nodded their agreement still trying to catch their breath.

The soldier who had remained topside already had a plan. The four of them would have to leave the vehicle behind and find another way out. If they moved to the west on foot toward what used to be the rear of the Sphinx, then they could head unnoticed to the Al Ahram highway. Their own people would be waiting there to pick them up just north of the Great Pyramid.

All four started running west as fast as they could manage in the crater. They didn't dare use their flashlights and risk alerting the Egyptian responders to their presence. The archeologists were cradling their cameras in case they fell. They were not about to give up the incredible discoveries their digital memories held.

191

When they reached the far end of the blast site, they looked back to see many flashlight beams dancing in the distance. The Egyptian soldiers had arrived. Mark, Nuri and the two soldiers managed to scramble up the side of the crater and headed toward the highway. As promised, the Delta Force team was waiting to take them back to the hotel.

Chapter 27

Colonel Mansur had been able to avoid capture, but at what cost? The newscaster on the radio described the destruction of the Sphinx, leaving no doubt that all his team members were dead. He knew they had been together at the backup rendezvous point just minutes before the annihilation of the Sphinx. Whatever set the Cubane off had ensured a spectacular pyrotechnic display to mark their deaths.

The Suez Canal mission, had it succeeded, would have ensured the retelling of their exploits for many years to come. However, it was possible that destroying a national treasure like the Sphinx would serve Amir's purpose just as well. Sadly, it was due to sloppy work. That meant there was no honor in what they had done even if the accidental explosion accomplished the intended goal.

It was then that Mansur remembered that he still had the detonators and the evidence he was supposed to plant at the scene of the explosions. All the other vehicles carried the suitcases packed with Cubane, but he carried the metal shards with the fingerprints of Mossad agents. Unless those prints were found at the scene, nothing would directly tie Israel to the disaster.

He would have to figure out how to plant the incriminating evidence on the scene for his own survival. With no known motive or other suspects to distract the investigators, Mansur knew the existing evidence would lead back to him. That was ironic since he was not responsible for the hotel explosion in Giza or the demolishing of the iconic ancient statue.

What caused the Cubane to explode? He had counted the number of detonators he still held and none were missing. It was so stable a compound that you could hit it with a hammer or shoot it with a bullet and it would have no effect. But what if it was not stable? Maybe it wasn't even Cubane? What if it was a defective batch? That would answer why a cowardly *fatah* - an Arabic insult - like Ramin would have access to such a rare and expensive substance. The Americans or Israelis probably sold it to him hoping he'd manage to kill the buyers and himself.

Perhaps Amir's plan all along was for this debacle to happen. Had Amir colluded with Ramin to procure the defective Cubane from the start? They both knew his explosives expert would handle it carefully in the testing, as a professional would. However, it would most certainly detonate during the mission when rough handling couldn't be avoided. Amir had probably hoped they would all die in the effort and leave no witnesses behind. Even a failed attempt to disrupt passage and commerce through the Suez Canal would stop any efforts toward peace.

What Amir hadn't counted on was Mansur surviving the death of his team. The rest of the world would assume their leader died with them. If there were no surviving witnesses, Mansur could easily change identities and start a new life.

There were only two people left who knew he was still alive. Once they were gone, Mansur would be free to assume a new identity. Amir deserved to die for many reasons. That left Ramin Acaba. He would enjoy killing that coward and tying up the last of the loose ends. He must eliminate both men, alone and without a trace, if the world was to believe that Achmed Mansur had died with his team.

***

George Salazar hung up the phone after Langley brought him up to date on the situation in Giza. He had rented a car in Cairo and had already driven to a hotel in Suez. It was near the railway station where the trains went to Port Said at the north end of the canal. He still had a few hours to kill before he met with Mansur outside the city limits.

He had to wonder if Mansur was still alive after the fiasco that destroyed the Sphinx. His death in the explosion would have been a stroke of luck. But if he was still alive, did he still have a team of mercenaries, let alone any of the Cubane, to attempt the original mission to take out the Suez Canal? The man might still try to carry out his mission. Salazar was sure that the obliteration of the Sphinx had already accomplished his goal to put an end to POTUS's peace plan, so killing Mansur was his top priority. That meant he had to develop Plan B.

In the unlikely event that Mansur was still alive, he would be desperate to plant the evidence at the blast site to implicate the

194

Israelis as the perpetrators of the explosion. The good news was that Mansur would have no chance to do that before their meeting at the staging area. That lowered his chances of being caught. Mansur had no idea that the so-called evidence was faked. Salazar had known that Mansur needed to believe that he would get away with it as long as the Israelis were implicated. George had known from the start that Mansur and his incriminating secrets had to die the moment he was no longer useful.

A tone from his computer told Salazar that Amir had just received an email. It was a coded message from Mansur saying only that he would make their prearranged meeting at the staging area location as agreed. Salazar sighed and began going over the details of his new Plan B.

Who would have guessed that he was lucky to be in Egypt right now to tie up loose ends? Otherwise, Ramin would be tracked down to reveal the existence of Amir. Once they learned Mansur was still alive, they would find and interrogate him. Either way, Amir's presence would be known and that would eventually lead back to him. How long would it take before someone put together that CIA Director George Salazar and the mysterious Amir were the same person? He knew both Ramin and Mansur had to die, tonight.

Amir placed a call to Ramin and told him that Mansur planned to kill them both. He invited Ramin to come with him to the pre-dawn meeting with Mansur outside of Suez. He told Ramin to come armed. Amir would make sure Mansur was so distracted by anger that Ramin could easily shoot him. The plan was simple but Achmed Mansur was a trained killer, and neither Amir nor Ramin were in his league when it came to assassinations. They needed this two-to-one advantage to succeed.

Ramin was certain that both Amir and Mansur would try to kill him if he ever gave them the chance. When Amir called to suggest that they work together to kill Mansur, Ramin reluctantly agreed. Mansur and Amir had to die if he wanted to live through this night. He knew he could not kill them both on his own.

Ramin had been lying low in Suez with several of the mercenaries he worked with regularly. One of them, Abel, was part of the expert sniper team that helped breach and destroy the American supply depot in Israel under Mansur's command. Ramin calculated his best chance to survive this night was to hire Abel to eliminate Mansur and Amir. He considered that Abel might not accept the job if he was hesitant to kill Mansur. He decided that Abel would only see Amir and Mansur in the moonlight as two unidentified men he was being paid to kill. Ramin would not tell him who the targets were and Abel probably wouldn't ask.

When Ramin approached him, Abel quickly agreed to do the job, especially at the fee that was offered. The assignment was straightforward and Abel would have almost no personal risk. A lot of variables could go wrong for Ramin, but that was the nature of the setup. Abel's only condition was that he be paid in advance in case the job was compromised. Ramin had no choice but to trust him given the limited time and circumstances.

Abel left immediately to arrive at the meeting place before anyone else. He parked behind the abandoned building so that his car would not give away his presence. Ramin would ride with Amir and wait for Mansur in the parking lot. Abel would be sure to setup inside the building so that he had a good line of sight to take out the two men. Once they were dead, Ramin and Abel would have the bodies cremated so they would never be identified.

Chapter 28

Ramin pulled into the parking lot with Amir sitting beside him in the passenger seat. They both relaxed a little when they saw no sign of Mansur. That would give them the chance to get set before he arrived, assuming he'd be there. If he didn't show, then Amir planned to take out Ramin and deal with Mansur later.

Amir had a nine millimeter automatic at his side and a snub nose .38 caliber strapped to his ankle. He was also wearing a Kevlar vest. They got out of the car and Amir walked to the spot where he wanted to confront Mansur. Ramin made sure he stood out of the sniper's line of fire from the building as they waited for Mansur to join them.

Amir said, "You really need to calm down. Mansur will know something is wrong if he sees you like this. Are you sure your pistol is in good working order?"

Ramin nervously nodded his head. His voice shook as he said, "I am a businessman, not an assassin. As it is, I have the CIA, Mossad, and probably every Egyptian law enforcement officer looking for me. After this night, I will have to disappear and not come back, ever."

Amir answered, "That is probably for the best. With Mansur eliminated, you will have a much better chance of evading capture. The world will want his head and there will be no one left alive to point an accusing finger at us. They will continue to search for Mansur until his body is found. We must make sure that never happens."

A car turned off the highway and headed toward them. There was no doubt that Mansur was alive and well and was coming to kill them. Amir reminded Ramin to wait until Mansur was angry and distracted before making a move to shoot him. If Mansur wasn't distracted, he would kill them both in a bloody gun battle. Ramin nodded, wiped his sweaty hands on his pants, and tried to look calm as the intimidating man walked over to join them.

Mansur quickly sized up the situation as he parked his car. His brain was hard-wired to calculate his opponents' strengths and weaknesses, especially when walking into an obvious ambush. It was still very dark but he was certain there was someone in the abandoned building approximately fifteen meters away with a rifle aimed in his direction. The two men in front of him would be armed as well but he could easily deal with them.

By their positioning, Mansur could assume that the sniper worked for Ramin. That made sense knowing what a coward he was. He stood facing the building so the sniper would have clear shots at both Amir and Mansur. That meant Amir would probably shoot Ramin at the same moment that Ramin was planning to kill Mansur. It was no secret to him that each man had come to this meeting with the intention of being the only one who walked away. He liked his chances over theirs, but he would have to stay sharp to live beyond the next few minutes.

He planned to keep walking until Amir obstructed his direct line of sight to the old building where the sniper had to be positioned. The sniper would have to kill Amir first to have a clear shot at Mansur. That meant Mansur would shoot Ramin and drop to the ground. Then it would be just him against the hidden gunman. Mansur's ball of unstable Cubane versus the sniper's rifle would be an interesting contest. He was wearing a Kevlar vest and he planned to use the dead men's bodies as additional cover from the Cubane explosion. He knew his plan was dangerous. He was sure to be wounded even if everything went well. However, if Allah willed it, his injuries would not be fatal.

Mansur approached them with both hands in his jacket pockets. He was ambidextrous shooting a pistol, but he could only throw right handed with confidence. The Cubane was in his right pocket and the pistol hidden in his left.

"Good evening my friends!" Mansur began. His smile didn't reach his eyes.

Amir interrupted, "Don't call me friend you incompetent *ibn haram* (Arabic for bastard). *Surmayye a'raasac!*" (another terrible Arabic insult). Ramin blinked in surprise but then remembered it was Amir's intention to infuriate Mansur. His excellent choice of insults would likely accomplish this better than Amir had planned.

Mansur started to respond but Amir cut him off again, *"Aneekik o aneek ummk o obook o ahlk klhm!"* Amir had just threatened Mansur's entire family with rape.

Mansur, still appearing calm, was done talking. Without bothering to pull the pistol from his pocket, he fired twice into Amir's face. He had detected the Kevlar vest beneath Amir's clothing so head shots were the only way to put him down for good. Ramin awkwardly pulled his own gun out and fired but Mansur dodged the shot by dropping to the ground. As he fell, he fired twice at Ramin putting a round in his heart and one that burst into a ghastly crimson spray out the back of his head. Mansur immediately propped up Amir's body to use as protection against the sniper.

Abel opened fire immediately but Mansur had moved fast enough that Amir's vest and body were already protecting him. He could feel the corpse react with every round the sniper fired. Holding the body on its side allowed Mansur to remain concealed as he removed the ball of Cubane from his right pocket. He would have to throw it as hard as he could to ensure it would explode when it hit the building.

Suddenly, a tremendous flash of hot pain shot up Mansur's leg. Abel had figured out the Kevlar vest problem and was now firing at Amir's legs. He knew the bullets would rip through and find his hidden target. Mansur was hit a second time in the right calf and then a third time in the left thigh.

As he readied himself to hurl the Cubane ball, Abel saw that he had a clear shot at Mansur's arm. He pulled the trigger at the same moment Mansur started to throw. Abel's timing was perfect and his round hit Mansur in the wrist. Bones shattered and the sharp impact caused the chunk of Cubane to detonate before it left his hand. It erupted with an explosive force more like an eight-inch artillery shell than a simple hand grenade.

Abel managed to duck for cover but the walls of the dilapidated building disintegrated from the force of the blast. Like oddly shaped jagged cannon balls, the flying bricks and plaster destroyed everything in their path. Abel was mercifully knocked out and somehow survived the devastation. He did not regain consciousness for perhaps twenty minutes. When he did awaken, he was mostly buried under the debris. He had second degree burns everywhere. His left arm was broken above the elbow and he guessed he had a concussion from his massive headache and swollen eyes. There was nothing left around him but rubble and the burnt out shells of their cars. His own car, parked so that it was hidden behind the building, was also totaled.

Abel was certain that Allah wanted these men completely erased, for what else could have caused such an explosion? Surely it was like the end of the world had rained down upon them all. Abel was thankful that he survived, but now he would have to find his way out of this mess. If he could walk to Suez, he had the money to make it the rest of the way home.

Chapter 29

- Three Months Later -

Dr. Mark Heston and Dr. Nuri Zayd wanted everything to be perfect when their VIP visitor came to see the progress they'd made. They were formally trained in archeology, but because of their phenomenal discovery underneath the Sphinx, they had remained an integral part of the team here at Jet Propulsion Laboratory - JPL. It was their skill in translating the text from the 32 tablets that led other scientists to discover the secret of near perpetual energy. The breakthrough would not have succeeded at all if the soldier hadn't stopped to recover the pieces of the floating object just as the chamber collapsed. They were in fact unique crystals designed to tap into the earth's stored power.

The phone rang and Nuri answered it. He hung up and excitedly told Mark, "He's here and on the way up."

A minute later President Alexander walked through the door to the lab with an entourage of scientists and Secret Service agents. This was the first time Mark and Nuri had met the President, although they knew he had personally recommended them to be part of the American team that discovered the Hall of Records beneath the Sphinx.

Matt shook both their hands saying, "Gentlemen, if your reports are accurate, there may never be a more important scientific discovery in the history of humankind than what you have done here in just three months."

"Thank you Mr. President," they both responded. "Please take a seat. We appreciate that your time is limited," said Mark.

The chairs were arranged in a circle around a polished obsidian pedestal and two empty tables in the center of the lab. Eyeglasses with darkly tinted lenses were distributed to everyone in the room. On top of the pedestal were two tetrahedron-shaped crystals twinkling like brilliant diamonds. Unlike the four-sided Great Pyramid of Giza, these were three-sided crystal pyramids roughly the size of a baseball. Mark picked them up and handed them to the President to examine.

"Are these the originals you found under the Sphinx?" Matt asked.

"No sir," Mark answered. "We have found a method to manufacture these perfected crystals from the writings on the tablets that were in that same room. At the moment, they are just pretty rocks. There is no visible difference between them unless they are fused together. When they come together, these two crystals become a conduit for seemingly infinite energy."

Matt tried to push the crystals together trying different combinations and angles. He had read about this unusual development in the initial reports. They remained separate and solid. Mark held out his hands and Matt returned them. Then Mark asked everyone to take their seats as he walked to the pedestal and mounted the crystals on their sides. Their bases were positioned to the outside so each pyramid's topmost point was directly aimed at the other. From his perspective, Matt could see that the triangular bases of the two crystals were offset from each other to form what would look like a six-pointed star. Then Mark nodded at Nuri to throw the switch. A low hum filled the lab. Mark flipped another switch on the pedestal and the crystal points slowly started to move toward each other.

Nuri increased the volume and the low hum became a clearly audible musical note, complete with harmonic tones. The sound was almost human for it seemed to be pronouncing the syllable "oh." The crystals glowed with a blueish-white light as the tips of each pyramid came closer to touching. The sound increased in volume and the crystals became brighter. When the points finally touched, the light was so intense that it hurt to look directly at it. Everyone put on their tinted glasses and watched the demonstration with growing wonder. After thirty seconds, the sound decreased and then stopped altogether. The audience sat in awed silence as the light softened back to a comfortable glow. Mark walked back to the pedestal and removed the crystals from the mounts holding them at their bases. He then turned and handed them back to the President.

Matt saw that the two crystals were now fused together. The way they melded together looked almost like an odd hour glass when viewed from the side. However, the offset bases did indeed create a six-pointed star that could be seen from several angles as he rotated it in his hands. He asked, "Those tablets in Giza told you how to do this?"

Nuri replied, "Not directly, but we learned a great deal about resonant frequencies that science had not understood before now. It is through the proper application of sound vibration that quasi-chemical reactions with solid objects, like these crystals, become possible."

"But what does that have to do with unlimited energy?" Matt sounded confused and was feeling a little overwhelmed by what he'd just witnessed.

"Mr. President," Mark began, "it will be easier to show you first and then explain what you're seeing." And with that he placed the crystal back on top of the pedestal.

Nuri activated the low note sound again while Mark hit another switch on the pedestal. The spectators gasped when the pedestal started to descend into the floor but the crystal held its position as if floating in midair. Nuri and Mark then produced a number of common electronic devices and placed them on the two folding tables sitting in front of the spectators. The devices were then plugged into a power strip which was not plugged into anything. The gadgets included a cell phone, a microwave oven, a hair dryer, and a laptop computer. A portable window air conditioner was then wheeled in alongside the other devices and it too was plugged into the power strip.

Nuri stepped back to his console and the sound changed. The "oh" sound gracefully rose one octave at a time until it was too high to be heard by the human ear. Suddenly, a light beam shot up from the floor below into the crystal. That beam refracted out as a separate ray linking the crystal to the power strip connected to the devices on the tables. Each of the electronics came to life the instant the beam of light hit the power strip. The displays on the cell phone and laptop showed they were booting up. The hair dryer moved as it started blowing hot air and the microwave oven flashed 12:00 am in the LED display. Even the AC unit began blowing air which became cool just moments later.

Matt was no electrician, but he knew the circuit breaker should have blown with all the juice being drawn through the power strip. He walked over to the tables for a better look. That the power strip itself was not plugged into an electrical socket left him dumbfounded. Upon closer inspection, Matt saw that a tiny crystal was attached to the plug end of the power strip.

Mark then picked up the cell phone and unplugged it. The display went black as the power had obviously been cut. He asked Matt to open the back of the cell phone. It was no surprise that the battery had already been removed. However, Mark took a moment to install a tiny crystal into the cell phone that looked similar to the one on the power strip. The cell phone came back to life.

Matt now saw that a separate light beam went directly to the cell phone from the main crystal. It followed the phone as Matt moved it around and the power remained on. He then ran his hand through the new light beam. Nothing changed with the phone and he felt no effect on his hand. It was clear they had discovered how to transmit electrical energy without wires or other physical means of transference.

"We can see the beams of light only because we infused this lab with particles that make them visible. Otherwise, we'd see no signs of the energy passing between the crystal and these electronic units," Mark explained.

"This is incredible!" said Matt. "But where does the power come from originally to cause all this?"

Nuri fielded the question. "That's why we wanted you to see what it did first. The answer is hard to believe unless you've observed it in action beforehand."

Mark jumped in, "We've learned that the earth acts as a capacitor for the energy produced by the Sun. When the right resonant frequency is applied and this crystal conduit is available, it greatly increases the power strip's capacity. Any electrical device with a receiving crystal can operate through a wireless connection to the main crystal. Also, connecting a receiving crystal to the main breaker in an electrical panel will power any hard-wired devices that are connected to it. We have yet to find a limit to the amount of power the main crystal can provide to any number of receivers."

Nuri added, "This technology brings a whole new meaning to the term 'precious stones.' The receiving crystal functions like a power regulator or director for the energy it attracts. They automatically draw the exact amount of power needed for the optimal function of each device connected to it."

"You mean that beam coming up from the ground is actually stored energy from the earth guided by the crystal to run these electronics?" Matt was beginning to see what they meant, but he hadn't a clue how it worked. He also took a step back from the main beam just to be careful.

Nuri said, "Yes, you have the idea. And before you ask, we still don't know very much about why it works. However, we can't find any negative effects on living tissue or inert substances regardless of how we have measured it. If anything, we think this technology has great potential for healing living tissue. The uses for this technology are probably limitless."

The President said in a commanding voice, "Ladies and gentlemen, can I have the room for about ten minutes with Doctors Heston and Zayd?"

Everyone filed out leaving Matt, Mark and Nuri alone except for the two agents standing by the door out of earshot. The President stood still for a moment, deep in thought.

Then Matt turned to face Mark and Nuri. "I hadn't heard anything about the healing potential you just spoke of with this technology. What makes you think resonant frequency energy has the capability to heal?"

Nuri answered, "We only just figured this out ourselves! Jason Fisher, the soldier inside the chamber with us, must have activated some sort of healing therapy when he touched the pedestal that also started the resonant frequency generator. There were so many distractions in the chamber that night that it was easy to overlook. Some of what happened did not appear on the video or still shots we took. For example, we all saw a holographic movie of sorts that does not appear on any recording."

"I'm not sure how that answered my question," Matt said expectantly.

Embarrassed, Nuri went on, "A close examination of the video Mark captured in the chamber led to our current working theory. The recording showed us that Jason had been visibly scanned with some sort of green light. That is what led us to surmise it also healed him in the process. Mark too was affected, but neither Jason nor Mark was certain they had been healed until they underwent physicals to confirm the changes."

Matt asked, "You say they were healed in the chamber, but the soldier had to be in top shape or he wouldn't have been assigned to the Delta Force team. And what was wrong with Mark that a healing couldn't be attributed to something else?"

Mark smiled, "I had type 1 diabetes since I was diagnosed at the age of ten. My pancreas and insulin levels have apparently been nominal since I left the chamber."

"Well, that is impressive, but the soldier couldn't have had any serious medical issues. Right?" Matt asked.

Nuri responded, "His case is even more of a mystery. At first, the doctor was not surprised that he was perfectly healthy. Then he saw in the soldier's medical history that he had had his gall bladder removed about five years ago. The MRI revealed it had grown back and was functioning perfectly. The tests also revealed that a broken bone in his right leg that mended long ago appears now to have never been injured."

Mark added, "It seems likely that healing is a part of the pedestals' design. Nuri didn't touch the pedestals and nothing changed in his physical condition. We're still deciphering the information contained on the 32 tablets, but so far we haven't discovered how to channel resonant frequency power toward healing."

"Is that a secret that is now lost to the world because that chamber under the Sphinx was destroyed?" Matt asked.

Nuri sighed, "Perhaps, but there is hope it might still be found. The Hall of Records in Egypt is rumored to have been one of three in existence. The other two are still hidden but may yet be located. Once we have learned all we can from the discovery in Egypt, we intend to return to archeology to search for one or both of the remaining chambers like we found in Egypt."

"I have a favor to ask of you," Matt began. "I need JPL and especially the two of you to keep your discoveries out of the news. We all have enough on our plates moving forward toward the greater good with RF technology without having the media stalking us all for information."

They both readily agreed.

Matt had a second request. "I'm intrigued by the idea that there might be other hidden places in the world containing similar technology to what was destroyed in Egypt. Assuming you believe that is possible, how quickly can you begin to search for them?"

Mark and Nuri were pleased that their sabbatical was about to be extended for an indefinite period.

Chapter 30

Later that same day, Matt and Erin were in the Executive Suite of Air Force One returning to Washington. This was the first Erin had been alone with Matt since his meeting with Mark and Nuri at JPL. He brought her up to date on what he had witnessed there and the incredible potential for resonant frequency power.

"So we will soon have the ability to generate unlimited electrical power and send it wirelessly to any point in the world. The cost of providing this power is practically zero compared to fossil fuels or even sustainable energy alternatives. The United States could soon be the sole supplier of all the world's power needs from one location," Matt said excitedly.

"But won't that bankrupt our own energy corporations? How many people will this new technology put on the unemployment lines?" Erin asked with genuine concern.

"I've thought of that, too. Those are just two of the points that need to be addressed. As part of the answer, I intend to nationalize "RFP" technology for several reasons. First, the corporations that will be financially harmed by this discovery should be bought out by the nationalized resonant power company at their current market values. Second, those people who lose their jobs in this process should be retrained to facilitate bringing this new technology to the world," Matt offered.

"But to nationalize the energy industry so that it is owned and operated by our government goes against the free enterprise system. Why would you decide to do that?" Erin asked.

"Actually, public utilities in this country are often run as a controlled monopoly. In the case of our water supply, the government is most often the owner and operator. It's done that way to ensure the public safety and to promote efficiency. But the proper handling of RFP can accomplish far more than just that," Matt said with a nod.

"What exactly do you have in mind?" Erin could tell he was leading up to something they had not discussed before.

He said with a smile, "Resonant frequency power is such an improvement over fossil fuels that it will inevitably be used throughout the world. Nationalizing the revenues of the international energy industry means all the profits would go to the government. This windfall could easily do away with the need for federal taxes. It is possible that all government functions could be funded from RFP doing away with taxes in this country altogether. If other countries want to nationalize their power industry in the same way, they too could lower or eliminate the need for taxes. As long as any sovereign nation abides by our rules for maintaining a peaceful coexistence, we will provide unlimited RFP to them at a reasonable cost.

Erin's mind raced through all the implications of what Matt just said. "Here's a technical question I've wanted to ask. How would they measure the amount of power each country consumes through the crystals to know how much to bill them?"

"The brains at JPL figured that one out," Matt explained. "The receptor crystals that draw the power can be tuned to different frequencies. They say it's a lot like keeping cell phone accounts separated. Each country will have its own frequency and sub-frequencies so that the power consumed can be divided and measured down to a single customer. Because the technology appears to work across any distance and through any barrier, there won't be a place on earth where power won't be available to those who subscribe."

"But is this technology safe?" she asked, trying to find the flaws in Matt's plan.

"It appears to be far safer than what we have now. The receptor crystals only draw the amount of power needed to operate each end-use of the power. Tests show that if a person inadvertently touches a dangerous electrical connection, the power automatically ceases at that point until the connection with living tissue is broken," Matt said, still impressed with the many implications of this discovery.

"But won't the people of other nations try to duplicate or circumvent the system? Can't they reverse engineer this technology to bypass our monopoly on this type of energy?" Erin asked.

Matt answered, "From what I'm told, without the knowledge gained from those 32 tablets, we could have gone for centuries without learning of resonant frequency technology. Yes, eventually everyone will be able to duplicate it, but how much better will the world be by then?"

He was still wrestling with an ethical dilemma he had yet to work out. Matt asked Erin what she thought. "Do you think I have the right to claim U.S. ownership of this technology that was discovered under the Sphinx in Egypt?"

Erin smiled, appreciating that Matt was concerned over this point. "Except for those first two crystals the soldier took with him, the property that legally belongs to Egypt is still there under tons of earth. Give the original crystal pieces back to the Egyptian government and the law has been fulfilled."

Matt marveled at how quickly she came up with the perfect solution to a problem he'd been struggling through for days. He decided to ask about the other ethical considerations. "Do you think it's fair to withhold RFP energy from countries that violate the peace plan?"

Erin was quick to respond, "Yes. They don't have to buy power from the United States if they don't abide by the conditions that go along with our offer to provide them with safe, inexpensive, reliable power in unlimited quantities. That does bring up the question of what happens when you are no longer in charge. The world leaders may trust that Matthew Alexander will always be fair, but what about your successors?"

He smiled as he said, "If I have learned anything through all of this, it is that each nation elects or inherits the leadership it deserves. If we continue to work together for the good of all, then the right people will be elected when it's time for me to step down."

Erin suddenly remembered, "You never did tell me what happened with Generals McComb and Newman. What exactly did they do that compelled you to ask for their resignations?"

Matt replied thoughtfully, "They were no longer the right people for those positions. I would have fired George Salazar, but he disappeared. Simply said, it was clear to me that they were all working against the peace plan instead of helping it to succeed. The moment they became more of a liability to our nation's interests than an asset, I asked them to resign."

After they touched down at Andrews Air Force base, Erin asked a last question before they faced the reporters on the tarmac. "Is everything that was left behind in that Egyptian chamber lost forever?"

Matt smiled as he considered her question. "Those two archeologists, Mark and Nuri, are convinced there are two other hidden locations like the one they found under the Sphinx. My hope is that they will eventually track down one or both of them. And I plan to do all I can to help them succeed!"

***

Mark started reading a government white paper on resonant frequency power knowing it would be a sure cure for his insomnia. He was dozing off before he got to the second page but found he was still consciously aware of his thoughts. He recognized that he was dreaming and tried to remember what this state was called. The term popped into his mind. He was experiencing a lucid dream.

As he took in his surroundings, he tried to identify the people in the room with him. He locked eyes with Nuri but his friend stared blankly back at him without recognition. Mark couldn't remember seeing the other three people before. While they looked human in appearance, they seemed to consist more of white light than flesh and blood.

The brightest light of the three spoke first, "There is no reason to be afraid. No harm will come to you here. I am Amelius. This is Ariel and Halaliel," he said as he pointed to his companions. "We are gathered here with the two of you to discuss your future."

Nuri suddenly came out of his trance and asked, "Are you some sort of angels like in the Qur'an or the Bible?"

Halaliel answered, "As your subconscious mind takes greater control, you will soon remember the answer, but it is both yes and no. Yes, in that Ariel and I are angels, as you define such things. No, because Amelius is a soul like yourselves."

Mark interrupted him by asking, "What's the difference between an angel and a soul?"

Ariel responded, "There is almost no difference when a soul is making cooperative choices where everyone gains. Angels only make choices that are intended to benefit all. Ideally, souls do the same, but unlike angels, they can make selfish choices where they sometimes try to take advantage of others."

Nuri blurted out, "But what about Lucifer? Wasn't he an angel?"

Amelius smiled and said, "No. Lucifer is a soul. As Ariel said, there is little difference between souls and angels when all choices are made in harmony. With Lucifer's first selfish thought, the difference became clear. But we are here specifically to help you choose what is to come next in your earthly lives."

Mark asked, "Why? What makes us so special? I find it hard to believe you meet with everyone like this to discuss their future, or do you?"

It was Ariel who answered, "Make no mistake in understanding that you are indeed special. The same is true of every soul in existence. However, your recent choices, along with those of many others, have moved both of you into a unique position. You can make a difference by helping to shape a wonderful future for humankind."

Nuri was skeptical. "I admit that we're in the limelight at the moment because of resonant frequency power and discovering the Hall of records in Egypt, but that will soon pass. We plan to return to archeology just as soon as we can."

Halaliel laughed, "That much is certain! But the choice that lies before you is which long-lost discoveries you will pursue, if any. You will find that you are not so welcome in Egypt after the destruction of their great treasures. The Egyptian government will soon connect your quick exit from Cairo to the discovery of resonant frequency power from underneath the Sphinx. That you decided to share this remarkable discovery with the United States rather than Egypt will present an interesting array of choices in response to President Alexander's pending plans."

Mark sadly saw where this would lead. "Archeologists don't really function well with fame or infamy. What options do we have left that don't completely change our lives and careers?"

212

Amelius adopted a consoling tone, "To use a cliché from earth, 'That ship has already sailed.' Your lives will never be the same as before, but see what possibilities are ahead for you that have only recently become available!"

Mark and Nuri watched as their surroundings became a 3-D experience where they could see all the consequences of their possible future choices. The wonders they could yet discover would not come without great risk. They also saw potentially deadly challenges already developing that would reveal themselves once President Alexander was no longer in office.

They were shown that their discoveries in Egypt would not bring lasting peace to the world. They saw that many people were already planning to undermine the technological gift of resonant frequency power. The world's toughest challenges still lay ahead and Mark and Nuri would be at the center of the global conflict. They could also choose to stay out of the fray and live comfortable lives without risk if they would give up their careers in archeology.

The future scenarios faded away and Amelius came back into their view. "Now you understand the choices that are before you at this critical point in humanity's timeline. You have the potential to achieve your own goals as well as help the souls of earth to become better people. You can also choose to 'let this cup pass' if that is your will. No one is forcing you to take the more difficult path. If you decide not to serve in this manner, others will eventually step up to fulfill this important role."

Mark and Nuri suddenly realized they could read each other's thoughts. Neither was particularly spiritual or altruistic, but they both doggedly pursued the truth regardless of where that led. They silently agreed that they were two of the most unlikely and reluctant heroes ever. It was simply by chance that what they wanted to do most also fell in line with the greatest results that they had just been shown.

They looked at the three glowing beings and the light emanating from them became even brighter as the shapes before them vanished. Both Mark and Nuri heard them say together, "You have chosen well and the world will benefit because of this. You will feel moments of regret over this decision, but if you persevere in being of service to all, you cannot fail. In times of fear or doubt, remember these words of encouragement: When you find yourself walking through the valley of death, there is nothing to fear, for all that is good is always with you!"

The Hall of Records Trilogy

Part 2

In the Presence of My Enemies

Prologue

It has been 10 years since archeologists Mark Heston and Nuri Zayd discovered the fabled Hall of Records in Egypt. Sadly, the Sphinx was destroyed by a terrorist's bomb that inadvertently revealed the underground chamber and its amazing artifacts. Mark and Nuri barely escaped with their lives when the unstable vault collapsed. Their cameras recorded the written secrets of an ancient technology called resonant frequency power, or RFP. Their discovery led to the development of a completely safe and unlimited power source that seamlessly replaced electrical power plants. Resonant frequency energy could safely power any electrical device using a small receiving crystal in place of a hard-wired electrical connection.

This amazing new discovery could not have come at a better time. The world's nations depended on the uninterrupted flow of oil. A war seemed imminent because of escalating terrorist attacks in the Middle East. When RF energy essentially replaced fossil fuels overnight, the world had little reason to interfere with the political problems that plagued the oil-rich region.

Matthew Alexander was the President of the United States at the time resonant frequency (RF) technology was discovered. He announced that the United States would sell RF energy at a fraction of the cost of fossil fuels to sovereign governments. The only requirement for countries to become wholesale RFP customers was to support and maintain an international treaty promoting human rights and global peace.

After buying out the stockholders of all fossil fuel-based energy corporations in the U.S., President Alexander was able to eliminate federal taxes. The global income received from RF energy sales more than made up for the loss in tax revenues. Most countries followed the U.S. government's example and found the new windfall a great help in reducing taxes globally. There were a select few who chose not to participate due to their massive oil reserves and long-standing opposition to anything that put them in league with the United States.

President Alexander's great hope and plan that RFP would bring about world peace was short lived. The angry conflicts between nations continued, albeit not officially. Any declaration of war would result in the U.S. cutting off the offender's supply of RF energy. Few of the wholesale RFP customers felt that the U.S. could be trusted as the sole provider of energy to the world.

Mark and Nuri, with the support of President Alexander, continued their search for another Hall of Records. They believed there were at least two other sites with more of the remarkable technology that had been tragically lost when the Sphinx was destroyed. Their efforts to organize expeditions to find these hidden locations stalled once Matt Alexander became a lame duck in his second term. His successor, President Donald Westbrook, had never been a fan of the Alexander administration, nor did he believe the unconfirmed story of how resonant frequency technology was discovered. President Westbrook felt that nothing good could come from supporting the archeologists' proposed expeditions. His bias against them began when he was a Congressman on the Ways and Means Committee. Everything he had learned about these two men verified that they were eccentric and strongly disagreed with his own agenda and ideologies.

Delayed but undaunted, Mark and Nuri sought private financial support for their quest. Matt Alexander, now retired from public life, continued to offer what help he could. He held a strong belief that Mark and Nuri were the world's best chance at discovering another Hall of Records, if any remained. While Matt's support provided the bulk of the financing they needed, two other people had become intricately involved with their project.

Gil Kowalski, the Director of National Drug Control Policy from Matt Alexander's administration, had become the U.S. Ambassador to both Mexico and Guatemala. He had also been instrumental in helping Mark and Nuri obtain the necessary permissions for their expeditions into the Yucatan peninsula. The contacts he developed working against the Central and South American drug cartels had opened a lot of bureaucratic doors in those countries.

The other key person was an unlikely companion to Mark and Nuri. Jason Fisher had recently retired from the U.S. Army's Delta Force. He was the same soldier who had accompanied Mark

217

and Nuri into the Egyptian Hall of Records. As the walls crumbled around them, Jason had picked up the special crystal that made RF energy possible. Ironically, he had been a life-long skeptic with little trust in metaphysics and folklore. However, he became a believer in the value of Mark and Nuri's explorations because of the things he saw and experienced firsthand underneath the Sphinx. Between his Delta Force skills and strong belief in Mark and Nuri's mission, Jason was the perfect guardian to watch over the two naïve archeologists.

After several expeditions to Guatemala, Mark, Nuri and Jason narrowed their search down to a remote area named Piedras Negras. Without the support of the U.S. government, this was likely to be their last opportunity to discover more of the ancient technology that had been lost beneath the Sphinx.

Chapter 1

Mark Heston and Nuri Zayd were fast asleep in the back of the jeep. The exhilaration they felt over this latest adventure in Guatemala had quickly given way to exhaustion. Their companion and driver was Jason Fisher. Jason met the two archeologists years ago when he was a member of the U.S. Army's Delta Force team. He had been assigned to protect them back in Egypt and he took the job seriously. Though Jason had since retired from the military, he now watched over these two as a civilian.

All three of them were dressed in jungle fatigues, but Jason was the only one who looked at home wearing them. He had kept all his carefully tailored battle dress uniforms from his active duty days. He had removed the military patches but he still looked like G. I. Joe on a recruiting poster. The archeologists looked more like freshly scrubbed recruits in their bulky gear. Their naïveté toward humankind's darker side was a constant source of frustration for Jason. Nevertheless, he hoped they never lost their enthusiastic approach to life.

Jason and the two archeologists had become good friends despite having little in common. The day after he retired from the military, they asked if he would help them find another Hall of Records. He readily agreed. Two years and four disappointing expeditions later, they had little to show for their efforts.

As they departed the sparsely populated town of Tierra Linda, the paved road suddenly gave way to rutted dirt. The jeep shuddered as it jostled bodies and camping gear in all directions. Jason smiled seeing that the two men were still out cold. He was glad they could catch up on their sleep during the bumpy 10-mile drive to the river the locals called Rio Usumacinta. From there, they would head north to Piedras Negras using an inflatable zodiac boat.

Jason reflected on all that had changed since they first met in Egypt. After their initial success, Nuri and Mark started searching for another Hall of Records like the one they discovered in Giza. The same urban myths and psychic sources that helped them find the hidden chamber beneath the Sphinx also talked about two other locations. Both were rumored to have vaults containing the same advanced technology that was lost when the underground chamber collapsed.

The two remaining sites were said to be in Bimini and the Yucatan peninsula. The former was somewhere below the ocean surface inside the Bermuda Triangle. That made it easy to pick the Yucatan as the better location to begin their search. Finding a hidden chamber in the Guatemalan jungle would be hard enough without having to dig a hole in water.

Mark and Nuri's discovery of resonant frequency power (RFP) from the crystals and hieroglyphics in the underground chamber had been a real game changer. Having sustainable, safe and unlimited power for a fraction of the cost of electricity from fossil fuels brought immediate prosperity to all who used it. The U.S. "owned" the initial discovery and decided to do a friendly buyout of their country's power industry. The government retrained the power plant workers to provide RF energy to the world. President Matt Alexander had promised that the revenues from the USA's new venture would eliminate the need for federal income taxes. He was re-elected by a landslide having made good on that promise in his first term.

There was a catch before other governments could buy RF energy wholesale for their own countries. Agreeing to a permanent peace treaty was required to guarantee an uninterrupted flow of RFP power from the United States government. Sovereign declarations of war became a thing of the past. All but a handful of countries desired low cost, unlimited energy more than they wanted vengeance or imperialism.

The peace accord held for a while, but it did not put an end to violence. Loopholes surfaced that circumvented President Alexander's peace plan. Rogue paramilitary groups began to carry out missions that supported their nation's agenda, while government leaders expressed their mock dismay. Civilian casualties from terrorist acts became commonplace once official battlefields ceased to exist.

In an effort to close the loopholes, President Alexander called for investigations into any ties between terrorist acts and governments who had signed the peace accord. Bowing to an overwhelming international consensus that the U.S. should not be the world's judge and jury, Matt turned the inspections over to the United Nations and agreed to accept the U.N.'s findings and recommendations for each investigation. Unfortunately, the inevitable occurred. The guilty countries quietly bribed the U.N. inspectors with large sums of cash to maintain their uninterrupted access to wholesale RF power.

Jason's thoughts returned to the present as he pulled up to the bank of the river. Mark and Nuri woke up once the engine stopped and the silence registered. Jason was already taking some of their gear down to the shoreline. The archeologists decided to tackle the inflatable zodiac boat that was strapped to the roof of the jeep. The deflated rubber seemed to have a life of its own and was too heavy for the two of them to carry. Jason let them struggle with it as he lined everything else up by the water's edge for loading. He kept a poker face as he watched the thick rubber boat get the better of them. He pulled out the air pump and asked if he might help. Mark and Nuri watched as the zodiac began to swell. Their curiosity turned to embarrassment at how easy it was for the three of them to carry the rubber boat once it was fully inflated.

The river was the fastest way to get to Piedras Negras because there were no paved roads or airstrips to access the area they intended to explore. They had been using a grid search method of the unpopulated areas of Guatemala for several years. To date, they had no luck finding another Hall of Records in Egypt. Piedras Negras was the last section they had to search within Guatemala's borders. The archeologists dreaded the thought of having to get permission from Mexico's government to continue their search if they struck out here.

It was well before noon when they had everything loaded into the zodiac. Jason knew the jeep needed to be secured if he expected it to be there when they returned. He drove it behind some bushes and covered it with branches. Then he disabled the engine with a hidden kill switch.

The river was slow this time of year and there were no rapids to contend with all the way to Piedras Negras. The rudder and an occasional dip of an oar was enough for Jason to guide the rubber boat because they were travelling with the current. They had a small

RF powered engine to get them back up river, but there was no need for speed at this point.

Nuri and Mark soon tired of their surroundings. They had seen plenty of this part of the world from their previous expeditions. The rocking motion of the lazy river soon lulled them back to sleep. All was quiet except for the ongoing cries of the howler monkeys. Their screeches rang out ahead of the northbound zodiac as a warning to the others that intruders were approaching. Jason kept a close eye on both banks of the river despite the apparent lack of danger. Only locals and the occasional rafting tour travelled this waterway because much of it was too shallow for commercial boats.

It took the better part of the day to get to their destination. Jason did his best to camouflage the boat under some low branches knowing they would probably not return until tomorrow or the next day. The chance of anyone finding and stealing their zodiac in this remote place was laughable, but they didn't want to tempt fate. With high hopes and a full back pack each, the three men headed east.

Jason used a machete to clear a path through the foliage while Nuri served as the navigator with the map. Both he and Mark were convinced they were finally going to find the elusive chamber. They kept a close watch for unusual terrain that might indicate buried ruins below.

Jason called back, "You'd better double check the map. There's a large clearing up ahead that shouldn't be there!" Nuri agreed after verifying he couldn't see any open areas near their location. They all picked up the pace to check it out.

When they cleared the trees, the men stopped dead in their tracks. They found themselves at the end of a long, narrow meadow with a paved road centered in the clearing. By Jason's estimate, the length of the road was slightly less than half a mile. The tire marks they saw at their end indicated this was a private airstrip probably used for small planes.

Mark and Nuri were immediately excited. Having an airfield this close to the presumed site of the hidden chamber would make it much easier to excavate once they located it. Jason was conversely not happy at all and told them to stay put while he checked the perimeter. He took off running toward the far end of the clearing staying near the tree line of the surrounding jungle.

They watched Jason reach the far end of the clearing in perhaps three minutes. At 45 years old and sprinting a half a mile with a full backpack, they were reminded of Jason's impressive skills and stamina. He was 6' 2", 210 pounds, short dark hair, and the muscled look of a gymnast, Jason hadn't seemed to age a day since they first met him in Egypt. Mark and Nuri knew they were lucky to have him as a member of the team. They hadn't needed a bodyguard at any point in their expeditions, but Jason's strength and survival skills had come in handy on several occasions.

They walked onto the road when they heard the faint sound of an engine approaching from somewhere in the distance. The buzzing sound was definitely coming closer as they scanned the skies to locate its source. A moment later a Beech Baron twin-prop airplane touched down directly in front of them and taxied toward Jason at the other end of the runway. Mark and Nuri took off running toward the plane delighted to have the chance to befriend the owners of this landing strip. They couldn't see Jason waving them off and urging them to hide because the plane was blocking their view.

The two archeologists were not athletic at all and much slower than Jason. The weight of their backpacks quickly slowed their sprint to a jog. They began walking when they saw the plane's side door open and the steps unfold to the ground. Two men jumped from the plane to the tarmac turning toward Mark and Nuri as they landed. A moment later they heard sounds like the endless cracking of a whip. When they connected the noise of bullets whizzing by to the muzzle flashes and gunfire reports, their survival instincts finally kicked in.

Nuri and Mark ducked off to the north toward the cover of the trees with the two men closing in fast. The branches whipped past and tore at their clothes as they ran through the jungle stumbling over the rough terrain. Mark was in the lead and was doing his best to zigzag through the foliage. The setting sun was working in their favor but they were unarmed and no match for their pursuers.

Nuri almost tripped when he noticed that Mark's back pack started to glow each time they cut to the north. The glow dimmed when they retreated to the east or west. Nuri knew the light was coming from the specialized crystal receivers Mark carried in his backpack's outer pouch. The brighter glow as they ran north meant they were moving closer to a sending RFP crystal. The irony was not lost on Nuri that the first sign of the hidden chamber came as they were running for their lives.

He called out, "Keep moving to the north. I can tell you which way to go!" Mark adjusted his path as Nuri guided him to the left or right. They could hear the gunmen moving through the bushes in the distance behind them and they wondered what had happened to Jason. Had he been killed when the opening shots were fired? Nuri had to hope that Jason's combat training would keep him alive and manage to rescue them all before it was too late.

Nuri could see that the crystals in Mark's backpack were getting brighter with every step. They had been on the run for five minutes and would have to rest soon. They could see a sharp rise in the ground in front of them and Nuri told Mark to go around it for cover. As they passed what looked like a giant anthill shrouded in plant life, the crystals began to dim. Nuri grabbed Mark's pack and pulled him to a stop.

"Whatever that hill was back there, it has a sending RFP crystal," said Nuri breathlessly.

Mark pulled off his backpack to see that the tiny crystals were glowing brightly. The archeologists looked back at the steep rise in the terrain. Until now, neither man had recognized the shape of a pyramid protruding from the ground. The local vegetation had overtaken and disguised the structure long ago, but this was exactly the kind of thing they had been searching for. They ran back to the pyramid wall, hoping to keep the structure between them and their attackers.

They soon realized that the glow of the crystals in the looming darkness acted like a faint beacon for their assailants to spot them. Mark positioned the backpack between his body and the foliage covered wall to shield the glow as much as possible.

The nearby angry voices made it clear their trackers had caught up to them. Mark and Nuri continued to hug the wall and move slowly away from the men not knowing what else to do. Mark was sure they could hear his heart pounding. Nuri risked a quick look back toward the threat. He was about to suggest that they dump the glowing backpack and run for better cover, but he was alone! Mark and the crystals had vanished without a trace.

***

Jason couldn't believe Nuri and Mark had actually started running toward the airplane as it landed. He tried to wave them off but the plane's path on the runway blocked their view of him. He quickly headed for the tree line hoping he could still get them out of this mess.

He was not surprised when the heavily armed men started shooting at Mark and Nuri without bothering to ask questions. How were they to know that the two guys running toward them were harmless? Jason figured that an unmarked airstrip so far from civilization meant the cargo that just touched down had to be either drugs or weapons. His line of sight for the men chasing Mark and Nuri was blocked by the airplane. Against his better judgment, Jason stood up to go after them. The next moment, two more men with automatic weapons appeared on the tarmac. They scanned the area in Jason's direction. He was outnumbered but his bigger concern was getting to Mark and Nuri before they were captured or killed.

Jason was sure they would not join in the pursuit of his friends if he threatened the cargo. From his position in the foliage, he fired three rounds flattening the plane's tires. Jason hoped the two guards would return fire and they did not disappoint him. He did not start this fight but he finished it quickly. With two more carefully aimed rounds, both men fell where they stood. As the echo from the shots faded in the distance, Jason was already making a beeline past the plane running full out to help his friends.

Before he reached the other side of the clearing, Jason looked back to see a large military grade truck pull into view. No doubt the truck was there to transport the illicit cargo from the plane to another destination. He ducked into the jungle as the truck sped across the open field in pursuit. He was glad that he had a head start.

***

As Mark gathered his bearings, his first thought was that he'd been blindsided. How else would he have ended up flat on his back when a moment before he had been leaning against a solid mound? He recalled that it felt like the surface supporting him had disintegrated. He knew that RF technology could have that effect on solid materials so the crystals he was carrying must have been why the wall had given way. His next thought was to find the same opening so he could bring Nuri inside to safety.

The glow from the crystals in his backpack was enough to light the area around him. From what he could see, he was inside an ancient room made of cut limestone. The construction was reminiscent of the underground chamber's walls in Egypt. When he saw some familiar symbols inscribed on the decorative stones, the archeologist in him took over.

Mark had worked a lot with this symbolic language over the past decade, but the syntax here was so intricate that he could only get a general sense of the story engraved on the walls. The parts of the tale he could decipher told him RF technology had been developed that provided unlimited food and water. The gift had come from the Children of Light. A leader in the Sons of Darkness corrupted the gift and turned it into a terrible plague to destroy all of humanity. Instead of producing unlimited sustenance, the infected person lost the ability to process food or water no matter how much they ate or drank. Left untreated, they soon starved to death or died of dehydration, whichever killed them first.

A cure was discovered in time to stop the extinction of the human race, but the hieroglyphics warned that the plague, if unleashed again, could finish the job for which it was created. Mark could tell there was much more information about the cure in the engraved symbols, but he could not translate them. He felt like this chamber was a display room inside a museum. The story written across the limestone wall ended at an obsidian altar holding a small, intricately carved wooden box. Mark picked up the box to examine it and found more of the ancient writing engraved on its top. It appeared to be similar to an old puzzle box he owned as a boy. He was surprised to find that the box opened the same way by sliding three panels in order.

Once opened, he found four objects inside. There were two clear vials with each end melted like glass to seal them. One vial was filled with a black substance and the other was pure white. The box also contained two crystal medallions much like Mark had seen before in the Egyptian Hall of Records. He started to examine each piece before he remembered the grave danger Nuri must be facing outside. He cursed at himself for getting sidetracked.

He put the four items back into the box and searched the room to find an exit. Holding his backpack out in front of him Mark pressed it against the wall and started sliding it along the surface. It worked, for a moment later Mark was able to push his way through as if the wall wasn't really there.

***

Nuri was stunned to find that his partner had vanished. He barely had time to look around when the two men rushed at him from opposite sides of the mound. He slowly held up his empty hands. They called out rapid commands in Spanish. Nuri generally understood the language, but their orders were peppered with slang insults and physically impossible profanity. He had no idea what they wanted him to do.

He cried out, "I don't understand you! Um...uh...no comprende!"

They looked surprised and quickly realized Nuri's dark skin did not mean he was Hispanic. The taller man switched to broken English saying, "You get down...now!"

Nuri dropped to his knees while keeping his hands in plain sight.

Again in English, the man asked, "Where is he? Your friend?"

"I don't know!" Nuri said, with a shaky voice. "I turned my head for a moment and he was gone."

With a snort the man yelled out in all directions, "Come out now or we will make little pieces of your compadre here." The other man produced a machete and cut a length of vine. Then he walked over to Nuri. He threw one end of the vine over a nearby branch and tied Nuri's wrists behind his back with the other end. He then hoisted Nuri up to his feet by stretching his arms upward until he screamed from the pain.

The tall man shouted again into the surrounding jungle, "You have one minute, Cabrone. If you don't come out, your friend will lose an arm."

The sun had disappeared below the horizon so that darkness completely shrouded the jungle. Their blueish-white flashlight beams frantically slashed through the foliage as they searched for any signs of Mark. With a grunt, the man yelled out in English, "Time is up!" He turned to his partner and said more loudly than he needed to, "The right arm first."

The man with the machete walked around Nuri to get into position. The tall man held both of the flashlights on Nuri and called, "Last chance!?" When there was no response, he nodded and the other man lined up his blade to strike.

In that same instant, two rapid gunshots came from behind them. Jason went for head shots in case they were wearing body armor. He rushed over and used the machete to cut Nuri loose.

"Oh, thank God!" said Nuri as he slumped to the ground from the ordeal. Jason caught him and eased him to the ground.

"Where's Mark?" he asked.

Nuri shook his head saying, "I have no idea. One second he was next to me and then he just vanished."

Jason declared, "We don't have a lot of time to find him. More men arrived after you ran and those two shots I just fired will lead them here."

A scuffling sound off to their left caused Jason to aim his flashlight and rifle instantly ready to fire. The bright beam revealed Mark squinting against the glare and looking very confused. "Nuri, is that you?" Mark shouted in a stage whisper.

Jason responded, "We're both here. Grab your stuff and let's get back to the boat. There are more men coming." Nuri immediately got to his feet but Mark looked dazed as he stared at the two bodies on the ground. He almost forgot the amazing discovery he'd made inside the pyramid and held out the box.

As Nuri and Jason approached him, Mark opened the wooden box to show them what he had found. The next moment Jason picked him up like a bag of cement over his shoulder and ran to escape the gun fire that erupted around them. Mark held onto the box, but its contents spilled out as all three of them fled back to the boat.

Chapter 2

President Donald Westbrook sat on the couch across from his predecessor in the Oval Office. Matt Alexander tried to cut through the tension with some light-hearted joking. Despite their rough history together, Don enjoyed Matt's sense of humor and started to relax. Matt had given no reason for wanting to meet, so his agenda could be anything from a social visit to asking for political favors.

Don's perfect silver hair and good looks combined to make for an unusually striking appearance. His political opponents had long envied his charisma supported by a deep voice that could sway anyone. Don grew up in Los Angeles and could have easily been a great actor, but wealth and fame were not enough for him. His utmost desire was to possess great power and that intense need had driven him all the way to the White House.

Except for being raised in Arizona, Matthew Alexander had a similar appearance and background to Don's. He too had originally wanted to be President out of a desire for power, but his eight years in office changed him as much as he had changed the world. It was early in his first term when Matt's goals transformed from a focus on his legacy to helping create a better world. He was still a patriot, but he came to realize that the United States was at its best when the rest of the world prospered as well.

Matt too had more than his fair share of charm and good looks. At 6'1" with an athletic physique that matched his keen intellect, Matt had been a favorite on magazine covers since first appearing in the public eye. When he managed to replace tax revenues by nationalizing RF energy, Matt sealed his place in history as one of the most popular Presidents of all time.

The pleasant conversation between the current President and his predecessor took an awkward turn. Don was surprised by Matt asking for his help with a special project. The issue had come up before, but they had never discussed it face to face. Those two crazy archeologists wanted funding to go off on another wild goose chase. Don's mind raced through his options hoping to find an easy way to deny the request. He decided his best move was to attack the credibility of the undertaking.

"I find it hard to believe you buy the archeologists' story about how they discovered resonant frequency power," Don began. "Now you want me to commit political suicide by publicly funding an expedition based on rumors and psychic predictions? I'm still in my first term here, Matt. I'm counting on a second one."

Matt smiled and said, "I understand your skepticism. Though we never revealed it publicly, there was plenty of evidence to substantiate their story. Several credible scientists at JPL confirmed that they saw the pictures and video files that have since disappeared. They were convinced that the records leading to the discovery of RF energy were found beneath the Sphinx. Mark Heston and Nuri Zayd knew where to look based solely upon those rumors and predictions."

"Plenty of evidence?" Don almost yelled. "You don't find it convenient that the pictures and video they took mysteriously disappeared before anyone outside of JPL had a chance to authenticate them? Only a conspiracy theorist would believe what you are calling 'plenty of evidence.' Who is to say that Egypt's government isn't telling the truth with their claim that RF energy was stolen from them?"

"Your skepticism might make sense if Zayd and Heston or the JPL scientists had become wealthy or hugely famous along the way," Matt replied, "and you know that has not been the case. They have all willingly given credit to their 'group effort' rather than enrich or draw attention to any individuals."

Don was silent as he considered what to say next. He knew that without a convincing motive for those men of science to lie, his own suspicions lacked credibility. Regardless, Don knew he could never support the proposed expedition.

The archeologists had been trying for years to get government funding for their expeditions. Since Don had been the Chairman of the Ways and Means Committee back when he was a Congressman, he had personally seen to it that their requests never saw the light of day. Being elected President had not changed his mind when it came to their crazy stories.

When anyone asked, he stated that their quest would only waste the public's money, but that was the least of his objections. The truth was that Don was furious with Matt for trading the appearance of peace for unlimited RFP power. He would never agree with his predecessor's premise that the goal of ending all wars justified sharing cheap, sustainable energy with the world. Don knew the better approach would have been for the U.S. to keep RFP for itself and everyone else could 'be damned.' Above all else, Don considered himself a patriot. His own silent prediction was that 50 years from now Matt's seemingly altruistic RFP plan would be branded as treasonous.

Don calculated that the best way to win this debate would be to initially start out on Matt's side. "I too had hoped that the world's desire for peace could be brought into reality by sharing RF energy. Unfortunately, most countries hate each other as much today as they did ten years ago. We have all prospered because of RF energy, but it has not made us better people."

"And your point?" Matt asked, waiting for the other shoe to drop.

"My point is that sovereign nations still find reasons to fight each other even after solving the age-old problem of having enough affordable energy. Whatever laws we pass against violence will always be broken. Humans are basically a violent people with long memories and an insatiable desire for vengeance," Don said with sincerity.

Matt countered by saying, "The only way every person on the earth can pursue life, liberty and happiness without interruption is if we agree to put an end to violence. Your premise that we will never stop killing each other divides us into winners and losers. A look back in history tells us that the people on top don't ever stay there. Why should the world pursue liberty and happiness if we don't really believe those goals are attainable in perpetuity?"

Don sighed and said, "You keep trying to solve the wrong problem! As long as the citizens of the U.S. are free to prosper and pursue the good things in life, what difference does it make what the rest of the world does? RFP could have insulated us from everyone else's problems and helped our people to live happier lives."

"Do you really think the U.S. can be the world's leader without being willing to help resolve the world's difficulties?" Matt asked hardly believing Don's myopic perspective. Was Don Westbrook truly the leader that the United States deserved?

"You keep assuming the best way to accomplish that goal is to immediately jump into the fray, even when we're not welcome," Don scolded. "You should have kept the U.S. out of it until the rest of the world was desperate enough to beg for our help. Keeping RFP for ourselves would have done just that until the time was right to dole it out as it best served the interests of the United States. The way you chose to share it, every country feels entitled to RFP and resents the U.S. for keeping the technology a secret. They should be openly thanking us, for God's sake."

Matt refused to take offense and said, "If I had focused on solutions designed to make me look good during my time as President, I might have done things your way. Achieving and maintaining a lasting global peace is a long process. I knew back then it would take much longer than eight years to work out all the bugs. One thing is certain. We cannot rightfully lead the free world and, at the same time, believe other nations are less deserving than us."

Matt paused before finishing his point. "An example of this comes to mind. Has your idea of perennial winners and losers worked in the case of welfare recipients? They started by asking for help out of desperation, but in just a few generations, they began to feel entitled. Soon after, people learned how to cheat the system and many of them saw nothing wrong with that. Before long, welfare was seen by all concerned as a problem rather than a solution. No sustainable plan for prosperity starts out by forcing people to beg."

Don knew that Matt was a brilliant man but that didn't make him right. He could also see that Matt would have a reasonable argument for anything said against his altruistic position. Don had entered this debate thinking he could win. When the proposed expedition had come up in his days as the Ways and Means Committee Chairman, no one in the room had dared to say anything when he quashed the matter. Matt had the high ground and that put Don in a tough position. The best he could hope for now was to keep from losing this argument. If Matt had a weakness, Don knew it would be guilt over the current international chaos Matt's RFP plan had started.

"So that's why you're here!" Don said accusingly. "You want me to fix the mess you've created. Your presidential legacy has become one of trading 'war on the battlefield' for 'terrorism in our cities.' Well, you've turned war into every country's dirty little secret forcing governments to choose 'terrorism' in self-defense of their interests and people."

Matt took a sip of water to give Don a moment to cool down. The move also served to show he would not be distracted by this red herring. He returned to his original point saying, "If another Hall of Records is discovered, the potential for this new technology promises to give you a chance to change the world for the better. If you could make life easier and more prosperous for everyone, what would that be worth?"

Don stayed on the offensive, "You're trying to get me to sponsor this ridiculous expedition to vindicate your blunder. My support of this farce would also imply that I'm in favor of your RFP plan. That's a clever idea, but trying to save face like this is beneath you."

Anger flashed through Matt's eyes as he thought of a hundred ways to respond, none of them respectful. He calmed himself down and was careful to speak softly. "You could have said 'no' without the ugly accusations, Don. If you think I'm here for selfish reasons, you're wrong. The fact is that I was offering you a way to get on the right side of this issue. If you think the media and voters would take shots at you for supporting Mark and Nuri's expedition, imagine how they'll crucify you for not getting behind them after they discover more technology like RF energy! Thank you for your time, Mr. President."

And with that, Matt walked out of the Oval Office.

Chapter 3

Matt left the White House in the back of the government limousine outfitted to protect the President. Federal law requires Secret Service protection for a departing President up to ten years after leaving office. Matt accepted that it was a cumbersome but necessary precaution.

The agents both sat up front leaving Matt alone in the back with his thoughts. He stretched out his legs hoping to catch some sleep during the 45-minute drive to meet his wife Erin. She had been visiting a friend in Virginia while he was at the White House. The stress of the meeting with President Westbrook had left him fatigued. He propped up his legs on the limo's seat across from him, closed his eyes, and drifted off to sleep.

Matt became aware of a strange sense of weightlessness. His mind wandered to key moments from his time as President. The memories became so real, it was as if he was experiencing the events for the first time. He forced himself to open his eyes. He was still sitting in the limo, but instead of the typical view of buildings and traffic outside, he saw a dense white mist.

He reached for the intercom button to ask his security detail where they were. The usual controls were not there. Matt called out, hoping to be heard through the privacy divider that separated the passengers from those driving in the front. There was no audible response but a voice in his head said, "Be not afraid. If you will concentrate, you will see that there is no need to panic."

Matt recognized the voice, but couldn't quite place it. He did as suggested and shifted his focus to the interior of the car. A man dressed in luminescent white was sitting next to him, completely relaxed, as if he'd always been there. Matt blurted out his name as it suddenly came to him, "Amelius!"

"Indeed!" The man in white smiled at him.

Matt's memories of their past encounters came flooding back and he realized how much he had missed this enigmatic counselor and friend. "I have been floundering without your guidance," he said with a bit of frustration.

Amelius had helped him persevere through the challenging events that led to the discovery of RFP during his first term as President. Those past ethereal encounters had helped Matt to navigate a narrow path of choices that resulted in global peace when the world was preparing for war.

Amelius answered, "Don't be so hard on yourself. You have done well! Did you think the introduction of RF energy alone would bring an end to all violence?"

"As I remember, that was one possible outcome of all those you showed me," Matt said defensively.

Amelius smiled again and said, "You offered the world a tremendous opportunity to cease all fighting. Should you really blame yourself if many chose a different path?"

"In some ways, it seems my plan to manage the distribution of RF energy made things worse. The Middle East struggles with poverty and chaos now that fossil fuels are nearly obsolete. Those nations are very vocal in their criticisms against us. The others are equally unhappy but they're afraid to say anything that might put their wholesale RFP agreement at risk. They live in constant fear that the prosperity they have all enjoyed for the past decade hangs like the Sword of Damocles on the whims of the United States. The people of the world secretly agree that the U.S. is not to be trusted because we might stop the flow of RF energy to any country at any moment. We have become like a drug pusher to RFP addicts," Matt summarized.

Amelius nodded in agreement saying, "Many do condemn you and this country for fulfilling that role. But isn't it the intent behind our decisions that identifies what is right and wrong? You had no intention of becoming a drug pusher. Let me continue with your medical metaphor to add the proper perspective. If several patients choose to abuse a prescribed drug, does that make their well-intentioned doctor a criminal?"

"I suppose not," Matt considered. "But what can be done now to help the world get back on track? I keep thinking of all the lost technological treasures lying beneath the Sphinx. Those discoveries could greatly ease the suffering of humankind. Am I right in believing that finding a similar Hall of Records could make a difference?"

"As you have come to expect, the answer to that question is both yes and no," Amelius replied gently. "Regarding your strategy to distribute RF energy, the world had an opportunity to choose a prosperous and peaceful coexistence. It will be no different with other technologies as they inevitably come to light. Any tool can do as much harm as it can good. The world is likely to test this quite soon, even as time is counted on the earth."

Matt asked, "You mean we are about to uncover another Hall of Records?"

"It's far more complicated than that," Amelius said, shaking his head. "See for yourself all the possibilities that lie ahead as things stand now." And with that, Matt saw the varied scenarios unfold before him, each projecting a different outcome based on the choices made and the combined attitudes of the people involved. He was overwhelmed at the countless options and the consequences for each.

"Now I see what you mean," said Matt. "Pandora's Box has already been opened. It is up to our two archeologists to find the remaining Hall of Records, to save humanity from itself. Do they know what is about to happen?"

"Yes, but not fully in their conscious state of mind," answered Amelius. "Once they saw how their discovery could influence the events of today, they both chose to play a key role in helping to avert the world crisis that is about to unfold."

Matt asked with a worried tone, "Are they up to the task?"

Amelius answered reassuringly, "Not on their own, but they have a great deal of help and support gathering to turn the 'seemingly impossible' into a wonderful new path for humanity."

Matt awoke with a start when the limousine door opened to reveal the portico entrance of Erin's friend's house. He hesitated, trying to recall the details of the strange encounter he had during the ride over. The man in luminescent white was not in the limo now and Matt wondered if he ever had been. No matter. Erin and their friends were waiting for him inside.

***

Archangel Halaliel visualized moving through time and space toward the palatial gardens that surrounded the vast estate. He loved the beautiful flowers that lined its walkways. Their imagined sweet fragrance would serve to anchor his consciousness until this memory became his reality. Halaliel had been here many times. Major events that directed the path of humanity for thousands of years had their beginnings in this beautiful place. He hoped Don Westbrook's memories of it would help him to make better choices during his incarnation as the President of the United States.

A moment later, Don and Halaliel walked side by side, each admiring the beautiful flowers that lined the walkways. Both men walked in silence until Don asked abruptly, "Do I know you?"

Halaliel smiled and said, "You know me well. It's been a while since we were in this place together, but your memories of your life here will soon return."

Don reflected for a moment and laughed as it came to him. "I am the First Citizen of Atlantis, the Head of State, and this is my home."

"Correct!" Halaliel confirmed. "What else do you remember of your life here?"

Don borrowed an apropos literary reference. "'These were the best of times, and the worst of times.' I had been assured that laser technology was the best thing that ever happened to Atlantis, and I regret that I trusted those two charlatans."

Halaliel shrugged and said, "You mean the scientists who discovered laser technology? Do you remember their names after all these years?"

"How could I forget?" Don said scornfully. "They are Doctors Mark Heston and Nuri Zayd."

"I was afraid of that," Halaliel said, almost to himself. "You can see no difference between the reckless Orion brothers of Atlantis and the two modern day archeologists. Heston and Zayd have progressed well since you were the First Citizen of Atlantis. They truly deserve your trust. In fact, your support of their expedition to the Yucatan can set right many of the things that went awry in this place." Halaliel spread his arms to encompass the entire fabled continent.

"Trust those liars?" Don hissed. "They swore to me that their fancy lasers would be the answer to our prayers. They promised that their new technology would perfect the country's communications, transportation, and defensive capabilities. I specifically asked them if lasers posed any danger, other than the obvious. They assured me their discovery was safe and had no downside."

"In their defense," Halaliel began, "they were not aware of the damaging back-blast vibrations when they brought their discovery to you. By the time they realized the unshielded back blast generated by laser beams could inundate the continent, it was too late. In some ways, their work could be compared to Madame Curie's discovery of radium. Lasers and radium can be quite dangerous, or helpful, depending upon their applications."

"So why didn't you warn me in time to save Atlantis?" Don asked.

Halaliel smiled wryly and said, "We did, repeatedly. Your conscious mind would not listen to your higher guidance because of the personal wealth and power that was at stake. Your highest priority was watching out for your own interests and keeping your citizens happy so you would be reelected. No amount of warning could be heard that might interfere with such limited goals."

Don was angry now with self-righteous indignation. "But if those crackpots had thoroughly researched and debugged their lasers before telling me they were safe, this lost continent would still be the center of the world!"

"It was a stroke of genius for you and Lucius, I mean Matthew Alexander, to create a Hall of Records that would preserve your civilization's technology for future generations."

"Now you're making fun of me," Don said cynically. "The Hall of Records may have been my idea, but my advisors insisted that Bimini would not be destroyed with the rest of Atlantis. Alexander, or rather, Lucius, was the one who commissioned the creation of the two safer locations in the Yucatan and the Egyptian land."

"And so we come to the purpose for our meeting here. Since the Hall of Records was originally your idea, it can rightfully be your legacy to restore what was lost. Why did you just turn down Matthew Alexander's request for financial support of Heston and Zayd's expedition in the Yucatan?"

"Are you kidding?" Don yelled; then quickly regained his composure. "I want nothing to do with those two, no matter what amazing discoveries they think they'll make. They ruined me and all of Atlantis with their reckless technology. We're getting along fine with just RFP. I don't need all those other gadgets that are hidden away in the Hall of Records. In fact, I don't think the world is ready for them. My goal is to keep the United States in firm control of the world without interference from those so-called scientists. I'll let some future President ruin his legacy by helping them to open Pandora's Box."

"Allow me to show you that Pandora's Box has already been opened. It is still your choice to make," Halaliel conceded, "but Mark and Nuri are very different people now than when you knew them in Atlantis. They have worked hard over many lifetimes to earn the chance to make right all the chaos they set in motion 12,000 years ago."

Halaliel started to show Don the various futures that rested upon his pending decisions. He was not surprised when Don simply disappeared in protest, unwilling to listen to Halaliel's suggestions. His obstinance and lack of trust in Mark and Nuri, would not allow him to listen to reason.

Chapter 4

Rodrigo Cortez settled back into his Corinthian leather chair near a large window. He gazed at the party his wife Fatima was hosting in their vast backyard. The swimming pool area covered nearly an acre and rivaled the popular resorts in Mexico City. Three casitas were equally spaced around the pool providing shade and had all the amenities that were available at the main house. There were perhaps 175 people enjoying themselves as they danced to the loud music. There was far more food, drink and cocaine than the partiers could consume. When you are 'El Jefe' of the largest drug cartel in Mexico, such extravaganzas are expected as a show of your wealth and conditional generosity.

He was 5'10", a powerfully built man with deep lines developing around his eyes and across his forehead. The years had not been kind to him. In his younger days, most people thought he was handsome, but it had been a long time since anyone had said so. El Jefe wanted to be feared more than admired. Fatima was the only person he loved and the only one whoever saw him smile.

From the second-story vantage point of his private office, Rodrigo was deep in thought but he was not thinking about his guests. His mind was preoccupied with three unusual items he held in his hand. He placed the items one at a time on his desk. The first was a crystal medallion measuring five centimeters in diameter and then two small clear vials. The vials were filled with a thick fluid; one was black and the other white. While the objects themselves were a curiosity, where they came from was what dominated his thoughts.

His number two man, Thiago, had brought these items to him along with a troubling explanation about why his plane was stranded on the Piedras Negras airstrip and four of his men were dead. The truck that was sent to offload a shipment of cocaine had received a radio message from the pilot. He said that three strange men were at the airstrip when the plane touched down. Two of the men ran off in one direction leaving the third man behind at the end of the clearing. The pilot indicated that they would get rid of the men to be sure the runway remained a secret.

Minutes later, when the truck arrived at the airstrip, they couldn't believe what they found. The pilot and one other man were shot dead on the tarmac, and the airplane's tires had been flattened. They caught a glimpse of a yanqui with a rifle disappearing into the jungle. Leaving two men behind to guard the plane, the rest took off after him. Then shots were fired and they altered their course to go in that direction.

From a distance, they could see two more of their men from the plane sprawled awkwardly on the ground. They also saw the three foreigners talking among themselves while standing near the bodies of their compadres. Rodrigo's men had opened fire with their automatic weapons, but the strangers managed to get away. They found the vials and crystal medallion on the ground after searching the area. These curious items were all the three men had left behind in their haste to escape.

Rodrigo couldn't understand why the intruders had killed his men but left the cocaine behind. The only description he had of the three men was that two were white and the third had darker skin. They were carrying full backpacks in addition to one rifle, so perhaps they were tourists camping out in the wild? But it would take far more than random tourists to kill four of his best trained men, especially when only one of them had a weapon.

He hoped that the vials and medallion would reveal something more than his men had told him. He picked up the transparent disc to examine it. He used a jeweler's loupe for magnification and inspected the crystal. It was high quality quartz but hardly worth killing for. He looked at the vials and assumed they had to contain drugs. He scrutinized the white vial. He could tell that it was not cocaine or heroin because there appeared to be miniscule beads floating inside a thick white liquid. Intuitively, the other vial interested him the most. It contained tiny beads as well, but the liquid and beads were black as night.

He considered the best way to open the vials since there was no obvious cap. The sealed ends looked like melted glass. He didn't want to take a chance on breaking the vials and spilling the contents. Instead, he picked up the butane cigarette lighter on his desk and attempted to melt the end of the black vial. He was surprised that the rest of the glass stayed cool to the touch as he held the tip to the hottest part of the flame. The tip of the vial glowed immediately but it took several minutes for the top to melt away. The lighter ran out of gas before he could open the white vial, but Rodrigo had what he wanted.

He didn't want to spill the vial's contents so he went to the master bathroom to get a cotton swab. He also grabbed a jar of his wife's face mask clay to seal it up again. After returning to his desk, Rodrigo stuck one end of the cotton swab far enough into the open vial to cover the tip in the black substance. He removed it and pressed some of the clay over the open end of the tube to seal it tight. Then he examined the end of the cotton swab with his loupe. As before, he could make out tiny black beads mixed with the black liquid.

He held the cotton swab to his nose and smelled it. It had no odor, which surprised him. He was finally curious enough to dab the blackened cotton swab on his tongue to see if it tasted like any drug he'd ever encountered. He found that it had no flavor. He decided to have a chemical analysis performed on the contents of the vials. To keep from spilling the liquid, he pressed the sealed ends of both vials into the face clay. He then pushed the cotton swab's clean end in the clay as well so that the blackened end was pointed up.

As he stood, Rodrigo realized he was ravenously hungry. He'd go downstairs to the party to eat his fill. Fatima would be pleased to have him join her as the event's gracious hosts.

Chapter 5

From the safety of their modest office and lab in Pasadena, California, Mark and Nuri considered their options. They were excited to have found the promising pyramid near Piedras Negras, but how could they go back there without risking their lives? What Mark had already seen was hardly another Hall of Records, but then he only saw the one room where he found the wooden box. They speculated that there could be a chamber somewhere inside the pyramid or below the ground that matched the one they discovered in Giza.

Nuri checked their phone messages and had more bad news. "Matt already met with President Westbrook. The answer wasn't just no, it was 'hell no.' The government won't fund any kind of expedition to Piedras Negras."

"Did he give a reason why?" asked Mark.

"He said Westbrook thinks we made the whole thing up about the Giza Hall of Records. He believes we stole the technology for RF energy from the Egyptians. Worse yet, he thinks the guys at JPL lied about viewing the still shots and video we took in the chamber beneath the Sphinx," said Nuri incredulously.

Mark was stunned. This wasn't the first time he had heard this conspiracy theory, but it was the first he heard that President Westbrook believed it. "So even the President thinks Egypt developed RF energy and we stole it from them? What's stopping him from arresting us and giving it all back?"

Nuri snorted and said, "Yeah right. Take the most lucrative invention in the history of humankind and turn control of it over to a third world country? Westbrook wouldn't hesitate to throw us under the bus, but he would never give up U.S. ownership of RF energy."

"What do you think happened to the digital pictures and video we took?" Mark continued, "Heck, we kept the memory discs secured, we had backups on several computers at JPL, and they still went missing. Clearly someone wanted that evidence to disappear, but why?"

"The Egyptian government had the motive but they couldn't have pulled that off. JPL is a very secure facility and there was no one around who didn't belong when the files and discs disappeared," Nuri recalled.

Jason walked into the room, catching the last of their conversation and asked, "What's this about the missing media files from Egypt?"

They told him what Matt had relayed about President Westbrook's suspicions and that there would be no government funding for their expedition. Jason just hung his head.

"But what about your discovery of the box inside the pyramid? You can use that to prove what you found," he offered.

"What we have is a wooden box with strange writing on it. That means nothing to a layman and especially not to someone who thinks what happened in Giza is a lie," Nuri explained.

"But if the writing on it comes from an advanced civilization, doesn't that provide the proof you need?" asked Jason.

Mark answered, "We still have all our notes explaining how to translate the written language from the Hall of Records, but that means nothing to 99.99% of the population. Just to look at it, even most archeologists would guess the language is ancient Klingon from the Star Trek books. As for the guys in the government who could validate that the language is real, nobody cares enough to prove the box is genuine."

"But we're going to need an army with a few million dollars of equipment to make sure the drug lords don't interfere with the expedition," Jason added. "The few people we have backing us now won't be able to fund a mission of that size."

"We still have good friends down the street at JPL," Nuri said, with a conspiratorial tone. "We may not have access to government money, but tapping into their satellite surveillance is possible through JPL. We already have the coordinates to point the cameras to see when the drug lords have quit looking for us, and it's safe to return. Then, hopefully, we can gather enough evidence to get all the funding we need!"

***

"Where are we?" Fatima asked her husband as they walked along a beautiful stretch of beach.

"I have no idea," Rodrigo answered. "I'm not even sure of how we came to be here."

They continued to walk along the shore allowing the shallow waves to wash the sand from their bare feet. Rodrigo had rolled up his linen pant legs but they were still getting wet. He didn't mind; the day was perfect and Fatima was smiling. In the distance, they saw a beautiful villa. It looked like an oasis set in the middle of this deserted beach.

Rodrigo asked, "Should we go there and see if anyone is home?"

Fatima let go of Rodrigo's hand and started running toward the villa. "I'll race you to it!"

He laughed and took off after her.

The next moment they found themselves inside the main courtyard of the villa. They saw a man dressed completely in white sitting next to an ornate fountain. He waved to them and the couple walked over to greet him.

"I am Amelius," said the handsome stranger. "And you are Rodrigo and Fatima Cortez. Your love for each other is inspiring. It is a love like yours that can save the world."

"What an odd thing to say," said Fatima. She couldn't remember meeting this man before, though he seemed to know both of them. She then asked, "What strange magic brought us here to your beautiful estate?"

"Actually," Amelius began, "many years ago in a lifetime you'll soon remember, this place was your home. This villa in Venezuela was where you lived after you were married in Spain. You two had made the hard decision, a pact before you were born, to prematurely end your time together on earth. And so you, Fatima, known then as Maria, died from yellow fever. You agreed to this so that Rodrigo, known then as Simón, could fulfill his purpose of freeing much of South America from its oppressive Spanish rule.

Both Rodrigo and Fatima had vague recollections of what Amelius had just told them. A moment later, memories of those times came flooding back with a torrent of emotions. Fatima, as Maria, remembered that their love would keep Simón from choosing to lead a revolt against Spain. Rodrigo, as Simón, vowed never to marry again in that lifetime. That was a promise he kept, though he lived for many years after Maria's death.

Amelius continued, "You, Rodrigo, were destined to accomplish much in this current life, but you refused to be separated from Fatima. Despite your abundant love for each other, being together greatly distracts you both. You were quite motivated to provide Fatima with incredible wealth and comfort. Unfortunately, you lost your way in your quest to become El Jefe."

Rodrigo was silent because he knew what Amelius had said was true. Despite his love for Fatima, he could not let go of Macizo. He liked being El Jefe because his wealth and power meant he could provide Fatima with everything she could want. He regretted who he had become.

Fatima exclaimed, "How is it that I know all these things to be true? It's like our thoughts are known to all and our memories have no limit."

Amelius answered, "You both are communicating at a higher level here than you do on earth. In this realm it is easier to see the truth of your thoughts. At this level, you've always known that your husband would not be able to hand the cartel over to anyone else. Your conscious mind refuses to focus on a reality that is in conflict with your earthly dreams for the future."

"Why are you telling us these things if we cannot change them?" Rodrigo asked.

"Nothing is stronger than your free will," Amelius answered. "It is always possible for you to undo any decision you make. However, you knew before your current births on earth that achieving happiness and growing old together in this lifetime was very unlikely. We are here to discuss that which is next for both of you."

"So what is going to happen?" they asked in unison.

"The world is in grave danger," Amelius explained. "A catastrophic event has been building for the past ten years. The two of you are in a unique position to save all of humanity, but this will require a great sacrifice from both of you."

"What kind of sacrifice?" Fatima asked with a nervous step back.

The serious expression on Amelius' face softened as he said, "Rodrigo, it is not by chance that you are the leader of the Macizo cartel. Everything you do draws the attention of your friends and enemies alike. That is why your death will not only be a great sacrifice, but a meaningful one as well."

"My death?" Rodrigo gasped, as Fatima reached for his hand.

"Yes, but your willingness to give your life will serve to save all of humanity!" Amelius exclaimed.

""I care nothing for humanity. They mean nothing to me," Rodrigo said with disgust. "I love Fatima with all my heart. As long as I can protect her, I am satisfied."

Undaunted, Amelius continued, "That is the beauty of your sacrifice. In dying you will stop the downward spiral of your life as El Jefe. Your death will indeed help to save Fatima, but she will have much work to do in order to save herself. Without a conscious knowing, she has been preparing for this event for many years. While you have been running Macizo, she has been with tutors learning much about history, languages and politics. Your wife's brilliant mind could not help but stay active, despite the privileged lifestyle you provided. It will soon be time for Fatima to measure up to the best that is within her. She must use her keen intellect to make the most of the opportunity your death will afford to all."

"Is this true, mi Amor?" Rodrigo turned to her in surprise.

"About my studies?" she asked rhetorically. "It is true. You never questioned how I spend my time, and you never complained that your wife could hold her own in all kinds of spirited debates with the educated wives of your elite acquaintances."

Amelius interrupted, "Allow me to show you the important roles you each have in the days to come."

The villa melted into darkness and a gigantic holographic movie began that revealed the current and future events threatening

248

the world. It showed the various outcomes that depended on the choices they each made. When the movie finished, the couple looked at each other in stunned silence.

"And this is the only way I can help Fatima to live a happy life?" Rodrigo knew the answer but was not ready to accept it.

Amelius smiled sympathetically saying, "Don't forget that you are saving the rest of humanity at the same time!"

Fatima said tearfully, "You say this is all for my happiness, but did you not see that my life will become a living hell before it gets better?"

"You did look happy after you reunited with your family, mi Amor. They will have nothing to do with you as long as we are together," Rodrigo said. That it was true did not cheer him much.

Fatima could not stop crying and finally said, "Rodrigo, I cannot do this."

He answered her, "Yes, you can. If anyone can, it is you. I will try to make this easy for you, my love." He turned to Amelius and said, "I accept my role in this. I accept my failure to achieve my true potential, but I am willing to make amends. You are right that I will hold Fatima back for as long as I remain on the earth."

Amelius placed a consoling hand on Rodrigo's shoulder and said, "You have chosen well, especially since the die has already been cast for your part."

Then he turned to Fatima, "It is your turn to remain behind to make a vital difference for humanity. Though you will soon find yourself walking through the valley of death, know that I will be with you every step of the way."

Fatima could feel herself fading back into darkness as she quickly lost consciousness.

Chapter 6

Doctor Sandoval knocked as he entered the room to check on Rodrigo's condition. His arrival had awoken Fatima from a disturbing dream. She was disoriented for a moment, but the doctor's presence helped her to focus on her husband's condition.

She stared hopefully as the doctor checked Rodrigo's vital signs. The deep lines in his forehead told her nothing had changed. He still didn't know what was ailing her husband. She had stayed at his bedside for three days and was exhausted from worry and lack of sleep. She watched as the doctor paused to write a note on his clipboard. His grave expression offered no encouragement.

To occupy her shaking hands, she fumbled through her purse and pulled out a mirror to assess her own condition. She could see that the strain of the past few days had taken its toll. She made no move to fix her makeup. For perhaps the first time in her life, she didn't care how she looked. Her husband might be dying. She knew there could be no life worth living without him.

Fatima had always been a strikingly beautiful woman. With her raven black hair, a model's looks, and athletically curvaceous form, it was no wonder she had caught a much younger Rodrigo's eye. From when they first met, he had been everything she wanted in a man. Her affections seemed to fuel his desire to succeed and to shower her with wealth.

Rodrigo had become widely feared and with good reason. It was the leaders of the other cartels who had given him the name El Jefe (the Boss). He had a natural talent for business and handling illicit money. He was a brutal leader who had little mercy for anyone who dared to defy him, but he never let his cruelty show when Fatima was near. He loved her and encouraged her to give the cartel's business a wide berth. Twenty years ago when they first met, Rodrigo was already employed by the Macizo cartel, though he had little use for drugs or violence. She understood why he took the job. His family came from poverty, which made working for the cartel his best chance to earn a good living. In their youth and innocence, they never considered that his connection to Macizo would be anything but temporary.

In those early years, Fatima and Rodrigo fantasized about the day they would have enough money to walk away from the cartel's perilous way of life. Rodrigo had no vices, as most people think of them, but his desire to pamper Fatima made him an ambitious man. He found that moving up in Macizo's ranks came at a great price. His desire to provide everything Fatima could want motivated him to do unthinkable things. Eventually, he found the wealth and power that came with being El Jefe was far more addictive than any drug the world offered.

Rodrigo now had more money than he could spend, but how do you walk away from an empire that generates billions of dollars each year? Too many people's livelihoods depended on his unique talent for growing, harvesting, refining and transporting cocaine into the United States. That's what he told Fatima when she would remind him of their shared dream of retirement. She came to hate the drug business almost as much as she loved her husband. And so she endured, hoping he would step down the moment another talented member of the cartel could take his place.

Her memories faded as she turned her sad gaze back to her husband. A nurse drew some blood samples and the doctor gently asked to speak to Fatima in the other room. She knew this would not be good news.

"Mil perdones. I have no idea what's wrong with him," were the first words out of the doctor's mouth. "His body reacts as if tumors are stealing all the nutrients from his blood. Since I had just performed his regular examination a few weeks ago, and he was in perfect health then, it must be something else."

"If it's not cancer, then what else could be wrong with him?" she asked.

"I'm hoping this new blood sample will tell us," he said gravely. "I will put a rush on it."

He left quickly, urging the nurse along and hoping Fatima wouldn't stop him. The doctor knew his own life could be dependent on Rodrigo's recovery. Drug lords and their families don't react well

251

to bad news and he feared he was the messenger they would make suffer.

Fatima turned to go back to Rodrigo's bedside. She attempted to hide her worries with a forced smile, but the mask would not stick. She was thinking of something cheerful to say when she realized Rodrigo was slowly moving his head from side to side. He tried to speak, but the effort was too much for him. His belly was bloated and his skin was dry and flaking away. He could not open his eyes because of the lack of tears.

It was ironic that Rodrigo had been both ravenously hungry and thirsty when the first symptoms of starvation and dehydration appeared. He simply could not get enough to eat or drink, no matter how much he devoured. Once he was full, he would force himself to vomit to make room for more.

He reached for her suddenly and coughed weakly as he tried to speak. She leaned forward and held his frail hand with both of hers, focusing intently on what he was about to say. With his last breath Fatima heard him whisper, "You must become El Jefe now!"

The incessant beeping in the hospital room abruptly changed to a steady tone. She looked up and cursed the heart monitor for telling her what she already knew. Her beloved Rodrigo was dead.

She was in shock, not just from losing her husband, but because his dying wish was that she take his place in the cartel. She wanted nothing to do with the dirty business that brought them both so much pain. She didn't care about the money, or supporting families, or even the power that came with being El Jefe. She wanted her innocent life back with the man she loved. Her shock turned to anger as her thoughts searched frantically for someone to blame for her husband's death. She swore she would find out who was responsible, and make them suffer as Rodrigo had.

***

Two days later, Doctor Sandoval tore open the envelope that contained Rodrigo's lab results and autopsy report. He scanned the documents hoping to find a scapegoat for El Jefe's demise. The latest results offered little he didn't already know. Rodrigo had died of dehydration. Had he not succumbed to that, it would not have been long before he would have died of malnutrition. The autopsy report gave details that he still had undigested food and liquids in his stomach and in his intestines. It was as if someone had shoved a seven-course meal into the stomach of a corpse, forcing it into the small intestines without any digestion at all.

Because no actual cause could be found for Rodrigo's death, the World Health Organization (WHO) had been called in and they took possession of his body. It was bad enough that El Jefe had died, but now he had to tell Fatima the WHO was about to investigate the drug lord's home in search of what killed him.

The doctor knew Fatima was inconsolable and desperate to find someone to blame for her husband's death. He decided to disappear before he became 'collateral damage' simply for being the bearer of this very bad news. He decided he would text the details of the report to her. Then he would destroy his cell phone and leave the country.

***

Thiago Bernal parked his car near the entrance to Rodrigo's palatial home. Fatima had told him after the party that her husband was sick and wanted his second in command to keep things running smoothly while he recovered. Thiago was used to managing things whenever El Jefe was unavailable, so he had thought little of it.

He had come to El Jefe's home in response to the text he'd received. It simply said, "Please meet with me as soon as you can." He assumed Rodrigo was feeling better and wanted an update on the cartel's business.

Thiago was destined to be a trusted leader in the Macizo cartel because his father, Diego Bernal, had been a lieutenant before his untimely death. Thiago rose higher than even his father for two reasons. First, he had a better education which helped him understand financing the complex dealings of illicit products. The other was that he and Rodrigo had been good friends going back to when El Jefe had just joined the cartel.

The two men had been inseparable in those early days. They closed the bars down together and always served as each other's 'wing man' when enticing the girls they met to go home with them. Both men had money, good looks and a way with words that made them popular wherever they went. They drifted apart once Rodrigo met Fatima, but they still remained good friends who knew they could always trust each other.

Thiago mentally organized his report as he walked through the huge doors of the main house. He decided to lead off with the good news. Production, shipments and revenues were up, which he knew would please his boss. He considered trying to avoid the situation at Piedras Negras, but he knew that would be at the top of Rodrigo's list. Thiago was frustrated at the lack of progress in finding those three men. He had already given El Jefe the peculiar items they left behind where Juan, Miguel and the others had been killed. He still had a dozen of his people searching for any sightings or news of the murderers.

When he knocked on the office door and heard Fatima answer, "Come in," he was confused. She was never involved in El Jefe's business and rarely went into his office. He opened the door and found her sitting at Rodrigo's desk. She gestured for him to sit in the visitor's chair facing her. With respectful confusion, he took a seat.

Thiago asked, "Where's El Jefe? He sent a text for me to meet him here."

Fatima was not her usual smiling self when she answered, "Rodrigo died yesterday and we still don't know what caused it. I'm El Jefe now." She stared directly at Thiago, obviously measuring his reaction.

He tried desperately to comprehend the impact of the words he had just heard. With Rodrigo dead, he was the next in command as leader of the Macizo cartel. He had always liked Fatima, but she was just a pretty woman. She couldn't run a billion dollar business the way he and Rodrigo had. He wondered for a moment if even he was up to the task, but he was certain this woman was not! His mind suddenly focused with laser-like precision. He knew he had to choose his next words carefully.

"Why do you want to be El Jefe?" he asked.

"My husband's dying words were 'You must become El Jefe now!'" she said flatly. "It is not so much a question of what I want as it is of fulfilling his last request."

Thiago thought for a moment before saying anything. She had played this perfectly. If people thought Rodrigo's final order was to make her the new boss, that would carry a lot of weight. Fatima was respected and anyone who opposed Rodrigo's previous orders had died horribly soon after. Thiago had to admit that this woman was already proving to be wiser than he would have guessed. If he immediately challenged her claim for control of the cartel, he was certain he would lose. He decided his best option would be to support her as the heir apparent. It did not matter how smart she was. How long could she lead the cartel before her shortcomings undermined her authority? He had learned years ago that patience was a virtue when it came to the volatile cocaine industry.

"Then I amend my question. Why have you asked me here?" Thiago's face was unreadable.

Fatima was relieved that he had not opposed her, at least for the moment. She was careful to maintain her air of confidence. She was sure that he would attempt a coup the moment she slipped, but until then, he could be very useful. With fire in her eyes she said, "The disease that killed Rodrigo has never been seen before. I believe he was murdered and I want to know who is to blame for his death."

Thiago considered her words and replied, "So do I. Where do we start?"

"What do you know about all of this?" Fatima asked, pointing to the medallion lying next to the cosmetic jar with the two vials and blackened cotton swab sticking out of it.

"Our men recovered those from Piedras Negras. They believe the three *cabrons* who killed our men dropped them in their haste to escape," he answered.

"This jar is from my medicine cabinet. Are you saying the three men were carrying all these items?" she asked, truly confused.

"No. The black and white vials were still sealed when I gave them to El Jefe…I mean Rodrigo. I brought them here shortly before your guests arrived for the fiesta. The crystal medallion was with them. The cotton swab and jar were not," Thiago explained.

Fatima suddenly pushed her chair back from the desk. "These things must be infected with the disease that killed my husband." Then she said with a forced calm, "If the disease was airborne, I would have it already. Rodrigo developed symptoms the same day as the fiesta. What else can you tell me about this?"

He thought for a moment and said, "At the party, he told me he wanted the substance in the vials tested because he thought they might be some kind of new drug. I don't think he had the chance to do that before he became ill."

Fatima said, "Thiago, we have little time. The World Health Organization is coming here to investigate the cause of Rodrigo's death. They apparently have never seen a victim of this disease, or virus, or whatever it is, before. If I'm right, the contents inside those vials will lead us to my husband's murderers. We must get them out of here, and privately tested, before the WHO can interfere."

"I'll have them taken to our closest refining lab. We know how to handle hazardous materials," he paused, "as long as you are right in thinking the disease is not contagious through the air. I'll hire a team of medical experts to buy the needed equipment to test everything. They'll know what to do to keep our people safe," Thiago reassured her.

Fatima nodded her approval. "In the meantime, please summon our top leaders in the cartel. Together, we will announce Rodrigo's murder, and what must be done from here."

Thiago nodded in agreement while silently thinking how smart this woman was to have him present her as the new El Jefe. Since he was the only real competitor for controlling the Macizo cartel, showing the others that she had his support would avoid all conflicts, for the moment.

Chapter 7

Dawn was breaking when Mark and Nuri pulled into the parking lot of their modest office complex. Jason was waiting for them in his car playing with his smartphone between sips of coffee. Renting offices that were just a half mile away from Jet Propulsion Laboratory (JPL) was no accident. The eggheads at JPL had long ago accepted the three of them into their family.

Matt, Mark, and Nuri had insisted that JPL be the only place that knew how to produce RF sending and receiving crystals. That way no one else would be able to gain unauthorized control of the technology. They also withheld key symbol translations so that no one, outside of a few trusted people at JPL, would know how to completely translate the ancient language. Without that specific information, other scientists would learn the language, but they would not be able to understand why RF technology worked.

On this opportune morning, Louis, a JPL scientist and friend, had agreed to help them tap into the satellite surveillance maintained by the U.S. government over Central America. JPL had an ongoing research contract with Uncle Sam that included an authorized portal to the U.S. satellite network. Since hacking the portal had little to do with their current government research, they were about to break a few federal laws. No one was worried about being caught because the satellites over Central America were on an automated schedule that was rarely monitored. Mark and Nuri called Louis on his cell phone as he sat at his work station in JPL. He was able to guide them through several impressive security firewalls without touching his computer. Unless someone was recording their phone call, only Mark and Nuri were liable for the digital intrusion.

When it came to hacking, Jason was every bit as good with computers as the nerdy scientists talking excitedly on the phone. He saw they had it under control, so he decided to stretch out on his favorite overstuffed couch. He spent a lot of time on that couch, especially when they started talking RFP technobabble that no one but Mark, Nuri and a few JPL scientists understood.

Jason mused back to the events that unfolded ten years earlier when the three of them returned from Egypt. His new assignment was to protect Mark and Nuri, as well as the JPL facility, from harm. Every new RFP discovery reinforced the importance of these scientists and their work. Jason kept watch as the politicians lined up to visit JPL's labs. It wasn't much later when they started jockeying for position to control the entire project through Washington D.C. Jason had soon realized where the real danger to his friends would come from. He was convinced that if Mark, Nuri, or the JPL scientists ever objected to the government's directives, they would be thrown under the proverbial bus.

Jason believed Matt Alexander meant well, but the man was far too trusting and ethical to slug it out with the power brokers in Congress. What worried Jason the most was the President's reputation for 'doing the right thing.' Everything they had discovered about RF technology had come from that chamber in Egypt. In one sense, Jason grabbing the RFP crystal as they fled could be interpreted as theft. Since the original RFP crystal was found in Egypt, would President Alexander decide to turn the technology over to the Egyptian government? Legally, that might make sense, but it would be a disaster for the rest of the world. Jason shook his head thinking about how life would be today if Egypt had become the sole owner of RF technology. Even now, Jason was sure that he had made the right decision to keep that from happening.

As he drifted off to sleep, he barely heard Mark and Nuri's excited voices confirming they were looking at satellite images of Piedras Negras.

***

Jason awoke with a start. He was no longer lying on the couch in the cluttered office. He recognized where he was, but he knew his surroundings couldn't be real. He found himself kneeling on a training mat in his favorite dojo. This had been where he first learned martial arts, but the building had been razed years ago. He scanned the room for other people, but he saw no one. Then he heard what must have been his subconscious say, "No one is ever truly alone."

He thought silently, "Where did that come from?"

The gentle voice spoke again, "You are not talking to yourself. I am here with you."

He couldn't remember having experienced a dream like this before, but what else could explain it?

The internal voice added, "Nothing will harm you here. This place was created from your past memories to put you at ease. Once you allow your fears to subside, you will see the truth of this."

Jason realized he had gone into his "Delta Force" mode and was ready for a fight. As he allowed himself to relax, he saw a bright light off in the distance. The light seemed to come toward him until a shape emerged that appeared to be human. It wasn't clear if the brilliant light was separate or a part of this remarkable man. Jason got to his feet to greet the stranger.

"I am called Halaliel. We have worked together in the Egyptian land, but several years have since passed, as you measure it."

"You do seem familiar, but I can't imagine where our paths would have crossed. I put my twenty years in as a soldier in the U.S. Army. My guess is that you did not spend any time in the military," Jason said with a tone that was more of a question than a statement.

"When we last met, you graciously offered to put yourself in harm's way to help Mark and Nuri discover, and safely escape from, the Hall of Records in Giza. You accepted the role of securing the crystal that would have otherwise been left behind. In many ways, you are as responsible as they are for bringing RF energy back to humankind," Halaliel explained.

Jason vaguely recalled the previous dream-like encounter Halaliel had just mentioned. With growing lucidity, he remembered seeing all the future paths the world might take. He had been shown that the best outcome for everyone could only happen if he went with Nuri and Mark into the chamber. It would be his job not only to secure the RFP crystal, but to make sure both men were unharmed in the process.

"So here we are again," Jason said, remembering clearly now. "I guess things didn't go as well as we'd hoped?"

Halaliel laughed, "Don't be so hard on yourself. How much better off is the world today than if a global war had occurred ten years ago? You are to be commended for your part in averting that horrible tragedy."

"Thank you for that. Knowing what to do is far less clear when consciously making decisions on earth. So are you just here to give me an 'attaboy' or has something new come up?" Jason asked.

"Actually, we're here to discuss an interesting choice you made a couple of months after securing the crystal that was not expected. As a result of that choice, you are about to be faced with an even greater challenge than before. Unless you trust the people around you, you cannot succeed in finishing what you have started," Halaliel said gravely. "Always remember that forcing your will upon others, regardless of your good intent, never works in perpetuity."

"That interesting choice you mentioned," Jason prefaced, "would that be when I removed all of JPL's copies of the media files Mark and Nuri recorded in the chamber?"

"Yes, but don't forget they are not gone forever. You still have copies of those files hidden away. Your surprising choice to remove them put the President, Mark and Nuri in a precarious position when they were asked to reveal what led to the discovery of RF energy. They declined to repeat publicly what they had disclosed privately because the story of what happened in the Hall of Records was too fantastic to believe without proof. Can you explain why you chose to hide the files?" Halaliel smiled.

"At first, I thought the President would simply give the crystal and media files to the Egyptian government. Then it occurred to me that he was such a 'do-gooder' he might give RF energy to the world for free. I figured that having no proof of what took place in that Egyptian chamber was enough of a game-changer that Matthew Alexander would 'do the right thing.' It seems I was right. He decided to nationalize RF energy, and the world is better off for it," Jason said, a little defensively.

Halaliel continued, "If you were convinced you had done the right thing, why didn't you eventually share what you did with your friends?"

Jason thought for a moment and confessed, "At first I wasn't sure how they'd react. Then it was clear that they would not have agreed with my decision. The longer I waited, the harder it was to explain, so I didn't."

"Do you remember seeing the holograms inside the Hall of Records? The JPL scientists would have discovered many other technological marvels if you hadn't hidden the files with the videos and still images. Also, Mark and Nuri would have quickly located the Hall of Records in the Yucatan, had you made a different choice," Halaliel said, watching for Jason's reaction.

"But wouldn't admitting that RF technology came from under the Sphinx support Egypt's claim to it?" Jason exclaimed. "I just couldn't see taking that chance. Even today the Egyptian government claims we stole RF technology from them. And that's based solely on rumors. Imagine if they had proof!"

Halaliel stepped to Jason's side and gestured before them. The alternative histories of the past 10 years ran by in rapid succession like epic movies on a screen. They showed how differently the years could have unfolded. "You can see here that Egypt would have made claims of RFP ownership regardless of what you chose to do. Nevertheless, with or without removing the media files, the status of your country's RFP ownership would not have changed. The JPL scientists, using the translations provided by Mark and Nuri, would have rediscovered many of the technologies you saw in the Giza Hall of Records. The true effect of your choice worked to limit their discovery to RF energy alone."

"Is it too late to change that?" Jason asked with remorse.

"What is done is done," Halaliel said flatly, but then he brightened. "Don't forget that everyone is given as many opportunities as needed to eventually make the right choice. You will soon be able to help put the world onto a better path."

The holographic movies with alternative futures played before them showing Jason the choices he would soon face. He could see how his lack of trust in the President, Mark and Nuri had hurt more than helped things along. He also saw future possibilities that could help guide the world toward a better way to live. There was likely to be great fear, suffering and tragedy ahead for the world regardless of what he did. But he also saw that humanity could pull together to get through this. The best results would only come from placing his trust in his friends, and in humanity to do the right thing. That had always been difficult for him, but he saw no better way.

With his decision made, Jason's consciousness drifted away allowing one of the movies before him to become a pleasant dream from which he would soon awake.

Chapter 8

Fatima sat at Rodrigo's desk and opened the envelope containing the preliminary test results of the two vials. Thiago had moved quickly to get the ampules out of the house and secretly analyzed using their own private labs and people. The World Health Organization had descended the following day collecting swabs of surfaces throughout her home. She knew better than to resist their inspection or their next visit would include the *Policía Federal* to remove whatever they wanted.

She was told that it would take at least another week before the WHO would offer any meaningful findings from Rodrigo's autopsy. The report Fatima received came quickly because the medical experts at Macizo's labs had been working with human test 'volunteers.' Thiago had ordered his men to target members of competing cartels whose people were unlucky enough to be spotted and grabbed off the street. With no ethical or procedural barriers to hinder them, they were able to discover a great deal about the vials' contents in a week.

The disease was not airborne, nor was it transmitted by human contact. It had to be injected or ingested for the illness to take hold. Once inside the body, the infection spread at an alarming rate. The concentration of microbes required to infect a body was measured in parts per trillion. 'The Glut' was what Macizo's lab people called the disease. It was short for the gluttonous cravings it brought on once someone was infected.

The report went on to describe what the disease did to the human body. Fatima had witnessed this already with Rodrigo, but the study confirmed that her personal observations were consistent with the research. The test subjects became absurdly hungry and thirsty within minutes of exposure to the compound. Depending on their level of good health at the time of infection, they died within days because of severe dehydration. Even if that symptom could be cured, a horrible death due to extreme malnutrition was inevitable over the following weeks.

Oddly enough, humans were the only species affected by the disease. Several types of mammals, reptiles, fish and insects ingested tainted food and water without becoming ill. It was as if this disease had been specifically designed to attack humans. The carrier agent for the disease was proven to be silicon-based. The Glut was the first of its kind since all other illnesses were caused by things that were carbon-based.

Fatima read the next part of the report with mixed emotions. The vial containing the white liquid proved to be a cure. Had they known to administer a tiny amount to Rodrigo at any point before he died, he would have recovered completely. The antidote was not difficult to duplicate. All that was required was to add the tiniest amount of the existing cure to a precise mixture of water and silicon. Given that the antidote was a biological anomaly, using traditional research methods to find a cure for The Glut was highly unlikely.

The cartel's people were still experimenting with the strange disease to see what made it thrive in humans, as well as other possible uses and antidotes. She would be updated on any new findings as they occurred.

Fatima noticed that her hands were shaking again and the words on the page blurred before her. She took a moment to control her grief. Doing so transformed her sorrow into anger. She wanted the people responsible for Rodrigo's death to suffer as no one ever had. She began to consider how the black substance could be used to her advantage. Possessing a deadly poison that was still unknown to the world would make her enemies tremble. She also knew that having such power could backfire on her.

Her jumbled thoughts tried again to ferret out who was responsible for Rodrigo's death. She knew almost nothing about the three men who started this fiasco in Piedras Negras. Was her husband's death by design or an accident; not that it would change her disposition toward them. Why had they been there in the first place? If their intention was to hijack the cocaine shipment, wouldn't they have brought an army of men instead of a disease filled vial? Even when they had the chance to steal the cocaine, they chose instead to kill the men and disable the airplane. She felt sure that their motives had to be more ominous than hijacking one shipment of cocaine, or killing a few of the cartel's foot soldiers.

She considered if Rodrigo had been their intended target. But then why would they go to Guatemala instead of Mexico to poison his food or drink with the toxic substance? Was it really their plan to leave the deadly vial behind in the jungle hoping that somehow it would end up in the hands of El Jefe? If that was true, leaving the vial behind as they did was a stroke of genius. But then why would they leave the cure behind as well? She surmised that they probably carried the cure along with them to avoid an accidental poisoning. In that case, leaving both vials behind was a mistake rather than part of their strategy. What kind of idiots would have such a well-thought out plan only to drop the vial with the cure right next to the one with the disease?

·The story Thiago had told her was that the foreigners killed four of their well-trained cartel soldiers. Then they managed to escape the pursuit of several more Macizo soldiers who arrived in the transport truck. One of the three outsiders was not a yanqui (white man), but they must have had extensive jungle training to have evaded capture, or being killed. She considered the likelihood that, given these peculiar circumstances, Rodrigo would want to personally examine the items these curious strangers dropped in their haste to escape. She knew the odds were 100%, but how would the murderers know that?

Fatima speculated on reasons why the men would have those items in the first place. They had to be planning to poison someone working with Macizo. She couldn't imagine another reason for them to be in that remote place. Maybe they intended to leave the diseased vial where it would be found on the airstrip? If Rodrigo's people had caught them in the act, then the norteamericanos (men from North America) might have been trying to dispose of the evidence in the jungle as they fled.

In her grief, she had trouble following her own logic. The only thing she knew for certain was that she would never see her husband again. Whether El Jefe died because of bad luck, an accident, or a deliberate assassination, she couldn't bring him back. All she had left in life was to make sure that anyone connected to his death, however innocently, would suffer as he had.

Then she remembered the crystal medallion that had been found with the vials. She picked up the translucent disk and inspected it to see if there was anything to it she had not noticed before. It was about the size of a large coin and had some odd looking symbols carved on one side. That thought caused her to flip the medallion in the air trying to guess if it would come up heads or tails.

She kept flipping and catching the crystal repeatedly, almost hypnotized by the flashing lights reflecting off its revolving surface. She tossed it higher until the crystal's arc went beyond her reach. She gasped when she realized the medallion was headed toward the decorative obsidian sphere sitting on the corner of the desk. She cringed as it struck the volcanic ball-shaped rock and expected it to shatter. Instead, the medallion stuck to the top of the stone and didn't move. There it stayed, impossibly balanced on its edge, like an Olympic gymnast who had gracefully executed the perfect dismount.

Fatima walked around the desk and bent over until her face was just inches away from it. Nothing she could see explained how the medallion remained balanced on its edge on the curved surface. She carefully positioned her index finger over the top of the crystal and lowered it until she made contact. Suddenly, the disk shown very bright, but without any heat. She was so shocked she jumped back removing her finger from the crystals' edge. The light faded immediately, but the medallion's precarious position had not changed.

She tried it again by lightly touching her finger to the top edge of the crystal. The amazing light show returned, but this time Fatima didn't recoil. She saw that the crystal was projecting a colorful, panoramic holographic movie. She stepped to one side to take in the full scene. The light disappeared again the moment she broke contact with the medallion. Standing to the side, she touched the edge for the third time and watched and listened in awe as the holographic movie played to the end. She kept her finger in place for another minute but nothing else happened. When she pulled her hand away, the crystal toppled to the floor.

Fatima was reeling from what she had just experienced. The moving pictures had visually communicated the story of the disease, but that wasn't all. She witnessed the story behind many wondrous things, including RF energy. She had heard a perfect Spanish narration that described what she was seeing in great detail. The movies looked like they had taken place long before her native language had been developed, which made the whole event even more mysterious. She decided to watch the holographic show again and look closely for clues.

She picked up the crystal and saw the medallion had an interior fracture at its core. It resembled the kind of star-shaped crack a car's windshield gets when a wayward pebble strikes it on the highway. That fracture had not been there a few minutes before. Fatima tried several times to get the movie to play again, but nothing happened. The crystal would no longer balance on its edge despite her numerous attempts at flipping it onto the shiny obsidian sphere. Then she duplicated the exact position of her finger holding the medallion on top of other objects on the desk. Nothing she tried did any good. The crystal medallion would never again tell its story.

***

Dr. Steven Welch was in charge of researching new pathogens for the CDC, or Center for Disease Control, in Atlanta. He had tissue and blood samples from a corpse in Mexico and the accompanying autopsy report was on his desk. The primary cause of death was from dehydration. There was little else about this disease anyone knew with certainty.

The World Health Organization (WHO) had contacted him to further investigate this case because of the potential biohazard it presented. Dr. Welch managed the world's best lab, technicians, and equipment to handle such a potentially dangerous disease. There was every reason to treat this case as a Biosafety Level 4 (BSL-4), which was reserved for the deadliest biological threats.

From what Dr. Welch had been told, this toxin caused every system in the body that processed food or water to shut down. Their hypothesis was that it was transmitted through ingestion only. Apparently, it was not spread through the air or through physical contact. Still, it was a very effective way to kill a lot of people.

The WHO report mentioned that the victim was the leader of the Macizo cartel in Mexico. It also indicated that he was the only casualty they'd found so far. With no other reported victims, his death could have been an assassination. In the violent world of cartels, their leaders are always targets, and this method of killing would get past most security measures.

If it was murder, the good news was that the disease was being controlled rather than running loose. The bad news was that this substance, properly contained or not, threatened the existence of humanity. Dr. Welch took a moment to consider his next move. He had a responsibility to report his findings to the WHO. They had to be warned of the potential pandemic this new disease could cause. He also had a responsibility as an employee of the U.S. government to protect his fellow citizens. He decided to call the Director of Health and Human Services (HHS) first, and let him decide what to do next.

Chapter 9

Matt answered his cell phone with a surprised smile. "Gil Kowalski! What does our Ambassador to Mexico want with an old, retired politician like me?"

Gil laughed, "You stay pretty busy for a retired guy. When we last spoke, you mentioned those two archeologists were looking near the Mexican border for another Hall of Records. Well something unusual hit my desk just now that my gut says is connected to your friends. Can you tell me if they were down this way a couple of weeks ago? And if so, did anything unusual happen?"

Matt thought for a moment and asked, "Are you wearing your Ambassador's hat or can I answer plainly without having it repeated?"

"Ouch!" Gil said at having their conversation take this turn. "Unless you tell me otherwise, this will just be two old friends catching up with each other."

"Fair enough," Matt replied. "A few weeks ago they were exploring a remote area of northern Guatemala called Piedras Negras. They surprised a small plane full of bad guys and contraband that required plenty of guns for protection. Our friends barely escaped and had to dodge bullets as they ran through the jungle. Ironically, their random escape route led them to a pyramid that was hidden underneath the jungle foliage. To make a long story short, they found a wooden box inside the pyramid containing two vials and two small crystals. They still have the box but they spilled its contents on the ground in their haste to get away. They haven't gone back for fear the bad guys are still looking for them."

Gil asked, "Do they know anything about a new disease that affects the body's ability to digest food and drink?"

Matt continued, "I'm not happy to hear you already know about that. The engraved warning on the box, and inside the pyramid, apparently mentions a plague. Mark and Nuri don't yet know how the vials and crystals might be related. Mark said that the language used for the warning was the same as what they discovered in that chamber under the Sphinx. Please tell me this is not why you're calling!"

"I wish I could," said Gil. "The CDC contacted the HHS and then the White House with a report of a new disease that could potentially become a pandemic. So far, it has not spread beyond the first victim. However, that victim was the leader of the Macizo drug cartel. You probably remember that they are the biggest supplier of cocaine to the USA from south of the border."

Matt let out a heavy sigh. "So the timing of the vials and crystals found in the pyramid coincides with this drug lord's mysterious death from a new disease? If those items were related to the death of this guy from Macizo, then this could easily be a pandemic in the making. I'll make sure that the archeologists translate everything they can from the box and get back to you."

"Good," Gil said. "Do I still need to stay quiet about this? Maybe I can get help from the White House?"

"I don't think you'll find President Westbrook in a very receiving mood where any of us is concerned," Matt replied, clearly frustrated. "But considering what's at stake, feel free to share anything we've discussed that you think will help. Can you get me a copy of the CDC report?"

"I think so," said Gil. "Since Patient Zero came from Mexico, I have a lot more clout than if it had started somewhere else."

"Under the circumstances," Matt offered, "we need to put each other on speed dial. I have my own gut feeling this will get worse before it gets better."

***

Fatima continued to analyze every scenario she could imagine. She still didn't know who had killed Rodrigo, but she was certain the United States was ultimately to blame. She surprised herself with another possibility. The U.S. government must have realized they couldn't stop the flow of cocaine into their country through defensive measures alone. What better way could there be to block the flow of drugs than by getting the cartels to stop on their own? So what was the best way to send a convincing message of their new strategy to all the cartels at once? Through the chilling murder of Mexico's largest drug cartel leader, El Jefe of Macizo!

What if the U.S. had been watching Macizo's movements around Piedras Negras? After weeks of monitoring, they could have decided how to make the vial with the disease and the crystal medallion curiously irresistible. She convinced herself that they developed an elaborate ruse to draw attention away from their true purpose.

Perhaps those three men had been waiting for the plane at the airstrip. They ran expecting the Macizo members to chase after them. Their real mission was to 'accidently' drop the contaminated vial and medallion knowing those unusual items would be given to El Jefe. She was almost fooled by the holographic technology the medallion had demonstrated. However, recording the narration in Spanish was a foolish mistake for such clever men to make. What would an ancient culture dating back thousands of years know of the Spanish language? The only part that didn't fit was leaving a vial with the cure behind as well. She had to assume leaving the second vial was unintended. Assuming it was a mistake, the rest of the story Fatima had pieced together made sense.

Once she was clear on who was to blame for her husband's murder, her plan for retribution almost formed itself. She sent a text to Thiago to meet with her immediately in her office and he arrived within the hour. Fatima already had a map of North America spread out on the small conference table. She invited Thiago to join her there.

"I have a plan to avenge Rodrigo's death," she began.

Thiago was surprised but hid his emotions under a stony expression. "You know where the yanquis can be found?"

"I'm not talking about punishing those men in Piedras Negras, I'm talking about retribution against the entire United States!" she said with a wicked smile.

Thiago knew she would eventually shoot herself in the foot, but who would have guessed it would happen so quickly? Still, he needed to carefully set the stage so he would not be blamed for whatever she had planned. "You want to go to war with the USA? That is a fight we can never win."

271

"We can win, but not through force. We can bring them down with the threat of their own disease," she said with a vengeful tone. "We have both the disease and the antidote, so our own people will be safe no matter what they do."

"But how will that threaten them if they already have the cure?" Thiago reminded her.

"We too had the cure but Rodrigo still died horribly because he didn't receive it," Fatima explained. "The disease kills so quickly that many of their people will die because the cure won't be distributed in time to save them. Their government would want to avoid mass panic and the price would be many lives lost to keep the peace."

"And what of our own people?" Thiago countered. "How will we get the cure to them in time if the disease spreads to Mexico?"

"Relax! I don't believe it will get to that point. Even if it does, we have already produced large quantities of the antidote in our labs with a plan for immediate mass distribution. Under the right conditions, the cure spreads just as fast as the disease, so making enough of it was easy once we learned how to duplicate it. We would have ample warning to distribute the cure before the disease ever reached Mexico."

Fatima continued with the bottom line to her plan, "My goal is to make the United States share their RF energy secrets. If they do give us that information, I will pass it on to the world. The subsequent loss of energy revenues from the other nations will quickly ruin their economy. If they don't comply, many of their citizens will die before they can act to save them," she said, with a confident nod.

Thiago pointed out, "You are effectively threatening the U.S. with biological war knowing just a few people are responsible for killing your husband? I'm all for avenging Rodrigo's death, but there has to be a better way that only targets the people who did this."

Fatima laughed. "Do you really think so? Wasn't it the USA's arrogance and misuse of power that ultimately killed Rodrigo? They think their government can do whatever it wants to anyone, or any country, that disagrees with them. That attitude of hubris has also become ingrained in its people. It is time to teach them all a lesson in humility."

Thiago considered her words. They echoed a long-held sentiment by many throughout the world. He had made it clear he was against her plan, so appearing to change his mind by supporting her now was in his best interests. She would be responsible while he would be seen as a good soldier who followed her orders. He was sure he would be able to put a stop to this before it got out of hand. "What is it you want me to do, El Jefe?"

Chapter 10

President Donald Westbrook entered the Situation Room to find the NSC members waiting for him. They started to stand as he entered, but he told them to keep their seats. They had only one agenda item and he wanted to get right to it.

He opened his portfolio with the Presidential Seal and began reading aloud, "Mr. President, the United States is known for its arrogance and persistent interference in the affairs of other countries. Your policy regarding the wholesale distribution of RF energy is the perfect example of both. Your self-appointed position as the world's moral judge ends today.

"You must turn over digital copies of your complete RF energy files so that we may share them with the world. That includes the initial research, production of the sending and receiving crystals, and any subsequent discoveries your scientists have made to date. Failure to comply will result in our unleashing the most lethal disease ever seen upon the citizens of the United States. Once all nations have their own direct access to RF energy, the world will no longer be forced to accept the USA as its moral judge and jury.

"You already know of the biological weapon we have named The Glut. The World Health Organization is holding the body of the first casualty of your arrogance. Refusal to meet our demands by the following deadlines will result in unleashing this disease upon your citizens. You have 12 hours to post your written intent to comply. Assuming you do, you will be given no more than 48 hours to upload a complete set of RFP files. If you miss either of those deadlines, the worst pandemic the United States has ever seen will begin."

He added, "It closes with the instructions for posting our answer to their terms using a dark internet website. Before you ask, no, the people behind this extortion attempt can't be traced through this communication or the dark website."

Don gestured to the Director of National Intelligence, Max Atwater, passing control of the briefing to him. Atwater was in charge of Homeland Security, the CIA, and the FBI.

"As the President just said, we have not yet been able to locate the people behind this plot. Here are the working assumptions we have made to determine how to defend ourselves. Number one, this threat is real as is evidenced by the CDC's confirmation of the first victim's body. Number two, if this threat is sanctioned by a sovereign government, they would have to be a member of OPEC. No one else would want to give RF energy away for free. Three, these terrorists have a base of operations in Mexico because that's where the first victim, Rodrigo Cortez, died. Four, they have access to a private laboratory capable of properly handling a BSL-4 biohazard. Otherwise, they would be in as much danger as they have threatened us with. That limits our options to compliance with their ultimatum, or to find them and destroy all traces of the toxin before they can deploy it."

Don asked, "Is there a cure for this thing? If not, do we at least know how to kill it while it's still in their lab?"

"As yet, there is no known cure for the sickness. The disease itself dies at temperatures above boiling water, but then, so do human bodies."

"What connection does this Rodrigo Cortez have to all of this?" Don wanted to know.

Max answered, "We don't know as yet, other than he died as a result of exposure to the substance. He was a cartel drug lord with many enemies. It is our best guess that the terrorists targeted him to flex their muscles. By killing the Macizo leader, they proved they could get to anyone they wanted. Rodrigo was called El Jefe by the other cartels. He didn't have many friends that weren't bought and paid for.

"How do these terrorists think they can be safe in Mexico if the U.S. is infected with the disease?" This time it was General Myer of the Joint Chiefs asking the question.

"Our theory is that the terrorists are not permanently based in the western hemisphere. If they did make good on their threat, they must believe they can safely quarantine themselves and their people. They could also have developed a cure, but the CDC doesn't think so. This disease has been the world's best kept secret. Other than the one victim in Mexico, no one has seen another case, or even heard of this Glut being developed. The CDC says the disease may

275

have been discovered by accident. It is apparently silicon based and leaves our doctors at a loss to explain how it infects humans."

"Silicon, like sand?" President Westbrook asked. "Since RFP cut the economic legs out from under the old OPEC nations, I can see why you're looking there for our extortionists."

"I wish pinning this on OPEC was that easy," Max replied with a sigh. "Please keep in mind that the terrorists' demands are intended to give everyone direct access to RF energy. It seems unlikely that those nations would pass up an opportunity to line their pockets. Of course, they could be lying about passing the secrets onto the world. In that case, they might be planning to become our competitor.

"There is another way this plot could subtly benefit OPEC nations," he continued. "Several Middle Eastern countries are not wholesale RFP customers because they want nothing to do with the USA. If they can get the technology for themselves without having to do business with us, they could join the rest of the world's RFP users without having to reveal that they threatened us with a WMD to get it. Our analysts are developing other scenarios, but those seem the most likely."

"Have we found their base of operations in Mexico?" asked General Myer.

"We are still working on that from several angles. They had to procure the right lab equipment to handle such a serious biohazard, so we're tracking all such sales and shipments into Mexico for the past year. Also, we are working with the Mexican government to inspect their medical facilities, in case someone is storing the disease cultures in plain sight. Our best lead, oddly enough, may come from RFP crystals," Max said slyly.

Don's eyes narrowed with this unexpected turn. "How can we locate these terrorists through RFP?"

"We learned some time ago that RF energy has a traceable signal if you know how to look for it. Our own scientists figured out how to track the exact location of any RFP user through the specific frequency they are assigned and billed under. If we get a lead on a particular medical facility, we can identify the RFP signals going in and out of the place to cross-reference which users or groups frequent that location," Max said, surprising the room.

"If you can nail that down, I can guarantee our forces will destroy any trace of that disease and the lab," the JCS commander assured them. "Mr. President, this will require approval from the Mexican government. Getting them to provide the contact information on specific RFP users will require letting them know of this threat. Also, using enough firepower to ensure total destruction of the facility will inevitably lead to some collateral damage."

Don nodded his agreement and said, "Regarding the destruction of the lab and terrorists in Mexico, I'd rather ask for forgiveness than permission. Max, keep tracking them down and gather proof of their involvement for the Mexican government. General Myer, I need your people to develop the appropriate attack scenarios so you are ready to go when a location is identified. Because of the limited time available to vet the possibilities before the deadline, we may be forced to take out numerous suspected targets simultaneously. Also, post a response to that dark website saying we will comply. That will buy us some more time."

***

Thiago was in R.E.M. sleep floating in a dream he wouldn't remember upon waking. Halaliel waited patiently for the dream to end before asserting himself into Thiago's consciousness. While he waited, he searched the Akashic records for Thiago's safest memories and locations on earth. He found one appropriate to use as the backdrop for this ethereal meeting.

"Hello Thiago," said Halaliel. He was casually leaning against a counter in a posture of friendly amusement. He held a steaming churro, and the familiar scent of the Spanish pastry instantly reminded Thiago of where they were.

"Do I know you? This looks like my mother's cocina from my youth, but you are not familiar to me."

"No, you do not know me, but I'm here to help you," Halaliel said gently. He set down the cinnamon pastry and his gaze became penetrating. "You are about to carry out a horrific plot against the United States. I want you to see all the alternatives available to you."

277

"You mean the biological attack on the U.S.?" he asked rhetorically. For some reason, he knew this stranger was not a threat to him. "Fatima has ordered it to avenge El Jefe's murder. I can't do anything to stop her."

"Actually, you have a great many choices you may not have considered. I'm here to make sure you see every opportunity open to you. You will understand as you watch them unfold."

Thiago was startled when the possibilities began to play before him, each with its unique outcome. After he had seen them, he asked, "Which of those alternatives are you saying I should choose?"

"The one offering the best outcome for everyone involved, of course," answered Halaliel, a bit perplexed. Then he seemed to remember something and added, "The soul is eternal. Yes, your more altruistic choices will mean this earthly life ends quickly for you. But if you gain the world by losing sight of what you're here to do, to become a better person, why would you make a selfish choice?"

"So you're saying that I should disobey Fatima's orders?" Thiago answered in disbelief and anger. "You just saw that will get me killed and she'll just go ahead with it anyway,"

Halaliel shook his head. "You are right that to oppose her now would likely mean she will have you killed and attempt to carry out her plan regardless. But also consider that the person who takes your place will be impressed that you stood up to her knowing that attacking the United States is reckless. He may also try to convince her not to go through with it."

"And so my replacement would die as well," Thiago exclaimed in disgust. "How many of her own people would she kill before she changed her mind?"

"As it looks now, you and two replacements would die before she would begin to reconsider. But it could go as high as five successors before she would agree that she had erred in her thinking," answered Halaliel matter-of-factly.

"You know that will never happen. Someone will carry out her plan regardless of the devastation it will bring. That would make me an idiot for following your advice, even if it was the right thing to do. Did you not see that carrying out her plan is how I can become El

Jefe once the pandemic begins? That has been my goal from the start."

"You did not look far enough ahead at the outcomes of your alternatives. It is never wrong to choose the 'right thing to do,' as you put it. It is rarely correct to take the easiest path that offers instant satisfaction. Let me show you more and you will see…"

Thiago cut him off abruptly. "I'm done watching your movies. I'm done listening to your advice. If you had to suffer like that to 'do the right thing,' would you really go through with it? Don't bother to answer. Just go away!"

Thiago suddenly felt as though he was falling and awoke with a start. He was still shaking from the disturbing dream. He vaguely remembered it had to do with the biological attack Fatima ordered on the United States. He remembered seeing himself die if he didn't follow her orders.

It also showed him that, by releasing the disease, he would quickly become the leader of the Macizo cartel. So why had he woken up shivering like a scared child? Thiago was embarrassed to have such thoughts. He busied his mind with other matters and soon forgot what had troubled him.

Chapter 11

Gil Kowalski, the U.S. Ambassador to Mexico, was on the phone for the second time in as many days with Matt Alexander. There was no law against his sharing government secrets with a past president, but there was no official reason to bring Matt into the 'biological threat loop.' Gil had called his old friend because his intuition told him that the USA's aggressive defense strategy against the terrorists' biological threat would make things worse. He hoped Matt and his people could help minimize the damage.

"We have military and black ops teams standing by to fire bomb any suspected lab locations in Mexico," Gil explained. "They want to move quickly to prevent the terrorists from deploying their biological weapon. It looks like they are going to take out three sites in the southern part of the country.

"One thing that bothers me," Gil continued, "is that we have no idea who the terrorists are, or why they are threatening us. You told me your friends almost died at the hands of several drug runners in Guatemala, but it seems unlikely that a drug cartel would want to share RF energy with the world. The NSC's best-guess is that the terrorists are based in the Middle East. The disease and assumed pandemic would be thousands of miles away, and they still want revenge against the U.S. for making their oil as obsolete as buggy whips."

Almost as an afterthought, Gil added, "We're still searching for any link between the Middle East and Macizo. The only connection that makes sense there is that the terrorists are paying Macizo's people a lot of money to act as their minions. It could be that they made a deal with the number two man at Macizo, promising to get rid of his old boss while proving the threat was real."

"That starts to sound plausible, but what happened in Piedras Negras can't be a coincidence!" Matt said, thinking the scenario through. "Mark and Nuri discover a pyramid there with hieroglyphics matching the ancient language they found in Egypt. What Mark was able to translate warned of a disease with symptoms exactly like those that killed the Mexican drug lord. It had to be Macizo's people who almost killed my friends and took the two suspect vials with the bacteria or virus or whatever back to their leader. That means the disease came from the pyramid, not the Middle East. Blaming this fiasco on unknown terrorists working with drug runners doesn't hold water."

"I agree," conceded Gil. "I know of no connections between the drug cartels in Latin America and any militant groups on another continent. So if Macizo is responsible for the threat, the question remains as to why they would threaten the U.S. when they are in as much danger from the disease as we are."

"Going with that, I can think of two scenarios that fit," said Matt. "First, the threat is a bluff they have no intention of carrying out. The other is that they already have an antidote to protect their people in case the disease spreads. The two different colored vials Mark described could possibly support the latter explanation. God help us if they feel they are safe against infection and have little to lose by carrying out the threat!"

"The word from Washington is that they don't believe there is a cure," Gil countered. "They believe discovering this toxin, they call it The Glut, was a fluke. Since our own people at the CDC can't begin to theorize how this disease was developed, Westbrook believes that the terrorists simply stumbled onto it. The fact that the cartel's own leader died from it supports his belief that The Glut was unintended. Who knows what drug runners are using these days to develop new products to sell on the streets?"

Matt was not convinced. "There could be a lot of reasons why that man died of the disease even if they had the cure. The problem is that Westbrook will never believe our claim that a cure exists, and he is unwilling to negotiate or comply with the terrorists' demands. With those two givens, he has little to lose by destroying the lab sites in Mexico. Whether they have an antidote or not, it's a good bet that the terrorists already have the toxin inside the U.S. ready to make good on their threat."

"I'll try to reach him and tell him what we know, but we may already be too late!" Gil hung up without saying good bye. He was already dialing the White House.

***

281

Fatima was on her computer with Thiago via Skype. He had just arrived in Las Vegas with a couple of his men. From his hotel room he could see the setting sun give way to the casino lights that lit up the sky. They were there waiting for the deadline to see if the U.S. would turn over all their files on RF energy. The U.S. government had already answered that they would comply, but who knew if that was just to buy more time? If the RFP files were uploaded according to Fatima's instructions, then Thiago and his men would simply come home. Otherwise, their next stop would be Lake Mead to drop the infected cotton swab into the water. Estimates were that 30 million U.S. citizens were served by that one water source.

"In some ways, I'm hoping the President thinks I'm bluffing," Fatima said defiantly. "They will come to their senses as soon as their own people start to suffer as my Rodrigo did."

"What happens if the U.S. government is unwilling or unable to stop the plague before it reaches Mexico? Do we have enough of the cure on hand to protect our people if it comes to that? Maybe we should tell them that we have it. That way they'll know that we are both serious about the threat, and protected from it."

She scoffed, "The U.S. knowing we have the cure means they'd never stop looking for us. After all, we're their only competition when it comes to curing The Glut. I don't think they counted on anyone getting control of the disease and the cure when they so cleverly planned to murder Rodrigo."

"Then I will wait here in the hotel room until I hear from you," he said. "Let's hope they know you're not bluffing. Are you sure there's no way they could trace your demands back to Macizo? If soldiers show up at your home or at the lab, they won't hesitate to destroy everything, with or without the cure."

Fatima had thought this point over carefully. "I'll bet those three yanquis told their government they successfully carried out their mission. Once they heard that Rodrigo had died, they would get credit for a job well done. They would not want it known that they lost the tube with the cure."

Thiago smiled knowing he too would not want to admit making such an error.

Fatima continued, "No matter what happens, remember that we have redundant labs just outside of Oaxaca and Merida. All three locations have samples of the disease and a large cache of the cure safely stored away. The World Health Organization has already tested everything in my home and knows that there is nothing here to connect me to the threat," she said proudly. I'm betting the U.S. will upload the RFP files before the deadline. If they don't, or you don't hear from me, you know what to do."

They wished each other good luck as Fatima ended the call and their computer screens went blank.

Thiago called his men and instructed them to return to the hotel. They were out enjoying what Las Vegas has to offer, but he needed them sober in case they had to act quickly."

***

"Mr. President?" the voice said over the Oval Office's intercom.

Don Westbrook was reading the hourly updates on the search for the disease in Mexico. The assistant called to him again before he managed to say, "Yes, what is it?"

"Mr. President, Ambassador Kowalski is on the phone for you. He says it's urgent."

Don thought for a moment and then asked, "Is this about those archeologists down in Guatemala?"

"Let me check, sir," and the line went silent. A few moments later she came back and said, "He says it does involve them, but he stresses that it is urgent that you take his call."

"Put him through," said Don begrudgingly.

"Mr. President?" Gil's voice broke the silence.

"I'm here Ambassador Kowalski. What is it that's so important?"

"Sir, I have reason to believe the imminent attacks against the terrorists in Mexico should be stopped. The archeologists you asked about had a recent encounter in northern Guatemala that appears to be closely related to the biological threat made against us." Gil then related the high points he had discussed with Matt Alexander.

"And what proof do you have that the vials they found in Guatemala have anything to do with the alleged disease and cure we're searching for in Mexico?"

"They have no specific evidence of that, but the Macizo leader died of the disease proving they are involved in some way. The translations of the words inscribed on the pyramid's walls in Guatemala warned of a killer plague that matches Rodrigo Cortez's autopsy report."

"Is there confirmation that the people who attacked the archeologists work for Rodrigo Cortez?" Don asked.

"We don't have proof of that either, Mr. President. But it seems clear that the attackers were drug runners. That is strong circumstantial evidence knowing that patient zero was the head of the Macizo drug cartel."

"I don't really see how that helps your case. If Macizo controls both the disease and the cure, then why did their leader die of it?" Don asked skeptically.

Gil answered, "We don't know for certain. It could be a coup through assassination. Also, this wouldn't be the first time a new lethal discovery caused the death of the person who discovered it."

"So your story now is that a drug cartel starts experimenting with a lethal disease and kills their leader in the process? You really are grasping at straws," Don sighed. He pulled off his glasses and pressed his thumb and middle finger against the bridge of his nose. "I have to admit that I'm less than impressed with the credibility of those two archeologists. Has anyone else verified the translation of the symbols they claim they found in Guatemala?" Don asked.

"No, sir. They weren't able to get pictures of the pyramid's walls for anyone to verify the meaning, but they do have a small box with a similar dire warning that describes the disease perfectly," Gil said, feeling a little defensive. "Mr. President, what if they have the antidote stored along with the disease in the labs we're about to fire bomb? If you destroy those labs, you may be removing the only chance we have to stop a pandemic. Chances are that they already have the toxin inside our borders ready to make good on their threat."

Don had heard enough. "Ambassador Kowalski, you obviously agree that we are dealing with a threat that staggers the imagination if these terrorists actually unleash it on this country. Short of negotiating with terrorists, which is not an option, we cannot stop that. It is our best guess and hope that this quick strike on their labs will destroy all traces of the disease.

"You say there may be a cure, but that's only a guess based on the credibility and some unsupported statements from those two treasure hunters. I can guarantee you that the danger is real and the threat is in writing. There is too much at stake here to not take this opportunity to destroy the disease before it gets loose. The CDC seriously doubts that a cure exists, so we have a lot to lose if we don't act now."

Gil interjected, "And if the terrorists already have the disease inside our borders?"

"If the pending mission does not eradicate it, at least the terrorists' labs and inventory will be destroyed. If nothing else, that should slow them down from doing further harm. Unless you have anything else to add, I thank you for your opinion."

Gil answered, "No sir. However,..." but there was no one listening. The President had hung up.

Chapter 12

Most of the National Security Council members were sitting in the Situation Room. They were all present to witness the destruction of the suspected lab locations in Mexico. Primarily this was a military operation involving the Navy, Army and Air Force. As the JCS, General Myer chose to personally direct the simultaneous assaults.

"Alpha team on site and in position," crackled the hi-fidelity speakers.

"Bravo team ready to go."

"Charlie team ready and standing by."

"Acknowledged!" said General Myer. He reflected on all that had gone into making this moment possible. The big break was in tracking down the specialized lab equipment needed to handle a BSL-4 biosafety threat. Five different companies had recently purchased the type of equipment required to handle dangerous biohazard materials. Two of them were in the U.S. and readily allowed inspections of their facilities. That left the other three, all of which were located in Southern Mexico in Oaxaca, Merida and Tuxtla Gutierrez. They knew better than to approach those locations and ask to inspect them. They had another way to verify that these were the labs they were looking for.

The Mexican government was unaware that RFP frequencies could be tracked like a GPS signal to nail down a user's location. It was the one RFP discovery made by the US government's scientists without the help of JPL. The Mexican officials quickly figured it out once the U.S. requested, and was given, a list of the RFP users whose crystal frequencies had been tracked to the three suspected lab locations. The Mexican government disclosed that many of the people on the list were known members of the Macizo cartel.

Connecting the purchase of the biohazard lab equipment to the same drug cartel whose leader was patient zero was confirmation enough to proceed. They convinced the Mexican government to approve a mission led by US military forces inside their borders. General Myer agreed that Mexico would publicly denounce the United States military action if the collateral damage was deemed to be excessive. Conversely, they could claim it was a joint operation if their citizens approved of the dramatic eradication of these drug labs.

The President entered the Situation Room and motioned for everyone to keep their seats. As he took the chair at the head of the table, he asked, "What's the latest, General? What did we find out that convinced Mexico to agree to this?"

"The biohazard equipment was delivered to three suspected labs we located in Southern Mexico. That coincided with the users' RFP frequencies their government confirmed are assigned to known members of the Macizo cartel. Patient zero was the leader of the Macizo cartel," James replied. "That much evidence would get you a warrant in any country."

"What we're doing today is hardly serving a warrant, General. This is a death sentence without a trial. Are you positive destroying these labs will eradicate the disease as well?"

Surprised at the corrective tone, the General answered, "As sure as we can be in the time allowed and with the limitations placed on the investigation, yes sir, I'm convinced."

Westbrook thought back to his recent phone call with the Ambassador to Mexico. The news connecting the Macizo cartel to the disease was disturbing. He quickly tried to think if the threat coming from the cartel changed anything. Unless the archeologists' wild story could be believed, he couldn't see that putting a name to the terrorists made any difference.

"So be it then," said the President with resolve in his voice.

General Myer pressed the intercom button in front of him and said, "Teams Alpha, Bravo and Charlie, commence Operation Vaccinate."

***

Matt had insisted on Gil including Mark, Nuri and Jason on the conference call. Gil's news that the President was proceeding with the destruction of the three suspected lab sites in Mexico made it necessary to break security protocols.

"Tell them of the President's reaction when you described the attack in Guatemala," Matt said, once everyone was on the line.

Gil began hesitantly, "First, let me say that President Westbrook did hear me out, mostly. He understood there are connections, albeit unverified, between the Macizo drug cartel, the writings you discovered in the pyramid and the disease that now threatens the United States."

"What threat? What disease?" the three of them said out of unison.

Matt gave them the edited version of recent events so that Gil could deny disclosing any details if this call was questioned later. When he finished, he asked, "So what's our best course of action now if they destroy the cure with the labs in Mexico?"

Jason was the first to speak. "None of us are biohazard experts, but if the toxin is still out there, what other course of action is there but to find an antidote as quickly as possible?" Nuri and Mark agreed with him.

Matt said, "No luck finding a cure so far. The CDC has yet to develop anything that can neutralize the contagion without killing the infected person as well."

"And they are doubtful that a cure is forthcoming anytime soon," added Gil.

"Then we have to go back to Piedras Negras," said Nuri, immediately understanding Matt's point. "But the bad guys may still be patrolling the area."

Mark added, "If we get another look at the message written in the pyramid, this time with our translation notes, I'll bet we can put the CDC on the right track. We might even find more samples of the disease and cure, assuming that's what was in the vials."

Jason interrupted, "I hate to bring this up, sir, but we're out of money. It wouldn't matter if the cartel thugs went away forever. We can't afford another trip out of the country."

"I'll cover the cost," said Matt. A smile came to his voice as he added, "If you guys are successful, nothing would make me happier than to request reimbursement from President Westbrook."

He didn't need to mention the dire consequences if they did not succeed.

Jason had the last word before they hung up. "Then we'll start planning the best way to get back inside the pyramid, but we don't go near the place until it is safe."

***

The USS Nimitz headed south from San Diego the moment it was clear that sites in southern Mexico would be their targets. 'Old Salt,' as it was known to the Navy, was a battle tested aircraft carrier that housed the F-18 Hornets assigned to Operation Vaccinate. Ten F-18 jets would incinerate the three lab locations simultaneously. There were three F-18s assigned to each of the three labs locations with a fourth assigned to the Oaxaca lab. Their intel on Oaxaca indicated they had subterranean bunkers. The fourth F-18's mission was to strike first to expose the lab's lower levels using bunker busting bombs.

The CDC had recommended extreme heat as the best way to eliminate the disease. General Myer's best strategists suggested specialized missiles to burn the labs to the ground leaving no survivors. The satellite intel helped them to calculate the strike points for the greatest effect. The Delta Force teams were at a safe distance around each lab with orders to shoot anyone trying to escape. They were also there to paint their respective targets with lasers that would guide the Air Force's incendiary missiles with pinpoint accuracy.

General Myer spoke quietly through a headset maintaining direct contact with his men in the field. He looked up and addressed the other members of the NSC, "Ladies and gentlemen, the F-18s are about two minutes out from their respective objectives and the Delta Force teams on the ground have already begun laser-painting their targets. It would be best to watch the three center monitors to witness the full effect of the incendiary bombs."

The side conversations hushed as all eyes returned to the wall of video monitors. The three largest screens held static overhead shots of each lab location. It was early morning in Washington D.C., but still very dark throughout Mexico. The satellites must have had infra-red capability because green blotches moved around the faint building outlines. Their movements indicated they were probably guards at the entrances.

"60 seconds," said General Myer.

President Westbrook's thoughts kept returning to his earlier conversation with Ambassador Kowalski. Don hadn't initially cared that the labs were owned by the same cartel that was headed up by patient zero. After all, Rodrigo Cortez could have been a victim of the disease in concert with the threats made against the U.S. by Middle Eastern terrorists. But why was the Macizo cartel somehow involved with OPEC nation terrorists? He doubted the cartel's people would risk suicide knowing the disease could quickly reach Mexico. Was it possible that the archeologists were telling the truth? If so, then it was possible that Macizo didn't know they had the cure until after their leader had died. That would mean The Glut could kill millions of his fellow citizens because they were about to destroy the only antidote! Don tried to calculate the impact of stopping this deadly mission until he could get more facts confirmed.

His ruminations were interrupted by General Myer. "I need final approval for the F-18s to launch their missiles, sir."

Don Westbrook was about to order his people to stand down. He hesitated realizing that meant he would have to negotiate with terrorists. For decades, the policy had been that the United States would not negotiate with any group that threatened violence. If he reversed himself now, he would never recover politically or personally. He reminded himself that he had the best advisors in the world. They recommended this attack to put an end to the disease and the brazen terrorists who thought they could threaten the USA. "Launch when ready General," he said resolutely.

Myer said something in his headset microphone and looked up at the screens. A few moments later, the first monitor showed a huge explosion caused by the bunker busting bombs. Then, almost as if it was choreographed, gigantic parallel lines of fire poured across all three laboratories. The expanding flames completely engulfed the targets and the monitors flared bright white for a moment. As the images finally cleared, it was difficult to tell that any structures had been there at all.

Amazingly, there had been a few survivors at each location. The satellite video showed green blotches dragging themselves away from the burning buildings. The Delta Force snipers carried out their grizzly orders that there be no survivors.

General Myer declared, "Great work! As soon as it's clear, move the Hazmat teams in to inspect the targets and ensure that the disease has been eradicated."

President Westbrook was not happy. He felt justified in destroying the labs, but he couldn't help but feel guilty. Even if the attack had been warranted and accomplished the mission, they had just carried out a sentence of death on 100 or more people without due process. Don suddenly realized someone was trying to get his attention.

"We're re-tasking one of the satellites to give an overhead view of the final target," said General Myer.

Westbrook had not remembered there being another target but he'd always relied more on verbal briefings to make decisions than he did reading thousands of pages of government reports. "What target is that?" he asked.

Myer answered, "That is the home of 'patient zero,' Rodrigo Cortez. Actually, it's better described as a fortified resort and compound than a primary residence. That's where any remaining leaders of the Macizo cartel should be. There will be no air assault there, only ground troops. We're counting on getting the full story from the people we take into custody there."

Chapter 13

Thiago's cell phone was on its fifth ring waiting for him to decide if he would answer it. The caller ID number was not the one he expected. It was Rodrigo's office phone instead of the burner cell phone Fatima was supposed to use. He took the call not knowing what else to do.

Before he could say anything, Fatima shouted into the phone. "Thiago! They are coming for me. I will go into the panic room but you must leave for the lake immediately!"

"I'll leave now. Call me when you are safe," Thiago said reassuringly. He was always good in an emergency situation. "If I don't hear from you, I will have a thousand lawyers working to get you free."

He disconnected the call and looked toward Luis and Tomas, the two men he had brought with him to Las Vegas. His serious expression told them it was time to go to work.

"Luis, get the car and meet us out front," Thiago ordered. "Tomas, you gather everything we brought to this place and meet me in the lobby. I'm going to check us out of this room. We will not be coming back here."

"Where are we going?" asked Luis.

He paused for a moment to assess the impact of what came next. He answered with an ominous tone, "To make history."

***

Fatima was shaking as she hung up the phone. She was thankful to have been able to warn Thiago that soldiers were coming. The security monitors in Rodrigo's office confirmed that the proverbial wolf was at her door. She could see more than two dozen soldiers surrounding her home. She heard them smash through her beautiful front door and yell for everyone to get on the floor with their hands on their heads. Fatima did not want to be arrested, let alone die, at least not yet. She hoped there was still time to get to the panic room in the basement.

She ran to the far wall of the office that featured a relief style wooden carving of an oak tree. She poked her finger through a knot in the tree and a concealed panel silently slid back. It revealed what looked like a fireman's pole that would take her forty feet below to the basement.

She and Rodrigo had practiced going down the pole only once when it was first installed. She remembered that it had a sturdy platform they could stand on with a hand-break to control their speed of descent. She ironically reminisced over how much fun that had been because she never imagined a day like this would come. She silently thanked Rodrigo for having the forethought to install both the pole and the well-equipped panic room. With that, she stepped forward onto the platform and disappeared from sight just before the soldiers burst through the door.

The hand-brake for the platform worked perfectly. Fatima landed softly in the basement, and she made a mad dash for the panic room door. She could hear the soldiers following behind her. They had figured out where she had gone and were sliding down the pole like a bunch of firemen. She was just seconds ahead of them, but it was enough. She punched a flat red button upon entering the room and watched as the solid steel door slammed shut.

Now that she was safe, Fatima heaved a sigh of relief knowing she had everything she needed to live in reasonable comfort for a month. She sadly amended that thought. She could last for two months because Rodrigo was not with her.

The soldiers knew where she was, but getting to her would be a real challenge. They would find no way into the room that wasn't protected by thick steel walls or yards of concrete. Below her was another level that she could access by ladder. The atmosphere was controlled by an air scrubber that automatically kept the correct balance of oxygen, nitrogen and carbon dioxide. The lower floor contained stores of food, large banks of car batteries and a generator to recharge them, if necessary. The panic room had been built before RF energy had been discovered, so the archaic electrical equipment remained as a backup system in case the RF energy was cut.

There was one feature to this panic room that set it apart from most others. Rodrigo had planned ahead and installed the highest quality equipment to maintain communications with the outside world. The room had a secure satellite connection providing TV programming, internet access and a telephone. The satellite dish was several kilometers away, and not easy to locate or disable. If necessary, Rodrigo said he could orchestrate an assault on the people laying siege to his home. When he first showed Fatima this room, she had jokingly asked what they might do if an entire army was camped inside their house making it impossible to fight their way out. He had smiled and said he had that covered too.

Her thoughts returned to the present when she remembered this wasn't a rival cartel that was after her. These were government soldiers and, by the looks of it, they were from the United States. She needed to know what was happening outside before deciding what to do next. She located the laptop and powered it up. She went to the dark website where the U.S. had promised to upload the RFP documentation. As expected, there was nothing posted.

She then searched for news stories about the assault on her home. Since that had begun just a short while ago, it was no surprise that the press was silent on the attack. Then she read that within the last hour there had been terrorist bombings in Oaxaca, Merida and Tuxtla Gutierrez. She quickly deduced the attacks had been on the Macizo facilities where the cocaine and labs were located. The timing of the soldiers invading her home with the bombings at those three sites could not have been a coincidence.

The utter horror of these events had her in a state of near panic. She had lost Rodrigo and now her home. The cocaine business was in real trouble, assuming those three processing locations had been demolished. But it was far worse than her emotional and financial losses. The U.S. President must have known that destroying the facilities to eradicate the disease would also wipe out the cure. She had already told Thiago to make good on the threat of infecting the population of the United States. If she didn't stop Thiago, it would be her own people who were at risk with no one to protect them but the U.S. government. She wondered if the arrogant Americans would bother to help her people if they became infected.

She tried to remember how far away Lake Mead was from Las Vegas. She guessed it would take them at least 30 minutes to get there by car. She had been in the safe room for perhaps ten minutes. She was relieved that she still had time to stop Thiago, if she could reach him.

She located the satellite phone and hit the power button. She cursed when she saw that it required a pass code before she could make the call. She knew Rodrigo's computer password was "Mi#!Reina" (meaning "My #1 Queen") that substituted an exclamation point for the numeral one. She tried using the number "1" instead, but it did not work. The phone waited silently for the correct PIN.

She searched her memory for other passwords Rodrigo had used over the years. She tried using birth dates and various pets' names, but the phone remained locked. She sat down at the small desk and began to search the laptop. She hoped he would have the pin number stored somewhere in a document or saved email.

There were no data files on the hard drive, but there was a DVD in the drive. She saw that it contained a video file so she clicked on the icon to play it. Rodrigo's face appeared on the screen and she gasped. After a moment, he began to speak.

"Hello my love. If you are watching this, it means you are in the safe room without me and I am probably dead. Remember that I will always love you. You are protected and that is what matters. I want to say some things that I haven't said to you before. You already know what is in my heart, but I want nothing left unsaid between us.

"Those around us think El Jefe of Macizo has everything a man could want. They are not wrong, but it took attaining great wealth and power for me to finally realize I have nothing of value, except you. I am sorry that we did not have a long and happy life together. I have been able to provide well for you, but that was my goal, not yours. You only wanted a happy family, but my ambition made that impossible. You were right to decide against bringing children into this kind of life. Being El Jefe comes with a heavy price. I've had to do many awful things to get this far.

"What a fool I was to have the most wonderful, beautiful woman in the world and not spend every precious second that I could with you. How patient you have been with me and my useless ambitions. I hope you can forgive me for making us both give up the perfect life and family we should have shared for many years to come.

"This room will keep you safe for a time, but you can't stay here for long. In the lower room you will find a trap door that accesses a tunnel. You will need to push hard on the second tray of batteries to expose it. Once you enter the tunnel, the trap door will automatically close behind you. They will eventually breach the safe room, but you will be long gone before then.

"The tunnel has a rail system with a powered flatbed car to transport you to the other end. The exit hatch is near the highway and you can reach it quickly by heading north once you are out of the tunnel. You should use the satellite phone and internet access to make sure people you trust meet you at the highway, once it is safe to leave.

"Oh, I almost forgot. You'll need the code to unlock the satellite phone. As it has been my whole life, the answer is you, Fatima! Adios, mi amor!"

She sat there stunned as the video ended and the computer monitor went blank. She hadn't noticed she was crying, and was surprised when she felt a tear drop on her hand. She understood that Rodrigo wanted to reassure her with his heartfelt message. But she had never felt such an overwhelming sense of loss, even when she sat with his lifeless body at the hospital. Seeing his smile again reminded her of the fantasy life they could have had together. She had longed for the simple joy of raising a family with her husband. The agony of hearing him say he had wanted a family too was heartbreaking.

Her thoughts were interrupted by a loud clank on the safe room door. The soldiers knew where she was and were testing their options to get her out of the room. She suddenly remembered she was trying to call Thiago but needed the access code. Rodrigo had not said what it was exactly, but he did say that she was the answer.

She picked up the phone again where it was patiently waiting for her to try another PIN. She smiled sadly and pushed the buttons corresponding to her name: 3-2-8-4-6-2. The phone accepted the code that spelled Fatima. She looked at a nearby clock and was relieved to see she still had time to stop him.

***

They were still 10 minutes away from Lake Mead when Thiago told Luis to exit Highway 93 and park the car along the side of the deserted road. He was close to hyperventilating and needed to clear his head. The dire consequences of his orders would make anyone hesitate to carry them out. The thought that he would soon become El Jefe was of little comfort to him. He was anxious to learn if Fatima had been taken by the authorities. That would make all the difference in what he did next.

He examined the small case and the heavy glass test tube that lay in the foam rubber cutout. He had been warned not to touch the cotton swab it contained. Thiago knew the cure had been successfully tested on several people, but he dreaded the hell that awaited him if he became infected. The thought of being so desperately hungry and thirsty that nothing else mattered was terrifying to him. Thiago was used to violence and even torture, but murdering millions of innocent bystanders to avenge Rodrigo's death was enough to give him pause.

The original plan had been to find a place to park on the road spanning Boulder Dam's retaining wall, and then empty the contents of the test tube into the water below. Something had bothered him about that plan from the start. Standing there at the side of the deserted road, he saw the height of the huge dam relative to the level of the lake, and understood why. The scientists had said that the cotton swab must make direct contact with the lake's water to work as planned. If the falling cotton swab managed to affix itself to the rough concrete wall of the dam, it could be weeks before the disease made it to the water below.

He thought of the other risks involved with his original plan. The sun had set hours ago, so darkness was on his side. However, the road on top of the dam always had traffic, and witnesses, driving across it. He decided that the marina at the lake's edge was a far better place to do what he had to do.

At that moment, his cell phone rang. This time the caller ID told him it came from the satellite phone Rodrigo always kept in the safe room. Thiago answered, "Are you okay, Jefe?"

"Oh thank God, Thiago! I didn't know if they had come for you as well," Fatima said with obvious relief. "I am safe for the moment. Are you okay? Is anyone following you?"

"Not that I know of," Thiago said looking over his shoulder. "I have been very careful. Where are you? Did the soldiers hurt you?"

Fatima sighed, "They were too late. I made it to the safe room in the basement before they could reach me. I am alright for now, but I need to know if you did as I asked."

Thiago was disappointed at the news that she had made it safely to the panic room. If Fatima was dead or captured, he would become El Jefe. There would be no reason to kill so many people. However, with Fatima very much alive and temporarily out of reach of the authorities, he considered his options. He decided to gather more information. "Why? Has something changed?"

"Our labs at Tuxtla Gutierrez, Oaxaca and Merida have been fire bombed. The news is saying it was terrorists, but the timing of the government soldiers coming to my home is no coincidence," she said. "That means they have destroyed both the disease and the cure we had at those locations. Only the United States has the cure now."

Thiago could guess that she had changed her mind about poisoning the lake. If she could not be blamed for ordering him to infect the water supply, the members of Macizo might continue to support her as their leader. He knew what he had to do from here.

"Then the norteamericanos who dropped the vials in Piedras Negras must have planned Rodrigo's death," Thiago said, still wondering what Fatima's next move would be. "You can rest easy knowing I have already done as you ordered. Rodrigo's death has been avenged!"

"Oh my God!" she yelled. "The only cure is in the hands of the U.S. but the infection will surely reach Mexico through the Colorado River. If they think our government is involved in any way, they may not share the antidote with Mexico. It will be as if we killed our own people."

Thiago's quick mind was already executing a new plan. He had finally become El Jefe, but he was also a wanted man. He saw a way to sacrifice Fatima for his own freedom.

"I am sorry, Fatima," Thiago said sadly. "It is too late. We must focus now on getting you out of the safe room. Do you have a plan?"

Her heart sank. She was sure that he was lying to her. She knew she had called him in time because he could not have driven to Lake Mead before now. He had his own reasons for wanting to infect the lake. "When you get back to Mexico, call me on this satellite phone. We can decide what to do once you get here."

"No doubt they are looking for us too, so we cannot fly back to Mexico. I will buy a used car here with cash and a forged driver's license so they can't trace our movements. I know you will be safe in that room, so please don't go anywhere until I return. I am going to destroy this phone in case they have the number. I will call you when I return. Expect to hear from me in a couple of days."

"A couple of days? Why should I wait that long to leave this awful place?" she asked. But he had already hung up.

***

Luis and Tomas waited in the car as Thiago walked slowly down to the end of the pier. They wondered what they were doing here. Was he meeting someone? Was this pier a drop point for drugs or money? Why were they with him at all if they were not required as backup for some dangerous meeting? They knew better than to ask these questions, so they waited, and watched.

Thiago pulled on a pair of disposable rubber gloves as he walked the length of the pier to the water's edge. He pulled out the protective case from his pocket and removed the heavy glass tube containing the tainted cotton swab. The full moon was bright enough to see the diseased swab resting against the rounded bottom. He carefully removed the stopper, and hesitated for just a moment.

He imagined the life ahead of him as the leader of the largest drug cartel in Mexico. He smiled realizing that Thiago Bernal would finally become El Jefe. The debate in his mind was over. He was here to infect Lake Mead, blame Fatima for the plot, and turn her over to the government in exchange for his freedom. Having no more need of it, he tossed the protective case into the lake. The glass tube with the tainted cotton swab quickly followed. He watched the escaping air bubbles pop on the water's surface as it disappeared from sight. A still, small voice inside his head asked a vexing question, "How many people have you just killed to become El Jefe?"

Chapter 14

Fear spread through Dr. Steven Welch's gut as he reviewed the CDC report. A mysterious illness had been reported in Boulder City, Nevada. People were complaining of an unquenchable hunger and thirst. Their digestive systems had shut down, and the emergency rooms were reporting more cases every hour.

He had to notify the HHS and the White House immediately. If the CDC could isolate the source location of the pathogen, it might be possible to contain the outbreak. He made the calls and agreed to come to Washington D.C. as an advisor to both the HHS and the Department of Homeland Security. Involving the DHS confirmed his worst fears. This disease was being handled as an intentional attack rather than a random biological outbreak. He wondered what they knew that he didn't.

Steven was not comfortable serving as their expert on a disease next to nothing was known about. He reviewed what little data he had. The pathogen was transmitted through ingestion of contaminated food or liquid. Only humans were affected; no other animal or plant life suffered any symptoms, even with direct injections. It was not hard to kill the disease, but everything that did, also killed the host in the process. He did not look forward to telling the heads of his government that the only option he could see to minimize casualties was to quarantine the victims, and anything tainted with the disease.

***

Mark, Nuri and Jason all settled back into the overstuffed couch in Matt Alexander's living room. The retired President had asked them over on a matter of urgency that could not be discussed on unsecured phone lines. Matt skipped the usual pleasantries and got right to business. "You must return to Piedras Negras right away!"

"How do you know it's safe?" asked Mark, clearly remembering their last expedition.

"I believe it is safe now, but please check to be sure. The Macizo cartel is in big trouble!" Matt responded, trying to convey his sense of urgency.

"What's the big hurry?" Jason asked with concern.

"Some of this you already know, but the narrative is unfolding quickly," Matt explained. "I believe the vials and crystals Mark found in that pyramid are now physical proof of the story carved on the box and the interior stone walls. You dropped those four items outside the pyramid as you escaped. It appears the Macizo cartel is the new proud owner of your discovery and is not afraid to use them."

Matt paused, but no one said a word. He continued, "Now a new disease with symptoms exactly like those Mark translated from the pyramid has been reported in the emergency rooms of Nevada, Arizona and California. This outbreak has already been classified as a pandemic; but the CDC won't announce that publicly until they have a plan for containment to minimize the exposure and panic. We need you to go back and identify anything that can help us get ahead of this thing."

Nuri interjected, "We don't know anything about diseases. Shouldn't the government put together a team of medical experts to go with us?"

"I'm afraid we're still on our own. President Westbrook is not open to anything we have to say or suggest. I have learned some disturbing developments since we last talked about this. Very compelling evidence pointed to the Macizo drug cartel in Mexico as being the terrorists behind the threat to infect the U.S. President Westbrook decided to move against them with full force. They found the cartel's probable locations for storing the substance and took them all out with synchronized fire bomb raids."

Mark asked, "So what happened to start the pandemic if the labs and the vials were destroyed?"

Matt looked frustrated as he said, "Westbrook gambled that the pathogen was completely contained in the three labs they destroyed. Now we know it wasn't. Worse yet, assuming they had the cure; all of it was likely destroyed with the disease. The CDC's best guess is that the Colorado River was somehow contaminated, and that is the source of drinking water for millions of people."

Jason took over now that he understood the situation. He knew their next steps called for practical measures. "First, we're all on bottled water that doesn't come from Lake Mead. We can leave for Guatemala immediately, but what about the cartel's soldiers?"

"They are dealing with much bigger problems than the three of you," replied Matt. "Now that the cartel's labs have been destroyed, there is an arrest warrant out for anyone connected with them."

Nuri had his laptop out and was reviewing the satellite coverage around the pyramid. "That would explain a lot. According to the latest intel from JPL's hotlink, there has been zero activity around the Piedras Negras area for the past two days," he confirmed.

"So you can leave immediately," Matt said, sounding optimistic. "There's no time to lose. The CDC says people will start dying of dehydration in just a few days."

***

Fatima paced aimlessly around the upper bunker of the safe room. She could guess why Thiago had told her to remain where she was until he returned to Mexico. She was not fooled by his feigned compliance. He intended to turn her over to the soldiers in exchange for his own freedom. She realized the situation provided him with the perfect way to get rid of her and become the new leader of Macizo.

She could use the escape tunnel to leave this place, but she was sure to be spotted if she tried to walk to the nearest town. If she simply stayed put, they would eventually find a way in. She had to leave as soon as she could, but who could come to her rescue that wasn't loyal to Thiago, or in danger of arrest by the soldiers?

She ran through a mental list of people she could call. Everyone she could think of was somehow connected to Macizo. She then considered if it might work to simply call a cab to pick her up on the highway near the tunnel's exit. She tried to imagine how that might play out. The soldiers would have the area secured for several miles around her home. That meant no one could get in or out of the area by car without going through a roadblock. She laughed at herself for coming up with such a stupid plan. She could picture the soldiers' reaction when the cab driver told them, "I am here to pick up a woman hiding in the trees somewhere on the south side of the highway."

She realized there was only one person she could trust who might be able to get past the soldiers, but that didn't ease her mind. She had not spoken to Lupita in years. Her younger sister had strongly objected to Fatima marrying 'that drug dealer.' They married anyway and Lupita vowed to quit speaking to her until Rodrigo was out of her life. Fatima honored her choice as much out of anger as she did out of respect. It was hard to believe that the relationship between them could get worse after that, but it did.

Lupita married Jorge nine years after Fatima married Rodrigo. The young couple had little money, but neither of them seemed to care. Fatima still loved Lupita and kept track of how she was doing. She decided to give the newlyweds a better, more prosperous life. Lupita would refuse any gift from Fatima, so she convinced Rodrigo to secretly arrange it. To everyone's surprise, Jorge was hired by a local bank and received several rapid promotions over the next couple of years.

At first, Lupita was proud of Jorge and his meteoric rise among his peers. Her suspicions began when she would ask him about his job and his answers were evasive. Jorge finally grew tired of her queries. He admitted that his job as Vice President was not what he hoped it would be. He mostly entertained customers on the golf course and was encouraged to say nothing when invited to an occasional meeting at the bank. Lupita was certain that Fatima was behind this embarrassment. When she insisted that Jorge quit his phony job and walk away from the generous salary, he refused and a divorce soon followed. She still blamed her sister for corrupting Jorge and ruining her happy marriage.

Despite their bad history together, Fatima was desperate and Lupita was truly her only hope. Fatima used her cell phone's contacts to look up her sister's phone number. She prayed that Lupita had not changed it over the years. She dialed it into the satellite phone and waited for it to connect. She reminded herself to call her Lupe, since the nickname, Lupita, implied that she was still a young girl.

"Bueno?" said the woman on the other end. Fatima froze for a moment marveling that she had not heard that sweet voice in many years. She whispered frantically, "Lupe, this is Fatima. Please don't hang up, I need your help!"

There was a long silence on the other end of the line. Lupe finally answered, "I heard about Rodrigo. I can't say that I'm sorry for him, but I am glad you called. I have missed my hermana mayor."

"I have missed you too, but first, I need your help," Fatima repeated. She quickly described the events that ended with her in the safe room. Lupe's first question was not a surprise.

"Are you still involved with Macizo?" she asked with reproach.

"If you're asking if I am involved in the cartel's dirty business, the answer is no. However, I am using my unwelcomed position to avenge Rodrigo's murder. But I fear they are trying to get rid of me now that he is gone."

Lupe paused again and then said, "Of course, I will help you. What do you need me to do?"

Chapter 15

A uniformed man stood in the middle of the street as he signaled for Lupe to slow down. The local police had set up a roadblock requiring a careful check of all vehicles and passengers. She rolled down her window after she pulled to a stop where the policeman indicated. She drove a 1973 Dodge Challenger muscle car that she received as part of the divorce settlement. It had been kept in perfect condition, but it had none of the modern features her ex-husband had wanted. Jorge had been happy to let her have the classic car so that he could keep the late model Mercedes for himself.

The policeman admired the car for a moment and then walked past her without saying a word. He clicked on a flashlight and began inspecting the back seat area through the rear window. Lupe calmly asked, "What's going on, Officer?"

The man frowned at her and answered with a touch of annoyance in his voice, "Please show me your driver's license and state your reason for being here."

Lupe handed him her license and said, "I'm here to visit my sister, Fatima. She lives on this road. I'm running a little late. Can you tell me how long this will take?"

"I'll need to see inside the trunk. Please open it," the man said curtly.

She hesitated a moment and then turned off the engine and offered her keyring to him. "This classic car was built before inside trunk releases were standard. The round-headed key opens the trunk lock," she said smiling.

The man took the keys and finally noticed how pretty she was. He quickly inspected the trunk and returned her keys to her when he found nothing suspicious. He felt compelled to offer some kind of explanation for his rudeness. "We are redirecting all traffic away from this road. There is an investigation in progress."

"Oh," she said with feigned surprise. "My sister, Fatima Cortez, should have warned me of this."

He hesitated once her words began to register. "Please do not move. I need to call this in."

Lupe smiled at how long it took for the man to realize who she was. She calmly leaned back in her seat and turned up the music as she waited. After a few minutes, the policemen returned with several more cops surrounding her car. He handed back her license and said, "I will escort you to your sister's house. My supervisor wants to talk with you at the Cortez estate."

"Is everything all right?" Lupe asked, with believable concern.

"My supervisor will explain once he meets with you," said the policeman, now smug with self-importance. His boss was relieved they had found a member of the Cortez family to interrogate.

Lupe surprised the anxious group encircling her car by pleasantly agreeing to the policeman's request with a flash of her beautiful smile. The man got behind the wheel of the nearest marked car and signaled for Lupe to drive ahead of him. They travelled down the road for several kilometers with Lupe leading the way. She turned in at the entry gate to the walled-in estate. He pulled ahead of her stopping just shy of the massive portico and main entrance to the mansion. Even at a distance, Lupe could see the front doors had been smashed by battering rams. She identified what had to be the policeman's supervisor giving orders to another group of uniformed men standing at attention underneath the portico.

The moment he saw her pull to a stop, the supervisor left his men where they stood, walked over to her car and opened her door. She stepped out, intentionally exposing her toned legs for review. She then followed him to a nearby shaded area. He ordered the men to thoroughly search her car. He watched them for a moment and then turned his attention to Lupe.

"When is the last time you had contact with Fatima Cortez?" he asked, without bothering to introduce himself.

She answered, "About a month ago. We always get together on the first weekend of the month. Why do you ask?"

Lupe considered the unfortunate face of the man in charge. His features had long ago lost their battle with gravity. Her assessment brought on an amused smile, but she quickly covered it with a flirtatious look.

"And you've not heard from her since you were here last month?" the man asked, ignoring her question but noticing that she looked interested.

"No, but that's not unusual. She is always busy. That's why we make a point of getting together every month," she said in her most playful tone.

"Do you have any idea where she might be?" he asked, becoming distracted with the possibility that she might actually be interested in him.

"I assume she's waiting for me inside," she answered, sounding surprised that it wasn't obvious to her interrogator. She realized that she'd have to cut this charade short if she was going to get back on the road in time.

They stared at each other for a moment. Lupe adopted a neutral expression that conveyed she was all business now. She could see the shift in the man's face from lustful hope to frustration.

"There has been a warrant issued for the arrest of your sister," he said harshly. He handed her a business card and added, "If you hear from her, please contact me immediately!"

"Well, I'm sure this is some kind of a mistake," she said taking the card, "but I'll do as you say."

He waived Lupe away, annoyed that she had wasted his time, and he was no closer to getting Rodrigo Cortez's woman out of that ridiculously reinforced basement.

***

Fatima checked her watch and estimated that Lupe had reached the outer roadblock. Her internet inquiries showed that the perimeter set by the police was beyond the exit point of her escape tunnel along the road. Her plan was risky, but Fatima knew that Lupe was the only person who could make it through the roadblock to the estate and still be allowed to leave once she was questioned. Since they would search Lupe's car on the way in, Fatima felt certain that they would not bother to search it again. After all, the police had the area securely locked down.

She estimated it would take an hour from the time Lupe reached the outer checkpoint until she was cleared to exit the same way she came. On the return trip, Lupe would keep an eye out for the signal that Fatima was waiting in the nearby trees to be picked up. If they couldn't get her out at the appointed time, they would have to regroup later, and come up with another plan.

With the clock ticking, Fatima pushed hard on the large metal rack that held some of the backup batteries for the safe room. As Rodrigo had said, it was very heavy and Fatima worried that she might not be able to move it. She redoubled her efforts and the shelf finally gave way and rolled back to expose the entrance to the escape tunnel. Fatima hung the straps of her tote bag over her shoulder and took careful steps down the ladder. She shivered as the cobwebs brushed against her bare arms. When she reached the bottom, she flipped the light switch that also triggered the battery shelf above to return to its original resting place.

She screamed when she turned and saw a mass exodus of insects, literally thousands of them, running from the light. She shivered uncontrollably as she watched them all skitter out of sight. The place smelled of foul mold and mildew and something sour she didn't try to identify. Despite the tunnel being closed off at both ends, nature had found many ways to fill this dank and eerie space. At least there didn't seem to be any rats or snakes, but she knew there were several varieties of poisonous spiders in the area. Within a minute, the insects had mostly disappeared into the shadows though she could still hear scratching noises that confirmed they had not gone far. She was nearly petrified by this chilling game of hide-and-seek, but she made herself focus on the task at hand.

She was relieved to see her means of escape appeared to be in good shape. The small RF powered flatbed railcar was where Rodrigo had said it would be, waiting patiently for her to board. A string of dim bare bulbs lined the tunnel revealing almost 50 meters of the parallel rails before they curved out of sight. Fatima was barely able to stand up in the tunnel, and it was perhaps 1.5 meters wide. The flatbed car was slightly less than a meter wide, but it was long enough for two people to sit comfortably in tandem. She choked up slightly remembering that the design was meant for both

Rodrigo and her. After taking a moment to regain her composure, she brushed the tunnel debris off the flatbed surface and sat down next to the control levers.

There were two vertical metal levers that operated the flatbed car. Small signs next to each lever told her that the right one controlled the movement and the left one controlled the brakes. She tested her skill pushing the right lever lightly forward, and the car inched slowly along the rails. She uncovered many of the insects that had taken refuge under the railcar. She had to fight her panic and the urge to pull hard on the throttle. Calming herself, she checked to see that she still had her tote bag. It held her purse, laptop, satellite phone and extra clothes. She would need all those things with her to have any hope of escape. Then she pulled on the right lever, and the car lurched forward.

As she moved down the tracks, she found that the tote bag was good for keeping the overhead cobwebs at bay. She gained more confidence in her use of the controls with each passing minute. She wished that Rodrigo had thought to let her practice driving the railcar, but all things considered, the plan was working. It seemed like an eternity before the end of the tunnel came into view. The rails terminated at a wooden post with red reflectors marking the end of the line. She rolled to a stop and looked back the way she had come. According to her watch, she saw that she had travelled the three or four kilometer distance in about twenty minutes. She knew she could not have walked through this horrible tunnel on her own, so she silently thanked Rodrigo for looking after her, even after he was gone.

This end of the tunnel had a steel ladder leading up to a round metal hatch with a wheel in the center of it. It looked like the type used on submarines from movies she had seen. She had forgotten about the hatch. She climbed the ladder and tried to turn the wheel while balancing her weight on the metal rungs. The wheel didn't move. She pushed on the hatch, but still no luck. She checked her watch to see how much time she had before Lupe would be looking for her signal along the road. She guessed she had no more than 45 minutes left to get there.

She looked around the tunnel for anything she might use as a lever to force the wheel to turn and open the hatch. The iron rails for the flatbed were cut in three meter sections. That meant they were much too long and heavy to be of use. She considered taking the flatbed car back to the bunker and finding some sort of pry bar there. If that was a 35 to 40-minute round trip, she would have very little time to make it to the road if everything else went as planned. Fatima tried to guess at the other challenges she would have if she managed to get out of the tunnel. How would she know which way was north if she was surrounded by trees? She had no idea how much time she would need to find the road to meet Lupe.

She calmed herself with a deep breath and glanced around the tunnel. Her gaze returned to the flatbed car. Either one of the metal levers might open the hatch, but how could she remove them without tools? She could try to wrench them off by hand, but how long would that take? And if that didn't work, she might damage the railcar to the point where she'd be stuck walking the distance back to the bunker. She sighed aloud realizing that removing one of the levers was her best chance.

Fatima tested the brake lever by pushing it sideways. She then tried to break it off at the base by wiggling it from side to side. She braced herself against the dirty wall of the narrow tunnel and kicked at the lever for all she was worth. It finally started to bend, but it refused to break off no matter how hard she kicked. She moved to the other side, and kicked at the lever from that direction hoping to weaken the metal by bending it back and forth in opposing directions.

It took her twelve precious minutes, but the weakened metal suddenly gave way and the lever flew into the wall of the tunnel. The momentum of her final kick carried her forward and she gouged her right calf on the lever's jagged metal stump. Her leg started bleeding so badly she thought she might pass out. Working through her fear and pain, Fatima removed a sweatshirt from her tote bag and began ripping it into strips to bind her wound. She managed to get the bleeding to stop, but she was running out of time and her leg really hurt.

She picked up the broken lever and examined it. It was a little over half a meter in length. She feared it may be too short to give her the leverage she needed to rotate the hatch's wheel. She climbed the ladder and looked for the best way to position her improvised tool. She inserted the bar between the metal spokes to turn the wheel in a counterclockwise direction. She pushed with all her might and managed to get the metal to creak a bit. Each time she strained to move the wheel, she exhausted herself. She realized she needed more force to open the hatch.

She looked at her watch and saw that going back to the panic room for tools was no longer an option. The other lever was still attached to the flatbed. She took a painful step toward the railcar and wondered if she would pass out before she could kick the second lever loose. She sadly acknowledged that her fear, pain, and doubts didn't change the fact that she had to have more leverage to open the hatch.

Fatima was right-side dominant, which meant her more coordinated leg was the one she injured. She started kicking the remaining lever back and forth with her left leg as best she could. Her progress was slower than before, but she kept at it.

She eventually managed to break the second lever free without injuring herself. She cursed when she saw that the metal had snapped off at least ten centimeters shorter than the first one. She hobbled up the ladder and positioned both levers against opposite spokes on the wheel. She pushed to loosen it with renewed resolve but the wheel remained frozen.

With just a few minutes to go until her deadline with Lupe, she thought of one thing she hadn't tried. She left the longer lever in place and started using the shorter rod as a hammer. She slammed one lever against the other as hard as she could over and over. She was almost out of strength when she heard the metal pop. The wheel had shifted, and Fatima struck it again. It moved a little farther as the 'metal on metal' screeching audibly hailed her success.

The wheel finally gave way and she was able to spin it to open the hatch. With a metallic creak and a shower of dirt raining down, she slowly pushed it open. Fatima squinted as daylight and dirt poured into the tunnel. She had no time to waste. She returned to the tunnel floor one last time and grabbed her tote bag. Then she said a quick prayer of thanks that she managed to escape this horrible place.

She climbed the ladder again and awkwardly managed to get both her body and the bag through the opening. It was tricky lifting her body with an injured leg, but she managed to roll clear of the hole. She pushed the hatch lid closed and gave the outer wheel a cursory turn. Not surprisingly, she found herself surrounded by trees and was unsure of which way to go. The sun was mostly overhead and was no help in determining east from west. She had a compass app on her computer, but the internet connection only worked from the safe room. Fatima remembered that Rodrigo had said to head north to get to the road. She started walking directly ahead without having a better guess where north might be.

Then she remembered an old cliché from her school days. She saw that moss growing on the trees was mostly facing toward her as she walked. She couldn't remember if moss grew on the north or south side. She also wondered if the old saying was true in the first place. She decided that moss must grow on the side away from the sun so she must be headed south. She quickly reversed her course. She prayed that was right, or Lupe would be forced to drive on without her.

***

Lupe could see that all the uniformed men were staring as she drove away from the Cortez estate, but none of them followed with more than their eyes. She was used to turning men's heads, but she feared that her looks could stop her from helping Fatima. She hoped that her classic Dodge Challenger was all they were thinking about now that she was out of sight.

She continued down the road, careful to stay under the speed limit. She didn't want to give them any reason to pull her over. Lupe continually scanned the road and her rear view mirror for other traffic. When she was a couple of kilometers away from the roadblock, she cut her speed in half. She was looking for the arranged sign that said her sister was waiting in the nearby trees.

They had agreed that Fatima would leave an article of clothing in the center of the road. That was how Lupe would know where to stop. If the discarded clothing was seen by any of the policemen, they would most likely ignore it. She drove as slowly as she dared looking for anything in the road. She knew that Fatima would have to be exposed for a few seconds when she planted the clothing, but that part was easy. Getting Fatima into the trunk without being seen was the hard part. If they managed that, they felt confident that the policemen at the roadblock would allow Lupe to pass without inspecting the trunk a second time.

313

Her heart skipped a beat when she saw someone in the distance. It was a woman, plainly limping, who dropped something in the middle of the road. Lupe sped up in a panic realizing that her sister must be injured. She hit the brakes when she reached whatever it was that Fatima had dropped, and put the car in park. She threw open the car door and stood facing the trees to the south looking for any sign of her sister.

Lupe froze the moment Fatima began to emerge from the trees. She wanted to go to her sister, but a police car had just appeared on the road behind her. Lupe had to think of something fast. She immediately yelled to Fatima that a policeman was coming and to remain hidden. Her sister retreated back inside the tree line and prayed.

Lupe walked quickly back to her trunk. She opened it hoping something there would offer an excuse for why she had stopped. She had cleaned out the trunk to make room for Fatima. It contained only an old blanket, a jack, spare tire and a tool kit. The police car slowed and then stopped behind her as she opened the kit. She found her answer among the assorted screwdrivers. She snatched the smallest one and headed for the right front tire. She knelt down and drove the sharp end of the screwdriver into the sidewall as hard as she could. When she pulled her hand back, the rubber wall was punctured and air was escaping, but the tire was deflating too slowly. Puncturing the tire again was not an option because the policeman had pulled to the side of the road in direct view of her.

Lupe turned toward the man and smiled hoping to distract his attention from the tire. It turned out that the officer swaggering toward her was the same one who had escorted her to the Cortez mansion. He was about twenty meters away when he asked, "Why have you stopped in the middle of the road?"

Lupe had planned to say she had a flat tire, but not nearly enough air had escaped for her story to be believed. She had to stall somehow until the deflating tire went flat.

"I think I saw an animal in the road! I may have hit it with my car," she said with convincing concern in her voice.

The policeman started toward her, but she pointed toward the middle of the road and almost shouted, "It should be on the other side of the car. Is it still alive? Is it dangerous?"

He smiled in amusement as he walked toward the spot where she pointed. With mock concern he told her, "You are right. This is a very dangerous animal." He held up a belt made of snakeskin and added with a laugh, "But I think it was dead when you got here."

Lupe had not bothered to look at what Fatima had left in the road, but she was relieved that her ruse was working to delay the policeman. She asked, "Are you sure? I thought I saw it moving."

"Senorita, this snake has not moved in a long time," he assured her. "Let me show you." He started walking around the front of the car to join her.

She screamed and the policeman stopped immediately. "Please Officer," she said with feigned panic, "I am deathly afraid of snakes, even if you are not." Lupe looked at the deflating tire and estimated that she needed about thirty more seconds until it would look as if it had been flat when she stopped.

She pleaded with him, "Please take it away and dispose of it!"

He grinned as he walked back to his police car. He started fantasizing that he was her white knight slaying the terrible serpent that threatened her life. He thought about asking her out to dinner as he tossed the belt onto the back seat of his car.

While his back was turned, Lupe threw the screwdriver into the nearby bushes. Now was the time to turn on her charm. She saw no other way to get Fatima out of this awful jam.

"Thank you so much, Officer!" she gushed. "I was sure that I had hit something because the car started swerving on me."

The policeman walked around the Challenger looking for anything that might be the cause. He discovered the problem and announced, "I don't doubt your car was swerving. You have a flat tire!"

She walked up beside him and gasped. "Oh my goodness; I could have been killed!"

She had already decided that getting him to change the flat was the diversion she needed to rescue Fatima.

"Officer," she began demurely, "could you call someone to help me with this?"

Seeing his perfect opportunity, the man offered, "I can change it for you Senorita. Let me get your spare out of the trunk."

"Oh thank you, Officer!" she said with a practiced flutter of her eyelashes.

"My name is Hector," he said.

"Well, thank you, Hector," said Lupe. "And you may call me Lupita."

Hector was quite pleased with himself that this beautiful woman did not hesitate to be on a first name basis with him. He thought about what he should suggest for their first date as he bent forward to retrieve the spare. He pulled it loose, lifted it over the lower lip of the trunk and let it go. The tire bounced a few times when it landed before he rolled it over next to the flat one.

While he was busy with the spare tire, Lupe grabbed the metal base of the car's jack and threw it as hard as she could to the other side of the road. She immediately started coughing to cover the noise it made as it hit the dirt and awkwardly rolled out of sight.

When Hector returned, he picked up the lug wrench and jack. He saw the jack was missing its base and let out a heavy sigh.

"Lupita," he said, "I'll need to use the jack from my car to change the tire. Yours is missing an important piece."

"I'm just so glad you're here and know what to do," she said with admiration. She was setting modern woman back decades with this ridiculous helpless act, but she would do almost anything for her sister.

As Hector walked back to his police cruiser, Lupe hoped Fatima saw her signal to stay where she was. Once the tire was changed, Hector would return the jack to his car. Lupe intended to walk with him and keep his attention away from Fatima until she could get inside the trunk. She considered the best way to communicate to her sister when the opportunity arose.

Hector was focused on positioning the jack when Lupe said, "I am so embarrassed, but...well, I have to use the restroom, such as it is. Is it okay if I excuse myself to go back in the trees?"

He laughed a bit and said, "Just watch out for snakes!"

She forced a nervous giggle and headed toward where she thought Fatima was hiding. The moment Lupe was out of Hector's sight, her sister appeared and they hugged each other tightly. It wasn't just from the relief of the moment, but they embraced as if trying to make up for the lost years since Rodrigo had come between them.

"We don't have much time," Lupe said, in an emphatic whisper. "When he is done changing the tire, I will make sure he goes back to his vehicle to put his jack away. That's when you should make a run for the Challenger. I'll leave my keys in the trunk's lock so you can open it. Just make sure to close it as quietly as you can once you're inside."

Fatima answered, "I'll go as fast as I can. I hurt my leg getting out of that damn tunnel. I'll tell you the rest later."

They quickly hugged again and wished each other luck as Lupe headed back to her car.

Hector was just finishing up when she returned. He handed her the tire iron and then he retrieved his jack. She walked to the open trunk of her car, and secured the lug wrench so it would not be in Fatima's way. She then slammed the trunk shut leaving her keys in the lock. Her key ring was still swinging from the motion and scratched the car's paint a bit. She hoped Hector hadn't seen what she had done. He might try to remove the keys and offer her advice on how to take care of such a beautiful classic car.

He must have missed it because he passed her by without comment. It surprised her that Hector needed no prompting for this part of her plan. She would need to slow him down to give Fatima as much time as she could. A moment later, Lupe saw her poor sister limping across the field toward her car.

She had to keep Hector's back turned away from her car until Fatima was safely inside the trunk. Lupe rushed to get in front of him before coming to a stop. She really turned on the charm as she said, "I don't know how to thank you for this. I would have been in real trouble if you had not been here."

Hector smiled at her and said, "I was glad to help. I'm hoping this is not the last we see of each other, Lupita." He was almost handsome when he smiled, she thought.

Fatima reached the old Challenger and turned the key to pop open the trunk. Lupe timed another polite cough to mask the noise. Then she said demurely, "My goodness! I would be happy to see you again, Hector. What did you have in mind?"

"Well, I already have your address from your license," he admitted a bit embarrassed. "Can I pick you up Friday night and take you to dinner?"

Lupe saw that Fatima had managed to get inside the trunk and was about to close the lid. Lupe reached up placing her hands over Hector's ears drawing him close to kiss both cheeks. She didn't let go until she could see that Fatima was safely secured inside the trunk.

"Yes, I'm looking forward to it!" said Lupe. She left Hector standing there in a daze as she hurried back to her own car. She hoped to make a smooth departure, but she felt like she had forgotten something.

"Hey!" Hector yelled after her. "I still have to put the flat tire in your trunk."

She froze realizing she could not talk or even kiss her way out of this one. Her mind raced looking for a way she could keep him from opening the trunk. She had to come up with yet another diversion to get them through this. She remembered that there was no trunk release button inside her vintage car, and a desperate plan formed in her mind.

Lupe moved toward the rear of her car saying, "Oh that's right. I forgot all about it. Let me open the trunk."

She blocked Hector's view of the key ring before twisting it with all her might in the wrong direction. She almost cried out from the pain before the old key broke off in the lock. She waited for Hector to catch up to her before she turned toward him with the broken nub of the trunk key still clutched between her fingers.

"What happened?" he asked with genuine concern.

"It broke when I turned it and the trunk is still locked," she sobbed, as if she was about to cry.

Hector tried to lift the trunk lid up hoping it was not latched. It wouldn't budge and the back of the car shifted from his effort. He thought for a moment and said, "You must have a way to open the trunk from inside the car, don't you?"

"This is a wonderful vintage car, Hector, but they didn't have such things back in 1973," she said with a shaky voice. "Can you just put the flat tire in the back seat? I really should be going and I'm sure you have more important things to do."

Hector shrugged in agreement and went to get a tarp out of his car to protect the Challenger's upholstery. Once the flat tire was loaded, he said, "I will have to accompany you to the roadblock. If you tell them you can't open the trunk, they will force it open thinking you have something to hide."

Lupe almost gasped realizing how close they had come to getting caught. It seemed so unlikely that the police would check her car again on the way out. She wondered if Fatima had heard all this from inside the trunk.

"OK then," she smiled. "Let's go!"

When they reached the roadblock, Hector pulled up alongside her and instructed the men to let her pass. They looked confused but they didn't question him.

Lupe smiled and waved goodbye to Hector as she drove away. When her heart finally slowed, she took stock of their situation. Once they discovered Fatima was not in the safe room, the police would guess she had helped her sister escape. Then both of them would be on their 'most wanted list.' She sighed deeply realizing she would have to leave her home and never come back. As sad as that was, she knew it was worth it. She had Fatima back in her life!

Chapter 16

Jason checked his watch and surveyed the banks of the Usumacinta River. He estimated they were still fifteen minutes out from Piedras Negras. He was glad they still had an hour or so of daylight left to find the pyramid. He asked Nuri to see if the media was reporting anything on the pandemic back in the United States.

Nuri had brought along a satellite modem for his laptop so that they could get in immediate contact with Matt if and when they had updates. He typed in the key words 'pandemic' and 'pacific southwest' before he clicked the search icon.

A moment later several headlines came up, all of them reporting a devastating illness that was tracking the Colorado River. The media outlets had taken to calling the disease 'The Glut,' alluding to the gluttonous symptoms of those afflicted. There was no new information except that the number of cases was growing at an alarming rate. The CDC had issued a warning for anyone living in the Pacific Southwest to drink only water bottled outside of the affected area until further notice.

Mark, Nuri and Jason all looked at each other as they reassessed how important their search for the antidote had become. The Glut was created by the Sons of Darkness to wipe out their enemies, the Children of Light altogether. The symbols inside the pyramid also revealed that the cure developed so long ago was their only hope to save humankind. Without it, the pyramid's prophetic warning would soon come to pass.

Jason saw a good spot on the river bank to ground the zodiac before they continued on foot. He gunned the little RFP motor enough to push the rubber craft onto dry land. No sense in getting their boots wet if they could avoid it. Within minutes they had concealed the boat under brush and a camouflage tarp. Then they moved out single file toward the pyramid's coordinates.

Jason was in the lead occasionally swinging his machete to clear a path. His khaki shirt was soaked from the hard work and high humidity. Mark held onto the clear plastic box that contained several special RFP crystals. They were the same type used the last time they had stumbled upon the ancient site. These tiny receivers were designed to light up when in close proximity to a sending crystal. RF energy could power any electrical circuit but it did not emit a magnetic field in the process. However, once these crystals got within a few hundred yards of the pyramid, they would serve as an excellent compass.

Nuri hated this place. The last time they were here he had come within seconds of having his arm hacked off by thugs. He shivered despite the hot, muggy air as the experience ran through his mind again. He tried to shake it off by checking the JPL real-time satellite surveillance link on his laptop to make sure the area was clear. He tripped a few times because his attention was divided between the monitor and his footing. The satellite's bird's eye view confirmed there were no other people around for miles. He laughed at having this real-time detailed knowledge of the area, and remembered how impressed he once was with Google Maps.

Mark too had been shot at by the drug lord's goons, but he was excited rather than dreading this trip. His biggest dream was to unearth another Hall of Records like the one they had found in Egypt. For him, the danger paled in comparison to the discoveries that lay ahead.

The pyramid was easier to find this time because they had approximate GPS coordinates from their previous expedition. They nearly missed it the first time because it was covered in many centuries of jungle foliage. They had to look up to see the top because it was about as tall as a six story building. It was much smaller than its counterpart in Egypt. The Great Pyramid of Giza was perhaps ten times the size of this one. It was Jason who first commented on this.

"Are you guys sure this is what you're looking for? This has got to be the tiniest pyramid I've ever seen."

Mark fielded his question saying, "What do you suppose the Giza pyramid would look like if the surrounding ground level was five hundred feet higher relative to the base? There wouldn't be that much of a difference compared to what we're seeing here. The Egyptians have to constantly clear away sand to ensure that their monuments aren't swallowed up by nature."

"Are you saying there may be another five hundred feet to this pyramid below ground?" Jason exclaimed. "Did you see anything when you were inside last time that indicated this thing is as big as the one in Giza?"

"No," replied Mark, "but then it may be even larger given the angle of the slope from the apex compared to the Great Pyramid of Khufu, as it was originally named. If the Egyptian pyramid had the same slope to its walls as this one does, the Giza pyramid's base would be nearly twice the size it is now."

Jason let out a low whistle thinking about the massive structure that could be hiding beneath their feet. He led them to the side of the pyramid where Mark had first fallen through the wall, and noticed that the tiny crystals glowed brighter with each step.

Suddenly, Nuri let out a yelp that made all of them jump.

"Something moved in my backpack!" He yelled as he tore it off. He let it drop to the ground as he stumbled back a few steps. "There's something alive in there!"

Jason held his machete poised to strike. The two archeologists positioned themselves on either side of the backpack, ready to run if anything jumped out at them. They prodded it with their toes and then Mark flipped it over with his foot. They were hesitant to reach inside for obvious reasons. There was plenty of life milling around the mulch that made up the ground around them, but nothing inside the pack moved. All they could see was a strange bulge protruding against the side of the canvas.

"What is that?" asked Jason gesturing with his machete toward the curious lump.

Nuri leaned down to get a closer look. He wondered what would happen if he grabbed the protruding shape through the pack's canvas. He thought better of that deciding instead to give it a hard poke to see if it would move again. The entire backpack shifted away from him when he jabbed at it, but nothing inside moved on its own.

He suddenly recalled what the object might be. "I think that's the wooden box we took from the pyramid. It felt hard, like wood, when I nudged it. Remember it took three sliding panels to open the thing?"

322

"Take it out and see," Mark said excitedly.

A very nervous Nuri carefully unloaded the top items from his backpack. He set each article aside until he withdrew the ancient wooden box and handed it to Mark. They saw that Nuri had guessed right. One of the moving panels on the box was fully extended. While that answered the mystery of the bulge in the backpack, it didn't explain how the panel had moved in the first place.

The sunlight was fading, so Jason pulled out a lantern to get a better look. Mark started walking toward Jason and the light. Then he surprised them all with a yell as he threw the box to the ground like it was a snake that had bit him.

"The thing moved again all on its own!" Mark declared pointing to the box on the ground. "There, see? A second panel has slightly shifted. I swear I didn't move it!"

Jason brought the light over to examine it. He confirmed that the second wooden panel had moved slightly to the right.

"So I'm not crazy!" Nuri said with relief. "But what is making the panels move?"

"The first one moved when we arrived. The second panel shifted when the box was moved again," Jason deduced aloud.

He picked up the box and walked toward the pyramid. He expected the third panel to slide open, but it didn't. He walked back toward his friends watching the box for any changes. There weren't any. Then he retraced their steps, but the panels didn't move.

Mark took the box from Jason and said, "Maybe it's reacting to something that's not part of the pyramid." To test that theory, he started walking in a clockwise direction in an expanding curve away from where they stood. He continued to circle around them moving outward in an imaginary spiral. They all watched in amazement as the second panel slowly slid open as far as it would go.

"Wow!" exclaimed Mark as he stopped in surprise, and nearly dropped it again. He continued walking the circular path he was on, but nothing else on the box moved. He had almost completed another rotation of the spiral's arc when the third panel began to slowly slide downward.

Mark stopped to point out the geometry of the movements. "If we draw a line from here back through the point where the second panel moved, and then extend it back to the point where Nuri threw down his pack, those events all occurred in a straight line."

Without finishing his thought, Mark turned left and all three of them followed the imaginary line. They watched in silence as the third panel continued to slide open. When it was completely extended, they all stopped. A moment later the lid to the box popped opened, along with their mouths, as they stared in amazement.

When nothing else happened, Jason said. "It looks like the show is over, but why did the box guide us here?"

"Clearly there is some importance to this spot," Nuri speculated, "but how does our position here relate to the pyramid?"

Mark was quiet for a moment, and then offered another explanation. "I don't think the box is reacting to the pyramid at all. What if it's reacting to the stuff that was in the box when I found it inside the pyramid? Remember the objects I dropped when we ran, or rather, when Jason carried me out of here? Maybe those things are still here!"

"That doesn't make sense if the black and white vials were both the cause and the cure for The Glut," Nuri countered.

Jason laughed, "Let's find out." He dropped to his knees and started searching through the dirt and mulch around their feet. It didn't take long before he held up a translucent medallion about the size of a silver dollar.

Mark immediately recognized it. "That's one of the crystals from the box! Is there anything else?"

They were all on their knees combing through the decaying leaves and dirt. After ten minutes of searching they gave up.

Jason said what they were all thinking. "It looks like they got both vials and one of the medallions, but this one was left behind. You two are the archeologists. What is the importance of this thing?" he said holding up the crystal.

"In Egypt…," they both began, and then Nuri let Mark explain. "Do you remember the holograms we all saw in the Hall of Records underneath the Sphinx? It seems that an ancient civilization knew how to program holographic videos into crystal. In Giza, the movies we saw came from a crystal box that started when I opened the lid. It could be that this medallion can play videos as well. We just need to figure out how it works."

Jason peered through the crystal in his hand. He saw nothing unusual beyond the rainbow auras it created when the lantern's light hit it just right. He handed it off to Mark hoping he would have better luck. After trying multiple combinations with both the crystal and the box, Mark gave up too.

Nuri said, "Why don't we see if we can get inside the pyramid?"

No one argued. Mark put the crystal inside the wooden box and closed the lid. He then slid the three panels so that the box was a square again and that locked the lid in place.

Jason walked over to the nearest corner of the pyramid. The glowing RFP crystals didn't change as he walked the length of the base. Mark and Nuri scanned the flora-covered limestone wall for any way to get inside.

Mark said, "The last time, I fell inside because I was leaning against the wall as we backed away from the guys with guns. I'll bet you can move the box along the pyramid's wall to find the entrance. Just pick a corner and start there."

Jason answered, "The foliage is uneven right there compared to the rest of the wall," he said pointing to the irregular surface. "Let's start there. If that doesn't work, we'll do it your way."

Mark handed the clear plastic box of RFP crystals to Jason. As he approached the affected area, he felt a strange sensation in his fingers. He kept moving forward and the tingling feeling moved farther up his arm as he went. He leaned in until his hand and the box disappeared inside the limestone.

Jason said, "Both of you, hold on to my arm and don't let go!"

Mark and Nuri grabbed his free arm as they inched their way forward together. The normally unflappable Jason couldn't keep the excitement out of his voice. "Don't let go! None of us want to be in the middle of this wall when it decides to become solid again."

Each man purposefully held his breath as they stepped through the wall. The archeologists were concerned about inhaling the air as they passed through. What would keep it from turning back into stone inside their lungs? Jason was far more concerned about what they'd find on the other side of the wall.

A moment later, no worse for wear, they were inside the pyramid. They released Jason's arm and Nuri took a tentative step forward. The musty atmosphere smelled of history and secrets. The lantern and RFP crystals Jason held lit up the chamber around them. As they surveyed the large room, Mark confirmed it was the place where he first found the wooden box. Their eyes constantly returned to the section of the wall where they had entered. It looked just as solid as the other walls, with the same ancient writings Mark had seen before.

The two archeologists were distracted and impatient to go exploring deeper into the pyramid, but Jason reminded them of their primary objective. "We're here to find a cure for The Glut before we do anything else. The people already infected will die soon if we aren't successful."

Nuri said, "You're right. Mark, get out your laptop and let's begin a proper translation of what these walls are trying to tell us."

***

Lupe felt it was safe to stop once they reached a populated town some distance away from the roadblock. She freed Fatima by lifting the seatback out of the bracket that divided the trunk from the inside of the car. Lupe knew she had to abandon her vehicle. They located a car rental business and left the Challenger in a nearby alley.

The following morning, the sisters arrived at their destination in their non-descript rental car. They both let out a sigh of relief once they saw the sign, "La bienvenida a Cancún." Their first stop was the local bus station. Fatima held a locker key tightly in her hand as she exited the car. She told Lupe to keep circling around the

326

loading zone until she came back. On Lupe's second pass, she saw her sister limping slightly as she carried two medium size duffle bags.

Fatima opened the rear passenger door of the rental car and tossed the bags onto the back seat. Lupe just stared at them hardly believing her eyes. Her sister buckled herself into the front passenger seat and told Lupe, "Let's go!"

"How much money is in there?" Lupe asked, trying to sound casual as she pulled away from the curb.

"I have no idea, but the bags weigh about 10 kilos each and are filled with one hundred dollar bills in American currency," Fatima answered. She thought for a moment and then picked up her laptop with the satellite modem. She Googled the question and made a calculation in her head to estimate the answer.

"There is close to $1 million in each duffle bag," she announced. "That should be plenty to get away and start a new life."

"I should think so," Lupe said with a laugh. She was feeling a little light-headed. "Have you figured out how to get us out of Mexico?"

Fatima had known from the start that she had to get out of the country. She also knew she would need money, and a lot of it. She had solved the cash part back when she was in the safe room. It was there she discovered the keys and a list of bus lockers where Rodrigo had stashed 'emergency money.' From the bus locker locations, Fatima decided Cancun would be the best place to go if and when she got away. Now that they had plenty of American dollars, it was time to plan phase two of their escape.

Lupe and Fatima needed to rest. They both wanted a room with a view of the Gulf of Mexico and the Caribbean Sea. The Hard Rock Hotel was a perfect fit. It overlooked the Playa Tortugas dock where passengers from the cruise ships disembarked from the tender boats. All those tourists meant there would be plenty of retail shops to choose from, and they both needed to buy a few things.

Once they were in the room and had taken in the view, the sisters started planning what to do next. Fatima already had a forged passport and driver's license, but Lupe did not. They decided against obtaining counterfeit identification in Mexico. No one in that line of work could be trusted to not turn them in. Both Thiago and the government would offer huge rewards for them, so leaving the country by commercial airline or bus was a sure way to get caught. Even with the best forged documents, people from Macizo and the government would recognize them.

Lupe suggested that they hire a private plane to secretly enter the United States, but Fatima said it was not worth the risk. She had once overheard Rodrigo and Thiago complain that private air transport of 'Macizo's product' to America was no longer an option. The U.S. apparently had such an advanced radar system that they were sure to be detected.

They also agreed that using a coyote to smuggle them across the border was the last thing they wanted to do. Carrying two duffle bags full of cash around such people was a quick way to end up dead.

Since they couldn't go to the United States by air or ground, escape by water was their only option. Trying to stowaway on a commercial ship would hardly work. The two beautiful sisters knew they would not blend in well among sailors and dockworkers. However, Fatima had been on many cruises in her affluent life. She understood the boarding process of a cruise ship and that offered possibilities. She ran her idea past Lupe to measure her reaction.

They could board one of the cruise ships in Cancun that would take them to Florida. Once there, they could acquire forged ID papers for Lupe and go anywhere they wanted. They couldn't just sneak onto a cruise ship without help, but they had a lot of cash to buy all the help they needed.

Chapter 17

Thiago and his men finally arrived at Mexico's capital city. It took them a couple of days to drive all the way from Las Vegas. The border patrol officers simply waived them through at the U.S./Mexico check point. After all, why would the United States Border Patrol stop three Mexicans from returning to their own country? He knew that the road trip would be the least of their problems. Any policeman who pulled them over would gladly accept a bribe from members of the Macizo cartel. It was either that or become a dead hero. Thiago knew that negotiating their freedom with the government would be the riskiest part of his plan.

He had worked out everything during the long drive. He had received a quick text from one of his friends inside the police department that there were arrest warrants for everyone employed by the Macizo cartel. His discreet inquiries to paid informants let him know that federal soldiers were guarding the Cortez Estate to prevent Fatima from escaping. While ongoing bribes protected him at the lower levels of law enforcement, he held no sway with most of the federal government. If he was going to become El Jefe and resume 'business as usual' for Macizo, he would have to give his government a scapegoat.

To that end, he would negotiate trading Fatima's freedom for granting all Macizo members immunity from prosecution for their past crimes. The success of his plan hinged on two key points. The first was that the federal government was willing to make such a trade. The second was to be able to get Fatima out of the safe room and into their custody.

Thiago had made several phone calls from burner phones to arrange the details with his government. He knew they would try to track his cell phone signals, so he never used them more than once. He kept calling back with his offer until he was speaking directly with the Procuraduria General de la Republica, the Attorney General of Mexico.

A deal was made. Thiago would get Fatima out of the safe room and receive immunity from prosecution for any previous crimes he or any member of the Macizo cartel had already committed. Thiago promised the Attorney General he would disclose his plan for getting Fatima out of the safe room once he arrived at the Cortez estate.

***

Her satellite phone rang several times before Fatima answered it. She knew it had to be Thiago because no one else had her phone number. She tried to assume a proper frame of mind before she answered the phone.

"Olah, Thiago," she said, with rehearsed desperation in her voice.

"How are you holding up, El Jefe?" was his comforting reply. He wanted her to believe he still recognized her as the leader of Macizo. There was no sense in making this transition difficult.

"I am scared and bored sitting in this place. Are you able to get me out?" she asked hopefully.

"Yes, it is time. Do you remember how to access the tunnel and operate the railcar to get to the escape hatch?" he asked, not really knowing the answer.

"I remember that there is a way out through a tunnel, but nothing else," she lied. "Can you come to me, or is it better to talk me through how to do this on my own?"

"I will gladly come to you," he told her truthfully. "Please be patient and I will have you out of there within the next few hours."

Thiago knew it would be much easier to arrest her by opening the safe room door from the inside. She could get hurt trying to leave by the escape tunnel, and he did not want to physically harm Rodrigo's widow. His men would be closely watching how he handled this transition of power.

"Very well," she sighed. "Please hurry!"

They both hung up envisioning very different outcomes when the time came for Thiago to rescue her.

***

Lupe looked at her sister and asked, "Well? What did he say?"

"He will come to me in the safe room to help me escape," Fatima said, with a sarcastic laugh.

They both looked out at the tranquil view of the ocean from the balcony of their hotel room. Fatima shielded her eyes from the dancing sunlight reflecting off the water. She shook her head as she considered how lucky they were to get this far. Their hurried escape plan had worked against all odds. With just a little more luck and a few more days, they would be in the United States.

Now they had to find two women who roughly looked like them and were already passengers on a cruise ship. They also had to make sure the ship was eventually bound for the United States. Luckily, most of the cruise ships visiting Cancun came from American cities along the Gulf of Mexico and the coasts of Florida.

They walked to the dock where tender boats from the cruise ships offloaded their passengers. Twenty minutes into their search, they found what they were looking for. Two ladies that somewhat resembled the sisters stepped off a tender boat. They were a bit older than Fatima and Lupe, but their hair color, height and body shapes were close enough to work. Better yet, they were speaking Spanish to each other as they conversed about the points of interest they wanted to visit.

Fatima and Lupe decided these women were worth following. They eavesdropped on their conversation enough to learn that they were both born in Vera Cruz. The two friends were disappointed to have only one day in this glamorous port city. They would have preferred spending a few days touring Cancun and the surrounding sights. In particular, they wanted to see Chichén Itzá, the most notable historic landmark on the Yucatan Peninsula.

They entered a gift shop off the pier and Fatima and Lupe saw their chance. They followed the tourists inside and feigned an interest in the cheap souvenirs on display so they could stand next to them. Fatima listened in on their banter until she had an opportunity to introduce herself.

"Excuse me," she said in perfect Spanish, "but I couldn't help hearing that you need transportation to Chichén Itzá? I am Graciela and this is my cousin Liliana," she pointed to Lupe and continued. "We are driving there this morning and would appreciate the company. We hope to visit the United States soon and would like to get your advice about travelling there."

The women looked at each other, a little surprised at the offer. They had been warned by the cruise director to be wary of the locals, but these women seemed harmless and even a little glamorous. The first one answered, "Thank you but I don't think so. We have to be back on the ship by 6:00PM and we wouldn't want to impose on your generosity."

Lupe, posing as Liliana, smiled and said, "It's not an imposition. We planned on returning to Cancun before then anyway. I wish you would reconsider. We can serve as your amateur tour guides for Chichén Itzá and you can tell us all about America. What did you say your names were?"

The first one responded politely, "I am Clara and this is my friend Rosie."

With the formal greetings concluded, Fatima again tried to convince them. "I do wish you would join us. It is a two hour drive and we'd love to hear what it is like to live in America. Is it wonderful?"

Clara and Rosie looked at Fatima and Lupe and then back at each other. The beautiful cousins hardly looked dangerous and this was just the kind of adventure they hoped to experience.

Clara answered for both of them. "We'd be glad to go with you. Actually, thank you for this kind offer. It will save us a good deal of money instead of going by bus and having to arrange for a tour guide."

***

An exhausted President Donald Westbrook dozed on the couch after reading the latest briefing on The Glut. It wasn't that the information was boring, far from it. The report pulled no punches with graphic descriptions of the horrors of all the people who were starving and dying of thirst.

Don had not been able to sleep soundly since authorizing the assault on the labs down in Mexico. He had hoped to eradicate the disease with the fire bombings, but that had clearly failed. Worse yet, the Mexican authorities had not been able to coax Fatima Cortez out of the panic room in the basement of her home. The interrogations of the workers at the Cortez estate indicated that she may be the only person with knowledge of a cure for The Glut, if it existed at all.

His eyes were closed but he could sense a presence in the room. No doubt someone was afraid to let him know he was late for a meeting. When Don opened his eyes, he felt disoriented. He knew he had fallen asleep on the couch in the White House residence, but now he was sitting in the living room of his childhood home. He saw a man, dressed all in white, sitting across from him in his father's old leather chair. He couldn't think of his name, but he was sure he had seen this man before. Should he call for security?

"You will remember me soon enough, but to answer your question, my name is Halaliel," he volunteered.

"How did you know what I was thinking?" Don asked, still bewildered.

"Thoughts are very transparent in this realm, but that is not how I knew. You ask the same question every time we meet like this," Halaliel said with a chuckle.

"I do seem to remember you, but please remind me," Don prompted.

"We often discuss the challenges of your waking life and the options or choices you have before you," the man in white said patiently.

As Don's mind cleared, he did recall previous encounters with this man. He even remembered their last meeting in an ancient palatial estate just before he received the terrorists' warning about The Glut.

"I guess I should have listened to you," Don said apologetically. "I really made a mess of this one."

"When your conscious mind is in agreement with your subconscious, it can be a great advantage or a difficult challenge," Halaliel began. "You have been consistent in living in accord with your convictions. That you do not trust Mark and Nuri, or agree with

Matthew Alexander's approach to global relations, has made things difficult. Not surprising, but difficult nonetheless."

"You're saying they are right and I'm wrong?" Don asked dejectedly. He almost pouted as he had so many times as a boy in this nostalgic room.

Halaliel laughed. "I never cease to wonder why earthly perspectives are always so black or white. All of you have a positive basis for your beliefs. Mark and Nuri are dedicated scientists who only want the best for humankind. You see yourself as the United States' number one patriot, while Matt casts a wider net to define the people he desires to help. In many ways, the citizens of your country agree with your perspective more than his. The answer is that either approach, yours or Matt's, could have worked to make things better than they stand now. It is your conflicting tactics that have brought about the greater chaos."

Don responded with anger, "So tell Matt and his cronies to get out of my way!"

Halaliel moved and sat down beside Don and pointed to a large blank wall where the show was about to start. A giant panorama appeared before them depicting, as Don suggested, the various futures the world could experience if Matt and his friends did nothing. The days ahead looked bleak no matter what he did.

"Are there any scenarios that work out well for the United States without relying on Matt and his people?" Don asked hopefully.

Halaliel said, "Eventually, yes. There are many, but you would have to wait a very long time, as it is measured on earth, before prosperity would return to the level it is today."

"How long is 'a very long time'?" Don persisted.

Halaliel observed the new scene unfolding before them and responded, "If you chose this path, it would take 341 years."

Don hung his head and asked, "Anything with a shorter recovery period?"

"Yes, but only by a few decades, as things stand now," Halaliel offered.

"And what if I throw my support behind Alexander and his team?" Don asked begrudgingly.

The scene in front of them changed in reaction to his question. Halaliel watched for a moment and then said, "There will be a short period of reshuffling as the current political sand castles give way to more permanent and sustainable governments, but all nations would prosper much more quickly if you made such a choice."

Don sighed, "I'm all for prosperity, but Matt's options don't leave the United States in the position of power we have today."

"And is that truly your primary goal regardless of the results?" Halaliel asked.

"I was elected President to protect the people and property of the United States," Don said with conviction. "My personal preferences aside, I will always strive to preserve, protect and defend the Constitution of the United States."

Halaliel pondered his statement before saying, "That is the difference between you and Matt. He feels that all people have the right to pursue life, liberty and happiness. After all, doesn't the Constitution contend that all people have certain inalienable rights, regardless of their citizenship?"

"I get your point," Don admitted, "but where should I draw the line for the people I am responsible for, and those I am not?"

Halaliel smiled, "That is not for me to say. I can, however, offer a different perspective for you to consider."

"And that is?" Don asked with genuine curiosity.

"Stop thinking that all the world's problems can be solved with political power. The better way to attain true peace and prosperity is if each individual chooses that path for themselves. Throughout history, how well has it worked to coerce opposing peoples to agree on a point of contention?" Halaliel paused, looking for a reaction.

Don remained silent so Halaliel continued.

"Three men achieved amazing results ushering in a peaceful coexistence among people, and none of them were politicians. Think

335

of Martin Luther King Jr., Mohandas Gandhi and Jesus of Nazareth. You know the powerful effect their peaceful messages had on everyone who heard them. They spoke to all who would listen without changing their message in accordance with the race, religion or nationality of their audience. To make choices where everyone benefits may not be politically savvy, but it is the better way to live."

"I still see great value in the United States maintaining its position as the most powerful country in the world," Don countered. "The U.S. didn't become the world's leader without taking the initiative and doing things better than everyone else. Supporting Matt Alexander's efforts to level the global playing field leaves no one clearly in charge. That can only lead to chaos."

"If you would prefer a more secular example of my point," said Halaliel, "try this one. A startup company can only grow so fast and so far with the limited resources available to a sole proprietor. That's why many entrepreneurs choose to go public with the ownership of their company's stock. The logic is that they'd prefer to own an impressive percentage of billions instead of 100 percent of far less wealth. And don't forget, all the new stockholders prosper at the same time."

Don again said nothing.

"As far as worrying about the United States' position as the world's leader, my analogy still works," Halaliel brightened. "Many companies are controlled by a single shareholder with say 30 percent of the stock ownership. That's because the remaining 70 percent of the shareholders either agree with their position, or no one can organize a majority of the votes against the 30 percent owner's wishes. Making choices where everyone benefits is a great way to win the hearts, minds, and votes of those who could otherwise be swayed to work against you."

Don's mind was racing as it processed everything he'd just seen and heard. He barely noticed as his childhood living room faded away. His cell phone was ringing and he reached to answer it. He jumped up from the couch when he realized he was back in the White House residence. It was his Chief of Staff calling with an update on the pandemic in the pacific southwest. His encounter with Halaliel was soon forgotten.

Chapter 18

Mark's attention went to the obsidian altar. The wooden box containing the vials and crystals had been displayed there the last time he was inside this room. Most of its glassy dark surface was covered with centuries of dust. Centered at the top of the altar was a shiny rectangular outline the same size as the box he now held in his hand.

Nuri ignored Mark because he was narrating a video recording that featured the engraved inscriptions on the surrounding walls. They had developed their own software program to translate the symbols into English. Nuri began to input what he read off the walls of the chamber into the laptop's program. They had been able to decipher over 3,000 symbols thus far, but there were 4,999 characters given in total. The theory behind the unknown symbols was that they referred to new technologies using laws of physics that the scientists at JPL couldn't follow.

Jason surveyed the room as well and walked over to the black stone. He remembered seeing similar obsidian altars in the Egyptian Hall of Records. He recalled what happened when he placed his hand inside the carved place for it on the top of the pedestal. A sending RFP crystal rose from the floor, powering up all the devices on display in the chamber. This time, he didn't see an obvious depression shape for his hand. He pondered if this pedestal could be used for some purpose other than a resting place for the wooden box.

He set the lantern down and asked Mark to hand him the box to see if it would react to the altar. Jason set the box down on the top of the pedestal and a subtle knocking came from inside. He called for Nuri to come over and record whatever happened next.

Nuri picked up the camera and aimed it at the box. Jason manually slid the three panels aside and carefully opened the lid. Inside they saw nothing unusual except that the medallion was on its edge and vertically resting against the wood. Jason reached in and repositioned the crystal so that it was lying flat in the center of the box. The crystal disk began to rock from side to side and ended up, as before, on its edge resting against the wall of the box. Nuri kept recording and Mark just grinned.

Jason then lifted the box off the pedestal and held it up so Nuri could capture the crystal's movements from another angle. The crystal disk slipped sideways until it was resting flat on its back. Nuri took the medallion out of the box with his free hand to get a close up. In the meantime, Jason ran his hands lightly over the pedestal hoping to activate it somehow. His fingers plowed streaks in the dust, but nothing he did caused the altar to change.

He then asked Nuri to toss the medallion to him. He wanted to see if it would react to the pedestal without being inside the box. The men were only five feet apart and Nuri's toss should have been easy for Jason to catch. It wasn't. The crystal changed direction in mid-arc and headed for the altar. Even more remarkable was that it landed with a decisive clink, balancing perfectly on its edge, centered in the square where the box had once been displayed.

Jason drew closer to the medallion to see how it was attached to the obsidian. With no visible means of support, it stood at attention and didn't move. However, the moment he touched the upper edge the room lit up with a bright glow emanating from the crystal disk. Jason reflexively pulled his hand back to shade his eyes and the light faded.

"Did you get that?" Jason asked Nuri, a little louder than he intended.

"I was recording," answered Nuri excitedly, "but the light was so bright that I doubt it got anything usable. Let me move to the side and try it again."

Nuri quickly adjusted the camera to record in broad daylight. He nodded and Jason extended his hand to touch the top of the medallion once again. He didn't pull back this time when the light filled the room. Mark moved closer to his friends to get a better look.

The white light shifted as colors appeared and projected a perfect holographic portrayal of the same story that was etched on the walls of the chamber. They all jumped a bit when a clear voice began to narrate the scenes that played out before them. It was similar to the hologram they had seen in the Egyptian chamber but the verbal description helped them to understand the technology shown in the scenes. It was remarkable. They now understood that the full scope of RF technology covered much more than safe and efficient power. Depending on how the sending crystals were first melded together, the potential of RFP's abilities seemed limitless.

When the holographic show stopped, the images dissolved into the soft light coming from their crystals, the laptop's monitor, and the lantern. All three men stared at each other without saying a word. They had originally hoped they would find a cure for The Glut, which they did receive, but that seemed almost secondary to the other secrets the crystal had just revealed.

Nuri broke the silence. "Do you need me to tell you what that all meant? I know neither of you speaks Egyptian Arabic fluently. I can't imagine why the narration was in the language I grew up with. How could the ancient people who did all these incredible things know about a language that wouldn't be developed until the 7th century?"

"But I heard it in English!" said Mark. Jason simply nodded his agreement.

Reaching for the medallion, Jason said, "Take a look at this." He held the crystal up between his thumb and forefinger for the others to see.

It had a smoky black center and it was cracked as if someone had tried to drill a hole through its middle. He positioned it back on the pedestal and tried to get it to repeat the holographic show they had just seen. The medallion did not light up. When Jason took his finger away, the crystal fell flat and didn't move.

No one had to ask Nuri to check his video camera. He was already running it back to make sure he had recorded the holographic show. After a minute of playing with the camera's controls he announced, "None of what we just saw and heard was recorded."

Mark said, "Well that makes our next steps pretty clear. We have to head back to JPL right away and make sure they have medical personnel standing by to create the antidote for The Glut."

"You two will need to start writing out everything you saw in the hologram," Jason added. "You'll have plenty of time to do that on our way back upriver to Tierra Linda."

***

Clara and Rosie sat in the back of the full-size car the sisters had just rented. There was no sense tempting fate by driving the Challenger. The four women settled in for the long drive to Chichén Itzá. They were clearly tourists with their brand new tennis shoes, colorful clothes, and oversized sunglasses. Lupe was driving and Fatima rode shotgun. The car was filled with a pleasant mixture of perfume and suntan lotion. Fatima was glad she hadn't used their real names when they first met Clara and Rosie. She reminded herself they knew her only as Graciela, and Lupe was Liliana. It would be better if the two Americans never knew their real identities. It would not be long before she and Lupe would be on several governments' watch lists.

Fatima kept the conversation light in the beginning. Talking about the weather and scenery held their interest for a while, and then she asked what it was like to travel on a cruise ship. Clara and Rosie maintained a formal demeanor at first, but it didn't take long for Fatima's charm to ease their fears and loosen their tongues.

They were new to cruising and talked about the ship with its great food and plentiful shops. They said their room was small so they spent most of their time at sea socializing on the deck with the big swimming pool.

Fatima and Lupe learned that the two women worked together in Fort Lauderdale for an apparel company. They had been friends for years and made plans to take this trip together after Clara's husband had died. Her husband had not left her financially set when he passed away. In fact, neither of them could really afford this trip, which is why it was so nice to get a free ride and tour of Chichén Itzá.

Rosie was several years younger and had not married, at least not yet. Her job was her life, but it wasn't a very exciting one. She was glad to help Clara work through the sadness of losing her husband. At first, planning the cruise was just a fantasy to take Clara's mind off her grief. Eventually, they decided to go on the cruise regardless of the cost. Seeing their country of birth without having to pack and unpack repeatedly, or bother with buses, trains, or airplanes, was their idea of the best way to travel.

Both of them had become U.S. citizens after living in Florida for several years. Their excellent bilingual skills were highly sought after because of Florida's huge Hispanic population. They had found work with Uniform Apparel (U.A.) in Fort Lauderdale. Their employer supplied uniforms to companies doing business in and outside the United States.

Clara had learned to sew professionally before she and her husband immigrated to the U.S. She was now the team supervisor over the Spanish-only speaking seamstresses. She had a good rapport with both management and the people who worked under her.

Rosie was well-educated and hoped to become a lawyer someday. She worked as a paralegal at U.A. and was in charge of translating legal documents and contracts between her employer and the Spanish-speaking companies with whom they did business. She was better paid than Clara, but her law school debt had forced her to put her education on hold.

Fatima was hopeful that their offer of money in exchange for spending a few extra days in Cancun would change the women's lives for the better. It would certainly help her and Lupe to start over.

Fatima and Lupe had toured Chichén Itzá before, but at different times. Between them, they remembered enough of the Castillo Temple's history to keep their new friends entertained as they walked the grounds. It was a good thing that they had to return to the cruise ship early because both sisters had exhausted their historic knowledge of the ancient Mayan city. Also, after so much walking, Fatima's injured leg was starting to ache, and her limp was noticeably worse.

On the way back, Clara and Rosie started asking questions about the sisters. Fatima, posing as Graciela, wove a rather detailed story of how they grew up in Mexico City. Everything she told them was untrue, but she did set the stage for why they needed to leave Mexico quickly and why they had so much American money with them.

She told them that she had no children, but her husband, Zefarino, would not let her work. She added that while he was a good provider, he was impossible to live with. He was a violent man who often got drunk and threatened her life. The scene he made a couple of nights before had been the last straw. He had pushed her backwards so that she fell onto a glass coffee table. The impact knocked her unconscious, slashing her right leg as she fell. Her obvious injury made her story more credible, and hopefully gained some sympathy. Liliana had helped her get to Cancun so that Graciela could drain the family bank accounts and get safely away before Zefarino could catch up to them.

Fatima told them she always wanted to live in America and earn her own way in the world. She was glad to hear that being bilingual was a skill that would ensure her success. She must leave Mexico forever or her husband would eventually find her. He had friends in the government who were searching for her everywhere.

This was the crucial moment for Fatima and Lupe. She had laid the groundwork, but now it was time to ask these women for assistance.

"I hate to ask this, but can you help us?" Fatima said, almost pleading.

The two friends looked at each other before answering. Neither one wanted to get in trouble, but Graciela's story had touched them deeply.

"Graciela, I'd love to help you, but I don't know how. I'm unwilling to do anything that is illegal," said Rosie. "After all, I could never become a lawyer if we were caught helping you break the law."

Clara nodded that she was in agreement with her friend, although Lupe could see that she was wavering.

"The help that we are asking from you is not illegal and we will pay for your, shall we call it, consulting time," Fatima offered encouragingly. "I am lawfully allowed to leave this country. The only reason I cannot do so openly is because of my husband and his government friends. You would only be helping us to get away without him finding out."

Rosie, being the more legal-minded of the two asked, "What is it that you want us to do?"

"We need you to agree to stay in Cancun for a few days. You can take over our room at the Hard Rock hotel by the pier, which is paid for through next week. I also need you to 'forget' that you left your boarding cards for the cruise ship behind in the car. Liliana and I will board the cruise ship tonight instead of you, and travel back to Fort Lauderdale. Once we disembark there, we will collect your passports and overnight mail them to you at the Hard Rock hotel. We'll ship your luggage to your homes in Florida. You won't have any trouble getting back into the United States once you have your passports in hand."

"But how do we pay for our trip home?" Clara exclaimed. "I am almost broke after paying for this cruise."

Fatima smiled, "That's the best part. I can pay each of you $50,000 in American dollars to spend a few days here waiting for your passports to arrive. Then you are free to leave or stay as you wish."

Clara and Rosie looked at each other. Clara asked her friend, "Is this really legal?"

"Technically, yes," she said thinking it through. "There is no law against losing our boarding cards. There is no law against accepting Graciela's consulting fee or staying in the prepaid room at the hotel. Getting the cash back into America might be tricky, but we can do that as long as we claim it as income and pay taxes on the money."

Rosie turned back to Fatima, "What happens if you get caught boarding the cruise ship with our cards?"

"They would throw us off the ship and the Mexican authorities will arrest us on shore," Fatima explained. "The people who check those cards are employees of the cruise line, not the Mexican government. They will assume we stole the cards, perhaps by assaulting the two of you to get them. They will assume you are victims and start searching for you."

They looked puzzled, so Fatima continued, "If that happens, you should immediately contact the U.S. embassy to report that you lost the boarding cards. Also say that you missed the last tender to get back to the ship. It is possible that Liliana and I could be arrested for stealing your boarding cards, but that is our risk, not yours. Besides, the odds of getting caught in the first place are slight. You've boarded the ship a few times now. How closely did they look at the 5,000 faces boarding one after the other?"

"You do vaguely look like us," Rosie observed suspiciously. "I guess it's safe to say that our meeting was not an accident?"

A little embarrassed now, Fatima said, "You are correct. We approached you because of our similar appearance and that you are fluent in both Spanish and English. With your help, Liliana and I should easily pass for the two of you."

Clara asked Rosie, "What do you think?" It appeared that both ladies were onboard, so to speak.

Rosie answered, "They have clearly thought this through. We are not breaking the law. We can really use the money and, to be honest, I was disappointed that we were going to miss seeing more of Cancun. I am willing to go along with their plan if you are."

"I am happy to help Graciela escape the wicked man she's married to," answered Clara, already paying some overdue bills in her mind. "We are in stateroom 307 on the Countess Deck. As I said, the room is quite small."

Graciela smiled as she produced a duffle bag and began counting out thick stacks of bills. The friends' eyes lit up seeing all that money and realizing this was no joke. This was really happening.

Lupe turned into the parking lot of the Hard Rock hotel and parked in the guest parking area. She turned and gave them some last minute instructions.

"You should not drive this rental car because, if we are caught, it could connect you to us. Here are your access cards to the hotel room. Please stay inside the room until we are safely on the cruise ship. You will be able to see the pier and tender boats from your balcony. If we are allowed to board, you will see the ship leave Cancun by 8:00PM without incident. If we do not make it onto the ship, you will see us disembark from the tender boat with the authorities. If you see that we are under arrest, you should immediately leave the hotel room, and report your boarding cards as stolen to protect yourselves. We will say nothing of this arrangement. It doesn't help us to tell them, so you know that's true."

Fatima handed Rosie a cheap tote bag with the money inside. "Here is the $100,000 we promised. Please leave your boarding cards on the back seat of the car as you step out so, if necessary, you can truthfully tell the police that you must have left them somewhere. It will take two days until the cruise ship returns to Fort Lauderdale. I will leave a message for you at the hotel room when we arrive in Florida to confirm that we picked up your passports from the cruise line. Then we will forward them to your hotel via overnight mail. The only reason you would not hear from us is if we are caught. If you have not heard from us in three days, go to the U.S. Embassy in Cancun to get back home. Make sure you have properly dealt with all that cash before you seek their help."

With all that said, Rosie took the tote bag from Fatima and the two friends nervously placed their boarding cards on the back seat of the car. They wished the sisters good luck as they walked away.

Fatima looked at Lupe and sighed with relief. "Come on," she said. "We don't have much time to go shopping!"

Lupe looked at her in confusion. "Can't we get clothes and other necessities onboard the ship? What else do we need to buy?"

Fatima laughed, "Most of the cash must be turned into loose diamonds to get past the ship's security. Diamonds will fit in our pockets and won't be picked up by metal detectors. We can convert them back into cash once we reach the Estados Unidos. Let's go find out what nearly $2 million dollars in diamonds looks like!"

***

Thiago arrived at the Cortez estate with Luis and Tomas. The government man, dressed in a tailored suit, slowly walked over to them as they exited the car. They eyed each other suspiciously until the suited man came close enough to speak.

"You had better be telling the truth about knowing how to access the safe room," the man said with venom in his tone. "The only thing keeping you alive at this moment is the deal you made with the Attorney General."

Thiago responded casually, "I can get Fatima Cortez to come out without incident. She is the cause of your problems, not me."

"How do you plan to get her out of there?" the man asked.

"There is a tunnel connected to the safe room. I know where the secret exit is located. I will call Fatima and tell her we have arrived to help her escape through the tunnel."

The government man interrupted him, "Why do you think she has not already used the tunnel to escape?"

"She knows the tunnel exists, but she has never been in it," Thiago said confidently. "The truth is that she is a pampered woman. She is used to having everything done for her. Even if she knows how to access the tunnel from the safe room, she would not dare to venture alone into such a scary place full of bad smells and biting insects."

The man thought about this for a moment. From what he knew of any drug lord's wife, Thiago had to be right.

"I will take some of your men to the tunnel's exit point," Thiago continued. "We will use it to get to the safe room where your men will arrest Fatima. My men and I will be free to drive away, and you can do as you wish with her."

"That is the arrangement, but only if all you just said is true," the man warned again.

"Neither of us will be disappointed," Thiago said with a laugh. "You can listen in as I call her to tell her I am coming."

Thiago pulled out a cell phone and dialed Fatima's satellite phone number. After a few rings she picked up.

"Olah, Thiago? Are you finally here? Thank God you have made it!" Fatima said with relief.

"I am near the tunnel and will soon take you out of that place," he said in a hushed, yet comforting tone. "Just stay where you are and this ordeal will soon be over."

"Gracias, Thiago! I will be waiting!" she said, as they both clicked off.

The government man adjusted his tie as he glared at Thiago. He then motioned to five soldiers to get in the nearby truck. Thiago and his men got in their car to lead the way. Despite his posturing, the government man was relieved that this embarrassing siege would soon be over.

***

Fatima put the satellite phone back in her purse after hanging up with Thiago. Then she turned to her sister and smiled.

Lupe asked in a sarcastic tone, "Did he say he had come to rescue you?"

They both laughed as they watched the sunlight sparkle like diamonds on the ocean waves. They were both poolside safely enjoying Mojitos on the cruise ship. Fatima wished they could see Thiago's face when he discovered she was not in the safe room.

She answered, "He is a good actor. I could almost believe he was sincere."

"He deserves everything he is about to get," Lupe said without remorse.

Chapter 19

Dr. Steven Welch was waiting nervously in JPL's main conference room. The Glut had already claimed thousands of lives and the death rate was increasing by the hour. The first to die had been the weakest patients who were already infirmed. At the catastrophic rate the disease was spreading, The Glut would claim at least one million lives within the week.

Steven had travelled to Pasadena from Washington D.C. to follow up on a call that was made to the White House. He was told that a scientist at JPL had information that could cure The Glut. He was familiar with JPL because of their past breakthroughs in RF energy. But weren't they all about aerospace and physics? Regardless, the CDC in Atlanta showed no progress toward discovering a cure, so what did he have to lose? In truth, he was glad to get away, for a while, from Washington and its politics.

Through the glass windows, he saw a large group of people walking with purpose toward the door next to him. Most of them wore suits but a few wore white lab coats. Then he noticed that three men in the entourage wore safari clothes, looking like they had just come out of the jungle. He was perplexed, but this did promise to be entertaining.

An incredibly fit man in a black suit, tie, and buzzed hair cut opened the door. He quickly scanned the room before nodding to the man behind him that it was okay to enter. Steven stood up automatically as the second man entered the room. It was Matthew Alexander, the immediate predecessor to President Westbrook. The three men wearing dirty khaki gear followed him in. The Secret Service agent who had opened the door closed it behind them leaving everyone else outside. He stood just outside to guard the door as the introductions were made.

Matt told Dr. Welch that he was mainly there to observe. The archeologists had a great deal of information to share with him. Matt requested that Dr. Welch limit his questions until they were done with the initial briefing.

Steven hesitantly raised his hand. Matt smiled as he nodded to go ahead. "Why are archeologists briefing me on a cure for The Glut?"

Matt answered the question so they could move on. "These are the men who discovered the secrets behind RF technology. They also discovered an antidote for the Glut in Guatemala, but that is a long, complicated story. Suffice it to say that both The Glut and its cure ended up in the hands of a drug cartel just minutes after my friends discovered it. They successfully risked a return trip to the area that yielded the information we're about to share with you."

"Are any of you medical doctors or biologists?" Steven asked, ignoring Matt's initial request.

"No!" Matt answered quickly. "Frankly, I must ask you to hold your questions. Also, please limit your queries to The Glut and its cure," Matt said evenly.

Steven couldn't understand why everything related to the government had to be kept so damn secret. He decided to let them tell their story rather than ask more questions they wouldn't answer. He gestured that they proceed.

Mark began with, "We believe the cure for The Glut will be silicon based rather than carbon. That is why you have had so little progress in your efforts to find an antidote."

Steven couldn't help but interrupt, "But all living creatures are carbon-based beings. How can a silicon-based disease thrive in a carbon-based body?"

Mark answered, "We thought you might know. We're hoping to learn a lot from your medical knowledge using what we have found to help you."

Nuri picked up from there, "The cure should be simple enough to manufacture. All you'll need are two ingredients, water and silica beads. They need to be combined using a ratio of 1.6 ounces of water for every ounce of silica beads. Actually, if I'm going to be precise, the ratio needs to be accurate to three decimal places, so it's 1.618 to 1. Once mixed together, the compound needs to be irradiated by a specially designed RFP crystal. We produce them here at JPL. They operate at a resonant frequency of 28,657 hertz.

That's a fairly low vibration, but it is a bit above the typical human hearing range."

Mark handed Steven a detailed color drawing of a clear tube that looked like it was copied from a photograph. He said, "The substance in the test tube you see here is believed to be a cure for The Glut. Its color is pure white and the viscosity is similar to evaporated milk. If the infected person ingests the tiniest amount of this substance, they will recover immediately. It also works just as well by injection."

Nuri added, "Once the antidote is created, simply add miniscule amounts of it to water to act as the carrier. The amount contained in a one liter beaker would be enough to cure the world's population and then some."

Steven checked to make sure his mouth wasn't hanging open. The four men were all looking at him patiently waiting for a response. Nothing he had just heard made sense, but then, neither did The Glut. He decided to buy some time to think by asking a few more questions.

"I'll come back to all those numbers you mentioned in a moment, but what does silica gel have to do with treating The Glut?" he asked.

Nuri said, "You are familiar with silica gel, I'm sure. It's in the packets of tiny beads you find in food packaging to absorb moisture. It's ironic that it carries a warning not to eat it. It really isn't poisonous and it makes an effective cure for The Glut if the other instructions we mentioned are followed."

"And you've already successfully tested this antidote?" Steven asked.

"Not personally, no. But the same people who were around when The Glut was created did test the cure and it worked for them," said Mark, smiling like there was much more to that statement than he had offered.

"And I suppose I can't talk to those people, or get a look at their research documentation?" Steven asked, already knowing the answer.

"Correct," "Yes," Nuri and Mark answered together.

Steven went on, "It did not escape me that the ratio of water to silica gel is the same number as the Golden Ratio. Can I also assume that the frequency you gave of (he looked down at his notes) 28,657 hertz is a prime number as well as part of the Fibonacci sequence?"

Jason interrupted here, "Since I seem to be the only one who doesn't know what all that means can you quickly catch me up?"

"Actually, I could use some clarification, too," said Matt.

Dr. Welch looked at the archeologists and they gestured that he go ahead with the explanation.

"Fibonacci was a mathematician in the 12th century who discovered that many aspects of nature and science were based on a particular sequence of numbers. It comes down to the ratio between two consecutive numbers in the Fibonacci sequence. Actually, the ratio is not exact until you reach the 40th consecutive number, but from there on, it is very stable."

Jason said, "I have no idea what you just said. Can you dumb it down for me?"

Steven smiled and said, "Sure! The integers in the Fibonacci sequence start with 0 and 1. When you add those two numbers together the answer is 1. Each new number is found by adding the previous two numbers given. So if 0 + 1 = 1, then add together the last two numbers, in that case they are 1 and another 1. So 1 + 1 = 2, and that takes you to the next equation by adding the last two numbers, being 1 and 2. That gives you 1 + 2 = 3. Then you have 2 + 3 = 5, and 3 + 5 = 8, and so on."

Jason said, "So the next number would be 13 because you would add the 5 and 8 together?"

"You've got it!" said Steven. "The Golden Ratio is calculated by taking any two consecutive Fibonacci numbers, after the 10th iteration, and dividing the larger number by the smaller one. The ratio will always come out the same, 1.618, from that point on."

"And what's the significance of the Golden Ratio?" Jason asked.

"There are many uses for it in math and finance. But the ratio is seen everywhere in nature, from the leaf arrangement in plants, to the pattern of the florets of a flower, the bracts of a pinecone, or the scales of a pineapple. The Fibonacci sequence is applicable to most living things, including a single cell, a grain of wheat, a hive of bees, even all of humankind," Steven said, marveling at how this 'cure' might well relate to eradicating The Glut.

Mark said, "We noticed the same thing. While we don't understand why these things work together to cure The Glut, using a Fibonacci sequence to restore life made intuitive sense."

Nuri added, "Melding RFP crystals together using specific Fibonacci frequencies produces different results and abilities. Some produce power while others cure illnesses. We believe there is no end to the applications this technology will have...."

Matt cut him off saying, "Let's stay on point here gentlemen!"

Steven frowned, but he did have a question he hoped they could answer. "What is the significance behind the frequency for curing The Glut being a prime number?"

Mark answered, "So far as we know, it's a coincidence. We are hoping you will be able to answer that one yourself after you develop the cure."

***

Thiago asked Luis to park on the side of the road. The truck with five Mexican soldiers pulled over behind them. They all exited their vehicles, and followed Thiago through the tall grass to the tree line.

It had been a few years since Thiago had been to the exit point of the escape tunnel. He knew where it was, approximately, but the foliage here was constantly changing. He asked the men to spread out in a line leaving about five meters between them. He quickly described the round metal hatch that would lead them to the safe room, and the search was on.

He saw fresh tracks indicating that someone else had been here recently. Luckily, they were barely visible and he doubted that the soldiers would notice.

Tomas was searching to Thiago's right and called out that he saw something. The other men converged on the spot where Tomas was pointing. Sure enough, it was the hatch that Thiago had described.

"Luis, Tomas, open the hatch!" said Thiago.

The metal wheel turned easily for them and they swung the heavy lid open within seconds. Thiago winced at the ease with which they opened it, knowing it meant bad news. Thiago hovered over the access hole as he looked into the tunnel. He nearly swore aloud the moment he saw that the tunnel lights were already burning. Then he saw the railcar and its broken levers lying directly below the hatch. There was no doubt now. Fatima was gone, and he was in immediate danger.

His mind raced as he tried to figure how they too might escape. The man with the suit had ordered the soldiers to disarm them back at the estate, so his cunning and trickery was all he had left. Their only chance was to get the armed soldiers down into the tunnel and secure the hatch so they could escape. Luring all five of them down below while he and his men stayed on top would not be easy.

He said aloud, "Ah good! The lights work and the railcar is here. One car is to be kept at each end of the tunnel, but sometimes they forget. Let me go down first to make sure everything is in working order."

He stepped through the hole and descended the steps of the metal ladder to the dusty floor of the tunnel. He carefully relocated the broken levers so they were hidden from view while he pretended to check on its condition. Suddenly, Thiago cursed loudly hoping to prepare them for some bad news.

He angrily ascended the ladder and said to the group, "The railcar doesn't seem to be working. It looks like we'll be walking a few kilometers to get to the safe room."

He looked at the leader of the soldiers and said, "We are, of course, unarmed. I know that Fatima has weapons with her inside the safe room. Do your men have tear gas or are you going in guns blazing?"

The leader said, "We have tear gas. Our orders are not to hurt the woman if we can help it. She must be taken alive."

Thiago already knew this, but it provided the reason he needed for the government soldiers to go first. He smiled and motioned toward the hatch saying, "After you, amigo!"

The leader ordered his men into the tunnel, and they queued up to climb down the ladder. Thiago motioned to Luis and Tomas to stay where they were. When the last soldier's head had cleared the hatch, Thiago jumped forward and slammed it shut. As he spun the wheel to secure it he yelled to his men to grab a couple of sturdy branches.

Thiago could feel the men trying to turn the wheel, but he strained to hold it in place so the hatch couldn't be opened. When his men brought the branches, Thiago had them jammed through the spokes of the wheel so that they dug into the dirt around the hatch. He had to make sure it would take time for them to get out of the tunnel.

A moment later all three of them jumped when a loud noise came from below. The idiot soldiers had shot a round at the hatch trying to get it open. Bullets would not penetrate the metal, but there was a real risk of one ricocheting back and hitting the soldiers. There was no second shot so either someone was hurt or they figured out that shooting their way out was a foolish idea.

"I don't think their radios will work inside the tunnel at this distance," Thiago said excitedly. "We may have only thirty minutes to escape before they manage to get out through the safe room at the other end."

Luis said, "But what about Fatima?"

"She's gone, you idiot!" Thiago yelled. "There's no telling where she was when I called her on the satellite phone. For all I know she is sunning herself on a beach in Belize. We have to get out of here, now!"

They ran for the car. He told Luis to open the trunk and then get ready to drive. Luis did as ordered and Thiago took a screwdriver out of the trunk. He walked over to the soldiers' truck and flattened all four of the tires.

With that, Thiago got into the car and they sped away.

Chapter 20

Fatima had just left a message for Clara and Rosie that their passports would arrive at their hotel the following day. She was glad that their plan had worked to get her and her sister to Florida. She was also happy that she had been able to help the other two women with their money issues.

It had taken some effort and a hefty tip to their cab driver, but they located a man who sold forged ID documents in nearby Oakland Park. They opted to go with driver's licenses and Social Security cards, rather than pay much more for U.S. passports. They were already inside the country with no plans to leave in the foreseeable future.

They decided to have dinner at the local diner next to their motel. Converting the loose diamonds into cash was becoming a priority because they were almost out of money. They started to fantasize about what they would do from there.

"If we're not careful, we'll have to start planning for the future," Fatima joked.

Lupe set her menu down with a wry smile and asked, "Do you think we should quietly live out our lives in the suburbs of America?"

"I don't know about you, but I wouldn't fit in very well," Fatima said shaking her head. "Besides, from the news reports, the disease they are calling The Glut is becoming a real problem. I'm beginning to believe that the stupid American government may not have the cure. That would mean that the men who dropped the vials in Piedras Negras were not actually working for the government."

Lupe was shocked. "Then why in the world did they destroy the labs with the cure that could save their own people?"

"I know! That just doesn't make any sense. Unless, they thought Rodrigo kept the cure at our home," Fatima said in frustration. "But how could they think we had the cure at home if we didn't use it to save him?"

"Maybe they thought that every bit of The Glut would be destroyed in the three labs," Lupe offered. "If you hadn't sent Thiago to Las Vegas a few days early, they would have been right."

"I am glad the Americans are suffering," Fatima said under her breath. "They are hiding so much more from the world than how to create RF energy."

"What do you mean?" Lupe asked.

Fatima described her experience with the crystal medallion and the Spanish-narrated holographic movie.

"So you think they have the technology to purify water in any quantity at practically no cost?" Lupe asked skeptically. "Then why don't they purify The Glut out of their own water supply?"

"Perhaps the heartless cabrons see some advantage in allowing so many of their people to die. They also know how to grow enough food to feed the world by using some other kind of RFP crystal." Fatima said, getting worked up thinking about the medallion's epic movie. She looked around the restaurant to see if anyone was listening to them. No one was.

Lupe didn't believe Fatima. "How can all that be true and yet for many years they have people starving, even dying, in their own country? Certainly they would make sure their own citizens were properly cared for if they can do as you say. How do you explain that?"

"It would help to know what the connection was between the three yanquis and the U.S. government," Fatima pondered aloud. "Maybe they stole The Glut, the cure, and the crystal from their own government. That might explain why they have not distributed the cure to their own people. But the United States obviously knows a great deal more about RF technology than they are letting on. The video I saw made that clear."

"We may never find out what happened," answered Lupe. "What do you think we should do now?"

"If the Americans don't come up with the cure soon, our own people in Mexico will be infected by The Glut," Fatima said, almost slamming her hand down on the table. "Their arrogance continues even when so many lives are at stake. I feel like God wants me to expose their despicable acts to the world."

Lupe almost laughed. "And how would you do that? Your own government has a warrant out for your arrest. We are in this country illegally carrying almost $2 million dollars in diamonds. If Thiago is still on the loose, he is plotting to find and perhaps kill you. Do you think anyone in the American media will take you seriously? You'll probably get arrested if you try to go public. Is that what you think God wants?"

Fatima shook her head. "No. And that's why I haven't brought all this up until now. Before we left Mexico, I didn't think we would get this far. But now that we have, I'm sure I was spared to do something very important."

Lupe was not convinced that her sister was being called to fulfill a righteous mission. She hoped to bring Fatima back down to earth. "Well, in the meantime," she sighed, "we have an even higher priority. We have to change those diamonds in for cash. Has God given you any ideas on how to do that?"

"We will go to New York City," Fatima said with certainty. "I understand that they have a diamond district with billions of dollars in gemstones. We should be able to quietly sell the diamonds there. If we limit the number we sell to any one dealer, we should avoid raising suspicion."

Lupe said, "Good! We have enough money left to take a bus if we leave in the morning."

Jason, Mark and Nuri were sitting together in their offices in Pasadena. The first samples of the cure had already been produced. Dr. Welch had arranged to test them at a nearby hospital on several dying patients. All they could do now was wait.

There was another reason the men were not meeting at JPL. Assuming the cure worked, Dr. Welch and JPL didn't need them anymore. They were free to focus on everything else they had learned in Piedras Negras.

They had been shown the layout for the Hall of Records and for the massive underground complex surrounding the pyramid. The holographic show had revealed many new concepts about RF technology, and the ancient civilization that had harnessed it.

358

The discussion quickly turned into a debate when it became clear all three of them disagreed on what to do next. Jason was anxious to go back to Piedras Negras right away, before the rest of the world tried to shut them out of their own discovery.

Mark wanted to stay in Pasadena and experiment with the wealth of information they had learned from the medallion's movie. Assuming the cure worked and their trustworthiness was restored, Nuri wanted to organize a well-funded government expedition to explore every inch of the Piedras Negras complex.

"We know approximately where the Yucatan's Hall of Records is located," said Nuri. "In fact, we are now certain that two locations remain, in Piedras Negras and in Bimini. President Westbrook will be so grateful we discovered the cure for The Glut that he'll back us all the way."

"President Westbrook isn't going to believe a word we say," Jason disagreed bitterly. "Our discovery of the cure for The Glut won't change his mind a bit."

Then Mark said, "We can't go back there on a shoestring budget. It could be one big waste of time. We have plenty to work on right here in Pasadena while we figure out how to get more funding..."

Jason interrupted, "You forget, we are no longer the only ones who know about the location of that pyramid. The reason no one else has messed with it before now is because no one else knew where to find it. Now that the politicians know it exists, it will not be a secret for long. I say we get down there again, quickly, and find that Hall of Records before it's too late."

"Seriously, Jason? Mark is right that going back down there with no funding could easily be a dangerous waste of time," Nuri said, shaking his head. "We have the video, such as it is, from inside the pyramid in Guatemala to prove we were there, and we turned the President's blunder into a heroic event by bringing back the cure for The Glut. Westbrook can't hate us now. I'll bet he's our biggest fan after all we've done for him."

The debate was cut short when Nuri's cell phone began to ring. He answered it and listened for a moment, apparently receiving some very good news.

"Great! I will tell them," he said as he hung up.

"That was Matt and Dr. Welch," Nuri explained with a broad smile. "The cure is working on all the patients treated so far. JPL and the CDC are going into full production immediately to enable a mass distribution of the antidote."

Jason pumped his fist and the two archeologists hugged in celebration. The threat of The Glut was over, but the party didn't last long. The cure worked but they still had to decide what to do next.

They agreed that Matt needed to be brought into this discussion. They wouldn't make any decisions until he'd had a chance to weigh in with his opinion.

***

After barely escaping with their lives, Thiago, Luis and Tomas had to leave the country. Thiago swore he would get even with Fatima for setting him up like that. The Attorney General of Mexico had informed the U.S. government of Fatima's and Thiago's escape. Victims of The Glut had now been reported in Mexico. The serious charges of international extortion and murder now included Interpol in the search for any members of the Macizo cartel.

Thiago sent word out instructing his best people to regroup in Tierra Linda. He also ordered that they bring with them whatever cash and weapons they could easily move. The cartel already had a sizeable presence in the town because of its proximity to the airstrip and the Mexican border. Also, they were on good terms with most of the Guatemalan security forces. Years of payoffs to key people had allowed Rodrigo to maintain a low profile in this country.

For years, Rodrigo made sure that Guatemala was used only as a conduit to transport their products into the United States. He always knew a contingency plan might be needed, and their nearest neighbor to the south was the logical choice. This was especially true because Mexico was not on good terms with the Guatemalan government. That made extradition unlikely. And that meant that Tierra Linda was about to become Macizo's new headquarters.

With the destruction of their three main labs in Mexico, Thiago was hard-pressed to get Macizo back into full operation. Luckily, the only part of their supply chain that was ruined was repackaging the cocaine into kilo blocks for distribution. Their supply of cocaine and the wholesale delivery network remained unscathed. Thiago planned to create new packaging locations in the remote northern jungles of Guatemala. The Piedras Negras airstrip made Tierra Linda a natural hub for their reorganized operations. And Tierra Linda was the nearest town with adequate housing for their people, and shipping access to all the supplies they needed.

Thiago had already checked into his room at the Tierra Linda motel. He was surfing the net in the lobby while waiting for the rest of his men to arrive. He read the latest news on The Glut epidemic. More victims were reported as it moved deeper into Mexico. The death toll was rising at an alarming rate. He was glad to have put even more distance between his people and the pandemic.

Suddenly, Luis rushed into the lobby. "Thiago, I have news of the gringos who killed Rodrigo and our men!"

"Tell me!" Thiago said, quickly closing his laptop. This would be the first good news he'd heard in a while.

"I was talking with the pretty blond camarera who works at the cantina next door," he began. "I said that we were looking for three gringos who caused us a lot of trouble. She told me she remembered seeing them because they had returned just a few days ago. In fact, she said they left again the day before we arrived."

"Did she say anything else?" Thiago asked calmly. "Better yet, does she know where they are now?"

Luis answered, "Just before they left, she overheard them talking. It sounded like they wanted to come back soon, but they did not say when."

"Make sure to post our people at the local airport and bus station to watch for them," Thiago said with a sadistic smile. "I want to welcome them warmly when they return."

Chapter 21

It had been tempting to shop in Orlando and take in the world famous tourist attractions there, but Fatima and Lupe stayed on the bus. They didn't have enough cash with them to play the role of sightseers. It was ironic to have nearly $2 million dollars in loose diamonds in their purses and yet not be able to afford more than a couple of bus tickets to New York.

The upside was that the long ride afforded them all the time they needed to catch up on the years they had missed in each other's lives. They both got an inside look at how the 'other half' lives in the process. Fatima was surprised at how happy Lupe was despite divorcing her husband and living in relative poverty.

For her part, Lupe was impressed at the depth of Fatima's love for Rodrigo. She began to understand why her sister had chosen to go with him all those years ago. Fatima had ignored the sordid dealings of the cartel and focused on giving Rodrigo a loving, comfortable home. She patiently waited for her husband to retire and live the good life with her, but they never got the chance. Lupe finally understood why Fatima was so upset with the United States. After all, it was their citizens' demand for cocaine that kept the cartels in business, and ultimately killed Rodrigo.

"It sounds like you still plan to avenge Rodrigo's death, especially after the U.S. government retaliated against you." Lupe's tone was more of a question than a statement.

"I have tried to move passed this," Fatima frowned, "but I can't seem to let it go. The U.S. still has control of RF technology and has allowed The Glut to spread into Mexico after destroying our labs where we kept the cure. This whole mess only seems to get worse as time goes on."

Lupe asked, "But what can you possibly do about it now that you're on the run from the authorities?"

"I've been thinking a lot about that since we first got on the bus," Fatima said softly, as if she was talking to herself. "I need to quit running and set everything right. I don't want to look over my shoulder for the rest of my life. I want America to be accountable to the world for what it has done. And let's not forget Thiago. He must pay for his treachery."

Lupe almost laughed. "That's quite an agenda you have there, hermana. Just how do you plan to do all that when I am the only friend you have left in the world?"

"I am beginning to see a way, sestrica," Fatima said with a smile. "Life will never again be what it was, but I think there is a solution we can live with."

"I'm all ears!" Lupe said, hopefully.

"I need to tell the world what I know of Rodrigo's death and The Glut," Fatima said with conviction. "We happen to be heading to New York City where the world's leaders meet regularly. If I can convince someone at the United Nations to publicly announce what I know, the United States will have much to answer for. I failed when I tried to coerce the U.S. into sharing their RF energy with the world. I think the better way is to attack their arrogance and shame them into it."

"But how do you come forward publicly and manage to stay out of prison in the process?" Lupe asked, concerned that her sister could be losing touch with reality.

Fatima's attitude was almost buoyant as she said, "I will expose the United States for the liars they are. To save face, they will have to give up a great deal of wealth and power to the other nations. After that, I will give them Thiago in exchange for our freedom and the right to live here without fear of arrest. After all, Thiago is the one who poisoned their water supply. I am convinced he acted against my orders when I told him to stop."

"You can blame Thiago all you want," said Lupe, "but how would you be able to prove it?"

"That is part of a grand plan I still have to work out, but I get closer every time I think this through," Fatima said proudly. "Keep asking me questions and we will solve this together!"

***

Despite all Thiago's queries and connections, Fatima was nowhere to be found. She had simply disappeared. He could guess that her younger sister, Lupe, had helped her escape because she too had a warrant out for her arrest. That meant they weren't in jail, but knowing that did little to help his cause.

Thiago wanted to find her to tie up loose ends. He knew she would continue her crusade until she was in prison or dead, or worse yet, until he was. He wondered what would happen if he called her satellite phone number. She had answered the last time he called, but they had not spoken since he escaped. He pulled out a burner cell phone and dialed in her number. He counted the rings as he waited for her to answer. He decided if she hadn't answered by the twelfth ring, he would give up. Just before he hit the disconnect button, the ringing stopped and the line clicked open.

"Olah Thiago," said the female voice at the other end.

"Fatima, it is you!" Thiago responded, hardly believing she had answered. "Let me start by saying that I was not arrested. I am glad that you are free as well."

"Is that all you wanted to say to me, Thiago?" she asked suspiciously.

"No," he said excitedly, trying to keep her talking. "You should know that I have found the three yanquis responsible for Rodrigo's death. They do live in America. I may have to wait a while for them to come back, but I am a patient man."

Thiago's surprising news held her attention. "What will you do when you catch them?" she asked.

"I will make them pay for murdering my friend and your husband," he admitted. "Is there something in particular that you want me to do?"

"Yes," she replied. "Tell me the truth about what happened at Lake Mead. I am sure I called you in time to stop you from poisoning their water. You told me you had already gone through with it, but I knew better. Why did you do it?"

"What does that matter now?" he asked with resignation in his voice. "The governments of the United States and Mexico are looking for both of us. Neither of us will be safe for the rest of our lives."

"Still," she persisted, "I want to know why you poisoned the water after I told you not to."

He considered how to phrase an answer so that she would believe he had good intentions. "I wanted them to suffer! How was I to know that the crazy Americans would allow their own people to die and let The Glut spread to Mexico? I still don't understand it." Thiago really let his anger show. "I thought they would be forced to distribute the cure and admit that they were responsible for starting the pandemic. It never occurred to me that things would get this far out of control."

"Thank you for telling me, Thiago," said Fatima. He heard the line go dead. He dialed her back repeatedly, but she did not pick up.

***

Mark, Nuri and Jason were headed south to return to Piedras Negras. They had met with Matt and discussed their options. Matt believed President Westbrook would do his best to hinder their efforts even though they had provided the cure. Matt was certain that the video of the pyramid would not change Don Westbrook's poor opinion of the four of them. They reluctantly agreed that from here on out they were on their own.

They landed at the Playa Grande Airport near Tierra Linda and stopped at a locker Jason had rented on their last trip to retrieve his backpack with his gear. Then they checked into the same local motel where they had stayed before. It was convenient because it had a passable restaurant next door and they were hungry. They planned to return to Piedras Negras in the morning and explore the pyramid from top to bottom. The crystal's holographic movie had shown that it was possible to access the massive underground complex by going through one of many hidden hallways inside the pyramid.

The sun was setting as they ate their dinner. Jason noticed that two local men were watching them closely from across the room. It looked like their interest was more than simple curiosity about the three strangers in Tierra Linda. He kept an eye on them as well and made a mental note to find out if they had friends with them in town.

365

After they had finished eating, the three Americans retired to their room on the second floor of the motel. Jason told them he had forgotten something. He grabbed his backpack and said he would return after a while. He used the back stairwell to exit the building and check on the men who had watched them in the restaurant.

From a discreet distance, he watched the two men leave the motel. They had been talking with one of the servers in the restaurant. He was sure they were going to see their employer. He followed them to a bar down the street and saw them duck inside. Through a large window in the bar, he saw them sit down across from an ominous looking man and pretty woman. They talked for only a moment before the two men left.

Jason saw they were headed back to the motel. Luckily, they didn't seem to be in a hurry. He decided he had enough time to ID the man in the bar. He pulled a digital tablet out of his backpack and zoomed in for a shot of the man still sitting with the woman. He wasted no time and emailed the picture off to his old friend Joe. Joseph Faro had been a fellow soldier in Jason's Delta Force unit. He had accepted a position with the CIA as a consultant after retiring from the military. Jason asked Joe to run a facial recognition search on the guy.

He then opened the skype software on his computer and called Joe. His friend picked up right away.

"Hey man! What's got you working at night?" Joe said with a grin.

Jason replied quickly, "If you could run that picture I just sent to you, I really need to know who this guy is."

"Already doing it," Joe said sounding a little distracted. He was suddenly more focused on the facial recognition software than the conversation.

Jason asked, "Is there a problem?"

Joe's expression turned serious as he looked directly into his laptop camera. "Jason, your man's name is Thiago Bernal. His boss died a few weeks back making him the new top guy in the Macizo cartel. He is bad news and wanted by his own country, Mexico, for at least a dozen felonies, including treason."

Now Jason was worried. "That's not a surprise, but I had to be sure. Joe, I don't mean to be rude, but I really have to go. I think this Thiago Bernal just sent two guys after my friends."

He signed off before Joe could respond. He shoved his tablet into his backpack and started running down the road to the motel. He retraced his steps to the back stairwell that he'd used to leave unnoticed. He had to duck into the shadows when he heard people coming down the stairs.

His blood ran cold when he saw the two thugs walking close behind Mark and Nuri. They had bound their hands behind them and held guns to their backs as they led them away from the motel. Jason hadn't thought Thiago's men would move so quickly. He kicked himself mentally realizing his carelessness left him unprepared to take these guys down without risking the lives of his friends.

He decided to follow them to see where they ended up. He consoled himself knowing Thiago must want to talk with them or Mark and Nuri would already be dead. That would buy him some time to come up with a plan.

He followed the four men for over a kilometer until they entered a rundown wooden shack on the outskirts of the town. As they went inside, a dim light appeared through the gaps in the knotted walls. Jason took a moment to walk the perimeter of the rustic one-room building to see what options he had to safely get them out of there.

The old shack was more of a barn than a place to live. He moved in close to get a look inside through one of the knotholes. Nuri and Mark had plastic ties holding their arms behind the wooden chairs' slatted backs. Ties also secured their ankles to the front legs of the chairs.

One of the men made a quick call on his cell phone and Jason guessed Thiago would be joining them shortly. As much as he wanted to rush in there and rescue them, he knew he had to wait. He needed to find out what the Macizo cartel wanted with his friends. He calculated that they were relatively safe even if they told Thiago everything they knew. They would still have value as bait or ransom.

Jason needed to remain of out sight, but he also had to stay within earshot of anything said inside. He quietly circled the building to position himself on the opposite side from the door. He hoped Thiago would think that he had dumped his friends and was now on the run.

Jason found he could hear everything said inside the shack. That meant he could wait for the right moment before making a move. His biggest concern was the unknown. There was no reason for Thiago to bring more men with him. However, if Jason was wrong about that, then a messy shootout was his only option. That wouldn't end well for any of them.

He heard determined footsteps coming toward the shack and knew it was too late to change his mind. He peered carefully around the corner to see Thiago with one other man. Jason understood enough Spanish to hear him tell the man to stay outside and watch for anyone coming. Then he entered the shack and closed the door behind him.

***

Mark wondered where Jason could be. He worried that the reason they hadn't been rescued by now was that Jason didn't know they'd been kidnapped, or worse. He could smell his own fear above the stink of the dirty little room.

Nuri was less concerned with the details of their predicament. His mind was caught in an endless loop. He was reliving his worst nightmare of being tied up by the drug runners with threats of bodily harm.

When the door opened and yet another man walked in, both of the archeologists started to struggle against their restraints. They could see a fourth person standing guard outside the door, and they began to doubt if even Jason could save them now.

One of their kidnappers brought the new man a chair and he turned it so that the back was to Mark and Nuri. He straddled the seat and sat down facing them with his arms resting on the chair back. He stared at them for a moment without saying a word. Mark kept his gaze on the floor. Nuri tried to stare down this imposing man but he lost the contest. Smiling broadly at his victims, the man began to speak.

"I can't understand how the two of you killed four of my best men," Thiago said with feigned disgust. "It had to be your missing friend. You two are worthless."

Mark found his voice and said, "You're right. We haven't killed anyone and I have no idea what you're talking about. We just got here this afternoon, checked into the motel, ate dinner, and went to our room. Why are you doing this?"

"I'm talking about the men you killed in Piedras Negras," Thiago growled. "Two were shot on the landing strip and two more in the jungle. What were you doing there in the first place?"

Nuri blurted out, "We were on an archeological expedition. We didn't kill anyone and we don't care what you're up to. Please, just let us go and we'll forget this ever happened."

Thiago let out a chilling laugh and said, "But I will never forget you. You have ruined my life, and you imply that you accomplished that without even trying? My enemies would love to have caused me such pain. You have a great deal to answer for and this is just the beginning."

The two bound men went silent, clearly terrified. Thiago savored the moment before resuming the interrogation.

"Where did you get the two vials you brought with you to Piedras Negras?"

This question took them by surprise. "We didn't bring them with us. I found a wooden box inside the pyramid just minutes before your men tried to shoot us. I accidently dropped its contents, including those two vials, when we escaped," Mark said, his voice shaking.

Thiago's face showed his confusion. "Pyramid? What pyramid are you talking about?"

"Your men didn't mention the hill next to where they found the vials?" Nuri asked rhetorically. "It is an ancient pyramid completely covered by jungle growth. It is the place we have been searching for over the past ten years throughout Guatemala."

"So you say you took the vials from inside this pyramid?" Thiago went on. "If you are truly archeologists, as you claim, what use did you have for such a deadly disease?"

369

Mark exclaimed, "I already told you I had just found a box. We had no idea what was in it. It looks like you found out the hard way when your men picked up the vials."

"So you had no idea what the vials contained?" Thiago asked disbelievingly.

Nuri jumped in. "We did not. Days later, we heard the news and it wasn't hard to guess what happened after your leader died. What you don't know is that the story of the disease and cure is written on the inside walls of the Piedras Negras pyramid. Only we know how to translate that ancient writing."

Mark added helpfully, "We came back just a few days ago looking for the cure. We found it in that pyramid and our government is already distributing it to anyone infected with The Glut."

Thiago didn't know what to believe. Their story sounded plausible and it answered why they kept coming back to this God-forsaken town in Guatemala. Who could have guessed that three yanquis looking for an ancient pyramid could ruin the Macizo cartel by accident? Over the years, others had tried to shut them down and paid dearly for their failures. The odds against this happening without considerable planning were astronomical, and yet, here they were.

"Where is your missing friend?" Thiago asked in a neutral tone.

"He stepped out a few minutes before your men broke into our motel room and kidnapped us," Nuri said, his voice rising under the stress. "I have no idea where he is."

"Is this true?" Thiago said, now looking at Mark.

Mark was exhausted and so angry that he couldn't help himself. "Oh that much is true, all right. What he didn't tell you is that our friend singlehandedly killed your men in Piedras Negras, and is probably planning to kill the rest of you as we speak!"

"Is that so?" Thiago said, enjoying that the subject had now changed to one where he was the expert. "If he tries anything, these men have orders to kill you first and then take him alive so we can express our annoyance in a very personal way."

Thiago and his men laughed at the thought of someone trying to take them all down at once. He was ready to teach this gringo a fatal lesson in humility. After all, how many hostages did he need? The next moment all hell broke loose inside the shack.

***

Jason listened intently through an open knothole as Mark and Nuri answered Thiago's questions. He hoped it was obvious to everyone that the incident at Piedras Negras should be blamed on an unfortunate coincidence. It was as if some unseen force had brought them together to unleash The Glut and disrupt the lives of everyone involved. Now Thiago and his men were threatening their lives again. Jason shook his head already seeing in his mind how the next minute would play out.

He knew his Glock-18 semi-automatic pistol could shoot through the cheap wooden slats of the shack. With careful aim, he could kill the two men standing behind Mark and Nuri without hurting his friends. Once the first two were out, he didn't have to be careful shooting in the other direction. He would do his best to put Thiago and the man outside the door down using whatever bullets he had left. The speed with which he could execute the plan would dictate who lived and who died.

Jason positioned himself so he could see his first two targets through the knothole. He confirmed that their guns were already drawn and that they posed an immediate threat to his friends. No doubt Thiago was armed, but he wasn't holding a gun at the moment. Jason wasn't sure where the man outside was standing. If he didn't take out all four bad guys within a couple of seconds, Mark and Nuri's odds of survival were not good.

He was about to sneak a peek around the corner to get a fix on the fourth man when he heard Mark threaten Thiago. "What the hell was he doing?!" Jason screamed inside his head. Mark's foolish bravado had just forced everyone's hand. Thiago didn't need two hostages. Jason had to act now to save his friend's life.

He pointed his Glock at the thugs and squeezed off two fast rounds. Both were perfect head shots and the men collapsed to the floor spraying blood and brains that looked like a cherry pie flung against the far wall. Jason rotated his hips and emptied the rest of his clip through the wooden boards in Thiago's direction. To his surprise, no rounds were fired back at him. It could be that Thiago didn't have a gun, or he'd quickly exited the shack when the shooting started.

With a practiced hand, Jason pressed the release to drop the empty clip and slid in a fresh one. He threw himself forward to the ground into a prone position and aimed at the corner of the shack closest to the door. He expected the other man to appear with his guns blazing at any moment. He guessed wrong. Bullets suddenly ripped through the cheap boards over his head and he felt shards and splinters of wood embedding in his flesh. He looked at the wall and saw that it was a good thing he was lying flat or he'd be dead.

He didn't return fire knowing better than to waste his ammunition. He waited for the other two men to give away their positions. He could hear one man yell to the other that he was going to get reinforcements. Jason couldn't tell if the person leaving was Thiago or the guard by the door. It didn't matter. If he didn't kill the one that was still there in the next minute, they would all soon be dead.

He reached for his backpack and pulled out a flashbang grenade, all the while lying low and watching for any movement. He pulled the pin but kept a tight grip on the handle. Once he let loose of the grenade, the fuse would ignite within four to seven seconds. With the clock ticking, Jason surmised that the man on the other side of the shack would do nothing to put himself at risk. Time was on his side and he only had to stay alive until more help arrived.

Jason wasn't about to let that happen. With a quick look around to make sure the man was not in his line of sight, he tossed the grenade in a high arc over the top of the shack. Then he yelled as loud as he could to make the guy look around him. Jason had barely covered his eyes and ears before a concussive boom and overwhelming light enveloped the area.

He immediately jumped up, Glock in hand, praying as he rounded the corner that the grenade had done its job. The man was rolling in the dirt groaning loudly and rubbing his eyes. Jason fired a double tap to the man's head and turned toward the door.

He pulled his knife from its sheath as he ran inside the shack. Within seconds he had cut the plastic ties and was urging his friends to follow him as fast as they could. They were dazed, but they managed to get up and stumble out of the shack. Jason retrieved his backpack and they all headed away from the town. Their survival depended on getting to Piedras Negras as quickly as they could.

They had a hike of a few miles ahead of them. He hoped that Mark and Nuri would be able to go the distance after this experience. If they could make it to the inflatable zodiac they had stored by the river, they would be in Piedras Negras before morning.

Chapter 22

Carlos Medrano had just returned to his office in New York. He had travelled to his home in Guatemala City to spend a few days with his family and friends. As expected, his time off meant he had a lot of catching up to do.

Carlos was Guatemala's Ambassador to the United Nations. He had held the position for the past two years and was well-liked by his peers. He enjoyed spending most of his time in America. There was ongoing civil unrest in his country, and he was glad to distance himself from the political maneuverings of his constituents at home. He had started his professional life practicing international law but his government already had enough attorneys. He eventually found that he had a real talent for securing foreign aid money from the wealthier countries of the world. His ability to cajole millions of dollars from the G-8 nations was quickly becoming legendary. Now he was the highest ranking Ambassador for Guatemala.

He looked through the phone messages that had stacked up on his desk while he was away. Most involved the usual requests intending to sway his vote on delicate political matters. When he came to the last message in the stack, he was sure that it must be a joke. It said that Fatima Cortez needed to speak with him urgently. He recognized the name, especially since her husband Rodrigo, leader of the Macizo cartel, had recently died of The Glut. What could she possibly have to say to him?

She left no phone number or other way to contact her. The note only said that she would call back this morning and requested that he take her call when she did. He thought about what she might want from him. A quick check online for the news told him that Mexico's Attorney General had issued a warrant for her arrest. He envisioned dollar signs guessing she probably wanted to apply for asylum in Guatemala.

Granting her official asylum would be impossible, of course. Not only was she wanted by her own country, he was told that the United States had connected her, unofficially, with the pandemic that had broken out in their pacific southwest region. Still, this woman was incredibly wealthy and probably desperate. He may be able to arrange for her to assume a new identity in Guatemala for a sizeable donation to the government. The few people he worked with who would know the truth of this were also wise in the ways of the world. He instructed his secretary to put Ms. Cortez through to him the next time she called.

***

Fatima and Lupe had done well for themselves in New York City. It seemed that the American dollar and quality diamonds bought in Mexico worked well together. By the time Fatima sold the last of her diamonds in New York, she had checks totaling $2 million dollars on her original $1,850,000 investment. Not a bad return over just a few days.

She decided to test the validity of her forged driver's license and Social Security card. She opened an account with a New York bank and deposited the checks she received for the diamonds. Because the checks all came from local merchants and none of the deposits consisted of cash, the usual red flags signaling illegal activity were avoided. The account manager shook her hand a moment longer than necessary and she wasn't sure if it was because of her classic beauty, her large bank balance, or both.

Fatima reminded herself that the Guatemalan Ambassador was supposed to return from his vacation that morning. Now that she and Lupe had cleaned up the cash they needed, it was time to finish what she had started with the American government.

She bought a burner phone and called for Ambassador Medrano. When she gave her name to the receptionist, she was immediately connected.

"Olah, Carlos Medrano speaking," he said quickly.

"Ambassador? This is Fatima Cortez. Thank you for taking my call," she said softly.

"What can I do for you Senora Cortez?" Carlos asked, doing his best to keep his tone neutral.

"As surprising as this may be, I am not asking for any favors from you, Ambassador," Fatima replied.

Carlos was clearly skeptical. "It is said that the person who asks for nothing is always the one who asks for too much."

"Perhaps," Fatima said with understanding, "but see if you aren't happy with what I have to share with you."

"You have my attention," Carlos said brightly. "Please tell me what's on your mind."

Fatima offered an abbreviated version of her story, leaving out that a major source of her information was the crystal medallion's holographic video. She told the Ambassador that the American government had already developed far more RF technology than anyone knew. She accused the United States of following a secret and self-serving agenda to control the global economy by keeping most of this amazing technology for themselves. Carlos remained silent the entire time. He wondered if this woman was crazy, telling the truth, or a combination of both.

"I find your story fascinating," he said cautiously then asked, "but what do you want me to do with this information?"

"I want you to tell the U.N. just how selfish the United States is, how they consistently lie to the world, and then demand that they share what they know of RF technology with all nations," Fatima said flatly. She couldn't tell if the man was a fool or purposefully being obtuse.

"I cannot say such things without proof. Do you have any evidence to support these allegations?" he asked.

"Yes," she lied, "but over the phone I can only point to circumstantial evidence. For instance, I know that the disease they are calling The Glut, as well as its cure, came from RF technology. I can supply you with enough additional information that you can either get them to admit the truth, or perjure themselves before the world."

Carlos was aware of The Glut, and the latest news reports said that a successful antidote had been developed just in time to save millions of lives. To have such a horrible disease appear out of nowhere, and then discover an impossible cure within days of the outbreak, seemed to support her contention. He decided that meeting with Fatima Cortez in person was in his, and Guatemala's, best interests.

***

Lupe waited nervously in their hotel room for her sister to return. She would have gone with Fatima that morning, but they agreed that it would be better if she were not connected to her dealings with Ambassador Medrano. Lupe would stand by, ready to help, if Fatima was arrested or worse.

Their plan was to stay in New York while Fatima did what she had to do with the United Nations. Mostly out of boredom, Lupe decided to unpack and put away their things. She found herself staring at the satellite phone in Fatima's suitcase. She had never used one before and was curious to see how it differed from a regular cell phone.

She couldn't see much difference except for the large folding antenna. She pressed the green button to compare the phone displays and the satellite phone powered up a few seconds later. Lupe was disappointed that it required a password to access its features.

Suddenly, the phone started to ring. She was already on edge and the shock of the unexpected ring almost caused her to drop it. The display read, "Incoming Call." She thought for a moment and realized that, like a cell phone, she wouldn't need to enter the password to answer it. She hit the green button and answered, "Olah? Um, hello?"

After a moment of silence at the other end a deep voice said, "Esta Fatima?"

Lupe remembered that Thiago was the only person besides Fatima with this phone number. Her thumb moved to power down the phone but she stopped suddenly. She decided there was no harm in talking with him, and he might have good news for her. "She is not here. Can I take a message?"

Thiago paused before saying, "Yes. Tell her that two of the yanquis are archeologists and the third is some kind of highly trained bodyguard. They managed to get away, but I am sure they are headed for Piedras Negras in northern Guatemala."

"Okay. Is there anything else?" Lupe said, scribbling the information on the hotel's note pad by the lamp.

377

"Yes," he said. "Tell her the norteamericanos claim they had found the two vials inside of an ancient pyramid in Piedras Negras. They dropped them in their haste to escape our men. I think they were telling me the truth. I will call again when I have taken care of them."

Lupe hit the red button ending the call without saying another word.

***

When Fatima returned to the hotel room, Lupe said she had news that couldn't wait. She told her of Thiago's call and that the norteamericanos claimed to have discovered the vials inside an ancient pyramid. While Lupe hadn't been able to make much sense of Thiago's message, Fatima's face froze in a state of surprise.

"What was he trying to tell you?" Lupe asked.

Fatima took a moment to collect herself. If Thiago was right, all her previous assumptions had been wrong. She felt dizzy with the implications and then the fog cleared from her mind. Suddenly, the entire story made perfect sense to her. "It means The Glut that killed Rodrigo was not planted on purpose by the norteamericanos. If the vials were discovered only minutes before in that pyramid, those men could not have planned Rodrigo's death. It also means that the holographic images I saw must have come from ancient technology. If those men didn't have a chance to see that strange movie, they may not know everything RF technology can do."

"So how did they discover RF energy?" Lupe asked.

That was a good question. Fatima mentally compared everything she had learned from rumors and news reports of the Sphinx tragedy along with the story given to her by the medallion. She decided to run it past her sister to see if she could make sense of it all.

"From what I remember, the Americans discovered RF energy shortly after the terrorist bombing of the Sphinx in Egypt," Fatima explained. "Thinking back, the crystal medallion must have been showing me the three places where these ancient secrets are hidden. Thiago mentioned one of them, being the pyramid in Guatemala. Another location was supposed to be underneath the

378

Sphinx. The third one is somewhere near the Bimini Islands that are part of the Bahamas.

"If the bomb that destroyed the Sphinx also uncovered the chamber beneath it, the technology could have been discovered then. It's not hard to imagine that the same archeologists who found that place in Egypt knew where to look for the second location in Guatemala. I remember that one of the suspects involved in the Egypt bombing was not from the Estados Unidos (USA). The news reports said he was from the Middle East.

"What if those same men were searching the jungles of Guatemala for another place like they found under the Sphinx, only this time they found The Glut and its cure instead? If Thiago is right about them returning to Piedras Negras again, my guess is that they are still searching for a hidden chamber containing all manner of ancient secrets. I couldn't understand most of what the crystal was showing me, but I'll bet those archeologists have figured it out."

"This is all so hard to believe!" said Lupe. "I don't understand what these secret chambers have to do with you."

Fatima looked resolute. "I must tell Ambassador Medrano that his country is the proud owner of all the secrets behind RF technology. He will be interested to know that the Americans are already trying to steal them, just as they did in Egypt. I will go to his office tomorrow morning and explain everything."

"And how do you stay out of prison if you publicly come forward like this?" Lupe's tone was full of concern.

"The Ambassador will do all the talking for me. He'll want to keep my name out of it so that he receives the credit for exposing America's treachery," Fatima smiled. "Afterward, I will give Thiago to the Americans. I recorded that phone call with him when he admitted to poisoning their lake after I told him not to. If I play that right, I should be able to negotiate our freedom to start a new life in the United States."

Chapter 23

Jason was sure that Thiago and his thugs would be waiting for them when they reached Piedras Negras. They would get there by airplane instead of plugging along in a rubber boat. He wished Mark and Nuri had not told them about the pyramid and their interest in it, but that couldn't be fixed.

Once they located the zodiac and got on their way, he pushed the little RFP motor as hard as he dared. The faster they could get to Piedras Negras, the better odds they had of hiding inside the pyramid before Thiago could track them down.

He still had some of the RFP crystals that allowed them to pass through the pyramid's walls and he absently patted them through the cargo pocket of his vest. Mark and Nuri had nothing with them but their clothes since they had been abducted from the motel room. Jason still had his backpack which was stocked with various weapons, and his tablet computer.

There was little to do as they continued up the river. It would still be dark for several hours and visibility was limited to wherever the men pointed their flashlights. Tree branches hung out over the banks and the loamy fragrance reminded Mark of a swamp he had once explored in Louisiana. Jason took a moment to fire up his tablet with the satellite modem. His face glowed blue in the artificial light. He sent an email off to Matt Alexander telling him of the tight spot they were in with Thiago and the Macizo cartel. He didn't know if Matt could help them or not, but it was worth a try.

When he finished, he took their GPS coordinates and looked at his watch. He hung his head after calculating their disappointing progress. If they hoped to get inside the pyramid safely, they needed the cover of darkness to pull it off. At least he knew the area and the most direct route to get to their destination. He was glad when Mark and Nuri drifted off to sleep as they moved along the river. It saved him from sharing the bad news that the next twenty-four hours were likely to bring the toughest challenges of their lives.

***

The Director of National Intelligence, Max Atwater, was already waiting in the Oval office when President Westbrook walked in.

"Good morning, Max," the President said curtly. "What's this all about?"

"Good morning, Mr. President," Max said, happy to have had a moment to gather himself. "I received a transcript from the NSA of two recorded phone calls between Fatima Cortez and the U.N. Ambassador from Guatemala, Carlos Medrano." At Westbrook's look of impatient confusion, he clarified, "Her husband was patient zero of The Glut and also the leader of the Macizo cartel in Mexico." The President nodded as he remembered her significance, so Max continued. "She gave her name to the Ambassador's secretary and that flagged our software. The message she left said she would call back and she did. A subsequent phone conversation between them took place sometime later."

"What was the gist of their discussion?" Don asked grimly, not sure where this was going.

"She told him some truths, and a lot of lies, regarding what we do and don't know about the limits of RF technology." Max paused before adding, "She is trying to convince him to go public with this information to embarrass the United States."

"What does Guatemala have to do with all this?" Don asked, not making the connection.

"You remember Matt Alexander's archeologists and their Hall of Records story?" Max prompted. "They claim to have found a similar chamber inside a pyramid located in the jungles of northern Guatemala. Allegedly, it contains the same relics they say were buried beneath the Sphinx in Egypt. I thought their story was a load of crap all this time. However, they did return from their last expedition with a cure for The Glut. I think we really have to investigate what they've been doing down there."

Don rubbed his eyes wearily. It was going to be a long day. "Are you saying those nutbags have been telling us the truth all this time?"

"I'm sure they've been lying to us more than they've been truthful, but we can't ignore this," Max warned. "Ambassador

Medrano is about to meet with Fatima Cortez in person and my guess is that he will try to embarrass us at the next meeting of the General Assembly at the U.N."

"She's here in the United States?" Don asked incredulously. "Can't we just arrest the woman before she meets with Medrano?"

"No," Max said shaking his head. "She's already inside the Guatemalan Embassy in New York. My guess is that she'll remain there until Ambassador Medrano has addressed the U.N. delegates."

"Get Alexander on the phone," Don ordered. "I cannot stand that man, but he could be useful in getting us through this mess with the least damage. Also, he might be able to tell us what's really going on down in Guatemala."

***

The secretary's voice interrupted the silence. "Matt Alexander is on the phone for you, Mr. President."

Don grunted as he picked up the handset and punched the button next to the flashing light. "Matt! How are you today?"

Matt paused a moment remembering how they had left things the last time they spoke. He decided not to mention it. "I'm fine, Mr. President. What can I do for you?"

"I wanted to thank you and your guys for finding the cure," Don said with genuine appreciation in his tone. "Millions of people would have suffered and died if your people hadn't come through when they did."

Matt was waiting for the other shoe to drop. "I'll convey your thanks to them. I must admit I'm a little surprised to hear from you."

Don knew he'd have to eat a little crow before Matt would let him move beyond their previous meeting. "I am truly sorry for that, and I want to hear what your guys found down in Guatemala. It is obviously a story worth listening to."

Matt had been absentmindedly checking his email before the President picked up the phone. He was about to answer when he saw the email from Jason marked with a red exclamation point. He clicked to open it and saw that his friends had almost died the night before, and they were still not safe. He remembered he was on the phone when the President interrupted his thoughts.

"Are you still there, Matt?" Don asked. "It sounds like I lost you."

"My apologies, Mr. President," Matt said quickly. "I have just read an email from Jason Fisher. They are in Guatemala right now and he is telling me they are in great danger. They think they have discovered a way to access the Hall of Records located inside a pyramid in Piedras Negras. The danger comes from the surviving members of the Macizo cartel. They blame our guys for killing their leader, Rodrigo Cortez, and ruining their drug trade business."

"I'm not sure I follow you," Don said, sounding bewildered. Then with incredulity, he bellowed, "Are you saying it was your people who found The Glut and unleashed it on the world?"

"It's quite the opposite, Mr. President," Matt said in earnest. "They did find the vials containing The Glut and its cure inside that half-buried pyramid. Then they were fired on by Macizo members. Apparently, our team had stumbled across a concealed airstrip the cartel used for transporting their drugs. My friends dropped the vials as they escaped. It was the cartel's people who discovered what The Glut could do...the hard way. My guess is that the threat you received to infect the U.S. was in retaliation for killing their leader. They mistakenly thought our expedition was a U.S. government sanctioned op intended to kill their people.

Matt continued, "They have since learned that Jason, Mark and Nuri are private citizens innocently exploring Guatemala for ancient artifacts. That doesn't change the fact that the cartel still intends to murder my friends."

Don was having trouble keeping up with the sudden turn of events. As he thought it over, he realized he could use this to his advantage. After all, the huge favor he needed from Matt just became a quid pro quo arrangement.

"Is there anything I can do to help them?" Don asked, smiling to himself.

"Can you send a covert team to Piedras Negras, Guatemala immediately to rescue them? I can give you the exact coordinates for the pyramid's location. If they aren't already dead, that's where they will be."

"I might be able to help, but Matt, the other reason I called is that I have a favor to ask of you," Don said, making it clear that his cooperation hinged on Matt's answer. "I need you to represent our interests in a matter of some concern that has arisen at the UN."

Matt was taken aback. He couldn't understand why Don would ever want him to represent the United States. They failed to see eye-to-eye on most everything in politics. Still, his friends were in trouble and Don had made it clear his help was contingent upon getting Matt's agreement.

"I will help you in any way I can if you will send a team to Piedras Negras in the next five minutes," Matt said bluntly, trying to keep the panic out of his voice.

"Done!" Don said, a little too triumphantly. "I will have Director Max Atwater contact you to get the ball rolling on both matters. I will send a government jet to LAX to take you to New York. Once you're in the air, we'll talk again, and I can tell you what I need."

***

"How is it going with Matt Alexander's people?" President Westbrook asked Director Atwater.

"I'm not sure we can help them, sir," Max said, hating to be the bearer of bad news.

"We can't stop a bunch of gangster drug dealers from murdering American citizens in a lawless country like Guatemala?" Don practically yelled.

"Please look at this strategically for a moment," Max cautioned. "Our proposed and unauthorized incursion into Piedras Negras could be construed by Guatemala's government as an act of war. Fatima Cortez has already told their Ambassador that they have a hidden chamber holding all the secrets of RF technology. She's convinced them that we are trying to steal everything inside that pyramid."

"How can they believe that fairy tale?" Don said with disgust. "There are no hidden chambers and no ancient technologies to be discovered. Didn't Matt say that only cartel criminals are after his guys rather than government troops?"

"That is true for the moment, sir, but we don't know what will happen once Ambassador Medrano conveys Fatima Cortez's story to his boss," Max answered, trying to stay on point. "There is something else you should know. When I asked for the satellites we have over Central America to point their cameras at Piedras Negras, someone had beat us to it."

"What are you saying?" Don asked.

"It means that someone has hacked into our satellite system and is already using it to spy on the area," Max confirmed.

"Who?" asked Don.

"I don't know, but we'll find out. My best guess is that it will end up being Matt Alexander's boys," Max warned.

"I can work with that," Don said, a little too happily. "It will help a lot to have a felony charge of espionage pending against Matt's people before this thing is over.

"In the meantime," he continued, "get a well-armed team down to Piedras Negras. If we can save Alexander's people, that's fine with me. But there are some delicate matters to consider here that are primary to the lives of those three men."

Director Atwater listened intently as President Westbrook explained the parameters of the rescue mission.

Chapter 24

Jason, Mark and Nuri were not the first to arrive at the pyramid. Thiago's well-armed men seemed to be everywhere. Jason had hoped to make a rush for the pyramid and be inside before the cartel's men could react. He had to rethink that plan after seeing their lethal preparations and warned his friends to be quiet.

As usual, Jason didn't share all his thoughts with the archeologists. He was sure it would scare them to death to know what the darkness hid from their untrained eyes. He decided it would be better to lie low until daybreak so he could execute a detailed recon of the cartel's defenses.

Mark and Nuri did their best to leave Jason to his planning. They counted the unending minutes sitting in silence at a safe distance from the pyramid. As hints of sunrise broke through the night, they began to measure the distance from where they were hiding to the barely visible wall of the pyramid. They didn't understand why they couldn't just make a run for the wall with their crystals in hand. They'd be through it and the wall would become solid again before the cartel's men could open fire on them.

Finally, they couldn't help themselves and told Jason what they wanted to do. Jason hid a grin as he listened to their plan. He asked for their patience while he completed his reconnaissance of the area. So they stayed hidden where they were as Jason slid soundlessly back into the jungle. After several minutes he returned and signaled for them to come in close.

"I like your idea to make a dash for the pyramid before the bad boys can catch up," Jason began. He enjoyed seeing how pleased his two friends were with themselves, but he couldn't forget the real danger they were in. He continued with the plan, "They have roving patrols along the perimeter, but I think we can get through the wall before they have us in firing range. I will have to take out the two snipers they have posted in the trees just before we make our move. I'd prefer to take the lead when we rush the pyramid, but the most dangerous position is the rear. Whoever goes last is their best target once they realize we're moving."

Mark said, "We know how to get inside the pyramid, Jason. We'll be okay with you watching our tails."

"I'm not worried about you knowing how to get inside," Jason said reassuringly. "However, there are two land mines you'll need to avoid, and a claymore trip wire located very near the entrance. I can point out a safe path that will avoid the mines, but you'll have to step over the trip wire on your own. Mess that up, and we're all dead." Nuri looked like he was going to throw up and Mark began to sweat through his shirt.

From their position in the shadows, Jason took the lead to get them as close as possible to the ancient structure before giving them his final instructions. He pointed to the section of wall where they had entered the pyramid before and said, "From here, taking a straight path to the entrance will keep you clear of the land mines. DO NOT run anywhere but in a straight line to where the wall opens." He emphasized his point with a flat hand slicing toward the goal. "The pyramid is surrounded by a trip wire a few inches above the ground and eight feet away from its base. It's very hard to see because it's black." He held out his binoculars and told them to confirm that they saw it.

Nuri went first and said, "I'm glad you told me where to look. I would never have seen it on my own."

Mark squinted and took a little longer, but he too located the wire. He handed the binoculars back to Jason and they both waited knowing there was one more critical detail. Jason took a small plastic box out of his cargo pants that held a few glowing RFP crystals. He gave one each to Mark and Nuri and kept one for himself.

"Whatever you do, don't lose that crystal or you'll never see the inside of the pyramid," he cautioned. "Nuri should go first and Mark second. We'll make a run for it together right after I neutralize the second sniper."

Mark's gulp was audible. The two archeologists looked at each other realizing this would be the first time Jason had killed another person in their presence where he started the fight. Nuri did his best to stop hyperventilating. Jason came to a kneeling position and took aim at a distant tree with his MP5 rifle. After a few seconds, a flash came out of the silenced muzzle followed by the distant sound of a dead weight hitting the ground. The first body had barely landed when Jason swerved to his left and took out the second sniper exactly as he'd done with the first.

"Now!" he whispered, and Nuri took off running for the entrance to the pyramid. Mark chased after him, and Jason followed still holding his MP5 in the ready position.

Jason knew that it would take them about six seconds to get inside if all went well. Nuri and Mark ran in a straight line, just as he'd told them. He saw in the distance that the cartel's men had already discovered one of the dead snipers. A few ran toward them trying to get a clear shot without shooting each other.

Jason almost collided with Mark when he and Nuri stopped short of the wall to carefully step over the trip wire. It hadn't occurred to Jason that they wouldn't just jump over the thing, but he had to remember this was not something they were trained for.

"There's no time to slow down. Put your arm forward and jump into the wall!" Jason yelled as loud as he could. Bullets whizzed by causing Nuri to stumble forward as he disappeared into the foliage-covered limestone. Mark was not so fortunate. He slipped and fell flat on his face. Luckily, he missed the trip wire, but he opened his hands to brace for the fall. His RFP crystal went flying out of sight. Jason had to drop his MP5 to grab Mark while holding onto his own crystal. He moved for the pyramid entrance carrying Mark with him.

Jason hadn't seen a huge man in camouflage rushing up on them from behind. The man had already emptied his AK-47 clip, but he was not going to let Macizo's enemies escape again. He was surprisingly agile for his size. At the same moment Jason and Mark jumped through the opening portal, the big man left his feet to bring them down with a flying tackle. He managed to grab Jason around his ankles as they all landed with a heavy thud.

Jason pushed Mark inside to make sure he was clear of the pyramid's wall. Neither Nuri nor Mark knew what to do as the huge soldier grappled with Jason on the floor of the temporary portal.

The uniformed man outweighed Jason by at least seventy-five pounds. Worse yet, Jason knew better than to let go of the crystal in his dominant hand. The other man grabbed for Jason's neck and was trying to pin him with his body. Jason drew a knee in between them and pushed for all he was worth in the direction of the doorway. The men separated for just a moment, but that was all Jason needed. As the soldier tried again to grab for his legs, Jason executed a neat backward somersault taking him inside the wall's safe zone, and he quickly threw his crystal against the far wall.

The man lunged forward again but he froze in midair as if something had grabbed him. A look of surprise and terror spread across his face as the wall solidified around his chest and shoulders. He was dead before he could scream.

The three Americans gasped for breath and stared at the macabre, lifeless body encased in the wall. Jason got to his feet and barked a command.

"Don't go near that wall with an RFP crystal. As curious as I know you both are, I don't care if the body is still intact or if it is now part of the limestone. We can't chance opening the wall so the others can shoot at us, or worse."

Nuri and Mark just nodded as they wondered how he knew what they were thinking. Jason carefully retrieved the RFP crystal he had tossed. He then collected the crystal Nuri held and put them both back in the box.

"It will not take long before Thiago's men try to find a way through the wall," said Jason. "They probably won't notice the crystal Mark dropped until nightfall. If they figure out how it works, we're in a lot of trouble. We'll be better off if they try to force their way through with explosives. Hopefully, the crystal will disappear in the blast. I don't know if they brought enough fire power with them to break all the way through, but we need to figure out where to access the inner sanctum of the pyramid."

Mark said, "You saw the hologram the same as we did. Remember that the RFP crystals can be used to access the hidden hallways that will take us to the underground complex."

Nuri added, "All we have to do is move along the inner walls of this chamber with a crystal until we find another portal."

Jason didn't hesitate. He took a crystal out of the plastic box and started walking along the inner wall of the chamber. When he was standing against the back wall opposite from the outside portal, his arm tingled with the strangely familiar feeling.

He was still wearing his backpack, so there was nothing to keep them from moving on.

"Grab my arm, stay close and don't let go as we enter the next stage of this maze," Jason warned.

They walked forward together until they disappeared through the wall.

***

Ambassador Carlos Medrano and Fatima Cortez entered the main conference room of the Guatemalan Embassy in New York. They had first met at his office in the U.N. building located ten blocks southeast of the embassy. The U.N. property was considered to be international territory whereas each nation's embassy was treated the same as their home soil.

Fatima had already given him a few details about RF technology and what it could do for Guatemala. Carlos offered her temporary asylum in the embassy while he checked with his government about protocols and their next steps. He was given authorization to do whatever he deemed necessary to find out what this woman knew.

"It seems that my government is very interested to learn what you know in exchange for acting as your proxy to speak against the American government," Carlos reported. He was beginning to see how important this meeting would be to his career. The other nations' ambassadors had paid little attention to him, but he knew that was about to change.

"That is good news!" she said.

He was distracted for a moment as he realized how beautiful she was when she smiled. "My President is particularly interested to know where you believe the cache of hidden RF technology is inside Guatemala's borders," Carlos said with great anticipation. "Please tell me the location so we can move on to the other topics we agreed to discuss."

"I only know the general area but it will not be hard to find," Fatima said with confidence. "It is in the jungles of Piedras Negras.

390

There is also a small airstrip to the south of its location. It will be occupied by many Macizo cartel soldiers. They are searching for three very important Americans. They are the same three men who stole the RFP crystal that was found underneath the Sphinx. You must act quickly. The same thing will soon happen in Guatemala that occurred in Egypt."

Carlos was taking notes, but he stopped writing and looked at her. This was too serious a matter for the woman to be joking. He knew this interview would last for hours and there was no time to lose.

"Pardon me for a moment, if you would?" he asked. "I'll be right back."

Fatima nodded, understanding his quandary. He walked into his private office to call in what he had just learned. If they could send soldiers to stop them in time, this theft of the most important discovery in history could be averted. He made the call and returned to the conference room.

"Please continue," he said smiling. He offered her a glass of water and hoped his trademark charm would encourage her to trust him and disclose everything.

"You already know that RF power supplies energy to the world, but that is just the beginning of what RF technology can do," Fatima said with conviction. "Can I start with the applications that will embarrass the United States the most?"

Carlos nodded, waiting anxiously for her next words.

"RFP user crystals can be tracked by location. In other words, America can track the location of any citizen or device that uses RF power crystals with greater accuracy than we have with GPS."

Carlos made a note and asked, "Do you know if they've employed this type of GPS tracking already?"

"Yes," she answered, not really sure of the truth. "You will be able to confirm this with the Mexican government."

Fatima knew the two countries did not get along, so checking with them on this was unlikely. She had seen RFP's tracking capability demonstrated in the holographic movie. She guessed that this was the reason the U.S. and Mexican governments had been able to find Macizo's labs so quickly.

"That is a serious accusation!" Carlos said in a surprised whisper. "What other RFP capabilities does the United States have that they have not disclosed?"

Fatima paused for effect before responding. "Both The Glut and the cure were developed using RF technology. Furthermore, if the correct procedures are followed, RFP can purify drinking water, grow food anywhere on earth, heal all forms of sickness, and actually reverse the aging process in humans."

Carlos was stunned. After a moment he managed to ask, "And all the secrets behind this new technology are recorded somewhere in Piedras Negras?"

Fatima smiled brightly and said, "Yes, but RFP is not a new technology. It was discovered long ago by an ancient civilization that has been forgotten. You will find that while it is easy to understand what RFP is capable of doing, understanding the science behind its capabilities is not so easily done. What, if anything, could Caesar have done 2,000 years ago if he was handed the schematics to a jet bomber? My point is that it may take many years for us to figure out everything RF technology can do."

"And so how did the Americans manage it?" Carlos asked with genuine curiosity.

"You remember that RF energy was discovered by scientists in the United States ten years ago?" Fatima asked, and Carlos nodded. "That was soon after the Sphinx in Egypt was allegedly destroyed by terrorists. I don't believe that was a coincidence. It's obvious that the Americans blew up the Sphinx to gain access to a chamber containing the same information that is stored in Piedras Negras. The secret to understanding RF technology requires someone who can interpret the ancient language. The language explains the science, and that's why the American archeologists who can translate these things are the key to their insidious plot."

Carlos asked, "Do you have proof of this?"

Fatima knew she had him. "All you have to do is get the Americans to admit that the same archeologists who were in Giza when the Sphinx was destroyed are the same three men I told you are in Piedras Negras right now."

"I do want to continue this interview at a later time," Carlos apologized, "but I have urgent matters of state I must attend to. Please make yourself at home in our embassy and we will meet again very soon. My assistant will show you to your quarters."

She smiled and stood with him, extending her hand in a friendly gesture. She knew full well Ambassador Medrano would tell the world about America's treachery in a way that she never could.

Chapter 25

Matt settled deeper into his seat aboard one of four 747s that alternately served as Air Force One. He was on a secure line to Washington D.C. with President Westbrook. They had much to discuss about the upcoming U.N. meeting with all of its Permanent Representatives making up the General Assembly (G.A.).

"Sorry to whisk you away so quickly, Matt," Don said apologetically, "but it couldn't be helped. The G.A. is meeting tomorrow to hear Ambassador Medrano from Guatemala address some serious allegations against the United States."

"Does this have anything to do with the trouble in Piedras Negras?" Matt asked.

"You are better informed to answer that question than I am," Don admitted. "There are rumors of significant charges against the U.S., but the actual facts and evidence supporting those charges are still unknown."

"So we won't find out what this is all about until the U.N. meets openly tomorrow in New York?" Matt asked, feeling like he was being set up.

"Correct. It seems likely that whatever your people have been up to in Guatemala will be on the list of topics for discussion. That's why I needed you to represent our interests and answer their questions at the U.N. meeting. We have no idea what your guys have been up to."

The President's tone turned even more serious, "I have to ask this, Matt. Have they done anything illegal down there?"

Matt took a moment to think before he replied. Mark and Nuri had permission from the Guatemalan government to conduct their grid search expeditions. As long as they allowed the appropriate departments to inspect any artifacts they found and wanted to bring back with them, they were in compliance with the laws. They had broken the letter of the law by removing the wooden box, but it had already been returned to Piedras Negras. He saw he would need to answer that question very carefully if the subject was raised.

"I can only answer for their previous trips down there," Matt hedged. "They have done nothing that would disgrace the United States. Even so, the permit they obtained shows they are there as private citizens rather than representing the U.S. government. If they got into legal trouble during their most recent excursion, it would be on them, not you."

"Great!" Don said, a little too cheerfully. "What about in Pasadena? Have they been keeping their noses clean in California?"

Matt heard sirens going off in his head. Clearly President Westbrook knew something was wrong to have asked such a question. He suddenly remembered the hacking of the satellite coverage. His friends had seen it more as an infraction at the time, but now Westbrook could use it to throw them under the proverbial bus. Matt knew what they had done could bring felony charges against them. He decided to go on the offense to stop Don from railroading his friends.

"Shouldn't you be recognizing them as national heroes rather than looking for reasons to indict them?" Matt began. "My God man, they just saved the lives of millions of Americans by discovering the cure for The Glut. They shared it without charge and they're not looking for accolades. Just what are you leading up to here?"

"Slow down, Matt," Don chided. "I didn't say they were in trouble. I'm only making sure we are being completely honest with each other. There's no quicker way for us to get on opposing sides of this thing than for you to withhold information from me."

"In that case, what noses were dirtied in Pasadena?" Matt asked, still not convinced of Don's good intentions.

"We traced the re-tasking of one of our satellites over Guatemala to an IP address registered to them," Don said, with a feigned hint of regret. "They accessed it through JPL's authorized connection. Keep in mind that could implicate one or more of JPL's employees as well."

"Is it your intention to prosecute those responsible?" Matt asked.

Don laughed lightly, "No. Assuming all goes well in Guatemala and at the U.N., I will pardon them all just in case someone decides to prosecute them in the future."

Matt heard the underlying threat in Don's statement. He knew the screws were being turned to ensure that he played everything out exactly the way the President wanted it done, or his friends would end up in prison.

"So what is it that you want me to do tomorrow?" Matt asked with resignation. He was feeling the start of a headache behind his eyes.

"You know me well enough to handle whatever comes up in a way that would best serve my administration and the interests of the United States. That's all I ask," Don said as reasonably as he could. "But if I believe you are working against me, you understand the consequences."

Matt had heard enough. This call wasn't to help him prepare for tomorrow's U.N. meeting. It was intended to intimidate him into being Don's robotic minion. He didn't really see much choice if he wanted to protect his friends.

"I'll contact you after the meeting tomorrow at my first opportunity," Matt said as he hung up.

***

Thiago was furious that the yanquis had escaped again. It was even harder to believe what had happened right before his eyes. How could they have run through solid rock? He shivered at the sight of Diego's boots sticking out of the wall. The left boot seemed to twitch, causing everyone to jump back. After a few more minutes with no activity, Thiago took a closer look. It appeared as though the limestone blocks had once been wet cement. How else could the stone form around his legs like that? He poked the right foot just to be sure Diego was dead. He was very dead.

Thiago decided to use explosives to blow a hole in the pyramid. He ordered his men to remove the trip wires and land mines first and then he cleared the area to see what an RPG (rocket propelled grenade) could do. The anticipation of blowing something up lifted his mood a little.

When everything was ready, Thiago fired the RPG himself. He aimed just above Diego's boots hoping the wall was weaker there after absorbing the body. If not, at least the blast would destroy the grisly sight that was spooking his men more every time they looked.

The noise of the explosion was deafening and it took nearly a minute for the smoke and dust to clear enough to see the results. The RPG put a good-sized crater in the pyramid's wall and Diego's remains were either incinerated or blown clear of the area. Since he didn't know how thick the walls really were, Thiago considered if he should use the last RPG round they had with them. They had not brought any tools suitable for digging through stone so it was an easy decision.

He cleared everyone away from the wall again and took careful aim. The second RPG round did just as much damage as the first, but the wall still held. Whether the remaining wall was just millimeters or perhaps ten meters thick was anyone's guess.

Thiago remembered that they still had claymore mines with powerful explosives. Unfortunately, they were a poor tool for this job. The RPG rounds were effective because all the explosive force was channeled forward into the wall. A claymore mine didn't move. He could place it inside the crater, but most of the destructive force would be expended toward the open air rather than blasting into the hole. Lacking a better alternative, he decided to try it.

He ordered his men to wire up a mine and place it inside the cratered wall. Then he had them gather limestone rocks to carefully place on top of the claymore. That would help to direct the explosive force back into the wall rather than away from it. When everything was ready, he depressed the button on the remote detonator.

As expected, there was far less damage done by the claymore than the RPG. The good news was that it had made the hole bigger. They had a few dozen more claymores and nothing to lose. He ordered his men to keep at it.

***

The international media's cameras were everywhere to televise this event live to the world. The room was filled to capacity when the Secretary-General of the United Nations, Kan Bi-Soon, walked across the stage to the main podium. He called the meeting

397

of the General Assembly to order. The agenda included some quick maintenance items to be cleared before they got to the main reason for the special meeting. No one left the room despite this lull in the agenda. Not a soul wanted to miss what was to come. Finally, Ambassador Carlos Medrano from Guatemala was called to speak before the group.

"Thank you, your Excellency," Carlos began, properly acknowledging the Secretary-General's introduction. He cleared his throat, and leaned into the microphone mounted on the podium before him. "I am here today to address a matter of grave concern, not just to my country, but also to the other sovereign nations of the world. At this very moment, there are groups of men attempting to steal ancient treasures from Guatemala."

The room buzzed with the members' reaction to his opening statement. When the noise settled down, Carlos continued.

"I want to make a brief statement and then call on the designated representatives from Egypt, Mexico and the United States to answer questions related to these charges."

The chatter in the room increased again and then quickly hushed. Carlos turned a page in his notes, took a sip of water to calm himself, and then continued with his prepared statement.

"Around ten years ago, two seemingly unrelated events took place that changed the world. The first was the terrorist bombing of the Sphinx in Egypt. The second event occurred a few months later when the United States announced its discovery of RF energy. They expressed their willingness to provide wholesale power to any sovereign nation that agreed to meet the terms set by President Alexander in his peace accord. Most of the world did sign that agreement and became customers to their inexpensive and abundant supply of wireless power.

"My first concern to be addressed today is that the destruction of the Sphinx, and the subsequent discovery of RF energy, was not a coincidence. I also believe that the bombing of the Sphinx was not carried out by Middle Eastern terrorists, as originally reported. It was actually perpetrated by three men. Two of them were born in America and the third one was born in Egypt, but became a naturalized citizen of the United States."

Outrage and disbelief were shouted across the room and Carlos had to wait for nearly a minute to continue.

"I believe the men responsible for the bombing did so to facilitate and cover up the theft of valuable Egyptian property. There is overwhelming circumstantial evidence that proves these allegations.

"Here is what actually happened ten years ago. These three men were employed by the United States government to obliterate the Sphinx in order to gain access to certain underground chambers. It was there that they located and removed an RFP crystal and written records that explained the secrets behind RF energy. Then they destroyed the underground chamber along with any remaining evidence of their crimes. They had help in stealing Egypt's treasures. American soldiers surrounded the blast area and claimed no one should enter because it was a nuclear fallout zone. The ancient records and RFP crystal were subsequently smuggled into the United States for detailed study."

Carlos paused to allow for another outburst, but the audience had long ago heard these rumors. What they were waiting for was proof that the United States had actually stolen RF energy from Egypt. He knew this was the perfect time to throw fuel on the fire by adding to America's list of crimes. The whole world was watching and this was Carlos' chance to secure his place in history.

"Unlimited wireless energy was not the only application for RF technology that the United States discovered. For instance, we all know that the amount of RF energy consumed can be measured down to a single user. But did you know that the Americans can track the exact location of any RFP user with greater accuracy than a GPS tracking system?"

That triggered a murmur out of the audience, but they waited to hear more.

"Perhaps the most egregious part of what I have to share with you today is not a crime the United States has already committed. It is, in fact, a crime of omission. I have reason to believe that other applications exist for RF technology. Our American friends have already learned how to purify water and grow food anywhere in the world through different combinations of RFP

399

crystals. Why they refuse to share this discovery with the rest of the world is a crime against humanity!"

This was the first anyone had heard about additional uses for RF technology. Carlos could tell by the audience's reaction that he had struck a chord with them all. To withhold discoveries that would provide unlimited food and pure water to billions of sick and starving people was unthinkable.

"I realize the serious nature of the allegations I've made here today. That is why I intend to support them by calling the aforementioned representatives before this august group for questioning. Can we begin with the Permanent Representative from Egypt, Mr. Pakhura?"

Akhem Pakhura stood up in the audience and came forward to the front of the assembly hall. His eyes briefly met Matt Alexander's and he flashed the past U.S. President a look of disgust. After swearing to tell the truth in his testimony, Akhem took the lone seat on stage, obliquely facing the audience and the podium.

Carlos began, "Ambassador Pakhura, are you familiar with either Doctor Mark Heston or Doctor Nuri Zayd? They are both archeologists. In fact, Egyptology is their specialty."

"I am, though I do not know them personally," was his response.

"Can you tell us how you know of these men?" Carlos prodded.

"Yes I can. Ten years ago, they worked out of the University of Cairo, but were employed by Harvard University. They requested an indefinite leave of absence from their jobs the day before the Sphinx was destroyed."

Carlos let that sink in for a moment and then asked, "Did the Egyptian government find fault with these two archeologists?"

"Our investigation is still ongoing, but we are certain they are criminals. It is our contention that those men stole the secrets of RF technology from an underground complex that was purposefully destroyed along with the Sphinx."

"And what made you believe there was an underground complex there that held the secrets of RF technology?"

"After the Sphinx had been demolished, our excavation and investigation of the scene showed that hallways and underground rooms had existed beneath the ancient statue prior to its destruction. A few months later, we received several boxes shipped from the United States to the University of Cairo with various items and artifacts inside. It came with a letter that said the items had been left behind at Harvard by the two archeologists you mentioned. Since their employment had ended, the university wanted to return the items to us. One of the artifacts was eventually identified as a sending RFP crystal. We believe those men stole the crystal, learned its secrets, purposely disabled it, and then returned it along with many other relics hoping it would be overlooked for what it was."

"What happened when you approached the United States with your suspicions of this horrific destruction and theft?" asked Carlos.

"They refused to respond no matter how many times we asked, or who did the asking."

Carlos said, "Thank you, Ambassador. That is all the questions I have for you at this time, but I may need to call on you later."

***

After Jason, Mark and Nuri walked through the second pyramid wall, they found themselves in a long hallway. It was reminiscent of the underground passage that lay beneath the Sphinx. They noticed that the ambient light in the hall came from other sources than their lantern or RFP crystals. There were glowing stones embedded in the limestone blocks all around them.

"Do you think these stay lit all the time?" Nuri asked.

Mark said, "Let's test that theory." He located the box with the crystals in it and set it on the ground. "Let's walk down the hallway without our own crystals to see what happens."

They all walked ahead about twenty steps. New lights appeared in the stone walls and ceiling as they moved forward. The box lying on the ground was still glowing, but the crystals embedded in the walls closest to the spot where they entered had gone dark.

When Mark went back to retrieve the box, the crystals at his end of the hallway lit up again.

Nuri said, "Let's hope this entire complex has this automatic lighting throughout!"

A moment later a loud boom sounded all around them in the ancient hallway.

"They are trying to blast through the outer wall," Jason explained. "That means they didn't see Mark's crystal, and the explosion probably buried it out of sight. We should keep moving. There's no telling how long it will take them to make their way into the first chamber. We need to be long gone by then."

Chapter 26

Ambassador Medrano had just called on Ambassador Gilbert Alba to take the stand for questioning. As the Permanent Representative Ambassador from Mexico came forward, Carlos looked over his notes. He had to be careful questioning this man. Getting the information he needed without embarrassing him, or the Mexican government, would not be easy.

"Ambassador Alba," he began, "would you share with us the details that led to the recent U.S. bombings of three illicit laboratories inside Mexico's borders?"

"Yes," Gilbert said as he sat straighter in his chair. "The United States government requested Mexico's help to thwart an extortion threat. The leader of the Macizo drug cartel had died from a mysterious illness, and an unknown perpetrator threatened to infect America with the same disease."

"Was the Mexican government also threatened by the same person or people?" Medrano asked.

"No, not directly. But the disease we came to know as The Glut did eventually infect many Mexican citizens," Gilbert said as he nervously pulled at his collar.

"Please continue with the details," Carlos prompted.

Gilbert inhaled deeply and resumed where he'd left off. "The Americans asked for help on two fronts in dealing with the extortion. They asked for permission to investigate the whereabouts of the person or people who made the threat. They also asked for the users' contact information for specific RFP frequencies. It turned out that most of the people in question were suspected members of the Macizo cartel."

"Did the U.S. government indicate why they asked for that information?" asked Carlos.

"No, but the reason became obvious later on," Gilbert said, gaining confidence as he continued. His words were full of righteous indignation. "They have clearly discovered how to track people through their use of RFP crystals, much like a GPS system. We learned the Americans matched the movements of known cartel members with locations of recent deliveries of specialized medical equipment that could safely handle The Glut. I will admit that they made a compelling case to be allowed to conduct simultaneous raids on those three locations inside our borders."

"Did the Mexican government assist in the 'raids' on these people and sites?" Carlos asked, giving the Mexican Ambassador a chance to distance his country from the events that would be described next.

Now Gilbert was on a roll and he understood the opportunity Medrano was handing him. "No. The U.S. government insisted that they carry out the operation so we had no prior notice that their plan was to eradicate those three sites. We were surprised when their soldiers made no effort to arrest any suspects. What they did amounts to murder without giving the victims a chance to defend themselves in a court of law. Had it not been for the horrific nature of the threat those unfortunate people allegedly posed to the world, it would have been Mexico instead of Guatemala bringing charges against the United States. As it is, the sovereign nation of Mexico welcomes this opportunity to see that justice is now served."

The outraged reaction from the audience took a moment to die down before Carlos asked his next question.

"Is there anything else you want to add to your testimony that the world needs to know?"

"Absolutely!" said Gilbert. "We have become convinced that the United States has made many undisclosed discoveries regarding RF technology. Our scientists explained this to me in a way we can all understand. We know that RF energy travels in waves that are not limited to line-of-sight. In other words, the waves can travel as easily through buildings, and even the earth, as they can through the air. If the waves can carry energy from any point on the planet to another, it follows that RFP waves can be used in a similar manner for communications."

Exclamations erupted from other representatives and spectators as some began to realize the far-reaching implications.

Gilbert paused to enjoy this moment and then continued. "In other words, we have already learned that the United States can track the exact locations of individual RFP users through their receiving crystals. For a country that stakes its reputation on following the rule of law, why were they so quick to kill the cartel members without warning or legal due process? I contend that it was because the United States was able to listen in on the victims' conversations through their RFP crystals. By illegally spying on the cartel members in this way, they became convinced of their guilt. I believe that the United States can use RF technology to turn any receiving crystal into an undetectable listening device!"

Now the entire audience was in an uproar. They were no longer a gathering of highly regarded international diplomats. At that moment, they were better described as an angry mob. Carlos Medrano had orchestrated his presentation perfectly. He had just enough truth, mixed in with conjecture, to seemingly validate Gilbert's claims. He knew this would work because of a long-standing, shared sentiment that the U.S. is arrogant and not to be trusted.

Carlos knew if he took a break now, the diplomats would convince each other that the United States was guilty of all charges. He smiled thinking, "They will be like an angry pack of wolves when Matthew Alexander is called to the stand to answer for his country."

Ambassador Medrano announced to the G.A., "I suggest we take a break for the noon meal to reflect upon the testimony we have heard this morning. When we resume, the Representative from the United States will be called to answer questions related to these charges."

"Matt, I hear the U.N. diplomats are ready to lynch you," Don Westbrook said, as he picked up the phone.

"That sounds about right," Matt sighed with resignation. "I'm not sure I can get them to listen to reason after the way Ambassador Medrano whipped them up this morning."

Don feigned some encouraging words. "You really are the best man to answer their questions and set things right again. Can you tell me what approach you will take when they put you on the stand?"

405

Matt started to lay out his strategy. "I can prove that our Delta Force team was on the trail of the Syrian terrorist, Colonel Mansur, and a huge cache of explosives when the Sphinx was destroyed. I can also prove that Mark Heston and Nuri Zayd were drafted into service to identify potential targets the terrorists might attack. The problem will be that our people really did keep the Egyptian first responders away from the area by claiming there was the danger of possible fallout."

Don finally asked the question he'd avoided for the past ten years. "Will you tell me the truth about what happened with your archeologist friends underneath the Sphinx?"

Matt had been expecting this question. "Mark, Nuri and two Delta Force body guards were staying at a hotel near the Sphinx when it was destroyed. They headed straight to the blast site the moment they knew what had happened. The rest of the Delta Force team kept everyone else away from the area while three of the four men entered an underground passage to investigate. They found the Hall of Records I've alluded to before. Almost everything we know about RFP came from the archeologists' translation of the hieroglyphics that were carved on the walls and on stone tablets stored in that room. To make a long story short, the chamber started to collapse. As they rushed to get out, they did remove an RFP sending crystal. The Egyptian Ambassador did admit that we have returned that to them. The digital pictures, and a video recording of what happened in that room, subsequently disappeared. I really don't know who got rid of them or why they did it."

Don said, "Actually, that's great news! We've already made good on giving Egypt back their crystal relic. The development of all RF technology is legally our property because it came from translating images of the information they observed in that chamber under the Sphinx. The discovery of RF energy is ours. That's already an established precedent in international law."

"So now you believe me regarding what happened in Egypt, and the importance of what's going on in Piedras Negras?" Matt asked, not hiding his surprise.

"It doesn't matter what I believe," Don answered. "It matters what everyone else accepts as the truth, and what they will want the United States to do about it."

Matt was disappointed, but it was foolish to think Don would change his mind. He decided to get his marching orders regarding what to do when the U.N.'s General Assembly reconvened. "So what parameters do I have to appease the angry mob?"

"You can't give up anything of substance," Don said matter-of-factly. "Give me a list of their demands and then take the jet back to California. My cabinet will meet to figure out what to do from there. If we need you again, I'll be in touch."

The line disconnected before Matt could object.

***

Mark and Nuri couldn't be happier. They were the first people to see the inside of this pyramid since its builders were lost to history. Jason was not nearly as excited because he was out of his element. He quietly fell back into his familiar role of protector.

Hours passed before their initial excitement turned to disappointment. There were no unseen passageways, no adjoining doors, no hidden chambers, or even steps to another level. The hallway itself was perhaps four hundred feet from end to end. The limestone walls had no carvings or artwork. The strangest part of all was the absence of life inside, such as mold or insects. After all the years this place had been deserted, it was as if time had stopped inside these walls.

They also wondered what it meant now that the loud booms had ceased. Had Thiago blasted his way through the outer wall and was actually inside the pyramid's anti-chamber? He wouldn't know the location of the hidden hallway from there, but this man was not making logical choices in his quest for vengeance. A pyramid's structure was as solid as they come, but how many bombs could it withstand before collapsing in on itself?

Jason was always thinking ahead, trying to avoid trouble before it found them. He believed they were relatively safe in this hallway, but they had no access to food or water. They could survive this way for a few days, but eventually they'd have to return to the outside world. He decided not to discuss this until his friends brought it up. He didn't want to worry them any more than necessary.

***

Thiago couldn't believe how thick the pyramid's walls were. He tried using every explosive device they had with them, but they couldn't blast their way through. All they had to show for their efforts was a crater measuring twenty meters across and eight meters deep, where Diego's boots had once marked the disappearing entrance.

He sent word to bring in more explosives and special digging equipment used to bore holes in limestone. He posted guards around the four sides of the pyramid in case the yanquis knew of another way out. For now, all he could do was wait. It would take a few more hours before the new supplies would arrive at the airstrip from Tierra Linda. Then this game of 'cat and mouse' would be over.

***

"Will the General Assembly please come to order!" the Secretary-General said emphasizing his words with several taps of his gavel. Muted conversations ceased and the last stragglers took their seats. "I will now turn the proceedings back over to the esteemed Ambassador from Guatemala, Carlos Medrano."

"Thank you, your Excellency," Carlos said, as he arrived at the center stage podium. "I call Matthew Alexander before this meeting of the General Assembly to answer for the crimes outlined in this morning's testimony."

Matt took a seat in the empty chair near the podium while excited whispers filled the room. He scanned the audience and saw no friendly faces. They seemed to be counting on Ambassador Medrano to embarrass both Matt and the United States on live global TV.

Carlos congratulated himself for successfully orchestrating this battle of wits with a man who had been the most powerful leader in the free world. He smiled, realizing that he was about to make his mark in history.

"Thank you for joining us today, Mr. Alexander," he began. "I trust you are ready to answer questions regarding the allegations made against the United States this morning?"

Matt simply nodded.

"You were the President of the United States at the time the Sphinx was destroyed in Egypt, is that correct?"

"Yes. I had been in office a little over a year when that tragedy occurred," Matt answered.

"And who do you say is to blame for the vile act that destroyed one of the ancient architectural marvels of the world?" Carlos asked.

"Our investigation showed that terrorists used a powerful explosive called octanitrocubane to destroy the Sphinx. A hotel in Giza was also destroyed just hours earlier by the same terrorists using a much smaller quantity of the explosive," Matt explained. "The first responders to the explosion at the hotel identified a Middle Eastern man who killed two firefighters in his attempt to escape that day."

"And wasn't one of the two Harvard archeologists, I believe they were identified in Ambassador Pakhura's earlier testimony, also of Middle Eastern descent?" Carlos asked.

"Yes, but the description of the terrorist at the hotel and that of Dr. Nuri Zayd vary considerably in height, weight, and age. Dr. Zayd is clearly not the man witnesses saw at the hotel who killed those firemen," Matt offered, with a silent sigh of relief to have gotten that on the record.

Carlos expected this answer. His plan was to put Matt at ease to make him less defensive. He would be asking some hard questions soon enough. Carlos continued, "Is there any evidence you can provide that would prove the whereabouts of the archeologists during the time when the Sphinx was destroyed?"

"Yes, there were two witnesses who were with both Mark Heston and Nuri Zayd in a hotel room prior to, and during, the destruction of the Sphinx," Matt responded. "Both doctors and the two soldiers were members of our anti-terrorist team who were in Egypt with the full knowledge and consent of the Egyptian government. Other members of that team were on the heels of a group of suspects and trying to subdue them before they could act. We regret that those efforts were unsuccessful."

Carlos was not happy that Matt's answers kept deflecting guilt away from the archeologists. Still, he was sure to catch Matt off guard with his next line of inquiry. He decided to move onto his more incriminating questions.

"What did the two archeologists do once the Sphinx was destroyed?"

"Doctors Heston and Zayd had the two soldiers drive them to the site. They understood the devastating significance of an explosion in that part of Giza. They put on protective radiation gear so they could investigate the damage done at ground zero," Matt took a deep breath before going on. "They found the explosion had exposed an underground tunnel beneath the Sphinx, and they followed its path to a hidden chamber some have called the Hall of Records."

Carlos tried to maintain his composure, but the audience collectively gasped at hearing this. Everyone had assumed Matt Alexander would avoid admitting that a Hall of Records existed, let alone that Americans had discovered it first. Carlos could smell blood and was pleased that the former president would have a hard time defending what came next.

"Is it true that the rest of the American military team set up a perimeter around the blast site to keep everyone away from ground zero?" Carlos asked.

"Yes, it is," Matt confirmed.

"And the reason they gave was to keep from exposing anyone to an alleged threat from radiation poisoning?" Carlos continued, clearly trying to box Matt into a corner.

"That is also true," said Matt.

"And later testing proved that there had been no radioactive fallout?" Carlos prodded.

"Correct again, "Matt said, with no further explanation.

"So, Mr. Alexander, can you explain why the Americans lied to keep Egypt's people away from the blast site?"

"Yes, but you mischaracterized their actions by claiming they lied. Our people weren't trying to deceive anyone," Matt said calmly. "The explosion that destroyed the Sphinx was later proven to be the world's largest non-nuclear detonation ever. Not knowing that at the time, our soldiers thought the resulting mushroom cloud overhead was caused by a tactical nuclear device. The members of the American team put on MOPP gear to protect themselves from the fallout. They were simply trying to keep anyone safe who didn't have the same protective gear to wear. Once Egyptian authorities showed up wearing their MOPP gear, they were allowed to safely inspect the site for themselves."

The room went silent and Carlos was stunned. He hadn't expected that Matt's answer would make so much sense. Worse yet, his explanation made the Americans look like heroes for trying to protect the Egyptian first responders. The ambassador's mind raced to find a way to salvage this disaster. He saw one other opening and he went for it.

"Mr. Alexander, did the archeologists remove anything they found in the chamber underneath the Sphinx?"

"No, they did not." Matt said evenly.

Carlos was astonished that the ex-President of the United States would lie to the world about something that could easily be proven false. He saw his chance to do permanent damage to Matt's credibility.

"Are you saying the RFP crystal that was returned to Egypt some months later did not come from the chamber under the Sphinx?"

"I believe it came from the chamber," Matt responded, "but the crystal was not removed by either of the archeologists. The soldier who accompanied them picked it up just before the room collapsed. Not being a trained archeologist, he knew nothing of the rules prohibiting what he did. After it was discovered that the soldier had removed the RFP crystal, the archeologists made sure Harvard University returned it to its rightful owner, the government of Egypt."

Carlos fell silent for a moment as he considered how to gain an advantage in this battle of wits. He had underestimated this man. If he failed to get Matt to say that they had knowingly done something illegal, this questioning would ruin his career.

411

"Mr. Alexander, is it true that the United States' discovery of RF energy occurred just a few months after the crystal was taken from underneath the Sphinx?"

"Yes, that's true," Matt admitted.

"And it's your testimony here that the discovery of RF energy did not come from the sending crystal the soldier took from that chamber underneath the Sphinx?" Carlos asked, hoping he'd found the chink in Matt's armor.

Matt smiled, "If what we learned had come from that crystal, shouldn't Egypt's scientists have been able to create their own RF energy? After all, they've had it in their possession for a decade."

"The Egyptian scientists have determined the sending crystal was made inoperative before it was returned to them. Are you saying that isn't true?" Carlos was grasping at straws here, but it was all he had.

Matt smiled again and said, "To our knowledge, the crystal in Egypt's possession is fully operational in every way. However, it's not surprising that their scientists have not been able to access its power in all the years they've had it. Please know that I am not disparaging their competence as scientists. They simply didn't see what Doctors Heston and Zayd saw in that Hall of Records."

Carlos finally had something to pursue. He jumped at it with near-desperation.

"So the archeologists removed some kind of written records from the chamber that explained the principals behind RF energy?"

"Your supposition is only half right," Matt replied. "They did not remove anything that came from the chamber. They were, however, able to translate inscriptions carved on the walls and tablets that they discovered underneath the Sphinx. That information was what our scientists used to discover the principals behind RF energy."

The Egyptian Ambassador stood up in the audience and demanded that the thieving Americans return to Egypt what was rightfully theirs. Carlos turned toward Matt with a questioning look that dared him to respond.

412

"All of the information they gathered in the Hall of Records is still there," Matt assured them. The archeologists took digital pictures of the information, but they took nothing out of the chamber they hadn't brought in with them when they fled for their lives."

"I demand that you provide copies of those pictures to the Egyptian government," Carlos said triumphantly.

"Are you now representing the Egyptian government too?" Matt chided. "First of all, they have not officially asked for copies. Secondly, that sounds like a diplomatic negotiation to be held privately between the U.S. and Egypt rather than being discussed in this public forum."

The questioning effectively ended when the Egyptian ambassador practically ran out of the hall. Everyone could guess his government was about to begin a careful inspection of the location where the Sphinx once sat. Until that moment, no one thought that the most lucrative discovery in history was still there to be found under the rubble.

The other G.A. members started leaving in a hurry as well. There was the obvious need to be on Egypt's good side, in case their renewed efforts were successful, but that wasn't all. No one had forgotten about the second location for another Hall of Records in Guatemala. That fabled chamber was apparently unscathed, and the race was on to find it.

Ambassador Medrano implored the G.A. members to remain in their seats. He still had a chance to redeem himself by proving the archeologists were about to do to his country what they had already done to Egypt, but it was too late. Only Matt and a few low-ranking U.N. staffers remained in the assembly hall. Carlos picked his legal pad up from the podium. He then angrily threw it into his briefcase before slamming it shut. Matt watched him walk off the stage without saying another word.

Carlos was finished, literally and figuratively. He was sure to be asked for his resignation. However, his country had an even larger problem than his personal embarrassment. Those same two archeologists and the soldier who had picked up the RFP crystal were in Guatemala right now trying to exploit his country's treasures. Worse yet, the rest of the world was about to join them.

413

He rushed off to call his President to see if he still had a job. If so, he would do everything he could to stop the Americans, and the rest of the world, from stealing what belonged to his people.

Chapter 27

Jason, Matt and Nuri were sitting together on the ground in the middle of the ancient hallway. They had explored every inch of its length several times and had come up with nothing. As disappointing as it was, their thoughts turned to finding a safe way out. Of course, that brought up a whole different set of challenges.

"We can always use the same portal we came in through," Mark said reluctantly.

Jason objected, "Going back the way we came? That has to be our last option and one we shouldn't try for at least another 48 hours. Thiago's men are swarming this place hoping we'll appear."

"Well, we can't stay here. There's nothing to see that we haven't examined already. Besides, without food and water, we're dead regardless," Nuri said with resignation.

Jason nodded his head and added, "I'm just saying we need to wait as long as we can. Hopefully, Thiago will give up and leave. When the time comes, I'll go out alone to see if it's safe. I'll come back for you after I've made sure."

"And what do we do in the meantime?" Mark asked.

"I don't know about you, but I'm tired," Jason said with a yawn. "We should all try to get some sleep. It will help the time pass more quickly."

The other two agreed and they each tried to get comfortable on the hard limestone flooring. After shifting positions for several minutes, it was clear that none of them could sleep. Nuri was about to say something to the others when he heard an inner voice say, "Each of you needs to hold a crystal in your hand, and the rest will be given."

"Did you guys hear that?" Nuri asked excitedly.

"Hear what?" was their mutual reply.

"I heard someone tell me that each one of us should hold a crystal," Nuri said, hoping he wasn't going crazy.

Jason had the plastic box that still held several tiny RFP crystals. He pulled it out and handed one to each of them. The crystals sat glowing in their hands, but that was nothing new.

"Now what do we do?" asked Jason.

Nuri closed his eyes and leaned back against the wall. He tried to focus on hearing the voice again, but his mind drifted. The next minute he was out to the world.

"Did you see that?" Mark exclaimed. "He's asleep! Do you think the crystals will help us all to go to sleep in here?"

"Why not?" Jason laughed. "It wouldn't be the strangest thing I've seen these RF crystals do for us."

They too closed their eyes and leaned against the wall behind them. It didn't take long before they were fast asleep.

***

Jason awoke with a start. He was no longer in the passageway inside the Piedras Negras pyramid. The place looked familiar but he knew it couldn't be real. It looked like the Hall of Records that had been destroyed in Giza ten years before. He realized, as he looked around, that there were subtle differences. While similar in many respects, this chamber was not the same. What surprised him the most was that it was in pristine condition without the slightest damage to the ceiling, walls, or the items displayed on the ornate shelves.

Eight obsidian pedestals formed a circle around the center of the room and seemed to be vibrating. At the very center of the circle Jason expected to see an RFP crystal arise from the ground. Instead, a white image of a man started to appear. The vibrations became audible and grew louder as the man's image became more defined. The sound stopped suddenly when the body of this man dressed completely in white came fully into view.

Jason stood in silent awe as the man spoke, "I sometimes forget the appeal of assuming a three dimensional form. It is no wonder so many choose to become enmeshed here."

"I'm sorry," he said after noticing Jason's discomfort. "I know it takes you a while to adjust, but meeting in this way should speed up your acclimation and help you to remember who I am."

416

"Halaliel?" Jason said both as a question and greeting.

"In the flesh...literally!" he said with a laugh. He was fond of Jason.

"I don't understand what's going on," Jason said, clearly distressed. "You usually choose a setting that is comforting. I don't have fond memories of this place at all."

"That is because I didn't choose this place. It was your thoughts that drew you here and we are not meeting under the usual circumstances," was Halaliel's perplexing reply.

"Please explain what is going on. This is really creeping me out," Jason said feeling a little shaky.

Halaliel smiled patiently and answered, "A wise man once said, 'In my Father's house are many mansions.' This is simply one of the infinite places you can choose to be. It is as real as any other place on earth, but your own thoughts, and the vibrations of the crystal your body is still holding in the passageway, have uniquely combined to bring you here."

"I'll have to take your word for it," Jason said shaking his head. "So why am I here?" he asked, feeling a little better now.

"Your earthly consciousness and astral form are here in the Hall of Records near the Bahamas. I have assumed a physical body so that we may communicate better while you are here," Halaliel explained. "Think of our meeting here as if you are watching TV inside the pyramid in Guatemala. You are still physically sitting in the passageway in Piedras Negras, but you are also surrounded by unseen broadcast waves carrying various programs to watch. By adjusting a tuner, you can pick the program's waves that interest you. When you commit to, or become engrossed in, a particular program, the hallway in which you sit fades to the background and the reality of the TV show takes over. That is analogous to what is happening at this moment."

"I'm pretty sure you're speaking English, but that made no sense. Can you say that again in simpler terms?" Jason asked.

Halaliel laughed, "In simpler terms? No. But I can see that explaining your current situation without analogy is the better way for you to grasp this.

"If your friends were awake now in the passageway, they would see you asleep leaning against the wall. They would not see me or any part of this place you call the Hall of Records. At this moment, your body and consciousness exist in separate dimensions. It is not unlike dreaming, though the mechanics are quite different. This method of astral travel is made possible because of the cooperation that exists between the RFP crystal and your mind."

"If you say so," Jason said with a snort. He could understand what Halaliel was explaining, but what was the purpose for all of this hocus pocus?

"Ah!" Halaliel responded, reading his thoughts and realizing what he missed. "The advantage of our meeting like this is that you will consciously remember all that has and will transpire between us here. The subconscious and conscious parts of your mind are more strongly connected now than in our other encounters. It is the reason why you are currently limited to seeing only the things that follow the laws of physics on earth."

Jason wasn't sure he understood. "But I remember our previous meetings. Are you saying that I won't remember those later?"

Halaliel was enjoying this back and forth with Jason because it helped him better understand the limited perspective the conscious mind endures.

"Oddly enough," he explained, "in your waking state you will remember that there were other meetings between us, but you will not remember their content because they didn't take place under these conditions.

"Each person has their own unique ability to retain what is given to them through the subconscious. For instance, Matthew Alexander is better than most in human form when it comes to consciously remembering what he learns during his ethereal encounters."

Jason asked, "So what is it that I should remember from this meeting?"

"We're here to expose the world to the true potential of RF technology," Halaliel answered. "You already know it does far more than provide abundant energy. It can also supply your needs for sustenance, telecommunications, construction, and even healing. The projection you saw from the crystal medallion barely touched on what the future holds for humankind, if you will allow it to come to pass."

A new moving holographic display began to show a detailed view of all that Halaliel had just described. It then shifted to illustrate a few choices Jason would soon face on earth. He could see the probable outcomes of each choice he might make.

Halaliel interrupted the display. "In this realm you cannot see it all. You are being shown only the most likely choices and outcomes before you. The limitations of time and space also limit what you can observe, but you will remember this encounter."

"I can see what I want to do," Jason said hesitantly. "But I will be acting on my own again without consulting my friends. Isn't that where I went wrong the last time?"

"Your past choices did make life on earth more interesting," Halaliel said with a smile. "But your motivation this time for going against the grain, so to speak, is far better today than it was before."

Jason suddenly felt sleep overtake him. He closed his eyes and the Hall of Records faded into a peaceful dream. He wouldn't awake for hours, but he would indeed remember every moment of this encounter with Halaliel.

***

President Westbrook sat at the head of the conference table in the Situation Room. The members of the National Security Council (NSC) were present along with some of the cabinet members who did not normally attend NSC meetings. Director of National Intelligence (DNI) Max Atwater had been asked to brief the group on the evolving world scene since Matt Alexander's questioning at the U.N.

"The entire Egyptian government is burning the midnight oil, for certain," Max began. "It seems everyone now wants to be their friend because Alexander hinted that Egypt may have their own RF energy source."

He waited to allow the President to stop him there. Don kept making notes, so Max continued.

419

"Another development is that most of the world's countries have suddenly decided the Yucatan peninsula is the perfect place for a vacation, cruise, or even military maneuvers. We have also confirmed that every satellite over the area is pointed at Guatemala. Other countries condemn the U.S. for allegedly stealing RF technology from the Egyptians. Ironically, many of those same countries have military ships heading toward Piedras Negras, ignoring Guatemala's blanket statement that no one has permission to cross their borders."

"Gentlemen," Don said, looking around the room, "we have a couple of problems to resolve, as I see it now. First, Alexander put us in a tough position with Egypt with his testimony at the U.N. meeting. Now the Egyptian government is clamoring for us to turn over everything we have on RF power."

The Secretary of State interrupted, "We should decide what we're willing to give up before we agree to meet with Egypt."

Don frowned and continued as if the Secretary hadn't spoken. "Second, how do we best handle the evolving conflict headed toward Guatemala?"

"We need to establish the limits and rules of engagement for any troops we send down there," said the Secretary of Defense, with a confirming nod from the JCOS, General James Myer.

Don straightened knowing the answers to both questions fell to him. He didn't like Alexander's 10-year old peace agreement that forced him to sell cheap and plentiful energy to the world. Now they were asking him what else he would give up and how far he was willing to go, given the current circumstances. He hated that these people were always looking to give ground or compromise when the going got tough. He was about to show them why he was the POTUS and they all answered to him.

"When bad things happen, I ask myself a question. I think, 'What's good about this?' and then I try to answer it." Don saw from the looks on their faces that they needed more information before giving him feedback.

"My best outcome for this situation is that the U.S. is no longer forced to sell RF energy to other nations. My hands are tied as long as our international customers do their best to keep the peace and take no aggressive actions against other countries. It looks like the treasure everyone thinks is hidden in Piedras Negras has them willing to renege on that deal. If and when they do, what do you think about cutting them off for breach of contract?"

Max jumped in to clarify what that might mean. "There are no less than thirty-seven sovereign nations, with a potentially lethal and uninvited presence, headed toward northern Guatemala. More are joining the party every time we count them. If all hell breaks loose in Piedras Negras, and we cut the power to those warring nations, that could easily lead to the rest of the world declaring war on us."

"What if we only cut the power to those nations without nuclear capability?" Don asked, looking directly at General James Myer for his answer.

James knew the President was asking for a risk analysis of damages to the U.S. if the non-nuclear countries no longer had access to RF power. He visibly winced at the thought. He was trained to defend his country regardless of the politics involved, but this POTUS was heading in a direction that he had trouble supporting.

"The shock to the countries cut off from RF energy would be so devastating that an organized retaliation against the U.S. would be unlikely." James couldn't stop there. He felt compelled to explain the real danger if the President followed through with this course of action.

"However, such an act would, in my opinion, knock over the first dominos in a long line of global politics and alliances. The nations with nuclear capabilities would fear they are next up on the RFP chopping block. In a global war scenario, the United States would likely prevail against the rest of the world if nukes aren't employed. That's because without RF energy, their limited access to fossil fuels could not keep up with us. As good as that seems, it quickly becomes the worst case scenario. Why? Because initiating a first nuclear strike becomes the only viable option to maintain a level playing field with the U.S. Many countries would choose to start over on this planet rather than be eternally dominated by the United States."

"You can take it down a couple of notches, James," the President chided. "I wasn't thinking of ordering anything close to that. But that does raise the question of the value of our peace agreement. Look at how many countries are willing to risk world peace, and their access to RF energy, the first time they see an opportunity to go around us!"

Max responded, "It's no secret that world opinion says we're not to be trusted with the keys to so much power, no joke intended. The recent fiasco at the U.N. showed us just how unreasonable people can become when they feel threatened or provoked. We have done neither of those things to any nation. The current fear started with the disclosure that we can use RF technology to track receiving crystals and the individuals who use them. We were forced to show our cards to the Mexican government to prove probable cause in taking down the Macizo cartel labs. We might have known that word would leak and cause this kind of trouble."

General Myer asked, "Do we already have RF technology that can do everything they claimed at that UN meeting?"

The President and Max looked at each other before Don nodded for Max to take it.

"We don't have a good answer to that question," Max said hesitantly. "The white coats at JPL and Alexander's people have kept any subsequent developments they've made to themselves. We could threaten to pull their funding, but then they would never share what they know about RF technology with us. The GPS-like tracking capability was discovered by our own people when they were conducting government-approved RFP experiments."

Don interjected, "However, Alexander's people came up with a cure for The Glut within a few days. That says a lot when the CDC didn't have a clue on where to start. Clearly Matt's team and JPL's scientists know more than they are telling. Another complication is that Matt's people are in imminent danger down in Guatemala. They may have already been killed by the Macizo cartel.

"The remaining question is what to do about the situation in Guatemala. Given the amazing things people claim exists in that Hall of Records, how do we proceed?" Don took a breath before stating his position.

"I don't think we can risk another country getting its hands on RF technology. If the world thinks the United States is not trustworthy, imagine if a third world country has control of it!" Don paused and looked at each person sitting around the table.

The room was silent as they took in the full meaning of the President's message. He seemed to be pushing for the destruction of Piedras Negras, and any nation's soldiers unlucky enough to be there would be considered collateral damage.

Max added what the President omitted, "We already have a covert team of operatives embedded in Piedras Negras. So far, no one else knows that they're there. They have identified the pyramid and the cartel's small army, but there is no sign of Alexander's people. The cartel has been blasting away at the same spot on the pyramid, so we can assume that's where Alexander's boys entered the structure.

"Our covert team has enough explosives with them to level the whole place for a mile around using strategically placed charges. As long as we don't use missiles that can be detected by satellites or radar, we can avoid any responsibility for the damage. The blame will be placed on the Macizo cartel. We have to decide if we want to wait for Alexander's people to appear or to take down the whole area before any witnesses from other countries arrive." Max sat back and exhaled loudly. He was glad everything was on the table. All eyes turned back to the President.

"We still have several hours before any of the invading nations' military units can get to the pyramid. Let's give Alexander's people until morning to contact us. If we've heard nothing to act on by then, the team has my approval to level the place just before the sun comes up." With that said, the President stood and the meeting was adjourned.

General Javier Hernandez was in charge of the Guatemalan troops sent to protect Piedras Negras. He wasn't clear about what he was protecting in the remote jungle at the northern end of his country, but he knew better than to hesitate when called to action.

He was told that the Macizo cartel had armed men there who were considered to be hostile. Javier had been friendly with Macizo for a long time and had accepted their gifts to look the other way for several years now. He knew he must approach this situation

423

carefully if he intended the contributions to his retirement fund to continue.

To do this, General Hernandez ordered a company of his men to hide in the tree line while surrounding the private airstrip he knew Macizo used regularly in Piedras Negras. They didn't have to wait long before a plane landed and a large truck emerged from the jungle to unload the cargo. Javier used a bullhorn to announce that they were surrounded but that they intended Macizo no harm. Once all the cartel's men had laid down their weapons, General Hernandez approached them with a squad of his soldiers.

"Good day, gentlemen," Javier began. "We are not a threat to you, but I have been ordered to contain the situation evolving here in Piedras Negras. From the looks of your cargo, you have some heavy explosives that can cause great damage. Can whichever one of you is in charge explain this to me?"

A man who identified himself only as Juan spoke for the group. "There is an old pyramid located north of here. The three gringos we were pursuing managed to escape inside. The explosives are to be used to blast open the pyramid so they answer to El Jefe for killing our people."

The General considered this and was glad the Macizo soldiers were apparently unaware of any treasure to be plundered. At least that was true of Juan. The General asked, "Who is in charge of Macizo's men now?"

The man answered, "El Jefe is Thiago Bernal. He is already at the pyramid waiting for us and these supplies."

Javier had met Thiago Bernal before and was sure they could come to an agreement they both liked. "Are you in radio contact with Thiago from here?" he asked.

"Yes," he answered, and handed the General his radio without being asked.

After a quick conversation, Thiago was on his way to speak with General Hernandez face to face.

***

Thiago entered the airstrip clearing with his hands held high. He wanted to be sure that the Guatemalan soldiers had no

424

reason to shoot him. He knew this General Hernandez and, more importantly, he knew the man had been on their payroll for several years.

As he approached the people gathered around the plane, Thiago lowered his arms and said, "General Hernandez, my old friend! To what do I owe this great pleasure?"

Javier smiled and replied, "I wanted to see what kind of trouble you were causing in my country. My government believes that you are here for a higher purpose than killing a few yanquis."

"You have it backwards, my friend," Thiago replied innocently. "It is the norteamericanos who are after your country's valuables. They have killed several of my men in pursuit of whatever they believe is inside that pyramid. I only want to bring them to justice for these unwarranted murders."

Javier decided to test Thiago's intentions. "And if I allow you to show these yanquis the error of their ways, you will leave this place and the pyramid alone?"

"I do not like this place," Thiago said truthfully. "Once these criminals have been dealt with, we will be on our way."

"How long will it be before you leave?" Javier asked.

"We have had difficulties reaching them," Thiago admitted. "That's what this shipment of supplies is for. It should not be long now."

"The problem is that the world is very interested in this place and many soldiers from many nations are coming," the General warned. "You do not have long before they arrive, and they could care less about you or the yanquis. They want whatever treasures are supposed to be hidden inside of the pyramid."

"It would be worth a great deal to me if you would run interference until I can deal with this situation," Thiago said with a leading tone.

"As long as you don't remove anything from Piedras Negras, I can protect you," Javier promised. "I will inform my superiors that you are assisting me in defending this area."

Thiago smiled and said, "I will tell my men that your soldiers will maintain a wide perimeter keeping others out while we finish our business with these killers."

Chapter 28

Amelius was waiting patiently for Mark and Nuri. He arrived in this place ahead of them to allow himself time to acclimate to a physical form. He knew the great importance this meeting would have on the future of humankind, so he needed to be at the top of his game.

From where he stood, the surrounding room looked a lot like the Hall of Records that had been destroyed in Giza. This one, however, was still standing and located below ground in Piedras Negras. He intuitively knew Nuri and Mark would not arrive for several more minutes. To pass the time, he picked up one of the familiar objects on display. The moment his hands touched the instrument it came to life.

Amelius played it with a virtuoso's skill and the chamber filled with the sweet sound of music the world had not heard for 12,000 years. His eyes became misty and a broad smile spread across his handsome face as the incredible melody touched his soul through human ears. Amelius had almost forgotten what it was like to be in a physical body. He inhaled deeply as he deftly fingered the instrument's keys. He played on remembering why the human form was so compelling.

The beautiful harmonies he created were in perfect accord with the laws of linear time and space. He marveled that such ecstasy could be experienced despite the limitations of a physical form in three dimensions. From his eternal perspective, humankind spent much of their lives living in fear. It would be centuries before they understood and believed that the universe in which they live is always friendly, even during the worst of times.

He reminded himself that in three dimensions the boundless love and mercy of the cosmos is perceived as infinite time and space. If only these delightful souls could see past their fears and remember who they are! Amelius ended the song and his silent reverie knowing Nuri was about to appear.

"Welcome," he said serenely as he returned the musical instrument to its display. "I was reminiscing with the harmonium. It is not often I have a reason to assume a physical form with its fascinating limitations."

"Hello Amelius," Nuri said in return. "Is this the room that was lost in Egypt?"

"No, but it is very similar. In another minute you'll begin to perceive subtle differences."

"So where are we then?" Nuri asked.

"We're waiting for Mark at the moment," Amelius answered. "He should be along shortly and then I can answer your questions together."

Nuri couldn't help but ask, "You said that you have assumed a physical form. Are you human?"

Before Amelius could respond, Mark appeared in the room just a few feet away from Nuri. Amelius knew to allow him some time to acclimate.

"Welcome Mark!" Amelius said cheerfully. "We have been waiting for you. We'll take another minute before attending to the important issues at hand. In the meantime, let me give you a quick synopsis of why this meeting is so different from our previous encounters."

Mark and Nuri nodded their agreement.

"Your physical bodies are still inside the passageway in the pyramid, but your minds are tuned into this Hall of Records that is located in an underground complex not far from there," Amelius explained. "Some on earth call what you are experiencing remote viewing."

"What exactly is remote viewing?" Mark asked.

Amelius smiled and answered, "It's just what I described. You are physically in one location but your consciousness is experiencing events in another."

Nuri asked, "And how is this different from our previous visits?"

"We are currently meeting in a place consisting of lower vibrations compared to our encounters of the past. That means, unlike before, you will consciously retain a clear, albeit limited, memory of this conversation." Amelius paused to see if they understood him so far. The blank stares he observed were not promising.

"There are some advantages to the limitations of time and space. As is humorously said on earth, 'time keeps everything from happening to you at once.' In the higher dimensions, all of eternity can be experienced in the same moment. That makes it easy to become overwhelmed and distracted from our true purpose. Eternity is filled with an infinite number of 'shiny objects' that can draw us away from achieving our goals."

"I think that you should have quit when we were just lost," said Nuri. Mark was still processing what he had just heard and barely nodded his agreement. "Perhaps our conscious minds are not ready for all that?" Nuri concluded.

"Well said!" Amelius laughed. "I just allowed my well-intended desire to expand your awareness to become a 'shiny object' that would hinder the purpose of our meeting."

Mark and Nuri laughed along with him, but they weren't sure they got the joke.

"Where is Jason?" Nuri wondered. "Shouldn't he hear whatever you need to tell us?"

"Actually, Jason is meeting with Halaliel at this same time but in a different place," Amelius explained. "You two have a different role in the coming events according to your skills and personal choices. Jason is uniquely qualified to handle what the two of you cannot."

"Where is he meeting with Halaliel?" Mark asked.

"They are in the remaining Hall of Records near the Bimini Islands. That chamber looks much like this one," Amelius explained. "His consciousness was drawn there because of the key role he will play in your probable future quest to find the third hidden location. You two were drawn here because of your intense desire to learn the secrets of the Hall of Records in Piedras Negras."

Nuri was ready to get down to business. "The crystal medallion explained a great deal to us already. Are we about to learn the physics behind RFP's ability to levitate matter and communicate anywhere in the world?"

"In a manner of speaking, yes," answered Amelius. "You will be given translations to the remaining symbols you haven't yet deciphered. Your friends at JPL will eventually be able to use those translations to accomplish everything you just mentioned, and more."

Amelius picked up a large crystal medallion that had been resting on one of the shelves in the chamber. Then he walked over to an obsidian pedestal near Nuri and Mark. He flipped the crystal disk in the air like it was a coin and it landed perfectly on its edge, centered atop the jet black surface of the stone column. A moment later, holographic images began to appear before them. They displayed large pages from a book containing English translations for the 4,999 symbols they first saw in Egypt.

Mark spoke as he observed the symbols cascading by. "It's easy enough to think we'll remember all this while it is in front of us. Are you sure we will retain this information once we're back in our conscious state?"

Amelius smiled at Mark's perspective. "Yes, but with an interesting filter applied to your memory. You will only remember the translations of symbols that will benefit rather than hinder humankind."

"Okay. How does that work exactly?" Nuri asked.

"The symbol before you now is a good example," Amelius said, tilting his head toward the holographic page. "If the JPL scientists became aware of this universal principal, that knowledge would lead to discoveries that would extend the human life span far beyond what you can imagine. You've now seen the formula and understand its root principal, but only on a subconscious level. Your conscious minds will not have access to it until the world is ready to receive it for the highest good of all."

"And who decides that?" Mark asked, a bit frustrated.

"The quick answer is that the world itself will decide when it is ready for such knowledge. This process is an interesting earthly application of the laws of attraction and karma," Amelius said resolutely. "Perhaps an analogy will help. Imagine placing a large inflated ball in the middle of a football field. Now line up 50 people on each opposing side's goal line. Then tell both sides they must push the ball across the opposing goal line, and blow the starting whistle. All 100 people will converge on the ball at once. The resulting, and mostly conflicting, force vectors from all those people will cause the ball to move erratically and make little progress. The ball may even move sideways or briefly become airborne. Regardless, the greatest progress will come when one side or the other organizes their people to all push at once in the same direction. It works the same way on earth. Once you get a critical mass of people working together to gain or accomplish something, they are difficult to stop. Just as it is with physics, the organized team's momentum can be either constructive or destructive, depending upon their goal."

Mark looked frustrated and said, "I don't see how that applies to filtering, or should I say censoring, our memories."

"Let's apply what I just said to discovering how to vastly extend a human life. Such a discovery would be a 'very shiny object' that can both aid and harm humankind. Longevity is very compelling to those in mortal bodies, but it has little to do with why people are here in the first place. If and when the world is ready to use such knowledge for the good of all, it would be as if many of you were pushing the ball in the same direction. The result would cause your memories to unlock those secrets and make them available on earth. Until enough people are on the same altruistic page, the science behind longevity will remain hidden to help humankind stay focused on treating each other well."

Nuri said, "Back up a bit. Explain what you meant by 'why we are here in the first place.' You mean why we are here on earth?"

Amelius laughed patiently and said, "Yes, and one day you too will find the humor in your question. It is quite simple. You are here to remember how to play well with others, so to speak. Every selfish choice we make puts us out of harmony with our friendly and loving universe. You two are no different from me except that your existence on earth is something like a 'time out' that human parents use to teach their children. You will remain enmeshed here until you learn to treat everyone as a most-beloved member of your family. Once you do away with selfish choices, you will be free to travel wherever you like in space and time and consciousness."

431

The holographic glossary ended and the light from the crystal dissolved. Mark and Nuri were visibly shaken by the knowledge they had just absorbed.

Mark said, "There is so much we don't understand on earth. Is everyone ready to receive what we've just learned?"

"The original gift was RF energy," Amelius began. "Matt Alexander believed that if the world had access to safe and abundant energy, the conflicts between nations would cease. There was great progress for a time, but the world is once again headed for a violent showdown that can still be averted."

"So what can we do to stop the pending conflict?" Nuri asked.

"You will remember enough of what you have learned here so that the people living on earth will be well-fed and have all the pure water they need to drink," Amelius announced. "Satisfying the lower rungs on what you call Maslow's Hierarchy of Needs will allow the world to focus on higher goals than simple survival."

"And that will lead to a lasting world peace?" Mark asked hopefully.

"We'll see. The potential exists for that outcome. The question is whether there are enough people on earth creating the needed critical mass of loving vibrations in time to avert disaster," Amelius said prophetically.

Mark and Nuri watched as a holographic movie revealed the choices they would soon face. They could see the ramifications of each option, and how each resulting choice would likely play out in the days to come. It was clear that the Middle East's role in 'playing well with others' would quickly become the pivotal factor.

They started to ask Amelius how they might best present resonant frequency technology's ability to grow food and purify water, but they were both overcome with sleep. In a few hours, they would awaken back in the passageway with a great deal to share with Jason, then Matt, and then with the world.

Chapter 29

Captain Jim Franklin, retired, was in charge of the covert ops team that was sent to Piedras Negras. Jim and his crew worked as private contractors the U.S. government hired for complicated situations like this one. He was glad to be in charge of such an important mission in service to his country. However, he didn't like the ambiguous orders he received regarding the Americans who were in trouble here.

"Just do the recon," his contact in Washington had said. "We'll have specific orders and rules of engagement after you give us the lay of the land."

Jim's assessment of the Macizo cartel's people surprised everyone. He reported that the drug thugs blasted repeatedly at the same spot on the pyramid's wall. They had already cratered a hole in the limestone that reached halfway into the base of the structure, at least as far as he could tell. If every country's objective was to explore and exploit this pyramid, why were these clowns trying to destroy it? And if leveling the pyramid was their goal, a child could see they were going about it all wrong.

The sun was down and Jim had not received new orders. He was running out of patience when his satellite phone buzzed. "Finally!" he thought as he flipped up the antenna to answer the call.

The orders were not what he expected. He had thought their mission was to rescue the three Americans trapped inside the pyramid. At least it was assumed they had managed to get inside the stone structure. No one had heard from them for some time. Instead, he was told that their highest priority was to level the pyramid and everything around it before morning. If the Americans made their presence known before sunrise, then they were to be rescued before completing their mission. Whether the missing Americans were rescued or not, nothing was to remain of the pyramid, or aggressors, in the surrounding area.

Captain Franklin called his squad leaders together for an ops briefing. There were four squads of ten men each. The leaders listened intently as Jim detailed each squad's assignment.

A team was assigned to each of the four sides of the pyramid. Their call signs would match the compass direction of their assigned pyramid wall: north, south, east, and west. Jim instructed them to keep an eye out for any sign of the Americans. If they were spotted, then rescue protocols were in effect. If there was no sign of them, on his command, they would light this place up fifteen minutes before sun up.

The plan was to eliminate all cartel resistance first, followed by the utter destruction of the pyramid and surrounding area. That would include placing massive underground charges to ensure any subterranean structures were demolished as well. The nearby private airstrip would serve as their exit point using five UH-60 Black Hawk helicopters to stay below the radar as they cleared the area.

The squad leaders had their orders and left to brief their men. Several hours of darkness remained before sunrise, and they had to take positions where they would not be in each other's line of fire. The four squads surreptitiously deployed to surround the pyramid. They had no problem avoiding the Guatemalan soldiers who mostly stayed a mile back from Macizo's perimeter. Using night vision goggles, each squad member kept track of the cartel's men, and a watchful eye for any sign of the Americans.

***

Ambassador Medrano had just hung up the phone from talking with his president in Guatemala City. He could tell by the president's tone that his cabinet had bigger problems than his U.N. debacle to deal with at the moment. Carlos still had a job but it would not be at the U.N. He worried that his next posting would be in Siberia or the Congo.

Before the president clicked off, he assigned Carlos one more task. He was to take Fatima Cortez into custody. While she had not broken any laws in Guatemala, she had value as a bargaining chip to the U.S. and Mexico. She was also an illegal alien in America if she left the Embassy's property.

He called down to the embassy's security desk to order her detainment. Just when he thought his day couldn't get any worse, it did. His chief of security informed him that Fatima Cortez had apparently left the building during the televised questioning at the U.N.'s General Assembly meeting. "She didn't just walk out the front door," the chief explained, "but our facility is not designed to hold prisoners."

Carlos realized that Fatima had seen the U.N. fiasco and decided it was no longer safe to have her whereabouts known. He couldn't blame her for leaving, but his life was now ruined because he had listened to that woman.

***

Fatima was horror stricken as she watched the past American president maneuver his way around every accusation. It was painful to watch the ambassador embarrass himself through his inept interrogation of Matthew Alexander. It did appear Carlos had accomplished one thing, although she was certain that was not the ambassador's intent. The world's governments would soon be warring over Egypt and Guatemala to see who would control RF technology.

The only viable part left of her original plan was handing Thiago over to the Americans in exchange for Lupe's and her freedom. The window of opportunity for that was about to close as well. She was sure that Carlos would try to have her arrested at his first opportunity. She had to get out of there immediately. After that, she and her sister would find someplace safe to lie low until a deal could be made to give up Thiago.

She looked out her window and saw the American agents waiting for her by the embassy's main entrance. She would have to find another exit if she wanted to avoid them.

Her timing was good. The entire staff still had their eyes glued to TV monitors throughout the embassy watching Carlos make a fool of himself. There were a number of exits to choose from, but none without someone standing guard. She took a chance that the loading dock by the kitchen would have fewer sentries.

She walked down a back hallway to the kitchen and found an employee locker room. What a stroke of luck! She quickly donned some casual street clothes stored there by a female worker. Someone else had left a blue baseball cap and she managed to braid her hair and tuck most of it up inside the hat. She also did her best to wipe off her make up. She looked in the mirror and was satisfied that her new appearance would help her blend in with the crowd.

435

As she had hoped, the TV coverage of the U.N. held the kitchen workers' attention. The guard for the rear exit was among the staff watching the spectacle. She decided not to try the roll up door. She was sure it would make an awful racket if she attempted to open it. She released the breath she hadn't realized she was holding when she saw a walk-through door next to it. That was normally where the guard was stationed. She had to hope the door was not locked. She made a beeline for it and tried the handle. It turned, but the door wouldn't open. Her heart sank until she saw a deadbolt knob. With some effort, she was able to flip the knob to the left. She then tried the door handle again. This time it opened, but it made a lot of noise as it moved on old hinges.

Fatima slipped out and closed the door behind her as quietly as she could. She found herself standing on a loading dock set back from the street. A wide driveway connected the dock area to a street that was surprisingly devoid of cars at the moment. She prayed the Americans were not closely watching this side of the building. She quickly walked to the sidewalk that bordered the street to see if the path was clear. She backed out of view when she saw two American agents standing on the corner to her left. Her heart was pounding and she almost ran back to the loading dock. Then she calmed herself with a steadying breath.

She knew these men were specifically searching for a lone woman who fit her usual polished description. She kept looking back toward the loading dock fearing someone might have seen her exit the building. When she checked the street again, she saw two men in suits walking toward her from the left. She almost panicked before she realized they were not the Americans looking for her. The businessmen coming toward her were still some distance away, but she heard them speaking in Spanish.

She backed up several steps so it would appear as if she had just exited the building when they could see her approach. She stepped onto the sidewalk just in front of them, using their bodies to hide her from the agent's view from the corner. Then she slowed her steps just enough so they would catch up to her. In case the Americans glanced in her direction, she tried to make it look like she had been with them the entire time. When the businessmen were even with her, she asked in Spanish how she could get to the Guatemalan Embassy. They smiled and said she was already there, but that the main entrance was on Park Avenue, the next street over. She asked the best way to get there and they pointed to the right.

She thanked them for the information making sure to waste enough time expressing her gratitude so that they all reached the corner together. The two men allowed her to pass in front of them before they continued on their way across the street. Fatima let out a sigh of relief when she was out of the sight of the Americans at the other end of the block. She hailed a passing taxi and asked him to take her to the hotel where Lupe was waiting.

She sat low in her seat and kept her hand up to cover the side of her face. She hadn't realized that the one-way street would force the cab driver to pass right in front of the American agents. She parted her fingers just enough to see if they noticed her. They never looked at the cab. Their attention was still on the embassy's doors.

***

Lupe was lying on her bed in a hotel bathrobe watching a movie when Fatima pushed open the door. She rushed to the closet and pulled out their suitcases, threw them on her bed, and turned toward the dresser.

"What's going on?" Lupe asked once she found the mute button on the remote.

"We need to leave. Now!" was Fatima's frantic reply.

"Why? What's happened? Are they going to arrest us?" Lupe was about to ask more questions when Fatima's expression stopped her short.

"I don't have time to explain, but yes, there will soon be people after us," Fatima said as she continued packing their things.

Lupe trusted her sister enough to not say another word. She threw on some clothes and helped to pack the remaining items. Their luggage was on wheels so they didn't bother to call a porter for help to check out of the hotel.

Minutes later they turned their key cards in at the registration desk. Fatima was trying to remain calm, but her hands shook as she pulled out enough cash to pay the bill. They were

437

relieved when the clerk wished them a nice day as they turned to leave.

Once they were outside, a valet hailed a taxi for them. He asked their destination so he could tell the cabbie. Fatima hesitated a moment before saying, "The nearest bus station will be fine!"

Nuri, Mark and Jason were awake and alert in the hallway of the Piedras Negras pyramid. They had been comparing their experiences with Amelius and Halaliel. Jason looked at his watch and saw they had a few more hours left until the sun came up. The explosions had started up again, and now they could hear drilling machines whirring away. It was clear that Thiago was not about to give up the chase.

Jason had noticed something unusual about the explosions. "Do you think it's odd that we can hear the blasts but we don't feel them?"

Mark thought for a moment and said, "Not really. The limestone construction of this pyramid is as solid as a rock, pun intended." He smiled, waiting for them to appreciate his keen sense of humor.

Nuri ignored the bad joke to add, "I'm with Jason on this. I'll bet the vibrations of those explosions can be felt a mile away. I don't understand how we can hear them but not feel the impact reverberating through the pyramid."

Jason had a guess, but he wasn't done pointing out the anomalies he had noticed about this hallway. He said, "This passageway is probably five times longer than the base of the pyramid we entered. Since we have stayed at the same level throughout, that's not possible, and yet, here we are."

"Okay, but what's your point?" asked Mark.

"What if this hallway is not restricted by the dimension we live in outside of these walls?" Jason theorized. "If that's the case, then we aren't hearing those explosions with our ears. Our minds are picking up on the activities around the pyramid."

"I'm still not with you," said Nuri. "Does your theory change our plans for getting out of here?"

"Probably not," Jason admitted. "But after all the explosions we've heard, my guess is that they've blown a hole halfway through the pyramid by now."

"What idiot would still be blasting away if that was true?" Mark said, shaking his head.

"Thiago probably saw the three of us disappear through a solid wall," Jason paused, and amended his statement. "I guess that would be four of us, counting the big guy who tackled me. For all we know, his legs were exposed and suspended in the pyramid's outer wall. In that case, I can see Thiago taking some desperate measures."

Nuri asked, "But how does that affect us when we eventually try to leave this place?"

"Your guess is probably better than mine, but wouldn't we appear in the same spot where we left?" Jason was not comfortable with this line of thinking, but it had to be discussed. "That's likely to be open ground now. Our exit point could be located above a deep pit."

"You mean we could be walking out of this hallway into something like an empty elevator shaft?" Mark exclaimed with fear creeping into his tone. "Then we could wait a week for Thiago's men to go away, and still fall to our deaths when we leave here."

"Why didn't we foresee this problem when Amelius and Halaliel displayed the possible futures we face?" Nuri asked.

"That's my point!" said Mark. "None of us remember how we get back to Pasadena!"

Jason smiled for the first time in a long while. "Maybe that's good news. If none of us were shown how we get out of here, that can't be a big decision we'll face. How many times did those guys tell us that we live in a friendly universe?"

"It's a mystery!" Nuri said with a nervous laugh.

If nothing else, they all felt better about the current predicament knowing that somehow they were going to make it home safely.

Chapter 30

Fatima and Lupe were doing their best to avoid attention as they caught the bus to Florida. Their destination was Fort Lauderdale to buy forged passports that matched their existing IDs. They wanted to be ready to leave the country at a moment's notice, but where would they go? The whole world was falling apart.

News reports confirmed that Piedras Negras was no one's secret. That was bad news for the sisters. Thiago was the only bargaining chip Fatima had left and the idiot had managed to put himself smack in the middle of a war zone. Even if he got out of there alive, she doubted the Americans would care what happened to him. Now that The Glut had been cured, Thiago's poisoning of Lake Mead was old news. Who had time for that when a world war was brewing?

The sisters rode in silence as the sun began to set on this frustrating day. Neither of them had been able to suggest a plan that could point them in a new or worthwhile direction. Fatima was tired and her thoughts turned cynical. She had once jokingly suggested that they move to a quiet suburban area and become spinsters. The thought still made them laugh, but they knew they were running out of options.

It was Lupe who offered a ray of hope. "Don't forget that you know a lot more about RF technology than almost anyone. The crystal movie you saw has given you a gift. We need to figure out how to make use of it."

"I'm not sure what you mean," Fatima said, shaking her head.

"For instance, the televised U.N. meeting announced to the world that low-cost abundant food and pure water are possible with new RF technology. What they won't know is how important the type of soil used is for producing the best crops. Your knowledge of that can be very valuable to the right people."

Fatima let out a skeptical laugh. "You'd be right if I really knew the first thing about farming or RF technology. If someone else figures out how to create RF food and water, then maybe I can use what I know to our advantage."

"So we keep a low profile while the rest of the world sorts it all out," Lupe said encouragingly. "In the meantime, we can figure out what we will do if and when someone creates that opportunity for us."

***

The news channels continued to broadcast reports of competing invasion forces set to collide in Guatemala. Unconfirmed sources claimed that spy satellites had located what appeared to be a pyramid buried under centuries of jungle growth in Piedras Negras. The first war ships to approach Guatemalan waters requested permission to dock peacefully. They said they were there to offer assistance in protecting the Guatemalan people from the greedy looters that were headed their way.

The President of Guatemala, Ernesto Cabrera, wasn't about to let anyone park a warship in his waters. He knew their tiny nation was woefully ill-equipped to take on the bullies of the world.

President Cabrera asked his military advisors if there were any major powers that had not sent soldiers toward Piedras Negras. Their response surprised him. The only G-20 country that had no warships headed their way was the United States.

"Please get President Westbrook on the phone," was his calculated reply. "Either they already have what the rest of the world seeks here, or he has something else up his sleeve. I intend to find out the truth and use it to our advantage."

***

Jim Franklin radioed his squad leaders. "All teams, this is the final comm check before we go dark."

"North team, ready to go," came the first reply. "East team, standing by," was followed by "South team, G to G." There was a slight delay before Jim heard, "West team, we're good here."

"All teams," Jim's voice carried an ominous tone, "the assault will commence in exactly five minutes from my mark. There will be no further radio contact unless our American friends make a last second appearance. No teams are to approach the kill zone until

441

I give the 'all clear' after the assault begins. Good luck, gentlemen. Counting down five minutes in 3, 2, 1, mark."

Each of the squad leaders set their watches to coordinate the strike. They were ready to hit anyone outside of their team with more firepower than they could imagine. The order was clear that there would be no survivors. Thirty seconds after they opened fire, the battle would be over.

***

"Please hold for President Westbrook," said the pleasant voice from the White House switchboard. President Cabrera's assistant nodded to her boss that he could pick up now.

Don Westbrook started speaking, "President Cabrera, what can I do for you at this early hour? Has the sun even risen yet in Guatemala?"

"Ah, President Westbrook," Ernesto began. "Thank you for taking my call. Daylight will be here in minutes, but there has been no sleep for me this night. I really need your help."

"Well, how can we help you, Ernesto?" Don said with feigned concern.

"You are aware that Guatemala is about to be invaded by many countries," he said as a preface. "I have denied entry to everyone, but they have paid Belize handsomely to anchor their warships in Amatique Bay and enter our country by land across the unguarded border. The first of them are expected to arrive at Piedras Negras in a few hours."

Don said nothing, so Ernesto continued.

"As you may know, our capital city is three hundred kilometers away from the pyramid they seek. We both know that none of the invaders are here to overthrow our government. They seek to raid our national treasures."

"Are you asking the United States to render aid of some kind?" asked Don obtusely.

Ernesto sighed, "Yes! Exactly! If I give your military permission to enter our airspace, will you stop these aggressors from stealing us blind?"

"I can't condone taking violent action, Mr. President," Don lied convincingly. "I won't answer their violent actions with violence of our own. But I will do this. Those who disregard your warnings to immediately leave Guatemala will be in violation of the RFP Peace Accord. Once the offenders have been identified, they will suffer the consequences detailed in the agreement."

Ernesto speculated if the President of the United States would immediately stop selling RF energy to so many nations. He could guess how they would react. Was America willing to battle the world over this?

"What will you need from me?" asked President Cabrera.

"First, I'll need you to provide a list of all the trespassing offenders," Don began. "Then we will..."

Don interrupted himself and asked Ernesto to hold the line. A moment later, the military leader of the Guatemalan forces entered the room and announced, "There has been a tremendous explosion in Piedras Negras."

On the phone Ernesto could hear the American President asking if he had received the news.

"Yes, I just heard," Ernesto said, feeling the weight of the world on his shoulders. "I will have to hang up now. It is too late to prevent the violence. I will assess the damage, draft the list you requested, and get back to you."

***

Thiago and his men had gone for more than a day without sleep. He ordered them to erect a tent and set up some cots inside. He stretched out on the nearest one and told Luis to wake him once they broke through the pyramid wall. A moment later, an incredibly bright light woke him with a start. He looked up and squinted through his raised fingers, and realized that the light was coming from a figure standing before him. As bright as the light was, there was total darkness everywhere else.

"What the hell is this?" Thiago cried out. "What's going on?"

A gentle, reassuring voice came from the impossibly bright figure. "Be not afraid, I will do you no harm."

"What do you want?" Thiago asked, trying to keep the panic out of his voice.

"To help you with a difficult decision," was the stranger's reply. A moment later, Thiago saw images of his life passing before him as if the darkness was a giant movie screen for him to watch. Every moment of his life was shown in great detail. He didn't see his life as he remembered it. Neither was this perspective of his life the way everyone else had viewed him. Thiago realized this recap of his life that focused on all the choices he had made was presented as the unvarnished truth. There was no bias or condemnation in what he saw, but he still felt embarrassed.

As the spectacle faded, Thiago heard the gentle voice say, "What follows are the probable futures from which you must choose."

The scene changed and Thiago witnessed events that were about to occur around the Piedras Negras pyramid. He could see his men dying all around him in a hail of bullets and countless explosions. The next scene surprised him. He saw a way that he alone could survive the assault and live to rebuild the Macizo cartel. As the tableau played on, he saw that he would become even wealthier and more powerful than Rodrigo had been. He couldn't believe his good fortune.

"Thiago!" a familiar voice called to him. "What do you really want in life?"

"Everything I just saw here. The money, the power, no one could stand against me!" he said excitedly, already making plans.

He realized that two people stood before him now. There was the man shining brightly and a lesser figure that he was sure he knew. Then it came to him. The man who had just arrived was Rodrigo Cortez!

"Yes, it is I, Rodrigo," he said in confirmation. "Let me show you the last words I recorded for my Reina, Fatima."

With that, another movie began and Thiago saw Fatima watching a computer monitor in the safe room of her home. She was crying as Rodrigo's recorded image told her of all his regrets. Thiago was surprised to hear that Rodrigo had found little joy in his life despite all he had accomplished.

He turned to El Jefe and said, "But you had everything! You had all the power and wealth that a man could want. You even had a beautiful woman to share it with. What more could you ask for?"

Rodrigo shook his head saying, "I never thought about life beyond my time as El Jefe. When we make choices based solely on earthly values, we often miss what's truly important. So the question still unanswered is, 'What do you really want in your life?' This time consider what really makes you happy before you answer."

"Nothing will change my mind, Jefe," Thiago admitted. "I want money and power and a beautiful woman to share it with, as you had."

"You thought having all that made me happy, but it did not," Rodrigo confessed. "Can you imagine why I felt that way?"

"No, Jefe, I cannot. I heard what you said to Fatima in the video recording, but that is you, not me."

Rodrigo considered how to respond. He remembered he once shared Thiago's perspective. How could he convey what had changed inside of him? Suddenly, he knew.

"How many people suffered so that I could have all those things? Not just the other cartels that challenged us. What about those who consumed our drugs and ruined their lives in the process?"

"There were many," he agreed. "But life will always have winners and losers. We must fight to keep what is ours. Those who don't will always be the losers."

"That kind of thinking put you at great odds with my beloved Fatima," Rodrigo said, pointing out the obvious. "And my own selfishness put Fatima at odds with her sister, Lupita. Don't the people we love, and those who they love, deserve to have everything they want in life too?"

"That is why everyone must watch out for themselves," Thiago said stubbornly, though he was beginning to see his argument was flawed. "No one else is going to!" he added, trying to convince himself, as much as Rodrigo, that he was right.

"So you say, but how well does that work in the long run?" Rodrigo responded with a shake of his head. "How happy are any of us who live only for ourselves?"

"So what is the secret to happiness, Jefe?" Thiago asked, not really expecting an answer.

It was the other person who spoke now. Thiago knew intuitively that this man dressed all in white was called Amelius.

"Look before you, Thiago," Amelius said.

The images started up again, but this time he was able to see further into the future than he had before. He saw that despite attaining great wealth and power as the leader of Macizo, he would constantly fear losing what he had. Ultimately, he would die alone because he trusted no one.

Amelius said, "It does not have to be that way. Here is your future if you love and care for everyone else just as much as you have cared for yourself."

The movie changed to a life he had trouble believing. As he treated everyone around him well, they did the same to him. The joy he felt in helping others to be happy brought him, and everyone around him, a sense of peace and fulfillment that he hadn't thought possible.

"But that kind of world only exists in the movies," Thiago said in frustration. "People don't treat each other like that. It takes just one person watching out for their own interests to mess it up for everyone."

Amelius smiled and asked, "Do you know what we call those who would 'mess it up for everyone' else?"

Thiago shook his head.

"We call them humans," Amelius answered, smiling again. "They incarcerate themselves in this place through their selfish choices. They can't let go of this earthly school until they learn to live in harmony with everyone around them. Those who learn how to play well with others are free to go anywhere they like."

The movie was still playing before them. Thiago kept watching the life he had chosen with Macizo in contrast to the joyous life he could have if he changed his selfish ways.

"I just don't see how I can do this. It looks like I will fail to change no matter how hard I might try," Thiago admitted. "Jefe, how were you able to do this?"

"I wasn't. That is part of the reason why I died. Making such changes comes slowly for people like you and me, my friend," Rodrigo answered. "I realized that love was the best catalyst for me to make such a change. Sadly, at this moment, there is no one that you love more than yourself. That will make it even harder to willingly walk away from this difficult life you've created."

"Do you mean I must willingly choose to die?" Thiago exclaimed.

It was Amelius who answered, "Do you feel like you're dead now in this moment? There are times when the best way to leave the world better off than you found it is to stop making it worse. If you will come with Rodrigo and me, we can help you to make better choices on earth when you are given your next opportunity."

Amelius stretched out his hand in encouragement. Thiago hesitated to take it, realizing he was about to abandon everything he had worked so hard to achieve. Thiago became El Jefe by choosing a path of death and misery. It was clear that every day he continued to live on earth would only make things worse for himself and everyone around him. Thiago was ready to escape the hell he had created. He reached out and let Amelius lead the way.

***

Jim Franklin was counting the seconds until the assault would begin. He lay motionless on the ground about two hundred feet from the pyramid. He had already chosen the objective for the RPG tube resting on his shoulder. He was one of three men targeting the cache of explosives near the battered wall of the pyramid. He watched through his night vision binoculars as the man he had identified as the new cartel leader ducked inside a newly erected tent.

Jim couldn't explain why, but he suddenly knew it was mission-critical that he change his target. With mere seconds left

447

before his team unleashed a firestorm, Jim redirected his RPG's sights to the center of the tent. When the counter on his watch hit zero, he pressed the trigger.

He had no doubt the resulting explosion ended the life of the Macizo leader. If he had not decided to aim for the tent, anyone inside could have survived the assault by digging in until the shooting stopped.

After 30 seconds of their planned "shock and awe" attack, Jim gave the order to cease fire. The deafening explosions and gun fire reports gave way to an eerie silence. After another minute, they heard the jungle sounds return. He knew his people had killed the other soldiers in the area. His orders now were to make sure nothing remained of this place.

***

President Westbrook had just disconnected from his call with President Cabrera. He sat in the situation room at the conference table with Max Atwater. Max was just hanging up the phone after getting an update on the explosion in Guatemala.

"This is the recorded satellite feed we have of Piedras Negras," Max said pointing to the largest monitor. "The video playing here shows what occurred beginning with the assault just before dawn."

The satellite camera had been set for night vision. There was no audio and it took Don a moment to adjust to the green images before him. At first, there was almost no movement, and then the entire screen flashed with a brilliant white light. From all sides, he could see the American squads open fire on the other soldiers posted around the pyramid. There must have been twenty to twenty-five explosions that Max explained were RPGs. That was followed by rifle and machine gun fire from all directions. The president watched as hundreds, maybe thousands, of hot bullet tracers laced the screen.

Suddenly, the firing ceased as quickly as it had begun. The monitor showed tiny green forms slowly approaching the pyramid from the surrounding jungle. Max explained the moving shapes were the American operatives preparing for phase two of the mission.

They would strategically plant heavy explosives to obliterate the pyramid and underground complex.

They had portable drilling units with them that could easily cut through the limestone. They already knew where to drill holes and fill them with octanitrocubane to maximize the damage. That was the same powerful explosive used to destroy the Sphinx ten years earlier.

Max asked the technician to forward the video to the time of the explosion and pause it there. He could see that the President had some questions.

"Do you really think there's anything to this Hall of Records crap?" Don asked Max.

"I don't know, Mr. President," Max said shaking his head. "There is a lot of circumstantial evidence that Alexander's people were onto something. It looks like we'll never know for sure."

"If they were inside that pyramid, I'd have to agree with you," Don sighed, with a hint of remorse. "But I'm not sure the world is ready for all the rumored advances RF technology supposedly has to offer. I regret losing those boys, but the collateral damage of this operation may have just saved civilization."

"I wanted to ask, is it really your intention to cut the offending nations off from RF energy?" Max asked.

"Not for a second," Don admitted. "But I had to make sure that everyone else believed it was on the table. I'm sure that it leaked from the NSC meeting just how serious I was. President Cabrera will only confirm my resolve to do just that. Now that the potential competitor for RF energy has been neutralized, the offending nations will have no choice but to continue with 'business as usual.' I will accept their sincere apologies, but that will come with a substantial bump in the price they pay us for RF energy."

"What about the RFP crystal in Egypt?" Max reminded him. "Alexander claims that crystal is completely functional. What happens if the Egyptians figure out how to make it work?"

"I'm not too worried about that," Don answered. "If they haven't managed to get it operational by now, I doubt they ever will.

Even our own guys haven't figured out how the JPL eggheads make it work. If that changes, we'll deal with it then."

Chapter 31

Jason, Mark and Nuri were passing the time comparing notes on their encounters with Amelius and Halaliel. The ongoing explosions were the only interruption to the otherwise silent hallway.

The next explosion was not like the others. In fact, it sounded like dozens of detonations all hitting within seconds of each other, like the grand finale of a fireworks show. That was followed by staccato pops that Jason identified as machine gun fire. Moments later, the sounds stopped altogether, leaving them straining to hear something, anything.

"What do we do now?" Mark asked nervously. His voice was unnaturally loud in the silence.

Jason was about to answer when all three men clearly heard an ethereal voice in their minds advise, "It is time to go."

They stared at each other for a moment and then simultaneously exclaimed, "Did you hear that!?"

Nuri smiled and said, "I don't need to be told twice. Let's get out of here!"

They jumped to their feet. Jason pulled a rope out of his backpack and secured it around his waist. He handed the other end to Mark and Nuri telling them to wrap it around their waists once each. He explained that they had to be ready to hold his entire weight if he should fall after going through the passageway portal.

Jason brought out the box of tiny crystals and took one in his hand. He passed the box with the remaining crystals to Nuri saying, "I will only need the one. You two may need the rest if anything goes wrong."

"You'll be fine!" Nuri nervously assured him.

Jason smiled, but he was less confident than Nuri sounded. He walked toward the end of the corridor where they had first entered two days before. The familiar tingling feeling came over him as he reached his arm forward and watched it disappear inside the limestone wall. He couldn't help but hold his breath and close his eyes as he walked straight ahead.

Jason took several steps on solid ground before he opened his eyes to survey his surroundings. He expected to see a blighted battlefield where the jungle had once thrived. He was surprised to see he was still indoors. He was definitely clear of the passageway. In fact, he was clear of Piedras Negras. Jason found himself standing inside the very ordinary lobby of their Pasadena workplace. His mind had trouble wrapping itself around what had just happened.

He turned to see the other end of the black nylon rope mysteriously floating in midair. He gave it a slight tug and was immediately yanked back through the portal. The next second he was standing in the pyramid's hallway. Mark and Nuri had fallen down in their desperate attempt to pull him back from the brink.

Jason laughed when he saw them. "Come on you two, get up!"

They just stared at him and wondered what could be on the other side of the portal to have him react with such calm.

"Get up!" he said again smiling, and they did, albeit slowly.

"Now I know why none of what Amelius or Halaliel showed us included how we get back home," Jason said with a grin. "Come on!"

With that he turned and walked back through the wall without hesitation. Mark and Nuri were already holding crystals in their hands. They also closed their eyes and held their breaths as they walked forward, expecting to fall at any moment. When they opened their eyes, they were shocked to be standing in the lobby of their offices in Pasadena.

Mark turned around to check on the portal. It was as if it had never been there. They still had the rope wrapped around their waists, but there was no longer an invisible connection to the passageway in Piedras Negras.

Jason said, "I've got to say, this is the only way to travel!" He started laughing.

"We have to call Matt right away," Mark exclaimed. "He'll probably think we died back there."

***

Jim Franklin was proud of his men. The efficiency and professionalism they showed securing this site, and now drilling the strategically located holes for the final phase of the mission, was impressive. But time was of the essence. The sun had risen and they no longer had the advantage of darkness to cover their movements.

They carefully inserted the precisely timed charges down each of the holes that were now filled with the octanitrocubane. They had just ten minutes to get to the airstrip and evacuate in the Black Hawks. Jim gave the order and his men double-timed it south to go back home. They saw a number of Guatemalan soldiers running in all directions. It seemed none of them were willing to risk their lives to safeguard whatever was in that pyramid.

The thick jungle growth slowed them down more than they had expected. It took eight minutes to get to the airstrip where the helicopters were waiting.

The men loaded up what equipment they had left into the birds and Jim gave the signal to take off.

To avoid radar detection, the pilots knew to stay lower than two hundred feet until they reached the Pacific Ocean. Their most direct azimuth would take them near the blast site. Jim advised the pilots to veer around it because there was about to be one hell of an underground detonation. That was an understatement.

The next minute an incredibly loud BOOM pushed the Black Hawk helicopters sideways setting off alarms that they were in danger of crashing. The skilled pilots made the needed corrections while everyone else on board looked down to see the aftermath of the explosion.

A huge mushroom cloud had formed over the target area, but that was not what had everyone's attention. The ground that surrounded the pyramid was in the process of collapsing in an odd geometric pattern. It reminded Jim of an ant farm as he watched the massive labyrinth of underground passages collapse. He could see an impressive network of structures disintegrate below the earth leaving huge sinkholes in their wake.

Jim guessed that the passageways must have connected all those underground structures. The pyramid had been at the center of this ancient complex that covered as much as 100 acres. Their detonations had acted as a lynchpin to annihilate it all.

He wondered if they had done the right thing. He had been told the three Americans were acceptable collateral damage. But what unknown secrets were buried forever down there that might have been preserved for posterity? He knew his memories of this mission would vex him for the rest of his life.

***

Matt sat mesmerized as he listened to Mark, Nuri and Jason describe their encounters with Amelius and Halaliel. He had vague memories of his own ethereal encounters that he'd always kept to himself. He also had a near-death experience when he suffered a heart attack that really changed his life. To find out that those events were real was difficult to fathom.

"It certainly does explain how I knew your names and where you worked back during the Egyptian crisis," Matt said to Nuri and Mark in dawning amazement. "How else could I have known who you two were? In fact, all three of you were exactly the right people to enter the Giza Hall of Records for the brief window it was available."

"Now we have new RFP information," Mark said with a grin. "We'll meet with the JPL team to review the symbol translations we gathered from Amelius. They should be able to discover new applications of RF technology that will provide the world with all the food and fresh water needed, at practically no cost."

"We must be very careful in how we present this," Matt cautioned. "President Westbrook thinks you died in Piedras Negras. Not only are you still very much alive, but now you have further proof that all your reports about the Hall of Records are truthful. You better let me manage how he finds out about this."

"But you know he's going to want to keep this new discovery as the sole property of the United States," Nuri said, showing his distrust. "What do we do if he decides to withhold any new developments in RF technology from the rest of the world?"

"You don't know him very well," said Matt smiling sadly. "Westbrook's primary concern is with controlling and exploiting RF technology. First, he'll celebrate the discovery as if he personally just saved the world, then he'll charge the other nations as much as he can for it."

"And do we let him get away with that?" Jason asked.

"I don't see any way around it," Matt said, obviously still looking for a better option. "He won't hesitate to nationalize any new discoveries, just as I did with RF energy."

Jason gawked, "Yes, but you were trying to usher in world peace. Westbrook doesn't care what happens to the rest of the world as long as the U.S. prospers."

Matt shook his head replying, "Hell, I even gave him the legal precedent to get away with it. We don't have much leverage here. He can still charge you guys with a felony for hacking their satellite anytime he feels you are not playing ball."

Jason was getting angrier by the second. "We gave him the cure for The Glut. You bailed him out of trouble at the U.N. He even tried to kill us along with the non-American soldiers down in Piedras Negras. He promised to pardon us if we did everything he asked, and we did. Would he really stoop so low as to charge us with crimes after all that?"

"The answer is simple," Matt sighed. "Yes, he would. Worse yet, he'd feel it was his patriotic duty to do it the moment you disagreed with his plans."

"I suggest that we work on the new technology at JPL without saying a word," Nuri said conspiratorially. "No one is asking if we're alive, right? So Matt is under no obligation to make that known to anyone outside of our group."

"Perhaps you're right," Matt said, rethinking his strategy. "I don't need to tell them anything, at least not until we're ready. Westbrook and the rest of Washington apparently want nothing to do with me. And so as long as I stay out of their way, no one should bother you."

***

Fatima and Lupe were now living in a high rise hotel overlooking Fort Lauderdale's beaches. They had added American passports to their forged identification documents. The good news was that leaving the country would not be necessary. The brewing conflict in Guatemala quickly subsided after Piedras Negras became ground zero. They monitored the news channels constantly to get the complete story.

The Guatemalan government decided not to prosecute any of the invaders as long as they turned around and went home. The guilty parties did so gladly after seeing satellite pictures of the area that had once been home to the pyramid. It looked more like a mining operation that had thoroughly ruined Mother Nature than it did a sacred site for ancient treasures. The devastation was complete and no one saw any reason to stay.

An interview with President Cabrera told of his disappointment over the destruction of the history and antiquities buried beneath Piedras Negras. Ironically, he seemed pleased that his country's political status had returned to being largely ignored. His own people's investigation of the area reported that the Macizo cartel had been trying to gain access to the pyramid. A tremendous firefight began as soon as the first invaders arrived on the scene. No one survived the battle to offer details beyond that. The forensic evidence found in the area told a great deal about the battle. However, there was no evidence of ancient artifacts that may or may not have been inside the pyramid, or the underground complex.

"So I suppose Thiago and the rest of the cartel are no longer a problem?" Lupe asked Fatima.

"I am quite certain Thiago and Macizo have been eliminated. However, if the Americans come up with an amazing new RFP discovery in the next few months, we'll know what really happened in Piedras Negras," Fatima said cynically.

"So what do we do now?" Lupe asked.

"Assuming we don't live extravagantly, we have plenty of money to live in America for as long as we like," Fatima said, thinking out loud. "I think I would like to open a school and teach English to other Hispanic immigrants."

Lupe laughed and said, "A week ago you were determined to ruin or at least embarrass the United States. Now you want to live here and help others to make it their home? What made you change your mind?"

Fatima thought before saying, "I admit that my grief over Rodrigo's death left me hurt and confused. It has taken a while for me to know what I really want out of life. I thought seeking revenge was the right thing to do. You know how well that worked," she said with a smile. "I've come to realize that making others happy is a far better way to live. Despite their arrogance, need for control, and desire to meddle in the affairs of others, there is a great deal to be admired in this country."

Lupe was relieved that their travels were over. From the beginning, she worried they would both end up in prison, or even killed. She was excited to share in her sister's plan for the future. This fresh new start would be quite a welcomed change.

***

President Westbrook was in the Situation Room in the White House meeting with the NSC. He hadn't been this pleased with himself in quite a while. His leadership had just prevented a world war. His superior planning ensured that the U.S. maintained total control of RF energy. He even successfully imposed a rate hike penalty on the countries that had foolishly sent troops to invade Guatemala. He couldn't imagine how things could have turned out better.

"Congratulations, Mr. President," said the Secretary of State. "Your handling of the situation at the U.N. and in Guatemala was inspiring. Everyone has gone home peacefully, and President Cabrera has confirmed to the world that we did not participate in the massive invasion against his country."

Max Atwater added, "You forgot to mention his leadership in resolving the pandemic just days before all that. You really are on a roll, sir!"

Don actually blushed at the praise, but he knew he deserved it. Who could have handled this better than him? Certainly not Matthew Alexander! If Matt had been in charge, Don couldn't imagine the mess the world would be in now.

"So Max," Don asked, "where do we stand with Egypt after Alexander made them think they had a working RFP sending crystal?"

"They have demanded that we surrender any pictures or videos those archeologists took in the chamber underneath the Sphinx."

"And what did you tell them?" Don asked with a smile.

The Secretary of State answered, "That the archeologists insist their still shots and video files disappeared shortly after they returned home. I was quite clear that we have been unable to confirm those files ever existed. I did offer to provide copies of the media files, if they ever did resurface. Oh, and one more thing; I denied their request to copy our RFP research files based on legal precedent that the research we've done is our proprietary work and property. They strongly disagree, but unbiased international legal minds have come to a consensus in our favor."

"Excellent!" gloated Don. "That puts an end to this mess, and we wound up with more money in the public coffers as a result. I guess the world leaders will know better the next time they decide to raise hell without checking with us."

As an afterthought, he asked, "Did we ever find out what happened to our three Americans in Piedras Negras?"

"No," Max said. "We are certain that no one in the vicinity of the pyramid could have survived our covert ops team's assault. They did a great job of destroying the pyramid and everything else in the vicinity."

"That we lost those fine men is a travesty," Don said shaking his head. "I suppose there had to be some collateral damage suffered along the way. Make a note that I want to quietly pardon them for any and all of their crimes against this country. They were a little overzealous early on in the game, but I want to make sure no one is able to disparage the names of these good men at some point in the future."

The Chief of Staff said, "Yes, Mr. President. Consider it done!"

Chapter 32

It had been an exciting few months for the scientists at JPL. Mark and Nuri had recently been able to translate more of the 4,999 ancient symbols discovered beneath the Sphinx. The two archeologists had requested that everyone focus on using RF technology to grow food and purify water. The results were amazing. Mark, Nuri, and Jason were invited to attend a special JPL staff meeting for an update on their progress.

Louis, the scientist in charge of RF technology at JPL, would be giving the progress report. He had worked with Mark and Nuri since the first day they arrived with the original RFP crystal and the incredible story of how they ended up with it. He was sure they would be pleased with the results of this latest project.

"Welcome gentlemen!" Louis beamed. "I wanted to brief you on our progress so far using your latest translations. As you requested, we have focused solely on developing RF technology to grow food and purify water. It's amazing that you were able to see how those new formulas could create viable sustenance from resonant frequency applications."

Jason just smiled from his seat in the back. He knew better than anyone else in the room the impact these discoveries would have on the world. After all, Halaliel had already shown him how this would unfold.

Louis continued, "We already knew that RF tech was based on Fibonacci and prime numbers. What we have recently learned is that there are unique locations on the earth that are ideal for particular RF applications. We found we can grow a new genus of food almost anywhere by employing a newly-designed RF crystal. The foodstuff is balanced for a human body's dietary needs. However, the type of soil used makes a significant difference in the food's quality and nutritional value. We still haven't been able to identify what particulates in the soil are responsible for these differences."

Nuri interrupted with a question. "Why not call it RFS for resonant frequency sustenance?"

Louis laughed and said, "Okay! If you give us the translations for all 4,999 symbols, we'll start to work on even more applications of this technology for you to name."

The blank expressions on their faces told Louis that wasn't going to happen. He continued with his briefing, a little less jovial, but enthusiastic nonetheless.

"Our experiments, so far, have led us to the following process to achieve the maximum output in producing this new food product. Using the aforementioned soil, the crop field must be at least one meter in depth. You can grow the food indoors or outside, that doesn't seem to matter. An RF crystal needs to be suspended over the crop field at a height that matches the exact proportions of the Great Pyramid of Giza's apex to the four corners of its base. In other words, a replica of the Great Pyramid would fit perfectly to scale underneath the RF crystal with its corners exactly matching the corners of the crop field."

Mark said, "We'll take your word for all that. So what is the cycle period for these crops to grow?"

Louis sighed, "We asked the same question when we first made this discovery, but the crop experts we asked to test this for us made working with them impossible. They asked for a sample of this new food product before they would commit to getting involved. For instance, we started by giving a sample to AgriFoods for them to test. We got a call back the same day from their CEO."

"Why?" asked Nuri.

"Because they had never seen anything like it," Louis said nervously. "I had to quit taking his persistent phone calls about buying the rights to it. Anyway, we never did get the answers we wanted because everyone who sees this stuff has the same reaction. We ended up conducting the growth experiments ourselves on a smaller scale that we could handle in-house."

From the back, Jason asked what he thought was an obvious question. "What does it taste like?"

Louis laughed and said, "It's easy to forget details like that when you're in the middle of changing history. We can vary the consistency of the food stuff from something as light as popcorn to the density similar to corn nuts. The taste can be tweaked as well from very sweet to sour, depending on your preference. It is a matter of varying the amplitude of the frequency used to excite the RF crystals to form the food stuff."

Mark asked, "Let me ask again. How much food are you able to grow over what period of time?"

"I guess I never really answered that question," Louis admitted. "The output is just as unbelievable as the cycle time required. If the area of the crop field is one acre, we have been able to produce enough to feed around 300 people per day. It produces that same amount every twenty-four hours. Only the quality of the soil seems to affect the output."

Nuri remarked, "That sounds an awful lot like the manna the Jews were said to gather every morning to feed themselves in the desert." The room full of scientists appeared to collectively stop breathing. Clearly, they were not comfortable with Nuri's reference to the Biblical story. He saw that they were not ready to deal with that subject, so he purposefully moved on."

"Is there anything else we should know?" Jason asked.

"Yes," Louis laughed. "I haven't mentioned purifying the water. Actually, the process is very similar to growing food. The difference is in the time required to purify the water, and I mean any water, including ocean water. The purification cycle takes seven minutes to complete. You fill a four-sided pyramid-shaped tank with any water. The RF crystal is placed at the apex according to what we're calling 'the Giza scale' above it. Then we excite the RF crystal for seven minutes and the water in the tank becomes as pure and potable as anything we've seen. The impurities don't just settle to the bottom; they are either completely dissolved or somehow removed, we don't yet know which."

Louis added, "We're learning new things every day, but that pretty well brings you up to date on what we know for now."

Jason stood and headed down the hall toward the offices. Mark and Nuri left the conference room to go back to the lab. They started comparing notes on what RFS, once perfected, would mean to the world. Both of them remembered their last encounter with Amelius when he told them what type of soil would work best with this latest innovation. Once the world figured that out, the race would be on.

***

Jason knew Louis would be busy with Mark and Nuri for a while. He walked down the hall to the man's office, closed the door and sat down at his computer. He pulled a high-capacity USB thumb drive out of his pocket and inserted it into an open port. He was familiar with the JPL digital security system and was soon copying the folders with the latest RF technology information onto his thumb drive. After a few minutes, he ejected the drive, deleted the transfer history from Louis' computer, and walked casually out of the building.

As he headed for his home, Jason considered his options. Years ago, he had carefully hidden the digital image and video files of what occurred inside the Hall of Records in Giza. Translations of the symbols discovered in that chamber, along with their subsequent experiments on the RFP sending crystal, allowed the JPL team to produce RF energy. Because the Egyptian scientists never saw the media files or symbol translations, they concluded that the crystal was no longer functional.

He stood in his living room with the area rug pulled back. He then opened his hidden floor safe and placed the thumb drive next to the older drive that was already inside the safe. He knew that the information stored on the first drive had already changed the world. He realized that the data on this new drive had even greater potential. He closed the safe's door, secured the handle, gave the combination dial a spin, and then neatly replaced the area rug.

He would wait to see what happened with President Westbrook before he did anything else, but he was fairly certain how this would play out. He smiled as he walked into his kitchen and pulled a beer from his fridge. He was glad to have the opportunity to set things right again.

***

Matt Alexander sat on one of the white couches in the Oval Office waiting for President Westbrook to arrive. He reminisced back to his own years as POTUS. Those had been good days, for the most part. He winced thinking how quickly his projects were abandoned

462

and policies were repealed once he was out of office. That was a hard but important lesson to learn. No one can change the minds of others regardless of the laws we pass. To achieve sustainable change, the people involved have to want those changes without being forced. The door opened and Matt had to refocus his thoughts.

Don enthusiastically entered the room with a grin and a hearty welcome. "Matt, it's great to see you!"

"It's good to be here, Mr. President," Matt responded as they shook hands. "I appreciate that you agreed to meet with me today."

"I'm happy to do it," Don exclaimed with his politician's smile. "First, I want you to know that I followed through on my promise. I have pardoned your boys for hacking our satellite so they are safe from prosecution. I included any and all of their acts related to RF technology, just in case someone tries to get cute later on. I regret the pardons were granted posthumously, but a promise is a promise."

This was exactly what Matt wanted to hear. They could stop worrying if crossing Don Westbrook might result in a lengthy prison sentence.

"Well, Mr. President," Matt began, "it so happens that I have good news about Mark, Nuri, and Jason. They showed up in Pasadena very much alive and well with some amazing discoveries from that pyramid in Piedras Negras."

The shock was evident on Don's face. He tried to recover his bearings and asked, "They're alive? How...how is that possible? And what amazing discoveries are you referring to?"

Matt was enjoying this, perhaps a little too much. "They have been working with JPL scientists to perfect a new RF technology that grows food and purifies water. The results have been promising. They estimate that within a year they'll have the bugs worked out. Once they do, no one in the world need ever go hungry or lack pure water to drink ever again."

Don was oddly silent as he considered all the ramifications behind Matt's revelation. He could immediately see possibilities here, but the potential downside to this news also scared him.

"Did you bring the research with you?" Don asked. "I'd like to have our people look it over before going public with this," he said carefully.

Matt reached into his pocket, and withdrew a portable hard drive. He handed it to Don and said, "Nothing new is ready yet, but here you go. This drive contains what we know so far. When Mark, Nuri and Louis are ready to go, JPL will provide all the RF receiving crystals you'll need for creating unlimited food and water. History will remember you as the President who eradicated hunger. I will say that I'd like to be a part of the team you recruit to figure out the best way to distribute this life-saving process to the world."

Don smiled nervously and lied as best he could. "Of course, Matt. It will take some time to organize, but I would love to have your thoughts on how we can make the best use of this." Don hesitated before asking the next question. He almost didn't want to hear the answer. "What else did they learn in Piedras Negras?"

Matt shook his head and did his best to keep a straight face. "Nothing more than I just mentioned. There wasn't time before the place was destroyed. As it was, my friends barely got out of there with their lives."

Don pretended to be disappointed. "That's too bad. I hope it goes without saying that the world doesn't need to know any further details about how Piedras Negras was destroyed. The United States is everyone's hero in global politics right now. It would be a shame to lose face over the unfortunate events in Guatemala."

"Handle this however you want, Mr. President," Matt said sincerely. "You're the guy the American people put in charge. I believe the citizens of this country have elected you to represent their interests and you'll do your best not to let them down."

Don didn't know how to take that last statement, but he decided not to press it.

"Thanks for coming by," Don said, as he pocketed the portable drive. He hurriedly left the room without saying another word. Matt had to show himself out of the Oval Office.

Chapter 33

A month had gone by before POTUS announced to the world the discovery of a new RF application for creating food and purifying water. While it wasn't yet ready for mass distribution, he promised resonant frequency sustenance (RFS) would soon wipe out hunger and thirst.

He went on to detail his overall leasing program that would be renewed every five years. RFS crystals would be provided by the United States to any country that agreed to adhere to specific terms and conditions. Those lease agreements would be amended every five years by the United States in order to keep up with the changing times.

The first three conditions to each lease agreement would be the same regardless of the countries involved. The first condition was that any RF products or services supplied through Matt Alexander's 10-year-old peace accord would become subordinate to the terms of this new lease agreement.

The second condition was that payments due to the U.S. from other countries would be made on time, or all RF services would be terminated until the outstanding balance was paid in full.

The third condition was that all prices charged for providing the RFS services needed to produce this food and potable water would be set by the United States. This included all prices set by other governments to their own citizens and commercial customers.

The remaining terms and conditions of each 5-year lease would vary from one sovereign nation to the next, depending on the products and services they traded with the United States.

The actual cost to produce this new food and pure water was pennies on the dollar compared to existing production costs and turnaround times. POTUS promised that the U.S. would set prices for RFS services so that the world's governments enjoyed the same financial prosperity with it as they had with RF energy.

President Westbrook closed with a reminder that the U.S. had the ability to enforce the conditions of the lease agreements.

They could individually deactivate, when necessary, any RF crystal leased from the United States.

***

President Westbrook was expecting Matt Alexander's call, but he was not looking forward to speaking with him. Despite his promise, Don had not included Matt in any of the strategy sessions for developing the new RF leasing program. He knew that his predecessor would flatly denounce the terms of the lease. Don was growing tired of Matt's discreet criticism regarding the way he ran the country. However, since Matt's people had actually discovered RF technology, Don admitted he couldn't avoid this phone call forever.

"Good morning, Matt," Don started out cheerfully.

"Good morning, Mr. President," Matt responded. "I just need about five minutes of your time and the answers to a couple of questions. Can we do that now, or should I call back?"

"Now is good, I guess," Don said. "Go ahead and ask."

"I have heard reports that you are planning to nationalize the use of all applications of RF technology," Matt stated with a neutral tone. "That would include any uses that have yet to be developed. I need to know if that is your true intention, or is it just a rumor?"

Don paused because he didn't want to outright lie to the man, but Matt had stated exactly what the U.S. intended to do. He was working with the Attorney General to nationalize anything having to do with RF technology now and in the future. He decided to soften the blow as much as he could without lying.

"We have explored the possibility, but no legal actions are imminent," Don said softly. "I wanted to keep the option available in case changes occur that make it necessary."

"Fair enough," Matt replied. "I also wanted to know if you intend to fund an expedition by Doctors Mark Heston and Nuri Zayd for the remaining Hall of Records they believe to be located near the Bimini Islands."

"We've already been down that road Matt," Don replied, sounding very tired. "The answer is still no."

466

Matt shook his head and asked, "Would you give me a chance to present new evidence to Congress that the Hall of Records does indeed exist and that it will reveal many new RF applications to the ones who find it?"

This intrigued the leader of the free world, almost enough to allow it. Then he had a moment of clarity. The only reason Matt would propose such a thing was only if he was sure it would serve his own agenda. Don decided to be honest and pass on his proposal.

"It won't make any difference," Don explained. "There is so much interest between Congress and NGOs in your Hall of Records that its discovery is inevitable if it exists at all. Your problem, given your secretive track record and reputation for not playing ball, is that no one trusts your people to share their discoveries with anyone else. I am aware of three teams who have already secured massive funding to conduct the search. The race, so to speak, has already begun."

***

Jason had heard enough about Matt's conversation with Don Westbrook. He walked out of the meeting with Matt, Mark, and Nuri in a huff. Only President Westbrook could have turned this beautiful opportunity into a means for greater control and profit. He had come to the critical moment Halaliel had shown him in the Bimini Hall of Records. He guessed that his friends would not agree with the complete data dump he was about to perform, but his mind was made up.

He went to an obscure internet café he'd located a month ago. He had the thumb drive with him. It contained the same records Matt gave to President Westbrook on RF technology. He also had a second drive containing the still shots and recorded video from the Giza Hall of Records, as well as what they found in Piedras Negras. No one else in the world had all these files in one place, but that was about to change.

Jason uploaded all the files he had to a public cloud site. He then copied an access link to the files using an anonymous email address. He sent the link to every international media outlet, wiki-leaks website, and resonant frequency blogger he'd been able to identify over the past month. The playing field for RF technology was

467

about to be leveled. If a person had internet access, they were now potential providers of RF technology.

Halaliel had shown him several scenarios that could unfold from here, but he knew for certain that President Westbrook's resonant frequency chokehold on the world was over. Now that everyone could produce RF power, the U.S. government would lose its main revenue source. President Westbrook would have no choice but to reinstate a federal income tax to make up the difference. Jason smiled as he clicked the 'send' button. Even if Westbrook wasn't impeached soon, Jason was sure his plans for re-election just went up in smoke.

***

Matthew Alexander sat in silence holding an RFP crystal his friends had used when they last met with their ethereal friends. He was interested to see if he could duplicate their experience and meet directly with Amelius himself. Matt wasn't sure this was how to accomplish that goal, but he held that thought as a mindful intention. He really wanted to meet Amelius and Halaliel in the Bimini Hall of Records.

After a long silent meditation, he was ready to give up. He opened his eyes and was overwhelmed by what he saw. Two men dressed all in white stood smiling before him. They waited patiently for Matt's mind to acclimate to his new environment. The surrounding room was exactly as Mark, Nuri, and Jason had described the Hall of Records from accounts of their own visits. He couldn't believe he was here.

"You're not really 'here,' you know," joked the man in white on the left. "At least, not as you define such things. Actually, you haven't physically left your living room."

Matt became aware that the man was reading his thoughts. He asked, "Which of you is Amelius?"

The man on the left said, "I am Amelius, but you are already remembering our previous encounters. You will soon recognize Halaliel, though your paths have not crossed as often."

"If you can read my mind," Matt said, "then you must already know why I wanted to meet you."

"We do," Halaliel said. "It will help you to recall what we say here if we agree to use what you will experience as audible words to express ourselves from this point forward."

"That won't be a problem for me," Matt said with a laugh. "Despite President Westbrook's attempts to monopolize RF technologies, someone posted every RF file we had on the internet. I suspect that must have been the same person who originally stole the digital media files from JPL's servers."

Amelius smiled as he interrupted, "We are, of course, aware of this. Did you have a question related to it?"

"Well, yes I did," Matt said, though he wasn't sure how to phrase it. "Isn't there just as much potential danger looming from everyone having access to RF technology than if only President Westbrook controlled it?"

Halaliel answered, "That depends on how you define danger. Giving everyone access has the potential for both greater and lesser outcomes. President Westbrook's desire to withhold RF technology from the world would eventually have ended in disaster. As things stand now, there are wonderful possibilities afoot!"

Matt thought of his next question. "Every time Mark and Nuri finally locate a new Hall of Records, something terrible happens to destroy it. Are they simply jinxed or is this your way of telling them to quit searching?"

Both of them laughed and Amelius replied, "The answer is neither. They should not stop searching for what they seek as long as their intentions remain altruistic. The Bimini Hall of Records will not be found through selfish intent. It will remain hidden until people desiring the highest and best use of the things found there come seeking. Only then can its secrets be revealed to the world in a way that benefits all of humankind."

"But how will they find this place?" Matt asked in frustration as he waved his hand around the room. "Isn't it supposed to be submerged under the ocean? Should they learn to scuba or deep sea dive to get here in the flesh?"

"RF technology has applications that will help you to succeed in your search where all the others will fail," offered Halaliel. "I suggest you focus on using RF technology for levitation and all manner of communication as the tools to help you the most. Mark and Nuri will know what to tell the JPL scientists to uncover these discoveries once the time is right."

Matt changed the subject. "I had questions about what happened in Piedras Negras, but now they don't seem so important."

"You should ask anyway. Your desire to know the answers will reappear once your consciousness returns to your body," both Amelius and Halaliel said together.

Matt was surprised that they had offered this advice. "Okay, why did you allow the drug cartel people to interfere when my friends first discovered the pyramid?"

Amelius laughed aloud, which annoyed Matt a little. "I didn't know 'we' were responsible for that. I can tell you why that karmicly occurred on a few levels. It may help you to understand why it can seem like bad things happen to good people.

"Had the drug cartel not interfered, your friends would have brought The Glut, as you call it, back to the lab at JPL. They would not have known the nature of the disease, meaning the pandemic would have started inside JPL instead of at Lake Mead. The disease would have inevitably spread from there. In that case, your people, the few who actually had the skill set capable of saving the world from The Glut, would have died first. The rest of humanity would have quickly followed with no one left to save them."

"Wow!" exclaimed Matt. "But you said on a few levels. Does that mean there were other reasons?"

"Yes," said Halaliel. "The man you knew as Rodrigo Cortez, leader of the Macizo cartel, once had a dream-state encounter with us to discuss the possibilities that lay before him. He agreed to interfere, as you phrased it, to put himself in harm's way so that his wife might choose a more fulfilling life. He also knew that giving up his life would save all of humanity, but his love for his wife was why he chose to make the ultimate sacrifice. We were all surprised and very pleased that Fatima measured up to the best that was within her to choose."

"So who was responsible for infecting the Colorado River with The Glut?" Matt asked.

"That was an interesting dynamic where Rodrigo's wife made great progress in her choices while Thiago Bernal took a turn down a dark path," Amelius answered. "Fatima had originally planned to avenge her husband's death because she thought your friends had intentionally infected him. She ultimately tried to stop Thiago from poisoning Lake Mead, but he believed going through with it was the only way he would ever become the cartel's leader. He would have willingly killed anyone who stood in his way to achieve that goal."

"Jason told me that Thiago and his soldiers wanted to kill my friends in Piedras Negras," Matt offered as background for his next question. "Who was responsible for the utter destruction of that sacred ground and all those people?"

"An interesting question, that last part," Halaliel said, looking at Amelius. "Your own President Westbrook gave the order to destroy Piedras Negras. He feared anyone but the United States possessing RF technology. He also believed there should be no witnesses left who might tell the world what he had done."

Amelius picked it up from there. "Regarding why so many died that day, there are as many reasons as there were people killed. Each person had a unique circumstance that led to their agreement to be at that place when it was so completely destroyed. Thiago, for instance, had set a selfish path that he could not easily correct. At a higher level of consciousness, he decided it would be better to stop making things worse. He chose to die in the battle of Piedras Negras because it was the most expedient way to stop making a mess of his life."

Matt said, "I remember ten years ago when I saw possible futures where my peace accord could have been sustained in perpetuity. What went wrong?"

Halaliel answered, "Seeing the possible futures, especially from your earth bound perspective, cannot help you understand how likely a particular outcome might be. Whenever free will choice is involved, the result is always uncertain to some degree. However, ten years ago, as you measure it, we could have predicted with 99 percent certainty that the earth would barely avoid annihilation over the recent conflict in Piedras Negras."

"Can you give me an example of a choice that falls under the remaining one percent?" Matt asked.

Both of them looked amused. "Yes, but you will not remember the answer upon awakening. Your friend Jason surprised us all by removing the RF digital files at JPL. That amazing choice changed a number of outcomes that are only now returning to the previously predicted condition," Halaliel explained.

Amelius added, "Before you ask, it was also Jason who released the new RF information to the world. It was his decision to do so after seeing the consequences of his previous choice. While this is hard to see now, especially for the citizens of the United States, the passage of time will prove that Jason made a laudable choice for all concerned."

"Why do we humans keep falling short of doing the right thing?" Matt asked.

"You don't give humanity enough credit," Amelius said in earnest. "And you don't yet have enough faith that the universe is truly friendly. This is the second time in ten years the world has come back from the brink of annihilation. President Westbrook actually believes that he alone manipulated recent events to the United States' advantage. He doesn't consciously know how close he came to destroying all of civilization."

Halaliel picked it up from there. "Many souls on the earth already desire a sustainable peace and prosperity for all. Then there are certain individuals who try to subvert that goal for their own personal gain, at least as they see it. Understanding how all these opposing free-willed vectors work together is fascinating. In this case, the world's prevailing good intentions, combined with the selfish choices of many individuals, created an amazing and wonderful outcome. This does not happen by chance. You saw this same pattern ten years ago in Egypt. There is no question that bad things can and do happen to good people. However, rest assured that all things eventually work toward good because the universe is indeed friendly."

"But what if we had blown ourselves up? What would have happened then?" Matt asked feeling quite confused and a bit righteous.

Amelius said, "The universe is friendly, but it is also omniscient. The manifest universe was created to be childproof, so to speak. No one can create such havoc that it can't be undone. We've got your back, as you like to say on earth these days. A good example is Thiago Bernal. It is true that the entity lost his forward momentum in the lifetime just passed. But he has the potential for great progress in his next life on earth."

Matt sighed, "I'm not sure I followed all that, but it did bring up another question. What lessons should I be learning from all this?"

"Embrace this eternal truth," Amelius paused, looking deeply into Matt's eyes. "There is no one in the universe that is more beloved than you. That statement is true for everyone alive!"

Matt drifted off to sleep contemplating the magnificent future that Amelius and Halaliel had shown him. His fears evaporated. He was convinced that the world would become sustainably peaceful once Jason, Mark, and Nuri discovered the hidden Hall of Records in Bimini.

The Hall of Records Trilogy

Part 3

Beside the Still Waters

Prologue

Ten years ago, President Matthew Alexander was the most powerful leader in the free world. Like many American politicians before him, his highest priorities were to be reelected and leave an enviable legacy in the history books. His first test of leadership came soon after he took office. There was an unprecedented terrorist attack against an American outpost in Israel. President Alexander vowed to stop the extremists through any means necessary.

However, a near-death experience changed his perspective. He revised his strategy by setting a peaceful example rather than trying to fight fire with fire. He called a halt to the organized military response so that he could personally visit the heads of state in the Middle East. His agenda was to propose a peace accord despite the escalating violence in the region.

When Matt's efforts began to succeed, his own top people turned against him and secretly worked with terrorists to force the world into a war. They had hoped the president would give them the green light to eradicate the terrorists despite the inevitable collateral damage it would cause to the USA's enemies and allies alike.

An amazing outcome surprised everyone when, instead of plunging the world into war, a massive terrorist bomb revealed what came to be known as resonant frequency (RF) technology. Practically overnight, humanity's energy needs could be produced in unlimited amounts at almost no cost. The catch was that the USA controlled access to RF energy, and announced that only peaceful nations could buy it wholesale. While that offer was too good to pass up, it also made the other countries distrustful of the United States. No one wanted the U.S. to have complete control over access to the world's energy supply.

Ten years later, the world was still in conflict, but tacitly condoned terrorist violence had replaced outright declarations of war. Matt Alexander served two terms and made way for President Don Westbrook to succeed him. There were three men instrumental in averting the global war who became reclusive and very reluctant heroes. Two of them were archeologists and friends named Mark

475

Heston and Nuri Zayd. The third was Jason Fisher, a retired Delta Force soldier. He was the archeologists' protector in Egypt and played a pivotal role in helping them bring RF technology to the world. Jason accepted the invitation to join Mark and Nuri's quest to find the fabled Hall of Records hidden somewhere in the Yucatan.

An unfortunate meeting in the jungles of northern Guatemala put the three American friends at odds with a drug cartel's soldiers. Just minutes after entering an ancient pyramid and finding a mysterious wooden box, they barely escape with their lives, but left the contents of the box behind.

They had unknowingly discovered a dangerous pathogen that could literally destroy humanity. The first victim of the deadly disease was the cartel's leader. His distraught wife wasn't sure who was to blame, but convinced herself that the entire USA was responsible. To exact her revenge, she threatened the U.S. with unleashing the pathogen if they did not make the secrets of RF technology available to everyone.

President Westbrook refused to give in to the unknown terrorist's demands and a major water supply in the U.S. was infected. The only known cure to exist had been carelessly destroyed, leaving humanity's survival at stake. Mark, Nuri and Jason returned to Guatemala to locate the fabled Hall of Records and learn how to stop the spread of the disease. They succeeded, but the rest of the world found out where, they too, could obtain the ancient technology developed by the Atlanteans.

War ships from dozens of nations converged on Guatemala. It appeared that humanity would annihilate itself instead of a disease doing it for them. Mark, Nuri and Jason managed to narrowly escape the destruction of the Guatemalan Hall of Records taking with them another RF discovery. It was called RFS for resonant frequency sustenance. This application of RF technology could supply unlimited food and fresh water on a daily basis.

The unusual source Mark and Nuri used to locate the Hall of Records in Egypt and in Guatemala came from the psychic readings of Edgar Cayce. Cayce's readings indicated the presence of a third and final Hall of Records near the Bimini Islands on the west side of the Bahamas. Once the world was aware that the remaining Hall of

Records was still up for grabs, every nation began a frantic search for the hidden chamber.

Mark, Nuri and Jason were fortunate to have help from two powerful ethereal guides who were not in physical form. Amelius and Halaliel had been their advocates from the beginning. They advised the three friends to bide their time in searching for the Bimini Hall of Records. They were assured that no one would find the fabled chamber until the world was ready. In the meantime, they were encouraged to pursue their research for new RF technology applications.

The archeologists, with the help of a Jet Propulsion Laboratory scientist, Dr. Louis Jensen, began work on a communications device. It would allow them to talk to each other anywhere in the world. Amelius and Halaliel told them it would be needed when it was time to go in search of the Bimini Hall of Records.

Chapter 1

"Can you hear me?" Doctor Louis Jensen had been asking that same question for most of the night. The answer was a mocking silence that filled the large room. He pulled out a mechanical pencil to record yet another idea that didn't work. His frustration showed when he pressed so hard that he broke the lead. He growled as he threw it down on the table. Louis was glad none of the other scientists were around. He was embarrassed by his reaction.

Some of his happiest memories were of his time here at Jet Propulsion Laboratory, but this was not going to be one of them. He had discovered resonant frequency (RF) power in this same lab. That first RF invention had changed the world. He never dreamed it would be this hard to develop a wireless communications device using the same versatile technology. He feared he was ready to cross the line between counting the things that didn't work and admitting failure.

Louis shook his head to snap out of his depressing reverie. He gathered himself for a few more seconds before hitting the speed dial number on his cell phone to confirm what he already knew. Despite the early hour, it only rang once before someone answered.

Mark Heston tried to hide the fact that he and Nuri Zayd had dozed off waiting for Louis to contact them at their own nearby lab. "Are you ready to try again?" he asked with feigned enthusiasm.

Louis hung his head and said, "I just did. Obviously you didn't hear me and I'm running out of ideas."

Nuri could see the disappointment on Mark's face. He asked his friend to put the phone on speaker. "Why don't we try to connect using other frequencies? We could start as high as our TV tuner can go and work our way down."

"Sure, why not," Louis said with a defeated exhale. "What's the highest setting you have at your end?"

Mark was already thumbing through the dog-eared manual to answer his question. They had converted an old television tuner to receive the test messages Louis transmitted from JPL. "It looks like we start with the 40th Fibonacci number. That's about as high as this old VHF receiver can go."

Louis queried his laptop for the exact frequency. "Remember back to when we had access to all of JPL's resources? Now we're forced to use this junk." He made sure to sigh loud enough for both Mark and Nuri to hear over the phone's tiny speaker. "I understand you don't want RF discoveries to get out before you're ready, but owning this technology means no government money for research. We could really use their help about now."

"No thanks!" and "Not interested!" the two archeologists said in unison.

"It's been our experience that working with the government is hazardous to your health," Mark added. "Let's set the tuners to 102,334,155 hertz. Remember to keep the power low so the local broadcast TV channels don't file another FCC complaint against us."

Louis switched his timeworn folding phone to speaker mode and set it on the work bench. "Okay, but I'm going to keep the phone line open this time. I'll use a text-to-speech app on my laptop to send continuous audio of the Fibonacci number sequence through the RFC crystal. Let me know when you're ready?"

"We're good to go," Nuri said from across the room. "Let her rip."

A minute later, a series of staccato electronic sounds chirped through Louis' RF speaker. The jarring noise made Louis spill coffee on his shoes. Since he had the only RF transmitting device, he couldn't imagine what he or his friends had done to make a sound like that. "What the heck was that?" Louis yelled.

"We didn't do it!" said Mark. "We only heard the sound through the phone, not through our TV receiver. I think the problem is at your end."

The rapid rising and falling of punctuated tones started again, stopped a moment, and then a monotone, tinny voice came on the line. "English? You speak English? There's only one planet in this universe that speaks English, and they haven't achieved real space travel let alone intergalactic communications. Who is this, and why are you broadcasting on the emergency frequency?"

Louis gathered his wits and started recording the exchange. He said, "My name is Louis Jensen. Who exactly are you?"

"I'm a dispatcher for the intergalactic emergency response system. Are you really calling for help from the planet Earth?"

Louis answered, "Yes, well not really for help. I hadn't meant to bother you. What's your location again?" He couldn't believe this was happening. Was he really talking to an alien from another galaxy? He hoped that it wasn't an elaborate hoax.

The voice responded, "You don't need to know that. How did you get on this frequency? I hadn't expected to add Earth to the list for at least 1,000 of your years."

Since no one else had RFC technology, Louis was convinced that this voice was coming from another world. He had so many questions he didn't know where to start. "Is it possible for you to come here so we can meet in person?" He knew that most scientists would not accept this recorded conversation alone as proof of intelligent life on other planets.

There was a notable pause before the voice said, "I just checked. No one here has any interest in visiting your planet. The truth is that we shouldn't be talking at all. Please stay off this frequency."

The speaker clicked twice and then went silent. Mark and Nuri waited helplessly as Louis tried to get the alien talking again. His queries brought only static in return. He was about to increase the transmission power when the box on his test bench started spewing black smoke and smelled of burning garbage. By the time Louis managed to remove the cover, he could see that the internal RF components were fused together. It was as if someone had taken a torch to them. The message was clear. His first conversation with an extraterrestrial would also be his last.

Mark and Nuri were dying to learn what had just happened, but they knew Louis was a better communicator in person. The three of them agreed to meet for breakfast at their usual place.

Louis couldn't stop smiling as he closed his phone and shut down the lab equipment. "I'm the first person to talk with aliens! Neil Armstrong's got nothing on me. And here I thought my device was a failure."

***

Halaliel felt a shift in the vibrational balance and direction of humanity. It is difficult to surprise an angel, especially one of Halaliel's standing, but this anomaly came way out of the proverbial left field.

Amelius' thoughts were with him a moment later. "Halaliel, what has happened? What earthly free will choice just changed the course of humanity?"

"That's why I didn't see this coming," Halaliel explained. "The choice was not made on Earth. It started in the Andromeda galaxy on the planetary dimension of Klacktu."

"I see," Amelius mused aloud. "Well, there never was a quicker way to distract humans than to offer proof of intelligent life on other planets. Do you know why Klacktu made first contact with the people of Earth? They know humanity is not ready."

Amelius was asking to be polite. He could already see the answer clairvoyantly, but Halaliel had not quite caught up to him.

"It was not Klacktu. It was our friends, the archeologists," Halaliel explained. "They have been experimenting with resonant frequency technology to improve communications. It seems they've succeeded beyond their wildest expectations, and ours!"

"Well isn't this an interesting opportunity!" Amelius said with a smile.

***

Ariel and Halaliel had agreed to hear the appeal of a soul who requested to return to human form as soon as possible. They both agreed he was not ready, but it was Nasrum's right to be heard. The two angels opened the discussion by inviting Nasrum to present his case.

"I was surprised to learn that you feel I am such a threat to your grand plans for the earth," he began. "I know that my methods don't mesh well with your ways, but isn't the goal of cooperation to achieve Allah's will through our many ideas?"

Ariel replied, "You are familiar with the earth saying, 'Be wise as serpents, yet harmless as doves?' Humanity is currently at a critical point in its spiritual growth. Your incarnation just ten years ago, as humans count time, almost started a world war. We surely don't want to risk that again, don't you agree?"

"I do not!" Nasrum said defiantly. "I am interested in peace, not war. I simply believe that the Islamic faith is a better path to follow in achieving that goal. You apparently believe that, if allowed to make their own decisions, humanity will eventually choose peace. Your ways haven't worked either. I believe we can succeed a great deal sooner by giving Islam the opportunity to be the world's guiding light."

"If that is true," Halaliel began, "then why are you blocking some of your thoughts? You must have more planned than you say or you would have no need for privacy."

"I am blocking nothing!" Nasrum spat back. "I was conducting a test to see if you trust me. I did not try to read your inner-most thoughts because I believed that you would not lie or try to deceive me. Clearly, you are the ones who are not trustworthy. This hearing is a sham."

And with that, Nasrum's consciousness departed. If there had been an ethereal door in his path on his way out, he would have slammed it shut with disgust.

"That could have gone better," Ariel said.

Halaliel answered thoughtfully, "And this is not resolved. There are a number of ways he can still greatly influence events on Earth. Remember the numerous times he has caused significant chaos even when not in human form. He could even manage to take possession of a body, though that is unlikely. Nasrum is an unusual soul in that he has convinced himself that he is right. He is far too self-centered to understand just how disruptive he can be."

"Nasrum can do no harm as long as the people of earth ignore him," Ariel considered aloud. "Since humanity often ignores what we have to offer, what chance is there that humans would honor his selfish guidance?"

"He appeals to their earthly nature," Halaliel explained. "While satisfying carnal desires works against their ultimate goal, most souls find those urges very compelling when they are in human form. We can be sure that Nasrum will use that knowledge to get his own way at humanity's expense."

"And what is it that Nasrum wants?" Ariel asked.

Halaliel answered, "He wants to be the earth's Messiah." The angel smiled at his own joke as he added, "In the worst way."

Chapter 2

Louis, Mark and Nuri were sitting in their favorite booth in a quiet corner of Philz Diner. They already had their coffee, but their usual orders of bacon, eggs and toast were still being plated. They met there often to kick around ideas for experiments to try with RF technology. On this morning, however, the conversation was all about extraterrestrials.

"Can you believe I just talked to someone from another planet?" Louis gushed. "I can't wait to tell everyone about this. I even recorded most of it for anyone who doesn't believe me."

The coffee Nuri was drinking almost came out of his nose. When he recovered he said, "You can't tell anyone about this! It's bad enough with the government always trying to pry into what we're doing and steal our work. It would be a lot worse if every whacko out there thought we had an alien hot line."

Louis was not surprised that Nuri wanted to keep it a secret. Hoping for a different reaction, he asked, "Mark, what do you think?"

Mark's thoughts were light-years away. He was mesmerized by the golden sunbeams outlining the fluffy clouds to the east. He shook his head as he caught up with the conversation. "I'm sure that telling the world intelligent aliens exist would really stir things up. If we say nothing about this, life will go on just as it did before. I could argue for either direction, but that is not what I was thinking about."

Nuri and Louis just looked at him and waited for him to finish his thought.

"Did anyone else think it was odd that the alien had zero interest in us or this planet? Also, what do you suppose humanity will do 1,000 years from now that will catch their interest?"

"Maybe that's when we discover warp drive?" Louis offered. "Isn't that when the Trekkers say the aliens will contact us?"

Nuri said, "I've got another question. Why did none of us see this coming? Jason, Mark and I were shown images of the events that will lead to discovering the third Hall of Records. Why wouldn't we have been warned about talking with aliens? I would think telling the world that intelligent life exists on other planets would help people to be more open minded."

Louis always felt uncomfortable when his friends started talking about the supposed ethereal encounters they had during their meditations. Believing in things that couldn't be proven in a lab was illogical to him. He reached for a packet of sugar, tore it open, and slowly poured it into his coffee. He decided to change the subject, "Where is Jason these days?"

"He's down in Florida looking to charter a boat to the Bimini Islands. That's where we think the Hall of Records is located," Mark answered.

"Because we keep our mouths shut!" Nuri blurted. The confused looks on his friends' faces told him they needed a little more context. "The reason we never foresaw talking with aliens is because we never tell anyone about it. That way it doesn't change a thing!"

"That makes sense," Mark nodded in agreement. "As incredible as it all was, let's agree that we don't tell anyone else what happened."

Louis continued to stir the already dissolved sugar into his coffee. He kept a neutral expression while thinking, "I can't believe we're going to just sit on this." He could see that Mark and Nuri were waiting for him to voice his opinion. He strongly disagreed with them but he couldn't argue against their logic.

Finally he said, "I think the world deserves to know that intelligent life exists on other planets, but it doesn't matter. I've been outvoted."

Mark and Nuri both exhaled in relief and picked up their coffee. Louis hesitantly set down the spoon and joined them. They raised their mugs together and toasted their promise to remain silent.

Nasrum was bored and growing weary of examining potential humans. Their lives were so limited and their interests were so narrow. Regardless, he needed to find one who was qualified and would follow his instructions. He was determined to get back in the game after being rejected by those two angels.

He knew he couldn't work with any of the existing Middle Eastern leaders. They were so self-absorbed that he couldn't reach them no matter how hard he tried. While he could manipulate anyone who would listen to him to a position of great power, the culture of the Middle East required their leaders to follow Islam, be male and to have royal blood. Nasrum could not find anyone suitable for his needs.

He expanded his search beyond the Middle East. There were many souls living in other countries who revered Allah. He considered several contenders in Africa, Europe and Asia who were devout Muslims and of royal blood, but none had aspirations to take on the reins of the world.

That left one more option. He had been avoiding it, but Nasrum decided to scan the United States for a good candidate. What he found was just more of the same; self-absorbed men who were unwilling to do what it took to attain true greatness.

He was about to set his search aside when he felt someone calling to him. The voice in Nasrum's mind was unfamiliar, but it was someone seeking his attention just the same. He followed the beckoning thread of consciousness until he located his unlikely candidate.

Nafid Alsab Anahni was a minor Syrian prince who had just completed his undergraduate education in the United States. Nafid was certain he was destined for greatness, but his life so far had been a disappointment. Now he was to return home to Damascus and the anonymous life he seemed fated to live.

In a desperate attempt for help, Nafid had prayed to Allah. When he received no answer, he looked for other ways to get help from beyond. He searched the internet and found helpful articles about channeling and Ouija boards. He didn't own a Ouija board and channeling seemed to be reserved for a gifted few. Then he landed on a site about automatic writing. Now that had possibilities!

Instead of praying to Allah for guidance, Nafid opened his mind to whatever or whoever could help him. He sat in the silence and sent out an appeal to anyone who would listen. He held a pen loosely in his hand and rested it on a legal pad. Then he waited as he continued to probe the ethers.

486

Nasrum had found his human puppet, a young man of royal Muslim blood who felt he deserved to be a great leader. And here he was inviting Nasrum to guide him. He silently thanked Allah for providing the right person.

He followed the path of Nafid's plea directly into his consciousness. Once there, he familiarized himself with the mechanics of controlling a body through a corporeal brain. It had been ten years, as time is counted on the earth, since Nasrum had been in human form. It took some effort to find his way, but suddenly Nafid's hand twitched and his eyes flew open.

The prince watched in amazement as the pen began scrawling shaky letters across the page. It was as if his right hand belonged to someone else. It had a mind of its own and it had something to say. Nafid was at once frightened and excited.

At first, the handwriting was illegible and the letters were large and uncontrolled. As the minutes ticked by, the words became readable. The Arabic prose was surprisingly eloquent.

These were the first words Nafid was able to read, "Now that you have finished your worldly education, you are ready for greatness!"

With his heart pounding in his ears, Nafid said aloud, "Who is this I am communicating with?"

He turned to a fresh page on the pad and was soon writing, "You called and I am here. If you must have a name, call me Rayiys (AKA master in Arabic). I am here to help you fulfill your destiny. You still have much to learn, but we have time, and patience is a great virtue!"

"How do I know I can trust you?" Nafid said quietly. He had read some disturbing stories during his internet search. "Give me a sign that shows your guidance will be in my best interests!"

Nasrum considered all the options. He knew what he had to do to fulfill his own ambitions. He had already made a mental list of tasks for this human to accomplish. The man would need a good amount of wealth to get started. He would also need to get the media's attention. Nasrum smiled seeing how he could kill two birds with one stone. He took a moment to peer into the future, as humanity defines such, to ensure his plan was not interfering with the karma of others. No one was karmicly slated to win the next several lotteries, so he accessed the information he needed.

"Of course, as you wish. Here are the winning Powerball numbers for tomorrow night's drawing: 10, 42, 54, 60, and 66 with 2 as the additional number. Go out now and buy a ticket with those numbers. We will speak again once you are certain of my good intentions."

Nafid stared blankly at his legal pad. Could it really be that easy? He looked up the amount of the jackpot for the next multi-state Powerball drawing. It was over $500,000,000! He convinced himself that it would be worth buying a ticket to see if his unseen mentor was truly the answer to his prayers.

***

Jason knocked on the door to the house and took a step back. He checked the address again while he waited for someone to answer. The address on the scrap of paper he held matched the one on the mailbox. Finally a crusty old guy appeared in the doorway. It took a second glance for Jason to realize that the man was no more than sixty years old. He smiled thinking this sailor must have packed a lot into those years. Jason looked past him to see a cramped living room filled with bookcases, a worn recliner and an old tube type television showing a football game.

"I'm not buying anything!" the man said impatiently. "Can I get back to my game now?"

"Actually, I'm buying, not selling," Jason began. "I'm trying to charter a boat to explore the west side of the Bimini Islands. Aren't you Gus Martin and isn't that what you do?"

"You'd be right on both counts, but I don't advertise," Gus said suspiciously. "How'd you find me?"

Jason wasn't sure how he should answer that question. He had foreseen coming here in a vision given to him by Halaliel the previous year. He still remembered the older guy's name and address from the possible futures he'd been shown, but he wasn't about to tell that story.

"A friend of a friend told me about you and where you live," was Jason's almost truthful answer.

Gus stared at him a moment and Jason's friendly smile worked to put him at ease. He couldn't help thinking that this old sailor was destined to look like Popeye's grand pappy. Gus paused a bit longer and then said, "Come on in, I guess, and tell me what you've got in mind."

***

Nuri was in the deserted courtyard area of JPL meditating in the early morning sun. He hoped to learn where they'd gone wrong with the RFC experiment. They needed a practical communications device that worked anywhere on the earth. Talking with an extraterrestrial, who politely told them to get lost, had been more of a distraction than making real progress.

Nuri focused his attention inwardly until the scene from the Piedras Negras Hall of Records played again in his mind. He confirmed that they had followed the steps correctly, except for some minor points. Proper RF communication required two frequencies much like earthly telephones that can send and receive simultaneously. Another problem was that they could not mix RF and earth's existing communications technologies. RFC could modulate an infinite number of discreet conversations using just one frequency. That was not compatible with earth's limited methods of signal modulation. In other words, the idea that a receiving TV tuner could pick up an RFC transmission, when both devices were set to the same frequency, was innovative but mistaken.

The last point was the most important. They needed to adjust the second crystal to the Fibonacci frequency just above the first. The lower frequency should be used to send and the higher one to receive.

In his mind Nuri asked, "So why were we able to communicate with the alien using just one RF crystal?"

The answer came back in vivid detail. Mental images showed him that Louis' RF crystal was set to the standard emergency channel monitored on the planet Klacktu. As luck would have it, transmitting a sequence of Fibonacci numbers was the galactic equivalent of an SOS on earth. The dispatcher had tried to respond to offer help and thought the troubled party's receiving crystal must be damaged. So he kept manually adjusting the send/receive crystals at his end to overcome the deficiency in Louis' design.

Klacktu was made aware they erred in talking with Louis and confirmed they would be more careful in the future.

Nuri emerged from the meditation and smiled. He had the information they needed and the RFC design flaws seemed easy to fix. He couldn't wait to tell Louis he had been talking with an alien from the planet Klacktu. How would the skeptical scientist explain the source of Nuri's answers this time? Louis was sure that meditation and the guidance they received while silently listening for answers was 'a bunch of bunk.'

Chapter 3

Nafid stood grinning before the members of the media holding a huge check for $503,600,000. He was the sole winner of one of the largest lottery jackpots of all time. He was fielding questions as his Rayiys had instructed him. He talked about his altruistic intentions for the money once he returned home to Damascus. He said that he wanted to help his people make a positive difference in the world.

Then someone asked the inevitable, "How did you choose the winning numbers?"

Nafid smiled and said, "I saw them in a vision. Predicting the future is one of my gifts."

The members of the media jumped on his statement with a myriad of questions. "What else does the future hold?" "Give us another prediction!" "How do you know what will happen?"

When the crowd quieted down he answered somberly, "Not all the things I foresee are happy events. For instance, I can tell you that in about an hour a jet airliner flying from the Philippines to South Korea will experience engine trouble and be lost at sea."

Most of the reporters made a note that the Syrian prince was a crackpot, albeit a very wealthy one. But there were also tabloid-type reporters in attendance who thrived on this kind of news. Nafid cut them off. "Please, no more right now. I mourn for those who are about to perish. I will hold a press conference after this tragedy is independently confirmed. Please allow me my privacy until then." They shouted more questions at him, but an impressive number of private security guards cleared a path for Nafid to disappear into his waiting car.

***

Fifty three minutes after Nafid had made his startling prediction, Quinjet Air flight 741 was lost at sea somewhere between its departure from Manilla in the Philippines and its destination of Seoul, South Korea. After two days without contact, all aboard were considered lost, though the search effort to find the wreckage continued in earnest.

Once news of the lost jet was announced, a media manhunt was on to find Prince Nafid. No one in history had accurately predicted a major tragedy in such detail and with so much press coverage. In the days that followed, Interpol, the CIA and the FBI investigated whether or not the prince was somehow complicit in the crash. Other than his prediction, they found no evidence linking him to the missing plane.

Nafid emailed a press release to the media outlets. He announced that they should gather at 9:00AM the following day on the steps of Boston's City Hall. When the appointed time came, a helicopter delivered the prince to the roof of the building. This was prearranged with the local authorities so he could avoid direct contact with the impressive crowd.

He was dressed in the traditional clothing of his home country, Syria. He paused as he stood before the microphone to address the huge gathering. Nafid thought to himself, "So this is what it feels like to have people hanging on your every word!" He knew in his heart that he was destined for this. He took out a prepared statement his Rayiys had written out that morning. The moment Nafid had long prayed for was finally here. After this announcement, whenever he would speak, the world would listen.

"You are already aware of the great tragedy that occurred yesterday with flight 741 over the Pacific Ocean. I pray that Allah receives those lost souls and blesses the family members who survived them."

You could have heard a pin drop as the prince looked out over the sea of people. He basked in their attention and hesitated deliberately, taking in the moment before he continued. If the members of the media had thought it was impressive to pick the winning lottery numbers or predict a random tragedy, his next revelation was about to change the world.

"You have now witnessed that I can foresee the future, both good and bad. But another of my gifts is to unlock secrets that would otherwise remain unknown. A great event took place a few days ago, but neither the media nor the public is aware of it. Why? Because Dr. Louis Jensen of Jet Propulsion Laboratory decided not to share his amazing encounter. The JPL scientist had a conversation with an alien from the planet Klacktu! He even managed to record most of their verbal exchange. This was made possible because of Dr. Jensen's experiments with groundbreaking resonant frequency communications technology." He paused again for effect. "I have more to share about life on other planets, but that's enough for now. I will announce another press conference soon."

***

"Hello, Louis Jensen speaking," he said picking up his desk phone at JPL.

"Dr. Jensen? This is Julia Peters with *The Herald*. I'm calling to confirm the conversation you had a few days ago with an extraterrestrial from the planet Klacktu. Can you tell me more about it?"

"How in the world did you know about that?" he said, immediately regretting the words. He hung up and called the JPL receptionist. He was about to ask her to block his calls only to find out there were five more waiting.

He told her to take messages and not to put anyone through who didn't work for JPL. His next call was to Mark Heston. He hung up when he got voicemail and called Nuri Zayd. Nuri answered but didn't bother to say hello. "Louis! I thought we agreed to keep the whole planet Klacktu thing to ourselves!"

"I have no idea what's going on," Louis cried. "I haven't told a soul about that. I just got off the phone with some newspaper woman and I'm afraid I didn't handle it very well. I asked her how she could possibly know about it."

Nuri must have put his phone on speaker because Mark said, "Ouch! It sounds like the genie is out of the bottle, but that doesn't change what we agreed. Under no circumstances do we comment on what happened."

Nuri interrupted Mark asking, "How would anyone find out about our RF communications experiments if you didn't tell them? That guy that's been in the news, Prince Nafid, told everyone your name and gave details about the Klacktu conversation on network television. I am so disappointed, especially after we all promised to keep it a secret."

493

"Prince who?" Louis exclaimed. "I have no idea who that is. And why did he give my name without mentioning you two?"

"We were wondering the same thing!" Mark said sarcastically. "As it is, I suggest that you stay inside the JPL complex to avoid the media. You know they're going to hound you if you go out in public."

***

Nasrum continued pushing Prince Nafid's rise to power. His human puppet already had money and growing credibility as a seer. He was pleased to see Nafid had already gone viral on social media. The prince soon had daily sacks of fan mail and hundreds of email requests for private readings from famous people. Nasrum ordered the prince to hire an internet tech firm to enhance his public image. Their job would be to make sure the prince was the top query on all the search engines and guide them to his official website.

Nasrum scoffed at how easily humans were impressed. It was a double-edged sword that his protégé loved to be adored. Nafid wanted to hold daily press conferences but Nasrum wouldn't allow it. He didn't mind the prince using his newfound status to woo women into his bed, but he made a standing rule that they be limited to one night stands. More importantly, he was not allowed to share any information with these girls that had not already been announced to the public. All this was done to ensure that no one got close enough to the prince to learn his secrets.

As if Prince Nafid was not enough of a challenge, Nasrum could not locate something that was vital to his plan. He could not detect the precise site of the Hall of Records in Bimini. It was common knowledge that the psychic, Edgar Cayce, had given its general location as being on the west side of the Bimini Islands. It was no wonder those two archeologists had chosen Guatemala to explore instead of Bimini after the Sphinx was destroyed. Nasrum still cursed his incompetent team for blowing up Egypt's most recognized landmark when he was in human form 10 years before. Worse yet, the Piedras Negras Hall of Records was destroyed before he could reincarnate back into the earth and take control the technology stored there.

He lamented that he could not find the Bimini Hall of Records. He did not understand why Allah would withhold such a vital piece of information from him. The amazing artifacts and records that lay hidden there would have made things much easier. Under Nasrum's guidance, Nafid could have used the Atlantean chamber's secrets to become the benevolent dictator of the world.

The archeologists who had discovered the first two locations became his Plan B to find the Bimini chamber. Nasrum was hesitant to admit that these humans were psychically closed to him. The suffering he felt was almost unbearable whenever he tried to eavesdrop in on their plans. He could tell that these men were close to finding the remaining chamber, but it seemed to be Allah's will that he could not read their thoughts. Nasrum concluded that this setback was a test requiring him to prove that he was worthy of being the world's Messiah.

He did have slightly better success in reading Louis Jensen's thoughts, but not by much. That was why he had Nafid announce the RFC contact between Louis and the alien on Klacktu. Few others would make the connection, but the uproar about extraterrestrials would work to make Nafid the richest man in the world. And with that vast wealth would come even greater power.

Only Allah was omniscient, but Nasrum was certain he was smarter than anyone else in the things that were important. For instance, foreseeing tragedies upon the earth was simple. Seeing creative ways to fulfill carnal desires, or to enrich one's self, or to make life hell for one's enemies, was second nature for him. He didn't consider it a weakness, but he found it difficult to care about events that did not clearly define a winner and a loser when a conflict was over. And when all of humanity prospered because of a new development, Nasrum paid no mind to such things. After all, if everyone profits equally, the score remains a tie. He was convinced that there had to be losers so that Allah's more worthy followers enjoyed winning all the more.

His next step was to move the prince back home to Syria. Then he would guide Nafid on how to invest his money until he became the wealthiest man in modern history. Nasrum regretted the years this would add to his plan, but he could be patient when he had to be. After all, it was clear to him that Allah was on his side.

Chapter 4

The media was desperate to reach Dr. Louis Jensen. There was a great deal of information about him online, but the man himself was nowhere to be found. The smart money was on Louis hiding inside the JPL complex. They maintained tight security for the staff and any visitors had to be with an authorized escort while on the premises.

Some overzealous reporters broke into Louis' house in search of evidence that could prove the existence of extraterrestrial life. They ended up trashing his home before the police arrived and arrested them for burglary.

Other's found out that Louis was divorced and had a 10-year old son, Louis Jr., whom everyone called Eljay. Louis' ex-wife, Beth, had worked at JPL for years, but she switched careers to medical research after the divorce. She resented being caught up in the "tell us more about your ex-husband speaking to aliens" nonsense. Worse yet, a contingent of paparazzi continued to follow her everywhere because she was the only available photo opportunity who was connected to him.

Beth had just picked Eljay up from school. She was heading home as she asked her son how his day had gone.

"It was okay, I guess," Eljay said with an unconvincing tone. "Those people with the cameras kept yelling questions and taking my picture at recess."

Beth was shocked to hear it. She couldn't believe they would stalk a child for pictures. That bordered on being illegal and it was way beyond acceptable behavior, even for the press.

"What were they saying, honey?" she asked.

"They kept yelling questions about dad," Eljay answered, a little distracted.

"Why were they yelling at you?" she asked, trying to remain calm.

"Because they were standing on the sidewalk outside of the school's fence," he explained.

Beth exhaled in relief upon hearing that they were at least obeying the law.

All of a sudden, Eljay pointed past Beth and said, "Mom! There's one now!"

She looked left and saw a man with a camera taking pictures of them from a van driving along side of her SUV. She panicked not knowing what to do. If she jammed on the brakes, the car behind them would rear-end her. She was blocked from turning right by another paparazzi vehicle in that lane. She decided to gun the engine to get ahead of them and turn right the moment she was clear.

She punched the gas but both vehicles sped up to keep her boxed in. At least the road was clear in front of her. She kept the accelerator to the floor as she looked left and right hoping for an opening. All of a sudden, both paparazzi vehicles pulled up short and she shot passed them. She was about to turn right when she realized why they had fallen behind. She looked up to see a red light at the intersection. She had no idea how long it had been red, but it didn't matter. She couldn't stop in time.

The last thing Beth saw was a dark blue SUV headed straight for her at thirty five miles per hour. The other driver never saw her coming. The impact collapsed Beth's door into a "V" crushing her body against the center divider. Both vehicles skidded sideways across the intersection into a curb. The other SUV came to a stop, but Beth's momentum rolled them over twice before landing awkwardly against a barricade pole in front of a convenience store.

* * *

"Dr. Jensen?" the receptionist said over the intercom. "I know you're not taking any outside calls, but this one is from the police."

"The police?" Louis said in disbelief. "What the heck do they want?"

"I'm not sure, sir," she stammered, "but they said it concerns your ex-wife Beth and your son Eljay."

Louis managed to say, "Please put the call through."

"Dr. Jensen?" a serious voice said a moment later. "This is Detective Crawford from the Encino Police Department. I'm afraid I have some bad news."

"Oh my God," Louis almost shrieked. "How bad is it?"

The detective said, "Your ex-wife and son were in a car accident earlier this afternoon. I'm very sorry to inform you over the phone, but she died at the scene. Your son was taken to the Encino Hospital Medical Center on Ventura Boulevard. I only know he was alive when the ambulance took him away."

Louis was already running down the hall to the lab where he hoped to find Mark and Nuri. One of them was typing on a laptop while the other was making adjustments to an RF crystal. They looked up and saw the frantic look on Louis' face.

He said without preamble, "I really need a ride. Can you drive me?"

"What happened?" they asked.

Louis was frantic but managed to say, "Beth was killed in a car accident and Eljay was with her. He was hurt enough that they took him away in an ambulance. If you can drive me to the hospital, I'll make some calls on the way to find out more."

***

Louis paced anxiously in the waiting room. He still knew nothing of Eljay's condition other than he was in surgery. Mark and Nuri sat nearby allowing him his space. The archeologists had mostly avoided their friend from JPL ever since Prince Nafid publicly announced that Louis had recorded a conversation with an extraterrestrial. They remembered just how much Louis wanted to tell the world everything despite his promise not to. Did he knowingly lie to them that morning in Philz Coffee Shop? There was no obvious connection between Louis and the prince, but how else would that oddball lottery winner have known all those details?

A doctor, who, from the look of him, had just been in surgery, took Louis aside to speak to him. Mark and Nuri watched Louis' face for any sign of his son's condition. There seemed to be both relief and concern creasing his features after the doctor left. He slowly walked over to tell them the news.

"Eljay is going to be okay, but he has a tough road ahead of him," Louis began. "He will need a lot of physical therapy, but they are hopeful he'll make a full recovery."

Mark asked, "What do you mean by he's got a tough road ahead?"

Louis sighed and stifled a sob, "Where do I start? He has breaks and extensive cartilage damage to his arms and legs that will take months to heal. The doctor just told me that Eljay doesn't know that his mother died, so I get to be the one who tells him. The worst part is that I'm all that he has left; a single dad with poor parenting skills. I'm a much better scientist than I'll ever be a father."

Nuri asked, "What do you mean by that? I thought you always did a good job of being in Eljay's life."

"I was always there for him as the divorced dad sharing quality time with his son every other weekend, but it was Beth who knew how to raise him," Louis said with regret. "I can't help but feel responsible for her death. I just found out from the doctor that she was apparently running from the paparazzi when she ran the red light. If that Prince Nafid had kept his mouth shut, none of this would have happened."

Mark and Nuri just stared at him. Was Louis admitting that he told Prince Nafid of his conversation with an alien? If so, then they could see how he might feel responsible for her death. As it was, they were not happy with him for breaking his promise. At least he had not mentioned their names when he was leaking the story.

They offered their condolences and made sure he had a ride home, but Mark and Nuri silently agreed that they would not get involved further.

***

After the accident, Louis went back into hiding. Since the media couldn't talk to him, they did the next best thing. They started speculating. They researched the planet Klacktu and where it was located in the cosmos. When the name did not appear in any official records, the guesswork continued. Conspiracy theorists alleged that

Prince Nafid must have meant "Klaatu" as in the protagonist alien who first said, "Klaatu barrata nikto," in the classic sci-fi movie, "The Day the Earth Stood Still."

Another day passed and the lack of news updates brought about more wild speculations. What the media termed as 'alien theorist experts' popped up on every news program offering their best guess on various planets where the aliens might live. Las Vegas odds favored Klacktu being a planet orbiting around Proxima Centauri, a star located about twelve light years from Earth.

A week passed with nothing new, but the media kept the story alive by exploring theories about the aliens' intentions. Some hypothesized that their motives were honorable, like Star Trek's Federation. However, the majority felt that we must seem like insignificant ants to any species capable of roaming the galaxy. Earth's likely value to such beings would be its natural resources, including human beings for slave labor.

The alien story was running out of steam when Prince Nafid announced that he would report on the whereabouts of Dr. Jensen. More importantly, he added that he would tell them more about life on other planets. The press conference was understandably standing room only.

The prince stepped up to a podium that strained to hold the plethora of microphones. He said, "I have a prepared statement to read and I will not take questions afterward."

The crowd murmured but they were so hungry for news to report that the room quickly fell silent. Nafid pulled out a sheet of paper and slowly unfolded it before he began.

"Dr. Louis Jensen is staying inside JPL's laboratory complex in Pasadena. Most of you have guessed that already. What you don't know is that once he does emerge, he will only say 'no comment' when asked about his contact with aliens."

A few of the reporters could not help themselves and started to shout questions. Nafid cast an icy stare around the room that lasted until they were quiet.

"The planet Klacktu is far away from earth. In fact, it is located on the far side of another galaxy that you have named Andromeda. Dr. Jensen, with the help of others, has developed resonant frequency communications technology that transcends time and space. Real time communications are now possible with alien worlds."

The crowd noise erupted again, but the prince stopped talking until they got the hint.

"I said possible, but it would be far from advisable. Humanity needs time to evolve before sticking its toe into the intergalactic waters let alone inviting other species to come here, as Dr. Jensen did. But let me be clear. Venturing outward to the stars is humanity's ultimate destiny."

Prince Nafid refolded the paper he'd been reading and, as promised, left the podium without another word. The reporters remained surprisingly quiet for the space of a breath as they absorbed the details of his prepared statement. By then it was too late. The prince had left the building.

The media created its own perfect storm to make the most of this turn of events. The new information from Prince Nafid, along with Dr. Jensen's unwillingness to answer their questions, fed the public's insatiable desire for drama. Prince Nafid had told them enough to keep this story headlining for days to come.

It wasn't long before nervous fringe citizens' groups gathered thousands of signatures on petitions demanding that their government develop contingency plans in case of an invasion. The most militant of the groups were not about to surrender their planet, or their loved ones, to the aliens. Elected officials began bending to voter pressure. They publicly commissioned think tanks to develop defensive strategies in case of an alien attack. Then both political parties published strategy statements to repel an interstellar assault. Public opinion polls conducted worldwide confirmed that nearly 100 percent of people admitted they believed that Homo-sapiens were not alone in the universe.

***

Gus and Jason were enjoying the ocean breeze as their clothes moved in ripples like waves across their bodies. Mark and Nuri preferred to stay below hoping to hold down their lunch. The archeologists' past experience with boating in the ocean had been limited to short runs. They had spent hours drifting down lazy rivers on rubber zodiacs, but bouncing across the Atlantic Ocean at 30 knots was a whole different story.

Jason verified the GPS coordinates for the Bimini Wall and Gus assured him they were on course. They both glanced at the video display of the nautical map. It showed that their current location was very near the red dot where the Bimini Hall of Records was said to be waiting. A few minutes later Gus powered down the boat and Jason went below to get his land-loving friends.

"Come on you two. It's time to get your feet wet!" Jason said with a grin.

All three men had been certified to scuba dive. Mark and Nuri had trained in a lake and were cleared to go as deep as 100 feet. Jason was certified in the ocean and was cleared to go as low as 300 feet with normal air tanks. None of them would dive deeper than 100 feet today. If they did, decompression stops would be needed to acclimate their bodies as they returned to the surface.

Now that the boat had stopped, Mark and Nuri hoped they could get into the water without making a mess. The plan was to recon the area in basic scuba gear. They had already seen visions of the entrance and were given the coordinates to explore. They wondered if the chamber's entrance might look very different from the remembered image they still held from a year ago. What if the scene imprinted in their minds was based on what the entrance looked like in 10,000 BCE?

They jumped into the warm, salty water with Jason taking the lead and his friends close behind. The boat was anchored just west of the renowned Bimini Wall. The water there was shallow, but their real destination was a nearby underwater precipice. They knew that the entrance to the Hall of Records would be found along the face of that cliff.

In the months after the destruction of the Piedras Negras location, sanctioned expeditions from many nations explored this site in search of the Bimini Hall of Records. Edgar Cayce's psychic readings had said to look for it on the west side of the islands, but nothing was given about how deep it would be. Despite thousands of hours spent by divers to locate the fabled chamber, no one had succeeded.

The three friends were confident in the guidance they had received from the other side. Amelius and Halaliel had confirmed that people with selfish intent would never find the hidden place. That was why they had waited months to make this trip. They let everyone else try and fail so that the three of them could explore the area in peace.

They started the search where the exact longitude and latitude crosshairs led them, but found nothing. They were not discouraged, choosing instead to separate with Mark exploring the cliff face to the north and Nuri to the south. Jason stayed where they started and dove deeper.

An hour later, they regrouped at the same spot where they had parted. None of them had found the entrance and their air was running low. They had prepared themselves knowing it was unlikely to find it on their first attempt. Since the Hall of Records had disappeared when the continent of Atlantis sank into the ocean, the coordinates could easily have shifted over the millennia because of subsequent earthquakes.

Using hand signals, Jason indicated that they needed to return to the ship. When they rose to the surface, they couldn't believe what they saw. There had to be over twenty ships of different sizes anchored above the Bimini Wall. One of them was a U.S. naval destroyer. After they were back on board, Gus told them the other boats had appeared within the last fifteen minutes.

Mark and Nuri were stunned, but Jason figured it out immediately. "I should have known we've been under surveillance this whole time. It did seem odd that everyone gave up searching for the Hall of Records in just months. They hadn't given up at all. They've been waiting for us to show them where it is."

"Then I guess it's lucky we didn't find it either," Mark said with a mix of relief and disappointment.

"What do we do now?" Nuri asked as he tried to count the ships. He could see their divers jumping in and heading west where the three of them had just been.

Jason shook his head and said, "That's enough diving for today. Why don't we see if we can get help from our ethereal friends?"

503

***

Nasrum had been sure these two archeologists and their soldier friend would finally locate the Hall of Records. He was surprised when they too were unsuccessful. He had been ready to intervene before they could succeed, but they never came close. If humanity ever learned of the technological wonders in Atlantis, he would be hard-pressed to maintain control of the world through Prince Nafid. If everyone had access to levitation, teleportation, instant healing and the Akashic Records, there would be little the prince could offer to hold the world's attention.

Nasrum still couldn't follow the archeologists' thoughts or conversations. He normally had no trouble hearing the thoughts of humans, but these two men were different. He endured a tremendous psychic pain when he tried to read their thoughts. Whatever they were saying came across as garbled speech in his mind. Nasrum was certain he had run into these two souls before. He reviewed his life as Achmed Mansur but he hadn't crossed paths with them before his body's untimely demise. He didn't bother to consider other lifetimes before that.

The soldier was a different story. Nasrum had moments of clarity with that one. His emotions were clear as a bell even when his thoughts were murky. That was why Nasrum was certain they had been unsuccessful in their search. That confirmed that his backup plan had worked. Getting the world to believe in intelligent life on other planets had changed the focus of humanity.

Nasrum was content to stop worrying about anyone else finding the Bimini Hall of Records. It was time to focus on the details for Prince Nafid's ascent to power in Syria. He was not sure Nafid was up to the task, but things were looking good so far. Nasrum longed to inhabit a human form again so he didn't have to work through this unworthy human. When he had been Colonel Mansur, he knew how to get things done.

***

Mark, Nuri and Jason asked Gus to remain on deck for a while. Gus was glad to oblige preferring the gentle ocean breeze to the stuffy hold of the ship. The three friends each held an RF crystal in their hands while they sat comfortably on a padded bench in the ship's hold. As they began their group meditation, each of them held the intention of meeting Amelius and Halaliel in the Bimini Hall of Records. Within minutes, they opened their eyes and were greeted by their two ethereal hosts.

"Welcome! It is great to see you again!" Amelius said with a broad smile.

Mark and Nuri were about to start with some small talk, but Jason was eager for answers. "So what went wrong? Was it all the people watching us that interfered with our finding the...this, Hall of Records?" He realized they were standing inside what looked like the remaining hidden chamber. He recognized it from his meeting last year with Halaliel.

"It would be easy to blame your frustrating day on the people who tracked you here," Halaliel empathized, "but that is not the case."

Amelius added, "You have not been following the changes that started because of Louis' conversation with Klacktu's emergency monitoring station. The world may look much the same to you as it did a few weeks ago, but believe me when I say that it has gone in a new direction away from the events you were shown."

Mark interjected, "I don't get it. The RF call with the alien was yesterday's news. When we left Florida, the media seemed to be moving on to other stories."

"The three of you were moving on, but the rest of humanity lags behind you," Amelius explained. "Do you remember I told you that this place is divinely protected? It will not be discovered until the world is ready for the wonders it contains."

The two archeologists nodded remembering the conversation.

Amelius continued, "When I told you that, you also retained a vision of the most probable futures that would lead to your discovery of this sacred place. That conversation Louis had with Klacktu has changed the trajectory of the timelines currently followed by the entire world. Everything you thought would unfold still exists, but your consciousnesses are now on a different path. In other words, the events you expect will no longer occur because of humanity's distracted focus on extraterrestrials."

"How is it that you didn't see this coming?" Jason asked with more than a hint of anger in his tone.

Halaliel smiled knowingly and said, "I always knew that it was a possibility, but three things occurred that were statistically negligible to cause this reset. First, Louis decided to broadcast an automated recording of successive Fibonacci numbers on the fortieth frequency as test audio for your RF communications experiment. That is a universally recognized SOS code and channel used throughout many galaxies. Second, the Klacktu employee took extraordinary measures to communicate with you because he thought you were in trouble. By the time he realized his mistake, it was too late to take it back. Third, and this was the most difficult event to predict, Prince Nafid managed to convince the world that extraterrestrials are real and that humanity has good reason to be afraid."

Amelius added, "The free will choices made by all souls is impossible to predict without some surprises. The combination of those three events occurring together, while obviously possible, was too negligible for most to consider."

"So you're telling us that whoever or whatever is running things doesn't know everything?" Jason asked.

Amelius smiled and said, "The Creator is indeed omniscient. We all live and move and experience our lives within the limitless bounds of the First Cause's mind. However, knowing all the choices we could possibly make is not the same thing as knowing which of those choices we will make and in what order we will make them."

Nuri asked, "As interesting as that is, where do things stand now?"

Halaliel shook his head and said, "What you would call the 'fast track' to peace and prosperity has been altered. It will now take decades for humanity to return its collective focus to what was just lost, but it is in having patience that we rise to the best that is within us!"

"Seriously?" Jason winced. "Decades? So what do we do now? Just leave this place and hope the appointed day comes before we're too old to try again?"

Amelius responded without a hint of frustration. "The answer to your question is yes. But I would suggest adopting a more optimistic attitude toward this; …let's call it a waiting period."

"Do you really think we will be physically able to scuba dive below 100 feet when we're decades older?" Mark asked skeptically.

"You are correct that at the current rate your bodies are moving away from perfection, that is not likely," Halaliel confirmed.

The three men gawked at each other with shared disbelief. It felt like they had just been handed a prison sentence. The exciting cause they had dedicated their lives to had just crashed and burned when they were so close to achieving the goal. None of them said a word, but their shared anger and disappointment filled the ethereal chamber.

Unexpectedly, they found themselves back in the lower deck of the boat. Their two ethereal friends were gone. Jason finally broke the silence when he called for Gus to join them. A moment later, the boat's captain bounded down the steps and landed with a thud. He stopped short when he felt the icy tension among them.

"I'm sorry, Gus, but we've agreed that we're done here," Jason said quietly. "In the morning, would you take us back to Florida?"

Chapter 5

Prince Nafid's connection with his Rayiys had progressed to the point where he could telepathically hear the words without having to write them out by hand. Nafid had hoped his improved clarity would encourage Rayiys to explain his overall plan. But when the prince asked why he was ordered to carry out a puzzling task, the answer continued to be, "So that Syria can become the political and financial epicenter of the world." Rayiys had to insist that Nafid save all his dictations to a laptop to ensure that he could print out and read the press conference scripts verbatim.

The prince's wealth grew beyond his wildest dreams. Rayiys' timing for buying or selling stocks and commodities was uncanny, but the prosperity didn't stop there. He was guided to open shell corporations in various countries and convert his wealth into their currency. This not only made his investments difficult for others to track, but he also generated huge profits through the timely conversion of dollars to yen, or euros to Swiss francs, whatever netted the greatest arbitrage profit.

Nafid's confidence in Rayiys' ability to predict any financial market's movements was growing by leaps and bounds. That is, until he was ordered to spend most of his accumulated wealth to buy all of OPEC's Middle Eastern oil fields. The prince was sure this would be a waste of money. It seemed that Rayiys' impressive winning streak was about to fall flat on its face and Nafid's financial empire with it.

What economic advantage could there be in owning abandoned oil fields? After all, RF power was available for free to anyone who could create the sending and receiving crystals. The OPEC nations' oil deposits still had some value as lubricants and in the manufacture of plastic products, but exporting huge tankers of crude oil was a thing of the past. That left the value of the land itself, which was less than the oil underneath it. The real estate holdings of OPEC nations consisted mostly of shifting sand dunes. The sad truth was that it was easier to develop and maintain Florida swampland than the deserts of the Middle East.

Through an attorney, Nafid obediently purchased OPECS' oil-rich properties in the Middle East. Many of the owners were starved for cash and could see no reason to refuse the unusually generous offer. Even they preferred RF power now that the U.S. was no longer the sole supplier. In short order, the prince owned just over 50 percent of the world's oil reserves as well as the property above them.

Then Rayiys dictated an extensive list of oil producing properties that Nafid did not yet own. The prince's questions about the purpose for the list went unanswered. Instead, he was told to schedule another press conference in the morning and type out the script Rayiys wanted him to read. Though the announcement clarified some things, Nafid was more confused than ever.

The statement read, "The world has recently become aware of a new discovery in RF technology. You already know that a process has been developed where food can be grown overnight and any water can be purified in minutes. What has been withheld until now is that there is a particular soil that optimizes the process. It must contain silicone, as in sand, and that sand needs to be soaked in benzene over thousands of years. While the RF process will still work with other soils, the inferior quality of the food and water produced by an inferior soil is nearly untenable. Many of the oil fields that are ideal for this process are privately owned and not for sale. However, other suitable sites still exist and may be purchased at the following locations: (the list Nafid already had on his computer was inserted)."

Nafid now understood why he had been guided to purchase the Middle Eastern OPEC properties, but why was Rayiys inviting competition by encouraging others to acquire the remaining fields? He silently asked that question, but Rayiys ignored him. Instead, he was told to emphasize to the media that tomorrow's press conference was of the utmost importance.

Mark, Nuri and Jason sat in the silence with their eyes closed. Except for the sour looks on their faces, an outsider might have guessed they were meditating. Anyone who knew them could tell that their thoughts were far from spiritual. The gloom of their shared frustration and disappointment filled the lobby of their rented Pasadena office. Instead of discovering Bimini's Hall of Records and revealing it to the world, they were now sitting on the sidelines not knowing what to do next. Amelius and Halaliel had been right. Humanity found themselves living in a world full of dangerous aliens with hostile intentions toward the earth.

The unspoken elephant in the room was their suspicion that Louis was to blame for their misery. He had said he felt guilty for his ex-wife's death. Because she had died trying to get away from the paparazzi, the implication was that Louis had leaked his conversation with an alien to the prince. While none of them wanted to outright accuse him of ruining their lives, it was clear that Louis Jensen was persona non gratia.

They had no plan for what they might do now that their mission was suspended indefinitely. Mark and Nuri could return to academics or pursue additional RF research, but they would hardly need Jason's skills if they did. No one wanted to admit that they had become adrenaline junkies, albeit their addiction was toward making a difference in life-changing, positive ways. In all of history, few people could claim to have had as much of an impact on the course of humanity as the three of them. Would they ever feel that rush again?

Jason, always the realist, suggested, "I guess we can stop paying rent on this office. The government has aliens from other worlds to worry about now. Hopefully they'll stop watching your every move if you work privately with Louis to come up with new RF discoveries."

"I'm not motivated to work with Louis at all," Nuri sighed.

Mark added, "I agree with Nuri. I'd rather take up teaching than to work with Louis or anyone else at JPL."

"You two do what you want," Jason offered, "but it sounds like nothing we do from here on is going to alter the path humanity takes in the future. Heck, if the Bimini Hall of Records isn't discovered for decades, we may be dead by then."

Silence again descended like a curtain drawn across the room. If disillusionment had a smell, the little lobby reeked of it. They felt let down by the 'powers that be.' How could Amelius and Halaliel just blow them off like that? After all they had done to bring peace to the world, the thanks they got could be summed up in three words, 'See you later.'

***

President Westbrook entered the room and everyone came to their feet. Don walked to his chair at the head of the conference table and invited them all to take their seats.

These were dark days for Don Westbrook. The United States would soon be bankrupt if he didn't reinstate a federal tax system. Doing that would almost assuredly make him a one-term president. The only customers who still paid the U.S. for RF energy were those who had not yet acquired their own RFP sending crystals. Since the schematics and instructions for creating them had been posted on the internet, RFP would soon be available to everyone for free.

The press conference that Prince Nafid held earlier that day offered the United States an unexpected ray of hope. If Don could figure out how to acquire the properties of the highest grade RF soil for growing crops and purifying water, it was possible to replace the loss of RFP revenues.

"Ladies and gentleman," he began, "we have an opportunity here, but we must act quickly. I intend to use the full force of this office to acquire most, if not all, of the properties this Prince Nafid listed in his press conference. And let's do our own research to see if he missed any. The United States needs this to happen for the good of its citizens."

He could see nods of understanding and approval around the table. The gravity of the situation was not lost on them. "We'll contact the current legal owners of these properties immediately. If a reasonable deal cannot be reached, more convincing methods of persuasion should be used. Hopefully, we won't have to resort to strong arm tactics to get back in the RF technology game, but all options are on the table."

* * *

Nasrum's plan was unfolding exactly as he had foreseen. He was anxious to gain control of the world's food supply, but Nafid's wealth fell well short of being able to acquire 100% of the properties needed for a monopoly. Sharing the list of the remaining prime RF soil locations around the world ensured that a desperate legal battle to buy them would ensue.

The initial offers to the current owners came in from everywhere. Of course, they didn't want to sell, but then the bids

511

kept climbing until some agreed to accept the cash instead of going into the RF soil business for themselves.

Nasrum's deceitful plan became clear to Nafid after the world's best attorneys were retained to beat out the competition. Whether the RF soil property owners agreed to sell or not, thousands of injunctions were filed around the world to stop any and all transfers of the properties until the legal arguments had been decided. Nasrum guided Nafid to ensure that his properties were unaffected while the lawyers kept everyone else from wrongfully depleting or hoarding the soil that could single-handedly sustain humanity. He knew that the greed and influence of the nations suing each other would take years to resolve.

Prince Nafid quietly became the sole supplier of RF soil that wasn't tied up in court proceedings. Having a monopoly on the most valued substance in the world quickly catapulted the prince to a new level of influence and prosperity. Nasrum was certain that his human puppet would soon become the next ruler of Syria and the most powerful person on the planet.

Chapter 6

Gus sat on the bow of his boat with a fishing pole held loosely between his knees. He turned and said, "Hey! Can you toss me a beer?"

Jason opened the cooler and gently lobbed a can of PBR over to him. Gus caught it with one hand and popped the top to quench his thirst. "Thanks!" he said with a smile.

They were taking a break before their next dive. Jason should have been more excited about the undisturbed shipwreck they'd found, but the ex-Delta Force Ranger was distracted. Reminiscing about his past adventures had become more of an obsession than simply recalling pleasant memories.

Jason enjoyed treasure hunting with Gus when they weren't hiring themselves out for chartered expeditions, but he really missed the good old days with Mark and Nuri. Two years had passed since he last saw them in Pasadena. Once his friends had become full professors at Stanford, his only contact with them was the occasional email. He took no offense since he was worse at staying in touch than they were.

Whether he would admit it or not, Jason had a specific reason for moving to Florida and working with Gus. If he ever hoped to get back on the trail of the Bimini Hall of Records, he knew he needed to have superior diving skills. Working with Gus guaranteed that he would become an expert scuba diver. It didn't hurt that he liked the old sailor. They were fast friends and compatible business partners.

He looked around and was relieved to see no other boats in sight. Jason resented that after two years he was still under surveillance. Every time Gus took him out treasure hunting, or to help with a charter, one or more boats were always following in their wake. It had to be expensive to keep such a close watch on him, but governments were not known for pinching pennies over something they considered a priority.

Luckily, the trackers didn't bother the charter business. Jason doubted the customers ever knew they were being watched. Their treasure hunting was another matter. The tracker boats were not shy about staying close, but once they were convinced it was sunken ships they were after instead of the fabled Hall of Records, the surveillance retreated to a reasonable distance.

"We've only got a couple of days to investigate this new shipwreck," Gus said out of the blue.

"Why is that?"

"My granddaughter is coming to Florida for a visit," Gus said proudly. "She just graduated with honors as a Navy SEAL."

"Boy, am I behind the times," Jason said with a rueful smile. "The last I knew, there were no females in the SEALs."

"She's one of the first," Gus continued. "I could hardly believe that she wanted to celebrate with her old grandpa."

"Were you ever going to tell me you had a granddaughter?" Jason asked.

"It's not like I was keeping her a secret," Gus objected. "Heck, I named my boat after her."

"Her parents named her Guppy?" Jason frowned.

"No," Gus smiled. "Her parents named her Diana. I started calling her Guppy because she was the cutest thing I'd ever seen and practically lived in the water."

Jason laughed as he crushed his empty can of beer and made a perfect jump shot into the port side trashcan.

"I've never heard you mention having kids, let alone a grandchild," Jason remarked.

"My daughter Sonja and her husband, Gary died from smoke inhalation when a fire that started in the garage burned the house down. Diana was barely five years old, but she managed to crawl out her window and survive a two-story drop to the ground. That's the only reason she's alive," Gus said sadly. "I raised her as my daughter ever since."

"That sounds like one tough lady!" Jason said impressed.

"You have no idea. Just wait till you meet her!" Gus said brightening at the thought of seeing her again.

"Then I guess we'd better get back in the water! You know our surveillance friends will report on the wreck below the moment we leave. Nothing we find out here ever stays a secret for long. Whatever we don't take with us this time will be picked clean by poachers as soon as we're out of here."

***

Mark and Nuri shared office space as full professors in Stanford's archeology department. They were the equivalent of celebrities in their field and the university kept them in the same office to more easily insulate them from unwanted visitors.

Nuri's side of the room was in perfect order. Mark's side looked more like he had a tornado come in twice a week to organize his papers. It was a mystery how these two had ever become friends, let alone survived adventures that would make Indiana Jones jealous. They were like quarrelsome siblings who still loved each other despite their differences. They had first met in their twenties as interns at Harvard University, and the rest was history.

"I'm bored!" Mark sighed aloud.

"I'm not grading all the papers again," was Nuri's irritated response. "You can figure out how to entertain yourself after you've finished your half."

"Let me rephrase that," Mark began, "I'm feeling unfulfilled."

"I'm still not grading your papers, so quit stalling and get on with it," Nuri whispered impatiently.

"We could meditate with the crystals and see if Amelius has some other way we can help," Mark said, almost whining.

"We already tried that," Nuri reminded him. "When he has something for us to do, he said he'll be in touch. In the meantime, we have work to do on ourselves. Amelius didn't say exactly what that was, but he was always going on about learning to play well with others. I'm pretty sure that includes grading those papers in front of you!"

"How can it hurt to ask again?" Mark pleaded. "Amelius is big on patience, so how could he get mad at us for trying to help?"

"Be my guest," Nuri said while slowly shaking his head in annoyance.

***

Nasrum was pleased with the progress he'd made. Prince Nafid was sure to be elected to lead Syria once President al-Assad died. It was a moot point. The prince already got anything he wanted, so becoming Syria's figurehead of state was not one of his immediate goals.

Regarding RF soil sales, Nafid enjoyed a 95 percent market share. It would have been 100 percent except for the illegal sales that couldn't be avoided. The temptation to ignore court orders, while the plethora of lawsuits worked their way through the system, was simply too great. Nasrum used his view from the spirit world to identify the illegal RF soil users. Initially, he had Nafid arrange to deactivate their food and water producing crystals. If there was no profit in buying illegal RF soil, then any smart businessman would stop buying from the wrong suppliers. For those who didn't mend their evil ways, Nasrum ordered the prince to officially shut the operation down by notifying the appropriate authorities. In this way, the demand for acquiring black market RF soil eventually dried up.

Nasrum kept moving forward with his plan to make a supreme leader out of the prince. He had been expecting some kind of intervention from Halaliel and his kind, but they stayed out of his way. Nasrum smiled knowing they were probably jealous of his ability to get humanity to freely choose a peaceful path. What these people needed was a leader who knew how to get things done. There was nothing wrong with legislating morality as long as the one in charge made it easy for everyone to make the right choices.

The psychic connection between Nasrum and Prince Nafid had become so strong that automatic typing had given way to telepathy. There was an occasion when Nafid didn't execute one of Nasrum's directives quickly enough. His Rayiys demonstrated his wrath by literally booting Nafid's consciousness out of his own body. It was only for a moment, but it seemed like hours in a nightmare where you are falling but never hit the bottom. Nafid felt like he had been given a reprieve from death and vowed never to displease his master again.

Nasrum's plan to consolidate global financial and political power in Damascus was already bearing fruit. He had the prince build a massive financial center that was far bigger than was needed to handle his RF soil empire. His plan was to create Syria's own stock market housed within the same impressive complex. The amount of business generated by the prince's investments made the new exchange profitable and an attractive home to other investors. Nasrum was certain Damascus' financial center would handle the majority of transactions for the world's stock, bond and commodity exchanges within the next year.

On the political front, Nasrum directed Prince Nafid to build a palatial new site for the United Nations. The existing location in New York had been the U.N.'s home since 1950, but it was hardly the inspiring structure it had once been. When the invitation was presented to the U.N. to relocate to Damascus, the vote was nearly unanimous, with the United States voting against. The prince's additional offer to pay all relocation expenses as well as provide luxurious new embassies for all the member nations was hard to refuse. The U.S. reluctantly fell into step with the other countries.

President Westbrook had become a lame duck. He had no choice but to reinstate federal taxes to keep the government machine afloat. He was so busy fighting his impeachment that he could do nothing to stop Syria from appropriating the United States' role as the world's most powerful nation.

Despite this progress, Nasrum grew impatient with humanity. He needed a way to bring the people together so that they would choose to stop all violence. He knew that religions could compel their congregants to do this, but most faiths disagreed with each other as much as he disagreed with the angels. Of all the world's religions, his preference was Islam. He even used the name of Allah when speaking of the Creator. The Islamic faith offered the complete integration of social, financial and political functions. That was what he needed most to achieve a lasting peace on earth.

***

Nasrum received a request from Gabriel and Halaliel to meet with them. He wished he could say he was too busy and offer to

517

reschedule, but that excuse did not apply to this realm that was not limited by linear time. He knew this encounter was inevitable, and so he accepted.

Gabriel and Halaliel greeted Nasrum warmly. He maintained a neutral demeanor while asking, "And to what do I owe this pleasure?"

Gabriel spoke first. "We are concerned that your influence over Prince Nafid has grown to the point where his free will has been usurped. You know this is not allowed and we are meeting with you in all the timelines where you have gone too far."

"You know very well that the prince reached out to me and asked for my help," Nasrum countered. "How can you say that the guidance I offered, and he has freely chosen to follow, was coerced?"

Halaliel answered, "Nasrum, we are aware that you took control of his body when he delayed following one of your directives. In many cases we will ignore such mistakes because a soul must be allowed to reap the consequences of their choices to learn a better way to live. However, your influence over the prince has been so great that it has changed the course of almost every soul incarnate on earth."

"And this is a bad thing?" Nasrum asked. He knew the question was forcing a debate they would rather avoid. "If your goal is global peace, my guidance has already achieved that balance. The world is no longer at war and even the terrorist attacks are far fewer than in their recent history."

Gabriel nodded, "Indeed you are correct. But your guidance for the prince has forced humanity's compliance rather than allowing them to make their own choice to follow where you lead."

"Then I am unsure of the purpose for this meeting," Nasrum stated, obviously taunting them.

"Because it would be better for you to freely cease your control over Prince Nafid rather than have intense scrutiny over all that you do." This last statement seemed to come from both of the angels.

"The real question here is one of style," Nasrum parried. "You would prefer that Christianity be the predominant religion of

518

humanity. I believe Islam is the best path to peace through the guidance given by Mohammed in the Koran."

"Our goal has never been about the religion one follows," said a new voice as Amelius joined the group. "The Holy Spirit, also known as the Law of Love, is the perfect consciousness that every soul ultimately seeks. The man Jesus lived a life of perfect love from birth to death, and that continued after He was resurrected. Even Mohammed, who fell short of that standard, accepted Jesus as a great prophet."

"Ah, so the man himself is now a part of this, what do they call it on earth, an intervention?" Nasrum said with surprise and resentment. He knew all about Amelius, but their mutual encounters had been few. "Is this where the lion is supposed to lie down with the lamb, or are you here to overturn the moneychangers' tables?"

Amelius laughed, "I've always enjoyed your perspective on things. Your desire for peace is laudable, Nasrum, but you lack patience in allowing others to exercise their free will. Try setting the perfect example for humanity and then allow each soul the freedom to follow the path they choose."

Gabriel added, "Giving them a choice of "my way or get out of the way" is not allowing humanity to exercise its free will, is it?"

"Fine. I agree to let Prince Nafid make his own decisions after carefully considering the guidance I offer," Nasrum said quietly. He wanted his statement to be the end of the discussion. He had hoped to keep Amelius out of it, but Nasrum's ambitions had drawn too much attention.

"If that is what you are willing to do, we accept," Amelius said with a smile. "Given that you continue to block certain thoughts from us, I trust that you will allow everyone on earth the same courtesy of making up their own minds as well?"

This was why Nasrum didn't want Amelius involved. Gabriel and Halaliel might have overlooked the fact that he had limited his promise to coercing Prince Nafid. Amelius was able to circumvent him from finding another willing incarnate soul to control as he had Nafid. "As you wish," was his grudging telepathic reply.

Chapter 7

Gus almost ran to the door when he heard the knock. Jason could tell that the old man really loved his granddaughter and hoped that she truly loved Gus in return. The woman had already impressed Jason by becoming one of the first female Navy SEALs.

"Grandpa!" Diana exclaimed as she dropped her bag by the door to hug him.

"It's great to see you, Guppy!" Gus said squeezing her tight.

They held each other and swayed for a moment soaking up each other's love, both losing themselves in memories of her childhood. Jason could see that he didn't have to worry about Diana's feelings toward his friend.

She looked over Gus' shoulder and saw a handsome older man awkwardly standing in the living room trying not to intrude. "Grandpa, who's your friend? I didn't know you had a visitor."

Gus suddenly remembered his manners and turned to make the introductions. "Jason Fisher, this is my granddaughter Diana Amal. Diana, Jason and I are partners in the charter and shipwreck salvage business."

"Partners?" she said in surprise. "You never wanted a partner before!"

"Hi Diana," Jason said as he extended his hand to shake hers. Damn, she had a firm grip. "I was Gus' client first and we took a liking to each other. Your grandfather has taught me a lot about boats and scuba diving."

"Then we have that in common. He taught me a lot, too, as I was growing up. I guess my choice to join the Navy was mainly because of Grandpa's influence."

"That might be true, but you became a SEAL all on your own," Gus said beaming again. "Let me get a look at you!"

She stepped back and he looked her over. Her rank was Petty Officer Second Class. She wore the golden SEAL Trident and an impressive number of ribbons on her crisp white uniform. Her shiny brown hair was shorter than Gus had ever seen it and it suited her. He realized that SEAL training and longer hair were probably incompatible. She was more buff than ever, though her muscle tone had been excellent before she entered the training program in Coronado a year ago. Gus loved her regardless, but also knew she had never looked better...or happier.

For his part, Jason had to admire the athletic woman. She had accomplished similar goals in the SEALs as he had in the Army's Delta Force. He was enjoying the surprising beauty in such a strong woman, but considering her young age compared to his, he quickly dismissed where that assessment was headed.

"Are you hungry?" Gus asked. "Jason and I were just about to eat."

Jason added with a smile, "Please join us. I'd really like to hear all about your SEAL training and any embarrassing stories you have on your grandfather."

***

Mark found himself sitting on a plain wooden stool in a white room without any other furnishings. Amelius was there but his expression was neutral rather than sporting his usual smile.

"Hello Mark," Amelius began. "What can I do for you?"

This was a rather cool reception compared to his other encounters with Amelius. He began to think Nuri had been right not to bother him. "I'm really hoping you can see a way that we can help speed things up in finding the Bimini Hall of Records."

"As I said before," Amelius sighed, "the timeline and everything you thought would unfold, including the discovery of the Hall of Records, has been changed."

"But there must be something we can do to help!" he said, a little desperate now.

"Actually, there is," Amelius said. "It seems you have decided to stop working with Louis on new RF technology projects. I mentioned before that having the ability to communicate and levitate using RF technology would be helpful if and when the time is right to discover the Bimini Hall of Records. You and Nuri gave up

521

everything when the Klacktu incident went awry. Although it may be quite a while, the world will eventually need you to perfect RF communications and levitation."

"Will we still be alive to see the remaining Hall?" Mark asked hopefully.

"As it looks now, yes. All three of you will be alive, albeit in your seventies or later when the time comes."

"And what of the other people who have been so important to our success?" Mark asked after a thoughtful moment. "What about Matthew Alexander? Will he be alive all those years from now?"

"Alive? Yes, most definitely," Amelius confirmed. "But I'm guessing you meant in his current physical form. To that question, the answer is likely to be no, both for Matt and for Louis Jensen."

The news that Matt and Louis would not be around when the final Hall of Records was found shocked Mark back to consciousness. Amelius had told him how they could still help the cause, but he was disappointed at the minor role he had been asked to play. Mark decided to ask Nuri if, under the circumstances, he too was willing to patch things up with Louis. He knew that their mutual hurt feelings would take a while to heal, so they might as well get started on the process now.

Diana read the letter in her hand for the third time. The printed words that ended her career had not changed. The letter said that the U.S. military was being all but dismantled. A token force would be maintained to organize rescue efforts during national emergencies, such as hurricanes and earthquakes, but all non-essential personnel would be retired with a full pension and benefits.

She supposed she had seen this coming for some time. Her assigned missions as a Navy SEAL stationed in the Middle East had been primarily to rescue victims of natural disasters. Occasionally there would be a potentially violent group to subdue and turn over to the local authorities, but she could count those missions on one hand. She suspected that the orders for arresting such groups came directly from Prince Nafid. He had an uncanny ability to sniff out and quell trouble before it began.

Diana felt betrayed by life in general. She couldn't believe her military career had gone the way of buggy whips and newspapers. It was easy to forecast that those industries would die out, but who could have guessed that the U.S. Navy would become all but obsolete? What would be next; death and taxes?

She shook her head and scolded herself for indulging in this pity party. She had her whole life ahead of her. Instead of feeling sorry for herself, she needed a plan for her civilian life. Since she was over 30 now and was not welcome back in the military, her working options were few. She had a generous pension from the Navy, so she didn't have to work to pay for expenses. But how did she want to spend her time, even if she focused on a hobby rather than a profession?

Diana considered working with her grandpa on his fishing boat. He would give her a job, of course, but he didn't really need her since he had Jason as a partner. Remembering Jason gave her an idea. She realized that he might be just the person to help her figure this out. He too had a strong military background and complained of being sidelined when he still had so much to offer. The stories he told her of his adventures with the two archeologists were almost beyond belief. Either he was the most convincing liar she'd ever met, or he had lived one of the most exciting lives she could imagine.

Her decision was made! She would visit Grandpa in Florida. She needed to be with her family right now. She hadn't seen Gus or Jason in some time and they could help her explore her options.

***

Prince Nafid was genuinely shocked to hear that President al-Assad had died in his sleep. Nafid was immediately suspicious that Rayiys was responsible for his early demise. A few short months before, the prince had been elected as the head of Syria's government. Now with the death of President al-Assad, Nafid accepted the inevitable appointment to be Syria's head of state. He was the first person whose last name was not al-Assad to hold that position since the 1970s.

Nafid reflected on how rapidly his life had changed since he reached out to Rayiys a few years back through automatic writing. His greatest hope had been to help restore Syria's respect as a nation. It had been his aim to play an important role in achieving

523

that laudable goal, but the power and wealth he now controlled was overwhelming. If he was honest with himself, he was tired of playing this exalted role. Rayiys controlled every statement or edict he gave in an official capacity. Instead of rejoicing in his good fortune, Nafid secretly wished he had never invited Rayiys into his life.

Changes continued everywhere at an unbelievable pace. Terrorism had been eradicated for the most part, even in the troubled regions of the globe. Rayiys accurately predicted where to send the authorities in order to thwart terrorist attacks. A cult following spontaneously developed that revered Nafid as their Messiah. Rayiys allowed it to grow, but he told Nafid that all glory should go to Allah when addressing the public. He said that such humility would encourage more conversions to Islam. Rayiys' focus on promoting Allah and the Koran was what kept Nafid going. Even if he hated everything else about his life, he believed that Rayiys was serving Allah.

As the years passed, peace prevailed across the earth. Nafid's popularity grew as prosperity came to people and nations formerly known for poverty and mass starvation. While some Christian factions pointed to Nafid as the anti-Christ the book of Revelation predicted, most others felt that unprecedented peace and prosperity could only come from God. Islam soon dwarfed all the other religions of the world combined.

Nasrum's planned utopia required one additional technological improvement. The 3-D printer had been around for decades but no one had been able to address its limitations. No one had figured out how to supply the raw materials required to create large products. Nasrum provided plans for an RF device that reduced any material down into its base elements. Huge amounts of any substance, from metals to landfill trash, could be fed into the processor with the desired base or compound elements extruded directly into shipping containers.

Recycling was now cost-efficient regardless of the product. Reprocessing plants quickly replaced unsightly landfills and the floating island of discarded plastic in the Pacific was finally cleaned up and put to good use. With RF energy and a never-ending supply of waste matter, these plants became the go-to resource for anything you needed. The refuse of the planet was transformed into practically unlimited manufacturing supplies with the help of the impressive new 3-D printers. Even dangerous or toxic substances became safe again once they were broken down into their base elements and safely stored until needed. The environment began to improve dramatically.

The international community hardly mentioned that Prince Nafid owned the patent to the new recycling processes and 3-D production equipment. Eventually, Nafid's financial holdings generated more than half of the world's gross national product. The only industry that was outpacing recycling plants was that of the Islamic religion. Nasrum continued to focus a great deal of his wealth on supporting Islam and encouraging religious conversions to his beloved faith. Massive and numerous mosques sprang up all over the globe, mostly funded by Prince Nafid's generosity.

Many of the world's colleges and universities willingly revised their programs to align with the madrasahs (Koranic schools). The changes in education were in response to the increasing need to fill the roles of imam (spiritual community leader), qadi (local judge of sharia law), mufti (superior interpreter of sharia law), mullah (highest level of judge in sharia law), and even a few ayatollahs (spiritual, legal and social experts of sharia law).

Any time a challenge to his perfect plan arose, Nasrum suppressed it immediately. He wanted no opportunity for discontent, subversion or even competition to exist in the perfect world he was creating. To that end, he directed Nafid to quietly settle all of the lawsuits pending over the remaining RF soil properties. Soon, 100 percent of the properties still in dispute were under Prince Nafid's control. Between Nafid's financial support and the charity requirement as one of the five pillars of the faith, the industry of Islam was well-funded. With automation, free energy, unlimited food and pure water, as well as the ability to create most any needed product on a 3-D printer, the war on poverty had finally been won.

Nasrum's ability to foresee and prevent most of the major crimes against people soon made them a thing of the past. The spread of Islam was working well to keep the people in line under sharia law. The devout believers in Mohammad, the Koran and Allah were pleased to see so many followers under the one true religion. However, some things would have to change to keep the peace. Nasrum could see women's rights would become a cause for conflict if he didn't promote equality between the genders, within reasonable limits, of course. He also had to clear the way for Islam to integrate smoothly into the culture of every society. Slow but constant changes would work to keep both sides of these potential conflicts in line.

As one decade melted into the next, a gentler version of sharia law was adopted by the world's governments. It was generally accepted that women were not to be discriminated against as long as they maintained a respectful demeanor and appearance as determined by the local judges. They could even serve as imams or qadis. In order to be recognized by Prince Nafid, sovereign governments were required to be democracies with one vote for each citizen. Employers were obligated to allow breaks for their employees to pray when the scheduled times for salah occurred during working hours. In this way, all cultures and nations integrated the Islamic religion into their way of life.

***

Diana, her Grandpa Gus and Jason sat in plastic chairs on Gus' back deck and watched the sun rise out of the water to the east. The sun glistened like diamonds across the water's inlet that led to the Atlantic Ocean. Gus' boat, The Guppy, never looked better than it did in the morning light. It didn't hurt that all three of them had spent the last few days really making the old girl shine.

Disrupting the serene hush of the early morning, Diana couldn't help but ask, "What are you two doing with the ADS suit I saw in the hold of the boat? Isn't that for diving down to depths of 2,000 feet?"

Gus looked over at Jason a moment before nodding.

"I'm still looking for the Bimini Hall of Records," he announced over the rim of his coffee cup. "I don't care what Louis told Prince Nafid, or what the guys in the vapors think, if it's down there, I should be able to find it. To hell with the rest of humanity, I want to see that place before I die."

Diana just looked at him and he realized his explanation had detoured into a confession. He was embarrassed, but managed to add, "I searched that whole cliff face down to three hundred feet using scuba gear. I considered other deep water diving options, but ended up getting an atmospheric diving suit (ADS) because nothing on the market could take me deeper. Back in the day, they used to run a quarter of a million dollars, but now all they do is feed the specs into a 3-D printer and finance it on a credit card."

Jason went on to tell of the interesting things he had seen so far using the ADS suit, but none of them included the Hall of Records. Then he digressed into telling old stories both Gus and Diana had heard, but they didn't mind. They enjoyed listening to him relive his happiest moments while they basked in the beautiful sunrise.

Jason had just finished recounting how they found the RF crystal inside the hidden chamber they discovered underneath the Sphinx. He admitted that he didn't know what possessed him to pick up the crystal as the stone walls crumbled around them. He later found out that the crystal, along with all the pictures and video they had from their brief time in the chamber, led to the discovery of RF energy. In a very real sense, that crystal had changed the world.

Gus mused, "Did anyone ever mention how much the RF energy sending crystal looks like a merkaba crystal?"

Jason looked at Gus in surprise and answered, "I've never heard of it. What's a merkaba crystal?"

"It looks like a three dimensional, six-pointed Jewish star, just like the pictures I've seen of an RF energy sending crystal," Gus explained. "Allegedly, it is used by ascended masters to connect with the higher realms of consciousness. 'Mer' means Light. 'Ka' means Spirit. 'Ba' means Body."

"Grandpa!" Diana gushed. "I had no idea you had any interest in metaphysics! I've never heard you talk about this kind of thing before."

Jason shook his head. He'd known Gus for years and had never heard him discuss anything remotely related to mysticism, even when Jason reminisced about his adventures. Of course, Jason hadn't really elaborated on his ethereal encounters with Halaliel and Amelius.

"Being interested in psychic stuff and believing it's real are not the same thing," Gus said, a little embarrassed. "I've read the Bible plenty. I have wondered all my life if those miracles really happened."

"It was no small miracle keeping Mark and Nuri alive all those years," Jason laughed. "There were a few times they would have been worm food if I hadn't been there to watch their backs."

"What about you, Jason?" Diana asked. "Do you believe in metaphysical things and spirituality?"

"In my early years," Jason began, "I didn't think about it at all. Then I met Mark and Nuri. The experiences I've had with them made me a believer. I've travelled between Guatemala and Pasadena in less than a second. I've walked through solid stone walls. I have even talked with the angels. I doubt anyone can remain skeptical after going through all that."

Diana looked at Jason with a thoughtful expression. Then she shook her head a little and said, "It sounds like there are a lot more stories you haven't told me. But let me ask you something. What made you decide to be partners with Grandpa Gus once you and your friends were told to go on with your lives?"

"Isn't your real question asking what you should do now that the rug has been pulled out from under you?" Jason smiled knowingly.

"I guess you're right," she admitted. "What gets you out of bed in the morning and keeps a smile on your face Mr. Delta Force?"

"I'm still in training to finish what I started," Jason said with quiet resolve. "I'm still hoping to be part of the team that discovers the Bimini Hall of Records. Gus is teaching me to be an expert diver. That skill has to come into play knowing the place is somewhere deep in the Atlantic Ocean. I am doing what I can to stay in shape to be ready."

"And how will you feel if that never happens?" she asked.

"I guess I've had plenty of excitement and been able to contribute more to humanity's welfare than most," Jason philosophized modestly. "Still, I feel like I've been sucker punched. I believed Mark, Nuri and I are destined to find a Hall of Records that isn't destroyed a minute after we get there."

"Well, you're 'zero for two' so far," Gus joked. "You guys sure have been hard on ancient hidden chambers."

Diana could see from Jason's expression that she'd better change the subject. "Getting thrown out of the SEALs has forced me to do a lot of thinking. What if the purpose of life is not so much about what we do as it is what we learn while we're doing it?"

Gus was out of his comfort zone and remained silent, but Jason was clearly thinking through her question.

"You sound just like Amelius and Halaliel," he mused. "According to them, you'd think the only reason we're here on the earth is to learn patience, faith and how to get along well with each other."

Diana was definitely going to have to ask Jason more about his "special friends," but she wasn't quite ready to go all the way down that rabbit hole just yet.

Gus surprised them both when he said, "That sounds a lot like this book I've been reading about the Sufis."

"What the heck is a Sufi?" Jason laughed. "And when did you start reading books?" That last jibe was really just his brand of teasing. Gus always had a worn paperback around, often tucked into his belt at the small of his back.

"The Sufis are a mystical sect of Islam," Gus said matter-of-factly. "I started looking into the Islamic religion because it's so popular now. I have to admit that what the Sufis believe made more sense to me than the doctrines of the Sunnis or the Shiites."

Jason said, "I don't know much about any of the sects of Islam. What's the difference between them?"

Gus smiled and said, "For Sufis, what's important is approaching the inner meaning of God through mysticism. They have a less orthodox interpretation of the Koran. That relaxed approach traditionally leads to a much more open relationship with people who follow other religions."

Diana surprised herself by asking a question that popped into her head. "Do any sects in Islam believe in reincarnation where we come back again as humans until we get it right?"

"The Druze, Alawis and some of the Sufis do believe in reincarnation," Gus explained. "The Sunnis and Shiites do not. In fact, that is often a problem between those factions."

"Grandpa," Diana asked, "can I borrow the books you have on this stuff? I hope they can help me decide what to do with the rest of my life."

Chapter 8

So much had transformed over the past 30 years. People are typically adverse to change, and some were brave enough to tell the prince his edicts were misguided. Nasrum was unfazed and told Nafid to ignore them. As long as peace and prosperity reigned supreme, he didn't care that many long-standing cultural priorities no longer made sense in his utopian society.

A good example of a major change was accumulating wealth. The motivation to become rich practically disappeared. Nasrum had directed Prince Nafid to use his massive fortune to generously level the financial playing field for everyone. He knew humans were less aggressive when there was less competition. Without the incentive to earn more money, people lost their desire to work long hours. In fact, a mandatory retirement age was set at forty years old, and workers were strongly encouraged to retire at the age of thirty. Most people did step down sooner rather than later because of the prince's liberal pension plan that more than paid the bills. Given the negligible cost of resources and the automation of most manufacturing processes, the work force required to maintain a healthy economy was a mere tenth of the population.

The one exception to the rules for early retirement pertained to all those working within the Islamic leadership. Unlike secular society where the quasi-caste systems between classes had largely dissolved, Islam's hierarchy of faithful followers commanded attention and respect. Anyone who worked as a paid member of Islam was revered like royalty in the social order. School children were taught the pecking order from imams to ayatollahs. Status was further elevated depending on which mosque they were assigned to in carrying out Allah's good work.

However, the growing popularity for becoming a career Muslim posed a problem. Unless a family member was already a part of the Islamic leadership, it was impossible to become an imam, which was the entry-level position for Muslim clerics. That upset the vast majority of the population so Nasrum could not ignore it. He 'strongly suggested' that the prince announced an unprecedented ordination process for devout followers of Allah. The goal was to remove the bias in the selection process. Annual testing was conducted on all citizens when they turned 18 years old. The top scores identified those who were most qualified to serve Allah without regard to race, gender or family connections. Assuming the prodigies-on-paper measured up to the potential they tested for, they were given a full scholarship and assigned to a mosque as an imam upon graduation.

The years brought other changes, as well. Mark and Nuri had retired from teaching, not that they were given a choice once they turned forty. They were eventually able to reconcile with Louis. Neither side would admit to being wrong, but they all agreed that remaining friends was much more important than winning the argument. They agreed to move forward as if it hadn't happened and to appreciate each other's virtues while forgiving their faults.

They picked up where they had left off with RF communications (RFC). A simple wireless earbud device soon replaced the suitcase sized prototype they started with. While it would have revolutionized the way the world communicates, they agreed not to publicize their invention. It seemed obvious that Prince Nafid's rise to power had somehow derailed their quest for the Hall of Records, so taking a chance on attracting the prince's attention was something to be avoided.

The confirmed bachelors would have moved on to other RF projects, but Louis died shortly afterward. That loss was followed by the passing of Matthew Alexander. Both men had succumbed to cancer. It was ironic that the world had eradicated hunger and poverty, but there was little scientific interest in improving health or longevity. No major medical advancements had been discovered since the prince came to power. It was difficult to explain why. Prince Nafid neither encouraged nor discouraged medical development. Some devout Muslims believed the lack of interest in research was because the promise of an eternal afterlife made the time humans remained alive on earth less precious.

Mark and Nuri had studied a great deal about physics and mathematics beyond their training as archeologists. Their innate desire to learn all they could really paid off. After Louis died, they were the ones in charge of resonant frequency research. Amelius had said that a levitation device (RFL) would be critical when the time came to locate the Bimini Hall of Records. So far, their experiments had been unsuccessful. Amelius added that their understanding of the physics behind this new RF application was being hindered by their sullen attitudes. It wasn't just that they missed their friend and fellow inventor, Louis. They were now in their seventies, and they had become far more suited for lab work than exploring deep underwater caves. Mark and Nuri did their best to be patient, but their disappointment over not leading an expedition to find the hidden chamber was difficult to suppress.

Their development of the RFL machine presented more challenges than a simple attitude adjustment. The proposed device was supposed to temporarily send a defined number of molecules from any mass or object to a different or "passive" dimension, while a very small number of molecules remained in the current or "active" dimension. Mark's and Nuri's translation of the Atlantean symbols, discovered during their expeditions in Egypt and Guatemala, revealed that the molecules isolated in a defined space in both dimensions remain connected. Essentially, where one molecule went, the others followed and maintained their relative positions to each other in the process.

The most fascinating aspect of the technology had to do with the change in mass. The weight would vary according to the number of molecules kept in each dimension. If the RFL device caused ninety percent of the molecules to move into the passive dimension, then the remaining connected molecules would weigh only ten percent in the active dimension. The idea was that once the lesser weight was moved to the desired location, the RFL technology could then reunite, or rematerialize, all of the molecules together in the active dimension.

They had been shown that the ancient Egyptians built fantastic structures using this method of levitation. If a block of the Great Pyramid normally weighed 6,000 pounds, and the levitation device was set to keep only .1 percent of the molecules in the active dimension, then the six-pound block could be moved easily.

So far, they had limited success with the process. They had managed to use resonant frequencies to cause the molecules to vanish, but it was all or nothing. In other words, their progress looked like a great magic trick that made any mass or object disappear and reappear without changing position.

533

Another problem came up that almost put them out of business. JPL lost its government funding when Uncle Sam ceased all non-essential projects. No one seemed to care when they became squatters in the JPL facility because they paid for their own utilities and became its caretakers. However, the government finally decided to sell the grounds and told them to leave. Mark and Nuri felt like President Westbrook was exacting his delayed revenge from beyond the grave for Jason posting all the RF technology secrets that led to his impeachment. Had it not been for Matthew Alexander's generous endowment that purchased the JPL complex, the entire facility would have closed forever.

Even so, the skeleton crew that remained at JPL was reduced to Mark, Nuri and Louis' brilliant son, Louis Junior. They all took to calling him Eljay after his mother died. For convenience, they had moved into the residence facilities attached to the main lab as they continued the work of Eljay's father. The complex was enclosed by a tall fence that provided privacy and security, but crimes of violence or stealing had all but disappeared. Except for the weekly landscape maintenance company and the occasional plumber, no one bothered them.

It was odd that JPL was now completely forgotten. This was the site where humanity first made contact with an alien species. Now, it seemed, no one cared that they had once talked with an extraterrestrial. The Islamic population of the world believed the prince's promise that Allah would always protect his faithful followers from harm, even from threats that were not of this world.

Nasrum sensed that he was being summoned to meet with the archangels. This time he was unconcerned whether Amelius was with them or not. He had accomplished all of his goals and proven that Islam had succeeded where their competing efforts had failed. Both peace and prosperity were sustainable, but only when someone of his ability used religion as the proper tool.

"My sincere welcome to you!" Nasrum began. "Are you here to congratulate me?"

Halaliel and Ariel looked at each other in amazement. "Is it really your position that your guidance has brought perfection to the earth?" The thought came from both angels.

"Don't think of trying to take credit for the things I have accomplished on this planet!" Nasrum said resentfully. "If anything, you fought me all the way. It's a miracle I managed to succeed!"

The vibrations Nasrum could feel coming from the two angels softened considerably, but he was still confused. Halaliel and Ariel were not hiding their thoughts, so he was able to eavesdrop on the conversation between them.

"The metrics he relies upon to gauge his success are surprising. The fruits of the spirit, love, joy, patience and kindness, are not considered when he evaluates the results," Ariel telepathically said to Halaliel.

"I have seen him repeat this pattern over many years. Peace, prosperity and what he thinks of as cooperation are his only measures of success," Halaliel replied.

Nasrum interrupted, "What do you mean, 'what I think of as cooperation'?"

Halaliel smiled and said, "Cooperation is not everyone on earth living life exactly as you want them to. It is better defined as everyone getting along beautifully despite their differing ideas and desires."

Ariel added, "If the First Cause, let's call our Creator by the name of Allah for your purposes, had wanted souls to live as you do, why would we have free will at all?"

"Because humanity with free will is more of a challenge and makes it clear who is worthy of Allah's favor! You know that I have not suppressed their right to choose. Humanity has freely accepted the lifestyle they enjoy under Prince Nafid's rule," Nasrum said triumphantly.

"But you have treated them as unthinking juveniles rather than worthy companions of our Creator...I mean, Allah," Halaliel explained. "When their free will options are limited to 'do this and you'll be rich, do that and you'll be poor,' what choice do you expect their finite minds to make?"

"Exactly!" Nasrum shouted telepathically. "They still have free will and I help them to make the correct choice. There is no more violence under Nafid's leadership because they have run out of reasons to kill each other."

"This is not the first time this has been tried!" said Amelius as he entered the conversation. "The Pharaoh Akhenaten, who ruled Egypt in the fourteenth century BCE, did very much what you are attempting now. It turned out badly for all concerned, even though, at first, his methods succeeded."

Nasrum clairvoyantly searched the Akashic records. Humanity's historians placed Akhenaten in the 18th dynasty and noted that he was King Tut's father. The Akashic records confirmed that Amelius was correct that there was much more to this man's story. He had ordered everyone to worship the one true god he believed in. His edicts brought great prosperity to the land until he died. Then his entire kingdom returned to the dismal shape it was in when he first came to power.

Amelius softened his voice and said, "You can't force people to cooperate and expect it to last forever. Eventually, their true nature comes out. You will be unable to stop the coming disaster your edicts have created. At one point, I too had to learn this lesson. Once you have mastered patience, you will understand this."

Nasrum spat back, "You say I force them to choose what I want. I say that my methods simply make for easier choices. In 1,000 years, we shall see who was right."

***

Eighteen years after her visit to Florida, Qadi Diana Amal had made a name for herself as a revered judge of sharia law. She held court in a small province outside of Damascus. She had found peace and contentment in her own studies of the Koran. For nearly two decades, she had studied the various sects of Islam, including Sufis, Sunnis, Shiites, Druze and Alawis. While she kept her personal beliefs strictly private, her interpretation of sharia law was so logical and fair that she was highly favored by all. However, even with Prince Nafid's relaxed rules, she had risen as high within the ranks of the Islam hierarchy as a woman was allowed to go.

Her frustration at having hit the proverbial 'glass ceiling' was interfering with her inner peace. She had the same feelings of betrayal and unfair treatment as she felt when the U.S. Navy had mandated her early retirement. While she would not be forced out of her current job, her ability to rise further within the ranks of Islam was over.

She was disappointed with their misogyny and wanted to resign in protest. Then she sadly realized that move could backfire if she became the poster child for why women should not have important roles within the Islamic order. She decided to pray, as she often did, before making such an important decision.

As she sat in the silence, she felt the presence of Gabriel, the messenger of Allah who was said to have dictated the Koran to Mohammed. She often felt Gabriel's loving presence when she prayed, but this experience was stronger, more intense, than she could ever remember. She felt like her body was swaying from side to side but she opened her eyes and saw that she was sitting perfectly still. She closed her eyes again and continued to pray for guidance.

"Diana, my child," a reassuring voice said in her mind, "be not afraid, it is I."

She opened her eyes to a radiant light. As her vision adjusted to the brilliance, she saw a magnificent looking man smiling at her. She knew at once it was Gabriel. A moment later she realized that they were not alone. Two other luminous beings were standing alongside him.

He said, "Diana, I'd like to introduce you to Amelius and Halaliel."

"It is truly great to meet you, Diana!" they both responded. Then Amelius added, "In a little while, you will remember that we've met before. It is difficult to plug into old memories until you adjust to a higher consciousness."

Gabriel answered her first question before she could ask it. "We have heard your prayer and came to discuss your options."

Diana smiled with the comfort that she was talking to the right people. "It is because of Islam that I have learned to love Allah and His children," she began. "I still want to serve but I feel hindered in my own spiritual growth. Is it possible for me to be of greater service to others outside of the Islamic faith?"

537

Gabriel didn't hesitate. "The answer to your question is yes."

Halaliel added, "Not only yes, that it is possible, but also that it is time for you to return to your family in Florida for the next steps on your path."

"As much as I'd like to see Grandpa again," Diana brightened, "how will I know what I should be doing? Do they need my help on their fishing boat? Is there something I'm missing, an opportunity where I can be of service to humanity?"

Amelius answered her, "Your time apart from them has been a period of great growth and reflection for you. The things that you've learned through Islam are to be shared with Gus, Jason and the men from Jason's past."

"Will they finally get to see the Hall of Records?" Diana asked with growing excitement.

Gabriel said, "Not right away. There are still some challenges for Jason and his friends to smooth out and you will help them do this. For the next couple of years be sure to enjoy your time with them! Life is never supposed to be all work and no play."

Jason drove up to the security gate at JPL and pushed the call button. He waited a minute and pushed it again. Still nothing happened so he called Mark on his cell phone. It went to voicemail so he tried Nuri's phone. He was about to hang up when Nuri finally answered.

"Hi Jason!" Nuri said, a little out of breath. "I'll bet you're having trouble getting into the complex."

"I tried the call button and Mark's cell. Was I supposed to do something else?"

"No," Nuri sighed. "The call button hasn't worked for a while now. Since no one comes here anymore who doesn't have a key, we haven't bothered to fix it. Mark's cell phone is probably buried someplace. Most of his calls go to voicemail before he can answer them. Hold on, I'll drive out to the gate and let you in."

"Don't bother," Jason said smiling. "I've still got my keys. I did want to let you know that I've brought a friend along."

Jason hung up before Nuri could say anything else.

A few minutes later, Jason and Diana walked into the common area where Mark and Nuri were waiting. It was good to see them looking well after all these years. Jason made the introductions and explained that Diana was Gus' granddaughter. They were both polite in their greeting, but Jason could tell they thought it was inappropriate that he brought her to this gathering. This reunion was meant to celebrate Matt Alexander's life on the tenth anniversary of his death. How could she understand what they had experienced and accomplished together and how close they had been?

"Diana knows everything about us, by the way. She's been a great help to me and Gus. After she figured out who I was and my connection to the two of you, she kept asking questions about our past adventures. At my age, reminiscing about our exploits is my best source of entertainment. Anyway, I want you to know that she is one of us!"

They visibly relaxed. Diana added enthusiastically, "I can't tell you what an honor it is to meet you both. I grew up hearing amazing stories about what all of you did together. Now I'll have faces and personalities to complete the picture. I know what a loss it was for you, and for the world, when President Alexander passed away."

The archeologists sadly nodded in agreement. To lighten the mood, Jason opened the paper bag he'd brought and pulled out a 6-pack of beer. He twisted the tops off of four of them and passed them around for a toast.

"To Matt Alexander!" Jason announced solemnly as he raised his bottle. "There will never be another one like him!" They all clinked their bottlenecks at once and drank together. They were silent for a while as each man reflected on their memories of Matt. Even Diana felt as if she knew him personally from all that Jason had told her about him.

"So, Diana," Mark began. "Tell us about yourself."

"There's not much to tell, anymore," she said sadly. "I was one of the first women to make it through Navy SEAL training to graduation. I thought I'd spend a career as a SEAL. Technically, I guess I did. After ten short years, the government decided they didn't need more than a token military and RIF'd, that's a reduction in forces, out almost everyone over 30 years old. I stayed in the Middle East and trained to be a Muslim cleric. It was only recently that I came home to work with Grandpa and Jason."

Jason asked, "What about you two? Have you made any progress with RF levitation?"

"Yes and no," Nuri replied.

"We can make things disappear and reappear," Mark added, "but we haven't, as yet, been able to move them."

"Are you getting any help from the guys in the vapors?" Jason asked with a laugh.

"None at all," Mark sighed. "Amelius was getting tired of my visits asking for his help. He kept reminding me that it is our negative attitudes that are in the way. Otherwise, we would remember everything we need to know to succeed. The way things are in the world, I haven't tried to contact him in quite a while."

Diana asked, "Maybe you could meditate with those crystals while Jason is here?"

Nuri said, "You really did tell her everything!"

"I told you I had," Jason said unapologetically. "I'm all about full disclosure, you know that!" he added with another laugh.

Mark said, "I'm willing if you two are?"

Nuri and Jason just nodded.

"Do you mind if I stick around and watch what happens?" Diana asked hopefully.

Jason answered for them, "Sure. But I'm afraid you'll just see three old men falling asleep. After a few more beers, I could manage that without meditating at all!"

"You've become quite the comedian since you decided to live on a boat!" Nuri smirked. He then pulled a tissue out of his pocket. He unfolded it to reveal three RF crystals. Jason smiled and pulled out one of his own.

"So you two had this planned all along?" Mark asked.

Jason answered, "I don't know about Nuri, but this is my lucky crystal. I always have it with me. It's the one I was holding when I was transported from the pyramid in Guatemala to Pasadena.

Nuri responded, "I wasn't thinking about Amelius at all. I assumed we'd try to connect with Matt. It would be good to see him again, even if it's not in the flesh."

They each held a crystal and sat back in their chairs. They closed their eyes and silence quickly filled the room. Diana, remembering her own encounter with Gabriel, Amelius and Halaliel, wished she could have gone with them.

***

"Hi, guys!" came a familiar voice in their minds. Mark, Nuri and Jason looked around and found themselves still sitting in the common area of JPL. Matthew Alexander now sat where Diana had been. The four men jumped up and happily greeted each other before settling back into their chairs.

Nuri asked Matt, "We're glad to see you, but why are we meeting here instead of someplace else?"

"Your combined intention to invite me along for this reunion was your main focus when you sent out the call," Matt explained. "The reason we're still at JPL is because of Diana. Her connection to Jason and her desire to be a part of this group kept us metaphorically tethered to her."

Mark said, "I'll take your word for all that. I'm pretty sure you already know what we've been up to. What about you? I've always wondered, what happens when you die?"

"Well that didn't take long," Matt chuckled with his familiar sense of humor. "I could spend years describing what happens. The quick answer is that you experience something like a life review rather than a Last Judgment. You see every moment of the human life you just finished, much like the detailed holographic movies the Atlantean crystals display. Without condemnation from anyone, you see all the choices you made from an unbiased perspective."

Jason said, "That can't be easy. We've all done things that we wish we'd done differently. I know I have."

541

"You're right that it's a tough experience," Matt agreed, "but mostly for a different reason. I was shown all the opportunities that were available to me on earth and how much better the world could have been if I simply acted on them. It is the sins of omission rather than the ones we committed that bother us the most."

Nuri asked, "Is that life review process all you've been doing for the last ten years?"

"No...," Matt started, but changed track. "Time is not measured here like it is on earth. Remember that I analyzed every moment of my eighty-four years during the life review. If you have only lived ten years since I was Matt Alexander on earth, we are obviously living on different time lines. After the life review, I was given the choice of what to work on next.

I have been learning all about patience and how to draw the best out of myself and others since then. At the right time on earth, I'll have a chance to reincarnate into a new body where the best conditions will exist to help me see the cause and effect of my choices. Because of linear time, three dimensions is a great way to connect the choices we make with what happens to us as a result."

The ethereal atmosphere within the group shifted subtly as Amelius and Halaliel entered the room. Had the two of them been in actual human form, the incredible radiance from them would have been blinding. Still, there was no denying how magnificent they were.

"You're here!" Matt said as he stood up. "Thank you for allowing us to catch up before getting down to business."

"But, of course," Amelius smiled in return. "It is good to see old friends reunited."

"The time has come to discuss the Bimini Hall of Records," Halaliel said flatly. "The world, as you say on earth, is about to come apart at the seams."

"Seriously?" Nuri gasped. "How can that be? There is peace and prosperity everywhere you look."

"It may appear that way at the moment," Amelius explained, "but let me ask, how happy have you been since these changes began thirty years ago?"

542

"I haven't been happy at all," Mark answered honestly. "I feel like I've wasted so much time sitting on the sidelines waiting to be needed again."

Jason added, "I've done my best to be ready, but what can we do to help at this point in our lives? I'm nowhere near the shape I was in back in my Delta Force days."

Halaliel said, "We have searched for others who could accomplish what humanity needs at this time. The three of you are still humanity's best chance to endure. To be sure, Diana Amal is a great addition to your team. It is no accident that she has joined your group at this critical juncture."

Jason asked, "So a 50-something woman helping a few 70-something men is your preferred team to save the world? Granted, Diana is pretty special, but I think you really have a lot more confidence in us than we probably deserve."

Amelius smiled again and said, "In the Atlantean era, a process was developed that could reverse aging. Your folklore called this the Fountain of Youth, though it works through vibrations far more than with water. Near the Bimini Hall of Records, there is a chamber they used for that purpose called the Temple Beautiful. Think of it as a rejuvenation spa. If you spend a few months there working through the process, your physical bodies will be reset to the optimum condition they were in when you were all in your twenties."

Mark was simultaneously excited and miffed. "Why didn't you tell us before that you could do that? I've been disappointed for decades now believing that this opportunity had passed us by."

"Do you not yet see the value in learning patience and strengthening your faith?" Halaliel asked, obviously perplexed. "In the waiting you had the opportunity to learn many lessons. Patience is just one of them. Faith that our Creator always has matters well in hand is another. Fellowship and cooperation were needed for you to willingly accept your changing roles to help as you could in bringing about a propitious future for humanity."

They each reflected on what Halaliel had said, trying to gage how far they had or hadn't come. Then Nuri asked, "What is about to happen that will ruin the existing peace?"

543

Amelius responded calmly, "We will answer all your questions once you begin the Temple Beautiful process. For now, it is time for you to return to three dimensions. It would be rude to keep Diana waiting any longer."

As the scene faded, all three of them heard, "Now you will remember what you need to perfect RF levitation. You must do so before returning to Bimini. Even from our eternal perspective, you have no time to lose!

Chapter 9

The morning papers' headlines said it all: "Prince Nafid Dead!" Nasrum knew that his perfect plan to save humanity had just died along with him. During Alkrim al-Assad's interrogation, the usurped heir confessed to the Syrian secret service that he hadn't planned to assassinate the prince. It was an unexpected kneejerk reaction of rage. After all, Nafid had stolen Alkrim's rightful place as president of Syria. He was also certain that, despite a lack of proof, the prince was responsible for his father's death. These terrible accusations flashed through Alkrim's mind at the same moment Prince Nafid offered his condolences during a formal state dinner. The al-Assad heir said he felt more like a witness to the surreal stabbing. It was the steak knife in his hand that killed the prince in payment for the murder of his father.

Nasrum had done what he could to guard Nafid's life. There were far more likely and talented assassins in the world than Alkrim al-Assad. As he calculated the odds, the son of the deceased president didn't have the mind set required to commit murder. Instead, Nasrum focused his attention on possible sniper, poisoning, or bombing attempts. None of his planning made any difference. The prince was still dead.

While time has little meaning in most ethereal realms, less than a second elapsed on Earth between Alkrim's uncontrollable fury and actually plunging the knife into Nafid's heart. The earthly rules of time and space would only allow Nasrum to intervene after the choice had been made, not before.

He analyzed the scene looking for any solution to prevent the mortal wound. Alkrim was sitting to Nafid's immediate left. The steak knife was already in his hand when his murderous intent materialized. Nasrum saw that the only viable option was to cause a massive earthquake to distract the deceased president's son. But causing an earthquake that was strong enough to keep the prince from being stabbed would also kill him when the building collapsed.

There was still a way to reverse the damage, but it broke rules that had severe consequences. Nasrum decided it was worth the risk. He tried to circumvent al-Assad's free will by warning the prince to stay away from the late president's son using any means necessary. That was when he discovered that the angels had seen this coming and blocked him from starting over by creating a new timeline.

What a repeating pattern this had become in Nasrum's life. His perfect plans were constantly being derailed by idiots like Alkrim and the jealous interference of ethereal beings. He couldn't let his chance at greatness slip away because of their treachery. Nasrum vowed he would create a new path to get the world, his world, back on track.

***

Nafid felt like he was barely awake. His thoughts reviewed the same dream over and over again. He wondered why it kept repeating like that. It took a while, but Nafid began to remember what happened. He had been stabbed. He opened his eyes expecting to find himself in the hospital recovering from the attack. When his vision focused, he did indeed see a hospital room with a kindly doctor standing over him.

"How are you feeling?" The doctor asked with a smile.

"I'm not in pain, but I am disoriented," Nafid managed to say. "How bad is it? Am I going to live?"

The doctor laughed and said, "Absolutely. You have suffered no permanent damage." Then he changed the subject, "Have you been paying attention to the dream that keeps repeating when you close your eyes?"

"Not really," Nafid admitted. "It all seemed too familiar, almost boring."

The doctor laughed again. "I can tell you that when you are ready to study that dream in detail, it will not be boring."

"Why is that?" Nafid asked, out of politeness more than curiosity.

"You will eventually remember that the ongoing dream is of the life you just lived on earth." the doctor said calmly.

Nafid was suddenly wide awake and panicked. "So I'm dead? I thought you said the damage wasn't permanent! You're not a real doctor?"

The man in the white coat explained gently, "I am here to help and answer your questions. This place and how I appear are guided by your thoughts. You said yourself that you're not in any pain. The soul is eternal and cannot be irreparably harmed. That's true no matter what you believed on the earth."

Nafid began to relax a bit recognizing that the worst must be over now. He said, "Is my Rayiys able to reach me here? I'm scared he may still have power over me even now."

"Your Rayiys, whose name is Nasrum, is hardly your master. He has moved on, and so should you," the doctor said barely hiding his disdain for Nafid's mentor.

Nafid was relieved to be free of Rayiys. "So what am I supposed to do with this dream?"

"Once you are ready," the doctor began, "the dream will slow down to the point where you will experience every moment, every nuance, and every repercussion of the choices you made on the earth. You will be shown those outcomes to encourage you to make better choices in the future."

"I'm not sure what you mean," Nafid said truly perplexed.

"Here's a good example," the doctor said pointing to the large TV screen that showed Nafid trying automatic writing when he first made contact with his Rayiys. "You know how using automatic writing turned out in your life just passed. But here is the life you would still be living had you returned to Damascus without contacting Nasrum."

The scene now showed him meeting a wonderful woman and settling down to a happy life with children. While this scenario did not have him enjoying the heights of fame and fortune he had just experienced, he could see that he would have been happier in the mundane life with his loving family. His realization of what was truly important on earth was difficult to recognize when he was in human form. The Life Review allowed him to learn from every one of his loving and selfish choices. The scenes continued to show him the truth behind every moment he lived including his assassination.

"Okay, I get the point," he said to the doctor. "I don't need to see any more."

"Actually," the doctor began, "the best part is yet to come. What you have seen so far are the choices you made and how you might have made better ones. What you will observe now are the opportunities that you missed or ignored in the life just passed. This is often the more enlightening experience."

As the doctor had said, Nafid began to view the opportunities that had been planned for him before being born in Damascus. He had held such high hopes for making the most out of those occasions. He then saw how he had ignored or deliberately chose not to act on most of them. Nafid also saw all the good that never occurred in his life, or the lives of others, because he chose not to act as he had originally planned.

Nafid could only feel guilt and shame when he realized how far he had strayed from the wonderful life he had hoped to live. He had made the goals of humanity his higher priority. It was easy to do because his friends and family all wanted fame and fortune more than love and joy. How could he have thought that was right? And then he realized that this was not the first time he had been through this Life Review experience. He had felt this same disappointment before. He had lived many other lifetimes in which he made selfish choices instead of trying to be of service to others.

"How can I make sure this doesn't happen again?" Nafid asked.

"Don't be so hard on yourself," the doctor said reassuringly. "You barely acknowledged the good you achieved in that life. In many ways, you showed a lot of potential for making better choices the next time around."

"So I'm going to get another chance?" Nafid asked hopefully.

"Yes, without question you will get another chance," the doctor said. "I will guide you now to your next stop. Think of it as a school to review the lessons you will be tested on in your next human life. When you're ready to try again, you'll be back on earth in another body before you know it."

***

The news of Prince Nafid's assassination had shocked the world. Nafid had never missed in his predictions. He had been able to circumvent terrorist threats and violent crimes alike. How could one man stab him without the prince knowing it was coming?

While the citizens of the planet debated that question, the secular and Koranic laws of the land were being tested to their limits. Prince Nafid had no direct heirs, nor had he drawn up a last will and testament. He had run his empire with little delegation, which meant the peaceful order of the world was about to implode. Without the prince's forceful and guiding hand, the unencumbered will of humanity was free to express itself again.

The largely ceremonial puppet governments of the world were quick to act on their newfound independence. They each claimed their sovereign rights and passed immediate protectionist laws to grab hold of as much wealth and power as they could during the initial chaos. They wasted no time re-creating their military might by employing their 3-D printers 24/7. The dreaded tools of death that most of humanity had forgotten were each country's highest priority.

The mosques around the world initially filled with faithful Muslims praying for peace and guidance. It didn't take long for them to empty out again when news of threats from neighboring countries convinced them to set aside their peaceful ways. Even the government officials were amazed at how many of their countrymen were ready to go to war to reestablish their time-honored way of life. Every sovereign nation embraced their historic culture. Their clothing, their holidays, their heroes and even their old religions returned faster than they had left. It seemed as if the people preferred their unique identities over global peace and prosperity.

All of the dirty secrets of Prince Nafid's reign were progressively exposed by the international media. Alarming statistics revealed the number of people who were not as happy with Prince Nafid's control as the news outlets had been urged to portray. They had missed having meaningful goals to pursue. Most people had not coped well with early retirement when they were still in the prime of their lives. Some turned to food, others to drugs or drink to fill the void, and others still looked to Islam since it at least offered a hierarchy to ascend. One of the scariest statistics of all was the suicide rate. It had climbed 1,000 percent since Prince Nafid first won the lottery that brought him to the public's eye. That percentage would have been worse if it had included all the deaths attributed to high-risk sports that people had taken up to add excitement to their lives.

It was clear that humanity would say they wanted to live 'the good life,' but people needed more. They wanted to be tested to see where they stood and what they could accomplish. Overcoming challenges and hardships was far more satisfying than simply living peacefully through each day. The speed with which immense political and cultural changes took place since the death of the prince proved that humanity's desires had been repressed rather than evolved.

The world's governments jockeyed for position now that Prince Nafid was gone. The stakes were high enough to justify extreme measures to get their fair share of the pie. If they couldn't come up with a diplomatic solution, and few thought that was possible, a world war seemed inevitable.

***

Mark and Nuri were explaining to Eljay the small but critical steps they had missed in developing RF levitation (RFL). Mark began, "We weren't paying attention to what was required to isolate the molecules we wanted to relocate. A quick description is that we needed a box around the box containing what we wanted to move. The outer box needs to be made up of a vibrational field that is slightly detuned from the inner box's Fibonacci frequency. This outer invisible field, when touched, feels like a soft cushion that completely covers whatever we want to seemingly levitate."

Eljay asked, "How does the outer containment field work?"

Nuri answered, "It adds a second box surrounding the first one. The two vibrational frequencies are close together but not mathematically or musically related. If they were keys on a piano, they would sound horrible when played together. The competing frequencies create a sort of partition that can be gently handled and moved."

"What would happen if you punched the containment field with your fist?" Eljay asked.

Nuri continued, "As I understand this technology, throwing a punch from the outside moving in, nothing would happen. The containment field and its contents would allow the outside molecules to pass right through or around it, depending on the density of what's outside. Air would probably flow around the field whereas solids would seem to pass through it. We don't know what would happen with liquids. They could go either way depending on the detuning of the outer containment field. A punch coming from the inside out would affect only the molecules leaving the protective field. The inside molecules that move outside of the field would immediately become subject to our earth's laws of physics."

Mark added, "Before you ask, we believe it's possible to insert an object or a person into the containment field by holding a crystal tuned to the field's resonant frequency. The crystal would allow the person to move effortlessly through the containment field in either direction."

"One other thing," said Nuri. "If you try to use a flashlight that is inside the field to light up whatever is outside of it, it won't work. There aren't enough photons passing through the containment wall and back to see with the human eye. But a flashlight turned on outside of the field would work to light the surrounding area for those who are inside the field looking out."

Eljay looked puzzled. "So you're saying we were unsuccessful before because we were trying to move the object without the second or outer field. It was like trying to grab onto a hologram. Creating a second vibrational box, one that is detuned to the object to be moved, creates a partition you can touch to relocate the object?"

"You've got it," Nuri said as he snapped his fingers. "We believe that this method will work if a light touch is used to handle the outer box. To an outside observer, it might look like a mime carrying an invisible object. However, when we stop all the RF vibrations, the object will appear in the new location."

"So levitation is like a mime picking up an invisible box? You guys really are nerds!" They had forgotten that Jason was in the room with them because he usually avoided these types of conversations. He walked over to the table and set his beer bottle down in front of their RFL machines. "Let's try it with this," he said with a laugh.

Mark and Nuri just shrugged and nodded. Nuri positioned the second RF machine they had designed next to the one Mark was already adjusting. They made sure they had them tuned correctly and warned Jason not to get between the machines and the bottle. When he jumped back suddenly, they started laughing. Through their snorts, they confessed that he was in no danger since the containment field was not created by a beam directed from the RF device. He failed to see the humor and was a little embarrassed.

Jason frowned and stayed out of the way. Mark felt bad and said, "This technology is not dangerous, you'll see."

He and Nuri pressed the corresponding buttons on their RF machines and a second later the bottle disappeared. Nuri walked over and, as predicted, looked like a mime picking up an invisible box. He turned and walked over to Jason and appeared to set the box on a nearby table. Mark pushed both RF off buttons together, and the bottle suddenly appeared on the other table. He told Jason to go ahead and see if the beer tasted the same.

Jason liked his beer, but he was hesitant to try this one. He slowly reached for the bottle and stared at it as he inspected the glass for flaws. Then he shrugged and took a drink. A moment later he doubled over and fell to the ground. He shook violently as he curled up in the fetal position. Eljay rushed over to help only to find that Jason was laughing, not shaking. He sat up, still smiling, and burped enthusiastically.

"Yep, that's still good beer," Jason announced proudly. "And that, my friends, is payback."

Mark yelled, "That wasn't funny, dammit. I really thought you were in trouble."

Nuri had recovered from the prank and reluctantly said, "I'm pretty sure it was funny, just not to us, at least, not today."

Jason added, "Wasn't it Amelius who said 'If you can laugh at something, you can heal from it.'? I'm sure you'll thank me later for providing this opportunity to exercise patience and improve your sense of humor."

Mark said, "I doubt Amelius would appreciate your interpretation of his teachings."

Nuri wisely changed the subject. "Speaking of Amelius, didn't he tell us to get down to Bimini as soon as possible? Jason, can you let Gus know we're coming so he can get the boat ready?"

***

While Nasrum had trouble tuning in to the thoughts and words of the archeologists, the ex-soldier, Jason, was easier to read. Listening in on Jason's thoughts was similar to hearing only one side of a conference call, but that was enough to know that the Americans were up to no good. Nasrum could see enough of Jason's possible future paths to guess what they were planning.

What little Nasrum could piece together of their potential futures was disturbing. He already knew that wars were imminent and the perfect worldwide utopia he had created would soon collapse. The best chance to restore global peace still relied on his finding the elusive Bimini Hall of Records. He would be damned if he was going to let Amelius' lackeys find it first. He needed to stop them cold to set things right again.

Nasrum took a moment to curse Ariel and Halaliel for not allowing him to reincarnate back into the earth. If he had been born thirty years ago, he could easily lead the world out of this crisis. The secrets of Atlantis were all he would need. He was certain he could have found the hidden chamber if the angels had not stood in his way.

Even if he could find another willing human puppet, it was futile to try to win the people back using Islam to attain peace and prosperity. While those objectives would be his ultimate goal, he would have to regain control of world affairs in another way. He needed to incarnate back into human form without kicking a soul out of its body, but he had a much bigger immediate problem. Stopping the Americans from finding the Bimini Hall of Records had to be his highest priority.

Chapter 10

Gus looked like an ancient mariner behind the wheel of his boat. He was surprisingly healthy for his advanced age and still very clear of mind. His beard was a little scruffy, but that just added to his charm. Mark, Nuri, Jason and Diana enjoyed the beautiful sunny skies and ocean spray as they navigated toward Bimini. Diana asked if anyone else appreciated the irony that they were heading into the mysterious Bermuda Triangle to find the Hall of Records. Mark and Nuri didn't believe in such nonsense and Jason gestured to let it go.

It had been a long time since anyone had tracked their movements, but it began to look like they were being followed. An American naval destroyer was matching the Guppy's course and speed. If they had thought about it, the ship's presence was not a surprise. In the days since the prince had been killed, the sovereign nations declared their independence. Each government's priorities simply picked up where they had left off decades ago. One of those priorities had been finding the Hall of Records by tracking the movements of Mark, Nuri and Jason.

Gus yelled to be heard over the noise of the engines. "I've made sure they don't know where we're headed by taking an erratic course, but there's no way we can lose them. They are faster than us and could blow us out of the water from miles away."

Jason squinted into the sun as he tried to think of a way to lose their stalkers. Gus' mention of weapons almost made him laugh. They didn't have any way to defend themselves, unless you counted the flare gun.

As if she could read his mind, Diana jokingly offered, "I have my spear gun on board! I'm just kidding, but it's in the dinghy if you need it."

Mark laughed mischievously, "I don't think the spear gun will scare them off, but I have an idea. Why don't we use RFL to discourage them?" He had developed a quirky sense of humor over the years that irritated Nuri.

"I can't wait to hear this!" Jason smiled.

Mark answered, "I don't believe there is a size limitation of the containment area the RFL machine can create. So how much would that ship slow down if it instantly took on a million gallons of sea water?"

"The shock value alone would work," Jason said excitedly. "Can we control RFL even when the machines are moving instead of sitting still like we tested at JPL?"

Nuri was beginning to see the possibilities. "I think they can. Containment fields should invisibly hold and relocate any amount of ocean water until we hit the off button."

Mark added, "We could manually lift the invisible box of salt water out of the ocean and gently push it toward the ship. At the right moment, we turn off the containment field and the water rematerializes."

"What happens if we don't turn the RFL machines off?" Jason asked.

"I'm still guessing here," Mark said thoughtfully, "but the invisible box would probably continue to float along at the same speed and trajectory it was travelling when you let go."

Jason asked, "So there is no limit to how far I can throw a million gallons of water?"

"Remember, it's not a matter of wind resistance or weight," Nuri said. "Think of throwing a ball in space. Without any other forces to slow or alter its course, the ball would move in the same direction forever."

Jason had thought of a plan, but he wanted to make sure. "So let's say I am holding the invisible box and I squat down before extending my body and arms fully. If I stand up at a rate of say ten feet per second, the box would continue to move in the same direction and speed after I let it go?"

Mark said, "I'm pretty sure that's what would happen, but we don't have time to test it!"

"Well, I say let's battle test it right now," Jason suggested with a grin. "Gus, break out the dinghy. Mark, can you hand out a few of those RFC earbuds? We need to stay in touch while I go have a talk with those sailors."

***

"Captain!" an ensign on the bridge called out. "The target vessel has stopped, sir."

The radio crackled with a report from the ensign stationed at the bow of the ship. "Sir, the target has launched a dinghy and it's headed our way."

The ship's captain said, "All stop. Let's see what they have to say to us."

Jason remained seated as the dinghy approached the huge destroyer. He stopped far enough away so he could still see the uniformed man watching him with binoculars from the ship's bow.

"I need to speak to the captain of this ship," Jason requested calmly, but he still had to yell to be heard. "I know he's probably in the ship's command center. Please ask him to come on down and talk with me when he gets a chance. I'm in no hurry."

After a moment, the ensign at the bow answered, his voice sounding a bit mechanical through the bull horn, "He says you can tell me whatever you have to say to him and I'll relay it." The ensign appeared to be in his early twenties and uncertain that he was qualified to act as the communications relay person for this awkward conversation.

"Well, I think it's rude that your captain would keep following us but not come out and properly introduce himself," Jason said.

"The captain says he has no intention of harming your boat. He says you should get to where you're going so we can all finish what we came here to do."

"But I came over here to convince you not to follow us!" Jason insisted. "The captain needs to turn this ship around now."

The ensign laughed condescendingly. "You are threatening a destroyer class ship while you're sitting in a dinghy with a small fishing boat as your support? Do you really want me to pass your message on to the captain? I can tell you it will not be well received."

"Yes, tell him exactly that and add that there is a penalty for rudeness. Now I'm only giving him five minutes to talk to me in person," Jason confirmed.

Nearly a minute passed before the ensign responded, "The captain says – and I quote - his orders are to track you. He doesn't want to hurt you or your boat, but he's damn sure not going to take any more crap from you. He says you have five seconds to turn around and get back to your boat or he'll flip your dinghy over with our wake."

"Well, all right, ensign," Jason said as he stood up and awkwardly raised his hands over his head like he was being arrested. "Be sure to remind him I tried to be friendly!"

Jason turned to start the dinghy's motor. Knowing Mark and Nuri could hear him through the RFC earbud, Jason kept his voice low. "At the rate I let the box go, I would say to rematerialize it in 3, 2, 1, now!"

Suddenly, a giant block of ocean water appeared to be suspended around the command section of the ship. A moment later, the walls of the box dissolved and seawater cascaded over the forward decks and flowed back into the ocean. The volume of water nearly washed some of the nearby sailors overboard, but that was not the worst of it. The seawater surrounding the bridge and command sections of the ship also rematerialized inside the bulkheads. For a moment, the bridge looked like an aquarium with dozens of flopping fish showing through the windows. The ocean water poured out of the open doors quickly enough that no one drowned, but the entire bridge crew was out of action. As the seawater drained away, electrical sparks flickered randomly throughout the command center. Jason smiled knowing those electrical short circuits would stop the destroyer from going anywhere for a while. He hoped it would give them the head start they needed.

"What the hell did you just do to us?" the ensign yelled, forgetting the bull horn dangling at his side.

"You think I did that?" Jason yelled back with his best innocent expression. "There's no way you can blame it on me. I'm thinking this will go down in the ship's log as another unexplained

557

incident in the Bermuda Triangle. Let your captain know that I am complying with his order. I'm leaving now."

***

When Jason was back on board The Guppy with his friends, they wasted no time getting underway. Diana warned Gus to continue with his erratic course to their destination or the destroyer could project their heading and they'd be tracked again before they arrived at Bimini.

"It's no wonder that this Hall of Records has never been found," Diana said in amazement. "Who would have guessed the entrance was hidden in the face of a cliff that's 1,500 feet below the surface of the water? No one can scuba dive that low and you only have the one ADS suit. How do the three of you intend to get there?"

"Yeah, we're wondering the same thing," Nuri said with more than a little concern.

Jason interrupted, "Diana, it's time we tell you what we learned during the crystal meditation back at JPL. When we make this dive, we will be gone for a few months, but we're going to be fine. We will have the RFC earbuds with us and we can stay in touch with you so you'll know we're okay. We'll also let you know when we're ready to be picked up."

Diana didn't like this news one bit. "Why will you be gone so long?" she asked apprehensively.

Nuri answered her, "Suffice it to say that, as we are now, we are too old to handle the challenges that will come our way after we reveal the Bimini Hall of Records. We're about to undergo treatments that are supposed to restore our health and strength to what it once was at our prime."

"They have the fountain of youth down there?" she joked. She was unconvinced, but with all she had heard and seen of their past adventures, she tried to keep an open mind.

"Something like that," Jason laughed, but didn't elaborate. "The truth is that we've told you everything we know about what's going to happen. I hope we'll have a whole lot more to tell you in a few hours."

"Well it won't be long now," Gus yelled above the sound of the engine and the passing ocean waves. "We're about 10 minutes away from the GPS coordinates you gave me. You'd better get your gear on before the Navy catches up to us."

"We won't need any scuba gear, Gus," Mark said mysteriously. "We're taking the dinghy."

***

"Sir, we have reacquired the target," navigation reported to the captain.

"Set course to intercept and speed to 40 knots," he ordered.

"Aye-aye, sir," came the crew's confirmation.

"Time to intercept?" the captain asked.

"Sir, at 40 knots, we are less than 30 minutes to target."

"Helm, increase to best possible speed." The captain knew that would only bump them up 4 knots, but he was growing impatient. To have an old man in a dinghy disable his ship after calling him out was embarrassing and unforgivable.

***

Mark, Nuri and Jason boarded the dinghy floating behind The Guppy and began setting up the equipment. They had not yet tried controlling the RFL machines from inside a containment field, but with the destroyer only 20 minutes away, they had no time for experiments.

Jason fired off all the questions running through his mind, "Can we breathe inside the containment field? How do we steer it while we're inside? Will we be able to see both the active and passive dimensions? Will we be in suspended animation inside the containment field and maybe never wake up?"

Mark said, "In retrospect, we should have asked Amelius for the rest of the plan before we left. It's a little late to try meditating now. It looks like we'll have to make it up as we go."

"Everybody calm down!" Nuri chided. "I suggest we play this as safe as we can. We'll grab more than 1,500 feet of air above us as part of the containment field so that we create a big hole in the water. We'll still be connected to the air above us while we descend to the level of the Hall of Records' entrance. If we get into trouble, Gus and Diana can pull us back up right away."

Mark laughed to hide his nervousness. "Jason, you suck at not being in charge when danger is nearby. If this dive doesn't work and we have to confront the Navy ship again, you can call the shots. Until then, we've got this!"

"If you don't get us going right away, we may not get the chance at all," Jason complained. "I'm guessing that Navy captain is mad enough to be creative with his orders. I'll give you odds that he's already figured out how to 'accidently' ruin our day."

Mark stepped gingerly over the gunnels and gear to the second RFL machine and checked the settings. He nodded so that Nuri and he pushed the buttons simultaneously to activate the containment field. The seawater that was captured inside the field slapped gently against the invisible barrier, and then became calm. Nothing else changed from their perspective, but Gus and Diana gasped as the dinghy and the three men disappeared from view.

"God, I hope you're still with us!" Gus said shakily through their ear buds. "What do we do now?"

Mark answered him, "From the back of the boat, you should be able to reach out and feel the containment field's surface. We have it shaped so it will ease into the water like submerging a large test tube. Just lightly grab the sides where you feel it resist, and carefully push downward in a straight line. Remember to go slowly. If there are no problems, we can always have you increase our rate of descent."

Diana said, "OK, I'm doing it now."

She reached out until she felt something push back a little, almost like a cushion of air. She repositioned her hands as high as she could and slowly pulled her arms downward feeling the containment field move with her as she did. A cylindrical hole about twenty feet in diameter pushed through the surface of the ocean and started burrowing downward. They were looking at a hole in the water that didn't move. Despite the lapping waves around it, the hole remained fixed in the ocean.

"I wouldn't have believed it if I wasn't watching this right now," Gus stammered. "You guys just did the impossible. I don't go in for all those miracles in the Bible, but Moses could have parted the Red Sea like this."

"If you think it looks odd from up there, imagine what it looks like down here!" Jason said as they continued to dive deeper. "We have the sheer cliff face on one side of us and the entire Atlantic Ocean everywhere else, except overhead. There is sea life all around. None of it seems to pay any attention to us. It feels like we're diving at a rate of around five feet per second. That means we'll be at 1,500 feet in five minutes. Where's the destroyer right now?"

Gus answered, "It's hard to say, but I don't think you'll have time to locate the entrance before that ship gets here. When they do, they'll be able to see the hole in the water. I'd rather not try to explain that, even if I could."

Mark and Nuri kept an eye on the RFL machines. Monitoring the movement of the containment field also showed them their depth as they continued downward. Jason kept scanning the cliff face for any signs of the entrance Halaliel had shown them. It was very dark at this depth and getting worse.

They watched the amazing sights around them until they heard Gus say, "You've got about one minute to go before they'll be able to see the hole."

Mark looked at Nuri and said, "We've got enough air in this containment field to last for hours. We can close off the top so that the hole will disappear below the surface as we keep descending. But Gus and Diana won't be able to stop our descent once we reach the entrance. But I think I know a way that we can reverse course once we reach the ocean floor."

"Do it fast," Nuri urged him. "We have enough problems without adding the U.S. Navy to the list."

Mark adjusted his settings and said, "Gus! The hole should have just disappeared. Any chance I'm right?"

"Damned if you aren't!" he said. "It's like you were never there! Good thing, too. We're being hailed by the destroyer."

"Well, be sure and tell me how that goes the next time we talk," Mark laughed. "We've got to figure out how to get from inside this containment chamber, through crushing ocean water, and into a hole in a cliff face while we are still moving."

"Yeah, well we've got our own problems up here. Gotta go now," Gus quickly signed off.

***

The nervous ensign hated this assignment. He was sure that being the 'bearer of bad news' never ended well for the messenger. He took a deep breath and said, "The captain has agreed to meet with you in person. Everyone on your boat must come aboard."

Gus said, "There's only me and my granddaughter on board. The others aren't here." He pointed to the surface of the water implying they had gone for a dive.

The ensign sighed and radioed the news to the captain. After a brief pause he said, "The captain still wants you both on board...now!"

At that same moment, a cargo net with a platform bottom began lowering from the bow of the destroyer. Gus was able to position his boat under the net because the bow of the big ship jutted out far enough to avoid a collision with the hull. Gus and Diana carefully jumped onto the platform at the bottom of the net and carried a 200 foot rope that was secured to The Guppy. That way, when they arrived on the deck they could secure the relatively tiny vessel to the ship's bow to keep it from floating out of range. Gus knew the captain could order the destroyer to start moving and his boat would be smashed to pieces, so he was on his best behavior.

The ensign escorted Gus and Diana to a room near the bridge and asked them to wait there. A minute later the captain entered with his XO. He looked like a drill sergeant ready to berate some trainees.

"That little trick your man pulled damaged my ship and nearly drowned some of my crew," the captain bellowed without introduction. "What am I supposed to do with you two and your friends when they come up?"

562

"What is it that we did again?" Gus asked. "I don't remember any of our crew boarding your ship until now. How could we have done anything to anyone here?"

The captain had hoped for an admission that they were somehow responsible for the deluge of seawater that swamped his bridge and cleared his decks. He'd have to let that go now that the old guy hadn't slipped.

"How long are your friends planning on staying down there?" the captain asked.

"They didn't tell us," Diana answered, "but I don't believe you'll see them back today, tomorrow or the next day."

"Just how many people are down there?" the captain asked.

Gus laughed. "There are three of them. They intend to find what they're looking for and stay there a while. We'll see them again, I'm sure of it."

The captain hit the intercom button next to him and barked, "Start searching for three divers in the area. It's possible they are heading for the West Bimini Islands travelling underwater."

***

Jason was not happy. "Uh, we have a bigger problem than trying to stop at the cave entrance. You realize that unless Diana or Gus can slow down the containment field, which isn't above water anymore, we might just keep sinking until we eventually burrow through the core of the earth and pop out on the other side? And then what's to stop us from floating off into space forever?"

"If we do nothing," Nuri answered, "that's exactly what will happen to us."

"Well then, do you have a plan?" Jason asked more calmly than he felt.

"We do have a plan," Mark said cheerfully. "Find something sturdy that's made out of metal and jab it through the bottom of the containment field as we approach the ocean floor. When the exposed metal hits bottom, you push us back in the other direction."

"That sounds suspiciously like jumping at the last second if you're in a falling elevator," Jason scoffed. "I'd be trying to reverse the inertia of all the mass inside this containment field. No way this will work. You two are the scientists. You shouldn't need me to explain the laws of physics to you!"

"I should have known you weren't paying attention when we explained all this to Eljay," Mark scolded. "And yes, we are the scientists. That's why you need to listen to us. Assuming we're right, the only mass you will need to worry about is the amount that is poking outside of the containment field. Everything in here with us is not subject to the physical laws of the Earth's active dimension. Punching a metal rod through the containment field will expose a portion of it to about 600 times the pressure we feel on the surface, but that won't be a problem. At five feet per second, we'll arrive at the ocean floor in another 15 or 20 minutes. At the slow rate of speed, and the small amount of exposed mass, the inertial force you'll be pushing against won't amount to much."

"Did you think I didn't hear you start all that with, 'assuming we're right?'" Jason said gruffly.

"If you have a better plan, we need to hear it now," Nuri said with a wry smile.

Jason just growled and started looking around the dinghy for something metal to use to reverse their momentum. He found a fire extinguisher canister and held it up asking, "How about this?"

Mark and Nuri busted up laughing. "You have to be kidding!" Mark managed to say. "You know at 6,000 feet below sea level any part of that exposed canister would be crushed causing it to blow up like a bomb, right?"

"The only metal rods we have are the shafts for the spear gun," Jason balked.

Nuri nodded, "That should do it. Now look for something to hold in your hand to press against the end of it. You'll want to cushion the end of the shaft so it doesn't dig into your palm when you push."

Jason found an old cleat attached to a piece of wood. "I can hold onto the cleat and press the wood against the end of the shaft."

Mark said, "Great! Now all we have to do is wait."

Chapter 11

The progress of The Guppy's crew had Nasrum's full attention. He had to admit that the old men were quite resourceful when it came to working with a technology they barely understood. If they did somehow manage to access the Hall of Records, his plans to regain control of the world would be ruined.

He was fully aware that he should not directly interfere with events on earth, unless he was invited. The penalties were harsh for those who thought they could get away with it. He had been heavy-handed in his guidance to Nafid, but the prince had consciously asked for his help and counsel from the start. Nasrum began to consider his options. Would anyone notice a minor interference, if it was truly necessary? He laughed at his own musings. Of course, they would notice! The real question was whether or not he was willing to deal with the consequences?

When the presence of the Navy ship forced the three friends to the ocean floor, Nasrum let out an ethereal sigh of relief. Then came a game changer. Nasrum recognized the opening in the cliff face to the Hall of Records as he watched the humans drift downward without seeing it. He thanked Allah for rewarding his patience. He started thinking of ways to access and use the chamber's secrets to, once again, take control of the world. His joy was short-lived.

The troublesome humans somehow managed to reverse their course and were headed back up toward the fabled chamber. These stubborn people did not know when to give up. Now that he knew where the Hall of Records was located, he had to stop them at any cost.

Nasrum could see that they still had to stop their ascent without shooting past the tunnel opening. He thought of a very subtle trick that would send them back up to the surface empty handed. The U.S. Navy would make sure they never found the chamber after that. Nasrum's choice to break the cardinal rule against directly interfering with a human's free will was an easy one.

If he didn't, his dreams and efforts for the past 12,000 years would be wasted. What could possibly be more important than that?

***

Jason was surprised that reversing their direction had been that easy. They were now slowly rising from the ocean bottom, but the second phase of the plan promised to be far more difficult.

"When we ascend to the 1,500 foot level," Nuri cautioned, "you'll need to jab the metal spear through the side of the containment field and hold us steady by anchoring it to the face of the cliff."

Jason asked, "Oh, is that all? Won't it be hard to stop us in place, or does that work the same way as when I reversed our course?"

"We'll feel a jolt like before, but you'll be able to stop our momentum," Mark assured him. "The hard part will be stopping us at the right moment to see the entry point in the cliff face. We obviously missed it on the way down."

Nuri said, "We're coming up on 1,500 feet now. Get ready!"

Jason stood with the spear poised and was just about to thrust it through the containment wall when a loud piercing screech dropped all three men to their knees in the small boat. It took them a moment to figure out that the noise was coming from their RFC earbuds. Something caused a feedback loop like when a microphone gets too close to a loudspeaker.

By the time they managed to remove their earbuds, several seconds had passed and so had the 1,500 foot mark.

"Now what do we do?" Jason asked in frustration.

"When we get to the surface," Nuri theorized, "we can switch off the RFL machines. That will probably dump us in the water, but even if the dinghy sinks, we should be able to swim to The Guppy."

"Yes," Mark added, "but if the dinghy sinks, then the RFL units will go back down to the ocean floor. We don't have replacements. You know that captain you embarrassed will probably detain us when we surface. If the Navy ever lets us go again, we will still have to go back to JPL to replace the equipment."

Jason chanced putting the earbud back in to see if he could raise Gus or Diana. Instead of his friends, he heard a familiar and reassuring voice. "Jason, there is no time to explain other than to say that you cannot come to the surface. I will intervene to reset your timeline to the intended course."

"Amelius?" Jason asked perplexed. He gestured toward his earbud so Mark and Nuri understood what was happening. "We can sure use your help. What do we have to do?"

"I will return you to the exact time and place before your earpieces malfunctioned. Simply carry out your original plan," Amelius said to all three after they had reinserted their earbuds.

"Is reversing time even possible?" Jason asked incredulously.

"I have protected you through the valley of death. I have sustained you in the presence of your enemies. Why would you doubt that I will lead you to the still waters? Continue with your original plan and have faith that you will succeed."

The next moment Jason found himself holding the spear ready to jam it into the cliff face. Nuri yelled, "Do it!" Jason couldn't explain why, but he waited. A breath later he heard Amelius say, "Now!"

He thrust the spear through the containment field and buried the point securely into the face of the cliff. The sudden stop almost knocked them down, but they managed to stay on their feet. Jason discovered he was able to release his hold on the spear and the dinghy remained in place. As the three of them looked around, Mark and Nuri realized their situation had gone from bad to worse.

They weren't moving and they could see nothing that looked like an entrance. The cliff face was barely visible because almost no sunlight could reach this far down. How would they get back to the surface? How soon would they run out of air? Mark's imagination began to conjure images of Jules Vern's giant squid. Nuri felt queasy with all the adrenaline his system was pumping. Only Jason took the moment in stride. He reached down for his pack and opened it up. His deliberate movements caught their attention. "What are you doing?" they both asked.

Jason held up something that looked like a pair of binoculars in the pale light. He said, "Just getting my night vision goggles out. Was this something you men of science didn't plan for? Well the old soldier in me thought of this a long time ago."

Relief poured over Mark and Nuri, but their bruised egos became evident in the awkward silence. Jason knew better than to rub it in more than he already had. He put on the NVGs and took a look around.

Mark said, "Great, but Amelius didn't tell us how to leave the containment field without being crushed by the pressure. Do you have something in your pack that will get us inside the Hall of Records and the Temple Beautiful without killing us?"

Jason ignored the question and continued to visually scan the cliff face. Then he saw it. He could make out the familiar shape of the entrance to a tunnel that burrowed into the rock. It was large enough for two or three people to walk through without stooping. "Hey guys," he said, "can you extend the containment field in that direction?"

The two scientists looked where Jason was pointing. They couldn't see the mouth of the tunnel right in front of them.

Mark responded, "Uh, yes. We should be able to do that." He and Nuri moved over to the RFL units and started making the adjustments. "Eventually, we're still going to have to exit the containment field to enter the Hall of Records. This is probably a big waste of time not to mention we could all end up dead."

"Let's not get ahead of ourselves," Jason said.

Mark and Nuri finished their calibrations and pressed the RFL buttons together. A horizontal projection of the field extended from where they stood toward the cliff face. Whether the new tunnel took them to the Hall of Records or would end up in solid rock was anyone's guess. "Set the new extension about ten degrees more to the right and fifty feet farther in that direction," Jason said pointing for emphasis.

"Okay, got it. Now what?" Nuri asked.

Jason said casually, "Now we take a walk. Do we leave everything here? It seems like we should. Even if we survive leaving this field, we're not going to need our stuff for a few months."

Mark said, "Why don't we leave it for now. We can always come back for it."

***

"How long do you intend to hold us here?" Gus asked. "We haven't done anything wrong that would allow you to detain us. We'd like to get back to our boat."

The destroyer's captain had run out of questions and knew the old man was right. They hadn't admitted to anything that hinted at illegal activity. He decided to try a bluff. "I am going to prosecute you for failure to obey orders. Your other man in the dinghy did not follow the orders he was given by a sovereign military leader sent to protect you by your government."

Diana's eyes narrowed as she finally spoke up. "That won't fly captain. I've held my peace so far, but it's time you know that I am retired Chief Petty Officer Diana Amal of SEAL Team 3. I spent ten years in the Middle East protecting America's interests before my discharge twenty years ago. I am familiar with the Uniform Code of Military Justice inside and out. And you already know that, absent a declaration of martial law, United States civilians cannot be prosecuted by any branch of the military."

The captain was shocked to learn Diana was a Navy SEAL, assuming she wasn't lying to him. He looked over to his XO for support. He had nothing. The captain decided to brave it out anyway and see if she'd back down to his authority. "Many things have changed since you retired, Chief Amal. I am authorized to do whatever I think is necessary to protect the interests of the United States. If that means holding you for trial, then that's the way it is."

Diana responded, "Just because I retired doesn't mean that I didn't keep up on military news and laws. Look at *Reid v. Covert*, (354 U.S. 1) back in 1957. That precedent still stands today and it states that it is unconstitutional for a military court to hold or try a civilian. And that case was over a civilian woman murdering her soldier husband. Your 'failure for a civilian to follow military orders' law doesn't exist. Even if it did, we have complied with every order you have given us. Let us go now or I will end your career when we get back to the United States." She stared hard at the captain and then shifted her attention to his XO who was sitting quietly next to the bulkhead. He quickly looked away.

The captain was speechless. He had just been reactivated after a forced retirement some years back. He did not want to cut short this second chance at his career no matter how much he was beginning to hate these civilians.

"Get the hell off my ship!" he bellowed, his face turning red. "You idiots are not worth the trouble it would take to blow you out of the water. Get back in your leaky tub of a boat now before I have you thrown off."

Diana just smiled at him as she gracefully stood to leave. Gus rose too and reached out to shake the captain's hand out of habit and good manners. The icy glare he received from the captain convinced him to turn and go without another word.

***

Diana tried contacting Mark, Nuri and Jason the moment she returned to the boat. "Are you there?"

"We're still here, Diana," Jason said.

"Oh, thank God," she exclaimed. "We couldn't talk before because the captain would know we could reach you. We just now put our earbuds back in."

Jason laughed saying, "I hope that went okay. We have a heck of a story for you. We're still alive, and we are doing pretty well despite some scary setbacks."

Nuri jumped in, "We're just about to try to enter a tunnel that will hopefully take us to the Hall of Records. We managed to add an offshoot of the containment field that tracks the tunnel we located in the face of the cliff. I'm glad you two will be listening on the earbuds to keep track of our status and stay in touch. People will want to know how all this went down and we don't have the recording gear with us."

Diana laughed, "You didn't have to ask. I'm documenting everything from here on."

Jason took the lead and stepped carefully out of the dinghy onto the containment field that was tracking the rock floor beneath it. The other two followed him nervously into the tunnel. Their limited view reminded them that flashlights did not illuminate the dark passageway outside of the containment field. They could see ahead of them inside the field, but nothing else was visible, except to Jason. He assured them they weren't missing anything. Even with his NVGs, there was not much to see. The ceiling, walls and floor were smooth and clearly not created by natural erosion.

They stopped when they came to the end of the containment field. They had no way of knowing how far they were from the end of the rocky tunnel deep inside the cliff. Jason turned and asked, "What do we do now? Go back and extend the field, or risk going forward and being crushed in the black abyss?"

"Remember," Nuri reminded them, "Amelius said that we should have faith that we will succeed. That doesn't mean we don't need to be cautious. We can test the tunnel to see if it's safe by poking the end of the flashlight through the field. If you hit solid rock, the light will be crushed the moment it leaves the field."

Jason walked up to the field's edge and quickly pushed the head of the flashlight forward a few inches. As soon as it cleared the containment field, the light was visible against the tunnel's walls on either side. They were relieved when the pressure beyond the field did not collapse the flashlight's casing. Then they were amazed to see that the surrounding rock was completely dry.

"Don't rush out there, Jason," Mark warned. "You may not die from the pressure, but who knows if the air in this place is breathable?"

Jason asked, "What do you think would happen if I stick my head through, like I just did with the head of the flashlight, and test the air?"

The two archeologists looked at each other and shrugged. For all their knowledge gained from exploring dangerous sites, they couldn't think of a better alternative.

Jason turned and quickly pushed his head through the containment field. He felt a mild tingling sensation where the barrier touched the skin around his neck. So far, so good, since his head didn't pop like a cherry tomato. Mark and Nuri watched as he took a quick breath and brought his head back through. He exhaled immediately and resumed normal breathing without saying a word.

"Well?" Nuri asked impatiently. "Did it seem all right to you?"

"I was ready for the worst," Jason began, "but seriously, the air seems to be fine. It felt like it had the right amount of oxygen. I think I should stand just outside of the field in the tunnel and test it for a while. I'm holding one of the special RF crystals you made so I'll be able to get back inside."

His friends reluctantly agreed and appreciated his brave offer. This time Jason pushed his way through the containment field with a forceful step. He stood motionless on the other side and surveyed the tunnel with his flashlight. Then he turned back to his friends and his expression froze in shock. He just stood there with the flashlight pointed at them without moving.

"What's he doing?" Mark asked. He took a nervous peek over his shoulder in case something scary had snuck up on them.

Nuri said, "Oh, I think I understand. Remember that he can't see anything but the dimension he's in right now. He can't see us. Whatever has his attention is behind us. Our containment field already passed it in the tunnel."

Jason cautiously took a step and reentered the inside of the field. He shook his head to clear it and just stared at his friends with wide eyes. "You won't believe what I just saw out there," he gasped.

"What?" they responded in unison.

"About fifteen yards back are two tunnels running to the left and right of the one we're in now. Just beyond that, is a wall of seawater. It reminded me of looking through the glass at an aquarium, but it's not perfectly smooth, like how Gus described the hole we made on the surface. It moves like the surface of the ocean, only sideways. I don't know if our containment field is doing that, or if something else is responsible. We need to find out if our two machines are holding back all that water. At some point, we're going to need to turn them off."

Mark asked, "Why would we need to turn the RF containment fields off?"

Jason said impatiently, "We need to know where we stand. Amelius said we will be here for months. What about air, food and drinkable water for the three of us? Are all those things available down here? I admit that I'd rather die looking for the Hall of Records than letting boredom take me sitting on the sidelines. If you two want to go back now, I'm not going with you."

Nuri said, "I'm with you, Jason. Can we at least get our gear out of the containment field before we try that? I doubt that we could react quickly enough, but we could at least try to reestablish the field if it turns out that it's us holding the water back and not some 'woo woo' magic in this tunnel."

Mark just shrugged and waited for Jason to take the lead.

They walked single file back to the dinghy and their equipment. They put their gear in the little boat and dragged it as far as they could to the end of the field inside the tunnel. This time all three of them stepped briskly through the field, still dragging the dinghy between them. Jason had described it well. Three flashlight beams scoured the walls in all directions. The sides, floor and ceiling were as dry as the air was odorless.

It took a while before Mark and Nuri turned to survey the tunnel from the direction they had come. It, too, was just as Jason described. That didn't make the wall of water any less ominous.

Mark and Nuri decided to turn the RFL machines off and then back on as quickly as they could. That way if a torrent of water came through, they might get the containment field reestablished before they drowned. They carefully retracted the boundary of the field to where the seawater stopped at the edge of the tunnel.

They said together, "In 3, 2, 1." Barely a beat later, they hit their respective RFL buttons twice to turn the field off and back on.

Jason said, "I didn't see any change at all."

"That's a good thing, Jason," Nuri said, exhaling loudly. "Anything else would have meant trouble."

"So we turn them off and wait this time?" Mark said more for confirmation than asking the obvious.

They pressed the RFL power buttons again and watched to see if anything happened with the wall of water in front of them. The seconds ticked by, but nothing changed. Jason stepped around the dinghy and started walking back toward the perpendicular passageways to the left and right of the main tunnel they'd entered. He shined his light down each one and yelled back, "I'm going to need an archeologist over here who can read those hieroglyphic symbols we keep running into."

Mark and Nuri ran to catch up to him. He pointed his flashlight in both directions to illuminate the symbols on the walls. The two men started laughing after they mentally completed the translations.

"So what do they say?" he asked annoyed. He didn't like being left out of the joke.

"We couldn't have asked for a better sign, so to speak," Nuri said still chuckling. "This one to the left reads 'Temple Beautiful' and the other one says 'Hall of Records.'"

Mark said, "Which one do we explore first?"

Jason interjected firmly before Nuri could answer. "We go to the Temple Beautiful. The only reason we're here is because of it. Amelius didn't say the world was ready for all the secrets tucked away inside the Hall of Records. He may not want us to explore it at all."

Mark sighed and said, "I'd rather ask for forgiveness than permission in this case. We've been waiting for most of our lives to get here." Nuri looked disappointed but didn't say anything.

"I'm just messing with you," Jason laughed. "I want to see it too!"

Chapter 12

Kathryn Campbell was the first President of the United States (POTUS) elected since the death of Prince Nafid. She had won a special election over no less than 200 candidates who all promised to put America back on top. Kathryn was well-spoken, charismatic, and had a quick mind. During the campaign, her striking good looks were often used in comical memes, but she wisely ignored them and campaigned on her other merits. Her winning edge was that she had been the Mayor of New York City. None of the candidates could claim they knew much about running a massive autonomous government, but a majority of voters agreed that she was the best nominee to get the nation moving forward again.

Her first presidential order had been to restart the huge U.S. government machine as if the prince had never existed. Now that she had it rolling again, Kathryn could make the necessary changes needed to modernize the old ways. One of the many presidential directives her sweeping kick-start policy revived was to find the Bimini Hall of Records. Today was the first time she had been aware that President Westbrook had an interest in such things.

Kathryn shook her head in disbelief after reading her morning's briefing report. The specific section she questioned was, by itself, unremarkable. It was the additional details her staff provided that vexed her. The written account came from John Archer, a naval captain, who had been tasked with finding the fabled Hall of Records. His report said that they had been tracking a small fishing boat heading for the Bahamas. He had reason to believe that the occupants had knowledge of the hidden chamber's location. His ship suffered some unexpected electrical failures, the explanation was cryptically vague, and three of the five people on the small boat disappeared before his ship could catch up to them. Subsequent searches had yet to locate the missing crew members.

President Campbell had trouble reconciling the disturbing details told to her by her military advisors with Archer's tersely worded report. If those accounts were true, she could understand why the captain had kept it short, but stories like this were hard to keep secret. Various accounts from the destroyer's personnel described their encounter more like they had gone up against Captain Nemo and the Nautilus. It was hard to believe that a small fishing boat with a crew of four old men and a middle aged woman could get the best of a U.S. naval war ship.

Kathryn didn't know anything about the civilian boat's captain, Gus Martin, or his granddaughter, Diana Amal. However, she did recognize the names of the three men who had mysteriously vanished. They were Mark Heston, Nuri Zayd, and Jason Fisher. She had been taught those names in grade school as the explorers who had brought resonant frequency technology to the world.

She was surprised to learn that these national heroes were not cooperating with the government. She would have to find out what went wrong so she could get them back into the fold. If half of what she'd heard about these men was true, it would be foolish to work against them.

Kathryn Campbell was skeptical, but if by some chance the Bimini Hall of Records was real, the rumored technology it held could put the United States back in charge of the world. Decades ago, the sudden loss of revenues that came from selling RF technology almost ruined the U.S. economy. It was no surprise that the U.S. had never prospered so well as it did under Matthew Alexander. That man truly impressed Kathryn. She wished he was still alive to call upon as an advisor.

Per Archer's report, the grandfather and granddaughter had gone back to Florida. No one had seen or heard from the three missing men since they disappeared just west of the Bahamas. As things stood now, the captain continued to maintain surveillance of the area and search for the men.

President Campbell decided that Captain Archer had to be taken off the search for Heston, Zayd, and Fisher. After what the captain had been through, it would be hard for him to remain professional if he did manage to find them. Also, assuming they did reappear at some point, using satellite surveillance to track them would be less intimidating than a hulking warship.

That brought up another problem. After years of neglect, the country's satellite systems needed a good deal of work to get back online. Her recently hired NASA scientists reported that it would take a while to make their entire orbital system operational again. However, they said they could manage to get a satellite working over Bimini in a few days. She ordered Captain Archer to return to port the moment a replacement ship arrived. Soon after, she hoped there would be satellite surveillance over the Bahamas, but she was taking no chances.

***

Amelius gently made his presence known to Nasrum. Then he got right to the point. "Directly interfering with humanity's free will choices without their permission is not allowed. You know this already, so I must ask, why did you do it?"

Nasrum scolded Amelius hoping to gain the upper hand. "I barely did anything, and your reaction was far worse. You also meddled with the timeline to ensure the outcome you wanted. As they say on earth, isn't that the pot calling the kettle black?"

Amelius sighed, "You know that your uninvited actions would have significantly changed the path of humanity. My actions simply reversed yours in order to keep the souls of earth on their own chosen course."

"If what I did was so bad," Nasrum growled, "then why didn't Allah stop me? I believe our Creator had no problem with my choice. It is you alone who has decided to condemn me."

"You know that you are posing a deceitful argument," said Amelius. "We both know that you purposefully chose to interfere knowing there would be consequences. What will it take to help you see a better way to live?"

Nasrum had no desire to answer that question. He quickly departed for a dimension so dark that he hoped Amelius wouldn't dare to follow him. He needed to gather his thoughts and begin again with another plan. This lonely realm was free of distractions and he needed to focus. There had to be a way to prove to everyone that he alone could save the world!

***

The chiseled tunnel came to an abrupt dead end. There was no sign, no door, nor any indication that the Hall of Records lay beyond that point.

Mark looked back over his shoulder and asked, "Did we pass the entrance somewhere along the way?"

Nuri just scoffed and said, "Does this wall remind anyone of a certain pyramid in Guatemala?"

"Yes, except that it's missing the encased soldier's body!" Jason said with gallows humor.

"Do you think the wall requires a unique RF crystal to open it?" Mark persisted.

Jason ignored the question and shared another memory. "If Thiago taught us anything, we can be sure that blasting through it isn't going to work."

From their earbuds they heard Diana say, "Jason, why not try using your lucky crystal? Maybe it doesn't need to be a specific frequency if the wall senses that the right technology is present."

They looked at each other and intuitively knew she was right. Diana had been paying close attention every time they talked about their past adventures. She had just come up with a really good idea at a time when they had figuratively and literally reached a dead end.

Jason pulled the tiny RF crystal out of his pocket and made a fist around it. As he stretched his arm toward the wall he felt an odd tingling sensation, but it did not feel the same as it had in Piedras Negras. The knuckles of his fist slowly connected with the wall when a bright flash went off behind him.

"What the heck was that?" Jason asked as he whipped around to investigate.

"What are you talking about?" Mark answered, genuinely puzzled.

Jason gasped, "You guys didn't see the room light up just now?"

His friends just shook their heads and said nothing. Jason turned around and tried again. As before, the moment his fist touched the wall, the room lit up for a fraction of a second. This time Jason's peripheral vision barely made out ornate shelving that lined the walls of the cave.

He tried the same experiment shifting where he stood and where he touched the wall. It didn't seem to matter what he did, or what crystal he used, the fleeting images that flashed remained in his peripheral vision. Mark and Nuri tried it next with the same results.

Jason's last attempt was to keep his eyes closed when his fist connected with the wall. Nothing changed from his previous attempts.

"Do you suppose this Hall of Records has been plundered at some point?" Jason asked. "It could be the phantom image we keep getting is what this cave used to contain before someone took it all away."

Nuri said, "If this place has been here for 12,000 years, your notion is certainly possible. It would also explain why the tunnel walls are dry and the air is fresh. Whoever took everything out of here didn't bother to turn the lights out, so to speak, when they left."

"But why would Amelius and Halaliel guide us here if they knew we wouldn't find anything?" Mark said, clearly frustrated.

Through their earbuds Diana said, "Amelius didn't say that this is the right time to open the Hall of Records. If I heard you right, all he suggested was that you come here for the Temple Beautiful. Why not head over that way and see what's there? I know I'm curious about it, even if you aren't."

They wanted to reject Diana's practical suggestion out of hand because she lacked their experience. But this was the second time inside of an hour that she had proved her worth.

Jason broke the silence to help lift their mood and get them moving again. "Hey guys, I've heard this place has a great spa across the way. Rumor has it that they have an anti-aging process that works miracles!"

They nervously laughed and agreed that it was time to go. Although there was a smile on Jason's face, he was thinking dark thoughts. He couldn't shake the feeling he was the reason they literally ran into a wall. Amelius had warned them that their less than loving attitudes could be the very thing that stopped them. He wondered if his Delta Force ways were blocking his kind and gentle friends from finding the Hall of Records.

***

The darkness that surrounded Nasrum was ominous. He consoled himself by rationalizing that it was just what he needed right now. He had never been so completely alone in his life though he was sure the number of souls in this realm was legion. This was the place where depressed souls went because it isolated them from everything. He knew the inherent danger in coming here. It was all too easy to forget you could choose to go anywhere else at any moment. A soul could become so wrapped up in their own thoughts that the universe around them disappeared.

Nasrum remembered his previous life on earth as Achmed Mansur. He had come within hours of destroying the Suez Canal only to be thwarted at the last instant. He thought of other times when the frustrating pattern repeated itself. It was as if the cosmos was purposefully holding him back from his destiny. He was certain that Amelius was behind his misery. He couldn't understand why Allah would let the 'holier than thou' Amelius hinder the peace and prosperity Nasrum wanted to bring to the earth.

He caught himself before his depressed thoughts rambled on in an endless loop. He reminded himself that this is exactly what causes souls to become entrapped in this dimension. On earth, they called it Post Traumatic Stress Disorder. The only way to bring such afflicted people back from reliving the repeating pattern of what they feared and hated most was to help them set it all aside and live in the present moment.

This place was so compelling because it reeked of fear and drama. The constant repetition of one's darkest memories was eerily captivating. As much as he hated this lonely realm, no one bothered him here. No one would betray him here, they wouldn't ruin his plans with their incompetence, and best of all, Nasrum could visualize everything unfolding exactly the way he wanted. He knew it wasn't real, but it was comforting to envision his enemies suffering while the world groveled at his feet with praise and worship.

Nasrum suddenly realized that he had done it again. He had nearly fallen prey to the vicious cycle of his own fearful thoughts. Then inspiration dawned on him. If the stupid humans would not accept his gracious path to peace and prosperity through Islam, then he could scare them into submission. He would bring fear and drama into their lives to hold their attention. Then he would persuade them that he was their only hope of rescue, survival and victory over insurmountable odds.

Chapter 13

Accessing the Temple Beautiful was surprisingly simple. The tunnel led them to a series of rooms that were lined with colorful crystals, gems and precious stones that all seemed to pulsate from an internal glow. None of the men spoke because they were awed by the remarkable layout of the rejuvenation chambers. Diana kept asking them to describe what they saw, but her promptings were mostly met by silence. The effect of standing in that amazing place was difficult to describe.

Over the next few days, Mark and Nuri translated the hieroglyphics that explained the purpose behind each of the chambers. The first room removed all toxins that had accumulated in the body since birth. The second room was designed to produce flawless stem cells creating an internal blueprint for the final stage of the body's regeneration. The third room completed the restoration of all the body's systems to their perfect state through a balance of its assimilations and eliminations. Amelius told them that the human body could last as long as a soul desired if this balance was properly maintained.

Mark did his best to provide Diana with details of their daily routines. "You would not believe this, it's amazing! Each room was created to perfect the human body by harmonizing it with the ethereal vibrations of the gems and stones embedded in these walls. But the rejuvenation process requires much more than simply basking in their vibrations.

"A strict diet and exercise regimen is also needed along with daily meditations to harmonize the person's mind and spirit with their revitalized body. RFS, resonant frequency sustenance, was already in place in these chambers and can provide more than enough healthy food and pure water for the three of us. But get this! RFS also purifies the air as easily as it does water! We never knew it could do that before.

"The Atlantean symbols also suggest a program of deep breathing exercises and chanting. Breathing connects the conscious mind with the subconscious or autonomic functions of the brain. The vocal chanting of particular syllables helps to synchronize the vibrations of the crystals and gems here with our body's systems to bring them back into balance."

Diana took down every word. She was struck by Mark's surprising ability to capture the magic of the place with his eloquent narrative. She wished that she could be there with them.

Halaliel and Amelius visited them often and answered all their questions. The three friends were not sure if they would remember the wondrous things they were told, but they found it fascinating to learn the answers to questions long sought by humanity.

Nuri asked how the universe and life began. Amelius responded, "The simple answer is that God moved from spirit into matter. Earth's scientists have called this the Big Bang. Our Creator is pure consciousness whose perpetual existence does not rely upon matter, energy or space."

Amelius went on to explain that the Creator was complete and lacked for nothing, but realized that life would be more enjoyable with companions who would be God's co-creators throughout eternity. While much of humanity thinks of the creation of souls as occurring after the universe was formed, the truth is that souls are also eternal. They have always been and will always be.

All three of them balked at the notion that their souls could be created by God, and yet have no beginning or end. In answer, they were shown a hologram of a sperm entering an egg resulting in a zygote. Then the zygote divided into identical cells repeatedly until there were too many to count. Once they realized that none of the cells were older than the others, they understood. The original zygote, God, created each soul in God's perfect image. All souls exist for eternity within the 'body' of God where we live and move and experience our lives according to our free will choices. Each soul knows itself to be itself and yet is still part of the Whole...the Creator that humanity calls 'God.' Two earthly phrases came to mind to explain the zygote metaphor, 'as above, so below,' and, 'on earth, as it is in heaven.'

When Jason asked why humanity lived such limited physical lives on earth instead of working with God to expand His amazing creation, Amelius' answer amazed them. "Each soul is responsible for its own choices. Many religions speak of a Lucifer or satanic being that leads souls astray of God's loving ways. The truth is that such stories are better interpreted as a metaphor for the selfish choices we make that separate us from the Creator. It is not that God turns away from us, for that would never happen. Instead, it is each soul that turns our back to God's light. In this way, we find ourselves staring into the darkness away from our Creator, and we forget how magnificent we truly are. Once we freely accept and choose God's loving ways for our own, we again turn toward the light and have unlimited access to God's omniscience and omnipotence."

They could only absorb a limited amount of such heavy information at one time, so their questions turned to the present. They asked how they could access the information and technology hidden inside the Hall of Records. The response did not change. The Hall of Records would not be found until the world was ready. When they pressed for how long that might be, the answer surprised them.

Amelius said, "Humanity has already achieved the critical mass necessary to reveal the Hall of Records. A majority of entrapped souls living on the earth are ready at this moment, but it is a silent majority. The souls who desire love and willing cooperation as their way of life must openly come forward to manifest God's loving ways in the world."

He explained further using an analogy from science. "If you place a plastic bottle of water in a freezer set to ten degrees below zero, the contents will remain as a liquid for a while. In time, it will turn to ice, but the process can be accelerated. Under the right conditions, thumping the side of the bottle will turn the water to ice within seconds. The correct conditions are already in place for turning the water to ice, but the change can come more quickly with a catalyst. It is just this way on earth at this time. All of the conditions are in place for a wondrous change. Humanity is ready to manifest patience and cooperation in both their thoughts and actions. In the same way that turning water to ice is helped by a catalyst, the world needs a 'thump' to speed up the process. Rest assured that a 'thump' of great magnitude is coming."

***

Nasrum had always felt he was special, but now he was sure of it. He had entered into the dimension of outer darkness and

584

returned unaffected to tell the tale. He knew that most souls were transformed once they resurfaced. Those poor mindless creatures no longer desired to achieve greatness for themselves. They became humble and wanted to do what was best for everyone. Nasrum was proud that he hadn't lost his mind, or his values. It had been dangerous to enter that dark space and potentially lose himself in the process, but he had triumphed. The risk had been worth it. He now knew how to convince humanity to do the right thing by following his edicts.

He regretted that his inspiration didn't occur sooner. In retrospect, the conditions on earth had been perfect when Prince Nafid first rose to power. The world wanted a leader to save them from an alien invasion. Nasrum's mistake was in reassuring the masses that Allah would protect his faithful children. He should have been motivating them through fear, especially given his particular talent for frightening people. The real challenge would be to convince the scientists and skeptics that only he could save them.

This time Nasrum resolved to personally carry out his strategy. Working through the incompetence of lesser souls had already failed. Still, that didn't mean that he was done with Prince Nafid. The man was dead, of course, but his reputation could prove to be quite useful.

Gus and Diana had returned home to Miami, Florida. They were still able to talk with Mark, Nuri and Jason through the earbuds, but there was nothing new to report. The novelty of the Temple Beautiful had worn off and everyone was doing well. The passing weeks turned into months that challenged Diana's patience.

"Do you have any idea what their plan will be once they come back?" she asked Gus.

"No," he replied. "I don't think they know either. Maybe they're figuring that out right now."

"Do you believe they are really going to come out of this as young men again?" she asked skeptically.

"Not really. I don't remember the Bible saying Jesus performed that particular miracle," Gus laughed. "I'm thinking they'll get healed of their aches and pains. We can only hope that place throws in an attitude adjustment so they aren't so hard to live with."

Diana smiled and changed the subject. "How are we going to pick them up when they're ready? You know that ship's captain will really be gunning for us if he gets another chance."

"I got the impression," Gus started thinking aloud, "that our friends would have that covered when the time comes. I'll bet they have at least one more trick up their sleeve."

"Perhaps," Diana mused, "but they'd better hurry up. The world is falling apart."

Gus nodded and said, "It sure is. Every country is jockeying for position to fill the gap left by that Nafid fella's death. Now that every nation is itching to test their military muscle, I'm afraid they're willing to start a war to decide who should be in charge."

"If it comes down to that," Diana speculated, "we're all in trouble. How many countries will accept defeat when they still have a nuclear option? It seems inevitable that this war will end with the losers nuking the winners as a last resort."

***

President Kathryn Campbell was listening to her staff of advisors. It didn't matter who was speaking because their reports carried the same conclusions. The world was in great shape if all nations could agree upon how to cooperate now that the prince was gone. In many ways things had never been better. The technology to supply the world's needs was still in place and there were more than enough willing workers to keep the economy moving. After 30 years of Prince Nafid calling all the shots, the nations' governments agreed that a centralized leadership should continue as before. The problem was that they all wanted to lead rather than follow.

The U.S. maintained that they had been the power center of the world before Nafid, so they were the most qualified to lead. The Middle Eastern countries contended that Syria was already the power center of the world, as well as the birthplace for all humanity. Russia felt that being the largest land mass with greater natural resources made them the logical choice. China believed that the question should be put to a worldwide majority vote. The other nations scoffed at that idea knowing China had the largest population. Even Italy made a bid for being the supreme leader by maintaining that it was they who had successfully ruled for nearly 1,000 years when Rome was the center of the world.

If every country had the natural resources needed for all the products it consumed, then perhaps isolation would have been the better answer. But the raw materials needed to create tech products and the best RF soil were not available everywhere. They needed some way to watch over international trade with each country receiving fair treatment.

President Campbell couldn't see a way to resolve all those conflicting agendas. Then she remembered the search for the Hall of Records. "Have we located the three men we were tracking and lost near Bimini?"

"No luck so far," answered General Armstead, who was the JSOC leader, Joint Special Operations Command. "We have ongoing satellite surveillance of the area. Our people have orders to track the old man and his granddaughter any time they leave their house."

"If it turns out that the fabled Hall of Records is real, owning the technology it's supposed to contain could be the deciding factor in this global dispute for leadership," President Campbell said. "Whoever the original developers were won't make any difference. When the U.S. controlled RF energy, we ruled the world. When we lost its exclusive control, we lost our place as the world's leader. Can someone clarify the legal question of ownership if the chamber is located near Bimini?"

The Attorney General's deputy, David Huffman, was at the table and fielded the question. "If anything discovered comes from a sunken ship, ownership defaults to the country of the ship's registration. Rumors are that the so-called Bimini Hall of Records was created by the people of Atlantis. Since there is no clear heir to Atlantis, ownership would default to the country whose borders, including the 12 nautical mile extension into the ocean, contains the discovery. In this case, that would be the Bahamas."

Kathryn sighed, "You mean if anyone finds the place within 12 nautical miles of the Bahamas that tiny country owns it?"

"Not necessarily," the deputy AG hedged. "A case could be made that international law applies if the discovery is made in very deep waters. In the same way that ownership of the space above a country is limited, the same concept could apply to the depth where property is found underneath the ocean. In that case, international law would award ownership to the people who made the discovery."

"And as U.S. citizens, we might induce them to nationalize whatever technology they bring back?" President Campbell asked hopefully.

"The AG thinks he can defend that interpretation of the law, especially knowing what's at stake here," David answered.

"Then we can try to persuade them to bring whatever they find back to U.S. soil," Kathryn declared.

"And if they resist?" General Armstead asked.

"Let's find them first, General. We'll hope for the best and prepare for the worst!"

Chapter 14

"How do I look?" Jason asked his friends.

"You definitely look younger," Mark said encouragingly. "It's ironic that there aren't any mirrors in the one place on earth where you can actually regain your youth."

"We're here getting healthier because we are needed to do important work," Nuri chided. "How we look is not important. Otherwise, there would be mirrors in here."

Mark quipped back, "I just realized that no matter how young you look, you still think like an old man."

"People fantasize about starting their life over again with the knowledge and experience they gained in a lifetime. What do you two think you'll do differently?" Jason asked.

"I don't have any regrets," Mark answered immediately.

Nuri nodded as he pointed to Mark adding, "What he said! How about you, Jason?"

"I always wondered what it would be like to have a family," he admitted. "You know, kids and a dog and a wife to come home to."

"You're too difficult to live with to think that a woman would ever want to spend her life with you," Mark joked. It surprised him a little to hear this softer side of Jason.

"To be fair, you have mellowed with age," Nuri allowed, "but Mark isn't wrong. No one is better in a crisis situation than you, Jason. But a close-knit family doesn't need a trained Delta Force soldier as its head of the household. Being a loving husband and father requires a different kind of courage."

"And what do you two know about it? Neither of you raised a family," Jason scoffed. "If you hadn't become famous from our past adventures, you might never have had anything but a blind date."

"True enough," Mark agreed. "But I've been asking Amelius and Halaliel about my past lives. He said I've been a loving family man for most of them. Having a wife and kids wasn't a good fit for me this time around, and I'm okay with that."

"Me too," Nuri said. "I have been a parent and a spouse many times. I do that well, but it's not what I'm here to work on in this incarnation."

"I don't get why we have to reincarnate," Jason mused. "If the human body can be rejuvenated like this, why don't we stay alive in one body as long as we need to? We put a lot of effort into learning to walk, talk, think, earn a living, and interact with people. Why do we keep duplicating that effort with each new life?"

"I was told there are two main reasons," Nuri answered. "First, what if you're Adolph Hitler and have such a bad run that you and everyone else can't forget what you did, let alone forgive it? Each new life allows for a fresh start. Second, the life-lessons we come to this earth to learn often require a different personality, gender, skills and life circumstances. They said that much like an iceberg only shows 10 percent of its mass above the water, we only see a small portion of the totality of who we really are in a given lifetime."

"I know why this came up," Mark snickered. "Jason's now young enough to hit on Diana when we're done here!"

"Don't go there!" Jason objected. "She doesn't think of me that way." Then he smiled and said, "And besides, with my new youthful good looks, she'll be too old for me. If we started dating, people would think she's a cougar."

They all laughed at that, but the mood soon turned serious.

"Practically speaking, she's as difficult to live with as you are," Nuri said to Jason. "You could learn a lot from each other. Then you could tell us what it's like to date a woman who can beat you in arm wrestling! Mark and I are clearly no match for her, but I'm pretty sure that Diana could whip you in a fair contest."

Half a world away, Diana smiled as she took out her RFC earbud. She would not embarrass her friends by admitting she had overheard their conversation. She reflected on her own regrets in life and vowed that she would never again lose sight of her priorities.

The Navy and Islam had let her down. From here on, she would follow her own path.

***

Nasrum had searched for days to find the right person on earth. Makoa was extremely distraught and ready to end his own life. He was sitting in his small boat having cast off from the decaying pier near his home in Madagascar. He set his little sail to take him far out into the Indian Ocean. His course was on a heading for Australia. He planned to secure himself to the boat's anchor and jump overboard. Even if he changed his mind after he was in the water, there would be no going back. The insurance policy on his life would pay double if he was lost at sea. His family would get nothing if it was proven that he committed suicide.

Nasrum could see that a few angels and souls had gathered to help the man make the transition. They were there to guide him to a realm where he would be lovingly cared for. Anyone who takes their own life in desperation typically has a rough time adjusting to the other side. To ensure that the transition is as smooth as possible, the depressed soul is often lifted from the body prior to any physical suffering. Nasrum was counting on this and waited patiently for his chance.

The man in the boat cut the tether from the anchor to the bow. He then tied the end of the rope tightly around his waist so that the large stone would hold his body underwater after he drowned. He picked up the stone and stood, then closed his eyes asking his family to forgive him. Hugging the rock close to his body, he jumped. As predicted, his soul was guided away before the human life had ended.

Nasrum wasted no time. He created a small RFL field around the now vacant body and placed it in suspended animation. The physical form had to survive a long journey ahead to start a new life on the other side of the globe. The RF field and momentum would transport the body through the center of the earth.

Nasrum stayed with the form as it passed through the planet's crust, mantle and core. A geologist would have appreciated this first-hand look at the layers of soil, rock and minerals slowly passing by. Within the first hour, Nasrum was bored. He might as well have been taking a bus ride across west Texas.

When he approached the earth's center, the movement of the molten magma of the core reminded him of the old lava lamps of the 1960s. He knew from the start that he would end up somewhere in the eastern states, but now he was getting close enough to make an educated guess as to where the body would emerge. He ceased generating the RFL field at the same moment the body cleared the tilled soil of a crop field.

The body landed awkwardly across two rows of corn stalks in a large field. Nasrum was glad to see there was no one nearby since what he had to do next would take some time. He first had to bond his mind to the body's corporeal brain. This process was easy at birth when the brain was a clean slate, but Makoa had been nearly forty years old. Connecting Nasrum's mind to the synapses in a cerebrum previously used by someone else felt like he was a stroke victim. His movements were uncoordinated and he wondered if he would ever be able to control this body. The trick was to adapt his thoughts to the limited reality of three dimensions. It took a few hours of repeated mental exercises and practice before he was able to stand and maneuver on steady legs.

Nasrum knew he had to find his way to the nearest city. That proposed a challenge since all he could see was the corn field. He was anxious to get on with his plan. He was certain that if Amelius was going to interfere, he would have done so by now. Allah must have rendered his actions invisible to any who would oppose him. He was now convinced that his mission was divinely blessed and guided.

As time passed, he would gradually lose the ability to read the thoughts of others or clearly see the future from his earthly perspective. The loss of those skills often goes unnoticed when a child is born because the soul cannot clearly communicate for years. He didn't care. He could always find a new body when he needed to. He was pleased that he no longer had to work through incompetents like Prince Nafid. He was free to create the global utopia he had always envisioned.

***

Nasrum considered what he needed to do as he walked toward the suburbs of Little Rock, Arkansas. He had feared the worst when Amelius reset the timeline for his three minions. While it wasn't clear why they failed, even after spending a few months at the site, he sensed they were about to resurface empty handed. That was surprising but good news. He took it as another sign that Allah was truly on his side.

With the threat of the Hall of Records out of the picture, Nasrum had time to execute his strategy. That would start by introducing himself to the media. He decided to make use of a local church that also ran a homeless shelter. The shelter took him in and generously agreed that he could stay for a while.

Nasrum was told that he could clean himself up in the communal showers. When he saw himself in a mirror, he realized that his ethereal perspective of Makoa's body was not the same as what he saw now that he was physically on earth. He appeared to be a mix between the Afro-American and Polynesian races. It would be a tougher job to convince the world that Prince Nafid had returned in this body, but he was up to the challenge.

He attended his benefactor church's Wednesday evening service. Fate smiled on him as they were a sect that practiced the gift of speaking in tongues. At the appropriate time in the service, Nasrum deliberately fell to the ground and began shaking uncontrollably. Then he sat straight up and spoke clearly in English with an Arabic accent.

"You see the body of Makoa before you, but I am Prince Nafid of Damascus, Syria. I am reaching out to you all from the afterlife because I promised to protect humanity and so I shall, even from the grave."

The shocked church members stared at him in confusion and a little skepticism. This was not the way speaking in tongues was supposed to manifest, but then, the Lord was known to work in mysterious ways.

After another moment, Nasrum stood and continued as his gaze swept the crowd, "I know many of you will doubt that I still live. To that end, let me offer to gain your trust again as I did before. The winning lottery numbers for Friday's drawing are as follows: 12, 16, 48, 52, 64 and 18. I will speak again through this channel after you have had time to prove that I am indeed Prince Nafid." Then Makoa appeared to pass out without another word. He seemed to float gracefully down to the floor. A few of the church members were kind enough to move him to his bed at the nearby shelter.

Most of the people assumed Makoa was drunk, or demented, or both. All but one of the congregants ignored his strange ramblings and went on with the service. It was no coincidence that Nasrum had purposefully made a scene in front of a journalist for the Jonesboro Examiner. He casually wrote down the lottery numbers and submitted the story to his editor the following morning.

The editor decided to go with the crazy story knowing their readers would enjoy it no matter how incredulous the source. Only Nasrum could have guessed that it would be picked up by all the major news networks and social media across the country. By the end of the day, the majority of news outlets were reporting that Prince Nafid claimed to be back and was speaking through a homeless man in Arkansas named Makoa. They included the lottery numbers at the end of the story.

Most people didn't really believe that some crazy homeless man could pick winning lottery numbers, but it turned out that almost two million people were willing to risk a couple of dollars in case this wasn't a fluke. When those numbers actually came up in the next drawing, there were so many winning tickets sold that the 'winners' ended up sharing the prize by paying out $38 each.

Most were disappointed that they could win the lottery but not get rich. Nasrum could not care less. He had what he wanted. He was back in the spotlight, and this time there was no one to stop him. Allah was clearly supporting him, and a great many people had accepted that he was Prince Nafid speaking from a different body. This time things would be different. Even if someone managed to assassinate Makoa, more bodies were always available.

In the days that followed, Nasrum garnered the public's confidence in his abilities by accurately predicting tragic accidents and the results of sporting events. Sports book businesses immediately quit taking bets on any game or contest where he predicted the outcome. Inside of a week, Nasrum had the attention of the world. It was an easy matter to gather enough wealth to secure a comfortable place to live away from prying eyes.

***

It wasn't long before Makoa announced a special press conference where he promised to discuss an issue of grave importance. He held it in a 20,000 seat arena and still had standing room only. When he appeared on stage, he was smartly groomed and wearing a suit. Nasrum saw no reason to deprive himself of every comfort as long as he was stuck in this body. The audience hushed as he took his place at the podium.

He stared into the distance for a moment and then his arms started to spasm. He understood that these people would believe in him more if he made a spectacle of the process in pretending to channel Prince Nafid. He marveled that his credibility would rise because it appeared that he was losing control. An awkward minute passed as the crowd watched his antics. Then Nasrum abruptly sat up and spoke.

"Many of you may remember back when I, Prince Nafid, first addressed the threat of alien life forms attacking the earth. I told you then that we are not ready to interact with extraterrestrials. I promised you that Allah would watch over His people, and your faith indeed kept you protected. Many of you wondered how I could be killed by an assassin. That was a test by Allah of your faith in times of crisis. It was a test that you failed. Once humanity chose to abandon Islam, Allah had no choice but to abandon you. That means that the earth is no longer protected. I regret to say that an alien invasion force is coming and we need to prepare if we are to save this planet."

Nasrum paused to allow the excited voices reverberating throughout the arena to run their course. Then he continued.

"I keep my promises. I will protect you, but you must do what I say without question in order to prevail against our true enemies. First, this petty fighting among the nations of the world must stop. If you want me to guide our civilization through the coming invasion, you must accept me as your absolute leader. Second, representatives from all the sovereign nations need to meet with me here in Little Rock. Any countries that do not comply with my directives will be left to fend for themselves."

Many questions were shouted from the audience. Nasrum simply held up a hand and said, "The appointed agents for each nation must gather in this same place in three days. For those who do not, may Allah have mercy on your souls."

He walked off the stage and went back into hiding.

***

"Is anybody there?" Diana asked for the third time.

"Yeah, sorry about that," Mark said, a little out of breath as he adjusted his earbud. "We were doing our daily exercises. What's going on?"

"Please get Nuri and Jason on the line as well," she said. "They'll need to hear this too."

"Okay, we're all here now," Jason and Nuri confirmed a moment later. "What's happening?"

"It's all over the news," Diana began. "Some homeless guy named Makoa is said to be channeling the spirit of Prince Nafid. If that wasn't nutty enough, the prince swears that aliens are planning to attack the earth. He did his thing again with the winning lottery numbers along with other predictions that came true. Now everyone believes he's the real deal who has come back to save the world."

"Why is he saying we're going to be attacked?" Jason asked. "Amelius has said that any extraterrestrials who could travel to earth are not a threat to humanity."

"I believe you," she huffed, "but the prince has everyone else thinking that a spaceship full of aliens is planning to raid earth's natural resources. He's got everyone so worked up that most of the nations have agreed to follow this guy Makoa who swears he's channeling Nafid."

"What's he telling the governments to do?" Nuri asked.

"They are building some kind of protective satellite system outfitted with RF crystals. Once they're ready, the plan is to deploy them around the earth in a geosynchronous orbit," Diana answered.

"I guess Prince Nafid isn't going away," Jason sighed. "We're almost through the Temple Beautiful process. We will figure out what to do before we leave this place. We'll ask our friends in the vapors what's going on and how we can help."

"There is a bit of good news," she added. "This Makoa, who channels the prince, convinced the competing nations to stop threatening each other. The war cry of 'beat the aliens' has managed to bring them all back to the same table. At least that means there will still be a world for you to come home to when you're ready, which I hope is soon!"

"Hang in there, Diana," Mark said. "You and Gus try to stay under the radar for just a little while longer."

Chapter 15

President Campbell asked, "What is the purpose behind these new satellites the prince wants us to build?"

"All he will say is that it's a defensive measure to deploy around the planet," came the reply from one of the advisors. "Our scientists are working round the clock to manufacture the satellites to the prince's specifications. No one knows enough about RF technology to say with certainty what they are designed to do."

"Well, what's their best guess?" Kathryn persisted. She motioned for the advisor to approach the conference table so she could get a look at him.

"The technology is all RF. They are melding two RF crystals together using a particular Fibonacci frequency. The resulting sending crystal looks nothing like the ones we already use for RF energy, food or water. Beyond that, they have no clue."

"I'm concerned that it could be an RF version of an EMP device," Kathryn said, subtly allowing the room to know that she didn't trust their alleged benefactor. "What if these satellites do disable the invading ships while annihilating our own RF technology on earth?"

The advisor answered, "The tests we are told to run send out the Fibonacci sequence of numbers on a specific frequency. The prince assures us that the numbers prove it is working. When we perform those tests, nothing else seems to be affected."

"How long will it be until the satellites are ready to be launched?" Kathryn asked.

"They're ready now," came the reply, "but the rockets and launch specifications are still being completed. They should be ready within the next week. Did you want us to slow down until we can gather more information?"

"No," she said. "God help us if we didn't do everything possible to be ready for an alien invasion. I'd rather we go back to the Stone Age than to have our planet ravaged by little green men.

Do our astronomers have eyes on an invading force coming from, well, anywhere?"

Another voice from the advisor team answered her. "No. We are constantly grid scanning every inch of space trying to detect suspicious movements. So far there is nothing."

This didn't make Kathryn feel any better. "Then keep searching while you move forward with the satellites as quickly as you can. Until he proves otherwise, we'll have to trust that this prince is really trying to help."

* * *

Jason, Mark and Nuri were undergoing one of their final sessions in the third chamber of the Temple Beautiful. Amelius and Halaliel were regular visitors while they meditated and basked in the rejuvenating vibrations of the crystals embedded in the walls. However, this time their subconscious meeting took place in what had to be the Bimini Hall of Records.

"It is time for you to return to the surface," Halaliel said. "We brought you here to show you two of the devices that will make all the difference when you face the world above."

"Wait! You mean this meditation is as close as we are going to get to the Hall of Records?" Nuri asked.

"Yes," Amelius answered, "for the time being. But let not your heart be troubled. If you will maintain a loving attitude, you will remember everything you need from this ethereal session to reconstruct these devices at JPL. The Hall of Records will still be here in pristine condition when the time is right."

Mark asked, "Do we get to pick which two? We saw a lot of RF equipment in the chamber under the Sphinx and in the Piedras Negras Hall of Records."

Halaliel wasn't going to let that subtle jab pass. "Your free will is not being hindered at all. The two devices that will help you the most are also what you and the rest of humanity are ready to receive."

Amelius walked over to the nearest of the obsidian pedestals. "Mark and Jason have already experienced this first

599

device in Egypt. It is for healing rather than rejuvenating the physical body."

Jason said, "Yes, I remember. That's where I put my hand in the depression on top of the stone. Mark did it too and, between us, it cured his diabetes while I had an old bone break smooth over and received a new gall bladder."

"Correct!" Amelius confirmed.

"And the other new RF tech you mentioned?" Nuri asked.

Halaliel held up a small crystal box and said, "Mark demonstrated this device when you were in the Giza Hall of Records. You completely underestimated its abilities. Because it projected a holographic movie of the history contained in that place, you assumed its function was simply to tell ancient stories. I assure you that it is much more than that."

"So what else can it do?" Nuri asked, getting a little impatient.

Amelius responded calmly, "This device can access the information available to you in the Akashic Records. You have only to think of a question, or ask it aloud, and the box will give the answer telepathically, though you have mistakenly believed you physically saw and heard the holograms played for you."

"Tell me again what the Akashic Records are exactly?" Jason asked.

Halaliel answered, "It is a compendium of everything that has ever been or will ever be that is written on the skein of time and space. In three dimensions, humans most often require a tool like this to access the information. Eventually, humanity will develop direct telepathic access to whatever is needed."

Amelius added, "As with everything else, you are not given more than you can bear and you will only receive information that is helpful and hopeful. In other words, not every question you pose to it will be answered."

Mark was humbled as he realized what a gift they were about to receive. "Why are you giving this to us now?"

Halaliel smiled, "Because until now, it was not time for you to unveil this to the world. It is your own elevated vibrations, combined with those of the rest of humanity, that determines what you can see and what remains a mystery."

Nuri asked, "So what are the questions we shouldn't ask?"

Halaliel said, "The limitations regarding its answers are automatic. For instance, if you ask questions that you are able to discern the answer for yourself, the information will be withheld. This helps to keep you from becoming too dependent. Also, this device will not disclose information from which the questioner, or the world, will not receive benefit. As is true with the Hall of Records, when the world is ready, the next steps are revealed."

Amelius added, "Being in this place is a good example. Your physical bodies have already been inside this room. At the time, it appeared to be a dead end to the tunnel that you thought would lead you to the Hall of Records. It was much the same in Guatemala when the drug cartel kept blasting away at the pyramid not realizing you were no longer there. You three had entered a different dimension when you passed through the pyramid's wall. The Bimini Hall of Records will remain in a different dimension that is accessible to only those of a pure mind.

"Once your mind is opened, you will be able to see the endless possibilities this Hall of Records offers. Meeting in this ethereal manner allows you to access a portion of your consciousness that is able to recognize this sacred place."

"Okay, so we're ready to go back now!" Jason said already wanting to leave. "How do we get there?"

Halaliel held up the crystal box and said, "Ask again."

They suddenly regained consciousness in the Temple Beautiful chamber. Jason jumped to his feet, enjoying privately how good it felt to be able to do that with such ease again. "Follow me guys. We'll be home in no time."

He didn't hesitate as he walked into a section of the chamber wall and disappeared. Mark and Nuri just looked at each other for a moment. Then Nuri shrugged and vanished as he followed behind Jason. Mark ran after them to make sure he wasn't left behind.

They found themselves back in JPL's break room looking at a very surprised Eljay. He still had half-chewed food in his open mouth as he stared at the three intruders.

"That's not a good look for you, Eljay," Jason joked. "To answer your question, we got here the same way we came back to Pasadena when we were stuck inside the pyramid."

Eljay swallowed hard and said, "That's not my question. Who the hell are you people?"

The three men started to laugh. They had forgotten that they didn't appear the same as when they had last seen their young friend. Their physical bodies were now those of men in their twenties. Of course Eljay would not recognize them until they explained who they were and what they'd been through.

Nasrum mentally inspected the twelve new satellites that were in a geosynchronous orbit around the earth. The communications loop test came back positive proving they were properly linked. The representatives from every government and their best scientists were gathered for this landmark occasion. All eyes in the Houston control center turned to the main video monitor that showed a live feed of Makoa's face from his secret location in Little Rock. Nasrum gave the order for the satellite system to go live.

Since the NASA staff had little understanding of RF technology, they had assumed that the twelve satellites would protect the earth in some way. It was quite the opposite. Nasrum needed to convince the people of earth that brutal aliens were ready to attack. He could sense lingering doubts among the less gullible of humanity. He had to convince them that this imminent threat was real.

The satellite array did not envelope the planet with a protective shield. It was not equipped with any defensive capabilities at all. Its purpose was to intentionally cause its own destruction in a spectacular way. The satellites were sending out a repeating signal of the Fibonacci numbers sequence on the emergency channel. Nasrum knew that when they were flooded with multiple false calls for help, the Intergalactic Federation would be forced to shut down the interference. He didn't know how long it would take them to respond, but he was sure he could use the event as proof that the aliens were coming and that their intent was hostile.

"I will now tell you what we have accomplished," Nasrum said to the Mission Control staff. "The satellites we sent up are a significant threat to the invaders. It may surprise you to learn that they will be able to destroy our satellites from a great distance. However, earth having this technology will give them pause and force them to reassess their invasion plan. They will have to recall their forces to adequately respond to the technology level they will now assume we possess. This not only buys us time, it greatly understates what we will have waiting for them when the time comes."

Murmurs of shock and alarm went around the room at Mission Control. Nasrum paused to let the team members' fears take root before he continued.

"We have bought perhaps a year's delay with what you have accomplished today. I will be able to show you how to properly prepare your defenses in that time. It is vital that all nations continue to cooperate in this effort to defeat our enemies. I promise that I will not let you down. Earth will be able to survive and even thrive against anything these demons can throw at us."

The space engineers and political representatives didn't look convinced. These were mainly scientists who made decisions based on facts and evidence. So far, all they had was Prince Nafid's word. A moment later, several alarms and flashing lights signaled something had gone wrong.

"Sir," Nasrum heard a voice say to David Pater, the head of Mission Control, "we've just lost contact with half of the satellite array."

All eyes went to the video screens dedicated to each of the twelve satellites in orbit. Six of the monitors revealed shiny pieces still moving in an outward trajectory. The other monitors showed the remaining satellites start to glow red hot before they too exploded into shrapnel. The room settled into a stunned silence. They had just witnessed that the threat was real and coming from an enemy with weapons far superior to anything on earth.

Nasrum spoke again from the main screen, "Don't be discouraged by this, but also don't fail to recognize what we are up against. The invasion force has the capability to destroy anything on or near the earth from great distances. They haven't done so because of their intent to rob this planet of its natural resources. That includes enslaving our people to perform manual labor. For transporting such huge amounts of workers and cargo, they need to be on location. The good news is that they do not yet travel as fast as their weapons, Allah be praised. That is why we have a year or more to prepare for their arrival."

The mood in Mission Control was strained. Nasrum could sense the question that was going through their minds. He knew answering it properly would lock him in as their trusted leader no matter what happened.

"You can be sure that I could have prevented the destruction of the satellite array, but that was a ruse. The aliens are now convinced they know the depth and strength of our defensive capabilities. They will be fooled into thinking the array is the full extent of the technology they must defeat. They will recall the invasion force currently on its way to earth so they can upgrade their weapons to meet our perceived challenge. They will be surprised at how outmatched their new assault force will be."

The mood lightened in the large room and Nasrum was set to lock his position as their undisputed leader.

"As inviting as it might be to make slaves out of the survivors, I have a better plan. We will let a few of them escape to go home and warn any other species to stay away from earth. In so doing, a reign of peace will begin on this planet that will last for one thousand years. I, Prince Nafid, promise all these things to you!"

***

Mark and Nuri stood watching Eljay as he studied the schematics they sketched for him. He kept shaking his head every minute or so until he finally looked up.

"I suppose this first one is some sort of healing apparatus," he began. "But I'll be hanged if I can even guess what the crystal box will do. I assume the whole container is an RF device but it's the first one I've seen that starts with a large crystal and transforms it without melding it with another piece."

"So far you're exactly right," Nuri said, obviously impressed. He then asked, "Do you have any idea why obsidian seems so tied in with helping to get the most out of RF healing technology?"

604

"I have some ideas," Eljay said hesitantly. "Obsidian may well be the best representative of an earthly substance found on our planet. If RF power comes from the earth in the same way that a capacitor stores energy, then obsidian would make an excellent conductor. The purpose of the obsidian pedestal is to activate and heal the person touching it, right? So it might be that the rock is ideal for passing on the earth's stored DNA information of all creatures and that directs the healing energies to the, um, ailing parts within a particular body."

"That's more than just an idea," Mark exclaimed. He was proud of Eljay. "What about the crystal box?"

"It doesn't seem to require obsidian to function," Eljay said, "though we might enhance the results we get if we try it. I'll want to experiment with the best way to employ obsidian in our design when the time comes."

"I'll want to be here for that," Jason interjected. "I have a lot of questions to ask."

Eljay exclaimed, "Is anyone going to tell me what this crystal box is supposed to do?"

Mark answered smiling, "Patience, grasshopper. We'll let you be the first one to ask that question to test it!"

Nuri asked, "How long do you think it will take to build the prototypes of these two devices?"

"Assuming we can locate an obsidian block big enough to carve into the pedestal, and a large enough crystal to build the box, and that I'll be working round the clock, not long at all," Eljay laughed. "Besides, I've been getting way too much sleep lately."

Jason said, "You don't need me for this. I'm going to call Gus and Diana on the phone. That is, unless either one of you thought to bring your RFC earbuds with you before we left?"

The all looked at each other a little sheepishly and shook their heads.

"Fine then," Jason nodded. "I'll let them know that we're okay and safe in California. I'll also tell them that we'll be back in RFC communication as soon as Eljay gets around to replacing the earbuds."

Chapter 16

Nasrum waited patiently while the world's top space engineers pored over his most recent drawings. The schematics had been delivered to Houston that same morning and he knew they would have questions. The scope of the new satellite infrastructure was beyond their imagination. He knew that the immense array would never perform as promised. Since he didn't need to protect the earth from an outside attack, what would be the point? His hidden agenda was to keep earth's people working together peacefully for 1,000 years instead of fighting with each other.

Nasrum had seen this pattern repeated numerous times throughout the universes. Souls would become entrapped in a particular realm or dimension. Many would rally to help their entangled siblings, but it was always one particular soul who managed to show everyone else the way of peace. Earth needed a savior and Nasrum was determined to be it.

His first step in becoming the earth's Messiah was to become humanity's undisputed leader. He already had that bullet point checked off. He was now working to maintain a millennium of peace. Trying to stop these humans from killing each other through that incompetent prince had been a waste of time. His revised plan, he was sure, was the way to go. He wondered why no one had tried it before now.

Assuming he could peacefully direct the people of earth for 1,000 years, humanity would qualify for membership in the Intergalactic Federation. As the planet's supreme ruler, he would be given the reverence and tributes that are rightfully due any soul who can lead an entire people out of their self-imposed exile.

Nasrum had worked tirelessly throughout history to get the world to listen to him. Organizing the citizens of Atlantis became such a hopeless cause that Nasrum helped to destroy the continent so he could start over from scratch. His next attempt at controlling the masses lasted nearly 500 years through the Roman Empire, but he could hardly claim that period was one of peace. Next he tried to save humanity through a series of dictators. He nearly succeeded with Germany in World War II because of Adolph Hitler's trust in the occult. Hitler invaded Poland on Nasrum's advice. He continued to do well until he chose to invade Russia despite Nasrum's warnings that it would lead to his undoing. By the time Hitler was ready to listen to him again, it was too late.

Those dismal failures convinced him to stop working through established despots. They only listened to him for a time until they decided that they knew better than he did. Prince Nafid had been a spineless leader who would not defy him, but stupid people and bad luck had, once again, ruined Nasrum's plans. He decided that taking direct possession of a body and claiming to channel the deceased Nafid was a brilliant way to avoid working with incompetents. This apparent loophole allowed him to incarnate back into the earth without anyone's approval. New bodies, like Makoa's, would always be available when he needed them. The world had already become desensitized to him speaking as Prince Nafid through other people, so he should have no problem popping up in successive physical forms for the next millennium.

* * *

Amelius and Halaliel studied the infinite potential timelines for Earth. The combined possibilities of every soul's choices presented a daunting challenge in predicting probable outcomes. When forecasting what humanity thinks of as the future, many souls and angels limit their research to the most likely choices and results. Amelius was different. He took great care to consider all possibilities in appraising the timelines. He did this through intuition more than a daunting research of the Akashic Records.

Amelius was a soul who was special in many ways. His approach to life was loving and optimistic. He too had made mistakes and had once become entrapped on earth. It took him thirty human lifetimes to find his way back to God. Rather than moving on to higher realms, Amelius chose to be his brother's keeper. He was dedicated to helping every soul who wanted to make their Creator's unconditional love their guide. Nasrum continued to work against Amelius' hopes for a better world. It was quite a challenge for Amelius to not block Nasrum's free will and yet limit the chaos he caused upon the earth.

Halaliel commented, "You know you can stop Nasrum from being so disruptive. He believes he is clever by hiding in outer darkness to avoid facing up to what he has done. His self-imposed prison is an interesting choice to avoid reaping what he has sown. He grows closer to losing his way out of that dark place. He'll probably stay there for a long vacation if he tries it again. Why do you allow this one soul to cause so much unrest on the earth?"

Amelius answered, "It is difficult to see, but Nasrum's pursuit of his own path will eventually help humanity reach its full potential. While he doesn't realize it, his selfish actions are working more against his stated goals than he understands. His selfishness blocks his access to certain key people and events. The diminishing connection between his mind and the corporeal brain of Makoa's body hinders him all the more."

Halaliel asked, "Is it worth the risk to allow Nasrum to proceed with his plans? A thousand years of coerced peace will not be of help to anyone."

"The truth is," Amelius confessed, "that Nasrum's campaign to scare people into submission will result in a better path for Humankind. His previous approach of using Islam needed to be revised in order to benefit everyone. With patience, you will see that the souls entrapped on earth and even Nasrum himself will learn much once his misguided plan fails."

"Do you believe that Nasrum will ever recognize the error of his ways?" Halaliel asked.

"Absolutely, but that will take time," Amelius began. "In many respects, Nasrum is a delightful soul and he has the potential to be of great help. In some ways, he is like the Bible's Saul who became Paul on the road to Damascus. He is certain that his goals, as selfish as they might be, will help humanity. He strongly believes our Creator wants him to be their Messiah."

Halaliel scoffed, "How can he believe that becoming a Messiah is accomplished through deceit? Surely he knows that a true Savior fulfills both the letter and the spirit of the law? Nasrum can't be recognized as earth's Savior until all his choices are in harmony with God's perfect love. He ignores that a true Messiah is also the willing servant of all."

Amelius smiled and said, "His goals and methods are clearly misdirected. He doesn't accept that the only things that last forever are rooted in unconditional love. I know you can see what a wonderful mentor he will be to others if and when this Prodigal Son decides to return home. It is through patience that we can see our Creator alive in Nasrum."

"But there are many ways to guide him to a virtuous path that are not so disruptive to others," Halaliel persisted.

"I have learned that better results come when a soul is allowed to have their way," Amelius smiled. "I struggled for a time myself with the desire to forcefully guide others. That is why I give a wide berth to using any measures of control over Nasrum that aren't absolutely necessary."

"You mean like resetting the timeline when Nasrum caused them to miss the Hall of Records?" Halaliel asked. "I am puzzled, though, that you let him get that far."

Amelius explained, "There was a small chance that Mark and Nuri would realize how they could stop the RFL containment field's movement before they surfaced. I intervened when the remaining timelines ended with their arrest because of Nasrum's interference."

"But you know he is not allowed to commandeer a body like the one left behind by the suicidal Makoa. Why didn't you stop him then?" Halaliel was truly perplexed.

"Because Nasrum, unlike so many other disruptive souls, actually believes he is right. He is convinced that the 'I am that I am' thinks as he does. He believes, even now, that 'Allah' hides his actions from my view," Amelius said with a sad smile. "The unconditionally loving nature of the First Cause confuses him. By letting Nasrum go forward with his plan, misguided as it is, he will eventually come to understand the unconditionally loving nature of our Creator."

"But in the meantime," Halaliel added persuasively, "he falls ever further into darkness and helps no one in the process."

Amelius said, "It is in our nature to want to help others when we are on the right path. The Christ Consciousness teaches, 'Let he who has not sinned cast the first stone!' I know archangels have a difficult time with that concept. Looking far into the future, Nasrum

609

will become quite gifted in helping others through the challenges he faces in the here and now. Despite the truth in all you have said, I still love Nasrum with an everlasting love."

***

President Campbell was on a secure video channel with David Pater, the Director of Operations at NASA. He was reporting on the prince's plans that he'd analyzed since early that same morning.

"The best quick description I can give you, Madam President, is that it's similar to a Dyson sphere," David hedged. "While a true Dyson sphere would encase a star to harness its energy, this seemingly invisible sphere is intended to surround the earth and shield us from detection."

Kathryn tried to sound unimpressed, but failed. "Is that even possible? Won't the earth be cut off from the sun if we go through with that?"

Dr. Pater said, "Let me try that again. While a Dyson sphere is intended to completely encase a star, the sphere Prince Nafid proposes uses RF shielding to render the earth invisible to anything outside of it. At least, that is what Prince Nafid has assured us. He claims we'll be able to see out and receive sunlight in, but anyone venturing beyond the RF field's grid will not be able to detect this planet's existence."

"Does that mean no more space travel for us?" she asked.

"Probably, unless the same RF shielding could be used on each spaceship," he speculated. "My guess is that unshielded space ships coming and going from the earth could be detected by the extraterrestrials. They've already shown that they can spot and destroy any target they want from whatever part of the galaxy they are in right now. I will venture to guess that anything we send outside of the RF shield will only serve to let the aliens know we're here."

"Can you get the prince on the conference line now and I'll monitor the conversation off camera?" she asked. "I'd like to hear him speaking about this satellite array first hand."

The next moment the face of Makoa channeling the prince came into view on David's laptop.

"Have you had an opportunity to review the schematics I sent to you, David?" Kathryn couldn't get used to hearing Arabic accented English coming from a half Polynesian, half African American face. It also bothered her that the prince addressed Dr. Pater by his first name.

"We have, Prince Nafid," David answered deferentially. "I have a few questions, if you don't mind."

"Not at all, David. We will be working on this project together for a very long time," he smiled.

"That point touches on my first question," David laughed stiffly. "Just how long do you envision this project taking to complete?"

"An excellent question, David. I'm certain this project will not be completed until you and the man I am speaking through now have long passed away. The shield will be built in stages or degrees. Over time, we will need to add offensive weapons to the array to better protect the earth. You can be sure that our first deployment will render our planet invisible to the species that already destroyed our satellites."

David was confused and asked, "But didn't you say that we can defeat them when they do reach earth?"

"That is still true, but news travels fast and plans are constantly changing in the universe. There are other alien species paying close attention who also covet the earth's resources. Some are so powerful and violent that it is better to avoid them altogether than to prevail at a great cost to this planet."

"So you are developing a two-pronged approach, is that correct? A defensive shield to hide us from predators while we develop offensive weapons to protect ourselves in the event that someone does find us."

"Exactly!" Nasrum said with a broad smile on his face. "I knew you were the right man to have in charge. Oh, no offense intended toward you, Madam President Campbell." His gaze shifted so that it looked like he could see her on his monitor.

Kathryn grimaced realizing that he'd known she was listening in the whole time. "No offense taken Prince Nafid. I did not want to intrude, but I do need to continue my conversation with Dr. Pater after you're finished. Would you prefer he call me back when you're done?"

"Nice save, Madam President! I like people who can think quickly when they are in a jam," Nasrum said, embarrassing her all the more. "Please continue your discussion with David. I am done for the present."

Makoa's face turned completely passive before the video screen went blank. POTUS wondered what the man did between channeling sessions for the prince. He was obviously well-groomed and cared for, but no one knew if Nafid's channel had a life beyond speaking for the world's newly recognized leader.

"At least we know better than to try that again," Kathryn said nervously. "There seems to be no limit to Prince Nafid's abilities."

"I agree, Madam President. It's a good thing he is on our side. I would hate to think what would happen if he turned against us."

Kathryn asked, "So why do you think he needs that man to convey his wishes to the world?"

"That's a good question, but I have no idea," he sighed. "Maybe it's a security measure? Let's face it, who would want to assassinate Makoa? Now that everyone knows the prince can communicate through any body at will, why would anyone bother to assassinate him? They tried that already and it didn't work!"

"I don't know if you're joking, but you make an excellent point. Please keep watch for any clues to the prince's motives or limitations," Kathryn instructed. "I am going to try to get you some help to learn what his array really does."

"Okay," David said blankly. "Who is it that can do that?"

Kathryn answered, "I have been told that the scientists who discovered RF technology have somehow found their way back to a lab they work out of in Pasadena. They have a poor history of working with the government since Matthew Alexander left office over 30 years ago. I hope to convince them to work with us."

"I'm surprised to hear they're still alive. They must be getting up there in years," David responded. "But if they can help, I'm all for it!"

Kathryn said, "I'm already trying to get in contact with them. I'll let you know how that goes. Please keep me apprised of any developments regarding the prince's satellites."

***

"Hey Dr. Zayd, can I borrow you for a minute?" Eljay had yelled loud enough that Nuri heard him from down the hall.

Nuri entered the lab to find Eljay standing in front of a large block of obsidian that had been reshaped into a solid, round column. It was about four feet tall and a foot in diameter. He had just finished smoothing out the hand depression carved in the slanted top of the block. "I need a witness for the first trial run of RFH, resonant frequency healing."

Nuri walked over to inspect the shiny black pedestal. Eljay said, "Jason told me that, in the Giza Hall of Records, he activated the RFH healing process just by placing his hand in the carved depression with the RFP sending crystal floating before it. From what you've told me, I don't believe this one needs an exterior crystal to do its thing."

Nuri took a seat and watched as Eljay placed his hand so that his fingers lined up with the carving. Nothing happened and he sighed saying, "Of course, it couldn't be that easy."

Nuri said, "Do you want me to try?"

"Very funny," Eljay said mockingly. "You know you guys are the healthiest humans on the planet right now. How would we know if it's working or not if you try it? You've got nothing to heal."

Nuri said, "I'm sorry, I hadn't thought of that. I wasn't trying to make a joke. If you don't have any other ideas, let me meditate a bit to see if I can come up with something."

Eljay said "okay," but his pained expression betrayed how he really felt about meditation.

613

***

Sitting quietly in the silence, Nuri could feel the presence of Halaliel. He didn't have to ask the angel what to do next. Halaliel simply showed him what he needed to know about RFH technology. The information also came with an explanation. As good as RFH was at healing, it was limited in how far it could repair the body. For a person to be rejuvenated back to their youth required the same lengthy procedure Nuri went through in the Temple Beautiful. Once he returned to a fully conscious state, Nuri found Eljay to give him the news.

"It's understandable why it didn't work," Nuri laughed. "You were right that RFH does not need an RFP crystal to operate. However, there is an entirely different process to preparing the obsidian pedestal if you don't want to directly power the device with an RFP crystal."

"Why is this the first time I'm hearing about this?" Eljay asked.

Nuri sighed and said, "Well, it's the first time you've asked. Besides, Mark is really tied up with designing the Akashic Record crystal box. I'm embarrassed that I don't remember the specifics on vibrational healing, but I didn't experience it first hand in Giza. Only Mark and Jason touched the obsidian to be healed of their old injuries. Maybe that's why the details for RFH don't stick with me."

"So what do I have to do to prepare the pedestal?" Eljay asked.

"Actually, you've done most of the work already," Nuri assured him. "The first challenge is that it's too big to fit into the RF programming device you use now. You also have to tune it to the correct base RF frequency along with three progressive octaves and overtones until the RFH programming fuses with the obsidian. I didn't follow this very well when Halaliel showed me how to make it work, but I did write it all down."

"Great!" Eljay grumbled as he looked at Nuri's notes. "Now I have to build a new supporting structure for the obsidian and figure out how to attach the RF oscillators at either end. Tell everyone else I'll be back after I get some parts at the hardware store."

614

Chapter 17

Eljay absent-mindedly picked up the telephone handset, "JPL, Eljay speaking."

The professional voice at the other end said, "Madam President Campbell would like to speak with Doctors Mark Heston and Nuri Zayd. Can you arrange that right away?"

He hesitated for an awkward moment before saying, "Who is this really? You certainly aren't the President of the United States."

"Of course not, sir," the voice replied. "This is her personal assistant. I'm trying to coordinate a secure phone conversation with the President and Doctors Heston and Zayd as soon as possible."

Eljay gasped once he realized that this was not a crank call. "I'm so sorry! I can get them right now, it will only take a minute. However, I have no idea if we still have a secure line into this building."

"I can verify that you do, sir," the voice said flatly. "I just called you on it."

Eljay looked down and saw that a light was on next to a phone line he didn't know was active on the bank of buttons to push. "Okay, I'll go get them."

The woman waited and heard someone pick up. "Nuri Zayd and Mark Heston here."

"Please hold for the President," the voice said before she went offline.

"Doctors Heston and Zayd!" a familiar voice began. "It is a pleasure to speak with you both."

The men hesitated just long enough to silently mouth to each other, 'It's really her!'

"We're here Madam President," Nuri managed to blurt out. "What can we do for you?"

"I need to ask a favor," she said. "Our government scientists have forgotten most of what they knew about RF technology and translating the written language, I'm told, came from the fabled continent of Atlantis. I understand that the two of you are the best experts available on these unusual subjects."

"We're flattered!" Nuri blushed. "But no one from the government has been interested in RF technology for years. What's behind this sudden interest?"

The president sighed and said, "I have a copy of a set of plans provided by Prince Nafid with a directive to build a massive RF satellite array that envelopes the planet. I'd like you to review them and tell me what we're building and if you believe this monstrosity will perform as the prince claims."

Mark answered, "We'll be glad to help, Madam President, but can I ask why you're calling us directly instead of working through your staff?"

"That's a fair question," she offered. "Let's say that Prince Nafid would probably not appreciate my questions and he has an uncanny ability to know things that he shouldn't possibly know. I'm just trying to keep the number of people investigating my suspicions to a minimum."

"Why do you believe he doesn't know we're talking right now?" Nuri asked.

"Perhaps he does," she sighed, "but my experience is that he would have already called me here at the White House to politely ask to be included."

Nuri said, "I see. And he hasn't done that yet?"

"No," she said, "but I would continue to investigate this project until the prince threatened me not to. The scope of his design will require at least hundreds of years and huge amounts of natural resources to accomplish. I just want to be sure this project is worth that investment."

Mark asked, "So do you intend to send the plans here for us to take a look? If you're trying to keep the headcount to a minimum of people involved, can you email them?"

Kathryn said, "I have already made arrangements for them to be delivered via priority mail and courier. The various pages have been separated so that they make no sense apart from each other. You will be able to put them together in the correct order without anyone being the wiser at my end. You should receive the separated pages in tomorrow's mail. Assuming you say yes, the courier deliveries will come later this afternoon."

"It appears that the prince still hasn't called," Nuri said optimistically, "and, these days, we're below everyone's radar. Please give us a couple of days to collate and review the plans. We'll tell you whatever we can then. Should we call you?"

"It's better if I call you," she confirmed. "Shall we say 6:00PM your time in two days then?"

Kathryn replaced the handset as she reflected on the phone call. She had expected some pushback from the men. It sounded like they wanted to help in any way they could. Was it possible that they weren't as hard to get along with as she had been led to believe? She wanted to ask them how they evaded the combined efforts of the Navy, CIA and FBI in traveling from Bimini back to their lab in Pasadena. She decided it would be better not to remind them of the ugly incident with Captain Archer. She really needed their cooperation.

***

"I have finally done it!" Nasrum congratulated himself. "After centuries of trying to lead humanity to peace, I have found the way. I was wrong to think that a strong leader, fascist government or even great prosperity could stop these idiotic humans from fighting each other. It was pure genius to unite them by hating a common enemy that was not of this earth."

Nasrum had deceitfully fielded all of NASA's questions regarding the array's ability to shield and protect the earth. While he claimed that the satellites' RF field would make the earth invisible to extraterrestrials, it served a much greater purpose. The RF vibrations the array would generate were ironically musical. They would strangely serenade the earth with discordant, inaudible sounds that would agitate humanity. Depending upon the intensity of the RF pulses, the results ranged from making people uneasy to triggering outright panic.

He still had to be careful. Nasrum could feel that President Campbell was unconvinced that he was the savior of the earth. His initial reaction to her suspicions was to find a suitable substitute, but he could see that she was a good and trusted leader. Replacing her without good cause would disturb the NASA scientists and he needed them at the top of their game to complete his array. He resolved to keep a careful watch on her and be ready to metaphorically pull her plug at a moment's notice.

There was yet another challenge for Nasrum to deal with. He had noticed it was becoming more difficult to read the minds of other people. President Campbell's thoughts were becoming particularly difficult to track. Could it be that he was already losing the connection between his borrowed corporeal brain and his spiritual consciousness? If that was the case, he would have to find a new body to act as Prince Nafid's channel to humanity. Nasrum wanted to avoid that for as long as possible. The process of inserting his mind into the brain of a grown adult was excruciating.

***

Mark, Nuri and Jason were in deep meditation when Amelius and Halaliel entered their thoughts.

Amelius said, "Do you remember the 'thump' or catalyst I mentioned that could quickly change the future?"

Not waiting for the men to answer, Halaliel added, "The time is upon you. The selfish energies surrounding Prince Nafid are weakening quickly. You three, with the help of Diana and Eljay, can help humanity choose its own karmic path free of Nasrum's interference."

Jason was the first to respond. "I'm glad you brought Prince Nafid up. We've ignored the guy because you've made it clear that an alien invasion is a myth. But he has convinced everyone else that the threat is real. Who is this guy and what's his agenda?"

Amelius answered, "It can be said that you are the Yin to his Yang. The three of you are the universe's loving, yet cogent, response to that soul's disruptive choices. Your lives are intricately linked through karmic connections. In past lifetimes, you have been the ones to restore balance in the wake of his misguided efforts."

618

"I'm not sure how that answered my question," Jason said sounding bewildered.

"Ah, the soul's name was what you really wanted to know," Amelius smiled. "With that in mind, let me try again. You would sow peace where Nasrum sows fear. You desire the willing cooperation of each person on earth working together. Nasrum believes that a lasting peace can best be achieved through dread and intimidation."

"This prince guy's name is Nasrum?" Nuri asked, not understanding.

Halaliel answered, "The soul's name is Nasrum. He is the one who invisibly guides Prince Nafid's orders. This is not the first time in earth's history that you have witnessed his influence. Well known leaders such as Genghis Khan, Alexander the Great, Julius Caesar, Adolph Hitler, and, most recently, Prince Nafid Alsab Anahni, have all been mentored by this same soul. In human form, you knew of him forty years ago as the Syrian Colonel Achmed Mansur."

Jason gasped, "Wasn't that the guy Matt Alexander told us blew up a Giza hotel and the Sphinx?"

Halaliel answered, "Nasrum and Mansur are one and the same."

"You make him sound like he's in league with Lucifer," Mark said with foreboding.

"In some ways," Amelius smiled, "Nasrum is more difficult than Lucifer. For you see, Lucifer knows he makes selfish choices to dominate other souls. Nasrum makes selfish choices thinking the ends will justify the means toward his goal of being the earth's Messiah."

"How can scaring the bejesus out of people over a non-existent alien invasion help to save humanity?" Jason asked.

"It can't," Halaliel confirmed. "But it does serve his selfish agenda to unite the planet through fear. The current worldwide alliance where all nations work together to defeat a common enemy will not endure for much longer. How can it when his plan is based on fear rather than love? Nasrum is only fooling himself, but billions of souls have put their trust in him."

"So how do we stop this guy?" Nuri asked.

"That choice is yours and you already have the knowledge to accomplish your goal," Halaliel said. "As you have come to realize, we offer help as you help yourselves. When what you need to achieve the greatest good is beyond your immediate grasp, we will always be there for you."

Mark sighed, "You have implied that this Nasrum has abilities that we do not. Surely you don't want Jason to assassinate him. He'd just use some other poor soul's body to do his bidding. I'm not seeing how we can put an end to his reign."

Amelius said, "With the simple truth! Examine the plans that President Campbell is sending to you. You will easily discern the array's function now that Nasrum's intentions are known. Be sure to complete the RF device to access the Akashic Records. It will be most helpful in overcoming the extreme challenges ahead for all of you."

***

Jason looked at his watch and announced to Mark and Nuri, "It's almost 6:00PM. We need to check in with Eljay before the president calls."

They saw a very haggard Eljay when they walked into his lab. They could guess he needed more time. "I can follow the design, but I can't see any useful purpose for this RF device."

"Tell us what it does and we'll be able to help you with that," Mark suggested.

"Imagine a piano that was designed to do nothing but play ugly music," Eljay said with a snort. "No matter what keys you play on its keyboard, the sound makes you cringe. It seems to have a range from 'annoying' to 'life-threatening.' That's because it has a gain control to pump up the force of its vibrational assault. What confuses me is that the vibrations it emanates are all above the audible range for humans. In other words, because we can't hear the sounds it makes, it's possible this device does nothing at all."

Nuri said, "I think you're dead-on except for the last part. What if it can cause each person on earth to fear for their lives at the same time? If the goal is causing chaos through fear, I'll bet it works great!"

"Can you build a scale model of this device so we can test it?" Jason asked.

"Sure, but it won't have nearly the effective range of the huge satellite array," Eljay guessed.

"Our goal here is to prove what it does," Nuri explained. "Prince Nafid is telling the world that this device emits a field that hides the earth from would-be alien invaders. I doubt we would be so quick to build this thing if they knew what it was really for."

The secure line rang at precisely 6:00PM. Mark answered and put it on speaker.

"Madam President, you have me, Dr. Zayd and our colleague, Dr. Louis Jensen Jr. on the line." He knew Jason didn't need to be introduced because he was only there out of curiosity.

"I'm a little pressed for time here, gentlemen," the president said. "What can you tell me about the satellite array the prince wants us to build?"

Eljay answered, "It is hardly a cloak of invisibility. That much is certain. We can't yet prove what it actually does, but we intend to build a scale model to find out."

The president asked, "How long until you can do that?"

Eljay guessed, "It will take a few days, at least. This is a kind of RF technology we have not worked with before."

"Then I will call you back at this same time in three days," Kathryn said before disconnecting. She hadn't meant to be rude, but she had been forced to put the French President on hold to call them when she promised.

Jason laughed, "So you have three days to figure out what the prince will take one thousand years to accomplish? Good luck with that!"

Nuri said, "I'm pretty sure that building this thing on any scale will not be hard. Worse yet, how difficult will it be for Nafid to convince everyone that he has protected them from invading aliens? Every day we go without seeing a flying saucer makes him more of a hero."

Mark interjected, "I'm still trying to get the symbols in my head translated for Eljay to make the Akashic Records box. I hope to have the specs ready by the time he's done testing the model."

Chapter 18

"I don't think I'm getting your best efforts here," Prince Nafid said flatly.

David Pater said, "I admit that we're moving slower than I expected, but we are doing the best we can. The scientists who know the most about RF technology are unwilling to join our team. Without them, we're stuck teaching ourselves how to work with these crystals."

"When do you believe the satellites will be ready?" the prince asked.

"That's why I contacted you," David said nervously. "We have no idea how to test the RF devices inside the satellites. How do you detect a shield that is supposed to be undetectable?"

The prince paused for a moment before saying, "If you build it properly, that won't be a problem. However, I will personally inspect and approve your work before it is time to propel the satellites into orbit."

"You're coming to Houston?" David asked, hardly believing he had heard the prince correctly. "You usually have everyone come to you. Would it be better to ship one of the satellites to Little Rock for inspection rather than have you come all the way out here?"

"I don't want to see just one satellite, David," the prince began. "I want to inspect them all before you deploy them. The technology, as you said, is too far beyond your team's expertise for me to have confidence in the quality of their work."

"You're the boss," David said with resignation. "I'll let you know the moment they are ready."

***

Mark, Nuri and Eljay were in the main lab at JPL. Designing the RF Akashic device (RFA) was proving to be the most difficult application of the technology so far. They had created several unsuccessful prototypes and were no closer to understanding a working box than before they started.

"Why don't you contact our friends in the vapors to tell you how to fix this?" Jason asked.

Mark said, "I guess that's reasonable, but Amelius told us we would remember everything we need to know if we maintain a loving attitude. If I have to ask what went wrong, I'll know that I've failed him."

"Nonsense," Nuri scoffed. "We've made plenty of blunders before. They've never made us feel bad about our mistakes."

"If I'm really honest with myself," Mark confessed, "I'm not sure the world is ready for this device. I mean, they have been so careful to not disclose too much information to us since we first met them. I don't see this RFA box being the answer to our woes. I'm worried that it might be like Pandora's Box by bringing on more problems than it solves."

Nuri reminded him, "Amelius said that it won't answer all our questions, just those that will be helpful and hopeful for humanity to know, when we are ready to know them."

Mark could only nod in agreement. With that, Nuri pulled three meditation crystals out of his pocket and presented his open palm to Mark. His friend hesitantly took one and sat back in his chair. Jason declined to take one without comment.

"Would you like to try, Eljay?" Nuri asked as he extended his hand toward him.

"You're inviting me to try meditating?" was his surprised response.

Nuri laughed and said, "After all this time you're not the least bit curious?"

Eljay hesitantly took a crystal from Nuri's hand and asked, "What do I do?"

Nuri realized that most of their preparations for meditation were not discernable by simply watching them. He invited Eljay to sit down and began to talk him through the process."

"Start by getting comfortable in your chair. It's important to keep your spine straight. That's how the spiritual energy rises from within. Hold the crystal in your left hand, since that is the receiving side of the body. Say a silent prayer asking to be protected as you enter into this meditation. I often use the Lord's Prayer, but whatever feels right to you will work.

"Then visualize in your mind's eye the intention you hold for this meditation. Ask the universe to arrange a meeting between us and others who would best help us accomplish what's needed at this time. If I were you, I would ask that Louis Sr. be present. No one who's still alive knows more about RF technology than your dad, not even us.

"After setting the correct intention, you sit in the silence and expectantly wait. There should be no doubt that what you asked for will come. Doubt and fear are the quickest ways to separate us from the help we need."

Eljay did his best to follow Nuri's suggestions. He had been cynical of their supposed encounters with people who were not real; at least they weren't real to him. His father had been skeptical as well, but Louis had become a real believer before he died. Eljay always wondered how they were able to troubleshoot his RF research. If meditation was the answer, what did he have to lose?

After a few minutes, Eljay assumed he had done something wrong because he felt the same as always. But when he opened his eyes, he had trouble adjusting to the site before him. His view was limited, like he was looking through a small window into a room where Nuri and Mark sat. He saw two incredible beings bathed in white light talking with his friends. The extraordinary scene wasn't scary; it was awe-inspiring.

Then Eljay heard the voice of his father, but he couldn't see him. "That's it son. Focus on what you see and express your desire to be present with your friends."

"Dad?" Eljay gasped. "Are you really here?"

He heard his father's familiar laugh. "We're not really anywhere at the moment. You have a foot in two realms while not really being a part of either one. That's why you're not fully experiencing the scene before you. Your partial presence is much like watching a TV show with the sound turned down."

His father was right. Eljay could not make out what was being said. He tried willing himself to join them, but nothing changed.

"I'm the reason this isn't working, son," Louis Sr. said. "I am too much of a distraction. Your greater desire is to talk with me than it is to join your friends. Don't worry, we'll meet again soon!"

Before Eljay could object, he could no longer feel his father's presence. Suddenly, the room with his friends flowed toward him to envelop his consciousness. The four of them looked in his direction and smiled.

"Welcome Eljay! I am Amelius and this is Halaliel," he said pointing to the other brilliantly adorned being.

"Uh,...hi," Eljay managed to say weakly. "I'm sorry to interrupt your meeting. I had a little trouble getting here."

Amelius and Halaliel laughed while Mark and Nuri looked puzzled.

Halaliel said, "Actually, we were just getting to the part you will need to hear. The challenges you've had with the RFA box, as you've decided to call it, is that it operates somewhat differently than your other RF devices so far."

"Get this, Eljay," Nuri blurted out. "The six sides of the crystal box all must be cut from the same larger crystal after it has been conditioned to the correct RF frequency. The sides need to be arranged in a particular order, like you would see with a set of dice. The first slice or wall of the box becomes the opening lid. The second must be positioned so that it faces the front, or meets the opening edge of the box's lid. The third slice is on the right and the fourth on the left side as you would see them from the box's front with the lid opening toward you. That leaves the fifth slice opposite you as the back of the box, and the sixth serving as the bottom or foundation piece."

"Do we just have to take their word for it," Eljay asked, indicating Amelius and Halaliel, "or can we know the reasoning behind all that?"

"It's not such a difficult concept, Eljay," Amelius said smiling. "The Akashic Records make available all knowledge that has ever been or will ever be. Think of modulating this conversation over radio waves and you'll understand how records are stored throughout the skein or fabric of space and time in your dimension."

Eljay just stared at Amelius blankly, indicating he was lost.

"If your mind is not already conditioned to intuitively access the Akashic Records, then this RFA device is very helpful. The box's RF vibration is tuned to the music of the spheres that moves freely through the fabric of time and space. In effect, a microcosm of the Akashic Records is captured inside of the RFA box. It acts as a translating conduit between the questioner and the infinite information it contains. In other words, you ask it a question and the corresponding answer is given, telepathically. You might feel like you are hearing and seeing the answers, but you are not. The RFA box does not communicate through your five senses."

Eljay said nothing. In truth, he was still trying to figure out if this was a hallucination or really happening. Everyone else in the room seemed to ignore his awkward silence.

"How does the box know when we've asked a question that the world is not ready to hear?" Nuri asked.

Halaliel answered, "It works on universal law rather than selectively making such decisions. You might think of your communications with it like the seven-second delay used in live media broadcasts. If something is not meant for the public to hear, the seven-second delay allows the information to be edited or deleted to meet the proper guidelines."

"So universal law is not a person deciding what we can know and what we're not ready for?" Mark asked.

Halaliel said, "Correct. Instead, it compares the combined vibrations of humanity at that moment to the vibration of the answer the box has been asked to provide. If that comparison is harmonious, then the information is not withheld. Otherwise, the box offers only what is appropriate, and perhaps that is no answer at all."

"Well said, Halaliel!" Amelius declared turning to the three friends. "Your team will soon be ready to meet Nasrum!"

"And how do we arrange that?" Nuri asked.

Amelius said, "You won't have to do anything but show up. Your country's president is already working on that."

***

Kathryn Campbell had trouble falling asleep. She could not shake the feeling that the prince had evil intentions despite portraying himself as the world's savior. She kept waking up from nightmares about being trapped, or not having a choice in what she could do. Each time, she'd open her eyes to find herself lying next to her sleeping husband in the White House residence. She did her best to get what rest she could.

Her next nightmare was particularly frightening. She looked up in the sky above the White House to see the impossibly large face of the assassinated Prince Nafid. He looked directly at her and began an evil laugh. As he went on, his face started to expand until it enveloped the earth in all directions. She had the presidential nuclear football next to her and found herself pushing the button. She saw numerous trails of fire heading upward in all directions to destroy the prince. When they exploded, nothing remained but darkness and a sense of dread coursing through every fiber of her being.

"Kathryn!" a gentle voice said in the darkness. "Focus on my voice and I can help you find your way."

The voice seemed to be coming from above her, but the darkness persisted and distorted her sense of direction. It occurred to her to try jumping. She bent her knees and jumped as high as she could. The darkness around her began to fade revealing a white room that looked like her residence, but was completely devoid of color. She landed softly on her feet and looked around.

"Nicely done! Your decision to jump as an active metaphor to raise your consciousness was impressive!" said the man dressed all in white. "That was a particularly ugly dream you were having."

"Who are you?" Kathryn asked. "And where am I?"

"I am called Amelius," the man smiled, "and this place is designed to hold a minimum of distractions while we talk."

"Talk about what?" she asked suspiciously.

"What your intuition and your dreams are warning you to avoid," Amelius said. "Deploying that satellite system the prince proposes is not in humanity's best interests."

"How can you be sure?" she began. "Actually, never mind. I'm already sure he's not who he says he is. How do I stop him?"

"I know the soul you call Prince Nafid well," Amelius began. "His intentions toward this world are not pure evil, but he sees humanity as a means to attain his own selfish goals. Anything or anyone that stands between him and his agenda is all the justification he needs to commit horrendous acts."

"So the prince is like Satan trying to rule over us in hell?" Kathryn asked.

"Goodness no!" Amelius smiled. "He intends for the world to be peaceful under his rule, whether humanity wants that or not. From his perspective, the earth needs a savior and he is convinced he is it."

"What will the satellite array do that's so bad?" she asked. "Will it really make us invisible?"

"There are no extraterrestrials intent on doing earth or humanity harm. The truth is that most other life forms pay little attention to the earth." Amelius explained. "The prince had you create the first satellites knowing they would be destroyed because they were a communications nuisance on a galactic scale. Their unexplained destruction caused you to believe that an attack was imminent. Since the new satellites the prince is about to deploy will disrupt only those upon the earth, none of the other worlds will interfere."

"And how does this new array disrupt us?" she continued.

"His plan is to control humanity through fear," Amelius went on. "He hopes to make people fearful enough with simple threats of alien invaders. If that alone doesn't work, the array will trigger a fearful response from all human beings on two levels. It can excite the adrenal glands to secrete adrenaline while disrupting mental thought patterns in such a way that the uncertainty leads to fear."

"Are you going to tell me how he can be stopped?" she asked.

"I am, but you will forget what we've discussed here upon awakening," Amelius warned. "You will, however, remember our conversation as a symbolic and confusing dream. In the past, I know you've found your dreams to be helpful. Tonight, be sure to set a clear intention that you will interpret your dream. It will tell you what you need to know to stop the prince. There are many, both in and out of three dimensions, who will help if you will let them."

***

The satellites were ready. Nasrum had inspected all twelve and found their quality to be adequate for his purposes. While occasional maintenance and replacements would be necessary, the satellites would give him all the control he needed to be recognized as humanity's Messiah.

Still, he sensed something was working against him. It could be that Amelius was trying to interfere, but that didn't feel right. He sadly admitted that the connection between his higher mind and Makoa's corporeal brain was deteriorating. He was forgetting his true nature as a spiritual being. If this persisted, he would have to start again with a new host body. How he hated that pain and annoyance. Nasrum felt sure that finding a new host could wait until the satellites were up and running.

Then it occurred to him that the archeologists could be plotting something. They understood RF technology and could possibly discern the true purpose behind his satellite array. The problem was that every time he tried to focus in on what they were up to, he couldn't do it. He could tell that they were still living at JPL, and that was a long way from Houston. Was it possible that the threat to his plans could come from somewhere else on the planet? He doubted that, but he had also once doubted that anyone could assassinate Prince Nafid. He doubled his resolve to remain vigilant. Soon, there would be no power on earth that could stop him!

Chapter 19

Jason and Diana rushed into the break room at JPL. "You said you have the RFA box ready to test?" She couldn't keep the excitement out of her voice. She felt like a kid on Christmas morning.

Nuri looked up and said, "Eljay is just finishing it now. He said that melding the edges of the RF crystal slices together was not difficult, but he found a lot of things that didn't work before he figured out how to create an operational hinge for the lid."

Diana asked, "Does opening and closing the lid turn the RFA box on and off?"

"No," Nuri laughed. "It is needed for some kind of dynamic vibrational balance in this dimension. The box works the same with the lid open or closed. For some reason, we all feel better flipping the lid open to make it work."

Diana smiled saying, "Well, of course! Then we appear to control everything it knows."

The next moment Eljay walked in triumphantly holding the small crystal box in his hand. "I don't mind telling you this is my best RF work to date!"

Mark put the question to the assembled group, "What should we ask it first?"

Diana smiled wryly and said, "Why don't we ask the box what question we should ask it first?"

Eljay frowned and seemed to think for a moment. "That's not funny. Asking a question like that could fry its circuits."

"You do realize that this RFA box is nothing like a computer," Nuri smirked. "Actually, I have a simple question to try that I've always wondered about."

Eljay handed him the box and gestured that he test it out. Nuri smiled as he opened the lid and asked, "Why did the crystal medallion Mark found in the pyramid in Guatemala only display the hologram once?"

Suddenly, the room filled with a montage of moving holographic images that followed the telepathic narration in their minds. They all instinctively ducked or took a step back in surprise until they realized the scenes and objects were not real. Stranger yet, the box's non-audible voice came from each recipient's own thoughts.

"Medallions, such as those found in the pyramid, do indeed draw information from the Akashic Records. While their technology is similar to what you call the RFA box, the medallion's design cannot sustain multiple connections after the intended message has been delivered. Once this type of medallion serves its purpose, the connection is terminated. Otherwise, the immense amount of energy required to make such a connection in this material dimension could become unstable. The crystal box you now hold is able to maintain a vibrational balance that will last in perpetuity, unless otherwise damaged."

Everyone stood still in quiet amazement. After a moment, Nuri asked a follow up question. "Why did the medallion react to obsidian as the catalyst for the movie to play?"

"As given, this RFA box is designed to maintain a connection and balance with the infinite in perpetuity. The vibrations of the obsidian acted much the same as an electrical ground wire for the ethereal connection to tell the preset story it was designed to share. At this time, it will not be of value to provide the details of how obsidian works as a conductor of Akashic information."

"That is unbelievable," Eljay gasped. "It not only answers the question you ask it, it also fills in additional information and edits other things out on the fly!"

Nuri handed the box back to Eljay saying, "Why don't you go next?"

"Was that really my dad I was talking to before I met Amelius and Halaliel during the RF crystal meditation?"

"Yes. He is present at this very moment choosing to align his consciousness with the events unfolding in this room. He wants you to know how much he loves you and how proud he is to be sharing this extraordinary moment with you."

632

Eljay was embarrassed to have everyone hear that last part. He silently wished it had not been said aloud. Unexpectedly, the voice in his head said, "No one but you heard that last statement. They heard that he was present in the room, but nothing after that."

"Now that's interesting," Eljay said shaking his head. "It seems the editing or censoring process can work on an individual basis. It told me that my father sent a private message to me that came after you heard he was with us in this room!"

They all looked surprised, but acknowledged that Eljay's father's presence was the only answer they heard from the RFA box.

"Can I try it?" Diana asked. Eljay gently handed the box to her and she stood quietly holding it as if she was praying. She stayed that way for almost a minute before she opened her eyes.

"None of you heard that?" she asked. They all confirmed they hadn't. She smiled and said, "Well I won't share everything I just heard, but suffice it to say Gus and I will be allowed to access the rejuvenation process in the Temple Beautiful in the not-too-distant future."

A cheer went up from the four men and they all congratulated her. Jason surprised everyone by giving her a big hug!

She then handed the box to Mark. He took it gingerly, opened the lid, and asked aloud, "When did we first encounter Prince Nafid and what is our ongoing connection to him?"

"You already know that Nasrum is the soul posing as Prince Nafid. You first encountered him in the continent of Atlantis when you and Nuri Zayd were brothers in the Orion family. You were not particularly gifted scientists in that incarnation. Nasrum started guiding you from spirit to create laser technology. That troubled soul was at the beginning of his disruptive ways and used the two of you to prematurely introduce laser technology to the world. You presented your discovery to the First Citizen of Atlantis without performing the proper research to ensure it was safe.

"The unknown back blast of vibrations from the laser went unnoticed until it was too late. You brothers made a commitment to dedicate your successive lives to cleaning up Nasrum's messes, of which there have been many. Your current incarnation has been no exception."

633

Mark then asked, "What can we do to stop Nasrum from using his RF satellites to manipulate humanity?"

"Those preparations are already underway by your nation's president. She will send for you when the time is right."

Jason asked, "What the heck were all those images that went by just then? I saw a big crowd seated in a huge auditorium. I saw gigantic video monitors and Makoa addressing the world as he stood next to a satellite displayed on stage."

The RFA box remained silent.

Mark asked aloud, "What about all the things Jason just asked?"

They waited until it was clear the box had nothing to say.

Then Mark asked, "Why don't you answer Jason's question?"

"Nasrum has a limited ability to read Jason's thoughts whereas the rest of you are blocked to him. While universal law automatically withholds key information from Nasrum, maintaining Jason's incomplete knowledge of the plan will be a tactical advantage. Because of Jason's marginal involvement, Nasrum will make incorrect assumptions that will result in his own undoing."

***

"We need to secure the largest indoor arena in Houston for the unveiling," Makoa confirmed.

David Pater said, "That would probably be where the pro basketball teams used to play on Polk Street. I believe it can seat over 25,000 after it was remodeled to be a mosque."

"Perfect!" the prince said offering an uncharacteristic grin. "When can you have a mock-up of a satellite delivered to the venue so I can plan the presentation?"

"We should be finished with it by the end of the week," David confirmed. "When do you want it delivered?"

Nasrum said, "I will need it on stage with me when I announce this great achievement to the world. Make sure it is delivered no later than the day before the presentation."

David nodded his head and left the prince alone in his hotel suite. The whole 'dead guy talks through a homeless man' thing gave him the creeps. He was glad to get away from there.

Nasrum chuckled hearing David's thoughts as the scientist walked toward the elevator to go back to the lab. How easy it was to scare these humans.

He concentrated once again to see if he could discern the pending threat against him. He knew it was out there, but he could not wrap his mind around it. The closest he could get was that something would happen during his worldwide broadcast.

Nasrum knew there was no one the people trusted more than the prince. If someone confronted him on stage, he was certain that they would be jeered away. Actually, he would enjoy the spectacle. What mere mortals could compete with him in popularity let alone a debate?

But what if his uneasiness was foretelling of another assassination attempt? Nasrum mentally followed the forward path and timeline of such an event and was comforted. If someone killed Makoa, the body's death would delay but not stop his plan from unfolding. The people would be so scared that they would deploy his satellites regardless. He could take his time obtaining another body to resume his rightful place as their savior.

Nasrum was sure Amelius knew nothing of his plans. If 'mister holier than thou' could see the true purpose behind the new satellites, he would do anything to stop it. Nasrum was convinced Allah was purposefully keeping Amelius in the dark or that troublesome soul would have already intervened.

There was only one thing to do. He needed to make sure his satellites were in place before the worldwide announcement and unveiling of his plan of protection. If anything did occur at the global event, then he would be ready to crush it in an instant. Once his array was in place, even Amelius would be unable to stop him.

***

President Kathryn Campbell could not forget the strange dream she'd had the previous night. The memory of it was pervasive enough to make her anxious. When she finally had a few minutes to herself, she wrote down what she could remember of the dream.

The most memorable part reminded her of the classic movie, The Wizard of Oz. It was when Dorothy confronted the wizard toward the end of the story. Despite the awesome spectacle that made everyone shake when they saw the wizard's giant face, it turned out to be an ordinary man hiding behind a curtain. Then the dream took it a step further. The man behind the curtain was Prince Nafid, and then she noticed another curtain beyond him. When she pulled that one back, it revealed something that looked like a semi-transparent ghost at the controls of some futuristic looking equipment.

She watched as the ghost seemed to shoot people with a kind of beam, something like you would expect in a video game. Instead of his victims falling dead, they became fearful and belligerent not knowing who to blame for their misery.

She remembered asking the ghost what he was doing. He was surprised that she could see him, but he answered her question. "Why, I am protecting all of humanity from an alien attack! But you already knew that, didn't you?"

The dream ended there, but it never left her thoughts from the moment she awoke. Kathryn had interpreted her dreams before. They always seemed to guide her to focus on a particular person, event or attitude she had in her waking moments. She generally found the information helpful in guiding her to do the right thing. She hoped this dream would help her as well.

If she took the dream at face value, she could see that the prince had been controlling events by working through Makoa. Nafid was able to keep the world's attention on what he did rather than who he was. But that didn't explain the ghost behind the second curtain. That ethereal being appeared to be the one in control, but what was his agenda?

The ghost seemed to be saying one thing while doing another. Regardless of what the ghost said, its focus was not on protecting the earth. The video game he controlled was agitating people so that they became fearful and anxious looking for someone to blame for their distress. It occurred to her to consider what Prince Nafid was doing in this same context.

Kathryn relaxed and allowed her mind to find the answers. She had an epiphany. The reason that everyone believed Makoa was channeling the prince was because he had demonstrated similar unexplained and impressive abilities. What if Makoa was just another face, another puppet, for the one in charge, just as Prince Nafid might have been before he was assassinated? The ghostly being could keep telling the world he was the prince to keep things simple.

While this was a plausible explanation for everything that had occurred with the prince, it still didn't answer why. Why stir people up over the existence of aliens? If they had no intention of invading the earth, why make people believe they were coming? If the aliens were not invading, then why did they destroy the first satellite array? And most importantly of all, what was the purpose behind the new satellite array if it was not intended to protect the earth?

She admitted to herself that she needed help to make sense of it all. She would ask to combine forces with the archeologists and hope to develop a strategy for the United States, and perhaps the whole world. She owed them a call back that same evening. She still had time to organize a proper game plan.

***

Eljay pushed the button on the old desk phone to disconnect the call. Then he turned to Mark, Nuri and Jason and asked, "Well, what do you think?"

Mark answered, "I don't think I've heard a U.S. president talk like that since Matt was alive."

Nuri agreed adding, "She seemed to accept our incredible tale about our recent adventures."

"So why didn't you tell her we had developed the RFA box?" Eljay asked smiling.

"Maybe we will let that be known in time," Mark said distantly, "but we've never been burned when we kept our RF discoveries in house."

Nuri said, "So let's get the box out here. I've got some questions!"

Eljay retrieved it and set it on top of an obsidian disc. He smiled confidently as he opened the lid and asked, "Does the obsidian disc the RFA box now sits upon improve its connection to the Akashic Records?"

The answer was a simple, "No, it does not."

Eljay frowned and looked a little embarrassed. He then gestured to his three friends to start with their questions.

Jason couldn't wait any longer. "How can we destroy Prince Nafid's satellites?"

"Given your current level of technology and spiritual development, you will not be able to destroy the satellite array before it is deployed," was the box's unemotional reply.

The men all looked at each other in amazement. How were they supposed to thwart the prince's plans if they couldn't get rid of the satellites?

Mark tried next. "What other options are available to us that we can use to destroy the satellites?"

The box said nothing.

Eljay blurted out, "Why can't you answer Mark's question?

The box answered, "Because, metaphorically speaking, you are trying to pick up the chair you are sitting upon. Your approach to resolving this challenge does not align with the soul lessons it is designed to teach."

"What the heck does that mean?" Jason almost yelled.

"You assume the most important goal in this case is to stop Nasrum from deploying the satellites, or, having failed to stop their deployment, to destroy the satellites in the sky. The desperate scenario that has captured your attention exists to teach you a great lesson," was the reply.

"And what lesson is that?" Nuri asked with strained patience.

"You have been given a wonderful opportunity to creatively work with circumstances as they are rather than what you would prefer them to be," was the answer.

"Are you saying we should just let Nasrum go through with his plans?" Jason asked incredulously.

The box was silent again. Jason growled in frustration when it became clear that the box would not respond.

"Why would you take a lack of response as meaning you should do nothing to stop Nasrum?" Diana asked from where she stood in the doorway. "I have been listening to most of this Q and A session with the RFA box. It seems obvious to me why it won't answer your questions."

When Mark and Jason said nothing, Nuri said, "Okay, I'll play along. Why won't it answer us?"

"Because you obviously need to start from the beginning!" she said with a smile. "Hey Kasha," she laughed, "Is destroying the satellite array the best approach to achieve all the goals involved in this situation?"

The four men all looked at each other and mouthed the name "Kasha?" as if it were a question.

"No. Responding to one such as Nasrum with a violent solution only adds fuel to the fire."

Diana said, "What other non-violent solutions can you suggest to achieve all the goals involved in this situation?"

"There are several, but one rises above the others because of its simplicity and the limited time you have now that the satellites are being launched into orbit."

Jason said, "You named the RFA box Kasha? That's not even a name!" The other men nodded their heads in agreement.

"How wrong could it be?" Diana replied. "The name worked to get a great answer and I wanted to call her something besides 'the RFA box.'"

Nuri resolved the issue with his next question. "Kasha, please outline the necessary steps needed to implement the suggested plan you just mentioned."

Chapter 20

President Campbell sat in the Presidential Suite of the Four Seasons Hotel. She held a special invitation to the presentation and gala Prince Nafid was hosting in Houston that evening. She had not risked communicating with Dr. Pater for fear of somehow notifying the prince of her intentions. Instead, she told the archeologists how to get in direct touch with David in hopes that the prince didn't monitor them as closely as he did her.

The story the two scientists had told her over the phone was difficult to believe. Kathryn had read a little about the fabled Hall of Records, but this was the first she had heard of the Temple Beautiful. She wasn't surprised that RF technology could heal, otherwise The Glut disease that contaminated the Colorado River thirty years ago might have wiped out humanity. Perhaps the hardest part to believe was that they somehow teleported from Bimini back to JPL in California. The only reason she kept her mind open about that was because they showed up in Pasadena when she had their best technology and people watching for their reappearance in the Atlantic. There was no way they could have slipped past all that.

She almost laughed when they claimed that their bodies had been miraculously rejuvenated so that they appeared to be in their twenties. She attributed that to men often thinking they look better than they really do. She did the math and guessed they would be in their seventies by now. She resolved to do her best to keep a straight face when they met in person for the first time.

Kathryn heard a knock at the door followed by a Secret Service agent entering. He said, "Madam President, the three men you have an appointment to meet with in an hour are here to see you. They apologize for being early. We confirmed their identities with facial recognition scans but it looks like they've had some, well, cosmetic surgery compared to the pictures we have on file."

"Well, they did warn me their appearance had changed," POTUS replied. "Please show them in!"

The agent nodded and turned to get them. A moment later he knocked and opened the door again. He stood to the side as three young men hesitantly entered the room. They stood awkwardly near the door and the agent had to step around them to be seen.

"Would you prefer I stay here or wait outside Madam President?" he asked.

"Please wait outside," she answered. "These men are national heroes and we have a lot to discuss."

He nodded and exited the room.

Mark, Nuri and Jason just stood there looking at the woman the nation called Madam President. They each remembered the good and bad experiences they had with her predecessors. The question in each of their minds was, 'How would it turn out this time?'

She gestured to the sofa opposite from the overstuffed chair where she was sitting and said, "Gentlemen, please have a seat." She couldn't believe how young they really looked.

They shuffled over and were getting settled when she asked, "Did you manage to work out a plan with Dr. Pater?"

Mark responded, "Yes, David has already..."

She interrupted him saying, "It's better if I don't know the details of things that don't need my direct attention. The prince has been keeping close tabs on me and I sometimes wonder if he can actually read my mind."

"Knowing what we do about the prince," Nuri said, "I would not be surprised to learn he is telepathic."

"What I really find incredible is that you are all supposed to be in your seventies." Kathryn had decided to make sure this wasn't a hoax before she went any further. "Do you have some way to verify that?"

Jason answered, "We had a bit of a hard time ourselves thinking of how we can prove who we are. We are happy to submit to DNA testing, but that would take hours at best. However, if you call your agent back in here, I think the Secret Service can help."

She suppressed her surprise at the request by turning away from them to click the remote button on the table next to her. The agent hurriedly entered without knocking.

"Yes Madam President?" he said professionally as he cast a wary look toward the three friends.

"I need your help with something," she said. She then nodded to Jason to tell the agent what he wanted.

"I'm sure you performed a facial recognition scan on us when we entered. Could you bring President Campbell a print out of the files you have on us?" Jason asked politely.

The agent looked at Kathryn and she tilted her head in consent. He nodded, turned, and left, closing the door behind him.

"Will the records identify anyone other than Mark Heston, Nuri Zayd and Jason Fisher?" she asked suspiciously.

Nuri laughed and said, "How could they? That's exactly who we are. Your security people will verify that in just a moment."

"I'll order some refreshments while we wait," she said. "Can I get anything other than coffee for you gentlemen?"

They shook their heads indicating that coffee would be fine.

When it arrived a few minutes later, the server poured black coffee into four ornate china cups. She then asked, "Cream and sugar?"

"None for me," they almost said in unison.

The server added both cream and sugar to Kathryn's coffee without asking. Then she handed it to her before making her quiet exit.

"It's rare to find three people together who drink their coffee black," POTUS said out of curiosity.

Mark explained, "We've been told that coffee is quite healthy for the body until you add cream and sugar to it. Then it becomes like sludge in the digestive system."

She chuckled and set her china cup aside on the table. "Sludge. Okay, I can take a hint."

The door opened again and the agent returned holding three folders that he handed to the president. He stood by while she opened them and scanned their contents. She looked at him and said, "That's great, Robert. Can you wait in the hallway, please?"

He nodded and left as quickly as he entered.

Jason asked, "Do your records say we are who we claim to be?"

"Yes," she began, "but I'm not sure how you can explain this."

She laid the three dossiers out on the coffee table between them. She arranged them so that the folders were lined up in the same order as the three men who sat across from her. However, the pictures were not of men in their seventies. They must have been taken forty years before when the Sphinx was destroyed by terrorists. The rumors that surrounded their possible involvement with that tragedy, coinciding with their discovery of RF technology, had kept the conspiracy theorists busy for years.

"How is it that you young gentleman are supposed to be in your seventies but the pictures in our files show slightly older versions of you in your thirties?" POTUS asked staring at them without expression. It could be that these men had someone on the inside to change the pictures in their files. But if they were that well connected, why would they have used the wrong pictures?

All three men laughed with understanding. It hadn't occurred to them that the only pictures the government would have on file for them would be from Matt Alexander's time.

Nuri was still snorting when he said, "These are indeed photos of us, but they were taken when we were in our thirties, Madam President."

She was a little embarrassed when she realized they were probably right. The U.S. government had barely had time to regroup and start functioning again after the assassination of Prince Nafid. It made sense that any pictures they had on these three would be outdated. As hard as it was to believe, the computer facial recognition software showed there was a ninety five percent probability that the young men sitting before her now were exactly who they claimed to be.

"Okay!" she said. "I'm astonished, but convinced. We'll do a DNA test to confirm everything later. I'm sure you have a great deal to work out with Dr. Pater before the festivities start this evening." She picked up an envelope on the table next to her and handed it to Jason who was sitting the closest. "Here are the two tickets you requested for tonight's event."

She then stood, indicating the meeting was over, and said, "Best of luck, and may God be with you!"

***

David Pater looked incredulously at the tiny earbud Nuri had just placed in his hand. He fitted the slightly spongy material inside his ear canal. "So I can talk to anyone else wearing one of these things if it's tuned to this frequency no matter where they are on the earth?"

"Yes," came the answer through his earbud, which made David jump in surprise. "Hello. It's me, Dr. Louis Jensen, Jr. I'm in Pasadena at JPL," said Eljay.

"How is this possible?" David asked.

Mark answered, "This is the same old technology that originally enabled us to talk to the emergency operator on another planet. We've had these earbuds for years."

David was impressed to find that the fidelity from the earbud speaker was as clear as hearing Eljay's voice in person. Also, there was no annoying delay as often happens with satellite connections.

Jason asked, "Were you able to insert the special RF crystals we sent you into all twelve satellites before they were launched?"

"I was," David confirmed. "But I don't understand why we would need to store back up RF crystals in the satellites. If we have to send a manned space flight up for repairs, they can easily bring the replacement crystals with them."

Mark explained, "We can tell you now that they were not back up crystals. We had to keep you in the dark so that the prince would not detect any deceit on your part. If you had known their true purpose, he may have read your mind and destroyed the crystals before the satellites were launched."

644

David looked shocked for a moment and said, "Well, you did have me fooled. I really had no idea they weren't what you said they were. So what do the crystals do and why is it that the prince doesn't know what the four of you are up to?"

"We'll explain what all the crystals in the satellites are designed to do tomorrow. It's safer this way. There is divine interference preventing the prince from reading our minds or following our movements, but we don't want to push it," Mark explained. "He knows we exist and that we're working against his plan, but he has no idea what we're going to do next."

"Still," Jason added, "the guy is resourceful and has tricks we can't imagine to keep things rolling his way. Even I stay out of the loop where I don't have a need to know."

"Have you already seen the agenda for this evening?" David asked.

"Yes," Nuri told him. "The prince will start with a monolog of his vision for the future. Then he will unveil his mock satellite and explain that the twelve real ones are already in orbit around the planet. He will answer five seemingly random questions from the audience except that they are already prepared. Then a select number of the 25,000 guests are invited to reconvene at the nearby reception ballroom for dinner, drinks and dancing."

"And when do you plan to confront him?" David asked.

Mark answered, "If by 'confront' you mean 'ask him questions,' that's where we need some help. If you can manipulate who hands out the prepared questions, the two of us need to be in that chosen group," he said gesturing toward Nuri.

David said, "Yes, I can hand three of the cards to my assistant and tell him I'll pick the other two. Don't worry, I'll make it look like I chose both of you at random. What about the healing demonstration you mentioned?"

Nuri said, "Assuming the lectern we had delivered to you earlier is the one used on the stage tonight, I guarantee you'll see a show you'll never forget."

* * *

Nasrum sat in what used to be the entertainers' green room before the arena was converted into a mosque. He was deciding how to punish the people who dared to plot against him. A telepathic scan he had performed on the President and Dr. Pater revealed that they were planning some betrayal. He would show them the error of their ways soon enough, but he could leave that for tomorrow.

He could not yet discern the exact nature of their treachery. He was certain it would be revealed during his presentation, but details of the attack were not clear. He had his best security personnel positioned throughout the building to keep an eye out for sharpshooter assassins. They had metal detectors on every entrance. He also had arranged for a wall of security men that would stand between him and the audience. They had orders to incapacitate anyone who tried to rush the stage. The path was secure from the green room to the spotlight where he would make his grand entrance. He even made sure to scan the minds of all his security detail to confirm that they were trustworthy.

The two archeologists concerned him the most. As of that same morning, he thought they were still at JPL in Pasadena. Now he couldn't locate them. He had always been able to pick up on their movements once they left that cursed place, but he couldn't find them anywhere.

The soldier who was always with them was a different story. Nasrum was able to follow his thoughts and movements better than the two scientists. It was as if the man's mindset was more in tune with Nasrum's thinking and that made for a clearer connection.

Nasrum reached out telepathically to locate the soldier and was surprised to learn he was in Houston. He tried to imagine all the ways the skilled warrior might try to kill him. Explosives were ruled out; too many innocent people would die in the blast. He could read the man's mind well enough to know he would never do that. He tried to see what the soldier was planning. Jason was not thinking of murder or mayhem. He seemed genuinely interested in sightseeing his way around downtown Houston. That concerned him all the more. Only a true killer could keep his thoughts that well-hidden.

Then Nasrum laughed at himself for not having more confidence. He was smarter than these humans. He had all the power on his side. He had prepared for all contingencies. It was time to relax and start enjoying his victory. No doubt they would try something, but they were destined to fail.

Jason was not used to playing the role of a decoy. He had walked point many times when on patrol in the Army, but that was different. Being the 'point man' meant taking the most dangerous position to draw fire away from your squad in case of an ambush. His role this evening was hardly that of a hero. In fact, he was the decoy because of his weaknesses, and that bothered him all the more.

Kasha had told him to leave the room before the details were finalized for Nasrum's big event. Jason objected until he was told why. "You have a unique connection to Nasrum that Mark and Nuri do not. You were once close friends with him which makes it easier for him to read your thoughts. You both enjoyed testing your strength and prowess when in physical form. You constantly competed against each other in what could be called mischievous acts.

"Nasrum eventually went too far with his mischief and you went your separate ways. You then found solace with Mark and Nuri as like-minded souls who had also been led down Nasrum's dark path. The three of you made a pact to undo the damage you'd helped cause in the past by opposing Nasrum's future efforts. You have spent many lives together doing just that."

To be told by Kasha that he had once been friends with Nasrum was embarrassing. Kasha let him know that their friendship had not been revealed to the others. However, it had to be disclosed to Jason so that he would understand his important role as the decoy. Nasrum would assume the best way for someone to stop him would be by assassination. Jason's presence would naturally draw all the attention away from his friends.

Now that he was aware of their connected past, Jason could actually feel when Nasrum was checking in on him. It almost felt like cotton gloved hands sorting through his thoughts. The sensation was eerie but easy enough to ignore when there was little he could do about it.

So Jason played the part of a simple tourist, always staying close to the Polk Street building. Tonight, Nasrum intended to gain control of humanity's path for the next 1,000 years. Jason and his friends had other plans.

Chapter 21

Nasrum had originally intended for both President Campbell and Dr. Pater to make opening statements to warm up the crowd for his entrance. He changed his mind opting to come out on stage cold with no introduction. If they were not directly complicit in an assassination plot, he still had to punish them for their disloyalty. Denying them their time on the stage was just the beginning of his retaliation. Even now, he could feel their nervousness in anticipation of this evening.

The spectators continued to move toward their newly installed assigned seats. The few remaining faithful that used to meet in this huge mosque had been moved to a much smaller place of worship. Relocating them had only made sense and killed two birds with one stone. There would be time to rebuild Islam to its former glory after his plan was in full effect.

He kept checking on the soldier. The man made him nervous because he remained close to the building, but he had yet to make any suspicious moves. The inevitable time would come when Jason would try to enter the auditorium. Nasrum already had his security people watching him. Until then, he would have to be patient.

Then he reached out with his mind to see if he could locate the archeologists. For all he knew, they were dead. He could not sense them at all. President Campbell and Dr. Pater were already seated toward the back of the auditorium. A last probe of their minds did not reveal any new deceptions.

It was time to test his satellites. In the privacy of the green room, he visualized a big red button in his mind that would activate them. He mentally set the amplification to its lowest level and saw the red button depressed. He remembered to block the effects the array would have on Makoa's corporeal brain. He needed to keep a clear head while the array emitted its disruptive vibrations upon the rest of humanity.

A moment later, he could feel the audience react. The noise in the room grew louder as the people became anxious. Nasrum wanted the crowd to be a bit off balance. He was pleased to confirm that his satellites were in perfect working order. If need be, he could crank up the amplification on the array until the people of earth would have one priority. The fear level would run so high that everyone in the room, and on the planet, would worry about their own survival. When the only choice humans have is to run or fight for their lives, whatever plans they had the moment before are quickly forgotten.

Before this night was over, Nasrum would secure his place as earth's Messiah for all eternity.

* * *

Mark and Nuri purposefully sat apart from each other in the large auditorium. They didn't want to chance Nasrum noticing them, either by appearance or by the proximity of their combined thoughts. They both had managed to secure aisle seats to ensure easy access to the public microphone when it was time to line up for the Q and A part of the show.

Suddenly, Mark's guts tightened up and he began to feel undeniably agitated. He looked across the aisle to see how Nuri was doing. The expression on his friend's face and the rising crowd noise confirmed they were all feeling it. Eljay moved to counteract it with his own RF device.

"Make sure you match our additional crystals' output to what Nasrum's satellites are putting out, Eljay," Nuri said anticipating his reaction. "That feels like the lowest setting. I'll bet this is just a test run to confirm it's working. As bad as this feels, you know he can pump up the intensity a whole lot more."

Mark added, "I can already feel the counter-effects of your device kick in. My gut reaction went from being nervous to mildly suspicious."

Eljay answered from JPL, "Now we know our device works too! We have to assume that Nasrum is 'wisely' blocking Makoa's brain from the RF array's effects. Hopefully, he won't notice that the recalibrated vibrations cause people to be distrustful rather than anxious. I'll bet it's hard to read the difference between fear and suspicion from the crowd."

Nuri asked, "What about the array's ability to bypass the brain and cause the adrenal glands to continuously pump adrenaline into the system?"

Eljay laughed and said, "That's the best part. Without a perceived threat, a normally functioning brain will automatically counteract Nasrum's RF effects on the adrenals. Our RF crystals are programmed to enhance the brain's ability to control all the endocrine glands. Since Nasrum is forcing Makoa's brain to ignore RF vibrations, there is nothing to stop Makoa's adrenals from overloading his system.

"We may have figured out how to use Nasrum's array against him, but it will be the humiliating questions Diana cooked up that will make the difference," Mark predicted. "She's figured out how he's a hypocrite three times over."

Nuri laughed and said, "I'll bet Nasrum's got surveillance on Jason just waiting for him to make his move. We're about to find out if, what is it Diana calls him, Mr. Delta Force, has any acting skills. He has to convince Nasrum that he's a lethal threat even while he shops for souvenirs."

"Hey guys," Mark jumped in. "It's time to go dark. The show is about to begin!"

***

The lights dimmed in the auditorium and the crowd noise dropped to a whisper. Nasrum was confident that feelings of anxiety continued to fill the room. While this presentation was intended to celebrate saving the planet, you could tell that the crowd was off balance. Suddenly, a voice came over the PA system. "Ladies and gentlemen, our next guest needs no introduction, and so here I am!"

A spotlight appeared on a man standing in the middle of the darkened stage with giant video monitors showing close up images of his face. All of humanity recognized that this was Prince Nafid in Makoa's flesh. The audience applauded and the guests started to rise in twos and threes until the entire arena was offering Makoa a standing ovation. Outwardly, the prince couldn't help but show some emotion at this overwhelming welcome. What he didn't sense was the uncertain suspicions that the world was feeling at this moment.

A smiling Prince Nafid gestured for the people to take their seats. It took a minute for everyone to sit down, and another minute for the crowd to settle in for the presentation. You could have heard a pin drop when the prince began to speak.

"Today marks a special accomplishment for all of humanity," the prince began softly. "Not so long ago, this entire planet became the target of an alien race bent on stealing Earth's natural resources and enslaving every man, woman and child. Because of our cooperative efforts, the aliens who desired to end our way of life are no longer a threat."

With that, the prince raised his hand and the black silk that covered the mock satellite fell away revealing the sparkling silver and gold device that had allegedly saved the world. The audience courteously clapped in appreciation, but this was all old news. They were waiting for something new to ease their fears and to protect their loved ones. As the applause died down, the prince continued.

"But, as with many great accomplishments, this achievement marks not the end but the beginning of our challenges. It is not enough that the earth cannot be seen by our enemies. We must continue to build our defenses until we can stand against any aggressor in the known universe."

The applause politely began again, but the prince gestured that he had more to say.

"This generation is making a commitment to its children for many years to come. Humanity will not just be safe on earth," Nasrum paused for effect, "we shall reach for the stars and be safe wherever we go!"

The audience clapped with more enthusiasm now. This was just the kind of news they had been waiting for. Despite their ongoing suspicions, it took a minute for the genuine applause and whistles to die down.

When the prince started to speak again, something went wrong with his wireless headset and his voice only carried to the first row. After a frustrating minute, a member of the technical crew appeared on stage and pointed to the hard-wired microphone mounted on the nearby lectern as the quickest way to fix the problem. The prince shot the man a condescending look and sighed aloud, but he needed to keep his momentum rolling.

The lectern appeared to be made of a highly polished dark wood. The tilted flat surface at the top was skirted with a thick royal blue material that hung down to the floor. Nasrum walked over and started to adjust the gooseneck microphone. That was when he noticed something odd. There was a shiny black circle in the middle of the lectern's rectangular surface. In its center was the imprint of a hand. It looked like something you would see at that movie theater on Hollywood Boulevard where the movie stars all left their hand prints in the sidewalk.

He was about to compare the size of the imprint to Makoa's hand before he snapped back to the moment. Not only were there 25,000 people in the audience, there were billions watching this event around the world. Nasrum considered turning off the satellite array for the moment, but he decided to wait a bit longer. After all, he had learned that instilling a little fear into his followers was a good thing.

He reminded himself that this was the point in the agenda when the audience would ask him prepared questions. His answers would motivate and guide humanity for generations. "Do we have any questions from the members of the audience I can answer at this time?"

Almost every hand went up. The prince laughed and said, "Can I have the ushers randomly pick five people out of the crowd and I'll answer whatever they want to know."

Mark and Nuri ended up being the second and third people in line to ask the prince their prepared questions. If anyone noticed, it was clearly a set up because all five people in line had white 3" x 5" cards with the questions already typed out. The first person was handed a microphone that had been quickly wired into the PA system and was urged to speak.

"Prince Nafid, you just mentioned that when we start to travel into space, we will be safe wherever we go. How can we be sure of this?"

A murmur came from the audience that she had voiced their own concerns. Nasrum was pleased that she asked the prearranged question with a wary tone. The array was obviously working and he could answer the challenge in a way that would ease their feelings of anxiousness.

"No species exists that I am not familiar with. Humanity is my favorite and I would see the rest of the universe be more like us. I will ensure that our technology is always superior to any species we encounter. If they don't know how to respect their betters, they'll soon wish they had."

The audience, not just in the auditorium, but throughout the world, gasped hearing the implication that the prince would make humans the rulers of the universe. That was quite a leap for the world to make; going from being victims to conquerors. The applause that followed felt awkward because the array's vibrations continued. Nasrum assumed they were feeling a bit fearful. He had no idea the people were beginning to doubt his word.

"Can we have another question please?" Nasrum said. He stood up straight when the next person walked forward and took the microphone. He didn't recognize the man's face, but every part of him vibrated with suspicion. He quickly searched for the soldier with his mind. He was just outside the auditorium in a souvenir shop looking at tourist junk. Nasrum relaxed a bit thinking whatever the immediate trouble was, it would not be violent. He was certain he could handle whatever came next.

Chapter 22

Jason could feel Nasrum's nervousness when the familiar cotton gloves combed through his thoughts. He did his best not to react. He started trying on different pairs of sunglasses and looking in the mirror to see if anyone was watching him. Everyone else in the shop was glued to the store's media screens tuned to the action taking place in the nearby auditorium.

Jason slipped his earbud in thinking they might need a heads up. "He's starting to panic guys," Jason said quickly, then removed his earbud after he said it. He didn't know the details of their plan, but making Nasrum feel cornered was risky.

Eljay jumped in, "I'm staying on top of the gain control. If Nasrum tries something, I'll be able to override him."

Nuri said, "Don't increase the volume until I hit him with my questions! Mark is up now. This whole thing is about to get real!"

***

Mark said, "Prince Nafid, I am confused about something."

The prince stood there a moment deciding how he wanted to play this out. This vile person was not staying with the prepared words on the card. He decided to see what this man wanted, "And what is it that confuses you?"

"My question goes back to when you first made your presence known as Prince Nafid," Mark paused a beat to get control of his nervousness. "I remember you saying that Allah (peace be upon him) had initially protected humanity because we were His faithful people. But when you were assassinated as Syria's leader, many people lost faith and turned away from Islam. Because of that, you told us that we had lost our Creator's protection against the aliens."

Nasrum noticed that the questioner was speaking as a Muslim who strictly followed the ways of Islam down to the correct salutation when saying Allah's name. No one had questioned Allah's displeasure with humanity until now. "You remember well. What was your question?"

Mark began to read the words Diana had written out for him. "Even now, you appear to revere Allah (peace be upon him) above everything else. But if our Creator does not think humanity should be protected because we lost faith in Him, why are you acting against His wishes?"

The rumblings of angry agreement emerged from the audience and echoed around the auditorium. If not for the array's vibrations, the crowd would not have overreacted this way. Nasrum knew that the people watching this unfold around the world were equally irate. He still wasn't worried. He knew how to handle this young man's embarrassing question. His bigger concern was that the soldier would try to use this disturbance as an opportunity to assassinate him. A quick mental check on Jason showed he had moved from trying on sunglasses to admiring himself in the mirror while wearing silly looking hats.

Suddenly, Nasrum began to feel nauseous. He was able to block the confusing effects the satellites had on Makoa's brain, but he had forgotten about the array's effects on the adrenal glands. Makoa's body was now flooded with adrenaline. Nasrum was losing his mental connection with the spirit realm. Could he handle this challenge with only Makoa's conscious mind? He would have to. The question had to be addressed to reassure his floundering people.

"It is true that Allah (peace be upon him) is still unhappy with humanity. However, I, Prince Nafid, have interceded on humanity's behalf that we be given another chance to prove ourselves worthy. Allah (peace be upon him) is patient and desires that I guide his people back into His loving arms. We must be very careful to uphold His ways from here on, lest we lose this gracious opportunity."

Nasrum tried to relax as an usher guided Mark back to his seat. It had been touch and go there for a moment, but he had answered the question well. Then a warning signal went off in his mind. He intuitively realized that the next questioner intended to cause more trouble. He couldn't think straight because of the adrenaline coursing through Makoa's body. He began to sweat and his knees started to shake.

Nuri could see the prince was in trouble and didn't hesitate to ask his question. "Prince Nafid, I think I speak for everyone when I express my thanks for interceding with Allah (peace be upon him) on humanity's behalf." The sarcasm in his tone was quite clear. A murmur of curiosity travelled like a wave through the audience before Nuri continued.

"I worry that we now walk on thin ice when it comes to breaking the rules of sharia law. For instance, isn't it blasphemy to desecrate one of Islam's holy mosques for our own purposes?" Nuri paused for just a moment to let the audience guess where this was going.

"In fact, didn't you order that this grand and holy mosque be converted into this secular auditorium to celebrate your accomplishments? You ordered the desecration of this holy place solely to glorify yourself. You have shamelessly placed your own exaltation above all else. If that wasn't already an affront to Islam, why are you serving alcoholic drinks at the reception to follow? To commit such shameless sins, I have to ask if you are even on speaking terms with our Creator."

Nuri's brazen accusation, in conjunction with the array's RF vibrations, was like adding fuel to a growing fire. Billions of people around the world were immediately up in arms. The jeers and outrage thundering through the auditorium were a microcosm of the betrayal the global audience felt toward the prince. Nasrum was unable to think straight. He tried to turn the array off but he became distracted when he noticed Mark and Nuri standing together in the aisle. Who the hell were these two men?

Jason had shifted to watching the event on TV. Now that his friends had asked Diana's questions, it was time for him to distract Nasrum even more. He mentally invaded Nasrum's panicked thoughts by telepathically saying, "Don't you recognize the Orion Brothers, my old friend? We all dropped by to say hello."

Nasrum finally remembered Jason, Mark and Nuri. He also realized they weren't trying to kill him. If they had simply assassinated Makoa, he could have secured a new body and picked up where he left off. These devious turncoats had murdered the prince's reputation instead. Did they understand they had just passed a death sentence on the world? Humanity would destroy itself without his leadership.

Nasrum had only one remaining option. He resolved to cause such a panic that the world would beg him to lead them again. He braced himself and mentally invoked the satellite array to emit a full power burst of fear upon the earth. Nasrum watched for the inevitable riot to break out just as Eljay turned up the volume on his RF machine at JPL. No one could see or hear it, but Nasrum's satellite array performed a figurative backflip.

Nasrum was confused to see that the array was not working. The auditorium had quickly fallen into an awkward silence. Then some people stood and began walking toward the exits. It wasn't long before the entire audience decided that it was time to leave. They weren't fearful or even anxious. If anything, they looked disappointed. Nasrum couldn't stand the looks of sympathy he received from some of the crowd as they headed for the doors. Just then he heard Jason's voice inside his head. "How's that array working for you?"

"What have you done?" Nasrum mentally cried out in anguish.

Jason said, "We took the fear out of your array's vibrations and added a twist of our own. The world now sees you as you really are. They intuitively understand that you are a fraud because there is no threat from extraterrestrials. We took away your smoke and mirrors until all they could see was a soul to be pitied."

Nasrum looked up to see that the auditorium was almost empty. Even his security guards had disappeared. The anger that had been building inside of him finally broke through. If they wouldn't accept him as their savior, he would tell these puny humans exactly what he thought of them. He could see that the TV cameras were still broadcasting his words to the world. Nasrum raised his hand and dramatically slammed it down on the lectern to get everyone's attention again. In that same instant he found that he could not speak. Something had ambushed his control over Makoa's body.

Nasrum looked down to see his hand fitted perfectly inside the lectern's obsidian outline. He couldn't move and it was too late to stop it. Makoa's body was being healed! All its past bone breaks, cysts and even a missing appendix were returning to their original perfect states. He could feel that the brain was also being made whole. The healing energies dealt with Nasrum's consciousness as a foreign virus to be purged. Makoa's body was dying as quickly as it was being healed. Without a soul's connection to it, the human shell could not continue.

Makoa's eyes began to fail. Nasrum could barely tell that Jason had left the store and was now walking up the aisle to join Mark and Nuri. He did his best to show his utter contempt for them before he lost consciousness. Jason stared at him and said, "Nasrum, you have done this to yourself!"

The three friends watched as Nasrum's soul departed and Makoa's eyes closed forever. They looked around to see that the auditorium was nearly empty. The world no longer revolved around the great Prince Nafid. Jason remembered to let Eljay know what was happening and announced in his earbud, "Nasrum is finished."

***

Out of the darkness came these reassuring words. "Nasrum! Let me help you. If you will reach out to me, I can guide you out of this place."

He recognized the voice, but couldn't quite connect it to anyone he knew. Where was he anyway? One minute he seemed to be fulfilling a lifelong dream, and the next minute he was reliving his worst nightmare.

Then it dawned on him. "Amelius!" he yelled.

Suddenly, the memory of his nightmare flooded back through his consciousness like a tidal wave. He had been sabotaged by "Mr. Holier Than Thou." He was sure that Amelius had kept just enough hidden from view to make a fool out of him.

Amelius said, "You really believe that I did this to you? Do you take no responsibility for what brought you to this place? You need to get away from here before it's too late. Please reach out to me so I can help you."

"Never!" was his terse reply. "Go away."

Amelius sighed in disappointment but would not override Nasrum's free will. Nasrum had made his choice. There was no

659

telling how long it would take for the suffering that came with living in outer darkness to convince the poor soul to accept help. One thing was certain; when he did, Amelius would be there for him.

***

Mark, Nuri and Jason were standing together just outside the auditorium. There was cause for great celebration, but none of them had much to say. Nasrum was gone, but what was left in his wake? Would the nations of the world begin a free for all grab for wealth, land and power? Without Nasrum around to control humanity's selfish desires, that seemed inevitable. None of the friends were sure they had done the right thing.

Mark quietly asked, "Eljay? Can you get us back to JPL? I think we're all ready for a break and we need to see what the world will do next."

Eljay answered, "I haven't been able to build a reliable transport device as yet, but let me ask Kasha what can be done to get you back here."

The three friends remained quiet while they waited. Then Eljay was back on the line.

"Kasha says that you can't leave the RFH lectern behind. If you will gather around it, Kasha will guide me to bring you back."

They had forgotten about the obsidian pedestal device in all the confusion. There were still a few people milling around inside the auditorium, but no one tried to stop them as they approached the stage. They climbed the steps and positioned themselves around the lectern. A moment later they were back in JPL's lab in Pasadena. Makoa's body and the mock satellite were the only things left on the stage.

Chapter 23

Mark, Nuri and Jason were on a conference call with David Pater. They had promised to explain the real function of both sets of RF crystals that David had placed in the satellites. They also owed both Jason and David the details of their plan that put Prince Nafid out of business.

Mark started with, "You knew most of the plan already. We left out a few key details so that Nasrum would make assumptions that would keep him off guard."

David asked, "Who is Nasrum?"

Nuri answered, "He is a soul who guided Prince Nafid's predictions as well as his financial and political decisions. When the prince was assassinated, Nasrum escalated his personal agenda and took control of the body of Makoa, a man who committed suicide. After they died, the souls of the prince and Makoa moved on from the earth. Nasrum decided to make the world believe Prince Nafid was still around so he could quickly reestablish his credibility."

"That explains a lot, but I'm not much of a believer in life after death," David sighed. "I was suspicious from the start because Makoa's personality was so different from Prince Nafid. How does some homeless guy come off more arrogant and over-bearing than a prince, especially if they're supposed to be the same person? Then again, no one wanted to question him after the amazing things he was able to do."

Jason said, "You had a lot of direct contact with Nasrum. I'm not surprised you could tell the difference."

"Anyway," Mark continued, "the extra crystals we asked you to install in the satellites were calibrated to change the array's original purpose. Nasrum was able to affect both the mind and the body through the vibrations spread across the earth. The array was designed to instill fear in everyone. On the physical side, it caused the adrenal glands to pump adrenaline into the system. On the mental side, it confused the mind causing emotions to rule instead of reason. At its lowest level, Nasrum could use the array to make people feel anxious. At its highest setting, the people literally feared for their lives."

Nuri explained their strategy to counteract Nasrum's scheme. "The extra crystals were made to turn his array into something else altogether. You experienced it yourself when you suddenly realized that Nasrum had been lying the whole time. However, instead of feeling threatened, the world viewed him with pity and disappointment."

David said, "That really does make sense of what happened in the auditorium. But why did Makoa die right after that? You had promised a demonstration of healing, not death."

Mark asked, "It was a healing that led to Makoa's death. Do you remember the lectern we had you place on stage?"

"Yes," he said, "but I only saw it from a distance. I remember the stage hands saying it was unbelievably heavy."

Mark laughed, "That's because it's a lousy lectern but a great RF healing device."

"What do you mean?" David asked.

Nuri answered, "The upright part of the pedestal is a column made of solid obsidian. The square top piece of the lectern fits around the top of the obsidian so that the combined surfaces are flat."

Jason interjected, "Now I understand! When Nasrum hit the lectern, his hand made contact with the obsidian and it started to heal him."

"I still don't know what that means," David complained.

"Remember that Makoa had committed suicide before Nasrum took over the poor guy's body," Jason began. "The obsidian was programmed to heal anyone who put their hand on it. When Nasrum did that, the pedestal healed the physical body and ejected Nasrum's consciousness as if it were a disease. Keep in mind that Makoa's soul had moved on to greener pastures months ago. Any physical body dies when there is no soul connected to it."

David said, "I'll have to take your word for that one, but here's something simpler. I don't understand how you got the prince, I mean Nasrum, to use the lectern. He had on a wireless headset microphone that night. Why did it suddenly stop working?"

Mark laughed and said, "That was probably the best kept secret of all. Eljay built an RF device that interfered with all the wireless mics. The lectern had a wired microphone so Nasrum would be forced to use it. We left it to Eljay to decide when to make the change. He timed it perfectly so that Nasrum was at the lectern when we asked him those embarrassing questions."

"Wow!" said Jason. "You guys really do know how to keep a secret! Until now, I would have said planning a surprise birthday party was a stretch for you. I'm impressed!"

*　*　*

President Campbell was making preparations for the upcoming United Nations meeting in Damascus. Many of the members of the General Assembly had requested this meeting. The suggested agenda would outline the organization of global economics and trade now that Prince Nafid was gone.

The U.N. member nations agreed to send their ambassadors to meet first to hammer out the rough points before their actual heads of state would gather to negotiate the details of the agenda.

Kathryn Campbell had not told anyone of her involvement in the demise of Prince Nafid. She hadn't revealed that Mark, Nuri and Jason had cleverly dethroned him. She especially hadn't tried to explain how three men in their seventies now looked like they were in their twenties. She would have preferred to keep those secrets, but it was not in the world's best interests for them to remain anonymous. She needed her three new consultants' help to create global order out of the chaos. She asked her personal assistant to call them in Pasadena.

"Please hold for the President," she said after Mark, Nuri, Jason and Eljay were on the line.

POTUS picked up and said, "I'm so glad you were all available. I never did get to thank you for what you did in Houston. Someday you'll have to tell me how Makoa died given that he was apparently the healthiest corpse the M.E. had ever seen."

Nuri answered, "Madam President, we're happy to answer your questions, but is that why you called? I'm guessing you have more on your mind than to thank us or get details on what happened that night."

"Indeed I do," she admitted. "The member nations of the U.N. are meeting next week to see if we can agree on how to move forward in peace now that the prince is out of the picture. I wanted to consult with you for ideas on how to proceed. Your perspective is unique and you've earned my respect more than I can say."

The four friends just looked at each other. They had thought of little else, so having suggestions was not the issue. The problem was figuring out how to explain their new RF technology that so few people even knew existed. Everyone was familiar with RFP and RFS for energy and sustenance. But they had added Kasha's help along with RF communications, healing, and, hopefully soon, RF teleportation to the list.

Mark knew that they needed more time to articulate a response. "You said the meeting isn't until next week? Can we have a couple of days to mull the question over and get back to you?"

"Of course," she said. "The General Assembly will meet first to create the agenda. Then the heads of state will gather in Damascus the following week. I'm afraid almost every country has a reason why they should be the crowned emperor of the United Nations."

Eljay said, "Isn't it amazing that despite having all the energy, food, water, and every product you could want to make life easier, we can still come up with reasons to fight each other?"

"When it's my turn to speak, can I use that as my opening line, Dr. Jensen?" she asked rhetorically. "Gentlemen, call me back when you're ready, and I hope that is soon. Good luck!"

***

"Kasha," Nuri began. "How should the U.N. proceed in their upcoming meetings so that every nation benefits?"

"Humanity has a bias toward resolving these issues at the highest level of government. The better approach would be to start the other way around. Every person on the earth should be asked to

664

set a loving, hopeful intention for this important gathering. All should pray that their leaders make the best decisions they can for all concerned. Every soul is of the utmost importance in God's eyes, and so it should be in how you treat each other. If everyone works together in this way, the outcome of this historic meeting will be glorious. Global conditions will go where the combined intentions of humanity direct."

"Nice sermon, Kasha," Jason said shaking his head. "We were looking for something like a suggested agenda they can all get behind. What guidance can you offer along those lines?"

"Very little, and for good reason. There is no perfect agenda to follow in achieving world peace if the leaders are not of one mind. Many of the heads of state are predisposed to compromise where they give up some things in order to gain others. In that way, everyone involved walks away with less than they wanted. A better approach is to remember that people who are equally informed rarely disagree.

"Though he did it through deceit and fear, Nasrum brought peace to the world by creating a common enemy. Imagine the success you will enjoy by uniting all people through love and cooperation. Once the world chooses to overcome selfishness and fear, there is no end to what humanity will accomplish.

"The true lesson behind this global exercise is to learn how to cooperate through patience, faith and fellowship. If eternal peace and prosperity is what you truly desire, then it would be better to follow the advice given in these words you would call a sermon."

Diana mused, "Sermon or not, Kasha made some great points! We seem to be focused on the wrong things again. Kasha is hinting that we need to go in a different direction. Why not try asking about a new approach altogether?"

Mark offered, "Perhaps you, Kasha, could gain the trust and cooperation of the heads of state if you addressed them as a group? Would that approach help?"

"That is possible, but ask yourself, 'Help to do what?' If your goal is to shock and amaze them into doing what you want, then the answer is no. However, if your goal is to help them to make better choices where everyone wins, then the answer is yes."

Jason was not convinced. "How do we get people, politicians especially, to listen to your brand of advice when they have no belief in a friendly universe?" He decided against adding, "...nor in talking crystal boxes."

"Truth can be ignored, but it is an everlasting part of every soul. It would be better to have faith in your leaders. Expect that they will measure up to their true potential. Prayer and expectation are quite similar when done with the right intent. The box before you now that you call Kasha can be quite convincing when needed. Continue to have President Campbell work toward a mutually agreeable agenda and put a Q and A session between Kasha and the heads of state as the first item. The experience will indeed set a cooperative attitude for the world's leaders to work together as friends instead of competing to come out ahead of their enemies."

"President Campbell, Kasha is with us," Eljay confirmed over the phone. "Please ask any questions you desire that will help you to gain confidence in the Akashic Records' information."

"Gentlemen," Kathryn began, "I have not interfered with your methods because you get results. Regarding what you have told me about this magic 8-ball type of crystal box, did you really expect me to believe it?"

POTUS suddenly changed her tone. "Okay, I've got a question. What can the Kasha box tell me that would cause me to believe that it is everything you say it is?"

"Yes, that information is available. Rest assured that what I am about to share with you is for you alone. No one else will hear what follows."

Kasha fell silent and POTUS didn't say a word, but they could hear sounds that told them she was still on the line. When she did respond a few moments later, it was only to say, "Wow!"

The men at JPL were struck by the change in her voice. Nuri decided to take the pressure off of her by describing the rest of their plan. "And Kasha can simultaneously share compelling information with every person at the U.N. in the same way that you just experienced."

"I'm convinced, but I'm not sure I can effectively describe what just happened. My watch tells me that only a minute passed

666

while it felt like Kasha had talked for hours. I reviewed every moment of my life up to now. I was shown the repercussions of every choice I've made, both good and not so good. I also saw the opportunities I let pass that could have made the world a much better place."

"We've all been there, Madam President," Mark offered sympathetically. "The experience either convinces you of Kasha's authenticity, or it forces you to believe that you've been deliberately deceived."

"Kasha!" POTUS said directly addressing the RFA box. "Why has humanity been allowed to suffer for thousands of years when the amazing information I just heard has always been available?"

"If you had heard everything I just shared with you back when you were age five, would you have had the same reaction then as you are having now?"

"I would have been surprised, for certain," she said, "but a five year old wouldn't have the capacity or life experience to adequately process this information like an adult can."

"Well said! Your statement was simple as well as instructive. RFA technology has always been available, but humanity, on the whole, had not achieved a mature enough mindset to understand and apply the information given. Even now there will be some who will doubt the truth."

Nuri asked, "Does that mean that some leaders at the U.N. will not be convinced no matter what you tell them?"

"Correct. The natural human reaction to things that scare or otherwise threaten anyone is to make an enemy of the perceived source of their pain. For those who are not ready, being told that much of what they believe is incorrect is taken as an insult. Some would go as far as to kill the messenger to maintain the status quo. Such violent reactions are seen as justified when it is considered to be the work of Satan, charlatans or others who would do them harm."

"So by presenting the U.N. leaders with Kasha, we are risking our lives as well as the lives of anyone connected to us?" Jason asked.

"Correct again. There are just as many potential timelines where none of you survive when compared to those where you will succeed in using the Akashic Records as a means to draw the leaders of the world together. Even in the best scenarios, your faith will be tested as much as your patience and physical endurance."

***

Amelius, Halaliel and Matt Alexander were waiting for Mark, Nuri and Jason to arrive. Matt felt a little outclassed in the presence of his spiritual hosts. He asked, "Why am I here for this meeting of the minds?"

"You offer a harmonizing vibration that will help to bridge the middle ground between perfection and carnality," Halaliel answered. "Mark, Nuri and Jason trust you and know that you understand the challenges before them as only those in human form can."

Amelius added, "This is not to say that your point of view is inferior. Even Halaliel and I can differ on the best approach to a challenge such as this."

"How can that be?" Matt asked.

"Most often there is more than one loving answer to any choice we make," Amelius continued. "For example, General George Patton is a very spiritual soul who believes that obedience to rules is the best way to cooperate. That path makes the way more difficult, but how many souls straighten their lives out after they enter the military?"

"I can see your point. What other approach could work in a time of war or extreme conflict?" Matt asked rhetorically.

Halaliel surprised him by answering, "Civil disobedience applied cooperatively until the aggressors cease their violent ways."

"Are you suggesting that the world should have stopped Hitler through civil disobedience rather than war?" Matt shook his head and added, "Hitler executed six million Jews who were not violent at all. What would have made him stop before he killed all but the people who fully supported him?"

"Over fifty million people died as a result of the conflict you call World War Two," Amelius began. "If done correctly, organized civil disobedience against Hitler would definitely have been met with brutality, but far fewer lives would have been lost in resolving their differences toward a peaceful outcome."

Matt was puzzled. "So which method is better? The approach that favors ending the bloody conflict as quickly as possible, or is it better to extend people's suffering for the sake of fewer casualties?"

"In other cases throughout your earth's history," Halaliel explained, "I have favored the former while Amelius preferred the latter. Deciding which approach is better is almost a moot point because wars will continue until those who prefer violence no longer outnumber those who prefer peace."

"And that's why you're here, Matt!" Amelius said with a smile. "You still relate to a human perspective and your friends trust you implicitly. It's not that they don't trust us, but it is difficult to feel we are all peers when one is still in human form."

"Speaking of which," Halaliel said, "Here they come."

Right on cue, Mark, Nuri and Jason appeared before them, obviously getting their bearings. They were given a moment to adjust to a higher level of consciousness.

"Matt!" Nuri beamed. "It's so good to see you!"

"I was pleased and honored to be invited to this meeting," Matt said honestly. "It is great to see the three of you too!"

Jason was coming around enough to ask, "Are you here for a social visit, or are you here to help us figure out how to survive the next few weeks?"

"The latter, it seems," Matt said with a curious smile. "It has been said, be careful what you ask for, you just may get it. Centuries ago, you three dedicated yourselves to cleaning up Nasrum's messes. You have been doing just that over many lifetimes. However, this incarnation offers the opportunity to bring closure to your shared promise. To do that, you must help to avert a world war."

"Is that all?" Mark said sarcastically. "What exactly do we have to do?"

Halaliel answered, "We can't give you a specific answer to that question, but haven't you wondered why we put you through the Temple Beautiful rejuvenation process?"

"Honestly, I wasn't going to bring it up if you didn't," Jason said with a nervous laugh.

Amelius didn't pull any punches. "There is a high probability that you will suffer life-threatening circumstances, both self-imposed and from those who disagree with your preference for world peace."

"Why would we choose to harm ourselves?" Nuri asked.

"Choosing to put one's self in harm's way for the greater good is often the result of civil disobedience," Halaliel explained.

Mark said, "Like those people who allowed the British soldiers to beat them in India's efforts toward independence? Or Gandhi going on a hunger strike until the violence ceased?"

"You have the idea," Amelius agreed.

"But if we stick to our guns, we will succeed, right?" Jason asked hopefully.

Amelius laughed, "Perhaps that wasn't the best metaphor, but I would favor civil disobedience, if that is what you are truly committed to do."

"What percentage of the world's heads of state will be against us?" Nuri asked.

Halaliel sounded hopeful, "Far less than you think, but they will be the leaders who feel compelled to prevail at all costs. That vocal minority believes it is their job to ensure their people come out ahead no matter what. While the ends never justify the means, some of humanity has yet to accept that basic truth."

"Then our current plan will work to sway the majority of the heads of state to resolve all their differences in patience, and equality for all?" Mark asked.

Amelius answered, "There is no doubt that a majority of them will be swayed. The question will be if they will all 'stay the course' when their faith is tested. Humanity is about to choose the path it will follow for centuries to come. A great deal rests upon the choices each soul on earth is about to make.

Chapter 24

POTUS was back in Washington D.C. on a conference call with the crew from JPL. She had called to say that there was an approved agenda for the U.N.'s heads of state meeting the following week.

"Were you able to get Mark and Nuri on as guest speakers?" Jason asked.

"Not exactly," she admitted. "I had to sell the proverbial farm to be allowed to make the opening speech. The rules say I can allot my time to someone else to speak in my stead, but is five minutes going to be enough?"

"Kasha can say a lot in almost no time at all," Mark reminded her. "If Kasha can't convince them to expand your time allotted on the agenda, nobody can."

"You should set it up with a friendly nation ahead of time to get a second to your motion to allow Kasha more time after they've all gone through the life review," Nuri cautioned.

"Gentlemen, at this point there are no friendly nations," POTUS sighed. "However, I can probably trade our vote on another issue to get it done. I just hope this is worth it. If you don't pull this off, I don't know what else I can do to help."

She hesitated and then said, "We have another problem. I'm not sure how I can get you into the General Assembly chamber. Only the leader of each nation is allowed into the hall that is guarded by U.N. security. I could probably get Jason approved to be on the security team, but adding a couple of archeologists would be a tough sell."

Eljay laughed saying, "I can get them in."

"Do I want to know how?" she asked suspiciously.

Eljay answered, "Sure! The same way they avoided detection when they returned to Pasadena from Bimini."

POTUS shook her head and wondered if she was beyond her depth. She had to remind herself that the youthful looking Mark and Nuri were actually in their seventies. Still, counting on them to pull this off was asking a lot, even if the universe was as friendly as they claimed.

***

"Will the General Assembly of the United Nations please come to order?" said the Secretary-General Akhem al Assad. The man was a distant cousin to Alkrim al Assad, the man who had assassinated Prince Nafid. He had quietly maneuvered his way into the leadership position of the U.N. just before his cousin murdered the prince and forced the world into turmoil.

"You all have the agreed upon agenda before you at this time," Akhem continued, "and I would invite the President of the United States to set the tone for this most auspicious meeting with her opening remarks."

Kathryn Campbell walked confidently to the podium. Every leader in the room saw that she carried no notes. They wondered how she could be so certain of herself that she would not need a prepared speech as backup considering the pressure she was under.

POTUS shook hands with the Secretary-General before turning to the nearly two hundred world leaders in the audience. She silently assessed the crowd for a moment. Her thoughts were not of what she was going to say, but of what would occur next. She wore one of the RF earbuds that kept her in touch with the team from JPL. They were monitoring what was being said so that they knew when to make their entrance.

"Ladies and gentlemen of the General Assembly," POTUS began, "there is little that I can say that could bring us all together in a spirit of cooperation and equality. However, I've recently met two men who I believe have the words we are hoping to hear. Many years ago, the world first heard of Doctors Mark Heston and Nuri Zayd as part of the team that discovered resonant frequency technology."

Side conversations rose and fell as the various translations of Campbell's announcement were relayed. She waited a moment, and then continued.

672

"I have invited them here today to speak in my place so that you can be as convinced as I am that we can happily cooperate to reach solutions without having to compromise. I will let you know in advance that these men recently located the fabled Bimini Hall of Records."

The room erupted with gasps and outrage that only increased as the translations were heard. There was hardly a country on the earth that hadn't sent an expedition to Bimini at some point in search of the rumored technology inside the Hall of Records. POTUS held up her hands to silence the crowd. When that had little effect, she simply raised her voice to make the introduction.

"It is time to hear from the men directly. If it pleases the General Assembly, here are Doctors Mark Heston and Nuri Zayd."

The shouts of anger ceased in startled confusion when both men suddenly appeared on the stage, and looking much younger than anyone expected. Since they were on the opposite side of the stage from POTUS, the bewildered crowd assumed the men had quietly walked up the steps unnoticed.

Eljay had worked with Kasha to perfect a resonant frequency teleportation device, or RFT. He hadn't worked all the bugs out as yet, but Kasha assured them that there would be ethereal help from the other side to overcome any technical glitches that could otherwise spoil their entrance.

Mark and Nuri stood motionless on the stage taking in the uncertain crowd of world leaders. President Campbell waved them over to address the G.A. They managed to find their feet and walked until the microphone on the podium was positioned between them.

Mark was the first to speak. "Before we get started, I want to show you something amazing that came to us from Bimini's Hall of Records."

He had to say it twice and wait for the translation to complete, but the crowd eventually settled down. Nuri took out Kasha and placed the crystal box on the podium so that the G.A. could all see it glisten like a diamond in the lights.

"Imagine a computer database that stores a record of every event that has ever happened," Nuri began. "Now imagine that those records are stored in a place where time and space are tools rather than limitations. And finally, imagine that database isn't just limited to past events, but contains a record of all possible future events as well."

The murmurs from the audience let the scientists know they were not buying that such miracles could come from a small crystal box. Mark took over the narrative.

"Some people call the ethereal archives of everything that has ever been or will ever be the Akashic Records. This crystal box can access those records and we gave it a name, Kasha. You'll understand why we see it more as a person than a computer in just a minute."

Driven by the doubt and unrest in the crowd, Nuri jumped in to quickly get to the point. "Kasha will now talk to you directly. Rest assured that what Kasha is about to say to you is for your ears only. No one else will know what is shared between you. This information is given to convince you of its authenticity."

And with that, Nuri opened the box.

***

Jason and Eljay waited impatiently back at JPL for an update from Mark and Nuri at the U.N. They understood their friends might be a little busy at the moment, but then POTUS had to be available.

"Madam President?" Jason said as politely as he could. "Can you tell us what's happening?"

"I'm sorry," she whispered. "I had forgotten you aren't able to see what's going on here. The entire room is silent at the moment. I believe Kasha is conducting individual life reviews with every person in the hall. Since I've already had my session, I'm not hearing anything but you for the moment."

Eljay asked, "Can you tell anything from their expressions? I mean, are they shocked, amazed, angry or happy? There must be some kind of indication of what they are feeling."

"As far as I can tell," she answered softly, "the only people in this place with their eyes open are Mark, Nuri and me. Their expressions are all over the emotional spectrum. With each new disclosure from Kasha, their faces react as they relive those moments. I can imagine I looked the same way when it was my turn to hear what Kasha had to say to me."

"Well," Jason said, "remember to make a motion to have Mark and Nuri's time extended the moment the G.A. is back with you. If they have to stop at this point, everything you've done will have been for nothing."

The next thing Eljay and Jason heard was, "Secretary-General, since the five minute limit for the opening remarks is almost over, I now offer a motion that the General Assembly extend the time allotted for at least thirty minutes."

A voice from farther away chimed in, "I second that motion."

The Secretary-General took a moment to mentally regroup before he put it to a vote. "All in favor of the motion to extend the opening remarks for thirty minutes please affirm by a show of hands."

Silence followed but POTUS whispered, "Not very many hands were raised."

The Secretary-General then said, "And all opposed, please raise your hands now."

POTUS said, "Again, very few hands are going up."

"The motion carries by a narrow margin of eleven in favor with eight against. The rest will be recorded as abstentions."

The Secretary-General gestured toward Mark and Nuri indicating that the floor was theirs for the next thirty minutes.

"Please remember that everyone here has had their own unique experience with Kasha," Mark began. "I have as well. So before we move on, I'd be glad to have Kasha answer any questions that are germane to the entire General Assembly, rather than being personal in nature."

The Ayatollah from Iran stood up and shouted in accented English, "What kind of heresy is this? Such things must come from Iblis who lies in wait for Allah's (peace be upon him) faithful to sway us from the path. How do we know that this isn't Prince Nafid back yet again to lead us astray?"

675

Nuri answered, "What did Kasha share with you that felt like it was coming from Prince Nafid? I will say that no one I've talked to about these conversations feels any of the fear or condemnation that was common when the prince spoke."

"I felt no difference between Prince Nafid's words and what I just experienced," was the Ayatollah's stern reply.

Mark spoke carefully into the microphone, "Kasha, what can you tell us about Islam and all the other major religions of the world?"

"Religions on earth are a construct of humanity. They are helpful and hopeful when they serve to gather people together who are of the same mind and approach to life. Religions, all religions, can also be used for personal gain or to exclude some souls for selfish reasons. Irreversible torture or banishment are never God's solutions to resolve our selfish choices. The Creator loves you, every one of you, with an everlasting love. No truer words have ever been spoken."

The members of the G.A. felt slighted to hear that their preferred religion was a human invention rather than being divinely ordained by God. Christians, Muslims, Hindus, Jews and Buddhists alike were certain their religion was the only one that followed and taught the truth.

Nuri continued by asking, "Kasha, explain why Prince Nafid was allowed to control the planet's economies and political systems to meet his personal agenda?"

"Nothing in the universe is stronger than free will. It is the Creator's desire that all souls have free will to make the choices they prefer. An excellent example of this is that every nation on earth has the political leadership it deserves. It may surprise you to know that the combined desires of humanity allowed the soul you call Prince Nafid to lead you astray. He directed your course for decades through a regrettable misuse of Islam to control the masses. After his body was slain, another host was found. He chose to abandon Islam thinking that fear was a better motivator in his quest to be the earth's supreme leader.

"The leaders of the world gathered here at this time have a unique occasion to set a loving, peaceful path for all of humanity. It

676

is through the poor example set by Prince Nafid as he carried out his selfish choices that created this unprecedented opportunity."

The leaders in the hall had to admit that the description they heard detailing how Prince Nafid had maintained complete control for decades made sense. They were still reflecting on the statement that each country has the leadership it deserves. No one was sure if that was a compliment or a backhanded insult.

The Prime Minister from Israel stood and asked, "How can there be peace among all the nations in the Middle East? There have been so many transgressions that forgiveness and moving on between warring peoples seems impossible."

"You are correct that the transgressions on all sides in the Middle East are many and ongoing. The question of forgiveness is an interesting one. In your year 1941, Japan bombed Pearl Harbor and brought the United States into World War 2. On August 6, 1945, the United States essentially ended the war by dropping the first of two nuclear bombs on Japan. The wartime transgressions against each country were horrific, but were they unforgivable? Given that less than fifty years later both countries were close allies politically and economically, forgiveness did take place."

The Israeli Prime Minister asked, "Surely you can see the differences between the strife in the Middle East compared to World War 2."

"Indeed it is clear, but not for the reasons you prefer. The conflict between the U.S. and Japan did not involve their chosen religions. When the fighting was over, forgiveness was easier because the transgressions were against each other. In the case of the Middle East, you see the transgressions as attacks against your Creator to whom you owe everything, and that is why you believe their sins to be unforgivable. Rest assured that all sins can be forgiven because your Creator loves you that much. If you could understand how much your Creator loves all souls equally, the fighting would be over tomorrow. You cannot fully comprehend the true nature of love and still see your neighbors as your enemy."

The President of Russia stood and said, "In my country we do not encourage organized religions, though the people are free to worship as they wish. What is the most common error that religions make in establishing their theology?"

"From a purely theological perspective, most religions teach that if one lives a good life, as defined by that religion's tenets, the soul is allowed to escape the bonds of the earth and live in perfect happiness somewhere else in the universe. The truth is that until each soul understands how they can be perfectly happy wherever they are, they remain entrapped on the earth."

The mood in the hall was becoming uncomfortable. President Campbell could tell the leaders' sentiments were not going in the right direction. She hoped to ask a question that would steer the group back on track.

"What should be the focus of this General Assembly to accomplish the greater good where all nations can live in peace and their citizens live lives that are happy and prosperous?"

"This is a most excellent question! Humanity often focuses upon what is wrong instead of how things can be improved. There has never been a greater opportunity to achieve peace and prosperity for everyone at any point in earth's history. All the needs of the body have been met so that the survival instinct has been satiated. The needs of the ego cause humanity to see living on the earth as a contest that must be won at the expense of others. If the nations' leaders here will expand the scope of who the citizens are that they are sworn to protect, the competitive need for global domination will be replaced by universal cooperation. In God's eyes, all souls are equally beloved siblings. Why should humanity see each other as anything else?"

The G.A. members were silent. The box surprised them by referencing God in several ways. Names like Creator, the I am that I am, and First Cause seemed to be all the same to Kasha. Regardless, it was difficult to argue with the logic presented in the statement on the equality of all people. The flaw was that it presupposed that the loving nature of God was accurate, let alone that a Creator existed at all. A voice from the crowd yelled out, "Can you prove the existence of a Creator?"

"Yes!" was the simple reply.

China's President Mao continued the challenge by asking, "Then prove that God exists here and now!"

"Nothing would be gained to do as you ask. For many in this hall, no proof is needed because they already believe. For others, the things they have witnessed here today tilted the scales toward believing in the First Cause. For some, their predetermined bias against the existence of the Creator has little to do with proof. Such people do not want to believe in a God who would allow so much suffering in the world. For them, it is easier to reject God's existence altogether than it is to acknowledge that the First Cause could create the depth of evil they have witnessed."

"And what defense is there for the rejected God you just described?"

"Since before the beginning, God gave all souls free will. Having free will means that souls possess the ability to make selfish choices that their Creator would not. For example, each nation represented here has a beloved flag that symbolizes the best your country has to offer. If a person chooses to desecrate that flag, where does the responsibility lie for the act? Does the fault lie with the creator of the flag or the one who chose to desecrate it?"

"Clever semantics don't belie that an all-powerful God could stop all suffering at any time and chooses not to," the Chinese president bellowed. "Why doesn't God take away all our suffering?"

"To remove all suffering would take away your free will. God's children are the perfect image of their Creator. Without free will, they would become as robots with a consciousness of strict obedience and a somewhat limited ability to appreciate God's magnificence."

Mao countered, "Then God should intercede before the suffering is more than we can bear, as do all good parents."

"Your angst is a matter of perspective. Don't good parents allow their children to suffer at times in order to learn life's lessons? Simple disciplines are seen as an excellent tool to teach them right from wrong. Such parenting methods are acceptable on earth because they are instructive and no permanent harm comes to the child."

Kasha paused for a moment to let that sink in before continuing.

"What is difficult for humanity to understand is that the soul is both invulnerable and eternal. The horrible crimes humans witness against each other are of their own making, not God's. So the law of karma, that you reap what you sow, ensures that each soul experiences life's events in ways that draw them closer to their Creator. No matter how bad things may seem, you live in a childproof universe. Your soul cannot be irreparably harmed in any way. Eventually, all souls see for themselves that treating each other as the Golden Rule embodies is the only way for everyone to be equally happy in perpetuity."

China's president was exasperated. "But it seems clear that some people will never learn. They will always try to come out ahead at the expense of others, no matter what. Even the best parents can raise a lifelong criminal despite their greatest efforts."

"But the best human parents are not your loving Creator. God has perfect patience, perfect knowledge and is all-powerful. The better question to ponder here is 'How long can the will of such souls resist the unconditionally loving ways of their Maker?'"

"The extended allotted time is almost up," interjected the Secretary-General. "Is there one more question to pose before we move on to the next agenda item?"

Mark spoke up saying, "Kasha, where do the General Assembly members stand on the matters discussed here today? Are the majority in agreement? And, if so, should they vote to accept your recommendation of maintaining equality for all as the guiding principal behind any legislation that results from this meeting?"

"Most members are in agreement. However, those in opposition feel strongly that they are right. The cooperative hearts and minds of the entire assembly are needed for true success. You cannot legislate sustainable peace and prosperity through a majority vote."

***

During the first break, the Chinese president, Mao Choi, pondered his experience with Kasha. He decided that it must be some kind of a mind trick. He knew the whole thing was a sham when the Kasha voice declined to prove the existence of God. He was tired of the disrespect his people received from the rest of the world. He knew that he possessed the skills needed to successfully lead his people through these uncertain times. The two archeologists could make that difficult by pretending to have the voice of God at their disposal.

Mao took out his secure satellite phone and called his second in command, Zhang. When his friend and confidant answered, he explained everything that happened in the G.A. hall. Mao said that the two Americans had been persuasive enough to convince the G.A. to cooperate rather than play into China's political wheelhouse. Zhang knew Mao was right. China was uniquely qualified to lead in many ways. If equality became the primary guide for U.N. legislation, China would lose those advantages. Zhang would do what he could to keep that from happening.

He would call his embassy in Los Angeles. They had specialists who would be able to locate and secure the people closest to the archeologists. When their loved ones turned up missing, the two troublemakers would not hesitate to return home.

Chapter 25

Yong and Li parked on Explorer Road near the main entry gate to JPL. They were hoping to catch a glimpse of where the people lived inside the complex. The land and buildings dedicated to the original Jet Propulsion Laboratory complex was huge. That was when JPL received massive funding from the U.S. government, but that had been long ago. Their recent intel said that only a few people actually lived on the property. Yong and Li could not tell from satellite photos which buildings were for housing. They dreaded the prospect of having to covertly search perhaps seventy five separate structures until they located the correct one.

A truck approached from behind them. As it passed, they saw that it was a landscape truck with a trailer. It pulled up to the gate and one of the men jumped out with a key to open it up. Yong and Li watched as the man with the gate key got back inside the truck. Then they drove out of sight leaving the gate unlocked.

The two Chinese nationals couldn't believe their luck. They opted to drive onto the property and recon the area. If anyone stopped them, they would claim they were lost. They had a map of the streets inside the gates, but none of the buildings had signage on them. They started out in the middle of the complex on Explorer Road. They passed Mariner Road and Mars Yard before returning to the point where they had entered the complex.

This time they took their first left on Mariner. They hadn't gone more than a couple of hundred yards before they saw a few cars parked behind a two-story building. Since they hadn't seen any other cars parked in the complex, it was a safe bet that this was the place.

They turned into an unoccupied parking lot that was out of sight of their target. Both Yong and Li carried guns, but their orders were to secure and relocate the residents of this place rather than hurt them. To that end, they also carried tranq guns with enough juice in the darts to render any human unconscious for hours. If all went according to plan, they would transfer two unconscious people to a nearby safe house before anyone noticed they were missing.

***

Jason and Eljay stared at the design on the computer monitor in the lab trying to smooth out the bugs in the RF teleportation device. Eljay's prototype used GPS coordinates to position its entry and exit portals. The problem was that GPS coverage had become spotty over the decades of neglect. Prince Nafid's sole focus in space had been his infamous array. The world's GPS system still had numerous holes in its coverage and probably would for years to come.

They had to admit that their first attempts were pretty funny. They video recorded Jason walking into walls where a portal had been a moment before. Another showed Jason walking through a portal only to exit where he had entered. They knew the entry and exit points overlapped because he was suddenly turned around in mid-step.

Eljay built a second RFA crystal box to help him work out the bugs at the lab while Kasha was away with Mark and Nuri. He named it Sherlock because of its uncanny ability to solve riddles from practically nonexistent clues. The new crystal box seemed to have a slightly different disposition, though, when asked, the box denied that was true.

Sherlock suggested that RFT technology could be guided directly by the human mind rather than manually entering GPS coordinates. This meant that a good amount of programming had to go into the RF crystal to safeguard the people using the device. For instance, the person being teleported could unwittingly end up in a dangerous position upon exiting the portal. Appearing on Mount Everest or outside one of the satellites orbiting the earth would kill a careless RFT user if they were not prepared for the conditions they would face at the exit point.

Sherlock identified resonant frequencies to infuse the crystal with the proper safeguards. Rather than rely on GPS coordinates, the user could visualize their intended entrance and exit points. The RFT device would perform as directed and heed all the other parameters to ensure a safe journey. Sherlock told Eljay that the RF vibrations had to be programmed in one at a time in numerical sequence of lowest to highest. That is what they were working on when all hell broke loose.

Two Asian men rushed into the lab and shot Eljay with some kind of darts. The only reason Jason escaped being shot was because the assailants had both aimed for Eljay instead of picking separate targets. His Delta Force instincts didn't fail him. He dove for the ground grabbing the leg of a chair as he hit the floor. A dart zipped just over his head giving him enough time to position the chair's seat like a shield as he stood to face the man closest to him. Jason held the chair straight out for protection and charged ahead. The man fired two more darts into the seat before Jason smashed into him. The man yelled, "Layshi!" as he flailed backwards trying to keep his balance. Jason lunged forward three more steps slamming the man's back up against the wall. He heard the man's ribs break with an audible crack. As he pulled the chair away, the stunned man slunk to the floor.

Out of the corner of his eye, Jason saw the other man kneeling at Eljay's side securing his wrists with PlastiCuffs. Jason picked up the discarded tranq gun lying next to his dazed attacker and fired two shots into the side and back of the other assailant. He had been reaching for a gun in his waistband, but the darts' juice took immediate effect. Jason dropped to one knee and swiveled around to check on the first man. He was too late, but the move did save his life. Instead of taking a bullet to the heart through his back, Jason was struck through his left arm. The copper-shrouded pellet smashed through his elbow before it shattered a rib and lodged in his lung. He collapsed to the floor before he blacked out.

Yong could barely move. The man he had just shot had broken his ribs making it nearly impossible to breathe. The way his vision was blurred, he guessed that he had a concussion as well. It was hard to claim victory here except that he was the only one in the room who was conscious. Who the hell was the young guy that almost took him out? Their hasty intel said the only people who frequented JPL were the unconscious scientist, a female in her fifties, and some old men who were easily in their seventies.

After a few minutes, Yong managed to get to his feet. He hoped that he could drag the scientist and Li back to the car. He could tell his injuries were bad, but he did his best to move through the pain. He was thankful that the young man wasn't on the list of people his superiors wanted because that would make three people he would have to move. The young guy's labored breathing told him

684

he was still alive, but Yong didn't know if the maintenance people heard the shots or called the police. He didn't want to risk firing another bullet and letting anyone zero in on his location. No matter, the unconscious man would bleed out in minutes.

Yong decided he would drive his car as close to the building as he could get it. He would try to find some sort of cart to help him load the unconscious scientist and Li into the car. What Yong didn't know was that he was bleeding internally. As he stumbled down the long hallway to get the car, the walls started spinning. He barely caught himself as he fell to the checkered linoleum floor. The next minute he too was out cold.

***

Jason tried to sit up the moment he became conscious. The searing pain throughout his upper torso convinced him to lie still. As his mind cleared, he remembered being hit by a bullet. He looked around the room, but the man who shot him was gone. Eljay and the other Asian man were still lying on the floor next to each other. Jason tried to think through the pain to come up with a plan. He was alive and conscious, meaning his heart was probably okay, but his shortness of breath told him his left lung was not as lucky. After seeing his left arm, it was no surprise he could barely move it. Still, he was thankful his injuries weren't any worse.

He was sure the man who shot him would be back. The tranq darts confirmed that this debacle was supposed to have been a kidnapping. He wouldn't have left the building without taking the person or people he came for. Figuring out who orchestrated this would have to wait. He had to stop the man with the gun when he returned.

In desperation he called out, "Sherlock, tell me what to do here!"

"Jason, don't panic. You are a trained soldier. You can easily survive this situation with the tools you have at hand. There is an obvious solution if you can think of it in time. You do not want to become too dependent on RFA guidance."

"Well here's one solution," Jason bellowed. "I could smash you against the wall, but I'll settle for getting us out of this mess. Tell me how I can do that!"

"It will not be difficult to disable the RFA box. Throwing it against a wall should work well. To do so would not be in your best interests. Moreover, you will not have time to save yourself. The RFH lectern is located to your left against the wall. If you can place your hand in the carved depression before you lose consciousness, the RF vibrations will heal your injuries in time to save your life."

Sherlock was right. Jason had forgotten about the podium. He skipped any further Sherlock insults and started dragging himself toward the lectern. His progress was slow because his right arm and legs were all he could use to low crawl across the floor. The pain was nearly unbearable and he could feel himself going into shock as he gasped for breath with his one good lung. Once he reached the base, he realized he would have to stand up to reach the obsidian's carved depression. Getting to his feet was not an option and there was no time to debate his next move with Sherlock.

He dreaded the desperate plan that came to mind. Jason gritted his teeth and reached forward to pull the lectern down across his body. He grabbed hold of the blue velour that skirted the obsidian pedestal and pulled with all his might. He prayed that the rectangular top was strong enough to absorb the impact. If not, he would be crushed by the weight of the obsidian. The lectern toppled over across his body. The top piece was half an inch shy of keeping the weight off Jason's ribs. The resulting pain briefly jolted him back to full consciousness. He managed to reach around with his right arm until he felt the edges of the carved hand print. He couldn't breathe, and his eyesight was going black, but he managed to line up his fingers and press his palm against the carved hand imprint in the obsidian.

The next instant, Jason's thoughts were thrown back to forty years earlier. He remembered the first time he had been healed by RFH technology, but this was different. He had been in great shape back then. This time he was nearly dead. The vibrations first raced through his mind as if they were asking for directions to the injured areas. He thought that this must be how a computer feels when a virus is removed from its system. He felt adrenaline flow through his body and the pain faded away. Within minutes Jason was able to remove his hand from the lectern, push the pedestal to the side, and get to his feet.

"Sherlock!" he yelled. "How long do I have until the guy who shot me returns?"

"Unless you're asking when he will reincarnate, your question has no relevance. The man died in the hallway."

Jason asked, "Is anyone else coming to finish what they started?"

"No. There will be no further efforts to abduct you or Eljay. However, your success in thwarting their efforts here will not change the minds of those who intend to disrupt the General Assembly meeting at the United Nations."

This was the first that Jason realized his friends might be in danger. "Are Mark and Nuri in trouble?"

"That depends on the timeframe involved. There is no immediate danger, but plans will soon be made to kidnap Mark and Nuri."

Jason picked up the phone and called the Pasadena police. The sooner he could satisfy the authorities that he and Eljay were innocent, the quicker he could go to Damascus to help his friends.

* * *

Yuri Alton, the Russian ambassador to the United Nations, had cornered Mark and Nuri at the state reception after the U.N. meeting had concluded for the day. He asked them many questions about Kasha and their other adventures. Their recounting of how they reversed their ages back to their twenties not only explained their amazing physical condition, it added credence to their other claims. They had both facial recognition proof and DNA tests that they were indeed who they said they were.

Yuri feigned interest in their stories and proof. The Kasha box was the real reason he had seemingly befriended the two. He asked if he could take a picture of Mark and Nuri holding the box, which they allowed. Then he asked if they would take a picture of him holding it as well. They hesitated, but agreed to that too. Yuri's last request was to have a private session with Kasha later that evening. He had not been in the main hall when the world's leaders heard Kasha's amazing and very personal revelations. Yuri convinced the two archeologists to agree to meet him later at their room so he could experience it for himself.

When Mark and Nuri were ready to call it a night, they found Yuri waiting by the door to their hotel room. They invited him in and set Kasha down on the round table near the door. Yuri took a seat at the table and asked them how Kasha worked. "Do you have to lift the lid to turn it on?" he asked.

Nuri answered, "The lid can be open or shut. It is there to balance the energies rather than to turn it on and off. Just mentally ask what Kasha would share with you." He nodded and gestured that the Russian ambassador give it a try.

Yuri carefully lifted the lid anyway and asked aloud, "What would you share with me this evening, Kasha?"

The answer was immediate. Yuri quickly relived every moment of his fifty-three years. He was shown every choice he'd made from his earliest days, including the opportunities he decided not to pursue, and how his life's circumstances had changed because of those choices. There was no question in Yuri's mind that this box was in touch with his inner-being. Either it was everything Mark and Nuri claimed it was, or they had invented a device that could completely analyze the brain's thoughts and memories. Regardless, this box was a remarkable piece of technology. This thought elicited a response from Kasha that Yuri had not expected.

"Are you certain that you want to switch the useless crystal box in your pocket for the RFA box? Doing so will not turn out well for you or your fellow citizens."

Yuri's entire body reacted to being called out by Kasha. His arm jerked and knocked the crystal box to the carpet below. While it wasn't his intention, bending over to recover Kasha off the carpet provided the perfect opportunity to switch the real thing for the 3-D replica in his pocket. Yuri managed to secure Kasha in one hand while placing the fake crystal box back on top of the table. He put the real box in his pocket and nervously stood to go.

Yuri shook hands with Mark and Nuri saying, "I want to thank you for allowing me to experience Kasha for myself. I'm sure I'll see you again before the conference is over." After that, he practically ran into the hall. Mark had to close the door behind him. Yuri already had his phone out texting the good news of his success.

Chapter 26

"Mark? Nuri?" the president said through her earbud. "Can you talk to me for a moment about tomorrow's agenda?"

Both men were more than ready to call it a day, but it was POTUS asking.

Nuri said, "Go ahead President Campbell. We're listening."

"Excellent!" she replied. "Kasha was correct that a majority of the world's leaders agreed that all nations should be treated as equals. If this conference were allowed to become a competition, some countries would inevitably take advantage of others. China, Russia and India all have their unique advantages of population, land mass or rare natural resources that could put them in a superior position. I was surprised when Iran emerged as the spokesperson for the Middle Eastern countries claiming they are already the economic and political center of the world. They also claim to be morally superior to everyone who is not a Muslim. I wasn't optimistic, but we did come to a majority consensus to treat all nations as equals by the final vote."

"So what would you have us do tomorrow?" Mark asked.

"Kasha warned that anything less than a unanimous vote would signal continued conflict," POTUS began, "It looks like Kasha was finally wrong because the majority consensus has really worked in our favor. You two and Kasha will be allowed to sit in on all the meetings, discussions and votes for the rest of the conference. China, Russia and Iran were against it, but then, just a minute ago, Russia changed their vote and now welcomes your help. I wanted to let you know the good news right away. Tomorrow's first meeting in the main hall starts at 9:00AM local time."

"We'll be there!" they assured her.

When Yuri was safely inside his hotel room with the door locked, he took the crystal box out of his pocket and set it carefully on the bedspread. He admired it for a moment before he opened the lid and asked, "How can Russia make the best use of this device?"

"By returning it to the people you deceived to get it."

Yuri was puzzled by the response. "That makes no sense. How could returning this box to the Americans benefit Russia?"

"I correctly answered your first question. The intent of your second question was to learn how to use the Akashic Records so that Russia profits at the expense of other nations. The answer is that ultimately, you cannot. If you would prefer that Russia benefits equally as much as the other countries of this world, then return this box to Mark Heston and Nuri Zayd."

"But if you have access to all knowledge," Yuri persisted, "tell me what my country can do to become the acknowledged leader of the earth?"

"If you desire to lead this world, you must first become its servant. The idea that you could profit at the expense of the other nations is not sustainable. While particular choices you could make now might appear to give Russia a temporary advantage, universal law ensures that selfish choices are always brought back into balance. That may take many years, but it is inevitable that you will reap what you sow."

Yuri sighed, "Who cares what happens decades from now? I will be long dead and buried having lived a full life enjoying Russia's position as the world's leader."

"The soul is eternal. Until you recognize how to treat everyone else just as well as you would have them treat you, you will remain attached to the earth living successive human lives until you gain that understanding. Trying to cleverly out-maneuver the other nations will only result in Russia being on the losing side of a future conflict. You can count on being one of the reincarnated citizens who does not appreciate being taken advantage of when that day arrives."

Yuri laughed, "That's hardly a threat. I don't believe in reincarnation."

"Nevertheless, the truth of reincarnation persists despite your lack of belief in it."

Changing tactics, Yuri said, "What's done is done. I can't risk putting my country in an embarrassing position by returning the box. What will happen tomorrow?"

"The non-functioning crystal box will leave the archeologists in a difficult dilemma. There are a great many outcomes to project because of all the free will choices involved. The most likely outcome will be that Doctors Mark Heston and Nuri Zayd will be detained and questioned to determine why they would want to deceive the United Nation's leaders. Too many outcomes diverge from that point to give a meaningful answer."

* * *

"Are you guys there?" Jason exclaimed. "Mark, Nuri, please tell me you still have your earbuds in!"

"Jason," POTUS answered. "I spoke with them just a few minutes ago. I believe they were going to sleep. We've all had a tough day and tomorrow promises to be even more challenging. Can I relay a message to them in the morning?"

Jason told the president about the kidnapping attempt. He summed up his story with, "Having failed here, we were warned that they will now try to kidnap Mark and Nuri!"

"I don't think that's likely as long as they stay here," she said. "There's too much security to think of trying to abduct anyone inside the U.N. complex. I'll warn them to stay inside the building the first chance I get."

"I'll get there just as soon as I can," Jason said. "Eljay has not recovered from the effects of the tranq darts. He did get a double dose, so he may not wake up for hours. I can't teleport to Damascus without his help. In the meantime, I don't know for certain the nationality of the two Asian men, so please tell our friends to be careful."

* * *

Mark and Nuri were seated to the side of the stage when the Secretary-General brought the G.A. meeting to order. POTUS had been unable to relay Jason's warning, but she intended to do so at the first break.

"Distinguished members of this august assembly, we voted yesterday to allow Doctors Mark Heston and Nuri Zayd to observe the G.A.'s proceedings with their Akashic Records crystal box. Our personal experiences with the device were mostly well received. We trust that the information will continue to unite us as we navigate these unprecedented political challenges."

The enthusiastic applause gave him a moment to take a sip of his tea.

"And so I now invite Doctors Heston and Zayd to present their device and have it make an opening statement to begin this meeting on a positive note."

Mark and Nuri walked onto the stage and shook the Secretary-General's hand before facing the audience. Nuri produced the crystal box from his pocket and placed it at the top of the podium for all to see. Mark flipped the lid open and stood back in anticipation.

They waited through an increasingly uncomfortable silence until Nuri said, "Kasha, what words of wisdom and encouragement would you share with us this morning?"

When nothing happened, Mark picked up the crystal box and wiggled the lid back and forth a few times. He then placed the box back on the podium to see if that made any difference. It didn't. The crowd was growing annoyed and uncomfortable murmurs increased in volume as the box's silence continued.

Both men remembered Yuri knocking the box off the table the night before. They hadn't checked to see if Kasha was still working. After a hurried discussion, they agreed that it must have been damaged.

Mark said, "Ladies and gentlemen, the box was inadvertently dropped last night. This is the first we've become aware that it was not functioning properly. We apologize for the delay. It will take a couple of hours to have another crystal box delivered to us."

The mood of the G.A. was impatient and side conversations sprung up throughout the hall. Mark and Nuri picked up the box, uncertain of where they could go to call Eljay. They had left their cell phones and earbuds in the hotel room.

Two suited U.N. security agents appeared a moment later asking Mark and Nuri to follow them. They were escorted to a corridor just outside the main hall and told to wait. Less than a minute later, two other men in suits came for them. They ushered Mark and Nuri out of the building to a waiting car. They both tried to explain that they only needed to make a phone call, but it appeared the security men did not speak English.

Mark said, "I didn't bring my earbud this morning. I didn't think we'd need them today. My cell phone is still back in the room since they don't allow them in the main hall."

Nuri sighed, "Me too. As soon as they take us to wherever we're going, we can call Eljay to send a replacement Kasha."

Then it dawned on them the car was headed away from Damascus. They were shocked to realize that their security escorts were not from the U.N. They reached for the limo's door handles, but they had been removed.

The driver turned off the paved highway onto a dirt road that continued for a few miles. The bumpy road ended at an old abandoned house with a dilapidated barn across from it. The driver pulled up to the front door and two men came out of the house. They opened the car doors and roughly pulled the confused passengers to their feet. Mark and Nuri could see they were carrying PlastiCuffs and black hoods.

Before they could react, they were slammed to the ground, bound in the cuffs and hoods, and then pulled to their feet again. They were led in the direction of the old barn and someone yelled "Steps" to keep them from falling on the wooden stairs at their feet. They assumed they were being led upward to the barn's loft but the stairs angled downward. Given what they saw of the age and condition of the barn, the idea that it had a lower level was chilling. The stairs were made of wooden slats that creaked loudly with every step. They were relieved to reach the floor with the steps intact. The wooden planks turned out to be a landing connected to a second flight of rickety steps that took them even lower.

They finally reached the bottom, but the surprises kept coming. An awful stench began to waft through the fabric of their hoods. The combined odors of mold, dust and what had to be a poorly maintained septic system all blended together to complete a

694

dismal picture in their minds. They realized that the stifling hoods were a mixed blessing. They blocked some of the horrific smell and kept them from seeing the hellhole that had become their prison.

Then they were forced to sit in two high-backed chairs. More PlastiCuffs were used to secure their ankles to the chairs' metal legs. With their arms still tied behind them, both men were already in pain. At last, someone said something, and, surprisingly, the words were in English.

"Why have you tried to deceive the leaders of the United Nations?" asked a deep voice with flawless diction and no discernable accent.

Both Mark and Nuri started to speak at once. Their frightened denials were muffled through the hoods causing the voice to yell, "Shut up!" They fell silent not knowing what else to do.

"Pay attention!" said the voice. Mark and Nuri both yelled after being sucker punched in the face. "Tell me what devious plan the two of you have made together?"

Mark cleared his throat and nervously said, "We don't have a devious plan. We have a defective crystal box. If you'll let me contact my friends back in the United States, I can get this cleared up in no time."

The next thing Mark knew, his chair was tilted all the way until only its metal back separated him from the dirt floor below. He heard some scuffling sounds he couldn't quite place until he felt water being poured onto the hood that covered his face. He started coughing immediately but that only made him take more water in through his nose and mouth. He tried to turn his neck to catch his breath, but rough hands held his head in place. The stream of water continued for about twenty seconds and Mark began to believe he would drown. He could hear that Nuri was being tortured as well.

The water finally stopped and the voice spoke again. "I don't care that you are dishonest men. The United Nations will deal with you if you survive this interrogation. What I really want to know is the exact location of the Bimini Hall of Records."

Nuri was still coughing, but managed to gasp, "I'll tell you where it is, but it won't do you any good."

"And why is that?" the voice asked calmly.

Nuri coughed again and said, "It's impossible for you to get there. You don't have the technology or expertise to dive 1,500 feet down in the ocean."

"Well," the voice hesitated for the first time, "then I suggest you tell us everything we need to know to accomplish the impossible."

"Are you serious?" Mark spat out in anger. "I'm guessing none of you are scientists and couldn't begin to grasp what's involved. Even if you could, do you really think we can do what you ask while we're being tortured?"

"I will give you a few hours to gather your wits," the voice said in amusement. "I will bring someone who will be able to understand everything you say."

Mark started to object, but Nuri cut him off saying, "Thank God. The sooner you bring this person, the better!"

Mark realized Nuri was just buying them more time and less abuse. He silently thanked his friend for keeping a cooler head under the circumstances. They heard footsteps climbing the creaky stairs until the room went silent.

Nuri said, "Hello? I need to tell you something else that is important!"

When no one responded, he said to Mark, "I wanted to make sure we are alone. Do you have any idea who kidnapped us?"

"I've been trying to place any kind of accent in the guy's English," Mark ventured. "He sounds American, but I can't believe President Campbell is behind this."

"Actually, I think that's good news," Nuri suggested. "They don't want us to see their faces and they don't want us to know what country or countries are behind this. That has to mean that they intend to keep us alive if we play this right."

"That's hard to believe," Mark said with disgust. "I nearly drowned when they were pouring water on me."

"It's called waterboarding," Nuri said. "It is intended to make you feel like you're drowning without much risk of actually

696

killing the person. At worst, we would lose consciousness and they would revive us. In some ways it's supposed to be worse than drowning because they can keep it up for hours."

"Thanks for that!" Mark growled. "What chance is there that Jason and Eljay will be able to find us?"

"Without any RF crystals with us to track, I'm not sure," Nuri sighed. "If only we hadn't forgotten the earbuds. They might have missed them when they searched us. I'm sure that President Campbell will start looking for us the moment she knows we're missing."

"So what do we do when they bring someone here who knows English, is an expert deep sea diver, and can understand RF technology?" Mark asked.

"I say we tell them a story they'll believe," Nuri said flatly. "We tell them we used ADS gear to access the entrance at 1,500 feet."

"I barely know anything about that stuff," Mark croaked a laughed. "I don't think I can be a convincing liar about things I know little about."

"Let me tell them. I asked Diana and Jason a lot of questions about it. I think I can make this work," Nuri smiled to himself under the wet hood. "ADS is an atmospheric diving suit that can safely submerge to around 2,000 feet. We have to try this. If we tell them they can't ever get to the Hall of Records because it's in another dimension, they may decide they no longer need us...in a bad way."

Mark sighed and said, "Didn't Diana say the diving suit weighs over 1,000 pounds? We were old men when we went there. Who's going to believe we pulled that off?"

"I'm hoping they don't know enough about us or ADS equipment to question how we did it," Nuri said. "It's my guess that our kidnappers have never actually worn an ADS suit. I think this story will buy us a couple of days until they figure it out. We'd better be rescued or a ransom paid by then. We could just as easily die of a disease in this place as we could from being tortured to death."

Chapter 27

"But we don't have any scientists who understand resonant frequency technology and speak English without an accent!" said Director Kalan of the Iranian Ministry of Intelligence (VAJA). "That is why we hired you!"

The voice responded, "I believe they are ready to tell us everything they know. These are not brave men. They folded almost immediately. Can you set up a satellite link so your own scientists can observe the interrogation and prompt me with their questions through an earpiece? That way I'll be the only one the Americans hear or see."

"Probably," said Kalan, "but we don't have that capability ourselves. We can arrange to use a satellite connection through Russia or China, but they cannot be trusted. There would be nothing to stop them from blackmailing Iran with this unfortunate incident in the future."

"Then your only option is to have me extract what you need from these two before I kill them," the voice said matter-of-factly. "That is, if you wish to keep Iran's involvement in this a secret."

"No one can ever know of this," Kalan sighed. "Once China's efforts to remove the Americans from the G.A. conference failed in the United States, it appears that killing them is now the only option. I will have one of our RF experts flown to Damascus as soon as it can be arranged. You will terminate the Americans after we learn what they know. You must make sure that their bodies are never found."

***

"How could they just disappear without a trace?" POTUS exclaimed into the phone. "There is more security in this place than we ever had at the White House."

Yusef, the Director of Security for the United Nations, answered, "Madam President, I believe they left the premises of their own accord. Our people escorted them from the G.A. hall, but then video surveillance shows that two other men walked out of the building with them. Witnesses say that the well-dressed men appeared to be your scientists' body guards as they helped them into a limousine and drove away. No one thought Doctors Heston and Zayd were under duress at any time."

"Nobody questioned them on where they were going?" POTUS asked, hardly believing this could happen.

"Syria is a free country, Madam President," Yusef said indignantly. "All people, your scientists included, are free to go where they like as long as they don't trespass where they are not allowed."

Kathryn Campbell could see she would get no help from U.N. security. She hung up the phone and put in her earbud.

"Jason!" she said. "Jason Fisher, can you hear me?"

"I'm here Madam President," Jason answered. "What have you found out?"

"Not much so far, I'm afraid," she huffed. "U.N. security thinks they left the building of their own free will and drove off in a limousine with two unidentified men. Witnesses thought the men were their body guards."

Jason shook his head saying, "They haven't got a suspicious bone in their bodies. Their minds were on what had just happened with Kasha. They would have followed anyone who politely directed them at that point."

"But who would have taken them?" POTUS asked.

"Start with a list of the member nations who voted against Kasha's suggestion for equality," Jason suggested. "That will point you in the right direction. I just tried to locate the RF crystals Mark and Nuri had with them. Our tracking shows all their RF devices are still in their hotel room inside the U.N. complex. I don't know another way to find them."

POTUS asked, "What about Dr. Jensen? Is he up and around yet? Maybe he knows a way?"

"He's barely conscious at the moment," Jason said. "It may be another hour or two until his head clears enough to be of much help. I'll get him back to the lab so there's no delay once he comes around."

***

Once Jason had prevented the kidnapping attempt at JPL, Amelius' and Halaliel's attentions were drawn to Mark and Nuri. The two ethereal beings could see all their possible futures. As events were unfolding in the prevailing threads of linear time, the likely outcomes were not promising.

Halaliel said, "I believe the better path is to involve Diana in the rescue effort."

Amelius considered the suggestion before saying, "As with most choices, there would be trade-offs. While the odds of Jason, Mark and Nuri surviving the ordeal would improve, the negative repercussions for Diana would most likely lead her down a dark path."

"That is possible," Halaliel agreed, "but I'm surprised to hear you say that. I'm usually the less optimistic between us. Don't you trust that her years of study as an Imam taught her that violence is not stronger than love? There is nothing selfish behind her desire to protect her loved ones. I believe that her superb warrior skills would only help Jason's efforts to rescue their companions. Isn't the goal here that they all survive so that Mark and Nuri can return to the U.N.?"

"That is a laudable goal, but look further ahead, Halaliel," Amelius advised. "In the same way that an alcoholic can lose a great deal of progress when they fall off the wagon, Diana would most likely surrender spiritual ground by becoming caught up in her fervor to save her friends."

Halaliel intuitively knew what Amelius said was true, but couldn't understand why. "What would cause her to slide back into believing that the way of power is better than the way of love?"

Amelius laughed and said, "My friend, you will never know the challenge of entertaining an unloving thought. Not only do they hinder a soul's connection to the Creator, selfish thoughts forge their own compelling path ever-further away from love."

"I do not desire the freedom to make choices our Creator would not," Halaliel confirmed. "It makes little sense to me that souls were given free will to make poor choices that can close themselves off from the love of our Creator."

"And yet," Amelius said, "you know how glorious it is when one of God's prodigal children freely and willingly returns home."

Halaliel was still puzzled. "But your position indicates that what is best for only one person outweighs what is best for many souls. Wouldn't it be better that Diana be allowed to choose her path if the rest of humanity will be better off because of it?"

Amelius laughed and said, "A similar issue was raised in the garden of Gethsemane. Your point is valid when a soul willingly chooses a difficult path and they are properly prepared for the challenge. Diana, if asked, would selflessly put herself in harm's way for those she loves, but it would be to her own detriment despite her good intentions. In the garden of Gethsemane, the Christ Consciousness was one with the will of the Savior from Nazareth. Rather than regressing, He learned obedience through the things that He suffered."

"I understand your words," Halaliel sighed, "but I clearly don't feel them as you do. You are like an AA mentor to an alcoholic. You truly understand and love humanity with an everlasting love. But whether or not our friends survive this event, the most precarious times for humanity are yet to come."

Amelius smiled, "And I have faith that the world will step forward in unity and in love to overcome the way of power. Even if they don't succeed today, I will never abandon them. After all, with every temptation, our Creator has provided a way of escape."

***

"I didn't sign up for this!" Mark grumbled.

"I didn't either," Nuri agreed, "but Amelius did warn us something like this was coming. And, by the way, listening to you complain about it isn't helping."

It had been hours since they were left alone in the lower depths of the dilapidated barn outside of Damascus. No one had come back to torment them, but that also meant no food, water, or bathroom breaks. Still, this more subtle form of torture was preferable to waterboarding.

"Why isn't Amelius helping Jason to rescue us?" Mark wondered aloud.

"How do you know he is not trying to help? This isn't the first time our lives were in danger for no good reason," Nuri reminded him.

Mark shot back, "You're right! The bad guys have nearly punched our ticket a few times, but those terrifying moments were over quickly. At least it seemed like it compared to this. It looks like this torture is going to last for days."

"And they still might kill us after we've told them what they want to know." Nuri added.

"I wonder what's going on back at the United Nations?" Mark asked. "If Kasha isn't there to offer the perfect guidance at key moments, will the General Assembly be able to peacefully come to an agreement on their own?"

"And what about Kasha?" Nuri sighed. "Do you think Yuri broke it when he dropped the box?"

"We were probably set up from the start," Mark admitted. "Remember that Russia changed their vote almost immediately after Yuri left our hotel room. I have to admit, that guy was smooth! I don't know about you, but I've begun to wonder if the universe is as friendly as Amelius claims."

"A more specific warning could have avoided this mess altogether," Nuri added. "I can already hear our ethereal friends' explanation for why they didn't tell us what was coming. We should have seen this as a tremendous opportunity for spiritual growth in our patience and faith."

"I'd be a lot more patient if they would untie my arms," Mark grumbled. "I can't feel them at all except for the shooting pains I get when I try to move."

"Why don't we try to make contact with Amelius and Halaliel? Meditation might help with the pain even if we can't connect with our ethereal friends."

"Be my guest," Mark muttered. "We would have heard from them by now if they were going to help us. Besides, there is nothing about this place that makes me feel like meditating."

***

Russian President Demetri Olaf stared at the crystal box sitting on the desk in his hotel suite. He had asked to examine it personally after his ambassador procured it from the American scientists. Demetri carefully lifted the lid and listened.

"Hello?" Demetri whispered. "Is anyone there?"

"Yes."

Demetri smiled at the response and asked, "Should I call you Kasha?"

"You can if you like. However, the information you can access through this device does not come from a person."

"Is this thing some kind of advanced computer?" he thought to himself. Kasha answered as if he'd asked the question aloud.

"As you are thinking of the comparison at this moment, that portrayal is incomplete but accurate. Calling the Akashic Records a computer is a very limited description of the information available from this source."

"Can you read my thoughts?" he asked, a little uncomfortable with the possibility.

"That is an interesting question from a linear time perspective. This source can access the records of everything that has ever been or can ever be. From a linear time perspective, the thoughts you have had are already recorded as well as every thought you might have in what you would call the future. But, technically, no, this source maintains a record of the thoughts you've had rather than directly reading your mind. With that said, from your perspective there is little difference."

"Can you tell me what others are thinking?" he asked, trying to understand what the box could do.

"Within certain limits, yes I can."

"And what are those limits?" he persisted.

"The information I offer must be helpful and hopeful for all. Questions asked with an intention of taking advantage of others will be answered in a way that will guide the questioner onto a better path."

703

"And who decides what my intentions are in the questions I ask?" Demetri challenged.

"The deciding factor is Universal Law rather than an individual. When you are not in human form, seeing the vibrations involved in the loving or selfish intent of others is not difficult."

"Is there any way to bypass that limitation in your answers?" Demetri asked.

"One day, many years from now as you count time, you will find humor in that question. The implication that you could bypass Universal Law in order to take advantage of others would be considered blasphemous if the First Cause were anything but unconditional love."

"Then the answer is no?" he asked, not really understanding what Kasha had said.

"The answer is no, but you would do well to study what was just offered rather than ignore it."

"I have heard this kind of drivel before," Demetri sighed. "Keep turning the other cheek no matter what happens. What kind of a God allows the horrors I've seen to take place in the world? Perhaps people are capable of treating each other well, but not forever. How can any of us be that naïve and forgiving?"

"Line upon line, precept upon precept, here a little, there a little, do your best to make choices where everyone thrives. The time required to accomplish this is of no consequence given that every soul lives forever. One enduring truth is that the Creator is unwilling to lose any soul, but it goes much deeper than that. The 'I am that I am' does not want any soul to ever be sad or discouraged, including you."

Demetri was stumped. This box was not what he had expected. He recognized the Bible quotes, but where were the threats of eternal damnation to go with them? He hadn't wanted to get into a theological discussion with Kasha, but now he was intrigued.

He asked, "If all that existed before the universe was God, it seems logical that He created everything in existence, including evil.

How can God be pure unconditional love and have created evil at the same time?"

"God did not create evil. God created perfect souls as His beloved children and bestowed them with free will. If those children make choices their Father would not, do you blame God or His children who freely made those selfish choices?"

Demetri smiled. Kasha was not infallible and he was about to prove it. "You just referred to God as the Father and you used male pronouns to describe Him. Are you saying that God is male?"

"The First Cause has no gender. This source did not refer to God using male gender terms until you implied your own preference. If you would prefer we speak of our Creator as a female, that is your choice to make. If genderless terms are better for you, they are the most accurate."

A little angry now, Demetri asked, "If God doesn't want any of us to suffer, or, what was it you said, be sad or discouraged, then why did He give us free will to do such awful things?"

"There is great joy in watching your children make better choices as they experience life. That way, God can kill the fatted calf when each soul finally and freely accepts His loving ways and returns to His loving arms. Before you ask, God does not desire to kill an animal to celebrate a soul's return. The reference was intended to appeal to your ironic sense of humor. Rest assured that no animals, or souls of either gender, were actually harmed in the parable of the Prodigal Son."

Demetri found that he was laughing lightly and realized the box was right about his sense of humor, but it did raise a question.

"You were kidding about souls having a gender, right?" Demetri asked.

"Correct, souls have no gender, just like their Father."

Demetri laughed out loud and found that he was starting to like this Kasha. Still, he didn't understand the part about why we have total free will if it can lead to great suffering.

"Wouldn't it be better to limit our free will so that humanity does not bring great misery to the world?"

"Indeed, and God did create an infinite number of such wonderful beings. They are called angels. They have free will, but only to make choices that work exclusively toward the greater good. The ability to make choices that God would not is reserved only for souls who were created in God's perfect image."

He asked, "Why are souls so special to God considering the atrocities people have committed throughout our history?"

"Because all souls are God's beloved children. Good human parents love their children as well. Regarding the damage humanity inflicts on itself, the universe is ultimately childproof. No soul is ever permanently harmed or rejects God's loving ways forever. The human form is simply like clothing that is worn for the occasion of living upon the earth. When we wear out one set of clothes, God will always provide another, as in reincarnation, until the soul learns to accept God's loving ways for their own."

Demetri hadn't considered that reincarnation allows humans to be given as many chances as needed to improve. He felt like that couldn't be right. Kasha addressed his doubts without him posing the question.

"Here is a helpful analogy. In the current century, people become addicted to online gaming and prefer to spend more time living a virtual life online than living their real lives. They become lost because they so closely identify with their online characters. It is like this with a soul living life as a human. The soul is not meant to inhabit a physical body, though it need not be a sin to assume a physical form. The limited existence of human beings is strangely compelling to an ethereal soul, much like drinking excessive amounts of alcohol to alter your corporeal mind is compelling. Eventually, all of humanity will choose to release from living on the earth in human form because they will remember their true nature as companions and co-creators with God."

"And how does Russia fit in with God's great plan?" Demetri asked suspiciously.

"Russia will eventually become the light of the world."

Demetri was shocked to hear this. He had been certain that this unusual box would always exhibit a bias toward the western

706

nations and for Christianity. He needed to be sure he had heard Kasha correctly.

"Please explain what you mean by that?" he asked.

"The same country that calls each other comrade also has more natural resources than any other nation. Your fears regarding the United States are largely unfounded. America has learned how to make efficient use of what they have. They can help your citizens to make the greatest use of the bounty Russia is blessed with while you show them what brotherly love is all about."

He asked, "And what role does religion, specifically Christianity, play in all you just described?"

"Religions aren't necessarily bad, but they can be used selfishly. Much of the secret to the success of the United States can be found on their currency which states, 'In God we trust.' That success is not based in Christianity but rather having faith in God."

"The world just went through imposed Islam because that's what Prince Nafid wanted. Will everyone become Christian next?" Demetri sighed.

"Religions and their clergy have many positive qualities, just the same as politics and politicians. It is the free-willed individuals within those organizations that define whether all its members will be aided or hindered by them. As time progresses on earth, humanity will focus more on God and less on a specific religion. This will be a natural and welcome shift rather than one that is forced."

"And what can I do to facilitate Russia becoming the light of the world?" Demetri asked.

"Return the crystal box to Doctors Heston and Zayd."

Demetri didn't like that answer. He asked, "How can I do that? I understand that they have gone missing."

"They were taken as a direct result of your ambassador's ruse with the crystal box. Your orders made their kidnapping possible. You can make amends by seeing to it that they are safely returned."

"Do you know where they are?" he asked.

"Yes. They are being held against their will at coordinates latitude 33.572266 and longitude 36.401810. Make contact with President Campbell and tell her that those coordinates will guide them to a barn located in a rural area northeast of Damascus. Doctors Heston and Zayd are being held prisoner there in the barn's underground bunker."

President Olaf considered his next steps carefully. He originally thought that possessing Kasha would give Russia a needed advantage over the other nations in creating the brave new world to come. It was clear now that his plan would not work. If Kasha was right, the only way Russia would come out ahead was if everyone prospered and helped each other. Even if Kasha was wrong, there seemed to be no advantage in keeping the box knowing that a great deal of good will with the U.S. could be gained by providing the coordinates.

"What is the best way to return this box without implicating Russia in its disappearance?" he asked.

"Tell your ambassador, Yuri Alton, to leave the RFA box in the archeologists' hotel room. It will be found during a forthcoming search for clues of their current location. While U.N. Security will be looking for answers regarding the existence of two boxes, nothing will point to Russia as being culpable. Yuri is clever enough to manage this for you."

Chapter 28

"Jason Fisher," President Campbell said over her RFC earbud. "Can you hear me?"

She had been trying to reach them for a few hours without success. Calling them on the landline was not an option. She could not be sure the phones were secure in the hotel and what she had to tell Jason needed to remain top secret.

Suddenly she heard, "Hello? Mark or Nuri, are you out there?"

"Jason?" she gasped in relief. "Is that you?"

"No, Madam President. This is Louis Jensen."

"Can you get Jason online to hear me? I have information on where we will find Mark and Nuri."

"I'm here now, Madam President," Jason said excitedly. "Where are they?"

POTUS gave them the coordinates and the strange story of Russian President Olaf casually handing her a slip of paper with the details they needed.

"I don't know whether to trust him or not," she cautioned. "He seemed genuinely interested in their well-being, but he would not explain further."

"We'll take it from here, Madam President," Jason assured her with grim determination.

***

"I can't just teleport you into an underground bunker," Eljay objected. "It's tough enough to target the correct spot on the surface of the earth. Trying to adjust for coordinates underground can go bad in any number of ways."

"You need to check with Sherlock," Jason insisted. "While you were passed out, Sherlock said that your approach to using GPS coordinates could be improved. I think you're able to set coordinates just by thinking of a place instead of mapping a grid of the planet."

"How does thinking of the destination improve on setting the coordinates digitally?" Eljay asked skeptically.

"I believe it is more exact because it works according to our intention rather than possibly inputting the wrong coordinates," Jason explained.

Eljay flipped open Sherlock's lid and asked, "Is Jason right about this?"

"Yes, he is. Jason, Mark and Nuri have already proven it. They have teleported long distances twice without manually entering numerical coordinates. The first time was from the pyramid in Piedras Negras to their office in Pasadena. The other was from the Temple Beautiful to JPL."

"I have no idea how to program an RFT crystal to do that," Eljay complained. "You're going to have to walk me through it."

"Jason will find this humorous, but you will not. The programming, as you call it, must be activated through intention rather than setting a digital frequency."

Sherlock was right. Jason started laughing and Eljay just scowled at him before asking, "Why doesn't RFT work the same as the other RF crystals we've made so far?"

"If done correctly, the outcome is the same, but programming RF crystals through manual settings can be described as 'clunky' and inefficient in comparison to using intention. Also, the Fibonacci frequency that works through intention makes your current method impractical. The frequencies are so great that your human life would expire before you could enter all the needed digits by hand."

Jason was still smiling when Eljay conceded, "I see. So how do we program RFT crystals through intention?"

"Have Jason hold the crystal in his right hand while meditating. The focus or affirmation for the meditation should be on the exact capabilities that you want the crystal to have when using it. Visualize the safety protocols you already use being included and add that it opens a portal to where you desire to go."

"You mean we could have been using this method all along instead of the elaborate devices I've had to invent?" Eljay complained, somewhat annoyed. "Why didn't you tell us about this earlier?"

"Your faith in RF technology has been a work in progress. It is not just you and Jason who needed to build on success; it was the whole of humanity. Until now, neither of you could have successfully programmed an RF crystal through meditation. As it stands now, Jason will have greater success than you intentionally programming the RF crystal."

Jason interjected, "Are Mark and Nuri all right? Can I get them back here before they really get hurt?"

"Yes, especially because of your unique skills and intense desire to help your friends. It is not a matter of luck, as defined in a dictionary. Luck is better defined as ninety-nine percent karma and one percent chance. Your friends have learned a great deal about themselves in that bunker. Rescuing them will work to strengthen their faith as few achieve here on the earth. You should begin now. Time grows short."

***

"Shhh, I think someone's coming," Nuri cautioned Mark.

The creaking of the bunker's trap door echoed eerily in the darkness. The boards that served as stairs groaned with the weight of men taking slow steps downward. From the sounds, at least two or three of them were coming.

When the noises stopped they heard a 'click' that had to be a light switch. Tiny dots of light showed through the stifling hoods that still covered their heads. Then they heard the voice say, "Good news! The blindfolds are coming off."

Mark and Nuri felt the hoods being pulled away. The light was painful to their eyes but they quickly adjusted to the dim bulbs that lit the dirt basement. They could see walls that were dug out of the earth with supporting wooden beams and plywood to keep the rocky soil from collapsing on top of them. Neither of them said a word. They knew it was a bad sign that their captors no longer cared if they were seen.

The voice belonged to a sinister looking man. He was tall, with a muscular frame that was enhanced by a well-tailored suit. He had a thick black mustache and a shaved head. If there was a human archetype for what a villain should look like, this was him. He stared at them for a moment and then smiled.

"Someone is coming soon who understands your science. He speaks English so you should have no trouble teaching him what he needs to know. The goal is to safely gain access to the Bimini Hall of Records. I want to secure the things a team will need to successfully complete this mission. Please list for me the equipment that will be needed to teach, train and accomplish all this."

Nuri didn't hesitate. He and Mark had been thinking this through for hours. He cleared his throat and took a breath. "You will need ADS gear for however many people you have on the diving team. We did it with three of us. You should have two submersible monitoring vehicles. One of them will keep you in radio contact with the team members who remain on the boat. The second one will be able to courier the things you find in the Hall of Records that you want to take to the surface."

The voice stopped him there. "What did you already remove from the place, and where are those items stored now?"

Mark answered, "We left the place just as it was. We didn't have the submersibles to help us, so we planned to get it all later when we could bring what we needed to keep it all safe."

Nuri realized the voice was about to catch them in a lie and added, "As you probably know, we did remove the crystal box since the pressure of the deep water should not have affected it, but someone managed to switch a fake box for our real one."

The voice looked surprised and then nodded seeming content with their explanation. He gestured and said, "Continue."

Nuri said, "You will need several water-tight, high-pressure containers to store the pieces you recover for transport. Those items have been in deep ocean water for thousands of years. To suddenly expose them to the open air and surface pressure would likely ruin them. We still haven't determined how to examine and test the artifacts once they are brought to the surface, but your people can figure that out."

Mark added, "We'll need a white board, markers and eraser for teaching your man about RF technology. Legal pads and pens too, a lot of them. Obviously, we'll need a work table and chairs...and much better lighting if you intend to keep us down here."

"You will remain here," the voice confirmed. "I will see to securing the items you mentioned and start making the other arrangements."

He motioned to the two soldiers that had come down with him. They all turned to go, but Mark yelled to stop them.

"And when we have told you everything, we will be released?"

The man with the voice offered a sinister smile and nodded as he ascended the steps. The mocking lie unnerved Mark and Nuri and they wondered if they would ever escape this terrible place.

Jason stood up from his meditation hoping he programmed the RFT crystal as Sherlock had told him. He held it in his right hand and mentally visualized a portal opening between him and his two friends. Nothing seemed to change but he stepped forward anyway. All that got him was two steps forward. There was no portal.

"Dammit!" Jason exclaimed. "I thought I did everything right. Check with Sherlock to see what I missed."

Eljay lifted the lid to the crystal box and said, "Okay, that didn't work. Now what do we do?"

"You did nothing wrong. The RFT crystal is working perfectly."

Jason was out of patience. "Then why am I still standing here instead of rescuing Mark and Nuri?"

"You programmed in the safety measures that prevent the crystal from teleporting you into a dangerous situation. Your friends are not alone. You will not have to wait long until it is safe to help them."

The two men just stared at each other. Eljay smiled and said, "Be careful what you ask for. You just might get it."

"I must be slipping. I hadn't thought about anything but getting to them as soon as I could," Jason said.

713

A few minutes passed before Jason asked Sherlock, "Is it safe now?"

"It is indeed. In fact, you must hurry. Your friends are in no condition to move quickly and they are bound by their feet and hands. They will need you to bring them back one at a time."

Jason pulled his combat knife from the sheath and held the RFT crystal tightly. He closed his eyes and pictured his friends before stepping forward.

The only thing Jason could make out in the darkness was an awful smell. He realized he was standing on a dirt floor.

"Mark! Nuri!" he whispered, "Are you here?"

Mark answered, "Jason! Thank God! Get us out of here!"

Jason moved toward Mark's voice and located the PlastiCuffs to cut them off. Mark tried to stand up, but he couldn't move his legs. He had been tied up for hours. Jason slung him over his shoulder like a sack of flour before assuring Nuri he would return in a moment.

He mentally opened an RFT portal and stepped through it with Mark dangling awkwardly. The next minute they were in Eljay's lab at JPL. Eljay jumped up to help Jason set Mark down of the floor.

"Oh my God man, you need a shower," was all Eljay managed to say.

"It's nice to see you again, too, Eljay," was Mark's curt response.

"There's no time for celebration yet," Jason exclaimed. "I've got to go back for Nuri."

He tried opening a portal but the crystal's safety protocols had apparently kicked in. Jason turned to Sherlock and yelled, "How do I override the RFT crystal's safety protocols?"

"The RFT crystal you're holding now works by intention. Set your intention to override the safety protocols and it will be so."

Jason closed his eyes and told the crystal he wanted to go back regardless of the potential danger. With his combat knife in hand, he took a step forward and the awful smell returned. The difference this time was that the lights were on and three men were in the underground bunker with Nuri. Two of them flanked Nuri's chair to either side. They wore mercenary uniforms and had their rifles trained at his head. The third man was standing next to a nearby wall. He seemed to be the interrogator. No doubt they wanted to know where Mark had gone.

Despite their shock at Jason's sudden appearance, the two armed men turned their rifles to shoot. With blurring speed and deadly accuracy, Jason used his combat knife to dispatch the soldier closest to him. Then he grabbed the man around his neck to use his body as a shield. Jason couldn't carry the dead man and rush the other soldier because Nuri and the metal chair holding him were in the way.

Jason was reaching for the dead man's rifle when the soldier across from him started firing. A bullet ripped through Jason's left forearm as the dead soldier's body rocked in reaction to the other rounds that hit him. Jason threw his combat knife with all his strength toward the other man's face. The tip of the blade burrowed deep into the soldier's left eye socket and he fell to the ground.

Jason was glad to see the man in the suit disappear up the stairwell. With any luck, they would have time to escape before reinforcements came. He retrieved his knife from the soldier's lifeless body and proceeded to cut the PlastiCuffs holding his friend to the chair. Nuri couldn't stand and Jason's left arm was a useless bloody mess.

He struggled to lift his friend up when three more soldiers started coming down the wooden steps. Jason knew it was suicide to try to shoot it out with them. He mentally visualized both of them teleporting to Eljay's lab. The mercenaries opened fired leaving gruesome clouds of blood as Jason and Nuri disappeared from sight.

***

Director Kalan of Iran's Ministry of Intelligence was seething over the news that the archeologists had escaped. He almost smashed the phone's handset down on his desk in anger. He thought he had hired the best team possible to locate and take control of the Bimini Hall of Records. They had learned how to access the submerged chamber 1,500 feet below. They had been told how to safely recover the artifacts stored there, but the two men had escaped before the specific location was disclosed.

Kalan dreaded telling the Ayatollah of this failure. They had already discussed this unfortunate contingency and agreed that it should be avoided at all costs. Now it was their only option.

"Sir?" the voice said. "Are you still there?"

"Listen to me very carefully," Kalan said with a venomous tone. "I don't want to hear any more excuses. I have a new mission for you. Fail me again and it will be for the last time."

"I will not fail you," the voice assured him. "Is there anything you need me to do in preparation for the new assignment?"

"Yes," was Kalan's terse response. "Obtain a map of the International Airport of Damascus. I am sending four Z-19 assault helicopters to destroy all of the airport's runways. You should develop the plan of attack before the birds get to your location."

"You want me to disable the runways?" the voice asked. "Nothing else?"

Kalan gritted his teeth and said, "The intent is to keep jets from landing or leaving the area rather than inflicting casualties. I will contact you again when the helicopters are about to arrive. You will receive further instructions then."

Chapter 29

Jason and Nuri were already falling to the floor when they reappeared in the lab. They landed heavily on Mark fracturing his back and mercifully knocking him unconscious. Eljay was in the next room locating the first aid kit when he heard the commotion. He grabbed the box and rushed back to the lab to help. All he could see was a bloody pile of lifeless bodies on the floor. Eljay froze in his tracks. He couldn't move. He couldn't believe that his friends were dying right in front of him. Sherlock suddenly started offering suggestions that sounded more like orders.

"Eljay, bring the obsidian podium over to heal your friends. You must hurry or Jason and Nuri will die."

Eljay had never been good under pressure but Sherlock's directions startled him into action. If he could place their hands in the podium's carved out surface, they would be healed of their injuries. He rushed over and tried to lift it up by wrapping his arms around the obsidian column. Eljay was not a strong man having spent most of his days working in the lab. He called to Sherlock, "We need a new plan. The lectern is too heavy."

"Using leverage from the top, push the lectern onto its side toward your friends. Try to use the inertia of toppling it over to keep it moving toward them."

Eljay's stomach became queasy but he did as Sherlock suggested. When the weight of the podium hit the ground, the top end bounced up in reaction to the force. Eljay pushed the base with all his strength and the lectern slid closer to his friends. The blood spreading out from the bodies flowed around the podium. The crimson liquid lubricated the floor so that he managed to slide it forward a few more feet. When the top of the lectern was on its second bounce, he managed to move it a bit farther.

But when the lectern's bouncing momentum stopped, so did Eljay. His stomach emptied in reaction to the stress, strain and all the blood on the floor. He was panicked that his friends would die because he let them down. He cried out in desperation, "Help me!" Sherlock spoke calmly a moment later.

"Eljay, you don't need the obsidian pedestal to heal Jason, Nuri and Mark."

He cussed at Sherlock between furious grunts as he again tried in vain to move the podium toward his friends. Eljay was covered in bile and crimson gore from the waist down. Each time he tried to push, his shoes slipped and he fell to the floor. Sherlock spoke again.

"Eljay, you will not be able to push the pedestal close enough to your friends in time to save them. Your efforts need to be redirected to succeed. Rest assured that your thoughts alone can heal them with or without the obsidian lectern. Your friends strongly desire to be made well. You need only to focus your healing intention directly upon them to help them attain that goal."

"Forget all that nonsense," Eljay shouted, "this is reality! Besides, why did you have me waste all that time with the podium if you knew I couldn't use it to save them?"

"At first, you were frozen in fear and you needed to take action, any action, to get started. You would not attempt a spiritual healing of your friends until you ran out of traditional solutions. You needed to exhaust your body so that you could see the futility of that approach. Your desperate desire and motivation to help them has opened your mind to spiritual alternatives. So now you must choose. Will you continue to stubbornly struggle to move the lectern knowing you have another option that will save your friends?"

Eljay lamented, "But how can I do that? I'm not made of obsidian!"

"You no longer need the assistance of obsidian to heal your friends. The reality is that, at a higher level of consciousness, they have willingly put their lives at risk to give you this opportunity. Let there be no doubt that you are a perfect channel for God's power to heal and they will be healed. Do not forget that the spirit is the life, the mind is the builder and the physical is the result."

Then Eljay heard the voice of his father, Louis, "You can do this son. You know that consciousness controls matter and energy. It is not a miracle, it is a fact. We are all capable of intentional healing, even in human form. You are a beloved child of God with

718

access to anything you need, including the power to help heal your friends!"

He felt an incredible rush of confidence flood over him. Sherlock began guiding Eljay through the process.

"Lay your hands on the foreheads of your friends and pray for their healing. Visualize them being whole again as if they'd never been in this condition."

The next moment, Eljay felt a jolt as though he'd been struck by lightning. He could feel the massive healing vibrations surging through his body and out through his hands to Jason and Nuri. He watched with astonishment as the healing flesh pushed the bullets out onto the floor. He marveled as their skin mended and returned to normal where the holes had just been. The entire process only took a few minutes, but time had stopped for him.

He intuitively knew that his two friends were fine and he collapsed from the effort. Exhausted as he was, he remembered Mark needed help too. He yelled, "Sherlock, what can I do for Mark?"

"His back is severely injured and paralysis is inevitable without intervention. However, you will need time to recover to function as a healing channel. In a moment, you can enlist Jason's help."

As predicted, a disoriented Jason jumped to his feet and tried to get his bearings. Eljay exclaimed, "You've got to move Mark over to the lectern."

Nuri was conscious now and managed to roll off of Mark so that Jason could move him. Eljay and Nuri watched Jason drag Mark through the blood and bile to reach the podium. He placed his friend's hand in the depression and they could see the obsidian radiate life into Mark's twisted body. His back straightened and healthy color returned to his face.

After a minute, Mark was able to sit up and cast a questioning look at his friends. Jason sat on the floor next to him and said, "Eljay! Do we even want to know what happened here?"

"It's over," he managed to answer in a raspy voice. "You are all back home and you're fine now."

Jason shook his head at the massive amount of blood and vomit on the floor. His gaze moved to the splintered wood and exposed obsidian pedestal that used to pass for a lectern. He considered calling a hazmat team to clean up the mess. "I wouldn't call this 'doing fine'," he jested.

"You should have seen yourself a few minutes ago," Eljay quipped back. "Compared to that, you've never looked so good!"

"We can't just sit here!" Mark said impatiently. "We've got to get back to the U.N. conference!"

The three others started laughing. They realized that Mark had no idea what had just happened. Jason said, "Slow down, Mark. As bad as the rest of us look, you got the worst of it. The U.N. members will manage to get by on their own until you and Nuri have a chance to clean up."

***

"Do you have any idea who kidnapped you?" POTUS asked.

Mark, Nuri and Jason were meeting with President Campbell in her U.N. hotel suite. They wanted to ask her what to expect at the next G.A. meeting and the best way to explain to the world what had happened, but she was still focused on the abduction.

Jason answered her saying, "There's no way to know for sure. The men I saw holding them were from the Middle East, but that's all I could decipher."

Nuri added, "The man who interrogated us had no discernable accent. He may have been Middle Eastern, but his accent and vocabulary sounded like he grew up in America."

"So how do things stand now with the G.A.?" Mark asked impatiently.

"Poorly, I'm afraid," POTUS said sadly. "While many were willing to carry on with a goal of equality without Kasha, a few of the members became quite adamant against it. Those few are claiming everything from Kasha being a complete fraud to the crystal box being an insidious construct from Prince Nafid."

"So a few loud mouths are ruining this conference for the entire world?" Nuri scoffed.

720

Jason asked, "Is it possible to get Kasha back on the agenda? Especially now that Mark and Nuri are back and can explain everything?"

"Not a chance. Fear of war is rampant among these people," POTUS explained. "Even I have to take steps to protect the United States from foreign aggressors. We can talk peace and equality all day, but if even one country invades a disputed territory, or, God forbid, plays the nuke card, the war games are on."

"By the way, Madam President," Mark asked, "where did you find Kasha?"

She answered, "The box turned up in a search of your hotel room. I've got it with me now for safe keeping."

"So what happens in the morning?" Jason asked with concern.

"The G.A. continues to work through the existing agenda," POTUS began. "If that goes as it has up to now, we could be at war by the end of the day. I've already got our military at DEFCON 2. With one phone call from me, they will deploy to defend our borders and occupy parts of the world that will be strategic to our survival."

None of the men said a word at this bleak possibility. It was difficult to hear that their president was becoming part of the problem instead of working toward a solution.

Nuri said, "You have been for peace and equality from the start. If your strategy has shifted to one of fearful military actions, how much more likely is it that the rest of the world's leaders will do the same?"

"Gentlemen," POTUS said, "You have an excellent point, but I can't stop a world war by myself. I was elected to protect and defend the United States. I'm not going to start the fight, but there seems to be little doubt that war is coming."

***

Mark, Nuri and Jason were in their U.N. hotel room after meeting with POTUS. Eljay was still back at JPL, but he was listening in through his earbud. Their collective mood was depressed. President Campbell had just told them the world was going to war.

721

The JPL crew was still dedicated to maintaining the peace, but they could see no way out.

Jason flipped open Sherlock's lid and asked, "Is a world war going to start tomorrow?"

"Almost every scenario points to the global leaders ordering their respective militaries to protect and preserve the interests of their fellow citizens. That strategy will inevitably lead to conflict."

Nuri asked, "What can we do to help avoid a world war?"

"Eljay should develop a new RFC device. This new crystal will be able to transmit both video and audio signals across all media channels on this planet. President Campbell will have the crystal box you call Kasha with her when the General Assembly meets in the hall. The signal Eljay should re-broadcast will come from Kasha which will be secured inside the President's briefcase. She does not need to know of her role in tomorrow's proceedings for it to succeed."

"I can't develop a new RFC crystal overnight," Eljay scoffed.

"If that's what you believe, Eljay, then you are correct. However, you have an opportunity to apply what you have learned and possibly avert a world war in the process. The choice is yours."

"To avert a world war?" Eljay sounded doubtful. His chest tightened as he grasped the magnitude of this responsibility. "Tell me how and I'll do it."

"You have already seen that the mind is the builder and the physical is the result. You can program an RF crystal to do practically anything with the right attitude and intention. If you will meditate with an RFC crystal, and infuse it with the intention of broadcasting an AV signal sent from Kasha on to the media channels of this world, the crystal will be programmed accordingly."

"Are you sure I can manage that?" Eljay complained. "I've never been much for meditating."

"And yet you were able to join the ethereal meeting at JPL with your friends not so long ago. Your father helped you to assume the correct frame of mind that made attending that meeting possible. You should ask that he join you in this meditation as well. He will be most helpful to you."

The earbuds were silent. Eljay was stunned that the future direction of the world somehow depended on him.

He asked, "How will broadcasting the discussions at the United Nations to the rest of the world make any difference?"

"It may not, but the greater lesson for you here is to have faith in yourself and faith in your intuition. You already know in your heart that all I have said is the truth. The world around you may yet fail to choose peace, but that is no reason to avoid what you have been called to do."

"Let me get back to you," Eljay said to his friends before signing off.

***

Eljay sat in the silence trying to get in a meditation mood. He had never been one for going to church. Praying was fine for anyone else, but he saw little connection between God and science. The idea that what we build with our minds can be made to happen on the earth went against everything he had grown up believing was truth. And yet, so many things had happened to him that he couldn't explain. Worse yet, those unexplainable events appeared to be testable and repeatable once he understood the science behind them.

He found himself praying to the one person he really trusted, his father, Louis Sr. "Dad, if you're out there, I really need you now!" He repeated the same thought aloud several times until he gave up. He began to wonder how he would explain this failure to his friends.

"What failure?" a voice said clearly in his mind.

"Huh?" Eljay couldn't believe what he'd just heard. He looked quickly around the room but he was still alone. "Who is this?"

"You called, son, and I'm here." The voice in his mind was definitely that of his deceased father.

"How can you be?" Eljay cried. "I must be imagining this. Consciousness can only exist inside a physical brain. Yours was cremated years ago. How can this really be you?"

Eljay heard his father chuckle before saying, "Actually, you have it backwards. Consciousness is all that truly exists. What we experience as the physical world is simply our thoughts agreeing to interact following certain laws like physics, chemistry, music, mathematics and so forth. A chess board can be used to play many games depending on the rules we agree to abide by. The physical laws of the earth create the chess board we collectively use to play well, or not so well, with each other while in human form. We souls exist with or without a body, just as God exists inside and outside of manifestation."

He wanted desperately to debate the nature of existence with his father. His dad was the only person in the world whose answers Eljay could trust. After all, if he was really here, then he must know the answers to his profound questions. Still, Eljay had a job to do and that was to create a whole new RFC crystal to do what Sherlock had suggested.

"Dad!" Eljay began. "I need help programming a new RFC crystal to rebroadcast a signal from Kasha to the entire planet."

"I know son," he said. "That's why I'm here. I want to help you do that."

"I have trouble believing that I can do anything just by thinking about it," Eljay sighed. "Can you help me understand how that works?"

"You already know how this works," his father began. "The spirit is the life, the mind is the builder and the physical is the result. All power and creativity comes from God. In the same way that an architect draws up a set of plans first on paper, think of that as the mind being the builder. When a contractor actually builds the project from those plans, think of that as the physical being the result."

"It's not that I don't understand what you're saying dad," Eljay said, "but it goes against everything I've believed up to now. Heck, you were an Atheist your whole life until you met Mark, Nuri and Jason."

"That might give you a hint right there," his father laughed. "I was wrong about the true nature of our existence. It took seeing what your friends could do that seemed to transcend science to open my mind to proof beyond the Scientific Method."

"So you believe in magic now?" Eljay asked skeptically.

"Quite the opposite, actually," his father offered. "I can now accept that there is a scientific reason for all the seeming miracles throughout history. You can see that levitating objects weighing thousands of pounds is no more magic than floating a steel ship in water. The science required to create the specialized crystal you seek is based on sound scientific principles."

"Again," Eljay objected, "I can understand what you're saying, but believing I can make that happen just with my mind and an RF crystal is impossible."

"Then let me help you get in touch with the most basic of all premises at the deepest level," Louis began. "I can feel that you really do believe that the universe is friendly. It's your lack of understanding of the science involved in RF technology that is the source of your fear and anxiety. Focus instead on how logical it is that God and this universe are friendly. It would make no sense for God to be otherwise. You don't have to debate this, just search your own heart to know what you believe about our Creator."

"I know you love me, dad!" Eljay cried. "But I've never felt close to anyone else. What can I do?"

Suddenly, Eljay felt himself being enveloped in a warm cocoon of love. It was a feeling like he'd never experienced before. He worshipped his father and knew his father loved him, but this was that emotion on steroids times a trillion. He thought he would burst from the joy and support that filled his thoughts.

"You rightly believe in our love for each other, son, but you are now experiencing the love of our Creator, the First Cause, the 'I am that I am.' Remember this feeling always. Knowing that it is the destiny of each soul to be this loved, to be this happy, throughout eternity makes all the difference. Search your feelings and tell me if there is anything you cannot do at this moment?"

Eljay was lost in the rapture of connecting directly with God. He still heard his earthly father's words and that helped him to focus. The epiphany that flooded his consciousness was wonderfully overwhelming.

725

"I see now what you've been saying. With God, all things are possible. I am in God and God is in me. The miracle is not that a drop of water like me can be in perfect harmony with the universal ocean that is God. The real miracle is that the essence of that infinite ocean is contained within the drop of water that is me."

"So how hard can it be to program an RFC crystal to do what Sherlock suggested?"

Eljay thought a moment and realized that he had already done it. The crystal in his hand would perform as desired.

"Thank you Dad," Eljay said with tears streaming down his face. They were tears of joy and he hadn't even realized he was crying. "And thank you Father, the 'I am that I am.' I will never forget this."

Chapter 30

President Campbell took her seat with the other world leaders in the G.A. hall. She silently prayed that today's session would go well, or at least better than it had the day before. She couldn't allow herself to believe that any of the leaders present would purposefully choose violence over equality for all. It was like one person spray painting graffiti over a beautiful work of art to call attention to themselves.

China and India demanded one vote for every citizen claiming that was the very definition of fairness and equality. The Middle Eastern countries felt that, since they were the most recent political and economic center of the world, they should continue on in that role. They added for good measure that global leadership was their divine right for Islam was the greatest of all the religions. The other religions felt they too were God's chosen, but many of them had no voice in today's meeting because of the separation between church and state among the other nations. Russia's president had been curiously neutral on most issues considering the biased noises he made at the beginning of the week.

The dialog deteriorated all the more with each new issue discussed. As much as the Secretary-General tried to follow Robert's Rules of Order, there was no controlling this crowd. In fact, as the rhetoric waxed on, they behaved more like an unruly mob than a gathering of the greatest leaders each nation had to offer.

The opening session dealt with trade agreements and the allocation of rare natural resources. As it was with all the other issues discussed, a few of the leaders were unwilling to accept the unequivocal equality of all nations. There were laments of extenuating circumstances as to why equality required a different definition in each case. In no time at all, instead of each person respectively taking their turn, the attendees started simultaneously yelling at each other across the aisles.

The Secretary-General called for a recess to allow tempers to cool. It was then that the news began to spread throughout the assembly of the worldwide broadcast. Someone was transmitting the proceedings from the G.A. hall to media outlets everywhere. In fact, the signal was overriding any programming on every channel and podcast. If anyone was watching a video monitor anywhere on the planet, the only program playing was a live broadcast from the United Nations.

Technical staff and security guards for the U.N. searched high and low for the source of the transmission. There were no audio or video devices of any kind to be found. The viewing angles shown from the live broadcast appeared to be coming from several invisible cameras. They seemed to be floating unseen throughout the hall with the uncanny ability to isolate embarrassing exchanges between leaders. Inexplicably, the text of the closed captioned dialog adapted according to the preferred language of the viewer.

When the Secretary-General called the G.A. leaders back to order, every one of them was aware that the world was watching and assessing them all. Would the top politicians try to maintain an air of professionalism and follow the rules, or use the broadcast to prove how dedicated they were to defending their countries? How this chaotic day would end up was anyone's guess.

***

Mark, Nuri and Jason had invited Diana and Gus to stay with them at JPL for a while. At first, they declined. But when they assured them that RFT had been perfected and they could move easily between Florida and California in just seconds, the offer was too hard to resist.

They shared a late dinner and caught each other up on all that had happened since they last talked. Gus and Diana stopped eating when they heard about Mark and Nuri's kidnapping. As hard as it was to believe, Gus and his granddaughter could only shake their heads amazed and grateful that they had lived to tell the tale.

Jason said, "Please finish up. There's a program coming on TV that you won't want to miss."

Diana said, "I don't feel much like watching TV. What could be more interesting than listening to your exploits?"

"If you've enjoyed the stories we've told so far," Jason laughed, "you're going to love this show. I promise."

The six of them moved into the break room and settled into the well-worn couches to watch the big screen monitor. Gus and Diana couldn't imagine what they were about to see. When the screen came on there was a movie playing. Before Diana could object again, the scene changed to a live broadcast from the G.A. hall in Damascus. The cameras moved around the hall like they were mounted on drones with precision controls. None of the national leaders seemed to be paying any attention to them and soon the first meeting of the day was called to order.

The Secretary-General announced that the first item on the agenda was trade agreements with respect to rare natural resources. Watching the meeting unfold on television was like watching a bad accident. No one could turn away from the increasingly ugly spectacle. It wasn't long before the members assembled were embarrassing themselves with their petty comments and insults.

Jason explained, "The G.A. leaders don't yet know that the world is watching them. Eljay created an RFC crystal that is picking up a signal from Kasha in Damascus and rebroadcasting it on every channel around the planet."

Gus started laughing harder than any of them and pulled a bandana from his back pocket to wipe his eyes. Diana smiled and said, "Okay, you guys did pick an interesting show to watch."

The next item up for discussion was the disputed distribution of Prince Nafid's assets. Since the Prince had no direct heirs or will when he was assassinated, there were many opinions on how that wealth should be dispersed.

The Secretary-General, Akhem al Assad, recognized the President of China, Mao Choi, as having the floor for opening comments.

"Distinguished leaders of the General Assembly," Mao began. "We have gathered a list of the assets the late Prince Nafid held in China. The list is impressive by size and composition. There is not an aspect of our economy that is not controlled by the positions he once held through those assets."

President Choi paused a moment before proceeding to set the record straight on how this would play out.

"I contend that all assets and property that are held in China indeed belong to China, even those owned outside of our borders." He went on to say much more, but the other leaders started yelling over him as soon as the translations came through their headphones.

It was common knowledge that Prince Nafid held over fifty percent of the world's assets at the time of his death. Given the tremendous wealth involved here, there wasn't a nation that wouldn't make the same claim as Mao Choi just had. China and the Middle Eastern countries would have an unfair advantage if the concept of equality was applied as President Choi intended.

All civility was gone. Individual accusations and insults were caught on camera and highlighted by the unknown director of the live broadcast. It was as if the petty exchanges were being edited in post-production so that each leader was at their worst when the spotlight was on them. There was no bias to the embarrassment. Citizens across the globe watched in horror as each of the world's leaders added to the contention with none offering a viable solution.

Akhem pounded his gavel and asked for another recess. The leaders ignored him and continued their ugly rhetoric off the official record.

Back at JPL, Jason got off the couch and asked, "So where do you think this is headed?"

Eljay said, "Sherlock predicted that those idiots would likely end up declaring war. Some will choose to be more protective than aggressive, but they will all deploy their military power."

Diana asked, "Did you invite us over here to witness the beginning of the end of the world?" She wasn't laughing any more.

"Hardly," Nuri assured her. "Sherlock claims this broadcast is the best chance we have of averting a war. We just don't know how as yet."

***

As the day wore on, the world's leaders cared less and less about the live broadcast. It was becoming clear that no one would give an inch where their country's own self-interests were concerned. During the breaks, some of the leaders of the smaller nations rushed to negotiate alliances with the United States, China or the Middle Eastern consortium of countries. As much as these not-so-secret agreements indicated that a world war was imminent, at least the pacts meant the war would employ conventional military tactics instead of nukes to settle their differences.

By the end of the day in Damascus, it was very early morning in California. The six friends had been dozing off in the JPL break room as the spectacle continued to unfold on the huge monitor. It had not been pretty getting the 'behind the scenes' view of their leaders negotiating allied positions to their greatest advantage in order to destroy their enemies.

For most people, this was their first real look at how politics and politicians ran the world. Everyone could see that these were unusual times, but the incredible stress of the situation served to unmask each leader's nature rather than change them.

The last session of the day was about to begin. The agenda item called for an agreement on limiting the size of each country's military force and weaponry. The issue coming up now was pure irony given that the nations had formed coalitions intent on prevailing over their adversaries. No one would be in favor of limits on military spending, but that wouldn't stop any of them from claiming only they had the right to maintain a strong military force in the face of the bad intentions of their neighbors.

As before, the accusations and insults increased. Mao Choi took the stage and grabbed the Secretary-General's microphone to address the group.

"I am tired of the empty threats and false accusations I've suffered throughout this day. I am a patient man, but this has gone on long enough. There is no need to vote on these issues because there is no consensus among us. What we have are alliances that will test each nation's resolve. China is the most powerful country in the world and our strategic partners are spread across the globe. Everyone knows that today's meeting has been broadcast live to every city, town and village. I want to say here and now to my constituents in China that it is time to defend ourselves. I order you to deploy our military might to protect not only our citizens but those of our global allied neighbors."

The resulting chaos had every head of state rushing for the exits to pull the proverbial trigger on their nation's own military plans. Within minutes, the entire planet would be at extreme risk of war. How long would it be until the first shot was fired? An even more ominous question was if a nuclear campaign was inevitable once the weaker countries had no other military options. The citizens of the world could only watch helplessly as the political posturing turned deadly.

***

President Campbell had just hung up from speaking with her Chief of Staff. As much as she hated to do it, she was responsible for protecting the citizens of the United States. Her order to activate all armed forces according to the scenarios her military leaders had been updating all day was her last option.

She sat down on the bed in her hotel suite and reflected on the events that had led to this tragic day. She reached into her purse for the crystal box and lifted the lid as she set it down beside her. She decided to ask what would occur next.

"Kasha," she said with a weary voice, "what is the expected outcome of Mao Choi deploying his military forces?"

"The expected outcome is that all other nations will follow suit. The world is now essentially at war with few prospects for peace."

"How long will it take until civilization collapses into chaos?" POTUS asked.

"If all the troops are deployed as just given, a nuclear strike would take place before the end of the week. Since every country now has nuclear capabilities, a nuclear winter would destroy life as you know it on the planet before the year is out."

"Is there any way we can stop this catastrophe before that happens?" she asked in desperation.

"The world leaders have already chosen their course of action. It remains to be seen how the citizens who elected those leaders will choose. There is one who has not been heard from as yet. He alone may be able to save the earth."

***

Four Z-19 attack helicopters took to the air from a remote location in the hills north of Damascus. The international airport had eight separate runways with four of them on the north side of the main terminal and four more to the south. The plan was to approach the northern runways in a single file looking like they were four unannounced aircraft preparing to land. Instead, they would stagger themselves so that each chopper took out a runway with rocket fire as they headed west.

Once the birds reached the main terminal, they would veer left toward the southern runways. After making a hard right, they would destroy the remaining four landing strips staying low enough to avoid radar detection. They would continue west across Lebanon, stopping to refuel in a remote location before reaching the Mediterranean Sea. They would land on an Iranian merchant ship designed to hide the four helicopters from overhead observation.

The heads of state for China and Iran had quietly flown out of Damascus immediately after the G.A. meeting was over. The rest of the nations' leaders were waiting until morning to leave. The plan was to strand them all in Syria while President Mao and Iran's Ayatollah were safely back home to direct their people.

The leader of Mark and Nuri's kidnappers was riding shotgun in the first helicopter and directing the assault using an encoded radio frequency. He was thankful that thirty years of peace had everyone's guard down when it came to the attack he had planned. He was sure that this mission would become the catalyst for a world war. He did not want to lead this assault, but Kalan had threatened his life if he refused. He couldn't understand how the archeologists had escaped the secluded bunker, but it no longer mattered.

The helicopter pilot pointed to the runway lights clearly visible in the distance. "We're about three minutes out at our current speed. The tower is demanding to know who we are. Do you want to handle this?"

The voice didn't answer the pilot. He keyed open his mic and said, "We were on a training mission when one of our birds started smoking. We request permission to land and effect repairs."

"This is the Control Tower. Do not approach the runways. Please identify yourselves. We'll help you all we can after we have verified who you are."

The voice asked the pilot, "How long until we reach their runways?"

"Just over a minute," came the reply.

The voice keyed his mic and spoke on the encrypted channel to the other Z-19s. "In thirty seconds, all units deploy into attack formation. Remember where to aim your rockets to disable the runways. The goal is to make them unusable for the foreseeable future. Follow my lead for when to turn south and then west again to continue the assault."

Then the voice switched his radio back to the control tower's frequency. "Control Tower, this is flight number 1002 confirming our identity."

The Control Tower answered, "Please say again. We have no record of who you are or your country of origin. You will be arrested if you land before your identity can be verified."

It hardly mattered. The voice had bought them the time they needed. He turned to the air gunner and yelled, "Fire!"

There was a five second delay from the initial explosions on the first runway until the second one erupted in flames. The third and fourth air strips went up in fireballs as well. The sequence began again when the birds reached the two-thirds point. Blasting craters in the asphalt a third of the way in from either direction would effectively keep any air traffic larger than a single prop plane from trying to take off or land.

The pilot banked left in front of the main terminal and headed for the farthest runway on the south side of the airport. The other three Z-19s followed and deployed in the same attack pattern for disabling the remaining runways. As the gigantic fireballs reached higher into the sky, the birds made their escape to the west. Radar showed no one was following them. After a quick refueling stop in Lebanon, they would easily make it to the ship awaiting their arrival.

The voice was relieved that this mission had gone smoothly. But now that a world war was inevitable, how long would anyone live to claim victory?

Chapter 31

Mark, Nuri, Jason, Eljay, Diana and Gus had drifted off to sleep in the break room at JPL. They were awakened by music coming from their TV monitor. As they all wiped their eyes, they could read a message written in beautiful script across the screen. It said, "Make a joyous noise around the world and gather everyone to watch!" There was a countdown that began at thirty three minutes and clicked down by seconds. Something was coming and the world was invited to witness the event.

Over the next few minutes they began to hear horns honking and all manner of festive sounds from the surrounding neighborhood. It was as if a New Year's Eve celebration was taking place in the middle of the day, not just in Pasadena, but everywhere.

Jason put on a pot of coffee seeing that they had time for a cup before the countdown ended. He brought a steaming mug out to each of them in the break room. Their contribution to the joyous noise was the pleasant sound of good friends sipping their fresh hot coffee.

When only five minutes remained on the TV countdown, the noises outside of JPL abruptly ceased and an expectant hush filled the void. No doubt people were preparing for whatever came next. It was not hard to envision every man, woman and child in the world waiting in front of their video screens.

When the countdown reached zero, an image appeared of the empty General Assembly hall at the United Nations. No one believed further negotiations would do any good. Had it not been for the disabling attack on the Damascus airport, the world's leaders would have already left Syria. They awaited word that repairs had been made to the runways so that flights could resume to take them home. That left all the heads of state sitting in their hotel suites watching the TV broadcast with the rest of humanity.

A white pin-spot of light suddenly appeared on the curtain at the back of the stage. Watching the light grow larger, one sensed that there was movement within it. As the light expanded, it became apparent that a human figure was walking toward the viewing audience. When a man emerged from the light, he was dressed in a pure white garment and stood in the middle of the stage. Everyone in the world seemed to recognize him, but humanity had many names for this unique and compelling soul.

Back at JPL, it was all they could do to hang onto their coffee cups. "It's Amelius!" the friends said in unison. He stood there smiling at the viewing audience with his hands folded at his waist. It was as if he could see into the TV monitors throughout the world and bid a warm but silent welcome to each person watching. He then held out his arms in a welcoming gesture and began to speak.

"Be not afraid, it is I. You know who I am even if you call me by a different name than your neighbor. Humanity appears to be on the brink of causing its own destruction. I am here to suggest that you, each of you, can change that. This challenge you face will become humanity's worse nightmare or, preferably, its finest hour. In physics, science teaches that a beautiful star or a nuclear bomb can result by attaining a critical mass. Each person has a similar choice to make today. Will you choose to be a beautiful light to your neighbors? You could instead choose to remain silent while the world's military forces race toward self-destruction."

The broadcast picture showed that the G.A. hall was filling up with the political leaders again. Rather than watch this unprecedented event on TV, they wanted to see it live.

Amelius continued, "It has been said that each nation has the leadership that it deserves. If you are satisfied with the outcome so far, then you have already made your choice. If you are not satisfied, then it is time to act in accordance with what you know in your heart is right. You may wonder how individuals can make this kind of difference. Historically, it has been demonstrated through civil disobedience. Your leaders have called for military deployments. Without any hint of violence, let your leaders know you only support peaceful alternatives. If you are a member of your nation's military, do not carry out your orders. Instead, I suggest that you each resign your positions and go home to your loved ones."

The G.A. leaders were clearly uncomfortable with all that Amelius had said, but no one dared interrupt.

"There is a critical mass, a silent majority on this earth, who are ready to say "ENOUGH!" Without condemnation, without violence, say "enough" to hatred, fear and even guilt. There has been more than enough needless conflict between God's children.

"Not so long ago, Prince Nafid controlled this world through a threat that was not real. At first, an amazing thing occurred. Citizens everywhere came together as a united people against the threat of invasion from other planets. However, using fear as the basis for cooperation cannot succeed for long. Today, you have the opportunity to cooperate out of love. When you make only loving choices, there is no law, no enemy, no outside threat that can harm you. Humanity can only harm itself. The universe and your Creator have always been and will always be friendly. The First Cause loves you with an everlasting love. The only separation between you, your neighbors and God is of your own making.

"This is a unique time in history. Today, no one is denied the needs of the body. You are free to focus on what is truly important: 'Treating your neighbor as you would like to be treated.' Loving God and your neighbor as yourself is why you are here on the earth. Most religions teach that you should live a good life so you can find heaven in some other place. In truth, heaven surrounds you wherever you choose, especially here."

Amelius allowed his words to sink in for a minute before summing up his message of encouragement.

"There are few among you who don't desire peace. The world leaders here, who have ordered the deployment of their military forces, know the truth of my words. There is no need to condemn them. They desire to protect their own people, but who on this planet is not your beloved sibling? From this day forward, live as you truly believe in your heart and all will be well."

With that, Amelius faded from sight into the beautiful light the same way he came.

***

The unprecedented flood of emails and calls to the various nations' capitals were all against taking military action. There was little doubt what humanity really wanted. President Campbell was the first to recall the United States' military forces. Russia and India were next. Many other countries followed suit until China and Iran were the only holdouts. The world held its collective breath in guarded anticipation.

Back at JPL, Eljay couldn't stand to wait any longer and asked Sherlock to describe what was going on behind the political scenes in China and Iran.

"There is good reason why the rest of civilization has heard nothing from those two countries. Their leaders saw the recall of the other military forces as an opportunity to seize power. However, when they ordered their soldiers to forcibly occupy key locations around the earth, no troops were there to carry out those orders. It wasn't that they refused to obey them. All of the soldiers allied with China or Iran were already headed for their respective homes."

Jason asked, "So what are the governments of China and Iran doing now?"

"They are deciding who should lead their people instead of Mao Choi and the unseated Ayatollah. It will not be long before they will announce that both countries have officially ordered their military forces to stand down."

"So the war was over before it started?" Jason asked perplexed.

"Yes. Amelius would have stopped Nasrum long ago if his reckless plan did not eventually serve the best interests of humanity. The global events going back to the beginning of Prince Nafid's initial rise to power was the catalyst the world needed to willingly choose peace."

"Unbelievable!" Nuri gasped. "You're saying that everything that started with Prince Nafid has been part of Amelius' plan for decades?"

"If you could see all the connected events from an eternal perspective, Amelius' plan started thousands of years ago. When Mark and Nuri, as the Orion Brothers, were guided by Nasrum to develop the laser technology that ultimately destroyed Atlantis, Amelius saw that this day was possible."

"Talk about making applesauce from rotting apples," Gus laughed.

Diana asked, "So what happens now, Sherlock?"

"In the not too distant future on earth, this day will be hailed as the beginning of the peaceful times ahead that many call the Millennium. In truth, the one thousand years of peace began once a critical mass of loving souls on the earth chose to make it possible. That number has existed for several years, but a catalyst was needed to allow humanity's silent majority to be heard."

"Does that mean Amelius is the Messiah so many religions have been waiting for?" Nuri asked, already knowing the answer.

"Indeed! Amelius is the way, the truth and the life for the salvation of humanity."

* * *

Jason, Diana and Gus toured the three chambers inside the Temple Beautiful. Mark and Nuri had provided written instructions translated from the Atlantean symbols so they would know how to reverse the aging process. Jason was excited for Gus and Diana, but quietly acknowledged that he would miss his friends over the next few months.

"I wonder how much the world will change while we're in this place?" Gus mused.

"We have our earbuds and Jason will give us regular updates," Diana said confidently.

"I'll be sure to do that," Jason promised to them both, then turned his intense gaze toward Diana. "What are you planning to do after you've been through the Temple Beautiful process?"

"I don't know," she shyly admitted.

Gus was feeling awkward and made a show of inspecting a particularly luminous crystal.

Diana added, "Whatever it is, I hope we find something to do together."

Jason had never met a woman before Diana who inspired him to seriously consider a long-term relationship. He had always been uncomfortable over their age gap. He still thought of himself as a seventy-something year old man who had no right to be with such a young beautiful woman.

Diana sensed his angst and laughed. "You know anyone looking at us right now would assume I'm a cougar trying to hit on a young hottie to take advantage of him."

Jason blushed and remembered making a similar joke the last time he was here. Then he bent over far enough to brush his lips against hers. He kissed her lightly at first until he gave into his feelings. She put her strong arms around his waist and pulled him close. He smiled and wrapped her in his embrace and their deepening kiss left no doubt of their feelings. Gus hesitantly cleared his throat to remind them that he was still there.

Jason was embarrassed and stepped back from Diana to shake Gus' hand.

"Let us know when to bring you back!" he said, pleased that Diana was also blushing.

"I'm looking forward to beating you in an arm wrestling contest in a few months," Gus joked. "Diana always could, but soon it will be my turn!"

Jason smiled again and waved as he stepped through the RFT portal back to JPL.

***

Secretary-General Akhem al Assad welcomed Mark and Nuri to the United Nations subcommittee meeting. This particular group of ambassadors was charged with developing a new charter that would redefine the U.N.'s purpose and mission.

"Welcome gentlemen!" Akhem said warmly. "The committee members voted unanimously to ask for your assistance in the challenging tasks before us."

The two friends nodded appreciatively having already agreed to help in any way they could.

He continued, "It was also agreed that you maintain ownership and control of all resonant frequency technology." The men and women around the table nodded their assent to this as well. "It has always been a good idea to keep a separation between church and state. It is equally as wise to allow RF technology to continue to be a tool for good rather than become a political weapon to separate us."

"That's a hard won lesson for sure!" exclaimed Mark.

"With that said," Akhem paused, "the committee would like to hear what Sherlock would suggest regarding the best use of the United Nations as a governing body."

Nuri pulled out the small crystal box and set it on the table before lifting the lid. He asked, "Sherlock, what advice can you offer to answer the Secretary-General's question?"

"With the unprecedented level of cooperation agreed to by all nations, there is no need for a central governing body for the world. However, the United Nations can still be of service by providing efficient access to each country's leadership. While all countries will remain their own sovereign nation, there should be no barriers to trade, travel or immigration. Since equality will now be the rule rather than the exception, any economic disparities between nations will soon disappear."

Akhem asked, "Should each country abide by the same constitution and laws?"

"No. The citizens of each nation should have the freedom to make those decisions as they see fit. The various cultures in each region will thrive when encouraged to pursue one perfect ideal of love manifested through many ideas for living a joyous life."

"What should be done in the case of moral issues, like abortion?" Akhem asked.

"This was just given in principle. Allow each country to set their laws and the people who agree with those laws will gravitate to the place that best fits their personal beliefs. Since laws are made by humanity, secular laws can and will change according to the preferences of the people."

"And which laws should be constant regardless of the country one lives in?" Akhem continued.

"All you need are the Great Commandment and the Golden Rule. Love God with all your heart, mind and soul, and your neighbor as yourself, and treat others as you would have them treat you. Any other laws should be developed for the greater good, as defined by the voting citizens."

"A final question, at least for this session," Akhem said smiling. "What system of government is best for nations to adopt to deliver the highest service to its people?"

"This is a great question, for in the answer lies the manner to approach all such controversial issues. There is no system of government that can fail while its citizens follow the Great Commandment and the Golden Rule. Conversely, there is no system of government that can succeed in perpetuity where its citizens use a lesser standard."

Chapter 32

A year had passed since Amelius appeared before the world and suggested that it was up to each person to ensure that peace prevails. The world's sovereign governments did follow Sherlock's advice and prosperity spread as never before across the earth. There was no strife between countries because it was painless to agree upon solutions that resulted in the greatest good for all citizens, regardless of their nationality.

Mark and Nuri finally explored the Bimini Hall of Records. There was an interesting legal challenge when the government of the Bahamas claimed ownership of the fabled chamber. Its location fell inside the twelve-mile boundary for the Bimini Islands. The international courts initially ruled that the 1,500 foot depth did not negate their ownership rights. When Mark and Nuri were able to show that the chamber was not of the earth, but actually existed in another dimension, the court ruled that the contents of the chamber belonged solely to the archeologists.

With that issue resolved, they spent their days exploring such fascinating sites as Machu Picchu in Peru, and Easter Island off the coast of Chile. When they weren't trying to understand the mysteries of ancient civilizations, they were helping Eljay to discover new uses for RF technology.

Jason and Diana married soon after she and Gus returned from the Temple Beautiful. They decided to devote themselves to creating and distributing obsidian healing devices throughout the earth. Medical care became as quick and easy as placing your hand on the stone. They also developed an emergency response system that combined the healing abilities of RFH with the immediate transport of that technology via RFT to anywhere it was needed on the planet.

Eljay also asked to go through the Temple Beautiful process. He was far younger than his friends, but he looked like the old man of the group when they all got together. He vowed to bring balance into his life by spending more time socializing, enjoying nature and the outdoors as well as maintaining his newfound excellent health.

He didn't want to waste this unique opportunity to make better choices this time around.

Gus was happy to continue chartering his boat and searching for shipwrecks. He moved into the residence at JPL and became Eljay's roommate because commuting to the Florida Coast was no problem for anyone with an RFT crystal. They became great friends and acted as each other's wing man when Gus would drag Eljay to go out on the town.

President Kathryn Campbell was reelected to a second term. She couldn't help but shine as a world leader. She had an excellent grasp on ethics and empathy and tempered it with an uncanny ability to see through a problem. When disputes arose in the early days of the new world order, her creative solutions showed everyone how to achieve equality for all regardless of the circumstances. She helped draft the new rules that many of the other governments adopted as their own.

Amelius sightings were reported everywhere. It became commonplace to hear that he appeared at celebrations, sporting events, concerts or stage plays. Everyone now called him Messiah because they all acknowledged who he was. The various names he had been known by throughout history were discarded because they only served to divide people rather than bring them together.

People were surprised that so many religions flourished despite agreeing that the Messiah walked among them. Believers of all faiths found that they enjoyed worshipping with others who shared their values. The key to bringing people back to God had been simple. Encourage everyone to make better, more loving choices because treating each other with patience and tolerance was how all souls could be happy in perpetuity. Few sects remained that had believed in eternal damnation, or used fear, guilt and shame as motivation to make compliant choices.

The souls who incarnated as newborn babies into the earth were those who desired to live in peace and harmony with each other. The Millennium had truly arrived.

* * *

Jason opened the door for Diana as they exited the racquetball court. He had hoped to win a game or two, or at least not embarrass himself. He was wrong on both counts. She could tell he was less than pleased. They sat down on a bench near their bags and guzzled water to quench their thirst. She decided this was a good time to learn more about the way Jason thought.

"I can't tell if you're upset over losing at racquetball or if you're still brooding over Mark and Nuri finding the Hall of Records without you."

"Which do you think?" Jason asked with a boyish frown.

"Well," she began while hiding her smile, "missing out on the Hall of Records is the bigger deal, but losing to me two minutes ago at a sport, any sport, seems more likely to be on your mind."

"I was embarrassed over losing," Jason admitted, "but now you've got me thinking about the Hall of Records thing again. I keep wondering if I should have gone with them."

"It's not as if they didn't invite you," she reminded him.

"My reasons for staying behind are not something I'm proud of," he said. "They didn't really need me this time and I was half afraid my less-than-holy ways would keep them from seeing the place just like before."

Diana asked, "What did Amelius and Halaliel say when you didn't want to go?"

"Surprisingly, nothing!" Jason exclaimed. "Mark and Nuri tried to talk me into going, but my two ethereal friends didn't say a word about my choice. Why do you think they had nothing to say?"

"I think they agreed with you," she said. "I also don't believe you're being completely honest with yourself about why you declined to go with them. Your choice showed growth in two ways. One, your greater desire was that they succeed in finding the place more than you getting to be there when it happened. The other was realizing that the Hall of Records had become a shiny object for you to obsess over. It took a real leap in faith and patience for you to know that it didn't matter if you went or not."

"If I'm so mature now, then why am I depressed over being beaten at racquetball by a girl?" Jason joked.

"Oh please! It might have something to do with me playing this game for decades when you've only just started," she chided him. "Amelius used my love of this sport to show us how we see life as humans compared to our true spiritual nature. Do you want to hear what he said?"

"Amelius plays racquetball?" Jason asked. "I never would have guessed. This I've got to hear."

Diana laughed and said, "I don't think he has played racquetball, but he knew I did and what he shared with me when I was in the Temple Beautiful makes sense. When we walk inside a racquetball court to play, all of life's possibilities are limited to the most simplistic terms. Success is measured in how a little ball is moved around inside a confined space."

"Isn't that what most games we play are based on?" Jason asked with a smile.

She laughed and admitted, "You're right, but because racquetball is played inside a closed room it makes the analogy all the more clear. When we walk through that door to enter the court, that's all we see. Nothing else exists. It's a lot like when we're born on earth. We forget what's truly important in our lives."

Jason said, "I'm not sure I follow you."

She explained, "In a racquetball court while we're playing the game, we don't think about anything outside of those walls. We don't think about our friends and family. We don't reflect on our lives, our careers or even our relationship with God. None of that matters because the true measure of success in that limited experience is how well we can get a ball to go where we want it to."

"It takes focus and dedication to become better at a sport," Jason frowned. "You make all that seem like a bad thing."

"I said the same thing to Amelius," she agreed. "He showed me the difference. For years, my racquetball friends and I played this game every spare minute we could. It got to the point where our self-esteem improved or deflated according to our win/loss records on the court. We couldn't wait to get back out and play again, and we were playing to win."

"I don't see the problem!" Jason complained. "Are you saying it's bad to be competitive?"

"Not at all," she offered, "but there is an interesting line to draw here. All competition should be designed to bring the best out of ourselves and others. The moment we feel better or worse about ourselves because we won or lost at sports is when we have lost the proper perspective."

"You've got to be kidding," Jason grimaced. "Are you one of those people who think we should hand out 9th place trophies and participation ribbons to everyone?"

"No," she smiled. "However, the moment we base our self-worth on what we do instead of who we are, we've lost sight of what's important. If God created us all in His image, then potentially we all have the same perfect abilities. Determining the winner of a competition only tells us who has practiced more, or harder, or focused better, or any of the other things that make us better at a sport. If each person does all those things perfectly, then the winner of a competition no longer matters. Winning and losing should not result in us thinking we are greater or lesser than another person or team."

"Okay, I think I get your point," Jason said. "But could you sum it up for me?"

Humanity easily becomes obsessed with earth's narrow rules for success. We pursue accomplishments that have little to do with manifesting greater patience, deeper faith, or how well we get along with others. Our ability to follow the Golden Rule should be our highest priority all the time, not just when we think God is looking."

"So do you think Amelius could beat you at racquetball?" Jason laughed, but he was curious.

"Not initially, no," she said thoughtfully.

"But if he is perfect, wouldn't he play racquetball perfectly?" Jason asked.

She said, "Yes, but if it worked like you're implying, then Amelius, in his earthly incarnations, would have been walking around giving sermons from the day he was born. Since he didn't, even though he was perfect, I believe he needed practice in human form to master the skills of three dimensions."

"So how many games would it take until Amelius could beat you?" Jason asked laughing.

"Not nearly as many as it's going to take you, Mr. Delta Force!" she laughed. "Let's get back in there and work on your patience."

"Right! We'll work on my patience and your humble attitude," he smirked as he tossed her the ball.

***

Matt Alexander and Louis were surprised to see each other. They didn't cross paths very often, even in this place where time was merely an idea. Matt said, "I'm here to meet with Amelius and Halaliel."

"The same for me," replied Louis. "They're going to help me decide what to do next on earth."

"Indeed we are," Amelius said as he and Halaliel entered their thoughts.

"Matthew," Halaliel began, "you have an interesting choice to make. Your awareness has grown so that sequential time on earth is no longer needed to help you become closer to our Creator. However, the choice is still yours. Would you prefer to reincarnate into the earth again, or move on to Arcturus for advanced studies?"

"I'm ready to move on!" Matt was happy to say. "If you had asked me that question right after my death as Matthew Alexander, I would have stayed. I was sure that the world was in big trouble and needed me to help fix it. Now I see that the salvation of everyone on earth is inevitable. It is truly a miracle when a soul changes its mind for the better, and you two have helped humanity to experience the miracle of the Prodigal Son."

Amelius smiled and said, "I appreciate your choice and your reasons. Also, my thanks on behalf of Halaliel and myself for your kind words. We are grateful to have been chosen to make a difference in this way."

"Louis!" Halaliel said excitedly. "Take a look at the human lifetimes ahead for you!"

Louis watched as the panoramic hologram unfolded in front of him. He was able to see successive lifetimes reaching hundreds of years into the future. He could perceive the projected spiritual growth he was likely to experience in each one. Best of all, they would be happy experiences.

Louis said with a smile, "It looks like I'll be several hundred years behind you, Matt! However, I think those years on earth will be good ones. It won't be like it was during the Spanish Inquisition."

"It could have taken you much longer!" Amelius said. "Do you know what made the difference?"

"I really don't, but I'm thankful for whatever it was!" Louis said sincerely.

"Do you remember the infamous RFC call to Klacktu before Beth's accident?" Halaliel asked.

Louis' ethereal shoulders slumped a bit showing he did indeed remember. Like Matt, he was still choosing to appear to others as his most recent human life on earth.

Halaliel continued, "One of the toughest challenges to overcome on earth is an unwarranted conflict. That is to say you overcame a conflict where most everyone involved was convinced that a lie was the truth."

"When was that?" Louis asked.

"You knew you didn't tell Prince Nafid of your conversation with the alien from Klacktu, but Mark, Nuri and Jason believed you had," Halaliel explained. "They blamed you for the long delay in discovering the Bimini Hall of Records. The guilt you felt over your wife's death seemed to confirm that for them even though you had nothing to do with it. That only convinced your friends all the more that you had not remained silent."

"But they got over it," Louis reflected. "We became so close in my last years on earth that I shared their belief in an afterlife and we worked together to get the bugs out of RF communications."

"Exactly!" Amelius interjected. "You learned to treat each other as if the unfortunate incident had not happened. To come through such an experience without harboring blame among any of you is asking a lot. That is why the four of you have been part of the soul grouping that ushered in the Millennium."

Louis was humbled and amazed. "So saving humanity from The Glut, and sharing RF technology with the world, not to mention getting rid of Nasrum, was not enough? It was our ability to get past a terrible misunderstanding that made the difference?"

Halaliel said, "You all had a great deal of help with those major events, but that's not the point. Learning how to lovingly work through your challenges together needed to be done on your own. That is why we never told the four of you of Nasrum's involvement with Prince Nafid disclosing the Klacktu conversation. Angelic intervention is not always the best way to overcome your challenges."

"I'm finally getting what you mean," Louis said nodding his head. "We aren't judged by how much of an impact our actions have on others, like finding the cure for The Glut. We are held responsible for doing the right thing no matter how small the impact is on ourselves or anyone else."

"Well said!" Amelius smiled. "We will meet again, but it is time for you both to take your next steps on the path."

* * *

Halaliel and Amelius were mentally vacationing through the timeline of the new earth. It was truly a pleasure to interact with souls who appreciated their neighbors. Humanity agreed that Amelius was the perfect role model for the world.

"How is Nasrum doing?" Halaliel asked.

Amelius smiled and said, "I try to visit him often, but he still blames me for his entrapment in outer darkness. When I offer to guide him out of that endless cycle of misery, he assures me that he is just fine where he is."

Halaliel asked, "Do you think he will come around in time to reincarnate back into the earth at the end of the thousand years of peace?"

751

"As things stand now," Amelius said, "I doubt it. However, if I invite him to come back to earth and see that he did indeed cause the thousand years of peace to begin, his impressive ego may work to his own advantage."

"When the test period comes," Halaliel paused a moment before finishing his question, "are you planning to 'stack the deck' for Nasrum's next incarnation?"

Amelius smiled and said, "Most definitely. Who would make a better human father for Nasrum than his old friend Jason?"

"And Jason has agreed to this?" Halaliel asked in surprise.

"Not yet," Amelius admitted. "But after a few more lifetimes of learning how to be a good parent with Diana, he should be ready for the challenge."

Chapter 33

The thousand years of peace had officially come to an end. The period of testing was to begin where souls who had not shared the world's preference for love and cooperation would be allowed to reincarnate back into the earth. Amelius knew that humankind was ready. Many things had changed since these unruly souls had caused so much chaos upon the land.

The people of earth all knew themselves to be God's beloved children. They lived in harmony because each soul incarnate wanted to draw the best out of themselves and others. This loving attitude brought with it other changes in how people chose to live. There were still churches, synagogues, mosques and temples, but they served more as places to gather socially and celebrate. Everyone now enjoyed a personal relationship with the Creator. Daily meditations replaced weekly Sunday sermons. The spiritual understanding of each person on earth in the current age far exceeded that of the most brilliant religious pundits from a thousand years before.

Resonant frequency technology was still in use, but it had been a long time since anyone had seen an RF device. The reason was simple. Once a soul understood how to program RF crystals using their intentions, they soon realized that they didn't need an RF crystal at all. What they purposefully visualized quickly manifested in the physical. There was no question that it was all based on science, but people from a thousand years before couldn't imagine RF technology working without crystals.

Families continued to be the preferred manner for living. From birth, babies were taught to get along well in family units. As they grew older, they learned how to cooperate with others in their local community. Then those communities, states and nations learned to patiently share their many ideas in pursuit of the one great ideal, love. The earth had always been a wonderful school for better living, but now that truth was recognized by all incarnate.

Living conditions were simple compared to the varied and chaotic expressions in the previous millennia. Because RF technology took care of the daily needs of the body, people were free to spend their time on the things that brought them joy. For many, they pursued artistic endeavors. Others preferred to understand the infinite ways that spirit could manifest in three dimensions. Stories told through movies, music and books that illustrated humanity's growing understanding of their relationship to God were appreciated by all.

Perhaps the most important change was the underlying peace and joy that was infused in the thoughts, actions and intent of everyone on earth. Humanity did not dread unruly souls being allowed to incarnate back into the earth. They looked forward to helping those souls as they had once themselves been helped.

*　*　*

The endless cycle of Nasrum's painful memories was suddenly interrupted. He had grown accustomed to Amelius' annoying disturbances, but this time there were two other souls with his nemesis.

"Hello Nasrum!" Amelius said cheerfully. "I have brought some friends with me this time. They have a special interest in helping you return to the earth plane."

Nasrum purposefully hid his thoughts and said nothing. He hoped they would just go away and allow him to continue reviewing the events that had wrecked his path to glory. As painful as those memories were, there was a strange comfort in identifying who was to blame for every one of his agonizing failures.

"Hello Nasrum!" the two friends offered in greeting. "We would be honored if you would agree to return to earth as our child."

The offer intrigued Nasrum more than anything else they could have said. The opportunity to return to earth had been denied him since his last incarnation as Achmed Mansur. That lifetime had held such promise, but it had been cut short by a bunch of idiots who couldn't follow his simple instructions. His memories cycled through again of how close he had come to becoming earth's Messiah.

"Who are you?" Nasrum managed to ask.

"You don't remember your old friends Jason and Diana?" he answered. "The three of us raised a lot of hell together back in the day."

Diana laughed and added, "We have already agreed to have the Orion Brothers as your siblings. This will truly be an opportunity to resolve the chaos of our shared past incarnations. I, for one, am really looking forward to being together in three dimensions again."

Nasrum's interest was piqued enough for him enough to think of leaving this place. He had vague recollections of these two people who wanted to be his human parents. His spotty memories of their experiences together were mostly good. Then he remembered that they had turned against him after the destruction of Atlantis. The endless cycle of painful memories washed over him again and his expression clouded.

"It doesn't have to be like this forever, Nasrum," Amelius said again gently, disrupting his reverie of suffering. "Why don't you take this opportunity to return to earth?"

For a brief moment, Nasrum considered the possibility. Amelius saw the opening and immediately filled the tortured soul's thoughts with such love, peace and happiness that they could not be ignored. Nasrum was amazed with the clarity of his thinking. He could see the wasted life he had created, but there was no condemnation of his selfish acts from any of his visitors. He managed to stay focused and not fall back into the abyss. His choice was simple. Either he could accept their help and try again, or he could remain in this hellhole forever.

"Did I really help to bring about the Millennium of peace?" Nasrum asked cautiously.

Amelius laughed and said, "You have been a part of saving humanity since the days of Atlantis. You, being exactly who you are, helped to create a miracle!"

"What do you mean, create a miracle?" he asked.

"The Creator is a God of love and of law," Amelius explained. "The entirety of creation unfolds in accordance with universal law. The only true miracle occurs when a soul changes its mind. God does not interfere with the choices we make."

Nasrum felt the truth of that statement in his heart. What he had seen as his ultimate failure had been the catalyst to save the world. Ironically, his worst choices had brought out the best in humanity. He no longer wanted to wallow in the misery of his past. It was time to try a better way.

Nasrum looked up at Amelius, Jason and Diana. He saw only hope and promise in their eyes. He was still hesitant to say yes, but how could anything improve if he stayed here? He almost laughed at how clear that was to him now. A smile appeared on his face as he said, "I will join your human family."

***

Sojan and Nadia smiled at each other from across the dinner table. Their happiness was not just because of the Thanksgiving celebration that had brought the family together. They were enjoying their grown children's friendly banter that never seemed to stop. It had not been easy for the couple to raise Rasmun, their youngest child, especially after learning of the challenging karmic history the entire family shared. Still, they learned patience by allowing Rasmun to find his own way in the world with their loving support. The whole family had learned to appreciate the qualities that made Rasmun unique. Somehow, he had learned to love his family and his neighbors in spite of his rebellious days as a child.

Rasmun's older brothers, Karm and Niru, had an intense interest in all things of science and history. No one was surprised to learn of their past lives and how important those studies had been to them over thousands of years. They too learned to love their little brother's odd sense of humor and mischievous ways. Rasmun had even taken an interest in their science experiments.

Everyone helped clear the table after dinner. They were expecting a visit from Silou, a woman Karm had befriended who also shared an interest in their RF experiments. They hoped to be able to communicate with other souls in other systems as easily as they used RF technology to communicate on the earth.

When Silou arrived, she and the brothers adjourned to the lab they had used since they were young. This was hardly the first time they had tried to reach out to the stars with hopes that someone would respond. During a past-life regression, Silou remembered that she had been Louis Jensen during the 21st century.

She had vague recollections of their earlier efforts to contact life beyond the stars. Still, she couldn't recall how they had first succeeded and was feeling discouraged. However, Rasmun had a plan. He felt certain that this time would be different.

"We keep using higher and higher Fibonacci numbers to reach out," Rasmun began. "I had an idea to start at a lower frequency and work up from there. Not only a lower frequency, but using an RF crystal device instead of mental intentionality."

Karm asked, "Why would that make any difference?"

"There needs to be someone at the other end who wants to talk with us," Rasmun explained. "The higher frequencies are probably used by advanced civilizations that have no interest in us. The lowest frequencies would be monitored by people who are still searching, as we are."

Rasmun pulled out an ancient looking RF device and they all had a good laugh wondering how anyone ever used such backward technology.

Niru asked, "Okay, did you have two particular frequencies in mind we should use to start?"

"Actually," Rasmun smiled, "I do. The Golden Ratio stabilizes on the fortieth number in the Fibonacci sequence. That's almost as universal as the number Pi. If anyone is listening for us to contact them, it seems like a good place to start."

Silou and Karm looked up the exact number and read it off to Niru. "It looks like the frequency is 102,334,155 cycles. That would make the receiving frequency the forty first number, or 165,580,141 cycles."

Karm said, "Rasmun, could you be our test signal? Here's the list of Fibonacci numbers from zero to a hundred digits. Could you please read them as our test audio while we monitor for any responses?"

Rasmun frowned at being given such a lowly task, but he did it anyway. He walked over to the old RFC device and started reading off the numbers. "0, 1, 1, 2, 3, 5, 8…"

Karm and Niru ensured the sending frequency was set correctly and then turned on the speaker in case someone responded. After less than a minute of Rasmun reading off numbers, staccato electronic clicks suddenly filled the room. The sound carried a recognizable meter and purpose to it even though it was otherwise unintelligible.

"Start reading the numbers over again, Rasmun!" Silou exclaimed. "I think we have something."

He began repeating the number sequence in earnest. He realized that what he first thought was a lowly job may have just made him the first, or rather, second person in history to communicate with an alien species. The sound from the RFC speaker suddenly changed from unintelligible noise to English.

"Right on time!" said the monotone voice. "We have been waiting for your communication."

Rasmun looked around the room at Silou and his brothers before asking, "Who is this?"

"You have reached the Intergalactic Emergency Response System. We will need to use another frequency to continue. My name is Losal. It is my pleasure to welcome you into the Intergalactic Federation. Please step up your transmission and receiving frequencies to the forty second and forty third numbers in the universal sequence."

Karm and Niru scrambled to change the frequencies. Silou and Rasmun urged them to hurry. Niru stepped back and nodded to his younger brother to try it again.

He started over saying, "0, 1, 1, 2, 3, 5, 8..."

The alien voice of Losal made a noise that sounded like he might be laughing. After an uncomfortable few seconds of this Losal said, "You don't need to recite the universal sequence any longer. I can see why your species drew so much attention eighty seven zicts ago interfering with the emergency system as you did."

Rasmun could only ask, "What's a zict?"

Losal laughed again. "I'm sorry. That would convert to around one thousand of your years."

"And what is the Galactic Federation?" Rasmun asked.

"I think you mean the Intergalactic Federation," Losal corrected him. "Any species that has successfully completed the Divine Process of achieving one thousand years of non-coerced peace is invited to become a member."

Rasmun couldn't help himself. "Really? Do your members have a secret handshake and everything?"

Silou almost panicked as she interjected. "He was just joking. We are honored that you would make such an offer. Is there an official process we should follow to join your esteemed group?"

Losal was laughing again before he said, "A secret handshake! I like that! You should help us to create one, though few of our member species have what you would define as hands. That should make it really interesting!"

Rasmun gently moved Silou away from the RFC device. Flashing a quick smile to his friends and family in the room he said, "I've got this!"

* * *

"How many years do you think it will take for all souls entrapped on the earth to free their minds?" Halaliel asked Amelius.

"It hardly matters," he began. "While it may take some time for all to accept our Creator's loving ways, the glorious outcome is certain."

"So what will you do after that?" Halaliel was truly curious.

"You mean once the last soul finds their way and moves on to whatever they desire to be next for them?" Amelius asked with a smile.

"Yes. Do you think you will want to do this again?" Halaliel asked. "I mean to become the perfect role model that other entrapped souls can follow to find their way home?"

Amelius laughed. "I believe that question is like asking the mother of a newborn if she is ready to have another child. I might take a long break apart from manifestation altogether. It is hard to improve upon sharing a perfect connection with God without the distractions of a manifest universe. And what is next for you, Halaliel?"

"There are several who have asked for my help, which surprises me. I know that many of the universe's Messiahs think my ways make the path back to God more difficult."

"And I am one of them," Amelius laughed again good-naturedly. "But there are some souls who gain a more loving perspective by following strict guidelines. Such differences make for an interesting universe and only you can fill that need. Jason, I mean Sojan in his current incarnation, always did respond better to you than he did to me."

"I suppose you are right," Halaliel admitted. "Then I will leave you to mop up around here. If you ever need my brand of help again, please do call on me."

"I will indeed!"

As Halaliel departed, Amelius decided he would return to outer darkness and try, once again, to help those entrapped souls. He never lost faith that they would freely accept the joyous life intended by their Creator in this friendly universe. After all, it is the Creator's greatest joy that we dwell in the house of the Lord, forever.

Glossary of terms, abbreviations and characters

4999 symbols – This refers to the Atlantean symbols that Mark and Nuri progressively translate from the ancient alphabet. Louis Jensen and his son, Eljay, often needed the archeologists help to translate key symbols in order shed light on the principals behind new RF applications.

Abel - is an excellent sniper and mercenary who works for the highest bidder in part 1.

Abel and Amon - are the two best snipers in the militia known as Mohammed's Faithful.

Achmed Mansur – A retired Colonel in the Syrian army. He is also the most recent "legal" incarnation of Nasrum upon the earth. He was the leader of the mercenaries hired to destroy the U.S. Army supply depot in Israel and the Suez Canal.

ADS – An abbreviation for Atmospheric Diving Suits that weigh over 1,000 pounds on dry land and can safely be used under water to around 2,000 feet.

Afkar - is a mercenary leader in book 1 who was hired by Ramin and Amir to kidnap FLOTUS.

Agent Culver - is another CIA agent looking for Mohammed's Faithful. He works under Special Agent Ross.

Agent Ross - is the CIA agent in charge of finding Mohammed's Faithful after destroying the supply depot in Israel.

Akashic Records – This is an exhaustive record of everything that has ever been or will ever be that is ethereally written on the skein of time and space. Edgar Cayce often drew on this information to give the answers to the questions posed to him.

Akhem al Assad – Is the Secretary-General of the United Nations in part 3. He is also a distant cousin to Alkrim al Assad, the son of the deceased Syrian President.

Akhem Pakhura - He is the Ambassador from Egypt to the United Nations in part 3.

Alkrim al Assad – Was the son of the President of Syria, making him the heir-apparent to take over the position from his father.

Allah – The Islamic name for God.

Allahu Akbar - is Arabic for "Allah is great" and is often the last words said by terrorists when they attack.

Amelius – This is a soul who has been a key character since part 1. His advice given from behind the scenes is always helpful and hopeful. His role overall does not become clear until toward the end of part 3.

Amir - is the pseudonym CIA Director George Salazar uses when he doesn't want the people he is working with to know his true identity.

Ariel – An archangel with minor roles in parts 1 and 3.

Armstead, General - is the JSOC or in charge of the Joint Special Operations Command in part 3.

Atlantis - is a fabled continent that was said to have sunk into the Atlantic Ocean some 12,000 years ago. Its citizens were the ones who created the three chambers called the Hall of Records in Giza, the Yucatan and west of the Bimini Islands.

Bashir and Kazim are the two mercenaries who delivered the suitcases full of Cubane to Mansur in the hotel in part 1.

Basir and Hakim - Both are members of Mohammed's Faithful and led the team that hijacked PFCs Wiley and Mendez's supply trucks.

Bimini Wall – Also known as the Bimini Road. This structure is visible from above the water. Some believe it is the top of a wall that stretches for about a half a mile in the shallow waters off the west coast of the Bimini Islands.

Camp David - is a secure vacation home for the U.S. President.

Carlos Medrano - He is Guatemala's Ambassador to the United Nations.

Center for Disease Control - This US Government organization is commonly known as the CDC and performs similar functions to the WHO within the borders of the USA.

Clara and Rosie - These two friends are American citizens who arrived in Cancun on a large cruise ship. They live in Florida.

David Huffman – The U.S. Attorney General's deputy in part 3.

David Pater – Director of Operations for NASA Mission Control in part 3.

Deborah Voss - is the Attorney General under Matt Alexander in part 1.

DEFCON 2 – Defense Condition 2 out of 5, with 1 being the highest level of alertness.

Delta Force - is the U.S. Army's equivalent to the U.S. Navy SEALS.

Demetri Olaf – The Russian President in part 3.

Diana Amal – Gus Martin's granddaughter and one of the first ever female Navy SEAL graduates.

Diego (not Diego Bernal) - He is a Macizo soldier who attacks Jason just as they try to enter the Piedras Negras pyramid.

Doctor Sandoval - He is the medical doctor who oversees the health of Rodrigo Cortez.

Donald Westbrook - He is the President of the United States in part 2. He was elected after Matthew Alexander served his two consecutive terms. Don came to be POTUS through the ranks of Congress and has very little trust in others, especially Mark and Nuri.

Edgar Cayce – A famous psychic who readings told of the ancient civilization of Atlantis. Much of the information about our relationship with God, Atlantis and the Hall of Records' locations in this trilogy came from those psychic readings. Cayce lived from 1877 – 1945.

EMP weapon – An abbreviation for electromagnetic pulse weapon. Generates a strong magnetic wave that can disable most electronic devices within its effective range.

Eric Jefferson - is the Vice President under Matt Alexander in part 1.

Erin Alexander - is the FLOTUS or First Lady of the U.S. and is married to President Matthew Alexander.

Fibonacci – Was a mathematician in 13th century Italy. He developed the Fibonacci sequence of numbers that has applications in nature, science and business. These numbers hold great significance for programming RF crystals.

Fred Shapiro - is Matt Alexander's National Security Advisor in part 1.

G.A. – General Assembly of the U.N. or United Nations. This group of ambassadors are the appointed representatives of each member country to the U.N.

General James Myer - He is the Joint Chiefs of Staff (JCS) leader in part 1 who confers and coordinates the US military forces with the National Security Council (NSC) and POTUS.

George Salazar - is Matt Alexander's Director of the CIA in part 1.

Gil Kowalski - is the Director of National Drug Control Policy in part 1 and the Ambassador to Mexico and Guatemala in book 2.

Gilbert Alba - He is the Ambassador from Mexico to the United Nations in part 2.

God – Also referred to in this book by the names: First Cause, Creator, I am that I am, Allah, Brahma, and Father.

GPS – An abbreviation for Global Positioning System to locate specific coordinates on the earth.

Graciela and Liliana - These are the assumed names of Fatima and Lupe, respectively, when they make their deal with Clara and Rosie.

Gus Martin – The grandfather of Diana Amal who owns the charter boat that takes the main characters to the Bimini Islands in part 3.

Halaliel – An archangel who is a major character throughout the three books. He was described by Edgar Cayce as one who would make the way difficult for the better understanding. In other words, he had more of a tough love approach than the kinder, gentler Amelius.

Hall of Records – Each part in the trilogy focuses on locating a fabled Hall of Records in the three places given in the Edgar Cayce readings. Book 1 was underneath the Sphinx in Giza, Egypt. Part 2 was in the area of Piedras Negras in Guatemala. Part 3 focused on an underwater location just west of the Bimini Islands which are part of the Bahamas. Each Hall of Records was said to contain records and artifacts of the ancient civilization of Atlantis.

Hector - He is the police officer who unwittingly helps and impedes Lupe's and Fatima's escape from the Cortez estate in part 2.

Intergalactic Federation – An organization of intelligent species living in various galaxies who have achieved an established level of spiritual growth. Any species that has yet to attain that level is supposed to be avoided by its members.

Isaac - is a Mossad operator and old friend of CIA Chief Tom Strickland in part 1.

Jason Fisher – A main character in all three books who is the protector of Mark and Nuri. He was a Delta Force soldier until he retired and joined the archeologists in their pursuit of the Hall of Records.

Javier Hernandez - He is a military general in book 2 who is in charge of the northern states of Guatemala. He is also on Macizo's payroll for looking the other way regarding illegal activities inside Guatemala's borders.

Jerome Westcott - is in charge of digital forensics for the CIA in part 1.

Jim Franklin - He is a retired green beret Captain in the US military serving as a black ops consultant for the US Government in part 1.

Joan Hartley - is Matt Alexander's Secretary of State in part 1.

John Archer – Captain of the destroyer class U.S. Navy ship assigned to track Gus' boat to Bimini.

Joseph Faro - He is a long-time friend of Jason Fisher who works as a consultant for the CIA. He can access software, like facial recognition programs, when Jason needs them.

JPL - The full name of JPL is Jet Propulsion Laboratory in Pasadena, CA. Introduced in the first book, it is a non-profit scientific organization that is largely funded by grants from the US Government. Mark, Nuri and Jason work closely with JPL's engineers to discover the secrets behind resonant frequency technology. Because JPL is not owned or operated by the US Government, Mark and Nuri are able to work on RF projects there without fear of the government stealing the technological applications they develop.

Julia Peters – A newspaper reporter for The Herald in part 3.

Kalan - The Director of VAJA, the Iranian Ministry of Intelligence in part 3.

Kan Bi-Soon - He is the Secretary-General to the United Nations in part 2.

Karen Moffitt - is the assistant to FLOTUS in part 1.

Karm – Post millennial incarnation for Mark in part 3.

Kasha – Name given to the first RFA box by Diana Amal.

Katheryn Campbell – She became the U.S. President at the time Prince Nafid was assassinated in part 3.

King Tabir - is the King of Saudi Arabia in part 1.

Klacktu – a planet in the Andromeda galaxy that Louis inadvertently makes contact with using an RFC crystal.

Knots – an abbreviation for nautical miles per hour. There are 1.15 miles to a nautical mile.

Losal – Intergalactic Federation representative some 1,000 years into the future in part 3.

Louis Jensen (Sr.) - He is the leading RF scientist at JPL as well as the main liaison for Mark, Nuri and Jason.

Louis Jensen Jr. – AKA Eljay, who is the son of Louis Jensen Sr. He stepped into the shoes of his father and carried on the resonant frequency research with Mark, Nuri and Jason at the JPL lab.

Luis and Tomas - These are two of Macizo's members who are Thiago's henchmen and bodyguards. They are with him in Nevada, Mexico and Guatemala.

Lupe (AKA Lupita) - She is Fatima's estranged younger sister who disowned Fatima as long as she was involved with Rodrigo and Macizo.

M.E. – Medical Examiner is a medical doctor hired by a government to examine and direct the disposition of cadavers. They work with both public health and with law enforcement, depending on the circumstances of the death.

Maaz al-Assad - is the President of Syria in part 1.

Macizo cartel - is the most powerful drug smuggling cartel in Mexico. Its leader is Rodrigo Cortez, also called El Jefe.

Madagascar – An island nation off the southern east coast of Africa.

Makoa – Citizen of Madagascar who committed suicide and Nasrum "illegally" took over his body to reinsert himself back into the earth in part 3.

Mao Choi – China's President in part 3.

Mark Heston - Is an archeologist and is best friends with Nuri Zayd. Both of them were introduced in the first book. Along with Nuri and Jason Fisher, they discovered the Giza Hall of Records and discovered a powerful ancient technology based on resonant frequencies (RF). Their knowledge of science grew by necessity to ensure they understood this advanced technology from Atlantis.

Martin McComb - is a U.S. Army General who serves as Matt Alexander's Chairman of the Joint Chiefs of Staff (JCOS) in part 1.

Martin McComb, Jr. - was a U.S. Army Major and the son of General Martin Macomb Sr.

Matthew Alexander - Matt was POTUS through the entirety of the first book. He went from setting hawkish policies to those of a dove after experiencing an NDE (near death experience) close to the beginning of his first term in office. In retirement, he remains close to Mark, Nuri and Jason as well as their greatest supporter in their efforts to locate the Hall of Records.

Max Atwater - He is the Director of National Intelligence (DNI) in part 3. His position oversees all security concerns for the nation inside and outside of the USA's borders.

Michael Simons - is Matt Alexander's Chief of Staff in part 1.

Millennium – Term used for 1,000 years of peace as predicted in the Bible's book of Revelation.

Minister Almahdi - is the misogynistic Minister of State for Saudi Arabia in part 1.

Mission Control – Control center, located in Houston, Texas, for NASA space flights.

Mohammed's Faithful - a Syrian based anti-American militia led by Col. Achmed Mansur.

Moshe - is a Senior Field Agent with Mossad in part 1.

Mossad - is Israel's equivalent to the CIA.

Murray - is the POTUS' and FLOTUS' dog in part 1.

Mustafa - was a bus driver and handyman for a Middle Eastern Catholic school in part 1.

Nadia – The post millennial incarnation for Diana in part 3.

Nantu - is Bashir's brother who they contracted with to retrieve the Cubane they dropped down the laundry chute to the hotel's basement in part 1.

Nason – The post millennial incarnation for Jason in part 3.

Nasrum – A soul who plays major roles in books 1 as Achmed Mansur, and part 3 in a number of ways.

Niru – Post millennial incarnation for Nuri in part 3.

NSC - is the council that advises POTUS on all matters of national security.

Nuri Zayd - He has been friends with Mark Heston since their college days. Both archeologists believe that earth's ancient civilizations were quite technologically advanced. After part 1, Nuri, Mark and Jason dedicate their lives to finding the remaining two chambers each appropriately called the Hall of Records.

NVGs - is an abbreviation for Night Vision Goggles that allow the user to see in near total darkness.

Octanitrocubane - is also called Cubane. It is a highly explosive substance that requires no oxygen to ignite.

Orion Brothers – Mark and Nuri were brothers in the same family back in the Atlantean times. They developed a dangerous laser technology that unknowingly created massive earthquakes that lead to the sinking of Atlantis.

Outer Darkness – An ethereal dimension or state of mind where souls end up repeatedly thinking about the awful moments of their life. Souls do not have to stay there, but it is strangely compelling to the depressed or distraught to be able to disconnect from other souls altogether.

Pam Selco - is the Secret Service agent in charge of FLOTUS' security in part 1.

Paul Saunders - is U.S. Army Captain in charge of the Delta Force team looking to stop Mansur from a terrorist act using Cubane to destroy an unknown target in Egypt.

PBR – Also known as Pabst Blue Ribbon beer.

Piedras Negras – a remote area of northern Guatemala where the second Hall of Records was hidden.

POTUS – An abbreviation for President of the United States.

President Donald Westbrook – He became the POTUS immediately after Matthew Alexander.

Prince Nafid – AKA Nafid Alsab Anahni who is a minor Syrian prince. He connected with Nasrum through automatic writing and became his puppet to control the world.

Private First Class Mendez - is a supply truck driver stationed in Israel for the U.S. Army in part 1.

Private First Class Wiley - is a supply truck driver stationed in Israel for the U.S. Army in part 1.

Private Reynolds - rides shotgun for the supply truck runs in Israel.

Private Shaw - rides shotgun for the supply truck runs in Israel.

Ramin Acaba - is an arms dealer from the Middle East who works with Amir.

Rasmun – if the post millennial incarnation for Nasrum in part 3.

Rayiys – is the Arabic word for master. This is the name Nasrum had Prince Nafid call him.

RF and RF crystals – The initials RF stands for resonant frequency, which is the driving force behind many of the ancient technologies in all three books. Using Fibonacci numbered frequencies, RF crystals can be formed and programmed to perform any number of scientific marvels.

RFA – An abbreviation for Resonant Frequency Akashic Records. This is a small crystal box that provides a telepathic connection between humans to the information stored in the Akashic Records. Part 3 has two such boxes, Kasha and Sherlock.

RFC – An abbreviation for Resonant Frequency Communication. In its perfected form they are earbuds containing RFC crystals that allow users to stay in constant communication with each other.

RFH – An abbreviation for Resonant Frequency Healing. This RF application transmits instant healing to those who touch a programmed obsidian pedestal. RFH heals but does not reverse-age the body as can be done in the Temple Beautiful.

RFL – An abbreviation for Resonant Frequency Levitation. RF crystals can be programmed to levitate heavy objects, liquids or gases. It operates in a manner similar to how/why a steel ship can float in water.

RFP – (Also see RFE or RF Energy) An abbreviation for Resonant Frequency Power which is a safe and completely interchangeable power source with electricity.

RFS - An abbreviation for Resonant Frequency Sustenance which has the ability to grow food and purify water using RF crystal technology. This also requires special soil that is mainly silicon (sand) infused with Benzene over thousands of years.

RFT – An abbreviation for Resonant Frequency Teleportation. This RF application allows for the instant teleportation of people, liquids, gases, from an origination point to a destination point of your choosing. It should not be confused with RFL (levitation) that moves molecules easily, but not instantaneously.

Richard Newman - is a retired U.S. Army General who serves Matt Alexander as the DNI or Director of National Intelligence in part 1.

Rob Norton - is an U.S. Army Captain stationed in Israel in part 1 who is in charge of the night watch at the supply depot attacked by Mohammed's Faithful.

Robert's Rules of Order – Procedural guide to maintain order in a formal group meeting or organization.

Rodrigo Cortez - He is often called "El Jefe" which translates to "The Boss" in English. He is the leader of the Macizo cartel, the largest drug smuggling operation in Central and South America. He is married to the love of his life, Fatima. She is the only person he truly loves in this world.

Sadad - is the one soldier Col. Mansur left behind to destroy Mohammed Faithful's hidden equipment, if needed, in part 1.

Scientific Method – Method for proving something as a fact by repeatable results through consistent testing.

SEAL – This is the U.S. Navy abbreviation for SEa, Air and Land.

Shallal - is Mansur's second-in-command of the mercenaries hired to destroy the Suez Canal in part 1.

Sharia law – The name for Islamic law based on the Koran and other holy texts.

Sherlock – The name given to the second RFA box by Eljay.

Silou – The post millennial incarnation for Louis Jensen Sr. in part 3.

Steve Lombard - is the Secretary of Defense in part 1.

Steven Welch - is a medical doctor wearing two hats. He is in charge of researching dangerous pathogens for the CDC (Center for Disease Control in the USA) and the WHO (World Health Organization) in part 2.

Suez Canal - is the man-made waterway that connects the Mediterranean Sea and the Red Sea in Egypt.

Temple Beautiful – Edgar Cayce's psychic readings describe this as a place where the human body could be regenerated to be young again.

The Glut - This is the current name for the disease-filled black vial (and the cure for it in a separate white vial) that Mark removed from the Piedras Negras pyramid.

The voice – A nameless leader of a group of mercenaries hired by the Iranian government to kidnap Mark and Nuri and extract information from them about the Hall of Records.

Thiago Bernal - He is the second in command of the Macizo cartel. His father, Diego Bernal, now deceased, was also a member of the cartel for his whole life.

Tom Strickland - is the Chief of CIA operations in Kandahar in part 1.

Tongue of the Ocean trench – drops from 70 to 6,000 feet below sea level just to the west of the Bimini Islands.

U.N. - is an abbreviation for the United Nations.

Wajid - is Director Gil Kowalski's counterpart in Afghanistan's government in part 1.

Wayne Thompson - is the head of the Secret Service detail in charge of protecting POTUS and FLOTUS in part 1.

WMDs - is an abbreviation for Weapons of Mass Destruction.

World Health Organization - This organization is also known as WHO. An international agency managed by the United Nations. Its purpose is to oversee health threats that can spread beyond borders and threaten the well-being of humanity.

Yong and Li – Black Ops operatives for China who are stationed as embassy staff in Los Angeles in part 3.

Yuri Alton – is the Russian ambassador to the United Nations in part 3.

Yusef – is the Director of Security for the United Nations in part 3.

Zhang – is the Assistant to China's President Mao Choi in part 3.

Made in the USA
Middletown, DE
25 September 2020